D1042865

"*Twelve Kings in Sharakhai* is a complex novel with crisp prose that is a joy to read." —Black Gate

"The protagonist, pit-fighter Çeda, is driven but not cold, and strong but not shallow. And the initial few scenes of violence and sex, while very engaging, soon give way to a much richer plot. Beaulieu is excellent at keeping a tight rein on the moment-to-moment action and building up the tension and layers of mysteries." —SciFiNow

"Complicated, rich, and endlessly fascinating."
—SFSignal

"Bradley Beaulieu has crafted a rich, fascinating world, filled it with compelling characters, and blended them into an epic tale that grabbed my attention on the first page and refused to let go. I look forward to more stories of Sharakhai."
—David B. Coe, author of *Rules of Ascension*

"I love epic fantasy for many reasons, not least of which is the fact every book is a portal to a whole new world. But when you read as much in this genre as I do, you sure get to visit a lot of them. That is why, when every once in a while I come across a setting that truly stands out, I sit up and take note. And Bradley P. Beaulieu's *Twelve Kings in Sharakhai* made me do just that." —The BiblioSanctum

"Fantasy and horror, catacombs and sarcophagi, resurrections and revelations: The book has them all, and Beaulieu wraps it up in a package that's as graceful and contemplative as it is action-packed and pulse-pounding."
—NPR Books

"Putting it simply, *Twelve Kings* is the best new Epic Fantasy I've read in *years*." —SFFWorld

Also by Bradley P. Beaulieu:

The Song of the Shattered Sands
TWELVE KINGS IN SHARAKHAI
WITH BLOOD UPON THE SAND
A VEIL OF SPEARS
BENEATH THE TWISTED TREES

* * *

OF SAND AND MALICE MADE

BRADLEY P. BEAULIEU

TWELVE KINGS IN SHARAKHAI

Book One of

The Song of the Shattered Sands

DAW BOOKS, INC.

DONALD A. WOLLHEIM, FOUNDER

1745 Broadway, New York, NY 10019

ELIZABETH R. WOLLHEIM

SHEILA E. GILBERT

PUBLISHERS

www.dawbooks.com

For my sisters, Kim and Dawn.
There's so much of you in these pages, and
especially in Çeda.
Your strength, your caring, your love of family.

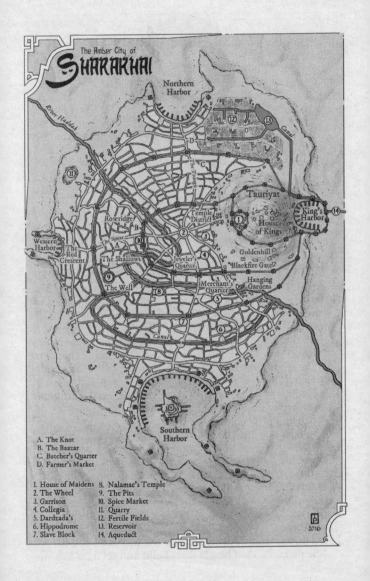

The Amber City of

SHARAKHAI

Northern Harbor

River Haddah

Tauriyat

House of Kings

King's Harbor

Roseridge

Temple District

Western Harbor

The Red Crescent

The Spear

The Knot

The Bazaar

The Shallows

Jeweler's Quarter

Goldenhill

Blackfire Gate

The Well

Merchant Quarter

Hanging Gardens

Canal

A. The Knot
B. The Baazar
C. Butcher's Quarter
D. Farmer's Market

1. House of Maidens
2. The Wheel
3. Garrison
4. Collegia
5. Dardzada's
6. Hippodrome
7. Slave Block

8. Nalamae's Temple
9. The Pits
10. Spice Market
11. Quarry
12. Fertile Fields
13. Reservoir
14. Aqueduct

Southern Harbor

2016

Chapter 1

IN A SMALL ROOM beneath the largest of Sharakhai's fighting pits, Çeda sat on a wooden bench, tightening her fingerless gloves. The room was cool, even chill compared to the ever-present heat of the city. Painted ceramic tiles lined the walls. A mismatched jumble of wooden benches and shelves that had clearly seen decades of abuse made it feel well loved if not well cared for. Were Çeda any other dirt dog, she would have sat in one of the rooms on the far side of the pits, the ones that hosted dozens of men and women. But Çeda was given special dispensation, and had been since winning her first bout at the age of fourteen.

By the gods, five years already.

She tightened her hands into fists, enjoying the creak of the leather, the feel of the chain mail wrapped around the backs of her hands and knuckles. She checked the straps of her armor. Her greaves, her bracers, her heavy battle skirt. And finally her breastplate. All of them had once been dyed white—the color of a wolf's bared teeth—but now the armor was so well used that much of the leather's natural brown shone through. *Well and good*, Çeda thought. It felt used. Lived in. Kissed by battle. Exactly the way she liked it.

She picked up her bright steel helm and set it on her lap.

She stared into the iron mask fixed across the front—a mask of a woman's face, cold and expressionless in the face of battle. Affixed to the top of the helm was a wolf's pelt, teeth bared, muzzle resting along the crown.

Echoing down the corridor came a voice that sounded old and hoary, a mountain come to life. "They're ready." It was Pelam.

Çeda glanced toward the arched doorway with the blood-red curtains strung across it. "Coming," she said, then returned her attention to the helm. She ran her fingers over the many nicks in the metal, over the mask's empty eyes—

Tulathan grant me foresight.

—stroked the rough fur of the wolf's pelt—

Thaash guide my sword.

—then pulled the helm over her braided black hair and strapped it tightly on.

As the weight of the armor settled over her, she parted the heavy curtains and hiked up the sloping tunnel into the heat of the noontime sun. The walls of the fighting pit towered around her, and above them, arranged in concentric circles, were the seats of the stadium. *It's going to be a good day for Osman.* Already there were several hundred waiting for the bout to begin.

Roughly half the spectators called the city of Sharakhai home; they knew the pits inside and out, knew the regular dirt dogs as well. The other half were visitors to the desert's amber jewel. They'd come to trade or find fortune in a city that offered greater opportunities than they'd had back home. It rankled that so many came here, to Çeda's home, and lived off it like fleas on a dog. Though she could hardly complain—

A boy in a teal kaftan pointed to Çeda wildly and called, "The White Wolf! The Wolf has come to fight!" and the crowd rose to their feet as one, craning their necks to see.

—the pits paid well enough.

A ragged cheer went up as she strode to the center of the pit and joined the circle of eleven other fighters. The money men in the stands began calling out odds for the

White Wolf. She hadn't even been chosen to fight yet, so no one would know who her opponent would be, but many still flocked to be the first to wager their coin on her.

The other dirt dogs watched Çeda warily. Some knew her, but just like those in the audience, many of these fighters had come from distant kingdoms to try their hand against the best fighters in Sharakhai. Three women stood among those gathered—two well muscled, the third an absolute brute; she outweighed Çeda by three stone at least. The rest were men, some brawny, others lithe. One, however, was a tower of a man wearing a beaten leather breastplate and a conical helm with chain mail that lapped against his broad shoulders. Haluk. He stood a full head and a half taller than Çeda and stared at her like an ox readying a charge.

In response, Çeda strode toward him and pressed her thumb to an exposed edge on the back of her mailed gloves. She pressed hard enough to pierce skin, to draw blood. Haluk stared at her with confusion, then a wicked sort of glee, as Çeda stopped in front of him and pressed her bloody thumb to the center of his leather breastplate.

The crowd roared.

A new flurry of betting rose, while the rest of the audience jockeyed for position against the rim of the pit.

Çeda had just marked Ḥaluk for her own, an ancient gesture that not all dirt dogs would respect, but these would, she reckoned. None of them would wish to fight Haluk, not in their first bout of the day. When Çeda turned away and returned to her place in the circle, all but ignoring Haluk, the naked anger on his face was slowly replaced with a look of cool assessment. *Good,* Çeda thought. He'd taken the bait and would surely choose her if she didn't choose him first.

When some but not all of the betting flurry had died down, Pelam stepped out from another darkened tunnel. The calls of betting rose to a tumult as the audience saw the first bout was ready to begin.

Pelam wore a jeweled vest, a brown kufi, and a red kaftan that was not only fashionable but fine, save for its hem, which was hopelessly dusty from its days sweeping the pit floors. In one of Pelam's skeletal hands he held a woven basket. As the fighters parted for him, he stepped to the rough center of their circle and flipped the basket lid open. After one last check around him to ensure all was ready, he shot his hand into basket's confines and lifted a horned viper as long as his lanky legs. The snake wriggled, swelling its hood and hissing, baring its fangs for all to see.

Pelam knew his business, but the snake made Çeda's hackles rise. Bites were rare but not unheard of, especially if one of the fighters was inexperienced and jumped when the snake drew near. Çeda knew enough to remain still, but foreigners didn't always follow Pelam's careful pre-bout instructions, and it wasn't always the person who jumped that the snakes chose to sink their fangs into.

As Pelam held the writhing snake, each of the fighters spread their legs wide until their sandaled or booted feet butted up against each other's. After a glance at each of the fighter's stances, and finding them proper, Pelam dropped the snake and stepped away.

It lay there, coiling itself tightly. The crowd shouted to the baked desert air, their voices rising to a fever pitch as each yelled the name of their chosen fighter. The fighters themselves remained silent. Oddly, the snake slithered toward Pelam for a moment, then seemed to think better of it and turned to glide over the sand to Çeda's left, then turned once more. And slithered straight through Haluk's legs.

Silence followed as a pit boy ran and snatched the viper by its tail, lowering it back into its basket as the snake spun like a woodworker's auger.

Pelam calmly awaited Haluk's choice.

The big man didn't hesitate. He made straight for Çeda and spat on the ground at her feet.

The crowd went wild. "The Oak of the Guard has chosen the White Wolf!"

Oak indeed. Haluk was a captain of the Silver Spears, and a tree of a man, but he was also a particularly *cruel* man, and it was time he learned a lesson.

Like jackals to a kill, the news drew spectators from

neighboring pits. The stands were soon brimming with them.

As the rest of the fighters exited the pit, a dozen boys jogged out from the tunnels bearing wooden swords and shields and clubs. Çeda, as the challenged, would normally be allowed to choose weapons first, but she followed ancient custom; she had marked him, and thus *she* was the true challenger, not Haluk, so she bowed her head and waved to the weapons, granting first choice to Haluk. Most would have returned the honor, but Haluk merely grunted and chose one of the few weapons meant for both him and his opponent: the fetters.

The noise of the crowd rose until it was akin to thunder. Some laughed, others clapped. Some few even stared with naked worry at Çeda, who had clearly just been put at a severe disadvantage by Haluk's choice of weapon.

The fetters was a length of tough, braided leather. It was wrapped tightly around one of each fighter's wrists, keeping them in close proximity and ensuring a brawl.

While glaring intently at Haluk, Çeda held out her left hand, allowing Pelam to slip the end of the fetters around her wrist and tighten it. Pelam did the same to Haluk, then took a small brass gong and mallet from one of the boys.

The pit was cleared so that only Çeda, Haluk, and Pelam remained.

The doors to the tunnels closed.

And then, after a dramatic pause in which Pelam held the gong chest-high between the two fighters, he struck it and stepped away.

There was slack in the fetters, a situation Haluk would quickly attempt to remedy—his best hope, after all, lay in controlling Çeda's movement—but Çeda was ready for it. The moment Haluk lunged in to grab as much of the leather rope as he could, she darted forward, leaping and snapping a kick at his chin. When he retreated, Çeda charged, a move he clearly hadn't been expecting. His eyes widened as Çeda grabbed his clumsily raised arm and sent her fist crashing into his cheek.

She could feel the chain mail dig deep into the fighting gloves she wore, but it was worse for Haluk. He fell unceremoniously onto his rump, his conical helm flying off and thumping onto the dry dirt, kicking up dust as it went.

The crowd stood and howled its delight.

As his helm skidded well out of reach, Haluk rolled backward over his shoulder and came to a stand, so quickly that Çeda had no time to rush forward and end it.

Haluk raised one hand to his cheek, felt the blood from the patterned cuts the mail had left in his skin, then stared at his own hand with a look like he'd disappointed himself. And then his eyes went hard. He'd been pure bluster before, trying to intimidate Çeda, but now he was seething mad.

None so blind as a wrathful man, Çeda thought.

Haluk crouched warily and began wrapping the fetters around his left wrist, over and over, slowly taking up the slack. Çeda retreated and pulled hard on the fetters, putting her entire body into it, making the leather scrape painfully along Haluk's arm. He ignored it and continued to wrap the restraints around his wrist. Çeda yanked on the fetters again, but he blunted the tactic with well-timed grips on the leather, the muscles along his arm rippling and bulging. He grinned, showing two rows of ragged teeth.

Çeda sent several kicks toward his thighs and knees, attacks meant more to test Haluk's reflexes than anything else. Haluk blocked them easily. She was just about to yank on the fetters again when he loosened his grip and rushed her. Çeda stumbled, pretending to lose her balance, and when Haluk came close she dove to her right and swept a leg across his ankles.

He fell in a heap, the breath whooshing from his lungs.

He grabbed for Çeda and managed to snag her ankle, but one swift kick from Çeda's free heel and she was up and dancing away while Haluk rose slowly to his feet.

The crowd howled again, many of the foreigners joining in, though they had no idea why. The Sharakhani knew, though. They understood why bouts like this were so very rare.

Haluk hadn't been defeated in more than ten years of fighting in the pits. Çeda had rarely lost since her first bout, and she'd lost none in the past three years. Everyone knew how widely the story of this bout would be told, especially if Çeda took him in so cleanly a fashion. Few would dare utter the tale within Haluk's hearing, but the entire city would be alive with it by the end of the day.

And Haluk knew it. He stared into Çeda's eyes with an intensity that reeked of desperation. He would not be so easy to take again.

As the two of them squared off once more, the crowd went completely and eerily silent. The only sound was of Haluk's ragged breathing and Çeda's strong but controlled breaths from within the confines of her helm.

Haluk took one tentative step forward. Çeda stepped away, snatching up some of the slack in the fetters as she went. Haluk did the same until they both held a quarter of the length in reserve, leaving them a scant few strides from one another.

Haluk took two measured steps toward her. He was trying to close the distance, but he was no longer reckless. He was cautious, as a man who'd become a captain of Sharakhai's guard *should* be.

Çeda kicked at his legs again, connecting but doing little damage. That wasn't the point, though. She had to keep him on his guard until she was ready to move in. She snapped another kick and retreated, but she could only go so far. Haluk had drawn up more of the fetters, so Çeda released some of hers. Haluk strode forward, taking up more of the braided rope. Which forced Çeda to release more. Until she had none left.

He drew sharply on it, keeping his center low, his balance steady, and Çeda was drawn forward until she was just out of his striking range.

The crowd began to stamp their feet, the sound of it reverberating in the pit, but otherwise they were silent, rapt.

Haluk pulled again, harder now that they were so close. And that's when Çeda moved.

Using the tension on the fetters to pull herself forward, she launched herself with a leap, straight into his body. In his surprise, Haluk grasped for her neck, but she slipped her forearms inside his and grabbed two fistfuls of his lanky brown hair. She wrapped her legs around his waist, twisted them around his thighs, and locked her feet around his knees, hoping to trip him up and end this once and for all.

He didn't fall, however. He was too big. Too strong. And he did exactly what she would have done. He rose up, preparing to slam her against the ground.

At the high point of his lift, she did the only thing she could: she clung hard to his neck and waist.

When they came down, they came down hard. Pain burst across Çeda's back and rump as Haluk's full weight bore down on her. Through her coughing and the ringing in her ears, she could hear him laughing. "Foolish move, girl."

He tried to lift away, but she'd locked her arms around his neck. Her legs hugged tightly to his waist. He was strong, but he had no leverage to break her grip. Again and again he tried to lift himself away from her to give himself room to punch, but each time he did, she began slipping her arms around his neck to cut off his blood. He would drop to prevent it, and then they were back, body to body, breath coming hard and fast, the very intimate duel continuing as each struggled for any small amount of leverage.

Once, when he lifted his head too far away, she crashed her forehead against his. The lip of her helm left a long cut against his skin. Blood seeped down his forehead, along his nose. It pattered against her steel mask, filling her nostrils with the smell of it.

Then, in a sudden and furious move, Haluk lifted, slipping a forearm across her throat, managing to pin her down.

Immediately the crowd was up, shouting, raging. But it all became little more than a keen ringing in Çeda's ears. She heard her own heart thrumming. Felt Haluk's arm tighten further.

It was a strong move, a *wise* move under the conditions, but he'd left himself open. She slipped her right hand down along his left arm, near his elbow, where she'd have the most leverage, and pushed. She let out a guttural cry while muscling his arm up, which had the effect of propelling herself down along his body, just enough to slip her head under his armpit and out of the lock.

He tried to slip his arm back under her neck, but before he could, she grabbed the buckles along the far edge of his breastplate and hauled herself away, and now she was half-way to his back. Exactly where she wanted to be.

She reached her left arm—the one tied to the fetters—up and over his head. The rope slipped neatly down along his face and across his neck. Immediately she tightened her grip and drew the fetters back.

Haluk knew what was happening—he tried to throw her off, at least enough to get his fingers beneath the fetters—but her grip was too sure. Still, he was a bull of a man. She grunted while gritting her teeth and arching her back. Her arms strained like cording on a ship's sails.

She thought surely he would have pounded his hand against the ground by now, giving up the match, or fallen unconscious, but he hadn't. He still struggled for air, his breath coming out in a desperate hiss, his mouth frothing from it. And then finally, all at once, his body went slack.

Çeda didn't hear the strike of Pelam's gong, marking the end of the bout.

But the crowd she heard.

Their elation could no longer be contained. They stomped their feet. They shook their fists. "The Wolf has won! The Wolf has won!"

Ignoring them, Çeda pushed Haluk onto his back and straddled his chest. She unwrapped the fetters and saw the blood drain from him, casting his face in a strange, deathly pallor.

His eyes blinked open. He stared into Çeda's eyes with a look of confusion, then took in his surroundings as if he had no idea where he was. The roaring crowd and Çeda's masked face soon registered, though, and a look of deep and inexpressible anger stole over him.

Çeda leaned down until they were chest-to-chest and whispered into his ear. "The next time you take your hands to your daughter, Haluk Emet'ava"—she pressed the thumbnail of her right hand into his side, in the depression between his fourth and fifth ribs—"it will go much worse for you." She leaned closer still and whispered, "The next time, it will be a knife in the dark, not a beating in the light." She rose, her legs still straddling him, and stared down into his eyes. "Do you understand?"

Haluk blinked. He made no acknowledgment of her demand, but there was shame in his eyes, a shame that spoke the truth of his crimes better than words ever could.

Like a wedge driving ever further into a thick piece of wood, she pressed her thumb deeper. "I would hear your answer."

He grimaced against the discomfort, licked his lips, and glanced to the cheering crowd. Then he nodded to her. "I understand."

Çeda nodded back, then stood and stepped away.

Pelam had watched this exchange with a glint in his eye that landed somewhere between curious and concerned, but he made no mention of it. He merely turned and presented Çeda to the crowd with a bow of his head and a flourish of his hand. As some howled and others collected their winnings, Çeda was surprised to see that Osman himself had come to watch—Osman, the owner of these pits, a retired pit fighter himself, the man she'd had to trick to earn her first bout.

How far we've come since then.

He stood with the crowd on the topmost row. He was one of the very few—along with Pelam—who knew her true identity. She had no idea how long he'd been watching, but surely he'd caught the end. She couldn't tell if he was pleased or not. Çeda gave an exaggerated nod to the crowd, but she and Osman both knew it was meant for him.

He nodded back, then tugged his ear, which meant he wished to speak.

To speak, and perhaps more.

Chapter 2

A SHORT WHILE LATER, after Çeda had completed her victory circuit of the pit—raising her hands to the cheering crowd—and retreated to the room she'd been given before the bout, Osman came to her.

She heard the two guardsmen intone, "Master Osman," in unison, and moments later the red curtains parted and he stepped inside the starkly appointed room. She heard the guardsmen shuffle farther down the hall, as they always did when she and Osman met.

She had already pulled her bracers off, but now she was unstrapping her white breastplate.

"Çeda," Osman said tentatively.

She ignored him, easing off her breastplate and standing, knowing she wore only her white tunic beneath, knowing the sweat on her skin would give Osman easy view of her form beneath. After setting the breastplate on the bench, she unbuckled her battle skirt, slowly collecting the heavy leather garment and setting it on top of the breastplate. She set one sandaled foot on the bench and tugged the tunic higher, exposing her thigh as she worked on the four smaller buckles on her greaves. She did the same with the other, and then with deliberate care cupped one into the other and set them both on top of the battle skirt.

Only then did she turn to Osman, who was standing several paces away, watching with no small amount of interest. He wore fine clothes—red kaftan, rich leather sandals, bracelets of yellow-and-white gold—but the vicious scar that ran across his face, from forehead, across the bridge of his nose, and down his left cheek, spoke of different days.

One of his thick black eyebrows rose as he stared. He seemed to want to smile, but didn't, perhaps waiting to see what she would do next. He was not the sort of man who could walk freely among the richer quarters of Sharakhai, but he was a master just the same. One could see it in how clean he was, how well cut his fingernails, how carefully groomed his short beard. He was a man who had risen from these very pits, but he was a pit fighter no longer.

He was not shy about taking in her form. He never had been. It was one of the reasons she liked him. She had long since tired of quiet, reserved men.

"What did you say to Haluk?" he asked.

She took a half-step toward him, acutely aware of the trail of sweat tickling its way down the small of her back. "My business is my own."

"He's not a man you want as your enemy."

She took another half-step forward. "Then it's good he doesn't know who I am."

"He'll come to me, you know. He'll offer me coin for your true name."

She doubted that. The laws of the pits may be unwritten, but they were ancient, not easily crossed, as she and Osman both knew. "He may," she said, "but you won't sell my name."

"Oh?" The smile that had been hesitant in coming was now in full display. There was no denying he was a handsome man, especially when he smiled at her as he was now. "And why is that?"

"Because if you did—"

She took one last stride. They were close enough now that she could feel the heat coming off him in the coolness of this underground place. She placed her thumbnail between his ribs, exactly as she'd done to Haluk, and pressed. Hard. He didn't flinch, as many men would have, but his breath was coming stronger now, harder.

"—you would seriously regret the decision."

His smile faded until it was a tarnished reminder of what it had been. "Is that so?"

"Never doubt it."

His nostrils flared as she released the pressure and allowed her callused fingers to trail down his chest. To his waist. To his hip. And then she let her hand fall free. She stood still, sharing a jackal smile with him, but nothing else.

For a time it appeared he would go no further, but then he stepped in and slipped his arm around her waist. Pulled her in tight and bowed his head to meet hers. His lips were warm as he kissed her. They pressed their bodies together, his strong hands running over her back, down her neck, pulling her in so tight it neared pain. Which she minded not at all.

She pulled him to the tiled floor, dragged his tunic up and over his well-proportioned frame. He gripped her thighs with strong hands and ran his fingertips roughly down her stomach as she pulled her sweaty tunic up over her head and threw it into the corner. A heavy grunt escaped him as she rose up, slipped him inside her, and dropped roughly onto his hips. She moved slowly at first, while his breathing became more and more labored, but then she moved with a growing urgency, rising and falling faster and faster.

He tried to pull her down toward him that their skin might touch, but she slapped his hands away. He tried again, and she pinned his wrists down, allowed her breasts to trail across his chest, ran her nipples slowly around his. She licked the scars that riddled his chest and arms and shoulders. She scratched his skin. Raked her fingers down toward the tuft of dark hair around his manhood.

She rode him hard, and for a moment, as she crested, all the aches and pains in her body became little more than faint memories.

As she lowered from her heights, she allowed herself to fall against his chest. Osman gripped a fistful of her hair and thrust into her as she bit his neck. She felt him release as well, felt his throbbing slowly ebb, felt his seed slick her thighs. And for a time the two of them lay still, their breathing falling into a steadily slowing rhythm that felt like the setting of the sun and the quieting of life over the desert.

When at last she lifted off his chest, she did not kiss him. She whispered no sweet words in his ear. She merely admired the landscape of his scars, wondering at the stories they told. She had often thought that this was as much a reason to be attracted to him as any other. *Here is a man skilled in the arts of combat,* she remembered thinking, *who knows how to debilitate, to harm, to kill. And if he knows those things, what might he know of the body's more subtle ways?*

She hadn't been wrong. He was as skilled as anyone she'd bedded—which admittedly hadn't been many. Although the emotions between them had never included love. At least not for her.

As Çeda ran her fingers lightly down his stomach, outlining the broadest of his scars, her closeness to him—as it always did sooner or later—became uncomfortable. She tried to hide it, but he noticed, and he'd always been a proud man, even if he wasn't proud enough to leave her once and for all.

"I've a task for you, Çeda," he said while shifting his hips, a cue for her to rise.

She stayed, provoking him. "I'm no servant to do your bidding, old man."

"So you keep telling me." He arched his neck, closed his eyes in pleasure as she squeezed him, but then, almost regretfully, his tone became serious. "It's a simple shade. Nothing more."

Çeda rose and from a shelf in the corner took a folded cotton rag. "If it were simple, you wouldn't be asking me." She wet the cloth in an urn in the corner and ran it over her body, collecting his seed from her thighs, then folding it and carefully washing away the sweat and dirt and blood.

For a moment, just a moment, she was glad of the handful of years she'd spent with Dardzada. He'd been a hard foster parent—and there were days under his care that made her want to beat him as mercilessly as she beat those in the pits—but there was no doubt he had taught her much, not the least of which was the herbs a woman might steep in boiling water to deaden a man's seed.

Yerinde forbid, she thought.

Osman sat up. "The shade is simple, but it's important it be done right."

"You're not listening." After drying herself, she pulled on her black thawb, then pulled the matching niqab over her head. "Send Tariq if you need it so badly."

Osman laughed. "Were it a brawl in a southern quarter tavern, I'd send Tariq, but not for this."

"Why not?" Çeda adjusted her veil, the beaten brass coins worked into it jingling as she did so. "Tariq can run a package as well as I."

He stood now and pulled his tunic back on. "This package needs to be run one week from now. At sunset."

Çeda paused for a moment, then continued her final adjustments to her niqab as if his words meant nothing. "One week from now is Beht Zha'ir."

Beht Zha'ir was a holy night. It came every six weeks—the night the twin moons, Tulathan and her sister, Rhia, rose together and lit the desert floor. It was the night the asirim roamed the streets searching for tributes and the Reaping King went with them. For Osman to ask her to shade a package—to do *anything* on that night—was bold, and for a moment she'd mistaken his desperation for a deeper understanding of her *other* pursuits.

"Does that mean you won't do it?" Osman asked, a bit too casually.

"I didn't say that."

"You'll need to speak more plainly, Çeda. My mind isn't what it used to be."

"I'll run your package."

"There will be two."

This was a message to be delivered in two parts, then; the key to decipher the message would be in one package, while the message itself would be contained in another. And since he hadn't mentioned anyone else so far, he was letting her choose the second messenger.

"I'll bring Emre," she said.

He considered this, nodded, and then reached into the leather pouch at his belt, pulling out a cinched cloth purse. "Your winnings," he said, casting it to her with a speed that made it clear he was testing her.

Quick as a hummingbird, she snatched it from the air. She weighed the purse in her hand.

"Plus coin for the shade," he said before she could say anything.

"Paying up front now, are we?"

"Half. You'll come by my estate for the rest." He said it gruffly, like an order, but there was a clear request in the way his eyes took her in, a subtle plea for her to come, perhaps spend the night.

After wrapping her gear in a tight bundle and slinging it over her shoulder, she strode toward the doorway with a distinct limp, wrapping the persona she used outside the pits around her like an old and favored shawl. To most she was simply a swordmistress, a woman who was skilled but for the injury to her knee, who could still show the children of rich merchants how to swing a sword or raise a shield. It suited her well enough. She enjoyed teaching, and it gave her all the excuse she needed to be seen near and within the pits.

She stopped when she came abreast of Osman. "Your estate."

He nodded.

"We'll see," she said, and then walked out and into the scalding city streets.

Chapter 3

THE NOISE OF THE SPICE MARKET swept over Çeda like a sudden summer sandstorm. It was raucous and biting after the quiet of the streets near her home. Hundreds of stalls occupied the great old building—one of the oldest in Sharakhai—a ramshackle mix of patchwork colors, milling patrons, and heated barter. Çeda had taken her armor to the rooms she shared with Emre, her oldest and closest friend, but even unburdened she retained her limp as she moved through the crowd, many of the stall owners sending her a nod or a smile as they filled small burlap bags with peppercorn or star anise or coarsely ground salt.

A girl with curly brown hair and bright brown eyes broke away from a group of children who were hanging about near the entrance. Çeda had known Mala for years, paid her from time to time for simple things, to act as a lookout, to collect a bit of information, things a girl Mala's age could do where a grown woman could not. It was surprising how often children were overlooked in a city that at times seemed overrun with them.

"Watch," Mala said, spinning and drawing a beaten old stick she used as a sword, then bringing it down across her body in a clean, sharp block. It was a move she'd failed to master for weeks now. If Çeda was truthful, it was still a bit clumsy, but it would come.

"Better," Çeda said, mussing her hair.

Mala frowned and skipped away, pulling her hair back while moving into a mock-serious pose, sword raised. Her sister Jein came soon after, and then more of their band, all of whom Çeda knew. They bore stick swords, and one even a proper shinai. To a child, they raised their swords as Mala was doing, hoping for a lesson. It wasn't something she'd ever reveal to her students at the pits, but she taught the children of Roseridge for free when she had the time. The trouble was, she didn't always *have* the time, and Mala and her pack could be an insistent bunch.

"Not now," she told them, slipping around one of the market's stout mudbrick columns and into the shade of the building proper. "Not now." They were disappointed, but it couldn't be helped. Çeda had business. "Tomorrow," she told them. "Tomorrow we'll dance." And then she was in among the throngs, working her way deeper into the market.

"Try, try," old Seyhan called as Çeda neared the four beaten tables that marked his territory within this mad place. He was handing out pieces of biscuit made by Tehla the baker. "Try, try," he called again, this time in Kundhunese to a tall, ebony-skinned woman and her servant, then once more in Mirean to a jowled man with long, thin mustaches.

Çeda snatched a piece as she came close, stuffing it in her mouth before Seyhan could frown at her.

"For *customers*," Seyhan said, shooing her away.

The bright flavor of cardamom and caramelized onion and lemon zest filled her, making her mouth water so much it pained her jaw for a moment. "I *am* a customer," she shot back.

"No, no, no," he replied, wagging his finger first at her, then at Emre, who stood a few paces away, untying a fresh bag of bright red paprika. "You get everything you need from *his* thieving hands. Don't tell me you don't!"

He was only joking. He let Emre take whatever spices

he wanted; oils, too. It was the one thing that saved their dishes from dropping below mere mediocrity and heading straight for inedibility. Seyhan was generous enough with his coin, too—he gave Emre a few extra sylval when the stall had bustling days like today—and yet Çeda was still surprised Emre had stuck with Seyhan for as long as he had. He was always flitting from this job to that. They always became *tiresome*—*I want something that interests me, Çeda, else why bother?*—as if jobs were nothing more than dalliances. But he seemed to genuinely like old Seyhan, and for that Çeda was glad.

She was saved from replying to Seyhan's accusations when a tall man with brown, leathery skin stepped close and took a piece of biscuit. After placing it carefully in his mouth and chewing as if his very life depended on the weighing of the spices contained within, the two of them began talking in Kundhunese, and Çeda moved farther along the tables, which had dozens of open bags of spice. *So many, from so many different places.* If the four kingdoms surrounding Sharakhai were a great wheel—Mirea, Qaimir, Malasan, and the Thousand Territories of Kundhun— then Sharakhai was surely its hub, and the spice market reflected this: a veritable palette of cultures from a thousand leagues in any direction.

Çeda was about to call out to Emre, who still hadn't noticed her, when two young women broke away from the crowd and approached him together. They were pretty Mirean girls. Creamy skin and exotic eyes and lustrous black hair. Sisters, perhaps, and clearly from a wealthy family—their rich silk dresses and bright jade jewelry spoke clearly of that.

"You came back!" Emre said, standing up straight and putting on the smile he often gave to women he'd only just met. He apparently thought it charming. His black beard was braided and hung down his bare chest, almost to the top of the wide tooled leather belt he wore, the one that matched the bracers on his muscled forearms. One of the girls smiled, averting her gaze, but the other stepped close, clutching a small silk purse in both hands.

She said something too soft for Çeda to hear, and then

Emre bowed his head to her and filled two bags with practiced ease, one with pink desert salt, the other with some bright orange spice Çeda had never seen before. Emre chatted with them as he worked, then held the bags behind the table while prolonging the conversation. As Çeda watched him, she wondered, not for the first time, why Emre never gave *her* that smile. He might've done so a few times before they'd lain together, but ever since, he'd treated her differently. He'd joke with her when they were around others, play like they were a couple when it suited him, but when they were alone, he never crossed that line.

The woman with the purse tittered. The other watched in silence with wide eyes, cheeks reddening.

Çeda should probably just leave him alone. She didn't really care who he shared his bed with—she didn't—but there was something about these women, sailing in from some distant port, wandering about the Amber City as if it were some long-neglected holding they'd finally deigned to visit. It chafed.

"Four months?" she said, loudly enough to be heard over the din of the market. She ignored the women as she stepped opposite Emre. "Four *months*, and now I find you *here?*"

The Mirean girls looked confusedly between Çeda and Emre.

Emre, however, glowered at her. He was trying to hide his annoyance and hoped he still had a chance to a chance to bed one of these women tonight. He might even have fancies of both at once. "I sent a note," he said as nonchalantly as he could manage. "Did the boy not find you? I said I'd fix whatever damage my mule did to your lord's dray."

As pathetic as his initial parry was, she nearly laughed. She enjoyed playing this kind of game with him, though they seemed to be playing them less often of late. "You did, but there's more to atone for than a split wagon wheel." She put her hand on her belly, cupping it in a gesture she'd seen so many women with child perform. "You did, after all, avail yourself of my lord's hospitality for some time. And there are the dead goats to consider."

The girls stared openly at each other now, edging backward, their eyebrows pinching, which was the most emotion that two highborn women from the northern kingdom were likely to share. Emre, meanwhile, burst into a fit of laughter. As the girls bowed their pretty heads and disappeared into the throng, Emre stared at Çeda. *"Goats?"*

"Dozens, dead by your hand!"

"Well, I'm sure they deserved it."

"Agreed," she replied. "They should mind whom they butt."

He gave a barking laugh. Seyhan, meanwhile, was speaking with a woman in a once-lavish abaya, one of his most loyal customers, a master chef for one of Blackfire Gate's richest lords. He frowned deeply at Çeda and Emre. "Go!" he said, shooing them away with fluttering hands. "You're worse than thieves, the both of you!"

As he turned back to the chef, Emre rolled his eyes and crawled under the stall. "He's got a shine for that one," Emre said, eyeing the old, bent-backed spice merchant.

"Seyhan?" Çeda asked, stifling a laugh. "Well, good for him!"

Emre began weaving through the crowd toward the scent merchants' old fort. "You don't know the half of it." Already the heavy breeze carried the scents of rose and jasmine and sandalwood, and more filled the air the farther they walked. "I defy you to name a man in Sharakhai who's more deserving of a bit of time stuffing the pigeon."

She slapped his arm. "You're disgusting." She glanced back at Seyhan, who was smiling at the woman again. "Could you imagine them, though? They're likely to have the Silver Spears at their door."

"Yeah, wondering who's being murdered."

A long laugh burst from Çeda, calling the attention of the crowd. When the patrons had returned to the business of barter and trade, Emre spoke in a low voice, only for her. "And the White Wolf, was she victorious?"

Her reply was every bit as prudent as his. "She did well enough from what I hear."

The relief in his expression was touching. "That's good," he said. "Is there another reason you came, then, other than to chase away the fine, smooth-skinned women of Mirea, that is?"

"Those thinly veiled harlots *needed* chasing," she shot back, "and can't I come just to see where your fortunes have led you this week?"

He slapped a hand over his heart. "You wound me! I've been at the stall for *ages*."

"Three months . . ."

"As I said, ages!"

Part of her wanted to laugh, but there was something about the fight with Haluk today—her near loss, if she was being honest—that was making her strangely sentimental. "We hardly see each other anymore."

After sidestepping a shoeless, sprinting gutter wren—a girl who reminded Çeda of running through the bazaar in the same pell-mell fashion—Emre bowed his head, allowing her the point. "Ships passing in a sandstorm."

She shrugged. She could hardly throw stones given how little time she spent in their shared home these days. "We should amend that."

He nodded, glancing back toward Seyhan's stall, which was all but swallowed by the crowd. "True, we should, but—"

"The master of the pits came to me today," Çeda interrupted, realizing she should wait until they had more privacy but wanting to know Emre's answer before she left the market.

"Oh?" Emre said.

"There's a bit of a run needed."

"A run?"

She leaned closer and spoke softly. "Through the shadows."

One eyebrow rose. "When?"

"Seven days," she said pointedly.

"Seven days," he repeated, glancing over Çeda's shoulder to the passing crowd. He leaned in too. "On Beht Zha'ir?"

She nodded, almost imperceptibly.

His eyes scanned the crowd as though he expected the Silver Spears to come rushing through the spice market to take them to Tauriyat, but the look soon faded and he met Çeda's eyes with a strange mixture of boyish excitement and poorly hidden fear. "It's been a while, Çeda."

"Like I said, we've seen too little of one another lately."

Emre leaned in closer, and said most earnestly, "Tell me true, will there be goats involved?"

She laughed. "No goats, gods willing."

"More's the pity." Once more, he bowed his head with a flourish. "And yet, despite your poor standing, I place my heart in your hands."

They passed through a stone archway and into the ruins of an old fort that had long since surrendered to the ever-growing market. The sun was high and shone straight down, making the perfume stalls seem to glow. All around, men and women stood beside bright glass globes filled with scented water. The bare stone walls of the fort's interior were stark, bordering on grim, but it didn't seem to hurt business any. It was the place one went to find the most wondrous scents in all the Five Kingdoms. Many high lords and ladies could be found here, running clear glass stoppers over their wrists, marveling at the scents applied. Young boys and girls wandered among the crowd, descending quickly upon newcomers. Each held dozens of strips of thin wood.

"Sir," they beckoned Emre, "the scent of cypress or fir or clove. What better to bring joy to the lovely dove upon your arm?"

"Dear lady," they called to Çeda, "amber for a woman as beautiful as those freshly polished stones. Or lavender. Or lemon balm. See for yourself; my master's scents are the finest in all the Great Shangazi."

Çeda beckoned one of them closer, a girl with jet black hair and intense eyes the color of unpolished jade. "Come, then, come." It had been years since she'd bought a vial for herself, and she had more than a bit of change filling her purse.

The girl ran up with a smile of practiced joy. "Now that I see you close, my lady, vetiver it must be, a thing to make you smile on a day filled with clouds, a thing to brighten—"

Çeda laughed, waving her hands to indicate she was

willing to try it and the girl could stop laying it on so thick. But before she could speak, a bustle arose from the far end of the enclosed fort, where several merchants stood near an expensively dressed man. The patron was not only tall, but imposing, and he wore bright red robes cut in the newest Malasani style—loose along the sleeves and tight down the body. He might be a lord of Malasan, or a caravan master, perhaps even a prince. Two women, young enough that they might have been his daughters, trailed behind him, chatting gaily with one another.

Çeda saw through them immediately.

They were careful, but she saw them scanning the space, measuring those closest before moving on to those farther away. They looked for weapons first, and then watched the faces of those gathered, as if memorizing what they saw. When the one in a flowing yellow dress spotted Çeda, she stopped for a moment. The two of them locked eyes, and Çeda suddenly found her heart beating like it did before a bout in the pits.

"What is it?" Emre asked.

Çeda shook her head and looked away lest the woman sense something amiss.

Emre's words died on his lips. He'd sensed it as well now—a strangeness, something surely yet inexplicably *wrong*.

Before Çeda could move, the sound of wooden wheels clattering over stone came from behind. Someone shouted, though what was said was lost in a terrible clatter of heavy wood as it rattled against the stones of the old fort. Çeda turned. The opening before her, the one she and Emre had used to enter the fort, had just been cut off by some massive contraption of stacked logs. The high sound of hammers pounding—metal on metal—came from somewhere beyond it.

Dust sifted down from above, rays of sunlight cutting through it. Conversation vanished like crows before a storm. Many simply stared at the barrier with looks of confusion or worry. But not the two women. One of them remained near her lord. The other ran for the only other passageway out of the fort, but before she'd taken two steps toward it, another massive set of timbers rolled into place, wedging itself almost perfectly into the opening. Again the sound of hammers pounding came from the opposite side.

The woman—how she'd hidden it from sight Çeda had no clue—was suddenly holding a dark sword in her hand, a shamshir made of nearly black metal. An ebon blade; a weapon only the Blade Maidens bore. The man must be important indeed to demand a pair of Maidens as escorts.

A shadow cast along the stones near Çeda's feet drew her attention upward. Far above, along the ramparts, were the sun-backed silhouettes of four men wearing black turbans and veils across their faces. They were muscling something up and over the edge of the stone walls.

Bladders. Massive, unwieldy, leather bladders, tipping end over end, falling from the ramparts down toward the crowd. They burst against the stones, splashing something clear and viscous over half the gathered crowd. The smell of lamp oil filled the enclosed space, choking the nose and throat and drowning out all others scents, even the perfume. The men had clearly been targeting the lord and the Blade Maidens; Çeda and Emre were far enough back to avoid being doused by the lamp oil.

Spice merchants, patrons, and hawkers alike screamed and shouted, eyes wide, staring around as if demons were about to spring forth from the stones. "Stand away!" someone called. "Stand away!" Though where one might do so, Çeda had no idea.

It had only begun to register who the men above were and what they meant to do when one of the Maidens took two long strides toward the far wall, ebon sword in hand. She launched herself from one perfume stall, which rattled as she leapt toward an exposed beam, a remnant of the floor that had once stood above them. Landing lightly on the beam, she used her momentum to launch herself like a sling stone. She flew toward a bare lip of stone and again propelled herself, leaping higher and higher and higher.

When her momentum slowed at last, she took one final leap. Arcing her body like a drawn bow, she drew a black-as-night dagger from somewhere in her right sleeve and drove it deep between two stones an arm's reach short of the lip above. A ringing sound like shearing metal resonated throughout the old fort.

By the gods, nearly forty feet in the blink of an eye, and she'd cleverly chosen a place where there was a wide gap between the veiled men. Two of them moved toward her while the remaining pair dropped one more ungainly bladder, again targeting the far left corner of the fort, where the second Maiden was using the tips of her fingers to test the stone. The bladder burst off target, but the Maiden ignored it in any case. She seemed to have found what she was looking for, for she stood and stared at the space her fingertips had just brushed. Then she took one stride forward, spun, and sent a vicious back kick against the stone, releasing a powerful shout, a *kiai,* that Çeda felt in her chest.

The wall shuddered, and a bit of stone crumbled away from the point of impact but didn't otherwise seem affected. She kicked again and again, each as powerful as the last, the stone flaking further and further. With each kick came another *kiai* that resonated somewhere deep inside Çeda.

Above, the veiled forms had moved to engage the suspended Blade Maiden, who was holding herself with one hand against the lip of the stone wall, legs spread wide, the sides of her feet somehow gaining purchase. The men wielded curving shamshirs against her, but the Maiden's ebon blade met their blows with frightening ease.

The gathered merchants and patrons were only now starting to understand what was happening. Children cried in fear, flocking toward their parents like goslings. A group of men were heaving their weight against the timbers in an attempt to push their way out, to no avail. A woman had taken out a studded cudgel, but seemed to have no idea what to do with it.

Amidst all the madness, the lord the Maidens protected stood with such tranquility it made Çeda go cold. A man from the eastern end of the city might demand an escort of two Maidens, but how rare for one of those lordlings to be so calm. The man met Çeda's eyes, perhaps sensing her stare.

That was when Çeda realized how wrong she'd been.

He was not merely calm, but serene, utterly sure he was in no danger whatsoever.

This man was no visiting lord. He was one of the Twelve Kings.

Not ten paces from Çeda, in the scurry and scuttle of the spice market, a King of Sharakhai stood, disguising himself as some wealthy lord, though why he would do such a thing she had no idea.

The King looked away, back to the swordfight above. The Maiden had gained the parapet and was now trading blows with the men. Their swords rang like a blacksmith's hammer, the sound amplified in the enclosed space. Meanwhile, the other Maiden was kicking the wall over and over and over, falling into some arcane rhythm Çeda couldn't understand but could somehow sense. The stone upon which she centered her attentions crumbled further, cracks forming around its edges.

Without knowing when it had happened, Çeda realized she had her kenshar gripped tightly in her right hand. She took one step toward the King, preparing to charge, to run the knife across his throat. She hardly felt Emre grab her wrist—the one holding the knife—hardly felt him spinning her around to face him.

"What are you *doing?*" he hissed. "You'll be *killed.*"

Çeda broke his grip with a sharp lift and twist of her arm. He tried grabbing her again, but she snatched his wrist and spun him into a nearby corner—the only dry space that remained. "Stay back, Emre."

She'd only just turned back around when something bright entered her field of vision from above—a torch, dropping like a sliver of the sun. The torch touched the spreading pool of lamp oil, and flames spread from the point of impact with a *whoosh.* It shoved Çeda away, and she cringed from it lest she be burned by the initial burst.

I can still reach the King.

Behind her, she heard the crash of glass, the splash of liquid over carpet and cobblestones, the sound of screaming as people caught fire.

I can still reach him.

But her feet wouldn't move as flame licked across the

fort's interior, racing over anything the oil had touched. A
cart went up in an explosive burst. The fire moved quickly,
hungrily, creeping up walls, slipping like thieves along the
seams between the cobbles. More carts were engulfed as
those trapped tried to back away, screaming, eyes wide as
new moons. The flames did not discriminate; they embraced man and woman and child alike in a steadily ex-
panding wave.

Flames now roiled between her and the King. They
were thick, but she could take one leap . . .

But no. Gods above, it was too far. The flames too fierce.

Bakhi's chosen, we're all going to die in these flames,
Çeda thought, and yet it was the girl who had offered Çeda
a strip of scented wood that truly brought Çeda beyond her
thoughts of revenge. The girl had remained in place, petrified, next to Çeda, but now she rushed toward one of the
burning men.

"Papa!"

"No!" Çeda shouted.

She grabbed the girl and drew her back, pinning her
writhing arms just as something wet and heavy draped
over them. A strong arm reached around her waist and
pulled them both back. The three of them fell to the cobbles.

A carpet, she realized. Emre had soaked a carpet with
scented water and thrown it over them.

"Papa!" the girl screamed, fighting even harder to get
away.

"It's too late," Çeda said, putting her hand over the girl's
eyes to save her from the horror. The girl continued to
struggle—and how could Çeda blame her?—but Çeda held
her tight, refusing to relax.

As Emre pulled the carpet low to protect them from the
growing heat, Çeda peered through the still-dripping
fringe. Wherever the oil had splashed or pooled, yellow
flames now coughed black smoke, occluding the air, making it difficult to breathe, even beneath the carpet. One
man tried jumping from a cart to one of the exposed
beams, as the Maiden had. He managed to grasp it, but
slipped and fell onto another cart, knocking several of the

glass globes, which fell and shattered, momentarily spreading the flames in hypnotic blue-green whorls. A woman tried to douse the flames on a young boy even while aflame herself. Some few closer to Çeda tried to copy what Emre had done until two men—both burning and screaming—began fighting over one of the sopping carpets.

In the corner where the King had been standing, the Maiden was shoving him through the hole she'd forced through the old stone. The flames caught up with her just as the King's legs and feet were lost from view. The Maiden had been doused so heavily by the splashing oil she lit like a newborn sun, but she didn't follow her King. By Goezhen's sweet kiss, she knelt down and replaced the stone she'd worked free to allow his escape. The fit was imperfect, but it would prevent the flames from following the King, who'd been doused nearly as heavily as the Maiden. Only when the stone had been set back in place did she roll away in agony.

Çeda stared at the black gaps around the stone. A King now lay on the other side, crawling away, vulnerable.

Her chance had come and gone in the span of moments.

Dear gods, the heat felt strong enough to burn them even beneath the carpet. The smoke became so thick it scoured Çeda's mouth and throat, and she coughed uncontrollably, which only served to make it worse. Those who weren't screaming were coughing as badly as she was; she worried that she and Emre and anyone else who'd managed to avoid the fire would die from the choking smoke. Through the fringe, she began looking for ropes among the stalls and wagons—perhaps she could tie it to a makeshift hook and cast it up to the ramparts—but moments later sounds came from the barrier behind them as the heavy wooden barricade rolled back and a dozen Silver Spears filed through the archway. They waved people out toward safety, helping some to stagger free of the blaze, throwing blankets over others in a vain attempt at dousing the flames.

Soon Çeda was lifted up and led out of the inferno toward the shaded aisles of the market proper, which now felt cold as ice. The girl came with her, shivering horribly, those green eyes staring up at Çeda with a wide-eyed numbness that echoed everything Çeda was feeling.

She and Emre were questioned by the Spears for a time, but Seyhan came and vouched for them both, and they were soon allowed to leave.

All the while, the only thing Çeda could think was what a coward she'd been. "You couldn't have done a thing," Emre said late that night when they reached their simple three-room home.

You're wrong, Çeda thought. *I could have killed a King.* "I can't talk," she said, heading for her own room, "not now."

She lay awake long into the night, replaying everything that had happened, what she might have done differently. The attack, she had no doubt, had been orchestrated by the Al'afwa Khadar, the Moonless Host. They were men and women from Sharakhai or the desert wastes who'd sworn to fight the Kings. She wondered how long that one attack had been in the making. Months, surely. Perhaps years. Not only would they have had to know that one of the Kings disguised himself to walk as a commoner among the streets of Sharakhai, they would've had to know his patterns as well. How often he went, by which routes, and how many would guard him.

It was times like this, when Çeda came near the Kings in some way, or returned to the foot of Tauriyat where her mother had been hung, that she felt so impotent she could scream it for all of Sharakhai to hear. The Kings left their House so very rarely. And here she had stumbled across one, almost defenseless, and she'd failed to honor her vow to her mother. Even if she'd somehow found the courage to try, she had no doubt she would have died at the hands of one of the Blade Maidens. They saw into the hearts of man. How could *she* hope to stand against them?

She fell asleep wondering when the King's response would come. Surely it would, and surely it would not be kind—the one thing that could be counted on in Sharakhai was that in the currency of vengeance, the Kings paid early, they paid in kind, and they paid with ample interest.

The next morning, as the Silver Spears continued their nightlong sweep through the western quarter for intelligence, Çeda heard a roar far to the west. She stood from her breakfast of bean salad and bread and threaded her way west from her home. The sound grew ever louder until it shook the foundations of the city. Soon she came to Hallowsgate, one of the twelve fortresses spaced along the city's outer curtain wall and the one situated due west of Tauriyat and the House of Kings, at the terminus of the street known as the Spear. Hundreds of Silver Spears were stationed along the wall, staring down impassively, their faces lost beneath the shade of their conical helms, sun shining brightly off steel-tipped arrows, ready against the strings of their short, curving bows.

Çeda could spare little thought for them, however. As she stared at the fortress walls, her world was reduced to the forms hanging by ropes from the battlements. Girls, Çeda realized. All girls. Two dozen. She counted them with morbid fascination. Their throats were cut, their bodies left to bleed down the sides of the tower like gutted rabbits. The bodies and the blood read like some ancient scroll: *Assail our walls,* they said, *and thine is the blood that shall flow; harm but one of our daughters, and twenty and four of thine own shall drown in their wake.* Seeing it so starkly written, Çeda realized it could be no other way. The Blade Maidens were the daughters of the Kings, after all—each and every one, firstborn of the Kings, taking up the blade at an age no older than these slain girls, to protect not only their own, but the city the gods themselves had granted their fathers.

Çeda stared at each body in turn, giving them a remembrance, a promise, especially the last. The little perfume girl with jet black hair and eyes like jade. What had *she* done to the Kings? Nothing. But she'd been there. She'd been present and had survived. That had been enough for the Kings to choose her. Or maybe it had simply been bad luck. A girl in the wrong place at the wrong time, not once but twice.

The anger and sorrow seething within threatened to overwhelm her—as it already had for so many others weeping at the tower's base. But Çeda refused to give in. She refused to cry. Instead, she stifled the rage, buried it deep inside her and let it burn with all her other regrets.

Then she turned and walked away.

She had no use for the dead, nor they for her.

Chapter 4

Sunrise over the Great Shangazi was an achingly beautiful sight—a burst of amber and ochre and rust, a panoply of shadows engraved against the lee of the rolling dunes—yet Çeda was blind to the beauty of it all, for her mother had gone deadly silent again.

Çeda was a skinny girl of eight hard summers, and she was sitting on a thwart within the confines of a skiff—a deceptively lithe skiff her mother, Ahya, had paid dearly to hire. The only sounds to fill the predawn desert were the sighs of the skimwood runners over the golden sand—that and the occasional *shush* as Ahya leaned into the tiller, sending the rudder to cutting the sand while the skiff leaned this way or that. The air was chill enough to make Çeda hug herself and shiver, but she said nothing of it. The desert's pledge of unending heat was rarely broken, and soon, whatever her lingering memories of the biting wind, they would be lost beneath the sun's brutal, unyielding stare.

Neither Çeda nor her mother had said a word to one another since their journey began. Çeda yearned to coax her mother into talking about the reasons behind their sudden and unexplained flight from the Amber City, but she had long since learned that to push her mother at the wrong time would have the opposite effect. Her mother could be incredibly mule-like that way.

At the very least she wanted to understand the fears that drove her mother so. And fear she did. Çeda could see it in her mother's bearing—as stiff as the thwart upon which she sat—and in the eagle-eyed way she watched the sands ahead, adjusting the tiller and occasionally glancing up at the sail but never looking at Çeda. Grim lines of worry and toil were etched into the corners of her eyes—eyes that were so often fierce, but on this strange day were heavy with exhaustion and a disquiet that bordered on panic.

As tired and worried as Ahya may be, though, she sailed onward, chin set stoically, her long black hair caught by the wind like a pennant set for war. Her mother was nothing if not driven.

For a moment, Çeda could think of little but the way Ahya, in preparation for another of her clandestine forays, had fallen asleep in their shared bed well before sundown the night before. Ahya's sleep had been fitful. Several times she'd called out Çeda's name, long and slow—*Chaaay-daaa, Chaaay-daaa*—with such sorrow it had made Çeda want to hold her mother and weep. She hadn't had the heart to wake her, but she had laid down behind Ahya, body to body, stroking her hair and wondering what wicked fears had been given life inside her dreaming mind.

Ahya had woken at dusk and left for many hours, returning only when the twin moons had set. She'd rushed into their hovel wearing her black dress and veil—not so different from what the Blade Maidens wore—and barked at Çeda to pack some clothes while she stuffed food and water into a bag, enough to sustain them for a day or two in the desert. Strangely, she'd also insisted on packing their books—the ones that had always moved with them from place to place, without fail. After changing into a dress that wouldn't get her killed were she to be caught wearing it, they were out and into the city with Çeda desperately wanting to know more.

In this, however, Ahya had trained her daughter well. They'd moved on short notice before—a dozen times at least that Çeda could remember—and Ahya had always insisted that Çeda remain silent until they'd reached a place where there was time to explain.

They'd gone to the sandy western harbor well before first light and paid good coin to hire this skiff, not to mention a healthy dose of prudence from the handsome, dark-skinned man who owned it. Ahya had struck a northerly course upon leaving the harbor, sailing them swiftly away from the Amber City of Sharakhai—the city whose cramped and twisted streets harbored endless thousands, the city that had instilled such fear in Ahya, she'd rushed them from their home in the starlit hours of the night.

"You went to the desert last night," Çeda said, unable to take the silence one moment longer. "Was it to collect more petals?" She said this knowing something else entirely had happened, but she had to get her mother to say something. Anything.

Ahya pulled on the tiller, making the skiff lean around a blunt black stone. "I went to the desert, but found no petals. Not this night." Çeda was going to ask what she *had* found, but her mother met her gaze and shook her head, an indication that she wasn't ready to speak. Not yet.

Only when they had navigated the last of the standing stones near Sharakhai, and the sand had opened up, did Ahya tie the tiller in place with two lengths of rope and face Çeda at last. She stared at her as *other* mothers looked upon their children—not with a frown, or with unkind eyes and a biting command, but with simple compassion; it was a thing Çeda so rarely saw she immediately understood that this voyage was far more serious than she'd guessed. Reluctantly, it seemed to Çeda, Ahya tugged one of her few prized possessions free from inside her dress: a silver locket, roughly the size and shape of a lantern's flame.

Her mother cupped the locket in her lap, hiding it from the wind. After prizing it open, she liberated two dried flower petals from within its folds, each white with a tip of palest blue. They'd been harvested by Ahya weeks ago from the night blooms of the adichara—twisted and wickedly thorned trees that only spread their flowers to the face of the twin moons. Her trespass was a thing expressly forbidden by the Twelve Kings of Sharakhai, but this wasn't what concerned Çeda; her mother had been liberating petals from the blooming fields since before she was born. Nor was it the fact that her mother was granting her a petal; she'd done so many times before, most often the day following the holy night of Beht Zha'ir. It was the fact that this was no mere fragment measured for a child, as it had always been before. No, this time it was an entire petal.

Why? she wondered. *Why now? And why here?*

"Open," her mother said, waving the petal near Çeda's mouth.

The petal eased her mind not at all, for it meant that Ahya thought this day important—important enough to give Çeda an entire petal; important enough to shape Çeda's life in some way—and it was with this realization that Çeda pieced together the clues at last.

"We're going to see the witch, aren't we?"

Her mother waved the petal again, ignoring her words. Afraid to disobey but every bit as afraid to comply, Çeda opened her mouth wide. With clear reverence, Ahya set one petal under Çeda's tongue while placing the other beneath her own. She watched Çeda carefully, though what she was hoping to see Çeda couldn't begin to guess.

Çeda felt the changes that always came over her, but this time to a much higher degree. Her tongue tingled. Her lips soon after. The skin of her face, the tips of her fingers, the soles of her feet. Even the place behind her navel—the place, her mother always said, where Çeda's shouts should come from when swinging a sword—came alive with the dizzying verve these petals granted. Her mouth filled with spit, forcing her to swallow constantly. Her hearing became sharper. The shush of the skimwood runners over the sand became raucous. Her mother's breathing sounded loud in her ears. She could hear the whine of a maned wolf pup far in the distance. She swore she could even feel the adichara trees that ringed the city, the trees from which her mother had harvested this very petal.

She felt more alive than ever before. As if she could take

down one of the mangy bone crushers she'd seen prowling the desert as they'd left Sharakhai by morning's light. As if she could leap from the skiff and chase the sister moons, follow them until they set along the edge of the world. There was nothing she couldn't do. And yet her mother looked at her ruefully, as if this were a test Çeda had already failed. Why, she had no idea. Her mother had often given her petals the morning after Beht Zha'ir, but there had been other times too: on the eve of Çeda's birthdays; on Beht Tahlell, the night the goddess Nalamae had touched her crooked finger to the sands of the Great Shangazi, creating the River Haddah and granting life to the desert; sometimes she even gave Çeda a bit of the petals when they danced with blades. Why, then, would she give Çeda a petal now and then frown when it filled her with golden light?

"Tell me," Çeda said, if only to shake that look from her mother's face. Ahya set her jaw stiffly, muscles working along gaunt cheeks. She was stubborn, but Çeda was her mother's child. "Are we going to see the witch?"

"Saliah isn't a witch," Ahya said finally, perhaps allowing that it was time for Çeda to know more of her secrets now that they were well out onto the sands and removed from those who might hear, including the King of Whispers.

Çeda begged to differ. Everyone knew that Saliah could peer beyond the day and into one's future, could cast spells if mood and need conspired to suit. Çeda smothered her biting reply, though. Her mother looked tense as the string of a tanbur—*more* tense, as if she might snap at any moment.

"Are you going to sell her petals?" Çeda asked, hoping it was true, and that they could leave quickly. For some reason, she now feared the future.

"Never you mind."

"I'm eight, Memma. I'm old enough to know."

With a reproachful look, her mother pulled her eyes away from the dunes ahead and stared into Çeda's eyes. She burst into a fit of nervous laughter, a thing tempered only by the feelings of dread and doubt that were clearly roiling inside her. Then the feelings seemed to break, and she leaned back and laughed, good and long, the sound of it bathing the bright desert sky. It seemed in that moment as if all the tension from the morning and from the night before shed from Ahya's frame and left her a woman reborn. She took Çeda's hand and kissed it three times. "Perhaps you are, Çedamihn, but I'll not tell you. Not yet. Not until I've spoken with her."

Çeda was glad to make her mother laugh—it was a beautiful sound, so seldom heard—but all too soon the weight that had been building along her shoulders these past many months returned, heavier than before, and Ahya was stiff on her thwart once more, hand on the tiller, watching the way ahead with grimly set eyes as the wind bowed the sail of their sun-bleached skiff.

"You'll be a good girl for your mother, won't you?" Ahya asked without looking at Çeda.

Çeda thought at first she was speaking of their visit with Saliah, but her look was much too grave for that.

In the span of a heartbeat, Çeda realized what her mother was planning to do. In the span of another, all thoughts of the desert witch vanished, and her world was reduced to herself, her mother, and this sandborne skiff.

Ahya was going to leave Çeda there. She was going to leave her with Saliah and go somewhere, a place from which she thought she might never return.

Çeda was desperate to press, to ask where she was planning to go and why she would leave Çeda behind, but just then all she wanted to do was show that she *would* be a good girl, so she nodded.

"You'll read the books I've given you," Ahya went on. It wasn't a question, nor even a request, but a fervent hope.

"I will."

"Practice what I've taught you of sword and shield. I've never said so, but we both know you are gifted. Never take that for granted. Do you understand? And if you ever have need, you'll go to Dardzada, and he'll help."

Dardzada was an apothecary who lived in Sharakhai's rich eastern end. Her mother took her to him from time to time, sold things to him—perhaps the petals she collected from the twisted adichara trees. The two of them would speak sometimes in the back room of his shop while Çeda was left to sit out front on a stool, told to *touch nothing*. He was always so cruel to Çeda, asking when she'd last bathed and telling her if she so much as looked at his plants he'd sell her to the wandering tribes. Why by the gods' sweet breath would her mother tell her to seek help from *Dardzada?*

Her mother must have known what she was thinking, for she went on. "He is blood of your blood, Çedamihn."

"He isn't, either!" Çeda said, hoping to trample the very thought with her words.

"He is," Ahya replied calmly. "And you'll understand that one day."

As they continued, Çeda begged herself to voice her fears, to ask her mother what she was planning to do. To ask her to stop. But she felt as though voicing them would make them real—that if she were to speak a word of it, it would make her mother do exactly what she feared most—and the more leagues that passed, the more she thought how foolish it would be to question her mother. Ahya had done dangerous things before, hadn't she? She often went out on Beht Zha'ir, a night upon which it was forbidden for anyone but the immortal Kings and the Blade Maidens to step foot in the streets. She had done so again just last night. She would leave wearing her black fighting dress. Some days she would come home none the worse for the wear, but on others she would return with cuts and scrapes and bruises that Çeda would dress under her mother's sharp instructions.

She'd flouted the laws of Sharakhai beneath the noses of the Twelve Kings for years and lived to tell the tales. She was a woman who knew what she was about, and she would come home safe. Tonight and every other night. Çeda knew it would be so.

Well after the sun had risen, a lone feature appeared on the horizon: a tall stone column that rose like an accusing finger pointing crookedly at a sky of cobalt blue. When they came nearer, Ahya pulled at the tiller and pointed them due west, and they chased the shadow of their sail several more hours. Çeda watched the horizon closely. She sat higher, wondering when it would appear.

And yet it was the chimes she noticed first. The chimes, so clear and musical, that lay just on the edge of hearing.

Like a dream, she realized.

They reminded her of her dreams.

Dreams she had forgotten until that very moment. And then, as if she were dreaming even now, Saliah's home rose from the sands. It was little more than a mudbrick house with a walled garden, but it looked magical out here in the desolate plains of the desert.

They stopped before they reached the solid stone upon which Saliah's home had been built, and then, in silent concert, Ahya gathered Çeda's bag of clothes and books, while Çeda drew the sail into an efficient bundle atop the boom. Ahya dropped the anchor—a heavy stone tied to a rope to keep their skiff from slipping away in the wind. Before stepping onto the rust-colored stone, Ahya picked up a fistful of sand. She raised it to her lips and whispered a prayer, allowing the sand to fall in a windborne stream. Whatever it was she was asking the desert gods to do, Çeda couldn't say, nor would she wish to. Such words were sacrosanct, meant only for the god to whom they were addressed.

Çeda reached down and picked up her own fistful of sand, lifting it and letting it sift through her slowly opening fingers. "Please, Nalamae," she whispered, "guide my mother, this day if no other."

Saliah was waiting for them near her door. She was a handsome woman. And how tall! She stood at least a full head taller than Ahya. In one hand, she held a crook with gemstones worked into the curling head; her other hand stroked the long braid of her hair, which hung over her shoulder and down her chest. She watched Ahya and Çeda approach, but she seemed to be looking *through* them, not *at* them.

"Who comes?" Saliah asked.

"It is Ahyanesh. And I've brought my daughter. May we speak, Saliah Riverborn? I bring to you a matter most grave."

"A matter most grave . . ."

"I would not have come otherwise."

Saliah considered as the chimes continued to ring from

the nearby garden. The time grew uncomfortably long, but at last, Saliah nodded and turned toward Çeda, her eyes staring well over Çeda's head, as if she couldn't see at all. She held her hand out, and although Çeda was afraid to take it, she did so, feeling compelled, though she couldn't explain why or how.

"Can you wander in the garden, little one?" Saliah asked.

"Wait—" Ahya called, her eyes wide at this seemingly innocent request. "Çeda?"

Saliah paused, tilted her head ever so slightly toward Ahya. "A matter most grave, you said."

"I did, but—"

"Then it must be Çeda," Saliah replied easily.

Ahya considered her daughter, then glanced to the garden wall, then stared at Saliah, her eyes imploring. "Why not me?"

"Because she is the one who will be wrapped in the cloak of your decisions. Because it is easier to sense hidden things when you look at that which lies nearest, not the thing itself. Go, now, Çedamihn. Let your mother and me talk." Saliah released Çeda's hand, then turned, regal as a queen, and strode toward her home. "Why don't you see if the acacia will speak to you?" She was soon lost to the deeper shadows of the entryway.

"Go," Ahya said with a frown, guiding Çeda by the shoulder and shoving her toward the stone wall and the archway that led to the garden.

Çeda didn't understand what had just happened, but she felt suddenly relieved to be free to wander. As worried as she'd been in the desert, Saliah's home felt like an oasis, a sheltering cave when the sandstorms came.

If anyone might help my mother, Çeda thought, *it would be Saliah.*

Çeda had wandered this place before, but as it had been with the chimes, the memories returned only after she'd passed through the arched entryway and into the garden proper.

It was wondrous. Outside, the desert had been quiet save for the chimes that tickled the very edge of her hearing, but inside, new sounds came alive. Birds with bright beaks flitted among the bushes and across the path that wound through them. They chirped and chirruped and called all sorts of songs to the inexplicably humid air. The orchestral sound made Çeda think of the River Haddah in the throes of spring, when the reeds were thick with nesting wrens and larks and wagtails. And the smells! Floral and fragrant and fecund. Valerian mixed with Sweet Anna mixed with the surprisingly acrid scent of golden-bells. And beneath it all an aged smell redolent of shaved amber. It made Çeda wonder if the world hadn't been born in this very place. It was wonderful, and did much to ease the dark mood brought on by the voyage here.

In the center of the garden towered an enormous acacia, its branches spread like a protective grandmother. Despite the way it dwarfed the garden's wall, the tree hadn't been visible until she'd passed through the garden's gate. Çeda walked to the base of it, looked up at its green leaves and the many-colored shards of glass that hung from its branches.

See if the acacia will speak to you, Saliah had said. Çeda knew Saliah would read the sound of the chimes when people came to her. But Çeda had no such abilities. *That* would take the skill of someone like the desert witch, someone who knew the inner workings of the world.

Wouldn't it?

Dozens of birds flew among the branches, but they never touched the chimes, nor the delicate golden threads that held them in place. The chimes were not low enough for her to touch, but she wished they were.

It felt blasphemous, but the urge to climb the tree was strong and growing stronger by the moment. Saliah had given her permission, hadn't she? Çeda swallowed, licked her lips, then stole a glance at the entryway. She could hear her mother and Saliah speaking softly, and with her senses heightened by the petal, some of their words carried.

"I've found four of their poems," Ahya said.

"Four is not twelve," Saliah replied.

"It is a start."

"It doesn't seem wise, despite what you've told me."

"Then show me another way!" her mother pleaded.

"It isn't so simple as you might think, and there is more to consider than mere Kings."

"So you've said. But the Kings must fall."

"I don't dispute it," came Saliah's reply.

"Then what else? What else can there be?"

Çeda lost some of the conversation as she rounded the tree and was startled by two yellow-crested birds fluttering from a nearby bush. She stared up through the branches toward the blue desert sky, watching the chimes catch the light in a thousand different colors.

"Take her," Ahya said. "Take her, and I'll return, or another will come."

"Patience," came Saliah's deep voice. "I would listen to the chimes."

Çeda heard nothing after that, and she had the distinct impression that it had been Saliah's will that had allowed her to hear as much as she had, and Saliah's will that had caused it to suddenly stop. This was, after all, her home, which meant much to those of godsblood. And there was no doubt in Çeda's mind that Saliah *was* one of those ancient people, descended from the first gods themselves. What else could explain her power?

Çeda waited for a time, peering up through the branches. She'd completed a full circuit of the tree. After one last huff of a breath, she jogged toward it, leapt off a round stone near its base, and swung herself easily around the lowest bough. She climbed higher, staying near the trunk to avoid the slim thorns of the smaller branches. As she neared the uppermost, she noticed the chimes were ringing differently. They sounded more urgent, somehow. More desperate.

She listened for some time, haunted by the changing notes that reminded her of the sounds the sandstorms made when they blew through Sharakhai. She hung upside down on a branch for a moment, but it suddenly felt very, very wrong, so she pulled herself up and examined the chimes instead.

She saw visions within their bright reflections. Momentary things, like silverscales flitting below the surface of a

river, there one moment, gone the next. She saw a woman's
callused hand, pierced and bleeding along the thumb. She
saw a beetle with iridescent wings land on a blindingly
bright flower. She saw a woman in a diaphanous orange
dress, dancing in the desert, sand flying high as she spun
and kicked. She saw ebon swords raised in triumph, women
in black fighting dresses charging over the dunes. She saw
a man with oh-so-familiar eyes wearing the elegant garb of
a desert shaikh. She saw this and much, much more, but
she understood none of it.

One vision, especially, confused her. She was standing
before a King. Or she thought he was a King. He had piercing eyes, wore a golden crown and fine raiment, and he
stood in a hall of endless opulence. The King's dark eyes
were intent, almost proud. He held a shamshir made of
ebon steel in one hand, with a mark etched into the blade
near the cross guard. The mark was a circular design of
reeds at the edge of a river. She could almost see the herons wading through it, hunting for scarletgills. The strangest thing about the vision was not the King, nor the sword,
nor even the fact of her in audience with one of the twelve
immortal rulers of Sharakhai. It was that the King was
holding the sword out for her to take.

She was so captured by this vision she didn't at first notice she was being watched. When she peered beyond the
branches, she saw Saliah's tall frame standing in the archway, staff in hand, through the golden threads and glinting
chimes. Ahya stood two paces back, her face expectant,
even hopeful. Saliah's face, however, was infinitely different. She looked neither angry, nor kind; instead she was
staring through the branches with an expression of awe, as
if she were gazing into the eyes of Tulathan herself.

Saliah held her right hand out, made a fist several times,
turning it over to expose the palm of her hand, then the
back, then her palm again. She swallowed and seemed to
regain a bit of herself. "Come down, child." Her words
mingled with the chimes, as if they were long-lost cousins.
"Come down now."

Unbidden, Çeda's limbs began to shake. She knew without knowing how that Saliah's sightless eyes had seen the

same things she had, but where Çeda was nothing but a bumbling child, Saliah knew how to read such things. The question was, what could she have seen that would upset her so?

With reverent care, Çeda wound down through the limbs, and when she dropped to solid ground, she saw that Saliah was crying.

"Is it true?" Çeda asked. "Will I wield an ebon blade?"

Ahya's eyes went wide. She swallowed hard, her gaze flitting between Çeda and Saliah. She was waiting for Saliah's answer but was clearly afraid to hear it.

Before Çeda could ask what was wrong, Saliah turned and strode toward her home. "There's no room for Çeda here."

Ahya glanced from Çeda to Saliah's retreating form and back, several times, a woman suddenly lost in a maelstrom. "Please," she called, "there is more we must—"

"Leave," Saliah repeated.

"If you could only watch her for a short while—"

Saliah stopped and spun. She thumped her staff against the stone. The sound of it was low, and it went on and on and on, as if the desert itself were nothing more than a vast skin drum. "There are many paths we might take in this world, and in the next, but for you, Ahyanesh Ishaq'ava, this is no longer one of them. Now take your child and leave this place."

Saliah turned and strode away, her form swallowed by the shadows of her home.

Leaving Çeda and Ahya alone.

Utterly alone.

Ahya turned numbly toward Çeda. It was strange how striking she looked just then. Piercing brown eyes, raven hair blowing in the breeze. She was not angry, simply dumbfounded. It seemed strange to say, but she looked as though her cares had been washed away, as if there were no true choices left, leaving the path ahead that much clearer. But then she snatched Çeda's wrist and dragged her back toward the skiff.

Chapter 5

TWO STORIES UP, on the edge of the mudbrick roof of her home, Çeda rested on the balls of her feet, watching the alley that ran drunkenly from her house, up through the center of the bazaar, and on toward the Trough, the city's central and largest thoroughfare. The wind might be gentle among the sheltered streets of Sharakhai, but up here it was strong enough to tug at the black thawb she wore, and the dust from the desert was thick enough that she'd pulled the veil of her turban across her face. Her mother's silver locket hung around her neck, a weight that this night of all nights tugged heavily on her heart.

The sun still glowed a brilliant and burnished gold along the western horizon, but the rest of the sky was a field of stars scattered across a vast cloth of inky blue. Most nights the city would be loud with the sounds of hawkers in the bazaar, of children running the streets, of wagons rattling along the Trough, but not tonight. Tonight the city was boneyard quiet. Tonight the city was boneyard still. For this was the night of the reaping, the night the asirim would steal into the city like dark hounds, baying and hunting for souls.

Beht Zha'ir came once every six weeks, when the twin moons were full, and when it did, the city transformed from a thing bright and alive to the cowering beast Çeda saw before her. Not a single lamp in the great city was lit. Not a single word was uttered. Neither was expressly forbidden, but none would risk them for fear of luring the asirim to their home. Even the highborn, who considered it the highest of honors to be chosen, would follow custom. They would stand vigil in darkness, praying silently to the desert gods for favor until the sun rose once more. Even on Tauriyat, the hill where the Kings lived in their palaces, no lights shone, and none save the Reaping King and his deadly Maidens would venture out.

And Emre still had not come home. He was out there, somewhere—who knew where?—perhaps in trouble, perhaps wounded. Perhaps dead.

"Hurry," she whispered, a word she hoped was carried on the wind to the gods of the desert themselves.

As she watched the alley intently, she wondered with a morbid and growing fascination whether the asirim would be attracted to Emre's fear. They might. She'd never strayed near enough to one of them to find out. She'd never even *seen* one. Not clearly, anyway. Just a shadow in the night years ago, a crooked form lumbering through the city like a wounded dog.

With full night so near, she could no longer see into the deeper shadows, and she would be unable to until the moons were higher.

"Nalamae's teats, come *home*, Emre."

And yet despite her pleas, the city grew darker, the moons crept higher in the sky, and the lane below lay achingly empty. She ought to go inside. She ought to wait. She'd be a fool to search for him on a night like tonight. She knew he'd gone to the southern harbor to pick up the package, but she had no idea where he might have gone from there. She couldn't abandon him, though. She would never do that to Emre.

The two of them had waited throughout the day for Osman to send word, for someone to give them the location for the pickups. She and Emre—both of them as edgy as they ever were when preparing for a shade—drank sparingly of water and pecked at a dish she'd made of saffron rice and raisins and pine nuts. Emre had whiled away the time, telling her of a Malasani bravo who'd come to the spice stall last night to try the vinegar peppers that Seyhan kept in clay jars beneath the spice tables.

"Said he'd heard of them," Emre had said with a cat's wide smile, his eyes distant. "He *demanded* one. Said I must give him the hottest peppers I could find. He left *crying*, Çeda. Crying and searching for anyone who would offer up a bit of water. But not a single one would, not even when he flashed gold."

Çeda knew that every spice merchant kept water behind their stalls, but they wouldn't have taken to a brash easterner pretending he knew more than everyone in the desert combined.

"They all smiled," Emre went on, "and said to him, *the gods' blessing be upon you, but I have none.* He left, and I tell you true, his face was bright as the sun, tears were streaming down his cheeks like a little boy who lost his mother. He's probably *still* crying from it."

Çeda had laughed ruefully, knowing the real reason the merchants hadn't spared the Malasani a bit of water. None of them would have breathed a word of it to Emre, but they all knew of his painful history with Malasani bravos. Still, as quiet as they might be about it, they would always take Emre's side. That they would surely do.

"You're cruel and petty," Çeda had said, "all of you."

But Emre had brushed off her disapproval like sand from the deck of a ship. "The Malasani can die a thousand deaths before I'd care about a single one of them."

And Çeda had left it at that, not wanting to tug on the stitches of a wound that, some days, still seemed half-healed.

Two hours before sunset, Tariq had come to their home, all cocky bravado, arms across his chest, talking down to them as if he owned Roseridge. Tariq was one of Osman's street toughs, a boy she and Emre had both run the alleys with when they were growing up in Sharakhai's west end.

"Two packages," he'd said. "Çeda goes first. Emre, you'll wait here until she's gone."

Tariq had ordered Emre to another room and given Çeda her assignment. She was to go to a distillery east of the city's northern harbor, and she'd soon set out wearing a long abaya and a hijab to cover her head and face—plus two sheathed fighting knives strapped to her calves should she run into trouble—which ostensibly left Emre alone with Tariq.

As soon as she'd slipped down an alley, though, she circled back. Neither Tariq nor Osman would be pleased, but she and Emre had long ago agreed that they would let one another know where they were headed in case anything went wrong. She climbed the narrow three-story building opposite their home and peeked over the stone lip that ran along the roof's edge. Emre had come to the window and leaned on the sill for a moment. His right hand hanging outside, he had pointed down—south—then flattened his hand like a sail, indicating the drop was in or very near the southern harbor.

She'd waited for Emre to stand and adjust the curtains, at which point she pointed up, north, and waved her hand like a leaf blowing in the wind, an indication she was headed to the rich green plantations fed from the Kings' aqueduct. She'd left for her pickup immediately.

Behind the distillery's ox mill she'd met a man of indistinct origin. His skin was dark like the Kundhunese, but his face looked more like the highlands of Mirea. He was a tall, distinguished sort, with dark clothes and midnight hair pulled back into a long tail. He'd given her a small ivory canister in a leather satchel, which she took to a hovel in the middle of the Shallows, an area with cramped streets and homes stacked upon homes, an area she didn't like staying in for any length of time, that very few in Sharakhai liked staying in for any length of time, even those who lived there. It was a dangerous place, but she reached the hovel in little enough time and was let in by an old, bony woman with wrinkles so deep she looked as though she'd been left in the desert to dry since the founding of Sharakhai. No sooner had Çeda stepped inside than the woman held out a grasping hand. She stared with a humorless, toothless grimace as Çeda held out the satchel, then snatched it away and shooed Çeda from her home. And that had been that, as simple as Osman had made it out to be.

These layers of subterfuge were not uncommon in the Amber City. There were many in Sharakhai who wished to speak to one another, to trade or do business, illicit or otherwise, but who refused to do so openly with the watchful Kings so near, particularly the King of Whispers, who, it was said, could hear one speak, particularly when you uttered words related to the business of the Kings. The men and women who played at these games of power knew that conducting business beneath the bright light of day was foolish, so they would hire men like Osman to ferry commands and money and conditions of trade, hoping, often successfully, to do business in the shadows instead, hidden from the watchful eyes of the Kings and their Maidens and, sometimes more importantly, the royal taxmen. And if it required that men like Osman be added to the ledger, well, that was just the cost of doing business in a city like Sharakhai. The risks might be considerable, but the chance to make money outweighed them.

And there was more to consider than mere money. The coin they paid to have someone like Çeda run their messages might be dear, but it provided a certain amount of insulation. If the Silver Spears or the Maidens managed to get their hands on one of the canisters, they would be unable to decipher the message inside without its necessary other half, and if they captured Çeda or another of Osman's shadows, she would know next to nothing. Even Osman himself—for his own protection as much as his patrons—would know nothing about the contents of the messages.

After leaving the woman's hovel, Çeda had walked away as though that were the end of it. Once out of sight, she slipped around the backside of a four-story tenement house, one of the few in the Shallows. It was grossly overcrowded—twelve to twenty in a flat—but she made use of an inset in the odd, blocky structure that was not only child's play to climb but hid her from prying eyes. Upon reaching the roof, she moved, swift and low, and lay down along its edge, watching the alley she'd just vacated.

This kind of spy work was a lucrative enough business, but it wasn't why Çeda had agreed to start running things for Osman. She liked keeping tabs on Sharakhai. She liked knowing who was talking to whom—an investment, she told herself, that might one day pay dividends.

Nearly an hour later, two men and a woman moved with purpose down the narrow street. Curving shamshirs in leather sheaths hung from their belts. Their light-colored thawbs and turbans blended into the mudbrick homes, and their veils hung free, twisting in the wind as they walked. They stepped inside the woman's hovel and left soon after, heading back the way they'd come. When they came to the nearest cross street, Çeda could see that the woman was carrying the same leather satchel Çeda had just passed to the old woman.

No sooner were they out of sight than Çeda descended to the streets and padded after them, through the Shallows, along the streets of the Well, and finally to Red Crescent, a neighborhood near the quays of the western harbor, the smallest and seediest of the city's four sandy harbors.

She hid in a recessed doorway when the three of them came to an alley. The woman, walking between the two men, paused and scanned the street behind her with a wariness that made it clear this wasn't her first time carrying packages. Apparently spotting nothing amiss, she followed the other two down the mouth of the alley.

Çeda gave them a bit of time—sensing their wariness would be heightened—then strode down the street, dusting her shoulder as she passed the alley, giving herself an opportunity to glance that way. Of the woman she could see no sign, but the two men were standing in a courtyard just beyond a peaked archway twenty paces down. It was no good trying to reach them that way, but there was another path.

She continued down the street to a bath house built for an ancient caravanserai that had once stood on this ground. Much of it had been torn down when the western harbor was built, but the bath house remained. The bath house alternated their days of patronage—women and girls one day, men and boys the next—and praise be to Tulathan, this was the women's day.

The attendant was a bored-looking boy wearing a blue kaftan. "The baths will be cooling by now," he told Çeda.

"It's all right," Çeda said, and handed two copper khet to the boy.

The boy shrugged, and with two clinks dropped the coins into a strongbox and handed Çeda a folded length of cotton. "Soap or pumice?" he asked, waving to a shelf that held a variety of each, for more coin.

Çeda shook her head and stepped toward the courtyard beyond the gates. As soon as she did, he went back to polishing a curving brass handle.

Four women and one young girl exited the bath house, laughing loudly as they took the steps down. Çeda headed toward the entrance, but the moment the group passed her, she strode with purpose to the corner of the ornate stone building. When she glanced back, the girl, the wind tugging at the ends of her long, damp hair, had turned to watch her. Çeda put her fingers to her lips, then ducked into the narrow space between the bath house and the wall that marked the perimeter of the grounds.

The two walls were close enough, and the brickwork rough enough, that she could easily gain purchase with hands and feet and press her way slowly up until she could grab the lip of the wall. When she reached the top, she heard a low murmur of voices coming from inside the bath house, but she could hear other voices more clearly now—the ones in the courtyard on the opposite side of this wall. She carefully lifted her head, seeing the three who had visited the hovel, plus one more. This man was tall and broad-shouldered. He wore a rich brown thawb, and two shamshirs hung from his belt. It was his forked beard, however, and the coiling tattoos of vipers wrapped around his forearms and wrists, that marked him as a man to be feared. His name was Macide Ishaq'ava, and he was the leader of the Moonless Host, a loose group formed from hundreds, perhaps thousands of members from the wandering folk, the twelve tribes that once ruled the entirety of the Shan-gazi Desert.

Everyone not simply passing through the city knew of Macide. Çeda had never met him, but she'd seen and heard of the types of things he left in his wake. The massacre at the perfume merchants' was but the most recent example. Years ago, the Host had reached a man who supplied a delicacy to the House of Kings: salted meat that came from rare mountain deer found in the southern ranges of the Great Shangazi. They'd poisoned it in hopes that the Kings would taste of it during their New Year feast. They hadn't, but eighteen of the highborn in attendance had, and they'd all perished from it. The Kings had not taken it lightly.

For the poisoning in their own house, they had poisoned dozens in return: men and women and children chosen randomly from the streets of Sharakhai—low born, recently come from the desert. The Kings had forced them to eat the same tainted meat, then thrown their bodies into the river so that all could see them on their way to the desert. Silver Spears lined the banks of the Haddah by the thousands, firing arrows upon those who dared to wade into the river to fetch the bodies.

In response, the Moonless Host abducted a young aspirant to the Blade Maidens, freshly chosen and not yet taken to the desert for her vigil. They staked her out on a sand dune and left her there to die. The Kings had found her and, in their rage, rounded up twenty-four girls—all roughly the same age as their young Maiden—and hung them by their feet on poles driven into the sand of the northern harbor. There they'd remained for twelve nights leaving them to die from thirst and exposure, the Maidens and Silver Spears watching carefully for anyone who would deny the Kings their message: that if the citizens of the city wouldn't give up the names of Sharakhai's enemies, then this is what would happen, blood for blood.

It was a vicious circle, fed at least in part by the man standing in the courtyard below.

Macide took the leather satchel from the woman and opened it, retrieving the scroll case hidden within. He examined it carefully, then turned the ivory rings that ran along its length to a certain combination, one that had surely been sent to him days or even weeks before. When he was satisfied, he cracked the wax seal at one end of the canister and pulled out a note written on parchment. Apparently pleased, he nodded and replaced the parchment inside the canister.

"Go," Macide said to the woman. "Fetch the second canister and meet me on the ship."

"Of course," she said, and then the four of them walked down the alley and were gone.

Çeda thought about following them, but she'd seen enough. She likely wouldn't learn more unless she could somehow get the parchment from Macide, but there wasn't time.

The sun was already low. Beht Zha'ir had nearly come to Sharakhai once more, and now that she knew the Moonless Host were involved, the urge to return home to make sure Emre had returned safe was strong and growing stronger. She had no real reason to worry, and yet she worried just the same.

Each and every step toward home had only amplified her fears, a thing helped not at all when she returned to an empty home. Soon the bright light of dusk had died along the horizon, and a chill swept over the city. The threat of the coming night grew like a festering wound, and all the while the threat of the asirim loomed ever larger.

Çeda was startled from her thoughts by shadows in the alley ahead. She stared, waiting breathlessly, but it was only a mongrel dog, followed closely by another, and then a third. They looked skittish, galloping along the street, slowing with hackles raised, then padding forward again. And then they were gone, leaving Çeda alone once more.

Emre wasn't coming, she realized. He wasn't coming because something had gone terribly wrong. She knew it as she knew the hot winds that blew through the desert. Resigned at last, she pulled the tail of her black turban from across her face and let it hang down her chest. With reverent care, she levered her silver locket open with her thumbnails, revealing a dried petal the color of bleached bone, with a tip of brightest blue.

It did not slip her notice how similar this all felt to the fateful day eleven years ago when her mother had taken her out on the sands. The day she'd visited Saliah, the desert witch. The day her life had changed forever. The day her mother had died.

Would her life change so much this night? Would she be forced to witness the death of another she cherished?

The petal felt light as moonlight as she picked it up and placed it carefully under her tongue. Jasmine and rosemary and mace mixed with the unmistakable floral scent of the adichara, the misshapen desert trees from which she'd harvested the petal. Her skin tingled. Her lips trembled. She heard a crisp sound, a wine-laced finger pulling a note from the rim of a crystal goblet. As she often did, she felt the blooming fields beyond the city, though this time it felt deeper, as if she could feel the hunger of the asirim.

In moments, her aches from the pits faded. Her hands shook. The very moons themselves seemed to shiver in the sky, and for a moment she felt as though she could feel the entirety of the city—every man, woman, and child as they huddled in their homes, fearful of the coming night, fearful of what would stalk from the desert and into this massive and wondrous city, born, however improbably, from the shifting sands of the Great Shangazi itself.

Çeda pulled her veil across her face and tucked the tail back into her turban. She gripped the hilt of her knife, a keen-edged kenshar, making sure it rested tightly in its sheath at her belt. She reached over her left shoulder and did the same with the wooden hilt of the shamshir strapped across her back. Then she leapt down to the exposed wooden beam that marked the space between the first and second floors and sprung forward, somersaulting down to the dry, dusty ground.

She struck a solid pace, heading through the old wall of Sharakhai—a wall that had long since been outgrown—and

down the winding lane toward the Trough, the broad street
that ran north to south, cutting the city almost perfectly in
half. From there, she would make for the southern harbor,
where Emre had been told to go. She'd not taken ten strides,
however, when a long wail settled over the city like a pall.
Another wail sounded soon after, higher and more desperate than the first. A shiver ran through her.

*By Tulathan's bright eyes, the asirim must be hungry
indeed to come so early. They usually don't come until well
after the moons have risen.*

Yet another wail, and it sounded like a laugh, as though
it knew she was out when she should have been locked safe
in her home.

The fourth sounded as though it were calling to her and
her alone. *Come*, it said. *Come, and we will lick thine skin.*

She ran harder, the vigor of the petal bearing her faster
than any man or woman in this city could manage. She
snaked her way through the empty stalls of the bazaar,
through the spice market beyond, and eventually came to
the edge of the Trough. She was exposed here, especially
under the brightness of Rhia and Tulathan, but none would
have the blankets over their windows pulled aside; none
would dare look out, not now that the asirim's jackal bays
were sounding over the city.

She passed the Way of Jewels, the Black Pillar, and Bent
Man, the ancient bridge that crossed the dry remains of the
River Haddah. Then, as she neared the slave block, she
abandoned the Trough for a shortcut to the southern harbor; a shortcut she and Emre had been using since they
were gutter wrens.

As she headed down a narrow alley, she trilled the call
of the amberlark: four rising notes followed by a long coo.
The calls of the asirim came louder. Some were close, she
realized. Very close.

One never knew the path they would choose. That fell
to the Reaping King and his whims. One never knew *how
many* would come, either. Some months it was a bare few;
on other nights their calls resounded throughout the city
from the rich eastern edges to the slums of the west end.

She trilled again, waiting, listening, fighting down the

urge to cower behind a barrel and wait for the night to pass as another asir called, this one much closer than the last.

Then she heard it, some distance away though clear enough—the call of another amberlark.

She knew it was Emre. But the call had been very weak, as if he'd barely managed it through his pain. Or fear. Or both.

The alley ended in a stone lip. Beyond was a canal that ran dry most of the year. The drop was steep, but she leapt with abandon, trusting to the adichara petal to strengthen her legs and dull the pain of her landing.

She trilled again, hearing no reply, but as she listened she *did* hear the sound of footsteps. They shuffled along the ground somewhere above her. She froze, breathless, sure that one of the asirim had found her.

Chapter 6

THE ASIR'S FOOTSTEPS ABOVE RECEDED, and Çeda's heart began to beat again. But then a hungry wail—an aching, utterly inhuman sound Çeda had never heard the likes of, even from the grisly asirim—broke the stillness. Çeda cringed, covered her ears with her hands. Somewhere, a door crashed in, and Çeda went rigid with fear. She couldn't catch her breath. A man with a croaking voice called fervent prayers to the twin moons with ever-increasing rapidity. "Choose me, Tulathan," he intoned, "that your light may shine upon me all the brighter. Choose me, Rhia, that I may serve the Kings in the farther fields."

Surely to that man, such prayers were not misplaced. In his eyes he would be would be a special place not only at the foot of the Kings, but of the first gods as well. So the Kannan, the book of laws penned by the Kings themselves, proclaimed. Çeda didn't know what to believe, nor did she care just then, for a moment later, a wet thud cut his voice short. After a time the footsteps approached her, as did an intermittent dragging sound.

Çeda crouched beneath the bridge. Made herself as small as possible.

She waited as the footsteps dragged over the stone

bridge above her. The shadow that fell onto the bed of the canal was close enough for her to reach out and touch, and it made her feel as though the asir could do the same to her. It never stopped its shambling gait, however, and it moved on, dragging the man it had been granted by the Reaping King out toward the blooming fields. Çeda's reaction was craven, but she couldn't think of the man's loss, only the relief at not being chosen as he had.

By the light of the moons she could see well along the canal but not what lay beneath the bridges. Those were nearly pitch black, and it took long, terror-filled moments for her eyes to penetrate that intense darkness. At last, she caught movement beneath the next bridge, only twenty paces farther on. It must be Emre. She wanted to go to him, but fear still rooted her in place.

Finally, when the dragging sounds had faded and her muscles had unseized, she ran low to the next bridge and, gods be praised, found Emre stretched out underneath, holding his side. In the moonlight a few paces farther sprawled a man wearing the simple clothes one would find in the desert and a turban that, even muted as it was beneath the light of the twin moons, was clearly red. Tattoos marked his forehead, the corners of his eyes, and the palms of his hands, tattoos that would tell—if one knew how to read them—the story not only of his life, but that of his family and his tribe. It was the turban, though, that marked him as someone from the desert. The tribesmen, if they chose to give up the life of wandering and settle in Sharakhai, were forbidden to wear red turbans or thawbs. Their women relinquished their bright red dresses and veils, embellished with beaten coins and golden embroidery. Any other colors were permitted, but red was set aside for those garbed for war. That was the price the Kings demanded for coming to their city, a sign that they had left their old lives behind, that their aggression lay behind them as well.

Why by the grace of the desert gods would one of the wandering tribes have come here? And why would he have attacked Emre?

She had no time to wonder further before a dark form

blurred before her very eyes. Something heavy crashed onto the dry bed of the canal. Another asir, she realized.

She shrank back into the shadows beneath the bridge. Her lips trembled as her mouth began to water at a strange, sickly sweet smell that filled the air. It reminded her of withered apples just starting to turn. It was all she could do not to turn and flee. But Emre was but a whisper away. She couldn't leave him.

The asir stalked forward and stooped down over the fallen man, running fingers with black nails over his chest. The thing had long, emaciated arms and legs, and its head looked somehow too large for its body. Its hair was stringy and hung in matted clumps about its shoulders. It looked, in fact, not so different from the starving children she had seen in the slums, except instead of the skin the color of ginger, the asir's was the mottled black of rotten fruit.

The asir leaned close. Çeda could hear it sniffing along the dead man's neck, and then, as quickly as it had come, the asir threw the limp form over its shoulder, climbed the nearby wall of the canal, and was gone.

Gods protect me, Çeda said to herself, waiting for the sounds of the asirim to fade. Then she knelt next to Emre and whispered to the darkness. "Emre."

For a moment she feared she was too late. He wasn't moving, and it seemed he was hardly breathing. If death hadn't already arrived, the lord of all things was surely on his way. But when she shook him again, he stirred and looked up at her. His eyes couldn't seem to focus. "Have you come to take me?"

"No, Emre. It's me. Are you all right?"

He blinked. His eyes narrowed in on hers at last. "Çeda?"

"Emre, are you hurt?"

His only reply was to raise his hand from his ribs and show her the blood that blackened his hand and forearm. Çeda was no stranger to blood, but her gut twisted in a thousand knots to see Emre like this, even more so from the look of innocence on his face, which reminded her of a boy not yet ready for the ways of the world.

"Can you stand?"

He grimaced and raised his arm. After she'd levered

him up to his feet and started to lead him away, he stopped her and said through gritted teeth, "The satchel."

"To the far fields with your bloody satchel."

"Get it, Çeda, or I'm as good as dead anyway."

It lay on the ground among the forgotten detritus of the spring rains. She picked it up—it was light, at least—and slung it over her shoulder. In a way it was good she had the satchel. It meant Emre had made the pickup at the southern harbor. He just hadn't been able to make the drop as planned. At least now she could get it back to Osman.

Together they headed southeast. It was the opposite direction from their home in Roseridge, but he'd never be able to climb out of the canal, and it only grew deeper the farther it wound toward the heart of the city. But ahead there was a log they'd seen a dozen gutter wrens levering into place in late spring—an easy way for them to get out if they ever needed it. Despite being an easy exit, the log was not overly thick, and it was difficult for Emre to find his balance. He resorted to straddling the log with Çeda pushing and supporting him from behind to get him up to ground level.

Once there, Çeda slipped Emre's arm over her shoulder. He sucked his breath through gritted teeth at the pain, but made no mention of it otherwise. He didn't have to. She could feel it in the way he moved, and she could feel his blood seeping through the light cloth of her thawb.

"We'll be home soon," she said, though it was far from the truth. At the speed they were going, it would take hours. She thought about stopping at someone's home, someone she could trust, and holing up for a day or two. But whom could she trust with *this?* No one. The chance of word spreading was simply too great, if not from the people she entrusted, then their children, or their neighbors, or their friends.

No, she had to get Emre home before the sun rose. Without aid.

As if sensing her discomfort, the asirim redoubled their calls, the long, mournful song of the dead for the living they were about to claim as their own.

Please, Rhia, guide me.

She'd no sooner pleaded to the goddess than Emre grew heavier. He was blacking out. The loss of blood, the effort of movement when his body wasn't ready for it. She tried to keep him up, and she might have been able to do so for a while with the petals' help, but what good would that do in the end? She couldn't carry him all the way home. She needed to find a cart—a mule too if she was able—and bring him home. She laid him down gently and turned to look for one. And that's when she saw dark movement ahead.

The blood drained from her face. Cold sweat gathered on her skin.

She should have moved faster. She should have carried Emre, taken him as far as she could before looking for a cart. But now it was too late, for one of the asirim stood in the road ahead, twenty paces away. Twenty paces, and it still seemed close enough to reach out and rake its blackened claws across her throat.

The urge to run was so strong that a child's whine escaped her. She wanted to flee, to scream, but she couldn't. She was rooted to the spot, as if a spike had been driven down through her and into the dry earth below.

The asir stalked forward, its head tilted like a desert lynx listening for prey. The golden crown it wore glinted with the movement. A crown! Why any of the asir would wear such a thing she had no idea.

It wore no clothes. Its skin was tightened and shriveled. It smelled like a charnel, but there were faint notes of fruit like fig and plum, which made it all the worse. Çeda gagged once, twice, the sound echoing in the emptiness of the street, but she remained as rigid as she could. As rigid as the stone beneath the desert.

When it came within arm's reach, it stopped. It leaned forward, sniffing the air. Tasting it. She could see its blackened skin by the light of Tulathan and Rhia, how tightly it was pulled over its bones. She could see yellowed eyes and tight, black lips pulled back to reveal receded gums and long, chipped teeth.

It blinked and frowned, jaw jutting forward. It seemed confused, though why, Çeda couldn't begin to guess. It stretched forward, jaundiced eyes widening as its hand reached for her face. She willed herself to move, to back away, to fend its hand away, but she couldn't so much as twitch as its desiccated fingers brushed her cheek, as they pulled the veil from her face. Never had Çeda felt more exposed. It sniffed her and then, almost tenderly, licked her neck where her blood pulsed most. She felt so very strange, like they were a twisted version of King and Blade Maiden. She dearly wished she could move or scream or fight, or feel anything but utter submission to this wretched creature. But she could not. She was well and truly trapped.

The asir began to speak. Or, Çeda *thought* it was speaking. It was difficult to tell. Its voice was soft as spindrift at first. She heard a word here. A word there. *Unmade* and *betrayed* and *fallen*.

But then she heard one distinct phrase. *Rest will he 'neath twisted tree . . .* And Çeda's breath caught in her throat. Those words . . . She'd seen them. Read them.

Her thoughts, and the asir's words, were cut off by the crack of a whip and another nearby wail, so close Çeda could feel the hairs stand up on her arms and the back of her neck.

The creature looked back the way it had come, then returned its attention to Çeda. It touched her forehead with an outstretched finger, pulled Çeda nearer, and kissed that very spot. Gods, she tried to recoil, but she was rooted in place. To be kissed by one of these creatures . . . It made her insides churn. And its lips! They were dry, but there was a strange warmth to them, a thing she hadn't expected, like maggots in a nearly finished meal.

The asir shuffled past, and slowly, as the sounds of its retreat faded, she was able to move again. Immediately, she pulled Emre to his feet and maneuvered him over a low wall. The wall marked the edge of a yard before a large, two-story home. At the center of the yard was a fig tree, and it was there that Çeda dragged Emre.

No sooner had she brought him to rest on the far side of the trunk than she saw forms gliding along the street. The moment Çeda saw them, her nostrils flared. Her breath came short and shallow. She felt like a maned wolf watching a desert hare, crouched and waiting for the right time to charge. It was a primal feeling, one born of fear and rage and impotence, one rooted in the bloody history of the lithe forms before her. It was a feeling she couldn't explain, nor even fully define, not even to herself, for these were Blade Maidens, black-robed and moving with the grace of a desert asp.

A dozen of them strode through the night, two by two, as if they and they alone ruled Sharakhai. Çeda couldn't help but think of the Maidens in the perfume merchants' fort, the ones who'd saved their King-in-disguise. Here were more, surely escorting King Sukru on his rounds. Indeed, such a large escort was justified after the Moonless Host had come so close to killing one of the Kings.

It comforted Çeda to know that the Kings might feel fear. And it made her dream. If only *she* might find herself closer to the Kings. The promises she might fulfill.

The very thought spurred a memory of a dark blade, of a river's edge, but it was so deeply buried it refused to fully surface. It left her feeling impotent and scared. They shouldn't have been caught out like this. They should be safe at home.

Her thoughts were broken by a tall form striding in the wake of the Maidens. He wore fine, bright clothes and a crown not unlike the one the asir had worn. He strode not with grace, as the Maidens did, but with the gait of the proud, the entitled. It was Sukru, the Reaping King, who legend said was the King who'd been granted the honor of selecting those whom the asirim would kill on the night of Beht Zha'ir. He roamed the city, marking those precious few who'd be given the honor. *How* was a matter unknown to most. Some said he cracked his whip against the door of the home he'd chosen and the asirim would take someone from within. Others said Sukru would peer into the darkness of the night—beyond doors and walls—and whisper the names of those he found worthy. Others claimed he wandered the city in the days leading up to Beht Zha'ir, disguised, and touched the skin of those the asirim should come for, and he wandered with them on this night merely to shepherd them through the city. Çeda knew the truth, though. She'd seen it with her own eyes years ago: Sukru marking a door with his bloody hand.

Behind Sukru came six Maidens more, each with a hand on the pommel of her sword. Çeda was nearly ready to offer a word of thanks to the twin moons—for Emre's sake if not her own—when one at the rear, the one closest to Çeda's position, stopped. She turned and scanned the yard, her eyes moving over the place where Çeda huddled with Emre. Part of Çeda *hoped* the Maiden would come. She wanted desperately to cross swords with one of them, as she'd dreamed so long of doing, but to do so now would be to throw away lives, hers and Emre's both. Whatever reason the asir may have had in sparing her life, she was sure the Maidens would not be so kind.

As if he'd heard her thoughts, Emre's breath caught. He stirred, and Çeda feared he would wake, that he'd call out.

But he didn't. And finally, bless the gods of the desert themselves, the Blade Maiden turned and continued in the wake of the others.

Çeda remained under the fig tree for a long while. She waited for the wails of the asirim to fade. Waited for Rhia, the golden moon, to trek across the indigo sky. Waited for Emre to rest. He was breathing easily, at last, and she would press her luck no further than she already had.

Finally, after Rhia had well and truly set, she woke Emre. His eyes fluttered open with a soft groan, and together they made their way through the city.

Tulathan had followed her sister, and the sun was brightening the eastern horizon by the time they reached home. Once she'd helped him up the stairs, she laid Emre onto his bed and set the satchel beneath it before fetching water and bandages. She made him drink as much of the water as he could before cleaning his wounds—two sword cuts across his chest and one on his left arm—and then set to stitching them. She was bone tired. The effects of the petal had worn off, and she was slipping down into the lethargy that always followed, and this time it was deeper than any she could remember.

The realization that she'd very nearly lost Emre sustained her, though. She set the stitches quickly and efficiently and then bandaged his wounds, and finally, after a kiss to his forehead—not so different from the one the asir had given her—she left him to rest. Only then did she allow herself to slink to her room like a beaten dog. She wanted nothing more than to fall into the embrace of her dreams, but there was a question that still needed answering.

She pulled back the horsehair blanket hanging above her bed. From the alcove hidden behind it she retrieved her mother's book. Along with the silver locket, it was one of the very few things she had to remind her of her mother's graceful hands, her winsome smile. Çeda used it to press the petals of the adichara. She flipped carefully to the back pages of the book and came to the one she was looking for.

As she stared at it, something inside her opened up and yawned, wider and wider, threatening to swallow her whole. She thought perhaps she'd remembered it wrong, that the words had somehow been a figment of her imagination— she'd been so caught in the spell of the asir, after all. But she *hadn't* misremembered. She *hadn't* made them up. Here they were, staring at her from the pages of her mother's book.

> *Rest will he,*
> *'Neath twisted tree,*
> *'Til death by scion's hand.*
> *By Nalamae's tears,*
> *And godly fears,*
> *Shall kindred reach dark land.*

Whatever was happening, Çeda didn't understand. Why by Goezhen's sweet kiss would this passage, this *very one*, be both written by her mother's own hand and spoken by that sad, pathetic creature? It made no sense. Over and over she read the words, then paged through the book to find more clues, but in the end she still couldn't unlock the puzzle.

With the light of the sun invading her small room, the exhaustion of the night caught up with her and she finally fell asleep, her mother's book clutched tightly in her arms.

Chapter 7

THE WORDS FROM THE PREVIOUS NIGHT echoed in Çeda's mind while she slept, and she woke hearing them still, though now it was a strange combination of her mother's melodic voice and the asir's dry rasp.

Rest will he 'neath twisted tree.

The desert wind was up and the day was warm. She could hear old Yanca across the way, coughing heavily from the dust, and beyond that the sounds from the bazaar, which was only a short walk down the lane. The day was already lively with hawkers calling, mules braying, a small bell jingling—Tehla giving sign that her loaves were fresh-baked. People would flock to get just a slice of Tehla's fresh bread, or they'd pay dearly for a whole loaf.

As Çeda sat up, the pains in her body came alive. She ignored them as best she could and retrieved a book from the shelf at the foot of her bed, an old history of Sharakhai, one of the more illuminating texts she'd found in her ceaseless combing of the stalls in the bazaar. The history spoke of how Sharakhai had been settled a thousand years ago, but not in any permanent way. Not at first. In those early days it was little more than an oasis, a place for nomads to gather water on their trek around the Great Desert.

Eventually, many of the tribes—even those that normally didn't travel to the heart of the desert—came to Sharakhai. Its central location made it a convenient place for the tribes to meet, to talk of their travels, to trade with one another, to sing songs and perhaps find husbands for daughters and wives for sons. The tribes did not believe in permanent settlements, and yet all too soon Sharakhai became one. Different tribes came at different times of the year, and so some would remain to trade with their sister tribes, planning on staying for a month or two. But for a few, months turned into years before they took to the desert winds once more, and their numbers grew with each passing season.

Soon, to the great dismay of the shaikhs, some from their tribes *did* settle permanently. Without ever meaning to, Sharakhai became a settlement, and then a city, and then one of the true powers in the desert, as strong or stronger than any one tribe. The shaikhs groused at this, but what were they to do? The reasons were sensible enough at first. A man was wounded and couldn't travel. A woman grew pregnant and promised to rejoin the tribe once the baby was born. When the shaikhs returned to Sharakhai they frowned and demanded their loved ones sail the sands with them, but for some the chance to rest in one place, to grow roots after so long on the sands, was too strong.

The city grew, and the protests of the shaikhs grew louder. Travelers from the north and south came, then from east and west, and the protests grew louder still. They demanded tribute from the lords of the city. They collected it when they gathered every year around Sharakhai, and the lords of Sharakhai, their ties to the wandering tribes still strong, complied. As trade grew, though, so did the city, and so did the boldness of its lords. Kings, they called themselves, one for each of the twelve tribes, and their tributes to the shaikhs began to dwindle.

As the tributes shrank, so did the power of the shaikhs, but the city of Sharakhai did not reckon on the number of spears and shamshirs that might be rallied to their cause. The shaikhs brought war upon Sharakhai, and there were many arrayed against the Amber City—far too many for the Kings to survive. But then came the night of Beht Ihman.

The Kings gathered on Tauriyat, the very hill where the House of Kings now lay, and they called upon the desert gods. They called to the moons above, Rhia and Tulathan. They called to dark Goezhen and his crown of thorns. They called to fickle Thaash and winsome Yerinde and stark Bakhi and gentle Nalamae. The gods came, and they listened to the Kings' plea.

Save us, the Kings said, *and what we have is yours.*

It was bright Tulathan who answered. *You shall have your city and your desert, too. But we require a payment, a tribute of our own.*

You have but to speak it, the Kings said.

Our price is dear, the goddess repeated.

Nothing is too dear for that which we ask.

Blood, Tulathan said.

Blood, said Rhia.

We require blood, said Goezhen.

This the gods asked, and this the gods received. Some brave few from Sharakhai, men and women who hailed from all twelve tribes, volunteered. They sacrificed themselves that the rest might live. It was a desperate act in a desperate time, but all would have been slain had the wandering folk had their way. Thus were the gods appeased.

They granted the Kings powers the likes of which the desert had never seen. And those who had paid the highest price became the asirim, servants of the Kings, bound to do their bidding and to protect Sharakhai from her foes. And so they did. They went at the Kings' command. The Blade Maidens took them out in the desert where they patrolled for enemies; and for those who took seldom-used paths, hoping to circumvent the tariffs demanded by the Kings, the penalty was death. The asirim were said to relish their duty, righteous in their anger toward any who defied the Kings' will, thereby ignoring the sacrifices they'd made on Beht Ihman.

But the gods were not content with the sacrifice of those few who became the asirim. In order for the Kings to ensure their power over the course of generations, more blood was needed. And so, in addition to heeling when the Blade Maidens called, the asirim returned to Sharakhai every six weeks when the twin moons rose. The asirim came for blood, and for many of the highborn—those chosen by Sukru and marked by his bloody hand—it was a great honor, for they deepened the legacy of the sacrifice those brave souls had made so long ago.

Çeda closed the history and opened her mother's book, hoping sleep might have ground away at the events of the prior night, allowing her to look at them anew. The book seemed wholly different now. A day before it had been a treasured possession; now it felt entirely wrong, as if her mother had stolen it from that dread creature. Which was impossible, of course, but even so, she couldn't escape the fact that the book was somehow connected to the asirim, or if not the asirim as a whole, then at the very least the one lost soul who had kissed her forehead with such strangely warm lips.

Rest will he 'neath twisted tree.

The twisted tree was surely the adichara, the thorny trees that grew in the desert. Few in Sharakhai would know this, however. Most had never seen the adichara up close, for such a thing was forbidden. Venturing into the blooming fields in daylight meant forfeiting one's eyes—a sentence harsh enough—but venturing there at night would lose one her life. Despite this, Çeda still visited several times a year, as her mother had done, to gather petals and press them for later use, when she needed them most. It was something she needed to do again soon, for she was beginning to run low, and even if she weren't, even if she'd hoarded the petals like some mad magpie, they began to lose their potency a few months from the vine.

The blossoms of the adichara glowed blue beneath the moonlight, and when they were harvested at that time—with both moons full—they gave one a strength and vigor that was granted by the gods themselves, even though the trees also had sharp thorns tipped with deadly poison. A single scratch could kill. And yet the poem claimed someone rested beneath them. The asirim? Some long-dead hero?

She moved through the pages of the book with more care. There were many stories within it, but the one whose pages held the strange verses told the story of Yerinde, the goddess of love and ambition, and Tulathan, the brighter moon, the goddess of law and order. The two had loved each other once, but this was the story of their downfall. Fickle Yerinde had loved all of the gods at one time or another, had lain with them as well. All except Tulathan. And so her desire had only grown. She wooed Tulathan, coaxed her down from the heavens to the earth below, and for a time Tulathan returned her love, but when she yearned once more for her place in the dark sky, Yerinde, feeling spurned, had taken her and secreted her away in the depths of a mountain fastness.

Rhia came to find her sister, and when she discovered what Yerinde had done, she freed Tulathan. Together they struck Yerinde down. Until that day Tulathan had been the smaller of the two, the weaker, but ever since then she'd been the brighter, the quicker to anger.

Çeda thought perhaps the story itself might relate to the asir, but if that were so, she had no idea what the connection might be.

Tehla's chiming bell pulled her from her reverie, and she realized she needed to check on Emre. She also needed to check in on her sparring class at the pits. She wrapped the book carefully in its white cloth and restored it to its hiding place.

He was still fast asleep. He didn't even move when she checked his bandages, a thing that should have been immensely painful. She felt his forehead and found him to be hot. Too hot. Poison, perhaps, or an infection. She had cleaned the wound last night as well as she was able, and she did so again, but she already knew Emre would need something more. She would have to go to Dardzada's.

Beneath Emre's bed was the leather satchel. Osman would be looking for this—or rather, whoever who had arranged and paid for the satchel's transportation would be looking for it. Perhaps the pickup had run afoul, and Emre had had to flee. Perhaps he'd been caught on his way to the drop-off. But why had a man from the desert tribes attacked him? Had he somehow stumbled across his attacker by mere chance?

No. Tribesmen came too rarely to the city, and when they did they traded during the day and left well before nightfall. If the tribesman was there, it was for a purpose, and Emre was now involved.

What to do now, though? The safest thing was to get the bag to Osman and find out where Emre was supposed to have taken it.

She glanced at Emre, then opened the satchel and found an ivory scroll case within. She shook it gently, but it made no sound. Bright yellow wax sealed one end, the end that would be opened, but before that could be done, a combination would have to be applied. Like the one Macide had opened the day before, the case had six ivory bands along its length, each of which could be turned independently. The combination would have been sent weeks or even months ago in anticipation of cases like this being couriered forward. When the rings were aligned properly, the top of the case could be lifted away and the contents removed. Otherwise, if the end was pulled with the wrong combination, a bladder of acid would be punctured, disintegrating the scroll within, rendering the message unreadable.

Two short whistles outside the window made her sit up straight. She put the scroll case back in the leather satchel and whistled back, matching the one she'd heard. After toeing the satchel back beneath his bed, she ducked her head through the woolen shades that lay across Emre's window. There in the alley stood Tariq. He wore white sirwal trousers and fine, dark leather sandals and a woven black cap he'd had since he was a child. He also had his shamshir at his belt.

The two of them stared at one another for a moment, then she smiled as if nothing were the matter and waved him up. Tariq gave her a rakish smile in return for hers and headed swiftly for her door. The moment he opened it and took to the stairs, Çeda ran to her room, grabbed her own shamshir, and set it down on the table where she and Emre prepared meals.

No sooner had she sat down than Tariq stepped inside. He turned away as he closed the door, trying to hide his reaction, but Çeda saw. He'd seen her sword, and a look of disappointment, or perhaps anger, had flashed across his face. She'd known Tariq since they were children, but he'd been under Osman's wing for years now. Even young as he was, he'd grown into one of Osman's most trusted men. And not without reason. He was brash, but also crafty, and wickedly good with a sword.

Tariq clasped his hands, the older way of praying to the gods. "Çeda," he said easily. "Where's Emre?"

Çeda nodded to the next room. "Things didn't go so well."

"I know. That's why I'm here."

"What do you know about it?"

"I know Emre didn't show."

"I mean the package, Tariq."

He smiled broadly. "I don't know anything about the package, Çeda." His manner was easy. Too easy. Osman had told him about the package.

"That's what I thought." Çeda smiled, every bit as broadly as he had.

"Does he still have it?" Tariq raised his eyebrows, and he tilted his head toward Emre's room as if he were readying to stroll on in whether she liked it or not.

"No," Çeda said.

"No?" Tariq echoed.

"But I know where it is."

Tariq's face turned cross. "And where by the gods' sweet breath is *that*, Çeda?" Tariq, normally so unflappable, was unsettled. She could hear it in his tone and in the way his eyes pinched. Whatever was in that case was important, and there was no way she was just going to give it back to him or even Osman. Emre had been chased and nearly killed by desert tribesmen, and none other than Macide Ishaq'ava had received the sister to Emre's case by Çeda's own hand. Whatever was going on was big, and she wanted to know more.

"I had to leave it."

"I believe I just asked where it was, Çeda, not for your thought process before making such a mud-brained decision."

"It's not . . . easily accessible. Not until tonight. I'll get it when it's safe and bring it to Osman tomorrow."

"Why don't you tell *me* where it is, and I'll go get it?"

"Didn't you hear me? It's not safe now." Çeda stood, as

if she wanted to be about her day. "Tell him I'll be by in the morning."

"Çeda"—Tariq's smile faded—"you know I can't allow that. Let me fetch it." He looked her up and down, an unreadable expression playing across his face. "Save us both some trouble."

He was right. She should probably just give it to him. But this was all too strange. The asir. The tribesman. The kiss from the crowned one. Besides, she hated being pushed, so fuck Osman, and fuck Tariq. They could have the case when she was damned well ready to give it to them.

"Don't worry that pretty little head of yours, Tariq. Osman cares that he gets the package, and he *will* get it, just not today." She pulled the chair back, away from the table, as if to give herself more room to maneuver. "So why don't you run back and tell him that? He won't blame *you* for returning empty-handed."

"Don't blame the messenger?"

"Exactly."

"The thing is, Çeda, they do blame the messenger, and I'm more than that to Osman. Much more. Come now. Don't be difficult. Let's go there together. Surely the two of us can overcome whatever concerns of *safety* you might have."

"I can't. I have things to attend to, Tariq."

Tariq's face grew cross. Normally he would put his hand on his shamshir and try to bluster his way through an argument. He was a dervish with a blade—everyone knew so— but Çeda was better, and he knew it. He was one of the few, besides Emre and Osman, who knew her identity in the pits. Give Tariq credit, though; none of the doubt he must have been feeling showed in his eyes, and none of it showed in his manner as he bowed his head to her. "Tomorrow, Çeda. First thing."

"Tomorrow," she echoed.

And then he was gone.

She probably shouldn't have pushed him that way, but he'd grown too brash since they were young, always pushing her.

She returned to Emre's bedside and poured more water down his throat. He drank but did not wake. His breathing came easier, which was a good sign, but his skin had never looked so pale. It was gray and ashen, and his lips were turning purple.

She reached under the bed, grabbed the satchel, and left their home. She was desperate to find out more about it, but Emre came first.

———◦———

Within one of Osman's deserted pits, Çeda's eleven students were lined up in two rows of five, with Amal—a young woman who, if not particularly aggressive, certainly had a knack for forms—standing before them, taking Çeda's place as instructor for the remainder of the class.

"You're doing well," Çeda said to Amal as she backed away toward the tunnel leading out of the pit. "Lead them through the nine dunes, then three laps around the pits. I'll see you all in a week."

Amal bowed her head and lifted her shinai to starting position as the others—all girls, ranging in age from five to thirteen years old—waved goodbye to Çeda. Çeda felt bad for cutting the lesson short, but there were too many things to do.

She left the pits and headed deeper into the city, then beyond the Trough until she reached Dardzada's apothecary.

Çeda could see his burly form through his half-shuttered window. He was talking with some man, a thin fellow who seemed jittery. Below the window, at a small table, three brass censers were laid out: one filled with myrrh, one with amber, and one with sandalwood. Appeasement for the desert gods, Bakhi in particular.

The very fact that Dardzada's home was built of stone and not mudbrick like the houses of the slums or the bazaar, lent a certain stature, and he'd been around long enough that he'd built a reputation. He knew how to find people. To most he was simply a man who dealt in herbs and unguents. But for a higher price, just as Osman could find shades to run your packages across the city, Dardzada could connect you with parlors that offered Yerinde's Kiss, a honey collected from the rare stone bees' nests far out in the desert, or a sniff of pollen from the adichara, or in very rare cases whole petals like the one in Çeda's locket.

Çeda never sold her petals—not to Dardzada or anyone else. She refused to even tell anyone but Emre about them. Being found with a single petal carried a sentence of death, but that wasn't why Çeda hid the fact that she collected them. Or at least, it wasn't the *only* reason. The petals, her trips out to the blooming fields, they felt like a secret she shared with her mother, and that was a trust she refused to break.

She waited as well dressed men and women walked along the street. Even a pair of Silver Spears passed on horses, clopping past, chain hauberks chinking, as cocky as they were oblivious to Çeda's half-crouched position in the shadows of the alley.

Half an hour later Dardzada's customer finally left. He caught Çeda watching him from across the street, and he frowned, as if by her very glance he'd somehow been exposed, but then he moved on. Çeda shouldered Emre's satchel and limped across the street. As she parted the beads that hung over the entrance, Dardzada—heftier than he'd been when she'd lived with him, especially around the middle—looked up from his ledger. He frowned at her, every bit as deeply as his patron had done a moment ago, then returned to the scritch-scratch of his writing.

She looked into his workroom and saw, brimming from an earthenware vase, a clutch of thick, green stalks with sharp thorns. "I need a bit of milk, Dardzada."

He looked up again, the space between his dark brown eyes pinching. He set down his black vulture quill and rubbed his hands over his brown-and-gold-striped kaftan. The top of his head was nearly bald. He was clean shaven, which somehow made him seem older, for it exposed the fatty rolls around his chin and neck. He took her in, noting the leather satchel under one arm. It felt for a moment as though he could see the hidden case within, but that was only her fears sparking fantasies.

"Are you hurt?" he asked.

"It's not for me," she said.

She might have detected relief, but it was gone so quickly she couldn't be sure.

"Then get it from someone else." He picked up his quill and began writing once more. "I've better things to do than patch up your beetle-headed friends from the slums."

"I can pay."

"I don't need your money."

"I'll mix it myself."

She heard a heavy-yet-resigned sigh. "Just hurry up about it."

She walked past him, through an open doorway, and into the workshop. The walls were lined from floor to ceiling with wooden shelves and drawers. He had hundreds of raw ingredients he used to make the tonics and elixirs and salves and unguents his patrons expected of him. Everything was exactly where it had been when she'd lived here. Dardzada had followed through on his promise to keep her after Çeda's mother had died. He'd been strict at first, but as he found it more and more difficult to control her, he'd become cruel, especially when she'd started running with Emre and the other friends she'd grown up with near the bazaar, so eventually she'd left and moved in with Emre and his brother Rafa.

Çeda took down one of the green stalks of charo from the earthenware vase and placed it thorn-side down on the broad worktable at the center of the room. After cutting off one end to expose the white flesh beneath, she used a rolling pin to extract the milk. This was one of the tasks Dardzada had always given her. She'd hated it then, but now, in a strange way, she missed it. It connected her to something besides shading and teaching swordplay and fighting in the pits. It connected her to the desert, and that always brought her back to her center. She milked three stalks, enough for four or five applications to Emre's wounds, which should be plenty. She used a dull-edged knife, slipping it across the workboard, scooping up the thick milk and scraping it into a glass phial. She took a phial of Dardzada's own healing remedy as well, a foul mixture of reduced oxtail broth, garlic, and boiled pistachio shells. It tasted rotten, but it would help Emre.

After stuffing them into the leather purse at her belt, she looked to the front and found Dardzada's nose still buried in his ledger. Quickly she spooned a bit of powdered nahcolite into a ceramic bowl and mixed in water until she could form a paste. Then she dabbed a cotton cloth into it and began rubbing it against her locket.

Making the silver shine was perhaps unwise of her—it drew too much attention, especially west of the Trough, in the Shallows or the Well, or even in Roseridge—but she didn't have the heart to leave her mother's last gift to tarnish. "Do you remember the book you gave me after my mother died?" she asked as she rubbed at the stubborn tarnish.

The sound of quill scraped against paper.

"Dardzada?"

"Have I not done enough for you this day?"

"My mother's book. Do you remember it?"

He shrugged without looking up.

"Did my mother ever speak of it?"

Now he did look up. "What?"

"Did she ever speak of it?"

"No, why would she?"

"Because it was one of the things she left me. I know she treasured it. I remember her reading it often late at night."

Dardzada's face softened. If Çeda didn't know better, she'd say he looked regretful. "She was a learned woman, your mother."

"Did she ever speak of the asirim?"

Dardzada rolled his eyes, dipped his quill in its well, and began scratching away at his ledger once more. "Everyone speaks of the asirim, Çedamihn."

"Yes." She finished her polishing. The locket shone like the first day she'd received it—the worst day of her life, the day Dardzada had given it to her. Çeda blinked away tears as she stepped into the front room. "Did she ever see any?" she asked as Dardzada scratched away.

"How would I know?"

"Dardzada, did she ever *see* any."

He must have heard something in her voice. He looked up and regarded her anew. "Why are you asking these questions? What's happened?"

He didn't know anything. She could see it in his eyes. "Nothing. Never mind."

"I'm no fool. You come to me the morning after Beht Zha'ir, begging for milk and asking of the asirim? Leave the blooming fields alone, girl. It isn't worth it. It got your mother killed, and it will get *you* killed as well."

"I didn't go to the blooming fields last night."

"No?" Dardzada sat up straighter and used his quill to point to her neck. "Tell me, Çeda, what do you keep in that locket of yours?"

She felt her face burn. "This is my mother's locket."

Dardzada laughed. "Indeed it is, and perhaps I should never have given it to you." He regarded her for a moment, surely seeing the hurt in her eyes, and then he returned to his writing as if she weren't there. "Out. Go. Take the milk to your precious Emre."

And she did, but it didn't keep his mocking laugh from haunting her through the hot city streets.

Chapter 8

Çeda wanted to return to Emre as quickly as she could, but there were other things that needed tending to first. She took a small detour on the way home and headed for the great bazaar, where she stopped at a fruit cart and scanned the crowd for a certain girl.

She handed over three khet for a handful of kumquats. "Never seen you here before," Çeda said to the fruitmonger, a squat Kundhunese woman with wild, kinky hair.

"Caravan here yestermorning," she replied in a thick Kundhunese accent, smiling as if Çeda had told her some witty joke.

"Where did you come from?"

"Yestermorning."

"No. *Where?* Ganahil? Aldamlasa?"

"Ganahil," the woman replied, still smiling her overly familiar smile.

Çeda took the fruit and moved on, limping her way through the bazaar's imperfectly drawn lanes, savoring the sweet taste and chewy skin of the kumquats. She watched carefully as she wove through the stalls, taking note whenever she spotted children running, especially the dirty ones, those unattached to adults. Just as she was popping the last of the grape-sized fruits into her mouth, she spotted a familiar group of children in the small plaza that surrounded the bazaar's central well.

Mala, her brown, curly hair flowing with the swirling wind, was standing with her sister, Jein, and a dozen other gutter wrens. Most were drinking their fill beneath the old pistachio tree by the edge of the plaza. Three of them were watching the crowd milling through the bazaar, choosing their marks with care, just as she and Emre had done almost every day when they were young, if not here in the bazaar then in the spice market or at the auction blocks or along the Trough. The city was always ripe the day after Beht Zha'ir, when dozens of raucous celebrations were held all over the city. After the rest and quiet—or for some, the unending stress—of the holy night, citizens and visitors alike flocked to the bazaar, to the spice market, to the unending food stalls, and coin flowed freely.

Mala's face lit up. "Çeda!" Then her face crumpled in disappointment. "But we've no swords!"

"No swords today, my sweet." Çeda waved her over, away from the other children. "Today, I have a job for you."

Mala smiled mischievously.

"Do you know Tariq?" Çeda asked. "Can you spot him in a crowd?"

She nodded.

"Good." Çeda crouched until they were eye to eye. "Come closer."

—◆—

Emre was still unconscious when she returned home, and he remained so while she removed his bandages and slathered the charo milk over his wounds. He coughed when she forced some of the elixir down his throat but then fell asleep again.

At least he's breathing easier.

Satisfied that it was all she could do for now, she moved through the room that served as hers and Emre's kitchen and sitting room and into her own room.

She slipped onto the chair at her desk, laid the satchel

before her, and pulled out the scroll case. The bright yellow wax was of a shade few bothered to buy, as it was expensive, but Çeda had long ago stocked up on several such colors.

From the hidden space behind the horsehair blanket above her bed, she retrieved a box and brought this to the desk as well. She flipped the lid back to reveal several deep compartments, one of which held a dozen sticks of colored wax. She tried three before finding two that were the closest matches. She'd mix them together and test it until she had the color just right. The wax was the least of her worries, though. The case also had the six ivory rings that she would need to set correctly before opening it. She couldn't even attempt to open it until she'd solved the combination, lest acid ruin the contents within.

She stepped into the sitting room and picked a wiry plant in a glazed cerulean pot from among the dozens she had sitting in the sun. After returning to the desk and setting the pot down with a thud, she ripped a healthy hunk of gray-green moss from the pot's bed. She was just setting it over the ivory case when she heard footsteps in the lane outside, footsteps that stopped near her front door. A loud ticking came, a sound like the river thrushes made when cracking snails with an anvil stone. After adjusting the moss, she moved to the window and pulled the curtain aside. Mala and Jein were standing there. When Mala caught the movement of Çeda's curtain, she reached down and dusted off her sandals. Then she walked with a deliberately fast pace away from Çeda's door. Jein followed, looking at Mala as if she were a beetle-brained fool.

Çeda sighed. She supposed it had been too much to ask for Osman to leave her alone until tomorrow. Jein was too young to understand, so Çeda had asked Mala to reveal nothing to her younger sister. The dusting of Mala's sandals meant that Tariq was on his way, and the fact that she was walking away quickly meant that Tariq was coming with haste. At best she had another few minutes.

She returned to the desk and set the moss back in the pot. Left behind, however, were dozens, hundreds, of bright red insects no larger than a speck of dust. Blood of the Desert, they were called, mites that lived in the roots of many desert plants. They were crawling all over the surface of the scroll case, over the images of jackals and leopards and falcons and other animals of the desert etched into the ivory rings. The mites tended to settle onto certain symbols, however, and soon it became clear what the combination was.

In order to avoid mistakes, the artisans who made such things would mark the correct etchings with a bit of kohl to make the work easier and to avoid puncturing the bladder of acid by accident. They would rub it off when they were done, of course, but the kohl itself was made from the soot of a specially prepared cloth that was burned slowly for hours. And from ghee. The mites, for whatever reason, couldn't get enough of ghee—something she'd learned while in Dardzada's care.

Çeda slid the rings into place as another ticking sound came, louder than before, and more urgent. Tariq was getting closer. She cracked the wax seal, pulled the top off the case and retrieved a tightly rolled piece of leather. She tipped the scroll case toward the light and looked down its length. Surprisingly, she saw no bladder of acid.

She could hear footsteps now. Heavy footsteps. The footsteps of a man, not a gutter wren like Mala.

Inside the rolled leather was a small velvet pouch. She tugged at the drawstrings and tipped the contents into her hand. And gasped.

The gemstone cupped in her palm shone like moonlight. It was transparent, but the light that glimmered faintly from within was gauzy, like the veil of the heavens. It was so delicate she thought it might give like a tuft of wool, but she found it to be solid, every bit the gemstone it appeared to be.

By Tulathan's bright eyes, what could it be? And what properties did it hold that it would be ferried across Sharakhai in such a way?

The footsteps stopped outside her home. She heard the latch rattle and the door open, and then someone took to the stairs.

She replaced the top of the case and then stuffed it and

the two sticks of wax she'd chosen into the satchel, which she slung over her shoulder. She was no fool. She knew Osman was no man to trifle with. No matter that she bedded him from time to time; he would not treat her kindly were he to learn of this.

After slipping the wooden box back into the alcove behind the horsehair blanket, Çeda moved to the window. The moment she heard Tariq's footsteps outside the entrance door in the sitting room, she pulled the curtains aside and leapt to the ground below. Mala was watching her from around a corner a few buildings up, but Çeda shooed her off with an urgent wave before turning and heading south so she could weave her way toward the bazaar. She didn't feel entirely comfortable about leaving Emre, but even if Tariq forced his way in, which she doubted he would do, he would do Emre no harm when he found nothing in their rooms.

She needed to borrow a bit of flame to reseal the wax before going to Osman, so she turned onto the main thoroughfare west of the bazaar and the spice market. The sounds of the bazaar were high today, the calls of hawkers interrupted only occasionally by the bitter cries of barter. And the smells were already filling the cool air, smells of galangal and mace and roasting meats.

She hadn't known where she would go until she'd arrived here. She'd head for Seyhan's stall, she decided. He kept several lamps squirreled away for late night selling. She'd borrow one and prepare the case and then she'd be off to—

Çeda stopped in her tracks. The sounds in the street, so distant a moment ago, suddenly filled her ears.

Osman was standing straight ahead of her, paying at a stall for a freshly grilled skewer of honeymeats and melon. He turned before Çeda could duck behind one of the closer stalls, and when he saw her, he smiled in a not-entirely-pleasant way and headed her way. "And there she is," he said before biting off one of the steaming pieces of lamb and chewing it.

Çeda smiled easily and gritted her jaw to prevent herself from licking her lips. "A strange place to find a man of good means."

He smiled easily, the old battle scars showing through his black beard in the afternoon sun. "A strange place to find someone who should have been coming to see *me*."

"I was stopping for a bite before getting ready. For tonight."

"Oh?" he asked, biting off a hunk of melon and chewing it noisily. He held out the skewer toward her. "Would you like some of mine?"

He'd no sooner said those words than two of his men broke away from the crowd and stepped past Osman to flank Çeda. Neither looked like much, but she knew of them, enough to respect their skill with cudgel and fist. If she were going to run, now would be the time. But she didn't.

Osman's reach extended far in Sharakhai—certainly to all the places Çeda might run. She had to face him, and now was as good a time as any.

"I've given up goat," Çeda said simply.

"Have you?" He slipped another hunk of meat off the skewer and began to chew. "And why is that?" he asked as his eyes glanced over Çeda's shoulder.

She looked behind and saw Tariq exiting the same alley she'd taken here. He was Çeda's age, but his cocksure attitude made him look like a little boy preening for the girls. She turned calmly back to Osman and looked him in the eye. "It's too gristly, Osman. Especially the old goats Avam buys. Gets stuck between my teeth."

Osman laughed grimly, attracting the attention of a few men walking past. He ignored them and allowed his stony gaze to linger on Çeda. "Am I an old goat, Çeda?"

She paused. Of course he wasn't. He was much more than an old goat. But she wasn't about to admit that here. Not like this. "If you need me to answer that for you, then perhaps you are."

For a moment there was hurt in his eyes, but it faded in an instant. Osman hadn't made it to where he was by showing weakness to anyone. He nodded to the bag slung around Çeda's shoulder. "Do you have it now?"

Çeda looked around meaningfully. "Don't you think your estate would be better? Let me come to you after I've—"

Osman threw his skewer into the dry dirt and pointed to

the alley, and immediately the men at Çeda's side took her by the arms and forced her there. Again she thought of slipping through their grasp, of fighting if she had to, but somehow this felt right. She'd been lying to Osman for years, and there was a part of her that was sick of it, so she let them take her into the deep shadows of the alley. Once there, Tariq pulled the bag from her shoulder and rummaged through it. He pulled the scroll case out and held it up to Osman as if it were a precious jewel fallen from the heavens.

Osman immediately snatched it from Tariq's hand and gave it to one of his other men, who secreted it away in a black bag hanging from his belt. Tariq's nostrils flared, and he looked to Çeda as if he were waiting to see if she were going to make mock of him, but then he bowed to Osman and stepped back, his hand on the pommel of his curved shamshir.

"Leave us," Osman said.

For a moment, no one moved, as if they couldn't believe their ears.

"Leave us!"

Tariq jutted his chin back toward the main street and headed there. The other toughs followed, but not before they'd passed knowing looks to one another.

"The scroll case was open," Osman said.

"It was," Çeda allowed.

"Who were you going to sell it to?"

"No one. I would never."

"Never?"

"Never," she repeated. "I've never sold anything of yours. What I've opened I did for my own benefit. No one else's."

"So you admit it then? That you've betrayed me before."

"Not betrayal, Osman. I did it . . ." She stopped, for the words wouldn't come. She'd been hiding her purpose from everyone—everyone but Emre—for so long, it was not just *difficult* to talk about, but nearly impossible.

"For your mother?" Osman asked. He turned his head to his right, toward Tauriyat, which lay hidden beyond a row of three-story buildings. "To do battle against the Kings?"

Çeda stood there, stunned. It felt as if Osman had cracked open her skull to have a look inside.

"Don't look so shocked, Çedamihn Ahyanesh'ala. Do you think your mother's story forgotten? She may have pretended there were none who cared for her—she may even have tried to convince you of the same—but there were those of us who did. Some of us very much."

The implications played through Çeda's mind, and one horrifying possibility came to her. "Were you and my mother . . . ?"

Osman was confused, but then he took her meaning and laughed. "No, Çeda, your mother and I were friends only, although she did me favors from time to time, and I her. Which makes your betrayal taste all the more bitter."

"What do you care if I've read a few notes? You hate the Kings as much as I."

"As *you?* No. I may find them distasteful, but they provide a certain amount of stability in this ever-changing city." His jaw worked. He shifted his weight from one leg to the other. "I can't let this go, Çeda. If I do, and the rest see it, then they begin to take too. And bit by bit the things I've built start to crumble."

Osman waited, perhaps expecting more, but Çeda merely stared at him.

"You've nothing else to say? No more words to explain why you've done what you've done?"

She stood there, silent and unmoving. What else was there *to* say? He was right. And she had known the risks all along.

"Very well," he said, and headed toward the end of the alley, where Tariq and the others were waiting. "Nothing broken," he said and lost himself in the crowd.

The men came for her, Tariq first. She thought of giving them a fight, if only to wipe that grin off Tariq's face, but if she did they'd only make it last longer.

She didn't give them clear shots, though. Tariq's fist came first. Then the others, and soon she was on the ground, and they were kicking her back, her legs, pounding her flesh like hammer blows. One came in so hard against the back of her head the world blossomed in stars and her arms went slack. Someone rolled her onto her back, and then more blows rained down on her face, her sides, her stomach.

When it was done, she heard someone moaning. It took her long moments to realize it was her. *She* was the one making those pitiful sounds. Well, moan she might, but she wouldn't cry. She refused to give Tariq the satisfaction. Nor Osman, if he was listening.

But when she looked around, she realized they were gone. For all she knew they'd been gone for hours. She had no idea how long she'd lain there in the alley, others walking by, perhaps wondering what she'd done to deserve such a beating.

She lay there for a long while, working her body gently to see if it was ready to stand. When she was convinced it could, she levered herself up like a newborn kid—all gangly limbs and staggered movements—and made her way back home.

She laughed as she hobbled her way along.

At least this time she didn't have to *pretend* to limp.

Chapter 9

WITH THE HEAT OF THE DAY baking the desert dry, Çeda's mother pulled on the tiller, adjusting the bearing of their skiff to skirt a large dune. The wooden runners hissed as the skiff leaned and then righted itself.

"I saw things in Saliah's chimes," Çeda said after a time.

Ahya merely shook her head, a numb look on her face. "What did you see?"

"A rattlewing," Çeda replied. "A bloody hand. I saw Blade Maidens, and a shaikh."

"And the ebon blade?"

Çeda paused. This was important to her mother. She could tell by the way she was trying to ignore her. "A King was giving one to me."

"Describe him."

Çeda tried, but the image in the vision was already fading. She did as well as she could, describing his garb, his imposing frame, the opulent hall in which he stood. Her mother kept her eyes focused on the horizon. She'd seemed haunted before, but now a look of resignation was stealing

over her. Çeda didn't like that. She didn't like it at all. "The
visions. They're all connected to one another, aren't they?"

A trick of the wind made their sail thrum, then it fell silent once more. "Yes," came Ahya's numb reply, "but it's
only one possible path, Çeda. Even Saliah can't always say
which aspects of the vision will come true." She spoke these
words with some small amount of hope, but Çeda knew she
was only doing so for Çeda's benefit. She believed in the visions, and she knew enough to interpret them better than
Çeda could. Çeda tried to get her to reveal more, especially
considering where they were going now and what Ahya
meant to do, but her mother would speak no more on the
subject, and eventually Çeda fell silent.

They reached Sharakhai well after midday. The city was
bustling, as it often was the day after Beht Zha'ir. But
Ahya didn't take Çeda home. Instead, they went straight
to Dardzada's. Ahya forced Çeda to wait outside while
Dardzada, wearing a striped thawb of brown and white—
and a frown for Çeda—locked the door so he and Ahya
could speak in peace. They left Çeda to sit on the dusty
ground outside the apothecary shop, watching the people
go by, few of whom took note of her sitting there. Night was
coming. It wouldn't be long now, and her mother would be
out again. There was something momentous she meant to
do and, unlike out in the desert, no amount of rationalizing
would diminish the fears Çeda harbored for her mother.

Çeda couldn't let her go. Not tonight. If she did her
mother might do something terrible, something she couldn't
take back. But what could Çeda do?

Ahya and Dardzada spoke for nearly two hours. The
effects of the adichara petal had long since worn off, and
Çeda was feeling shaky. Despite the heat, she shivered.
Her gut churned, slowly eating away at her insides until she
was crying from it.

The passersby took more note of her. "Are you well,
child?" some would ask. "Is there ought I can do?"

An ancient woman with a gnarled cane stopped and
with great effort knelt and hugged Çeda to her chest.
"Have you lost someone, dear one?"

Yes, Çeda thought, *I've lost my mother.* But she told her No, and the woman moved on.

When she could stand it no more, Çeda stole into the apothecary from the rear entrance and listened at Dardzada's bedroom door, where he and Ahya spoke in low tones.

"Are you sure you wish to do this?" Dardzada was asking. She'd never heard him sound as though he were pleading before—Dardzada was a man more used to barking orders than begging favors—but here he was, sounding as desperate as Çeda felt. "It isn't too late. I can speak to the Matron. She has the ear of one of the Kings. We could wait a day or two and see."

"That sounds reckless, and you know it."

"More reckless than what you're planning?"

"I won't jeopardize all we've done for a woman we know so little about."

"She's been faithful."

"She was a Blade Maiden. That's more than enough reason to pull at the tiller and steer well wide of her." A pause. "It's getting late. Has the draught steeped enough?"

The sound of clinking came, of glass on glass. "Yes, it's ready, if you still mean to go through with it."

"Will I have time to say goodbye to her?"

"Yes, it takes time. Once you leave, repeat the story we agreed upon, and soon it will be your only story."

A tinkling sound came, then the gurgle of liquid.

A short while later, footsteps came toward the door. Çeda backed away as quickly as she could, but her mother saw her before she could sneak through the front door. "Come," Ahya snapped at Çeda, apparently both unsurprised and unoffended by Çeda's guile. When Çeda came close, she crouched until the two of them were staring one another in the eye. A smell followed Ahya—part floral, part fetid—and her eyes were red, but they were also distant, unable to focus, as if she were under the spell of the black lotus. "You'll stay with Dardzada," she said.

Çeda was already shaking her head. "Please don't go, memma."

Her mother gripped Çeda's arms and blinked several

times, as if she'd had too much araq and was having trouble ordering her thoughts. "Be good for him, Çeda."

"Memma, no!"

Her mother stood, seemed to wrestle with her own sense of clarity, then focused on the front door, her intent clear on her face. Dardzada emerged from the back room, stalking toward Çeda as Ahya slipped like a ghost toward the door.

She turned and managed to focus her attention on Çeda. With great effort, it seemed, she took two strides toward her, knelt, and took Çeda's hands in her own. "Be good for him"—she kissed Çeda's hands—"and remember what I said in the desert." Then she stood and began walking away.

"No!" Çeda cried. She grabbed her mother's wrist and tugged, refusing to let go. "Please don't! Please don't go!" Her mother was trying to wrest her arm free, though in a strangely listless manner, and then, before Çeda knew what was happening, Ahya raised her arm and slapped her across the face. Çeda staggered back, stunned, and Dardzada grabbed her by the shoulders.

After one pained look at Çeda, Ahya turned and left Dardzada's home, the bell above the door jingling as the darkness consumed her. Çeda tried to wrest herself free of Dardzada's grip, but did so only halfheartedly. Her mother wouldn't listen to her pleas, not when she was so intent on leaving.

She'll be all right. She knows what she's about. But the words were hollow. She would fool herself no longer, not now that her mother was gone.

"Go upstairs," Dardzada said, shoving her toward the rear of the shop.

Çeda moved numbly to the stairs and took them up to the landing. Along the wall, beneath two windows, now shuttered, was a pallet with a hastily thrown blanket on top. She lay down, faced the wall away from the stairs, and clasped her hands.

Please, Nalamae, guide her. Please, Nalamae, guide her. Please, Nalamae, guide her. She prayed these words over and over, begging the goddess to listen.

Dardzada climbed up the creaking stairs and retired to his room without another word to Çeda. She heard his snoring some time later, but Çeda couldn't sleep. The night wore on, moment by excruciating moment, Çeda willing the sun to rise, for her mother to return. But the night ignored her pleas, becoming interminably long.

At last the light of the rising sun wove in between the slats of the shuttered windows. She stared at the slanted beams, listening intently for the sound of her mother's footsteps on the beaten wooden walkway outside Dardzada's shop; for the rattle of the door opening downstairs, but those sounds never came. Instead she heard the city awakening. The clop of mules and the clatter of cart wheels. The scrape of footsteps as people moved about. The sound of brooms as people swept the nightblown sand from their porches.

And then there came a *tick* against the shutters above her. It was followed by another. And a third.

"Çeda!" came an urgent whisper.

She got up and opened one shutter carefully, lifting it slightly to prevent it from creaking. Outside in the street below stood Emre, her closest friend and one of the few she'd kept as her mother had moved from place to place every few months. He was barefoot and wore his loose trousers and baggy shirt. The morning was chill, but you wouldn't know it from looking at him. The cold never seemed to bother him. For a moment, her heart was glad, but then she saw the look on his face.

Emre was nine, a year older than her, but just then he looked like a toddling child, scared of a world he didn't understand. "Çeda, you have to come." He looked to his left, toward Tauriyat, the hill in the center of Sharakhai that bore the House of Kings on its curved back.

Çeda wanted to tell him no, that she had to wait for her mother to return. But that look sent her gut to roiling so badly she thought she was going to be sick.

She heard the sound of approaching footsteps but was so lost in worry she didn't at first understand what it meant. Dardzada was stomping toward her from his bedroom. He pulled at her hair and yanked her away from the window, then pointed at Emre with one fat arm. "Begone, Emre, or I'll come down there and whip you myself."

Çeda heard no response. Emre wasn't afraid of Dardzada, but he wouldn't provoke him, either, especially not when Çeda would suffer the brunt of his wrath. Çeda watched as Dardzada swung the shutter closed. She had to go. She couldn't remain here.

By the gods' sweet breath, the look on Emre's face . . .

Dardzada would probably take a switch to her backside for it later, but she didn't care. She darted for the stairs. Dardzada stormed after her and tried to grab her—"Çedamihn, stop!"—but she was too quick. She was down and through the shop and out into the street in moments, and then she and Emre were running together, the two of them glancing behind from time to time. As they reached Highgate Road, Çeda saw Dardzada one more time. He was standing in the street, staring at her with a look of deep regret. And then he was lost from view.

By silent and mutual agreement she and Emre slowed. They couldn't keep up the mad pace they'd set in the beginning, but they ran as quickly as their lungs and their burning legs would allow. Emre said nothing further. He was clearly scared to. And Çeda didn't ask, for she was just as scared to know the truth. *More* scared. She knew something had happened to her mother. She just didn't know what.

Ahya might have been taken by the Blade Maidens, or by the Kings themselves. Perhaps she was being held for trial. All of that might explain the strange visions she'd seen in Saliah's chimes.

But she knew it wasn't so. If it were, Emre would have already told her.

So she kept running, her strides soon outstripping Emre's. Her fears built within her, imagining the worst, until they were ready to burst from her throat in an unending cry. And still she was utterly unprepared for the scene that met her.

Tauriyat stood at the center of the city. Twelve palaces were built upon it, all of them interconnected by bridges and tunnels. Collectively they were known as the House of

Kings. A towering wall ran around Tauriyat, and into it were built two main entrances: one at the sheltered harbor to the east that held the ships of war, and one to the west that opened into the heart of the city. Emre led her to the westward entrance.

The towering gates were closed, but atop the wall Çeda could see four Blade Maidens. Each wore a black fighting dress with a turban and veil hiding her face. They stood with bright spears in hand, staring not at the great courtyard at the foot of the gates, but out over the city, as if they could see beyond the dawn to the days and the dangers ahead.

"Stop, Çeda," Emre said when he'd finally caught up to her. "They'll be watching those who come for her."

He grabbed her arm, but she shrugged it off. She barely heard his words, for to the right of the gates, along the wall of Tauriyat, stood a gallows, and from it hung one lone form: Ahyanesh Allad'ava. Her mother. She'd been hung from her ankles, naked, her throat cut. Çeda tried to walk toward her, but Emre stopped her again. She stood, numb, but otherwise ignored him.

There were markings on her mother's hands and feet. No, not markings—cuttings. They had cut ancient runes into her mother's skin, and upside down, so that those who saw her could read them. Çeda knew what they meant. Her mother had taught her well in letters, if in little else.

Whore, read the cuts on her hands. *False witness,* said the ones on her feet.

And on her forehead was a sign Çeda had never seen before, a complex design that looked like a fount of water beneath a field of stars.

She should scream. She should cry. But the truth was, this felt as though everything—from leaving home in the early hours, to what happened at Saliah's in the desert, to this—had been preordained, as if she were merely turning the final page on the book of her mother's life. It had always come to this, she saw now.

The forehead symbol troubled her. "What does it say?" Çeda asked, more to herself than Emre.

"You know I can't read," he mumbled softly.

She studied that symbol, committing it to memory. Each curve. Every angle. The depth it cut into her mother's skin. The blood that left haunting patterns along her eyes and forehead and unbound hair.

She would never forget it. She couldn't if she tried.

Something clattered behind the gates, and they groaned outward. It sounded as though Tauriyat were some great beast waking from its midnight slumber. With the jingle of tack and the clop of hooves, rank after rank of Blade Maidens rode out on their tall horses.

"Come *on*," Emre said, tugging her arm.

At first, she refused to go, but as the horses neared, Emre became more insistent.

Before following him, Çeda stared at the tall towers of the House of Kings and spat on the dusty street. Then she ran down the narrow alleyway with Emre, where the horses couldn't follow, and they wended their way back toward Dardzada's.

"You shouldn't come," Çeda said when they were coming close. "He'll beat you for sure."

Emre smiled, for her sake. "Only if he catches me."

"I'll get anything he doesn't give to you."

With that, Emre's smile vanished. His brown eyes stared into hers with an honest, compassionate look Çeda had rarely seen from him, from this boy who liked to smile and joke too much. "I loved her too, you know."

Çeda nodded. "She loved you as well." She kissed him on the cheek, and then struck a solid pace toward Dardzada's shop.

The stout apothecary was waiting inside, but he wasn't angry. He merely stared at her as if he knew what had happened, as if he'd known since last night. All of it. Her mother leaving, her death, Çeda finding her this morning. He'd known, and he stared at her as if this were all as the gods had decreed, and there was nothing he, nor Ahya, nor Çeda could have done about it.

She didn't much care what he thought, though.

She went upstairs and lay down on her pallet. She heard Dardzada gathering his things a short while later, and then the front door opened and closed, and the hustle and bustle of the city washed over her.

And then at last she cried, the feelings of loss starting to blossom now that she was alone. Her life with her mother had always been one of change, the two of them moving from place to place around Sharakhai, never keeping friends for long. But Çeda had always had her mother. How she'd loved the times that they'd read to one another. How she'd loved the trips they'd taken out to the desert. How she'd loved the sweet coconut lassi her mother had made for Çeda on her birthdays, and the way they'd dance with swords for hours.

Now what did she have? Dardzada?

She had nothing. She had emptiness.

What could she have done to stop all this? There must have been *some* way. Perhaps if she'd been better behaved at Saliah's. Or if she'd pleaded harder with her mother. Perhaps she could have delayed her departure. Or made her stay. Another night, things might have gone differently. Another night and, breath of the desert, she might still have her mother.

Gods, why did her last act have to be that slap across Çeda's face?

Tears fell as a thousand scenarios played through her mind.

Long into the night, she prayed for this all to be a dream, to wake up and find it all to have gone away.

<hr />

She woke to someone nudging her shoulder.

It was Dardzada. He was sitting on a chair by her pallet, holding a small leatherbound book with a chain draped like a bookmark through its pages. From the chain hung a beautiful silver locket. Her mother's locket. These were her mother's things.

"She wanted you to have these," he said, holding them out for Çeda to take.

Çeda didn't want them. It felt as though accepting them would make her an accomplice to her mother's death.

But that was foolish. The book was a collection of

poems and stories her mother had cherished. And the locket was the one thing of beauty her mother had allowed herself. She rubbed the painful, salty crust from her eyes, took them both, and pulled the locket around her head, felt its lovely, sickening weight against her chest. The book she opened gently and thumbed through, reading several lines from her mother's favorite poem.

> *Rushes withered,*
> *River dry,*
> *Warbler shivers,*
> *'Neath winter sky.*

"The Maidens will be looking for those who knew your mother," Dardzada said as he relaxed the bulk of his weight into the simple wooden chair, "but Ahya hid her trail well, and the city guardsmen who patrol here—I've known them for years. They'll pass us by if I pay them well enough." He smoothed his brown beard. "And I do. I will."

"Do you expect me to thank you for it?"

Dardzada's eyes brightened. They were angry, but not for his own sake. "You should thank your mother, for her steps have been taken with care these many years. The friends she's made are fast. They won't give her up. And soon, if we've any luck at all, the House of Kings will lose interest in chasing ghosts and be satisfied with the example they've made today."

Çeda wanted to be sick. Her mother had been reduced to an *example*. An example for whom? Why? She thought again of the strange symbol carved into the skin of her mother's forehead.

"Why did she do it?"

"What Ahya did, she did to protect you."

"But why?"

"I won't reveal those things to you Çeda. They got your mother killed."

"You have to tell me. She was my mother."

"I'm sorry, Çeda. I owe your mother much, a debt I'll repay you in her stead, but I don't owe her that."

She couldn't help but think of her mother's final hours.

What they must have done to her. "They'll know of me." Clutching the book to her chest, she shifted away from Dardzada until her back was propped against the wall. "They'll come for me now, won't they?"

"No. She will not have told them about you. You'll be safe, I think. We'll all be safe."

Dardzada had allies, she knew, men and women the Kings would kill if ever they learned of them. She'd heard her mother speaking about them, speaking *to* them, over the years. These were the people Dardzada was referring to when he said *we*: the undying soldiers of the Moonless Host, as one of memma's friends had once referred to them.

"How can you be so sure?"

"I'm sure."

She wanted to know more, but she knew Dardzada wouldn't tell her, and that asking him would only convince him that his instincts to hide the information from her were correct, so she remained silent, running her hands over the cracked leather cover of the book. Dardzada got up a short while later and waddled his way back downstairs.

Late that night, after he'd come and gone a few times, she heard him climb the stairs and go to his bedroom. The door closed with a soft click.

Hours later, deep into the night, she heard him crying. It went on for a long, long while, much longer than Çeda would have guessed. Dardzada had always been so mean to Ahya, so brusque and quick to anger. Had he *loved* her?

A fine time to show it.

Çeda waited for his cries to soften and go silent, then a while longer for his snores to fill the house. Only then did she get up and creep downstairs. She left his home and walked into the cool night. She shouldn't be out. She shouldn't risk the chance of the city guard or the Maidens seeing her. But she would not hide. She would not skulk. Not tonight. She would see her mother one last time, and if the Kings found her, they could do with her what they would.

She wound down to the city's main thoroughfare, the Trough, and followed it to the Spear, the wide street that held the most expensive shops in the city and led to the very gates of Tauriyat.

The moons were high—bright Tulathan and her sister, golden Rhia, near her side—and by their light Çeda could see that the gates were closed. She saw a Maiden walking the wall. Çeda waited until she had passed from sight beyond the buildings of the grand square, then strode across the courtyard and stood before the gallows.

From beyond the city, from somewhere far in the distance, came the howl of a maned wolf. Another joined it, and another after that. They lifted Çeda's spirit even as she stared at her mother's form, still hanging in the dry desert air. The lanky wolves had always seemed like family to Çeda. Children of the desert, like Çeda and her mother.

Soon the wolves fell silent, and Çeda was alone. She whispered no words of farewell. That wasn't why she had come. Instead she pulled her kenshar from its sheath at her belt—a knife her mother had given her two years ago, on her sixth birthday. She drew it across the palm of her right hand. The cut burned but no more than her heart burned for the loss of her mother. After slipping the blade back into its sheath, she ducked beneath the gallows' platform and scrabbled to the spot directly beneath Ahya's body. Using her bloodied hand, she gathered up a fistful of sand from the dark circle she found there—sand caked with her mother's blood.

"Blood of my blood," she whispered, then crawled back out from under the platform and walked calmly to the center of the courtyard, Maidens be damned.

From this vantage Çeda could see Tauriyat in its entirety— or as much as one could from outside the walls. Lanterns lit the road that wound its way up the mountainside. Like the winding branches of an acacia, the road split and split again, each branch wending its way to one of the twelve palaces. Lights from hundreds of windows twinkled, and Çeda wondered what they might be doing now, those Kings, while her mother swung in the wind.

Staring up at the lights, giving each house her undivided attention, Çeda raised her fist to her lips, squeezing the clumps of bloody sand she'd gathered. As it sifted through her fingers, grinding painfully into the cut, she spoke, but she spoke no plea to Nalamae—she had called on the goddess twice already, and she had failed Çeda utterly.

"This I vow, O Kings." She did not whisper; she spoke plainly and clearly, as if the Kings were standing there before her. "I am coming for you."

In the desert, the wolves renewed their calls, higher and more urgent than before. More and more joined in until dozens seemed to echo Çeda's vengeful words.

As the last of the bloody sand pattered against the ground at Çeda's feet, Çeda said, "I am coming for you, one and all."

Chapter 10

EMRE DREAMED.

He dreamed of a howling that spread through the shadow-cloaked streets of the Amber City. He dreamed of dark skies and rolling thunder.

He was running down the Haddah's dry riverbed, snaking his way along it, hoping to stay ahead of the dark forms slipping through the night. They stood on bridges above him, watching, cloaked in shadow. They allowed him to pass, but as soon as he had, they jumped down to the riverbed and began running with the others. A handful gave chase, then a dozen, then a flood of long-limbed asirim, some running like men and women, but most galloping like jackals. Their howls drove him onward, not because they sounded like feral beasts, but because they sounded so human. There was pain in those cries. Anguish. A lament for something they had long sought but never found.

The closest of them scratched at his heels. Another swiped at his legs, nails tearing skin and gouging flesh. The third caught his clothes and dragged him to the ground in a heap.

The weight of the asir bore down on him, but it was fear that petrified him. He couldn't move, not as the asir rose up, its lanky hair swinging, not as it pressed its long, grime-covered fingernail into his chest, not as it pulled back its lips, revealing a boneyard smile that caught Emre's breath in a dead man's rigor.

The nail pressed deeper into his skin. He felt it parting his bones, touching his beating heart. He felt it brush against his very soul.

"You should have saved me," said the asir.

And then he realized he'd seen that face before. Beneath the dirt, beneath the blood, beneath the decay evident in the tears and open sores in his skin, Emre recognized him.

Rafa. His brother.

Bakhi's guiding hand, please, no!

His brother only smiled, then pressed his fingers ever deeper, cleaving flesh and bone until his hand was gripping Emre's heart.

* * *

Emre woke, drenched in sweat.

He lay in a room of faded, chipping plaster that revealed patches of the ancient brickwork behind it. He tried to sit up, but stopped at a bright, burning pain along the left side of his ribs and lay back down.

"Nalamae's teats, who let the oryx in to stab me while I was sleeping?"

He probed the area, feeling sharp pain beneath the thick bandages wrapped across his chest and, slowly, he began to understand the state he was in, and the fog of his dream began to recede. Like a song from one of the deadly desert sirens, each painful press of his fingers drew forth memories, *real* memories of what had happened in the night, teasing them bit by aching bit from the cloudy recesses of his mind.

He recalled reaching the southern harbor well enough, and speaking to a man in a black turban and veil. The turban had been tied loosely, and the folds were strange, as if such garb were new to him. A man posing as a Sharakhani, perhaps.

A Qaimiri? he had wondered. *Mirean? Some Malasani dog?*

He recalled taking the leather satchel with the scroll case inside and leaving the harbor. More than this, however, was lost to him. It was as if he'd stepped into a doorway to another land after taking that satchel, his time there lost in the vagaries of that place.

He tried to sit up again and got farther this time, but the effort was so painful it made his ears ring. Only by carefully rolling onto his uninjured side and pushing up with his arms was he able to reach a sitting position. Even this made his skin go clammy.

After sitting there for some time, breathing and listening to the distant sounds of a smith's hammer working some forge-brightened alloy, he rocked himself forward onto wobbly legs and stood. Bright stars danced across his vision. Running his dry tongue over lips that were cracked and bleeding, he shuffled over to the table just next to his bed and took up the ewer of fresh water and drank his fill.

Bless you, Çeda.

The water made his gut ache, but he still felt better for having downed as much as he could manage. He took tentative steps toward the arched doorway to the sitting room, then parted the hanging beads, head pounding in time to the smith's relentless hammer, and slowly but surely made his way toward Çeda's room. He was so dizzy he nearly called out to her, but how pitiful would he look, already cared for by her—perhaps even *saved* by her—and now calling out like a fainting child?

Finally the feeling of dizziness passed, and he made it to her doorway. "Çeda?"

He parted the thick curtain that lay across it, and found her lying on her bed, facing the wall. She didn't stir as he made his way in. He tried to pull the chair from the corner, but his ribs screamed from that simple effort. He switched arms and tried again, scraping it loudly until it was sitting across from her bed. Even though maneuvering into that chair felt as though molten gold were being laid across his wounds, he could feel how well his wounds had been

tended. He didn't need to take the bandages off to know
how expertly she had stitched his cuts. He'd seen her do it
before, once on his own leg, sliced on a stone while climbing over the city's ancient inner walls, and countless times
on herself when Çeda had stitched her own wounds from
pit fights or others in the back alleys of Sharakhai. And
sometimes from her forays out into the desert.

You're every bit as bad as your mother, he used to tell
her. *And what of it?* she would shoot back with a grin that
made it clear how very pleased she was by the comparison.

"Çeda?" he asked when the pain subsided sufficiently
that he could talk without sounding like a wounded lamb.
"I know you're awake. You breathe like an ox when you're
asleep."

"You *smell* like an ox," she said to the wall. "Always."

He laughed, but his laugh died quickly for the pain it
caused.

Her words had come out strangely, as if she'd downed
too much araq the night before and was still coming around
the river.

"Çeda, what's wrong?"

She remained motionless for awhile yet, her chest rising
and falling as if she were deciding how to answer, but then,
like a capsized ship slowly righting itself, she rolled herself
over, wincing with every movement.

"Çeda! By all that's holy, what happened?"

Her left eye was swollen with a blood-crusted cut running along her brow. Her lip was swollen even worse, and
her clothes were dirty and torn, blood showing through in
several places.

"Went to the pits. Tried fighting a set of stairs." She
tried to smile, but it came out like a grimace. "Didn't go
so well."

"No jokes." Ignoring his own pain, he scooted the chair
closer to her bed. He looked her over, his hands opening
and closing of their own accord, an expression of the impotent feelings raging within him. Her blanket covered her
from the waist down, but he could tell by the way she was
curled up that she'd been beaten everywhere. As the mag-
nitude of it sunk in—Çeda, the White Wolf, beaten like

headstrong mule—his anger burned brighter. "Who did this to you?"

She drew breath, but the pain was clearly preventing her from breathing deeply. "I wish I knew. Because if I did, believe you me, I'd piss in their oats."

"I said no jokes. What *happened?*"

"What would you like me to say, Emre? I was a fool. I was heading through the Shallows, and someone jumped me. A couple of someones, I guess. Never got a good look at them."

"What were you doing in the *Shallows?*"

The Shallows was a swath of land just outside the western reaches of Sharakhai's ancient walls, land that had long ago been swallowed by the ever-expanding city. It was undesirable land, though, and so had never been settled properly. It was nestled in a gentle curve of the River Haddah, land that tended to flood in those rare times when heavy rains came to the central desert. It was filled with ramshackle hovels, one piled on top of the other, a forgotten place where the lowest in Sharakhai went to scrape a living. It was a dangerous place, not leastwise because many of those who lived in the Shallows were fresh from the desert. They were members of the wandering tribes who had given up their nomadic life to find fortune in Sharakhai. The trouble was that the city had neither forgotten nor forgiven the treachery of the tribesmen, how they fought years ago, how some *still* fought to destroy Sharakhai and return control of the desert to the shaikhs. The Kings had long allowed any from the desert to come to the city, because doing so weakened their numbers. But no one in Sharakhai made them welcome, none save their brothers and sisters in the Shallows.

"I already said it was foolish, didn't I?"

"*You* were beaten in the streets?"

She groaned, looking embarrassed. "There's always someone stronger, Emre. Someone quicker."

"We'll find them, then. Someone will talk if we lay out a bit of coin."

"You know very well that they won't. No one in the

Shallows is going to talk to you or me or anyone else, so get it out of your mind now."

"Why were you even there?"

With supreme effort, she pulled herself higher until she was leaning against the headboard. "I was taking a short-cut. Now leave it alone."

Emre sat back in his seat, grimacing every bit as much as Çeda.

Çeda looked at him and suddenly started to giggle, and when he looked at her, confused, it turned into a full-fledged laugh—how he loved the sound—and then she held her ribs, grimacing and laughing at the same time.

"What?" he asked.

"We're quite a pair, aren't we? Like two beaten dogs."

He chuckled at that, and in return she laughed even harder, though it was clearly causing her pain. Despite the pain, it felt good, the two of them, sitting here like this. They hadn't talked—truly talked—in what felt like months.

"And what of you?" she asked when their laughter had died down. "Do you remember anything from the other night?"

He shrugged. "I made it to the southern harbor and met a man there, near the two-story warehouse, the one with the wind chimes."

"Did you see his face?"

He shook his head as he fought to remember more beyond that early meeting. "He wore a veil. I don't even remember hearing his voice. I spoke the words Tariq had said to, and he handed me the canister. Simple as that."

"And then?"

He tried to remember, but the memories of that night were still lost to him, and the more he tried, the more confused he became. "I can't recall." He focused on her then. "It was you who saved me, wasn't it?"

She answered him with a sober nod. "I found you along the Haddah with a dead tribesman nearby."

Her words reminded him of his dreams—lying there in the dry riverbed, the asir atop him, pressing its claws deeper and deeper into his chest.

The dream was like a doorway leading to his memories—
his *real* memories—of that night. Like a scroll being unrolled
for the reading, more and more was revealed. The things
he'd done, the cowardice he'd shown . . . Little wonder it had
reminded him of his dead brother.

"Emre? You remember, don't you?"

He looked at Çeda, not really seeing her, instead seeing
a man lying on the ground, pleading with Emre to help
him. But he hadn't helped. He'd stared as if made of stone.

"Emre, talk to me."

He couldn't tell Çeda the truth. Were it anyone else,
someone he didn't care so much about, then perhaps, but
not Çeda. So he did the only thing he could do: He lied,
mixing in just enough truth so she wouldn't suspect.

"I was headed north from the harbor, and near Yerinde's
fount I heard someone following me. I ran, but there were
two of them ahead." He shook his head, feeling angry with
himself. He should never have allowed himself to be caught
so easily. "They trapped me near the ruins of Nalamae's
temple. I fought them, cut one across his legs, but not before
I'd been cut myself. I ran and took to the canals, hoping I'd
lose them, but one of them found me." Emre stopped, the
true memories of the night's events echoing the lies like
macabre shadows. "We fought and . . ."

"What is it?" she asked, and when he didn't respond,
she reached out and took his hand.

However warm her hand might be, it did little to banish
the chill running through him. "It's just that I've
never . . . I've never killed anyone, Çeda." It wasn't *the*
truth, but it was *a* truth, and for now, that would have to do.

She squeezed his hand. "They would've killed *you*."

"I know." He stood up from the bed with an awful grimace. "Can I get you anything?"

"For what?"

"For anything."

"No. Nothing." Çeda frowned as her gaze flitted from
him to her bedroom doorway. "Why? Where are you
going?"

"I need to get out of the house."

"Absolutely not. Your stitches, Emre."

He stopped at the archway. "Just up to the bazaar and back, I promise. I just need a bit of air."

She looked him up and down, then gave him a sharp nod.

When he made it to the door and grabbed the handle, he heard Çeda say, "Mule," from the other room, more than loud enough for him to hear.

He smiled and opened the door. "Ass," he shot back, and closed the door behind him.

Chapter 11

CEDA TRIED TO SLEEP, but that look on Emre's face . . . He hadn't merely looked afraid; he'd looked *haunted*. By what, she had no idea, but she could tell he hadn't told her the whole story, which made her feel all the worse for lying to him as she had. But how could she tell him the truth?

Yes, Emre, I opened the canister you'd promised to deliver safely and was caught by Osman doing it. You're welcome.

No matter that it had been partially due to worry over Emre that had driven her to open the case. It was still a betrayal of Osman's trust in Emre, and Emre's trust in her.

After a while—forcing herself to a state of relaxation that also served to minimize the pain—she got up and poured herself a good helping of water from the large ewer she'd filled the day before. After removing her clothes—the ones she hadn't had the strength or the will to take off the day before—she washed slowly and carefully, cataloging her wounds along the way. She had dozens of aches and scrapes and bruises, some deeply painful at the moment, but she'd received worse in the pits. The ribs she'd thought cracked seemed to be whole, if very tender.

It was the marks on her face that were the worst, for

they made a public statement. Few enough knew that Çeda had been working for Osman, and fewer still would know of Çeda's betrayal, but for those who did, Osman wanted a visible reminder of what happened to those who crossed him, even those as close as Çeda had been to him.

It was well over an hour before she finally managed to dress herself in a purple jalabiya, wrap herself in a black niqab, and veil her face. It was a rich dress, one she'd worn only twice since buying it a year ago, which was exactly why she chose it today. The fewer who recognized her over the next few days, the better. She didn't want to answer questions about it, and she didn't want anyone asking *Emre* questions about it, either.

She might have waited, given herself a chance to heal, but the stone she'd found in the canister, and the desert tribesmen that had tried to intercept it . . . it was all so strange, and she refused to let it rest.

She considered waiting for Emre—he should have been back before now—but it was clear he wanted time alone. Let him have his space, she decided, as she headed out toward the bazaar. She glanced up at the sun while walking gingerly down the alley. Gods, she'd completely forgotten. Her second class met this afternoon. She'd send word. Osman or someone at the pits would probably inform them of her absence, but she owed them a message with her apologies.

The crowd was not thick today, but there were enough wandering the lanes that she wasn't conspicuous as she wound her way toward Tehla the bread baker's stall. Tehla was crouching down, staring into the glowing red interior of an ancient brick oven that looked as though it had been built from bricks left over from the world's making. Using a flat wooden peel, she expertly rotated four loaves of bread, turning the side that needed the most browning toward the low-banked flames.

When she stood, she started at Çeda's presence, and then smiled easily, her relief showing as she spun the peel with an experienced twist of showmanship and set it into its holder alongside the oven. "I've got some loaves nearly ready, and two are unspoken for. Or if flatbread is more to your taste, I've got some laced with fennel and coriander, and another—"

She stopped, for Çeda had pulled down her veil, just enough for Tehla to see more of her face.

"Nalamae's teats, Çeda, what's happened?"

Çeda merely smiled. "Never you mind, my sweet. That's not why I've come."

"Are you sure? I could fetch Seyhan. He sells a few poultices along with his spices." Çeda merely shook her head, and Tehla nodded. She knew that Çeda had lived in Dardzada's home for a time, and that being so, Çeda would know how to make anything that Seyhan could manage and much more besides.

"I've come to ask about your brother," Çeda said.

"Yosan?"

"Davud."

Tehla's face pinched as the hot desert wind kicked up, lifting the roofs of the tents throughout the bazaar and tugging at her lazy curls. "What would you want with Davud?"

"I have a few questions I'm trying to answer. He's still apprenticing at the collegia, isn't he?"

Tehla's look of confusion transformed into a bemused smile. "He is, Çeda. He is. But why—"

"Can you get a message to him?"

Çeda remembered Davud as a boy. He'd been an utter terror around the bazaar. Always running around, tipping over barrels, stealing bits of mince pie when he thought no one was looking, even running small scams on the visitors to the bazaar, a thing none of the vendors took a shining to. It had earned him more than one beating from the stall owners, a thing his father had grown angry about at first, but had eventually been reconciled to as long as no one beat him too badly. Even Tehla herself—one of the kindest women Çeda had ever known—had taken a switch to his backside more than once.

But no one would deny that Davud had always been bright. When he'd finally got it into his skull that he'd eventually lose a finger or an eye to the Silver Spears if he didn't stop, he'd started working at the family stall. Realizing he had a knack for numbers, his father gave over the money handling to Davud, and while he worked, he would tell stories, grand stories from poems he'd read. Everyone heard them from their parents, or from the storytellers up and down the Trough, but Davud had a way with words, and with drama. He remembered the tiniest details and would use nuances of voice and gesture to play out the piece in ways even the poet might never have thought of. Some even said he told stories better than old Ibrahim—a thing no one would tell Ibrahim to his face—and his skill became renowned. And one day it got him noticed.

A master from the collegia's scriptorium had come to try the honeymead biscuits he said he'd heard so much about, and instead of moving on, he'd stood there in his white, ankle-length habit, listening to Davud tell his story. When the story was done, he'd remained for a long while, and when Davud asked if he'd like to hear another, he'd merely shook his head and said he'd heard enough. He left soon after, and Davud had been disappointed, but the next week the master had returned and asked Davud's father if he'd ever thought about entering him into the collegium historia.

"We've no money for the collegia," he'd told the master.

The master, a man named Amalos, had merely bobbed his head and smiled. "Let me worry about that."

The change in Davud since then had been remarkable. Çeda hardly recognized the young man who strode in to the tea room she'd chosen for their meeting. The tea room itself was far enough from the bazaar that she doubted she'd see anyone from Roseridge, yet near enough to the Trough and the collegia that no one would raise an eyebrow if they *were* spotted together.

Davud had grown. He had always been tall for his age, but now he was taller even than Emre. Where Emre was muscular, though, Davud was slender. He had bright brown eyes and a brighter smile, but more than this, he was composed and respectful, so different from his younger self. He stopped at the front of the house and spoke politely with the host, bowed his head at the host's answers, revealing bright teeth as he smiled, and followed him to the low table where Çeda was sitting. She wore a cream-colored

abaya and a matching shemagh that covered all but her
eyes. His smile widened when he spotted her.

As he wound his way through the patrons, ceiling fans
turned lazily, squeaking ever so slightly over the roar of
conversation. The fans—a must for the poshest establish-
ments along and near the Trough—were powered by some
ingenious, belted contraption commissioned by the owner
to keep a breeze moving over the teahouse patrons. Many
in the teahouse wore outlandish clothes—merchants and
visitors especially. But their custom of wearing layers of
heavy cloth would last no more than a week or two in this
heat-baked city, little matter that it would be considered
immodest in their homeland.

When Davud reached Çeda's table—the one farthest
from prying ears—he bowed most formally and said, "A
good day for old friends to meet!" He motioned to the table. "May I?"

"Of course," Çeda said, hiding a smile. Davud had been
smitten with her when he was younger, and it was clearly
still the case. *A thing I'll need to watch for. I want information, but it won't do to have him mooning after me.*

Davud folded himself onto the pillows opposite Çeda,
that wide, boyish smile still on his face. His smile vanished,
however, when she pulled back her shemagh, revealing the
bruises and cuts on her face. More than a week had passed
since the attack. She was still sore in a few places, especially her ribs, but she was feeling much better after taking
the time to let herself heal. She'd also stolen a few sips of
Dardzada's foul draught, what little she thought she could
spare from Emre's supply. It tasted like jackal shit, but
there was no denying it helped the body heal. The bruises,
though, were lingering. She'd thought of leaving her face
hidden, to keep Davud from worrying, but it would be a
rude gesture, and she didn't wish for Davud to become uncomfortable when she was asking so much of him.

"Çeda, what happened?"

She waved away his concerns. "A disagreement with a
particularly surly tree branch."

"A *branch?* A bough is more like it, and its older brothers as well!"

"Well, in their defense, I *was* in a rather fiery state of mind. Likely I startled them."

Davud laughed, his look of concern fading. Çeda patted the pillows next to her, and he shifted so that the two of them were side by side, backs to the wall, each of them now with a wide view over the entire bustling room—an arrangement that let them keep their voices low and speak in relative privacy. But she was doubly pleased he wouldn't also be able to stare at her bruises every second of their meal.

A young boy wearing a bright blue kufi came and stood next to the table, waiting patiently for Davud's selection.

"Order anything you like," Çeda said over the din. "They have wonderful teas, dozens I haven't even tried, from all corners of the world. And the owner's husband is a wonderful chef. He has these pastries with berries that make your tongue tingle when you bite into them."

"Her tea smells wonderful," Davud said, motioning to the beautiful inlaid teapot sitting before Çeda.

"Orange peel with cinnamon and mace," the boy replied easily.

"And do you have any of those lotus seed buns?" He held out a hand, forming a circle with thumb and forefinger.

The boy nodded, and when Davud held up three fingers, the boy bowed from the waist and fled to the back of the house. He returned a short while later with Davud's tea, a painted porcelain cup, and a plate of three small pastries that were pasty white, perfectly round, and looked more akin to poisonous white mushroom caps than sweets you'd willingly pop into your mouth. But pop Davud did, stuffing the first one in whole and chewing it with relish. "Have you tried them?" he asked between the sticky smacking sounds.

She shook her head. "They look foul."

"They're from Mirea," he said, and stuffed the second one into his mouth, "and they're wonderful."

When Davud had wolfed all three sweets, the two of them sipped their tea as the sounds of the teahouse enveloped them. "I've never been," Davud said, taking in the room. "It seems the Trough has new tea rooms and cafes and smoke dens sprouting up every week."

"That's because it does."

"Which in a way is nice, isn't it? Where else in the world can you get lotus seed buns and kefir and paella and grilled lemon octopus all in the same restaurant, much less the same city?"

"The city provides," Çeda said, the words traditional when discovering yet another new wonder in the byways of the Amber City.

"That it does, including more than its fair share of mystery." Davud tilted his head toward her and lifted his brows conspiratorially—once, then twice, then a third time.

Çeda tried to hide a smile, until a pent-up laugh escaped her. Davud was still young, only sixteen, if she remembered true, and yet he seemed twice his age. She knew his time at the collegia had changed him, but she'd had no idea just how much.

"Mysteries that need solving," Çeda replied, giving him her best impression of a collegia master's frown.

"Yes. About that . . ." He paused, watching not Çeda but the neighboring tables.

"Easy conversation causes less distraction," Çeda said softly.

His cheeks reddened at that, but he still bowed his head incrementally toward her before speaking, "I searched a bit for the stone you mentioned, on my own at first, but I was getting nowhere." He licked his lips, showing a bit of his age at last. "So I resorted to speaking with Amalos, as I mentioned I might."

"I hope you were discreet."

"Of course I was," Davud replied. "He doesn't suspect that it was for anyone but me."

Çeda reached out and took his hand. "I cannot stress it enough. The collegia has strong ties to the House of Kings. If anyone there got wind of this . . ."

Davud nodded and lowered his voice until it was all but a whisper. "Don't worry. Amalos has little love for the Kings."

Çeda squeezed his hand. It was something he probably shouldn't have told her, but she was glad he did. Knowing who had ties to the households of the Kings was a life and death matter for many in Sharakhai.

"In any case," Davud went on, "I told him I'd read about

a diaphanous stone in a text. And I wasn't lying! I just didn't share *why* I'd been reading the text in the first place. And besides, trust me in this, if nothing else; Amalos loves sharing the knowledge he's collected. Little wonder, too. The things he knows amaze me. So if you ever have need of information, you'll let me know."

Çeda nodded. "And what did he say, our good friend Amalos?"

"Well. That's where things become a bit difficult. There are several types of diaphanous stones, all of them very rare. Two of the three types Amalos was aware of come from mines in the mountains of Quanlang province in Mirea, and we suspect the third is from there as well, or from lands beyond. The Queen of Mirea safeguards the locations of those mines very carefully, lest anyone attempt to steal into them, or worse, gain control of them outright."

"Are the mines themselves important?"

It was Davud's turn to give *her* a master's frown. "You never know what might be important. Amalos mentioned it to me, so I mention it to you. Now, the first stone is called mind's flight. It's a stone that's relatively small, and polished to a high sheen, and when swallowed, is said to give one the ability to hear the thoughts of those around you."

"*Hear* their thoughts?"

"So the story goes, though it comes with a great price. The imbiber inevitably dies within hours of taking it."

"What good is a stone that kills the one who swallows it?"

"A fair question, and you can see why it would only be used in special circumstances, but Mirea's queens have been known to employ them in the past. Her agents volunteer for it and pass their discoveries to another, who records them carefully."

Interesting, Çeda thought, but if it were truly that rare, why would one be found here, and who would willingly offer themselves up for such an assignment?

The answer was obvious, of course. There were many in the Moonless Host who would sacrifice themselves for their cause.

"And the second?"

"The second is called a breathstone. It is not swallowed, not initially, anyway. Instead, it is given blood."

Çeda sipped her tea. "You'll forgive me, I hope, when I say I have no idea what you mean."

Davud laughed. "Don't feel bad. Neither did I. Amalos wasn't sure exactly how, but it apparently is fed the blood of the living, at which point it is prepared for its true purpose."

"Which is?"

"When forced down the throat of the dead, they are brought back to life. How long it lasts I cannot say. Minutes, no more than hours, is my guess, but while in this state, the dead can speak, at least until the magic of the stone and the blood wears off, and they slip back to the land beyond once more."

"That's grisly business, Davud, flirting with the domain of the dead."

"You haven't heard the worst of it. The third is called a saltstone. It can be swallowed, but is more often sewn beneath the skin of the forehead." He touched the center of his forehead, just above the bridge of his nose, cringing as he did so. "There it slowly dissolves, bleeding away memories, slowly but surely, until none are left. Within a week or two, there is nothing left of the victim. They become books filled with empty pages. They have neither thought nor emotion. More importantly, they are completely and utterly docile."

Çeda shivered. "What use would they have for such things?"

"The Mireans do not believe in killing as punishment, even for brutal and bloody crimes. They believe one's soul always has a chance at redemption, so they avoid death whenever possible. But there are times when the offenses are so unforgivable that action must be taken. There have also been times in their history where the games of kings and queens has led to the use of the saltstone. In retribution, or even love."

"Love?"

"Of a sort. A very twisted sort, I'll agree. There is one story in which a king, finding his queen to be too unruly, made her docile by use of a saltstone."

Çeda shivered. "That's grisly."

"Not to mention unspeakably cruel."

"And how can these stones be told apart?"

Davud raised his cup and took a long sip of tea, savoring it as though it would help him forget the cruelties perpetrated by the use of these strange artifacts. "Little is known about their physical attributes, except that they are as you described—transparent to some degree with white striations running through them. A mind's flight stone, however, has flecks of gold running through it. Did your stone have such?"

Çeda shook her head. "Are the flecks large? Easy to see?"

"I don't know."

Çeda hadn't seen anything like that. Then again, she hadn't been looking for it, either. "Let's assume it isn't a match. What about the others?"

"Amalos said that the text he'd read of saltstone specifically said it had a milky consistency to it."

Çeda shook her head, relieved in a way to rule that one out. "This one was very clear. There was white, but it was more like trails of smoke than milky."

"That leaves the breathstone. There were few enough texts that mention it, but, strangely enough, it is the only one whose use is forbidden by the Kannan."

The Kannan was the set of laws as written by the Kings and handed down to the Sharakhani. All who lived or came to Sharakhai obeyed them. The Kings had written the laws of the Kannan four hundred years ago, after Beht Ihman, the night the Kings had saved Sharakhai from the might of the gathered tribes, but it had adopted many of the strictures within the much older Al'Ambra, the laws the desert tribes had been using for thousands of years.

"Why not the others?" Çeda asked. "Why not forbid them all?"

Davud touched his fingers to his forehead, a sign that begged forbearance, in this case from any gods who might be listening. "Who can know the mind of the Kings?"

The Kings, Çeda thought. *The Kings can know.*

These smaller mysteries aside, Davud had done her a

great service. Outside the teahouse, he hugged her briefly—
Çeda wincing slightly from the pain it brought—and left
for the collegia, while Çeda wandered the streets of Sharakhai, soon finding herself walking along the Trough. She
fell into her old rhythm of walking with a limp, made all
the authentic since her left ankle was still tender from the
beating she'd received. She told herself she was simply
walking, that she was allowing her body to take her where
it would, but the more she wove among the wagons and
horses and carts and crowds, the more the sounds of the
city washed over her, the more she realized she was headed
toward one place in particular. Toward one *man* in particular. And why not?

The breathstone—if that was what it truly was—was a
mystery that needed solving. Emre had nearly died for it.
And if Mirea was involved in some way, then there was a
good chance the Kings were involved as well. As much as
it pained her to admit, she had done little to harm the
Kings in the years since her mother's death. She had been
a mere child then, barely able to avoid sinking beneath the
sands of the city. She had seen the Kings from time to time.
She had gone out of her way to learn what she could about
them, but it had always felt so insignificant in the grand
scheme of things. The Kings had painted a picture of themselves that was difficult, if not impossible, to see through.

She'd always thought there would come a day when an
opportunity would present itself. It had never happened,
but she hoped this might be her chance, somehow, and
she'd be damned by the gods before she would let this go,
not until she'd exhausted every possibility.

She wasn't looking forward to this meeting—Osman's
memory for those who had harmed him was long—but if
her mother had taught her anything, it was that problems
were like termites; they should be dealt with quickly and
directly. Ignoring them would only allow them to multiply
and spread, making it all the more difficult when you set
yourself to rooting them out once and for all.

Chapter 12

ÇEDA FOLLOWED THE TROUGH as it curved around the bulk of Tauriyat and the House of Kings. After that, it ran like an arrow due north, ending mere yards from the sands of the harbor.

The harbor was busy, as it often was after Beht Zha'ir. Ship caravans often timed their departures to reach Sharakhai a day or two after the holy night, hoping to profit from the celebrations that followed. A score of sandships were moored at the docks, some flying the red pennants of Mirea, others the ochre and brown of Kundhun. There were also three small caravels, docked next to one another, that flew no pennants at all. These were ships of the desert tribes. Few of them sailed to the city these days, especially with the number of sanctioned trade caravans being attacked by the rebel tribes, but there were still a handful of shaikhs granted favored status by the Kings of Sharakhai.

After dodging past a wagon stacked high with bolts of bright cloth, Çeda headed along the quay that curved like a new moon along the bay's inner edge. Three dozen piers reached out from the quay like combs into the sand. At the quay's western terminus stood a tower made from bright white stone, its twin standing sentinel at the bay's eastern edge. These were the northern harbor's lighthouses and, just like the southern harbor and the royal harbor to the east, they were lit every night except Beht Zha'ir, guiding ships into the harbor. These two lighthouses, unlike the others, were run by Osman—one of the many ventures he'd gotten into years ago, after buying the pits.

As Çeda strode along the boardwalk, her eyes were drawn toward the entrance to the bay, for just then a caravel with two lateen sails was gliding easily over the sand in the gap between the lighthouses. The harbormaster stood at an open pier, waving red flags to signal the caravel there. It adjusted course, the rudder kicking up sand in a tail. The crew was already working to pull in the sails, and eventually the caravel came to a rest fifty paces from the dock. A train of a dozen mules, led by the harbormaster's young son, trudged out to meet her. A massive rope was hooked to the mules' harnesses, and the young man called *Hyah! Hyah!* and whipped the mules onward, towing the ship to her assigned dock.

"Oh ho!"

Çeda turned. Ahead, sitting in the lighthouse's desert-dry yard, was a flatbed cart with a scrawny mule harnessed to it. An ancient man with leathern skin and a wide-brimmed hat sat crooked as a crook in the driver's bench. He smiled as Çeda approached, showing five yellow teeth standing proud as gravestones.

Çeda was in no mood to joke, but Ibrahim's smile was so genuine she couldn't help but return it. "The moons shine on you, Ibrahim. How is your gem of a wife?"

"Gem?" His face turned sour. "A piece of coal is more like it."

"If she's coal, then she burns as bright as the sun."

"That's why I wear my hat," he shot back, flicking the brim.

"Because you can't bear her beauty?"

"Because I can't stand the sight of her."

Despite herself, Çeda laughed, but she stopped when she saw Tariq standing in the doorway, watching their exchange.

With deliberation, she faced Tariq and unwrapped her shemagh from around her head and settled it over her shoulders. She wouldn't have Tariq thinking she was hiding anything from him. "Good day, Tariq," she said easily.

Tariq walked past her—giving her a sidelong glance that was half bravado, half disregard—and headed for the wagon. Çeda stepped into the tower, momentarily sunblind in the darkness. Her eyes adjusted and she saw Osman's tall form climbing down the stairs that hugged the tower's inner wall. He wore a long golden kaftan and red sirwal trousers tied off halfway down his shins. His beard was ragged and unkempt, making him look like one of the sea gods Çeda had once seen illuminated in a book, except Osman seemed contemplative today, more diplomat than wrathful deity.

She'd always thought this a strange place for Osman—a man of means—to spend his time. He could easily have others do this for him, but he liked the lighthouses, he'd told her once when they were lying together in bed. "They make me think of other places," he'd said, "what they're like, the people who live there, how they live differently from us."

"You could go there, you know. There's nothing stopping you."

But he'd merely shaken his head. "I'll never leave Sharakhai, Çeda."

"And why not? You're a young man yet."

He'd pinched her at that, but then he'd grown serious. "I love this city too much to leave her. But it doesn't stop me from wondering."

By the time Osman reached ground level, Tariq had returned carrying one of the barrels over his shoulder. For a moment, the three of them stood there, eyeing one another. The muscles along Tariq's jaw worked, but that was the only sign of his mood. Osman didn't seem pleased, exactly, but neither did he seem angry.

"I thought it was made abundantly clear," Osman said, "that you're not welcome here any longer."

"We need to speak." Her speech—Rhia be praised for small favors—no longer sounded as though she'd just been beaten in a back alley, but she was still painfully aware of Osman's looking at the wounds on her face.

"We have no business with one another. Not any longer. Now go, Çeda, or does Tariq need to give you another lesson?"

"That would be unwise," Çeda replied.

"And why is that?" Tariq asked.

She turned to him, ignoring Osman for the moment. "Because I deserved that beating. I may even have deserved worse, but I'm not willing to take another. Not from you, not from anyone else." Tariq bristled, but before he could reply, Çeda turned to Osman. "There are things you need to know about that night."

"Anything I need to know, I'll learn from Emre."

"He was unconscious for most of it, Osman. And there are things I've learned besides."

"About what?"

"About the contents of the case."

Osman's face showed the same look of betrayal he'd had in the alley before he'd ordered her beating, except now there was something more deadly in his eyes. It seemed to take some effort for him to tear his eyes from her, to pick up one of the two dozen barrels stacked inside the door, and begin climbing the stairs. "Bring a barrel with you."

For a moment she and Tariq stared one another down. "You know, Çeda, one of these days, there'll be no one around to protect you from yourself."

"And you think you'll be there to see it, Tariq?"

"If the gods are kind, I will." He laughed, as if he'd made some sort of joke, and then sauntered to a small room at the back of the lighthouse.

Çeda hefted one of the heavy barrels and followed Osman. Up and up they wound—twelve flights if it were one—and by the time she reached the top, she was well out of breath. She hadn't worked herself hard since the beating—she knew her body well enough to know when she could push and when she couldn't—but she was pleased at how good her joints felt from the movement. They were tight yet, but ready for more. Osman was breathing heavily too, though not as heavily as she would have guessed. In fact, he'd hardly broken a sweat.

"Twenty years from the pits and still in fighting shape," Çeda said.

"I might lug a barrel or two around, but fighting? I left that all behind, Çeda. I have others to fight for me now."

She moved to set the barrel on the stack with the others, but Osman shook his head and pointed to the curving iron stairs that led farther up. He went first, swinging open the trapdoor that led out and into the blazing sun. She squinted against the brightness and followed, and when she reached the roof, he kicked the door closed and moved to the massive lantern that stood at the center. The glass globe atop the lantern had a lens built into it, such that when the globe was swiveled back and forth, a bright beam would sweep over the desert, signaling ships at night or during a sandstorm. The wick—a weave of coarse, sooty horsehair—ran down into a brass tank. Osman unscrewed the cap on top of the tank and set it aside, nodding to Çeda and her barrel. As Osman stepped back and stared down toward the harbor, she pulled the cork from one end of the barrel and began carefully pouring the oil into the tank. Its pungent scent filled the air as it *glugged*. When it was done she corked the empty barrel, and replaced the cap. And then there was a hand around her throat and she was flying backward, the sky tilting up to fill her vision.

Her arms flung outward to catch herself, a bare moment before her body slammed against the stone roof of the tower, rekindling the pain of her wounds. Osman had a fistful of her hair and was using it to drag her slowly but surely toward the edge of the parapet. She kicked and thrashed, her fingers scrabbling against the stone as she fought for purchase—something, anything, to prevent being hauled to the edge like garbage for the offal pit—but Osman had all the leverage he needed to drag her up and halfway over the roof's stone lip.

When she felt herself leaning out over open air, she went rigid, she was so frightened of being thrown downward. She clutched at his arms, grabbed his kaftan, but he could drop her whenever he wished, and they both knew it.

She glanced to one side, saw the distance she'd fall

before crashing against the unforgiving earth below. Breath of the desert, they were high up.

The gods as her witness she'd never seen Osman look so furious, veins bulging, spittle flying from his mouth as his breath came heavy. When he spoke, however, he did not yell. He did not shout. He spoke instead with a quiet intensity that scared her far more than some violent outburst ever could. "First you break into a canister that wasn't yours. Then you admit to doing it many times before. And now you tell me you've continued to look into the affairs of *my* patrons? *Mine*, Çeda! Not yours! This is none of your affair!"

"It became my affair when Emre was nearly killed for the canister he went to pick up."

"Emre knows the risks, as do you. Or have you forgotten?"

Years ago, she'd taken a blood oath to protect any and all of Osman's packages she was entrusted with—with her life, if necessary—and Emre had done the same.

"I remember, but there's more to it this time." She tried to gain a grip on the parapet, but Osman maneuvered her away from it. "Don't you care that one of your own was attacked? That he was nearly killed?"

"I care, Çeda, but that's none of your concern."

"*Emre* is my concern. Did you really think I would let it go after he was attacked? I can't go after them, but I can look into the package, if you'll let me."

His hand was still tight on the back of her head. He shook her violently, his expression desperate, like a fighter in the pits who knew the end was near. "What am I supposed to do with you? Why do you always have to be so fucking stubborn?"

Her stomach was spinning, but she stared coolly into his eyes, knowing that to show fear now might convince him to release his hold and be done with her once and for all. "I am what I am, Osman. That's why you allowed me to fight in the pits. That's why you hired me to shade for you." He pushed her further. "There were tribesmen there! Did you know that?"

The muscles along Osman's neck tightened like cordage. "Of course I did."

Çeda was confused at first, but then she understood. *Emre, you bloody ass.*

She hadn't mentioned it to Tariq. Emre must have gone to Osman the other day, when he'd said he'd just needed to clear his head. "Did he tell you an asirim took one of the tribesmen?" He didn't reply, but she could see in his face that he hadn't known. "The asirim were thick in the streets that night. Surely you heard them. One of them hauled a dead tribesman up, threw him over its shoulder, and carried him away while I watched."

Osman's eyes narrowed. "Why?"

"I don't know. Perhaps it liked the smell of him. Perhaps it was hungry. Or perhaps it thought he had the canister Emre was sent to deliver. Did you know there was a breathstone in the case? Do you even know what a breathstone is?"

"Aren't you listening?" He shook her, and her left leg slipped over the edge. "I don't *need* to know, and neither do you!"

"Osman, listen to me. Do you remember when I first started shading for you? You said that you'd ripped the reins of the shading business from Old Vadram. You said he hadn't sensed the winds changing, that he'd been caught in the storm when the Silver Spears had decided they no longer needed to abide by old agreements."

"Vadram was half senile by that point. He'd been ignoring the crumbling ruins of his empire for years."

"And you?" Çeda asked. "Are you going to ignore the storm even when you see it billowing up along the horizon? Do nothing until the sands are howling over Sharakhai?"

His fists were shaking by this point, not from exhaustion, but with rage and worry. For long moments he kept her right where she was, but she could see the fire draining from him. His shoulders slumped, and his expression changed to one that made it clear he already regretted what he was about to do. Releasing a long sigh, he pulled her up and shoved her away from him. "What's a breathstone?" he asked as he stood, brushing the dust and dirt from his forearms and clothes.

"They're given to the dead," she said as she stood and faced him. "Fed to them, after which they wake for a time.

In that state, they can speak, at least until the effects of the stone wear off."

"And how long is that?"

"Bakhi only knows," Çeda replied. "Bakhi and perhaps whoever sent it to Macide."

As she said these words, she prepared herself for Osman's reaction. She expected him to shout with rage. To call her a meddling child. Perhaps even renege on his ill-considered bout of mercy and toss her over the side of the lighthouse. What she didn't expect was for him to work through the implications of what she'd said, smile resignedly, and then begin laughing, low and long, until it had grown into a full-throated affair that half of Sharakhai could hear.

"By the gods, you tailed whoever collected your canister," Osman said when his laugh died down at last. "Çeda, we don't take *sides!*"

"No, *you* don't take sides! Macide is a viper."

"He may be dangerous to the Kings, dangerous to others who oppose him, but not to his allies. We have little to fear."

"You're wrong. He's dangerous to his allies as well. You don't know what the Al'Afwa Khadar are like."

Osman shrugged his shoulder, as if he were loosening his aching body after a bout in the pits. "I know them better than you. Macide is merely focused. He's driven. I can admire a man like that."

"He's *too* driven, Osman. Like a mule with blinders, he plods onward, regardless of what happens around him, regardless of who he tramples."

An incredulous look overcame Osman. "He is driven for the blood of the Kings, Çeda. Isn't that what *you're* after? Isn't that what you've been striving for since your mother died? By all rights you should be allies!"

Çeda spit onto the roof in the space between them. "Macide and I will never be allies."

Osman ignored her words. "What happened to your mother, Çeda?"

"I can't tell you that," she said. The words sent a pang of regret through her, not because of any disappointment

Osman might be feeling, but because of how poorly she'd managed to fulfill her promise to avenge her mother's death. There were days that she wished she could go back and stand by her mother. She would fight by her side, and *die* by her side if that was how the gods willed it.

As they stood there in silence, the sounds of the city dreamlike in the air around them, a change came over Osman. His gaze softened. "I could help you." She'd never seen him like this. He'd always been the hardened warrior, putting on a strong face, never showing weakness. Even when they'd made love, he had been intense, rarely letting his guard down—perhaps for her sake, perhaps for his own.

Suddenly she deeply regretted what she'd done to him, even more so than when he'd first caught her red-handed with the canister in the streets near the bazaar, and it made her realize what her answer had to be. She'd known long ago that—Emre being the lone exception—she couldn't share her secrets. If others knew, it increased the chances that the Kings would discover her, and through her, her friends and those she loved. As much as she believed Osman *would* help her, she shook her head and said, "This isn't your battle."

At this, the stoic expression Osman usually wore returned, and he walked to the edge of the roof, holding his hands behind his back and surveying the cityscape of Sharakhai.

Çeda moved to his side as the hot desert wind tugged at her clothes. Directly ahead, far to the south, was the southern harbor and its two lighthouses, and to her right, past the line of the winding Haddah and the tents of the bazaar and the slums, lay the western harbor, the one that held the smallest of Sharakhai's ships. To her left was Tauriyat, with its own harbor—King's Harbor, with the ships of war, impregnable walls, and a titanic pair of gates at its entrance. A dark line ran from the mountains to the walls of King's Harbor—the city's aqueduct, which fed the tree groves and plantations and the man-made lake that occupied a wide swath to the northeast of Sharakhai. The Haddah and Sharakhai's numerous wells kept much of the city in water, but the aqueduct was vital, bringing so much precious water from its deep mountain reservoir. It had allowed Sharakhai to thrive and grow, even in times of severe drought, into the sprawling and wondrous beast that lay before them.

From here it was easy to see Sharakhai's old walls. They circled the more affluent areas around Tauriyat—places like Goldenhill, the temple district, the collegia—but also the traditional heart of Sharakhai—the auction blocks, the bazaar, the spice market. The city had long ago grown beyond those walls, reaching out into the dry desert, especially westward, where many of the poorer in Sharakhai lived in hovels and ramshackle homes and tenements. Çeda felt fortunate to live where she did, near the old walls and the bazaar. Roseridge was at least moderately safe. Other districts were both crime- and disease-ridden, unable to afford the private constabularies that patrolled much of the rest of the city or the requisite bribes for the Silver Spears.

"What do you suppose the Moonless Host would do if they succeeded, Osman? What do you suppose they would do if the asirim suddenly vanished, leaving Sharakhai defenseless?" She paused, waiting for the point to hit home. The asirim came for their reaping each night of Beht Zha'ir, but the Blade Maidens also used them to protect the interests of the Kings. Whatever Çeda might feel about them, she had to admit they had always provided a stabilizing influence in the desert, preventing not only the wandering tribes from attacking Sharakhai, but the four neighboring Kingdoms as well, all of which had coveted Sharakhai for their own over the centuries since its birth. "They'd pick up the war that ended when the Kings took power," Çeda went on. "They'd raze the city and return the Shangazi to the ways of the wandering tribes."

"Do you really think so?" Osman asked. "It's been four hundred years, Çeda. The mindset of the tribes has changed, even for those in the Moonless Host. Macide may be wicked with those swords he carries, but believe me, he's just as sharp with a pen and a ledger. He has to be. It takes money to supply his host, to feed their horses and repair their ships. It takes money to find men who can supply him with a breathstone. Macide would no more tear this city down than he would the wandering tribes. There's too much he likes about both. He just wants the Kings to be gone, to let the tribes live as they wish."

"What I hear is a man who doesn't wish to know what's happening in his own city. Who makes guesses when he should be learning more for himself."

"It isn't my city."

For some reason, standing here like this with Osman, the whole of the Amber City laid out below, she felt closer to him than she ever had before. She wished she could love him. She wished she could stand by his side and rule some small piece of this place with him. He'd made the offer before, to marry her, but she had never been tempted; or perhaps it was her promise to her mother that held her back, for she knew that to join hands with Osman would mean abandoning her hopes of harming the Kings. Osman was too protective of the things he considered his own. The day they crossed the threshold of his home as husband and wife, she would become beholden to him, and sooner or later, he would insist she leave her vows unfulfilled.

"You love this place," Çeda said. "You love it as much as I do."

"That isn't what I meant."

"I know. Sharakhai is in the hands of the Kings. And if not the Kings, then whose? Macide Ishaq'ava's? The desert shaikhs?" Far into the distance, vultures were circling. Somewhere below them—not visible even from this vantage point—were the blooming fields, the places where the twisted adichara grew, the places from which the asirim rose each night of the dual moon. The places to which they returned after their long night sowing terror. The fields ringed the city, demarcating a border that the gods of the desert themselves had pledged to protect. "Tell me who sent the stone to Macide, Osman. *You* would risk too much looking further into it with your own men, so let *me* look in the shadows. I'll be discreet, you know I will, and I'll share whatever I learn."

He continued to watch over the city. Then his gaze turned to Tauriyat, where the House of Kings lay. He stared at it for some time, as though he could peer through the walls to see the minds of the Kings themselves. "Part of me thinks the Kings will never leave this place. The gods themselves granted them the city, and control of the desert with it."

"You would leave it to chance, then?"

Osman turned to her. He looked her up and down, not as a lover, but as a man judging a warrior for the pits. "There's a tourney being held at the pits in two days."

"I know."

"Will the White Wolf fight?"

"The Wolf is wounded," Çeda said carefully, "but she may scrap with the other dirt dogs."

"It would be good if she did." He strode toward the trapdoor and swung it wide. "She might just learn a thing or two." And then he took to the stairs, leaving her alone with the vastness of Sharakhai.

As his footsteps receded, Çeda remained where she was, considering his words. She looked out past Roseridge, to a section of the city known as the Well. Osman's pits were there, a group of seven arenas where men and women fought for money. From here they looked like a dirty blossom, dropped and forgotten by the gods.

She didn't understand what he intended. Not yet. But she knew, as everyone in Sharakhai did, that this coming Tavahndi was one of the biggest fighting days of the year. Did he mean to test her in some way? Play some petty game in which she had to win in order to get the information she desired?

If that were so, then so be it; and woe betide the dog with the ill fortune to face her.

Chapter 13

"EXCELLENCE?"

Ihsan, the Honey-tongued King of Sharakhai, looked up from his desk and found the gaunt form of Tolovan, his vizir these past three decades, standing at the door.

"He's arrived," Tolovan said. "I've taken him to the veranda."

Ihsan nodded, and Tolovan turned and left, his long indigo abaya trailing behind him.

Ihsan dipped his quill into the ink-stained well near the ledger that was open before him and finished penning the last of the morning's appointments. From an aged bronze well, he scooped a small handful of fine white salt and sprinkled it over the still-damp page. When it dried, he lifted the ledger, forcing the salt into the gutter between the pages, then tilted it, pouring the grains into another, nearly empty well. This salt, stained gray from the black ink, he would use later, with his meals. The notion that he supped upon his words was not merely a comfort. It gave him a sense that they were a compact, an agreement between himself and his own past. It was why he was so very meticulous about recording his days, his plans, his meetings with the other Kings, and so much more.

And yet, before he rose, he made no entry for this coming meeting, nor would he do so later when he'd returned to his apartments. *From the eyes of god and man alike are some things best left hidden.*

With his thread-of-gold thawb barely brushing the travertine floor, he made his way to the ground floor. There two doors were opened for him, allowing him entrance to the wide veranda that overlooked Sharakhai's southwestern quarter and the endless desert beyond.

Only one table was set out. A table with two chairs. A sturdy man with a trim beard and moustache stood beside one of them. Mihir Halim'ava al Kadri, son of Shaikh Halim, Lord of the Burning Hands. Mihir wore a red turban, a thing forbidden to the populace of Sharakhai but overlooked for the visiting son of a desert shaikh. Orange tattoos marked the olive skin along the bridge of his nose, his chin and cheeks as well, and especially the palms of his hands. Unlike the other tribes, the Kadri left the backs of their hands unadorned, marking their palms instead. When Mihir saw Ihsan approaching, he bowed, and then raised his open hands toward Ihsan. *When we come in peace,* the gesture said, *you may read our tales, but when we come for war, we reveal nothing, for our palms will grip our blades.* It was a gesture that stood in stark contrast to his red turban, which, while in the past might have indicated a man preparing to tread the paths of war, had changed in recent decades to one of almost childlike impudence. To the shaikhs and their emissaries it meant that they stood apart from Sharakhai, that no yoke rested across their shoulders, but to Ihsan it looked as though Mihir were clinging to a lonely rock in a storm-swept sea.

"Tauriyat welcomes you," Ihsan said, bowing his head in return.

"My father sends his regards to the King of Sharakhai."

"Hardly *the* King." Ihsan took the open seat and gave one quick wave of his hand for Mihir to take his.

When Mihir sat, Ihsan gestured toward the doors, and immediately servants came bearing platters filled with grapes and pickled vegetables and grilled flatbread and smoked goat cheese—a fresh import from Qaimir—and

bowls of hummus and herbed olive oil and a paprika-dusted
eggplant puree that the kitchen knew Ihsan was favoring
of late. Glasses were filled with a yellow tomato juice, fil-
tered thrice so that it was crystal clear and glinted in the
summer sun. As a box of deep-grained wood was opened,
Mihir's eyes widened. The servant used a pair of silver
tongs to lift chunks of ice from the confines of the box and
drop them delicately into the glasses of juice.

"More?" Ihsan asked when the servant had half-filled
his glass with ice.

"No, thank you," Mihir was forced to say, lest he look
like a desert dog who'd never seen ice.

Which he probably hadn't. But clearly appearances
must be maintained.

"You've come a long way," Ihsan said after sipping some
of the tart juice. "The Burning Hands are well to their
summer hills, are they not?"

Mihir sipped at his juice, watching as the servants set
down the last of the food—freshly baked goat cheese and
caramelized garlic tarts—and left them in peace at last. He
tore off a piece of bread and dipped it into the pureed eggplant, savoring it before speaking. "We'd only just arrived
before I set sail for Sharakhai."

"So late."

Mihir chewed noisily. "There was good hunting in the
plateaus below the mountains. Antelope. Goat. Dogs by
the dozen."

Ihsan opened his palms to the sky. "The gods will provide."

Mihir smiled, then took another long sip of the chilled
tomato juice. "Bakhi is kind."

For a time the two of them ate and looked out over the
city. The sounds of Sharakhai came to them—immense
crowds, a ringing bell, hammers on stone—but it was soft,
as if the city were apart from Ihsan's veranda, separated by
the veil of dreams.

Industry, Ihsan thought. *Growth*. How different from
the world Mihir must be used to. He came from the desert
and a nomadic lifestyle, moving from place to place to
place, each dictated by centuries of tradition and war and

the occasional whim of their shaikh. It was a life as foreign to Sharakhai as the strange-crescent-shaped fruit Ihsan was eating. And yet young Mihir had come with news of the Amber City, or to be more precise, with *news that might affect Sharakhai*, as Mihir's father had put it when he'd requested this meeting.

Mihir seemed nervous. He seemed to want to be about his business, but Ihsan waited until they'd had their fill. He would not give Mihir the impression that he was eager for his news, whatever it might be. At best he would be ceding ground for no gain; at worst it would be tipping his hand.

"And how fare the Kadri?" Ihsan asked as he stared out to the desert. Well beyond the borders of Sharakhai, a sandstorm was rising. It looked to be headed this way.

"Very well, your Excellence. Very well indeed. The ships you gave my father last year have served us well. We've started trade with the southern Kundhuni villages, as you bade us. My father sends his thanks once more."

Without taking his eyes from the horizon, Ihsan waved his hand as if what he'd granted them was nothing. In the grand scheme of things, it was anything but. It was a promise. A promise the Kadri and three other shaikhs had made with the Kings of Sharakhai, to accept ships and horses and steel and the smaller trade routes it was no longer practical to police. The Blade Maidens had a hard enough time watching the primary trade routes for pirates and delivering the Kings' justice to those they caught, to say nothing of the smaller trails that led into the Shangazi from Kundhun and Malasan especially. The prime concern of the Kings over the past few decades had been ensuring that caravans could not bypass Sharakhai or the few caravanserais that could collect taxes. *And a fine job we're doing of it.*

The asirim, so tightly controlled in centuries past, were straining at their leashes. Some would bow to the will of the Blade Maidens only when King Mesut, the Jackal King, Lord of the Asirim, intervened. Some few had still refused, a thing that had never happened before. They'd been killed, of course, but it all made policing the pirate paths through the desert ever more difficult.

"It is but a passing thing," Mesut had told the gathered

Kings when they'd confronted him with the fact. "A storm passing through the Shangazi."

One can die from desert storms, Ihsan remembered thinking. *The Shangazi is not nearly so tenderhearted as you might wish us to think.*

Like the leaves of an acacia blowing over the tops of the dunes, it had been these signs, and dozens more, that Ihsan had seen. And they worried him. Sharakhai would no longer be able to control the borders as they had two centuries ago, or even two *decades* ago. So why not turn it to their advantage? Why not draw some of the shaikhs to their side and make it look as though the Kings were magnanimous.

It had worked better than he could have hoped. This very meeting was a prime example. Even two years ago, a shaikh would never have sent his son to deal with the Kings. He would have sent a vizir, and they would have demanded the Kings' envoy meet them out on the vast pan of the desert.

But here was Mihir, meeting with one of the Kings, perhaps not entirely trusting but willing to extend his hand in an offer of peaceable and mutual gain. And with even a small handful now willing to do so, the other tribes would, at the very least, give pause when considering whether to harm the interests of the Kings.

Across the table, Mihir downed the last of his drink, closing his eyes for a moment as the chill liquid coursed down his throat. Then he turned to Ihsan, his hand still lingering on his empty glass.

Here it comes at last, Ihsan said to himself.

"My Lord King," Mihir began, "I've come with news from my father."

"You wear a look most grave for one so young," Ihsan said, feigning concern. "What is it your father wishes us to know?"

"There are stirrings in the desert."

"Stirrings."

"Yes, your Excellence. There are rumors of men and women gathering."

Ihsan looked as though he were greatly surprised. "Gathering for what?"

"They gather to band as one. A tribe of tribes."

"The Moonless Host?" Ihsan asked.

Mihir nodded, clearly embarrassed. Not, Ihsan was sure, because that growing opposition included many from the Kadri tribe. No, it was because years ago Mihir might have joined them. Ihsan could see it in his eyes, the fire behind them, the rage at being sent here to treat with the Kings when he wasn't entirely sure he didn't want to draw a knife across Ihsan's throat.

"The Al'afwa Khadar have long sought to bleed us, young Kadri. Pray tell, what makes this different?"

"Their numbers are nothing like what we've seen in years past. They think Sharakhai weak, a peach ripe for the plucking. A foolish notion, but the words of Macide and his father, Ishaq, have begun to sway the young, the impressionable."

"And have members of your own tribe joined their ranks?"

Mihir seemed to choose his next words with care. "Your Excellency is wise. I'm sure you can guess the answer."

"Then I'll admit to some confusion. Have we not formed an accord with your shaikh? Have we not done so with many other tribes?"

"You have," Mihir allowed. "But memories do not die lightly in the desert."

Do they not? Ihsan thought.

"For some," Mihir said, stepping into the silence, "there are cruelties that cannot be forgiven."

"And what of your father?" Ihsan prodded. "Are there not cruelties that he cannot forgive?"

"My father has more to consider than his pride alone."

"And what of you, son of Halim? Are there not cruelties *you* cannot forgive?"

Mihir took a deep breath. "Forgive me, your Excellency, but have I done something to offend you?"

Ihsan painted on a most surprised expression. "Offend me?"

"You are aware, I have no doubt, of the circumstances behind my mother's death."

"That was indeed unfortunate, but the asirim . . . When

their blood is upon them, there's little to be done. The Kadri of all people know it is so."

A dozen years ago, King Husamettín, the King of Swords and Lord of the Maidens, had taken five hands of Blade Maidens, twenty-five in all, and a dozen asirim to put down a series of continued attacks against the northwestern caravanserais. He had followed their trail, and it had led him to a large encampment of three tribes, the Burning Hands among them. Husamettín had not been kind.

Mihir's mother, Syahla, had been wounded—a scratch from the blackened nails of one of the asirim—and had died a slow and painful death. Halim had come to the Kings, begging for a draught that might help her, an elixir, a salve, a laying of hands from one of the Matrons from the House of Maidens, or even from one of the Kings themselves. Ihsan had seen him and had refused his request, not once, but three times.

"The Kings cannot forgive such affronts as you committed these past years," Ihsan had said to the bereaved shaikh, "but you may find that in time such things may yield new paths."

Halim's eyes had been fire that day, but in time, as Ihsan had seen, the fire burned out of him, such that when Ihsan had approached him, Halim had been grudgingly receptive, and then open to a treaty with Sharakhai.

How he'd convinced his people to follow, Ihsan had no idea, but he could see from Mihir that it had not been easy.

Mihir stood, his chair scraping loudly. His eyes were now fierce, as his father's had been when Ihsan had refused his request, but these were the eyes of the young, the brash, eyes brimming with the callow bravado that had brought so many low. "The Moonless Host is gathering," he said. "Best you look to your borders, to the darkened dunes, to the streets of Sharakhai."

"To our very streets?"

Mihir ignored the condescension in his tone. "This is the last of the message from my father. The Host have had business in Sharakhai. My father heard word of their receiving a package beneath your nose, a thing that would lead to your downfall, if the whispers are to be believed, and he sent men to intercept it, to show his good faith. *That* is what my father has done. *That* is what the word of the Kadri means."

"And what did they find, these men?" Ihsan asked, leaning back in his chair and staring up at Mihir with a calm every bit as cool as the drinks they'd just enjoyed.

"We do not know," came Mihir's reluctant reply. "Of the two who were sent, one was found dead. The other is missing."

"What does your father believe the Moonless Host were sent?"

"We are unsure, but my father wishes me to tell you that we will continue to search. If we learn more, word will be sent."

At this Mihir gave Ihsan a half bow with one fist cupped in the opposite hand, not a declaration of outright hostility, but certainly its distant cousin. It was so far removed from the expression of greeting he'd used earlier—palms outward—that Ihsan nearly smiled. It seemed there was fire in young Mihir after all.

Without another word, Mihir strode from the table and toward the doors of the veranda.

Tolovan stepped out and looked to Ihsan—ready to do whatever his lord bade him—and when Ihsan shook his head, Tolovan let Mihir pass and then struck a measured pace toward the table where his King was still sitting.

"And how did you fare with the desert's young son?"

"It's interesting, Tolovan."

"Interesting, my Lord King?"

"Interesting. When one casts a net, one never knows what one might catch. But cast it often enough, and eventually *something* lands within it."

"Something good, I trust."

"It's rather too soon to tell." Ihsan stood, looking over the half-eaten fare. "Too soon indeed." He said these words, and yet he smiled as he stood and strode purposefully toward the palace.

Chapter 14

SEVEN YEARS EARLIER...

ÇEDA KNELT NEXT TO THE UPSTAIRS WINDOWS of Dardzada's apothecary, peeking through the slats of the shutters out to the street below, where three women in brightly colored jalabiyas—emerald and saffron and goldenrod—were walking down the street chatting gaily with one another. These women came every week, always at the same time, ostensibly to buy tonics for their skin, but in reality to buy *ral shahnad*, summer's fire, a hallucinogen made from the distilled essence of a rare flower found only in the farthest reaches of Kundhun. Çeda had been living with Dardzada for four years now, and already she'd seen many drugs of choice come and go. She knew, for she was the one who went through the painstaking work to prepare them. Dardzada might have perfected the formula, but it was her hard work that granted these women their eyes-aflutter dreams.

In the alley across the street, a boy poked his head out, staring up at her window. It was Emre. The women were just passing the alley, and when they walked past, Emre slipped into their wake and walked with a bow-legged gait, nose lifted high, arms swaying ridiculously. Çeda giggled but was horrified when he continued past Dardzada's shop. At least he stopped acting the fool, but if Dardzada saw him, he would know Çeda was up to something.

Çeda waited until she heard the women entering through the door directly below her window. She heard the floor creaking as Dardzada walked from his workroom to greet them, and immediately one began regaling Dardzada with a story about a beautiful horse, a gift she'd imported for her daughter's twelfth birthday. Upon hearing their voices fade—Dardzada often took his regular customers into the garden behind the shop for a cup of tea—Çeda opened the shutter wide, slipped out and onto the sill, then dropped down to the dusty street, rolling to make as little sound as possible.

She was up in a moment, and she and Emre were sprinting down the street. She socked him on the arm as they ran.

"Ow! What was that for?"

"For being such an idiot. I told you not to make a fool of Dardzada."

"I wasn't making a fool of *him*. I was making a fool of those women. Did you see the way they were walking? As if they could snap their fingers and the entire quarter would come running just to be the first to fall at their feet!"

"The entire quarter just might."

"That isn't the point." He socked her back, then sprinted ahead.

She quickly caught up and pinched his ear, then the two of them made their way, laughing, to the nearest stone steps down to the Haddah. It was spring in Sharakhai, and the river was swelling. It was going to be a rich fishing season if the rains kept up. Old Ibrahim said the river might even flood.

"Has the look of it," Ibrahim had told Çeda one day while fishing over the edge of an old stone bridge. "Just you see if it doesn't. Ibrahim remembers." He'd tapped his noggin below his wide-brimmed, sweat-stained hat. "Ibrahim knows the signs."

"What *signs?*" Çeda had asked.

And Ibrahim had turned to Çeda, his face pinching like

he'd bitten into a Malasani lime. "Never you mind, girl. Never you mind."

Çeda and Emre wound their way along the Haddah. Near the city's center, the bank was little more than a paved walkway that had been built for the more affluent of the city, the river flowing along a canal below. There were hundreds of people out, groups of the rich, some sipping rosewater lemonade and leaning out over the balustrades to look into the clear water below, others strolling and talking quietly. Çeda and Emre were given the eye by a few Silver Spears patrolling the promenade—they even followed the two of them for a short time until it was clear they were headed upriver.

They passed beneath Bent Man, the oldest and bulkiest of the bridges spanning the Haddah. The traffic along the Trough was lively, but through some trick peculiar to this place, the sounds seemed dull and distant. Soon the larger four- and five-story stone buildings gave way to squatter constructions, and those gave way to hovels. They had entered the Shallows, where crowds of men and women were out washing clothes. Children splashed in the water. Even a few herons waded along the edge of the reeds, their sharp beaks darting down to catch mudskippers.

A gang of seven or eight gutter wrens were playing at swords in the water, practicing the motions of *tahl selhesh*, the dance of blades, while wading in the shin-deep water, but they stopped and lowered their wooden practice swords as Çeda and Emre approached. Several began moving toward the bank but stopped when Çeda and Emre placed hands on the knives at their belts.

They continued through the northwestern quarter of the city, passing through a wonderland of trilling birdcalls and jumping fish and buzzing insects, all of it so foreign to the way of things in the desert ten months out of the year. *Is it like this in Malasan, where you can't walk half a day without running across a new river? Or Mirea, where it rains every week?* Some might call her a liar when she said it, but Çeda wouldn't like to live in such places. The desert was in her blood, through and through. The very thought of leaving it made her laugh.

"What?" Emre asked, looking at her as if she were mad.

"What?" she shot back.

"You just laughed. At nothing."

"So what?" she said, still smiling. "You look like an ox's ass all the time, and I don't make fun of *you* for it."

He tried to punch her arm again, but she was too fast. She ducked the blow and sprinted away, Emre chasing after. To the annoyance of some enjoying the river, they flew along the banks, screaming, until they were exhausted from it.

Near the edge of the city, Emre pointed and said, "There, behind those bushes."

After stepping behind the bushes with the flaming orange flowers, they dismantled a carefully constructed pile of stones. Within were the two packs she and Emre had brought here several days before in preparation for the journey. It felt good as Çeda shouldered hers. They had supplies for a few days, though they only planned to be out until the following morning.

When they'd passed the edges of the city at last, and entered the desert proper, Emre asked, "You sure you want to do this?"

Çeda eyed the way ahead, squinting against the brightness of the sun as it glinted against the flowing river. "Of course I'm sure."

"Why did your mother go to the blooming fields?"

Emre was being sly. He had wanted to know for a good many years now, but he'd waited until they were halfway to the blooming fields to ask her again.

It worked, too. Çeda reckoned it wasn't fair of her to keep it from him any longer. "She came for the blooms."

"I know. But why?"

She wasn't surprised that he'd guessed about the blooms—what else could she be going all that way for, after all?—but she was embarrassed that she knew so very little about her mother's life. Surely Ahya had planned to tell her one day: about the petals, why she collected them, what she meant for Çeda to do with them. She'd merely been caught before she'd had a chance to do it. Çeda had made the mistake of asking Dardzada about it a few months back. He'd not only refused to answer, he'd barked at her never to ask of it again. When she *had* asked a second time he'd beaten her for it and locked her in her room to think about how badly she'd disappointed him. He'd kept her there until the following evening, bringing her only bits of bread and water, telling her it was worlds better then she'd get from the House of Kings if they ever caught her.

She hadn't asked him about it again—she was no fool— but his actions had done nothing to quench the fire within her. If anything, it had thrown fuel upon it. She'd left it alone for far too long already.

She'd made plans with Emre over the following weeks for this very outing, planning when they would go, how she would sneak away from the apothecary, what they would bring. The only thing she *hadn't* worked out was how to tell Dardzada when she returned. She knew he'd be angry— knew he'd be a good deal more than angry, in fact—but she was nearly thirteen. She would make him see that she was becoming her own woman and that he could neither hide her from the world nor the world from her.

"She gave me the blooms sometimes," she told Emre while hopping along a series of rounded river rocks. "She'd take them herself, as well."

Emre tried to follow in her footsteps, but slipped and splashed in the water, twisting his ankle along the way. "When?" he asked, hissing and limping the injury away with embarrassment.

"On holy days, but rarely those the Kings prescribe, only the days the desert tribes celebrate the gods or the making of the desert."

"But why give you *petals*, the very thing the Kings love most?" He caught up to her along a wide bank of smooth river stones. Ahead, the river ran straight until it curved to the right around a rocky promontory upon which an abandoned tower sat sulking like a long-forgotten grave. "Why take adichara blooms, like the Maidens?"

This was a question Çeda had been struggling with for a long while, even before her mother's death. She'd asked, but had never been answered, at least not to her satisfaction. "I think she took them because the Kings would deny them to her. She gave them to me for the same reason. That which the Kings forbade, she did. That was her way."

"Was she one of the Moonless Host?"

"No," she said immediately. "She didn't agree with their ways. She thought them too brutal."

"But if she meant to kill the Kings—"

"I don't know if she meant to kill them."

"But her death . . ."

"Yes, I know, but I think she'd been caught off-guard. Maybe she meant to take something from them."

Emre scoffed. "You don't believe that."

"No, not really, but it might have been. I don't know. Maybe I'll never know."

Emre paused, and when he spoke again, it was with a quiet intensity. "Then why not leave it all alone?"

Çeda looked at him, aghast. "Because they *killed* her."

"I know. But people die every day, Çeda."

Çeda stopped in her tracks, waiting until Emre stopped as well and faced her. "Go back if you don't want to help. I'm fine on my own."

"No," he said. "I want to go."

"You just said you want me to stop!"

"No, I didn't." Emre looked completely confused, and more than a little scared. "It's just . . ."

"Just what?"

Emre didn't respond. He wasn't even looking at her anymore but over her shoulder. When Çeda stared at him, confused, he jutted his chin at something behind her.

She turned and saw a wolf's head, just above the river-bank. It approached until it was standing at the very edge, looking down at them. It was little more than a pup, and by Rhia's kind fortune, it was *white*. Its muzzle was gray—as were the tufts of darker hair along the mane covering its withers—but the rest of it was snow white.

She'd never seen such a thing. Never even *heard* of such a thing.

Emre had picked up a rock to throw at it, but Çeda grabbed his wrist. "No!"

"They're mangy," Emre said.

"They're beautiful." She took out one of the lengths of smoked venison she'd stolen from Dardzada's larder.

"Don't *feed* it."

"Why not?" she asked as she tossed it up to the embankment.

No sooner had it landed than another maned wolf came padding up to the edge of the bank, this one the normal tawny color with a blackened mane and muzzle. Another followed, and another after that, and more, until there were eight in all. These were adult wolves, each standing every bit as tall as Çeda.

Despite her words, despite her feeling that these were noble creatures, Çeda's hands and arms quivered like a newborn's. Her teeth began to chatter. She had no idea why. She wasn't scared. Not really. They were just so wondrous.

Two more pups came, the same size as the shorter white pup, which was as tall as Çeda's waist.

Emre reached for his knife, but Çeda hissed at him. "Don't. They're smart, Emre."

One of the wolves was itching to leap down. It ranged back and forth along the riverbank, looking down toward the rocky ground below. Another snapped up the venison and chewed, its head jerking forward as it swallowed. The rest, hackles rising, watched the two hapless humans, as if each were waiting for the next to attack.

The white wolf, though, didn't appear to be paying much attention to the pair of them at all. It nipped at one of the adults' legs, then harder until the larger one reached back and bit it on the snout. Immediately the white one turned and loped off. The adult let out a strange yelp, almost like the cry of a yearling child, and then ran off after the pup. The others soon followed, leaving the one that was keen to leap down. This one—a beast with many black scars around its head and withers—lowered its head and growled, teeth bared, then it too turned and galloped after its brood.

"We were stupid to bring only knives," Emre said softly.

"What would we have done with swords against a bloody pack of them?"

"A far sight better than anything I could do with a rat sticker like this." Emre held up his knife, staring at it as if he'd just realized how short it was. "Gods, what just *happened?*"

"I don't know, but Bakhi has clearly smiled upon us. Let's not make him a fool."

She started to head upriver, but Emre grabbed her wrist. "We're not ready for this."

"*I* am." And she yanked her arm away and kept walking.

She didn't hear Emre following, and for a moment she thought it might be better if he *did* head back to Sharakhai, but when she heard the crunch of the stones as he followed her, she was glad. As eager as she was to see the blooming fields, she didn't want to see them alone.

They continued well beyond midday, following the river several leagues out into the desert. They were sheltered from the oppressive heat by the river, which was cool along the banks, and when they grew too hot, they'd stop and splash water on themselves, cup water into their mouths until they were no longer thirsty, and then continue on. They came to a fork, where a small stream fed the River Haddah. Çeda chose to follow the stream, reasoning that it might make for easier walking as they came closer to the blooming fields.

They followed it for several hours more.

"Where do we stop?" Emre asked.

"There," Çeda said, pointing to a tamarisk tree in the distance. "They've got to be close. We'll climb the tree and look for them."

The broad-trunked tree was some distance from the stream, so they drank their fill, topped off the waterskins in their packs, and left the streambed, making a beeline for the tree. When they reached it, Çeda unslung her pack and handed it to Emre. After a quick climb she was able to see far along the amber sands. To the east, she spotted the white sails of ships moving in the distance: a caravan, drifting over the sands to some distant port—who knew where? Çeda might not want to leave the desert, but she would love to ride aboard a sandship one day, travel the Great

Desert and see the wonders she'd heard and read so much about.

Northward, wavering in the desert heat, she thought she saw a smudge of black. There was another west of it: The blooming fields.

Her fingers tingled. She'd never been, but she'd imagined so many things, and she wondered if reality would be anything like her dreams. A part of her was nervous about seeing them, but another part was glad this day had finally come.

When she climbed down, she paused, noticing a flat stone nearly swallowed by the roots on either side of it. The stone was the size of her hands placed side-by-side, and engraved upon its surface was a complex sigil.

"What is it?" Emre asked.

"No idea," Çeda replied, squatting down and trying to wrest it free. She had no luck, and they quickly moved on, heading for the nearest of the fields. As the sun lowered, throwing splashes of color against the cloudy western sky, they crested a low dune and saw a mass of trees spread out before them. When viewed from afar it was clear the trees were laid out in a very rough line—southwest to northeast—but as they trudged closer, they could see how erratic the spacing was. Like an island of black stone in the desert, inlets and islets and lakes of sand were hidden within the twisted groves.

Small forms like hummingbirds flitted to and fro above the adichara, and several flew toward them.

They were the açal. Rattlewings. Beetles as big as Çeda's thumb with wings as wide as the spread of her hand. Their shells were iridescent black, and their wings were a glimmering shade of purple, but the wickedly curved mandibles were a muddy, bloody red—a color that marked many insects in the desert as poisonous.

Many flew past before circling around and coming toward them once more. Then one landed on Çeda's arm and bit her.

She screamed in fright and pain and flung her hand at the beetle, but it had already flown up and away. Another came toward her. She swatted it away as one of them bit Emre.

The two of them retreated, but more of the rattlewings were now swinging past them. A veritable cloud of them floated in the air ahead, swinging back and forth, effectively blocking their way.

It was when Çeda turned back to look for an escape route that she noticed the carcass. Within the fields of adichara was the body of an oryx. She could see its distinctive black stripe running along its length, its white underbelly and its long ribbed horns. Much of the creature was wrapped tight in the arms of a tree, as if it had wandered into the grove and been strangled to death.

As she and Emre backed away from the rattlers, swatting at them when they came near, Çeda spotted two other oryx among the adichara, beetles swarming out from within their dead carcasses.

"Stop backing up!" she shouted. Gods, the thought of being slowly eaten by them, of becoming a home in which the rattlewings could lay their eggs and multiply. "They're herding us toward the trees!"

Emre glanced back, eyes wide with fear. Whether he understood or not, she didn't know. But he took his pack and held it before him like a shield. Several of the beetles attacked *it* instead of *him*, but more swept in and stung him on the thigh and shoulder. He swatted them and took a step back as the cloud continued to thicken. "What are we going to do?"

Çeda slipped her pack off and aimed it toward the beetles as Emre had done. "This way!" she said, trying to run to her left, but the buzzing black insects were quick to block her path. Another swept in and stung Çeda's ankle. The arm where she'd been stung first was in terrible pain.

Emre shouted again and swatted maniacally. *"What are we going to do?"*

"I don't know!"

Çeda caught Emre's expression, a perfect mirror of her own. He was terrified, frightened for his life. As was she. Her breath came rapidly now, the poison already beginning to spread through her arm, causing a deep aching sensation when she tried to swat the beetles. They couldn't go on like this, and they both knew it.

Hands shaking, his movements jerky and erratic, Emre pulled a blanket from inside his pack. He was crying with pain now, shouting at each new bite.

After one last desperate look at Çeda, he threw the blanket over his head and shoulders. Holding the pack before him, the blanket blinding him, he screamed and sprinted away across the sand.

The rattlers attacked, swooping in, many getting caught against the blanket. But many slipped *beneath* the blanket, stinging him over and over again. She didn't know if Emre had meant for it to happen, but most of the rattlewings followed him, leaving a thinner cloud with her.

"Leave him alone!" she yelled, running after Emre. "Leave him alone!" Tears streaming down her face.

The beetles ignored her cries and came for her, though not nearly in the same numbers as for Emre.

The sun had set, and the desert was cooling which, more than anything else, may have made the rattlewings peel off, one by one, and drift like dark clouds back toward the adichara. Emre didn't care, though. Either that or he didn't notice. He kept running, now screaming more from pain than fright. And Çeda followed, feeling small and foolish over the sacrifice Emre had made for her.

Eventually all the beetles were gone, and still Emre ran, though it was now more of a limp, a strangled gait that barely kept him from falling to the sands.

"Emre, stop!" she called. "They're gone."

She didn't know whether he heard her or not, for soon after he simply collapsed, the sand billowing where he fell. She dropped to his side and pulled the blanket away.

And saw the travesty the beetles had made of his skin.

Dozens of bites marked his face, arms, and legs. His torso and back, thank the gods for small favors, were blessedly free of the puckered wounds, but the rest . . . Dear gods, they might be enough to kill him.

She'd never seen the rattlewings before and had heard of them only once or twice in passing—Dardzada talking with a client, perhaps, or maybe it had been Ibrahim the storyteller, or Davud, the annoying boy in the bazaar who couldn't keep his mouth shut. Her own wounds felt painful enough—her skin was swollen and reddened—but that in itself wouldn't kill. It was the constriction against her heart that worried her most; it felt as if it were being pressed inside a box too small to contain it, and if *her* heart felt sluggish, what would Emre's be like?

"Emre?"

He moaned, opened his eyes, fixed them on her with something akin to recognition. "Did I scare them off?"

A bark of nervous laughter escaped her. She brushed his hair to one side, then got her waterskin out and gave him some of it. The rest she used to wash his wounds. Then she applied a salve meant to help against sunburns. She had no idea if either would help, but they might, and right now, easing the effects of the poison was more important than preserving their water. It was clear, though, that they would need more. And there was no way that Emre would be able to walk. Not like this.

By the time she was done, it was nearly dark. The stars were out. Only a strip of gauzy violet light still hung in the west. She needed to get back to the stream. There was water there, and she'd seen Sweet Anna along the way, and goldenthread, too. She could make a poultice from them.

"Emre, can you hear me?" She wrapped both blankets around him and left the strap of his waterskin wrapped around his right wrist, left the pack open near his left in case he grew hungry, then she leaned forward and spoke softly in his ear, "I'm going to get some help, Emre."

"From your mother?"

She almost cried. "No, Emre. My mother's dead." She stood and regarded him one last time.

"Tell her I miss her."

"I will," she replied, and then turned and loped toward the stream.

Chapter 15

THE MORNING AFTER SPEAKING WITH OSMAN, Çeda went to Emre's room to change his bandages and found him sitting up, trying to pull on his boots. "No!" she snapped, rushing to his bed. "You've already pulled some stitches, Emre."

"I can't stay in this bed any longer, Çeda."

"Emre, you've been out too often." By Rhia's bright eyes he was pale, even after a week of Dardzada's remedies. "Lie *down*."

When he didn't, she took him by the shoulders and forced him back onto the bed. His skin was clammy. She thought he'd taken a turn for the worse—an infection, perhaps, or the less threatening loss of blood and dehydration. But when she was finally able to pull back the bandages, his wounds looked much better.

As Emre rested and drank more water, his color returned, but the look on his face was still grave. Something in him still seemed deeply pained. In his *heart*, she knew, not his body. "What is it, Emre?"

He took a sharp breath, wincing from the pain of it, and said, "What day is it?"

"Devahndi. Nine days since Beht Zha'ir. Why?"

He shrugged. "It all still feels so real, like it happened just last night."

"That's natural," Çeda said.

He picked at the brown blanket across his legs. "I'm sorry, Çeda."

"Sorry for what?"

"For putting you in danger. You shouldn't have come after me."

"We take care of one another, remember?"

"And yet you're always taking care of *me*." He grinned as if he'd made a particularly dark joke.

She'd never seen him look more haunted. "What's wrong, Emre?"

He looked up. He shivered, then shook his head. "I'm just shaken, is all. How about you? You never told me what happened that night."

"I told you, I found you in the riverbed. You don't remember?"

He shrugged. "I remember some. Tell me the rest."

And so she did, recounting her evening, how she'd found him, how the asir had taken the tribesman. She stopped there. She didn't want him to worry over the asir and the sickeningly warm kiss she'd received. But he took her wrist as she was trying to spread Dardzada's healing milk over the cuts along his ribs. "What is it?"

She really didn't want to tell him, but here she was, hoping he would tell her what was troubling him while keeping secrets of her own. She had to trust him, so she took a deep breath and let it out. "One of the asirim stopped me." She paused, shivering, remembering that kiss. "He wore a crown, and he spoke to me."

"It *spoke* to you?"

She finished with the salve and placed a length of fresh cotton over the wounds. "Stay," she said as she stood and went to her room to retrieve her mother's book from its hiding place. She returned to Emre, turned to the poem written in her mother's hand, and held it out for him to see.

Rest will he,
'Neath twisted tree,

'Til death by scion's hand.
By Nalamae's tears,
And godly fears,
Shall kindred reach dark land.

"He *spoke* those words to me, Emre. How could the same lines be in this book?"

Emre gritted his teeth while pulling himself higher in bed. Then he regarded the book more seriously. "It *spoke*?"

"Those very words."

"But you'd taken a petal, hadn't you? You know they give you dreams."

She could hardly believe her ears. "And?"

"Maybe you *thought* you heard it. Maybe after you'd slept—"

"I heard what I heard, Emre. He was as close to me as you are now."

"But you said—"

"Are you listening to me?" She snatched the book away from him. "He *spoke* those words!"

"All right!"

She stared at the book, realizing she'd torn a page, and a black fury rose up inside her. She'd *torn* one of her mother's pages. She smoothed it carefully back in place, cursing herself for a fool, but as she did, she saw something, and her anger dwindled.

There were marks in the gutter of the pages, so close to the folds of the book she'd never seen them before. There were three of them.

"Çeda, what is it?"

"Wait," she mumbled, flipping through the book.

"What?"

She ignored him, finding more. Four marks on one page. Six on another. Two here and one there. It couldn't be co-incidence. It couldn't. But what could they mean? She saw no relation to the poem at the back, no indication they were connected in any way.

"Çeda, what *is* it?"

With a forceful exhalation, she turned the book toward him and pointed to the marks she'd found.

Emre squinted. "Did Ahya make them?"

She was about to snap at him, but that was only her residual anger talking, her anxiousness. The marks were made with a similar brown ink as the poem, but they seemed to be made with a different pen, or a different nib. "I don't know."

In the end, she couldn't puzzle it out and didn't have time to think about it just then. She put the book back in its hiding place and made ready for the day. "I'll be back later," she told Emre as she leaned into his room, her practice armor in one hand, shamshir in the other.

"And where are *you* headed?"

"To the pits. I need to loosen up."

"Loosen up? You were beaten bloody a few days ago!"

"Nine days, Emre."

"And you're not still sore?"

"Sure I am," she said, rolling her shoulders and feeling the burn, "but that's when it feels the best."

<hr />

Çeda stood before a stout wooden door, listening as the crowd beyond it stamped their feet in time, a slow and heavy beat, a demand for violence and blood. The air smelled not only of sweat and blood, but fury and fear. It infused this place, the dark tunnel behind her, the door before her, the fighting pit that lay beyond. She ran her fingertips over the wood, then bowed her head to it. "Thaash guide my sword."

She took a deep breath and released it, the sound loud in her iron-masked helm. Before a fight she would often think of her mother swinging from the gallows in the morning breeze, of the marks the Kings had left upon her hands and feet. *Whore. False Witness.* She would think of the strange symbol on her forehead, a thing that had taken on a different meaning for her. She used to think it some epithet the Kings had placed on her, some ancient rune now lost in time, but now she wasn't so sure. Now it felt like a clue, part of the mystery surrounding her mother, the book, the asirim. It made everything feel different. It made this *fight* feel different.

Beyond the thick wooden door, the crowd roared. Her opponent's door had just been opened, and from the way the crowd chanted—a barking that sounded like the jackals of the desert—she knew she was facing a foreigner.

"Çeda." She turned and saw Pelam walking up the dark tunnel toward her. He wore his long red kaftan, his sweaty brown kufi, and his long, dour face. As the door began to rise on its pulleys, Pelam nodded toward it. "Watch him. He paid much to bout with you."

Çeda returned his nod and turned back toward the door as it rose fully, revealing the pit. As she stepped out, the straps of her leather battle skirt slapping against her thighs, the volume of the crowd above her intensified.

"The White Wolf!" they yelled. "The White Wolf!"

"Show him!" others shouted. "Teach him what it means to cross swords in Sharakhai!"

Around the edge of the pit, a ring of men and a handful of women were seated. This bout took on a much different complexion than her last, against Haluk. This was a tourney, and as such it attracted the best fighters, which in turn attracted royalty, ambassadors and dignitaries, merchantmen and merchantwomen. They wore bright clothes and brighter jewels and used fans or horsetails to fend off the flies. Some few—those who wished to hide their identity—wore veils or burqas decorated with coins or silver bells that jingled when they moved. Behind those rich patrons, standing five rows deep on progressively higher levels, the crowd was not so extravagant. They wore shemaghs on their heads and long, loose thawbs of simple cloth and simpler colors—but still, they had paid handsomely to watch the tournament with the finest warriors.

Ten paces away from Çeda stood her opponent, a Qaimiri man, handsome, and perhaps ten years her senior. He was taller than she, though not by much, and well muscled. His oiled skin glimmered beneath the sun, and he wore a leather kilt and sandals. He did not pace or flex as many young fighters did. In fact, he had the bearing of a lord, or perhaps a lord's son. She wasn't surprised to see a well bred

man from Qaimir; they were drawn to the pits like dung
beetles, especially the rich or the spoiled. They considered
themselves the nobility of the fighting world, and yet they
heard about the pits of Sharakhai and the warriors who
could be found there and felt themselves somehow threatened. Many came only to test the Sharakhani, thinking it
would be easy, thinking their high birth or training would
help them. And there were times when it did, but more
often than not they were little more than pretentious no-
bles come to steal a bit of pride from the desert city that
boasted the best sword arms in all the Five Kingdoms.
They soon learned there was a reason Sharakhai had never
fallen to outside forces. They discovered that the children
of the desert trained in sword, shield, and spear from
the time they could walk. It was no mere interest, a thing
done for tradition's sake; it was as much a part of life in
the Shangazi as hunger, as thirst, as heat from the ever-
watchful sun.

As Çeda faced the Qaimiri, she watched his eyes for any
hint of hunger for their coming battle, but there was none.
He merely nodded to her and turned to face the edge of
the pit toward Osman's box. This one would be a challenge, she could tell. She was rarely wrong about such
things, and she found herself bouncing on the balls of her
feet, hoping she was right.

Osman, wearing an emerald kaftan and an embroidered
vest, stepped to the edge of his box. After their talk at the
lighthouse, she thought he would have summoned her before the match, but he hadn't, and now there was nothing
to do but fight and hope he hadn't changed his mind about
feeding her information about Emre's shade. He took up a
horsehair tail and dipped it into a brass ewer of water. The
moment he did, the crowd quieted, though shouting could
still be heard from other nearby pits.

"Bakhi's luck be upon you," Osman boomed as he lifted
the tail and swung it like a whip, first toward Çeda and
then toward the Qaimiri, spraying them both with water
drawn from the well beneath Bakhi's temple. Then he
looked to Pelam and nodded before sitting regally in his
carved chair. As the crowd began to shout, louder than

before, Osman turned to a man sitting next to him, a lord from the House of Kings who often came to the pits.

Behind Çeda, a dozen of Osman's boys trotted out from the darkness of the tunnel bearing swords and whips and shields. The Qaimiri was allowed to choose first. He took up a long, straight sword, one made after the fashion of his homeland. Çeda took a shield, oval in shape, barely larger than her forearm. As she fitted it onto her arm, the green-eyed Qaimiri picked up a round shield not much larger than the one she'd chosen.

Çeda was then allowed her second selection. As the Qaimiri had chosen a longsword, she chose a shamshir, the very heart of martial art in the desert.

The crowd laughed and stamped their feet and howled.

The Qaimiri seemed somehow pleased by this reaction. He didn't smile, but there was a brightness in his eyes now, a thirst for battle every bit as deep as Çeda's. He backed away as Pelam held a small gong between them and struck it.

The Qaimiri immediately rushed forward, trying to catch her off guard. She danced away, keeping her shield at the ready. He didn't swing his sword, but instead tried to use his shield to bull her up against the wall of the pit. She was too quick, however. She spun away, and he was forced to begin swinging.

She blocked his first few blows, which were tentative, meant only to test their range and gauge her reactions. She let him think she was slower than she really was, barely catching his swings before they struck her head or chest.

And then he overextended. Not by much. But it was enough for her to beat his sword away with her own, step forward and block his shield with hers, and cut him along his left side.

He pushed her violently away as the crowd howled and clapped in time, wanting more.

Blood ran from a shallow cut along his thigh. The swords of the pits were not sharp, but neither were they dull. The point of most bouts was not to fight to the death, but the threat was always there. One wrong move, one miscalculation, and one could lie bleeding on the sandy floor, watching the blue sky above, helpless as Bakhi came to escort you to the farther fields.

She thought surely the Qaimiri would be angry, but if anything, he seemed calmer. Amused, even. "That won't happen again," he said, his voice low like the strum of an oud, his accent thick but understandable Sharakhan.

"We'll see," she replied, then struck hard, blocking his hurried sword strikes with her shield.

But then he regained his balance and started raining blows against her. They were not overextended or misbalanced, as they'd been moments ago. They were precise, and she could tell she'd misjudged him. The placement of his feet, the compact yet powerful swings, his quick reactions—they all spoke of an expert swordsman, one who took his craft seriously.

She smiled, and this time it was genuine. But then, over the Qaimiri's shoulder, she saw someone enter Osman's box: a man with skin as pale as snow. He was led directly to Osman, who stood and kissed his cheeks.

Çeda locked swords with the Qaimiri and bulled her shield into him, sending him flying backward.

It had done nothing to harm him, but that wasn't her intent. From within her mask, she looked up at Osman's seats. The pale man had the almond eyes and strong cheekbones of a Mirean, and his ivory hair was pulled back into a tail that trailed down the back of his blue silk shirt. As he sat, Osman saw Çeda looking. He gave her a quick nod, his intent clear.

As the Qaimiri closed once more, she realized this was the man who'd contracted Osman to deliver the canister—him or one of his servants. It was the clue he'd decided to grant her, despite his normally tight compact with his patrons. She understood now why he wouldn't tell her at the lighthouse. This was the most he could bring himself to, the closest he could come to outright betrayal.

The Qaimiri delivered a flurry of blows, and this time she couldn't stop them all. The sword slipped past her guard and bit into her battle skirt, hard enough to pierce leather and skin, both. Hissing, she skipped away.

The crowd cheered, but not so loudly as before.

Foolish, Çeda. Foolish, foolish, foolish.

The crowd might want her to win, but they liked a good match as well, and they appreciated skill when they saw it.

She was limping from the wound to her thigh, and the Qaimiri used it to his advantage. He pressed, sending quick jabs toward her head, her shins, anything to keep her moving. And once, when she moved too slowly, he snuck in a vicious strike to her left shoulder, then beat her sword hard. Her arm went numb from the elbow down and she lost her grip.

The crowd gasped. A bare few clapped, but more snapped their fingers, making it clear they expected better of her.

The Qaimiri came on again, hoping to press his advantage, but this time Çeda was ready. She limped more than she really needed to, using her shield to block his sword strokes. She caught him glancing up at Osman's box more than once, perhaps anticipating the favor he'd receive if he won the bout.

He refocused but seemed off-balance somehow. When he committed himself to a strong downward strike, she beat it to one side with her shield and feinted as if she were going to slip past him. He was ready, which was what she'd been hoping for. As she spun back to center, she allowed the shield to slip down along her arm. She caught the leather grip, grabbed the top of his shield with her free hand, and whipped her own up and over it, catching him across the crown of his head.

Immediately she loosed her hold on her shield—which tumbled over his face—and gripped his shield with both hands. As the crowd rose to their feet, stamping louder than ever, she drew him away from the wall with long, powerful strides. He stumbled from the sudden violence of her movement, then she pivoted, pulled the shield across her body, and dropped to the ground, dragging him as she went. With his arm already caught in the shield straps, he was whipped off his feet. His sword tip, which he'd been trying to bring to bear against her, caught on the ground and spun from his hand.

He crashed to the dusty earth, and she had his shield.

She held it down, hoping to keep him pinned, but he let his arm slip out and rolled away, reaching for his blade as he went. She tried to block him, but he was too quick, and she was forced to take up *his* shield, lest she be left defenseless.

Both back on their feet, the cheering crowd was divided, some crying, "Sharakhai!" while others howled, and still others called out, "Qaimir!"

The Qaimiri faced her, the cut along the crown of his head spilling blood down his face. His eyes, however, looked up yet again toward Osman's seats.

Çeda struck, hoping to catch him while he was distracted. She blocked a few weak strikes, meant more to fend her off than anything else, and then she realized.

The Mirean. The man who'd come to speak with Osman. Çeda had been distracted by his presence. And she realized that the exact same thing had happened to the Qaimiri. His glances to the box hadn't been for Osman. They'd been for the albino. He'd come searching for him as well.

The thought so captured her attention that—while fending off three quick thrusts from his sword—she didn't see him ready himself. After the third of her blocks, he timed it perfectly. He bull-rushed into her, sending her flying backward. She fell unceremoniously against the pit floor, dust rising as she slid into the pit wall and struck her head on the stone.

Quick as an asp he was on top of her, one foot pinning her shield and trapping her arm, his sword at her throat.

The crowd fell silent.

Çeda's lips thinned into a miserably straight line. Grudgingly, she slapped the ground with her hand.

And Pelam's gong rang.

The match was over.

Chapter 16

THE AREA AROUND THE PITS was known as the Well. On a normal day it was one of the oldest and most cramped sections the city, but now, with so many leaving the pits, the streets were positively choked. Çeda pushed her way not only through the raucous crowd and the carts selling roasted pistachios and honeyed rosewater and thousand-layer sweets but also through the occasional circle where pit-goers had stopped to regale one another with stories of the fights they'd seen. With the sun setting, Çeda chose a darkened archway in which to wait, and she watched carefully for the man she planned to follow. She wore a striped hijab and a matching thawb, well made but threadbare, one that would fit in easily in this section of the city.

Among the throng, near the fighters' entrance, she saw several dirt dogs leaving—seven or eight men and a few women, all of them bloodied and bruised. They were immediately swamped by a small crowd of waiting admirers. In ones and twos, the dirt dogs peeled away, their admirers circling them like flies.

Coming down the stairs from Osman's private box were four Mirean soldiers, each of them tall and muscular, their hair pulled up into a topknot. As they scanned the crowd below, their hands on the pommels of their gently curved swords, Osman's own guardsmen—two hulking elephants chosen as much for their foul tempers as their skill with the studded cudgels swinging from their belts—stepped aside to let the Mireans by, but the lithe Mireans in the tight-fitting armor didn't go far. They waited as their white-skinned lord finished talking to Osman near the edge of the pit. After bowing politely to one another, the Mirean took the stairs down and headed east toward the Trough, his guards flanking him.

Young Mala stood in a nearby alcove, wearing a simple blue dress, her hair tied in a sloppy braid. Çeda nodded toward the Mirean men, and Mala nodded back. Instantly she was lost in the crowd, her sister Jein and three other children followed her, darting through the pit-goers like fish among the cattails.

Çeda waited a long time, then longer still. The light of dusk faded. Osman and Tariq left the pits together, the two of them chatting softly. Osman didn't notice her standing in the darkness of the narrow archway. Tariq, however, did. He looked right at her, then turned away and followed Osman.

The crowd continued to thin. More fighters left. And still there was no sign of the Qaimiri. Soon, the small plaza outside the pits was empty. She must have lost him. Or maybe he'd left through the exit on the far side.

When she'd nearly given up, he stepped out from the pit. He was limping badly, but he'd remained until the end. Which meant he'd made it to the third and final match of the day. He might have won, which would give him a chance to return tomorrow for a final fight and a large prize, but something told her he hadn't. He wouldn't. Because for some reason he'd only come to spy on the Mirean.

He walked into the darkness of Sharakhai after sunset. As slow as he was moving, he was easy to keep up with, but Çeda still gave him wide berth. He headed east, then south, in the general direction of the southern harbor, along a road that hugged the banks of the Haddah. Just before they reached the Trough, he seemed to disappear into a patch of dark shadows to the right of the road.

Çeda picked up her pace, padding quietly over the well-packed dirt. She watched carefully, and saw, at the last moment, a gleam of steel in the archway of an arbor overgrown with ivy. She stopped in her tracks but left her kenshar in its sheath at her side.

"Come no closer," came his voice from the darkness.

"I mean you no harm," Çeda said. "I've only come to ask your name and your business in Sharakhai."

"That's much to ask."

"Just your name, then."

"My name doesn't matter."

"Your name for mine?"

"You are the White Wolf, and that's all I care to know."

Çeda paused, suppressing a cringe. "Who?"

"You know very well who. I recognized your gait. It marks a person as well as their face or their name. Better, because few think to disguise it."

Stupid, Çeda. In her rush to catch up to him, she'd abandoned the limp she usually used outside the pits, not realizing he'd been paying attention. "Then it appears you have the better of me already. Come, are you so afraid that you can't even part with your name?"

He paused. "I saw the way you watched Osman's guest. You're meddling in things you shouldn't be."

"The moon-skinned man?"

"His name is Juvaan Xin-Lei. He's a caravan master from Mirea."

"I may be many things, but I'm no fool. Juvaan is no caravan master."

"He is. His family have owned that route since Mirea first began sailing the seas of the Great Desert. But you're right. He's much more than that. He's an emissary of Queen Alansal as well."

Tulathan's bright eyes, this was getting complicated. "And *her* business in Sharakhai?"

He shifted his feet, then stepped forward, sheathing his knife in one fluid motion. She could see his face now, lit in the dying auburn glow of the western horizon. "I've said too much already."

When he turned to walk away, she said, "I found a canister sent by Juvaan."

The Qaimiri stopped in his tracks and turned slowly back to her. "You what?"

"A canister, sent by Juvaan and meant for the Moonless Host. Interesting, is it not, that the Queen of Mirea and the Moonless Host are linked?"

An intensity had stolen over the Qaimiri that told her she'd struck the mark.

They were interrupted by a woman farther up the street shouting for her boy. A young voice called back moments later, and was quickly teased by several others for running to his memma.

"Tell me more," he said.

She crossed her arms, a self-satisfied grin stealing over her as she did so. "I don't know how you do things in Qaimir, but in Sharakhai, we trade."

The Qaimiri considered, and she thought perhaps he hadn't taken the bait after all. When he spoke again, though, she could hear the boyish curiosity in his voice. "A bargain, then. Your story for mine?"

"Done," she said.

"You first."

She was tempted to protest, but something told her that offering trust would be the right move here. He seemed honorable in a way that many were not. "A friend of mine was paid to deliver that canister. He nearly died in the attempt. That's enough for me to investigate who sent it."

"What's his name, your friend?"

"Irrelevant," Çeda countered.

"I thought we were here to trade."

"I don't betray those I love."

"So you love him, this boy?"

She knew he was toying with her, but for the moment she didn't care. "He's no boy, and of course I love him. He has protected me since we were children, and I him."

"And where would he have taken the canister?"

"As I said, it was destined for the hands of the Al'afwa Khadar."

"How do you know?"

"Because I delivered its sister to an old woman in the Shallows. It was later picked up by their agents and delivered to the hands of Macide Ishaq'ava himself."

At this, the Qaimiri stiffened. "Do you know where he is now?"

"No."

"You must have some idea."

"I have none. I saw him in the streets of Red Crescent, in an alley behind the bath house."

"Are you of the Al'afwa?"

There was a distrust in his tone that hadn't been there before. She measured her next response carefully, knowing that this was not merely important to the Qaimiri, but paramount. "I am not."

He seemed to weigh her words for a time. When he spoke again, his voice had lost its edge. "What was in the case?"

She debated lying, but this was her chance to learn more about it, about Macide's plans with it. "It contained a diaphanous stone."

"Describe it."

"As large as a grape. Nearly clear with cloudy white bands running through it. Light as air."

"White, you said?"

"As snow in the mountains."

"And the sister case. Did you open that as well?"

"No."

"Why? Why open one and not the other?"

"I had delivered the first before knowing its importance."

"Does Osman—"

Çeda raised her hand. "Enough," she said. "I've given you all I'm willing to trade this night." The sun had now fully set. Only a band of pale light remained on the horizon, which left the Qaimiri little more than a swath of jet against a field of kohl.

"Are you saying there will be another night?"

"I'm saying nothing of the sort." *Cheeky bastard*.

"Fair enough." And yet he paused a good long while before speaking again. "In return, I'll tell you a tale, if you're willing to hear it."

"I am."

"Sharakhai and Qaimir have many interests in one another, yes?"

"Of that there can be no doubt."

"And many travel from the Shangazi's southern borders to this very place, the Jewel of the Desert?"

"They do."

"Well, two years ago a large caravan came to Sharakhai. It brought wood and wine and grain. It brought finely crafted urns and bolts of supple cloth. It brought calves and foals and songbirds. It even brought crates of ice packed in fresh summer straw for the Kings to cool their drinks." As the Qaimiri did when telling tales, he slipped into a singsong voice. Çeda had overheard such tellings in teahouses throughout Sharakhai, but she'd never thought much of it. Then again, she'd never been the sole intended audience. Here, standing before this man in an alleyway, she found herself deeply drawn into his tale, hardly realizing it was happening. "The masters of Qaimir traded their goods for spices and tabbaq and the wicked steel swords this city can produce. But this was no ordinary caravan. There were dignitaries there to treat with the Kings of Sharakhai. There were Lords of Qaimir. Some even brought their families. They had come to trade, true, but they were there to see the wonders of Sharakhai as well.

"And they did. The caravan stayed for fourteen days and fourteen nights, and when they set sail once more, the Kings of Sharakhai sent royal ships with them to trade with Qaimir. The two caravans sailed as one, eleven ships taking to the endless sands of the Shangazi for the southern harbor of Nijin, but before they could reach even the first caravanserai they were attacked by the desert tribes. Twenty small ships—cutters and sloops and the like— attacked three days out from Sharakhai. They brought the ships of the Kings down first. In this they were both efficient and savage. The ships from Qaimir, however, they toyed with. One by one they took them down until only one remained. The largest. The one that carried royalty and their families. That ship was grounded when her runners were taken from her by chain traps hidden in the gutters of a sandy vale.

"The men were killed first, but not all of them. They left as many alive as there were women and children. These men were lined up like cattle, like slaves. The women and children were lined up as well, across from the men." The Qaimiri paused. He swallowed so hard Çeda could hear it in the relative silence of the night. "Each man—" He paused again. "Each man was asked to choose between his own life and that of one of the women or children. One by one, the men gave themselves that the innocent might live, their red blood staining the golden desert floor. But when it came to the final man—the final man by luck only, mind you—a woman charged forth. She ran screaming toward the leader of the tribesmen. Before she'd taken three steps, an arrow drove through her, and she fell, sand spraying where her knees struck the dunes, her hands clutching uselessly at the silted earth. The leader, a shaikh with a forked beard and golden rings and tattoos of snakes twisting around his arms and wrists, went to her as the man screamed and tried to reach the woman. She was his wife, you see, and though their daughter stood watching, her eyes wide with horror, he was still willing to give himself that his wife might have a chance at life. The shaikh judged that the woman had made a choice in the man's place, and he killed her with one swing of his sword."

Çeda had heard of the Bloody Passage. Most in Sharakhai had; that had been the point of it, after all, a declaration by the Moonless Host, claiming the desert as theirs. She knew the man he was talking about as well. The shaikh with the forked beard was no true shaikh at all, though it surely pleased him when outsiders thought him so. It was none other than Macide, the man with the forked beard and the snake tattoos Çeda had seen take the canister she'd delivered to the Shallows. She understood now why the Qaimiri had tightened upon hearing Macide's name, why he'd been so intent on knowing if she was one of the Moonless Host.

"When it was done," the Qaimiri went on, "the shaikh left her there. The woman spilled her blood, and lay lifeless upon the unforgiving sand. 'Go,' the tribesmen said to the man. 'Take your women. Take your children. Take your cargo if you will.'

"'But we have no ship! No water! You said you would let them live!' the man cried to the shaikh, who merely stared with dispassionate eyes. 'And I did. The rest is up to the Great Mother.'" His words came slowly now, as if he wished to leave them unspoken. "And then the tribesmen left. All of them. Leaving the broken ships, leaving the cargo, leaving the women and children and this lone man from Qaimir. He did what he could, he and the women. They made a skiff from the remains of the ship's runners. They traveled south, trying to reach the nearest caravanserai, but the going was too slow, and they had scavenged so little from the remains. All their supplies had been taken or destroyed. For three days they traveled, and one by one the children died. Then the women, some from the dry desert air, others from the sun and exhaustion.

"He lost his daughter a day before they were saved. By Tulathan's bright smile, *one day!* He saw her die, and he wanted to die with her."

Goezhen's swift sword, he was the one, the lone man to survive the massacre. "She was your child," Çeda said.

He nodded. "Her name was Rehann, and my wife, may she walk with our daughter in peace in the farther fields, was Yasmine."

No one deserved to see his wife cut down before his very eyes, to see his child die slowly of thirst as he made his way toward shelter. "My heart fills with salt for your loss," she said, unable to think of anything equal to the depth of his sorrow.

He seemed to harden at her words, as if they were a beacon, bringing more of the tale into relief. "Only four survived. Two of the women, one boy, and me. I returned to my King and told him my story. I begged that I be allowed to return to the desert, to hunt those who had committed this unforgivable crime. And so I did. I gathered ships of war and hunted the tribesmen. I knew their ships.

A thousand years could pass, and still I would remember the cut of their sails, the lines of their hulls. When at last I found three of them traveling alone, I took them down, but not before I questioned one of their number. It was not the shaikh, but another I remembered from the slaughter. The tribesman did not speak easily, even when tortured, but at last the truth was out. Or enough of it to lead me back here to Sharakhai where it all began. The tribesmen had been paid, I learned. Paid to attack the Kings' caravans. The presence of the Qaimiri ships had simply been an unfortunate accident."

Dear gods, an accident. So many dead because they'd had the misfortune of sailing with the royal fleet of Sharakhai on that particular day.

He looked at her, more shadow than man. "I've been following his trail ever since. And that canister might have told me more."

"But you know it came from Juvaan. Why not go to him?"

"Juvaan will pay for his part in this. The events that led to the Bloody Passage reek of his scent and that of his Queen, but I cannot lose sight of the fact that he is but one piece on the board. There are many more, and I must uncover them for my King."

"And the stone?" Çeda said. "Do you know what it is? Do you understand its nature?"

"I've a feeling *you* do."

"I didn't ask what you thought *I* knew. I asked what *you* knew."

"It's difficult to tell without examining it myself, but I suspect it's a breathstone. And yes, I understand its nature. Among other things, it can be used to speak to the dead."

"Do you have any idea who it will be used on?"

"None at the moment."

"You have no idea why Juvaan might have given Macide such a stone? No idea who they would wish to speak to?"

"None," he said coolly, "but I'll confer with my liege, King Aldouan." She saw him tilt his head in the darkness. "It occurs to me that the two of us might have more to trade in the future."

"We might," she allowed.

"Then how can I find you?"

She believed his offer was made in earnest, but she wanted him nowhere near her home. "Where I live, you would be noticed, something neither of us can afford."

There was a note of humor in his voice as he said, "I'd not come wearing the garb of a dirt dog."

"Even still."

"In that case, do you know Hefaz the cobbler?"

"Everyone knows Hefaz."

He stepped back into the deeper dark. "Then you know where to find me. But be careful. This is bigger than both of us. Chances are it would be better if the White Wolf left it alone."

"I can take care of myself."

"Perhaps you can," he said, stepping further into the darkness. When he was almost out of earshot, he said, "Ramahd."

"What?" Çeda called.

"My name," he said. "My name is Ramahd."

And then he was gone.

Chapter 17

RAMAHD AMANSIR GRITTED HIS TEETH against his bruises and pains as he stepped down from the dock and into one of the sleighs lined up for patrons like him, those unwilling to walk over the grasping sands to the docks at the center of the harbor.

The driver wore a kaftan and a dozen necklaces strung with fire-dried peach pits that clicked and clacked at the slightest movement. He turned to Ramahd and touched his hand to his forehead. "And where might I bring my Lord this night?"

Ramahd handed him a sylval. "To the inner docks."

It was dark, but by the light of Tulathan, Ramahd could see the sleighman's eyes light up as he slipped the silver coin into his purse. "A bit of a night cruise then?"

"You have a silver there, which is more than enough for a silent ride, I trust."

"Oh, that it is, my Lord." The driver clucked his tongue and touched his whip to the horse's flanks, and immediately the horse began plodding over the sand, the sleigh's runners gliding easily over the harbor floor. "That it is."

As they rode, the southern harbor's outer docks and the vast variety of warehouses and teahouses and brothels dwindled from sight, as did the sounds of reverie. Hundreds of foreigners mixed with locals in a festival that had culminated in a parade along the Trough, a great drum circle, and celebration on the sands of the harbor. There were still some few running about the harbor itself, many clearly drunk—caravan men and women and the like. Most were wary of the urchins that waited beneath the shadows of the docks, but those too drunk or too new to the ways of the Amber City didn't know they could be robbed in the blink of an eye, or worse, struck over the head by one of the older ones then dragged beneath the docks to be robbed or raped or slain at the urchins' leisure.

The sleigh made a beeline for the central docks. Though her northern sister was indeed large, the southern harbor was massive—four or five times the size and large enough to house two hundred ships along the outer rim of quays and docks and another two hundred in its center, where a series of docks had been built for long-term storage. Foreign ships of state were often berthed at the inner docks. All four nations that traded directly with Sharakhai—Qaimir, Mirea, Malasan, and Kundhun—had one or more ships docked there at all times. The wealthiest caravan masters, or at least the shrewdest, would often stay in Sharakhai for weeks at a time, waiting to buy those goods that would fetch the best price back home or wherever their caravan's terminus was.

Ahead, the silhouettes of the moored ships rose against the cascade of stars in the southern skies. Dozens upon dozens of them, from all across the Shangazi. The sleigh slid to a stop near a set of stairs leading up to the great maze of piers and sand and ships. Another sleigh, this one filled with eight men and two women—rough and tumble sandsmen, the lot of them—was just unloading while singing a Malasani drinking song both loudly and poorly. When one of them paused unsteadily at the foot of the stairs and watched as Ramahd's sleigh came to a stop, the driver turned to Ramahd, his peach stone necklaces clacking as he softly spoke, "Shall I go round the other side?"

"I'll be fine," Ramahd said as he stood and lowered himself carefully to the sand.

The driver looked to the bravo doubtfully, then shrugged. "You know your business. Ask for Hoav if you ever have need." And with that he was off, the horse's hooves plodding through the sand as it followed the other sleigh into the night.

Ramahd trudged toward the stairs, where the Malasani was still standing.

"Where you headed?" the bravo asked.

There was a day when Ramahd might have engaged him, pushed him just to see how far he'd go, to see how sharp his sword was, how swift his arm, but he was tired. Two days had passed since his bouts in Osman's pits, and his aches lingered. He'd fought three bouts that day, each one layering more wounds, more aches, and he didn't wish to add more, especially not for a drunkard and his nine drunk friends. He wasn't in the mood to trade words, either. He had little patience for fools and less for drunk ones.

So he strode up to the bravo and stopped only when they were face to face.

And said nothing.

He stared into the Malasani's broad face, into his reckless, callow, overconfident eyes. The Malasani blinked away his liquor for a moment or two, then puffed himself up like a peacock. But Ramahd didn't move. He held his stare, waiting, wondering what the bravo would do. And the more he was forced to endure his cocksure attitude, the more he hoped the man *would* do something.

The Malasani's comrades had reached the dock, not even realizing a conflict was brewing, but three of them had stopped and were watching the silent exchange.

"Come on," one of the women called in Malasani. "A bit of the bones, you said."

Slowly, the bravo's jaw lost some of its tight aggression, and then, like a cask of wine tapped for revels, his nerve drained away. He glanced to one side, then back to Ramahd, and finally he turned and spit well wide of Ramahd and strode up the stairs. The lot of them were soon gone.

Ramahd shook his head and made his way to the dock that held the two Qaimiri ships of state, one a massive

galleon that had arrived several weeks back as part of a
delegation that had come to Sharakhai to celebrate the first
exchange on a new trade route with Malasan. The other
was a sleek yacht with extraordinarily long runners made
from the highest quality skimwood. Ramahd headed for
the yacht, the *Blue Heron*. It was the pride of House
Amansir, named after his family crest, a heron wading in
calm water. Ramahd had sailed it to Sharakhai two weeks
before. He'd never made the journey faster.

By the bright light of Tulathan, he could see his first
mate, Dana'il, one hand behind his back, standing at the
ready near the ship's lone hatch. "My Lord Amansir," he
said with a bow of his head and a smart clap of his heels,
which brought the six crewmen to their feet. They clapped
their heels as well, each facing Ramahd from wherever
they happened to be on deck.

"At ease," Ramahd said as he took the short hop down
from the dock.

Dana'il relaxed to some small degree, while the others—
elite men, each and every one—returned to the business of
readying the ship for the coming night's sail. Dana'il waited
with an expectant look.

"You're smiling, Dana'il."

"I am, my Lord."

Ramahd knew the one and only thing that might cause
Dana'il to beam like this. "You found him?"

"We did, my Lord. Near the western harbor, as you'd
said. He's hiding in a cellar beneath a tannery. Its owner
has long been a sympathizer here in the city."

"Is he there now?" He might very well call off this voyage if he was.

"No. Macide left with Hamid near nightfall. Quezada
was forced to retreat for a time. Neither Macide nor Hamid
have been seen since."

"They're crafty."

"Aye," Dana'il said soberly. He knew that better than
most. He'd nearly been killed the last time they'd engaged
the Moonless Host. "We can't be sure, but we believe Macide only recently began using the cellar."

So he might feel safe in using it for a week or two yet.

Ramahd stepped forward and gave Dana'il's shoulder a friendly squeeze. "The gods have shone upon us at last. This is better news than I could have hoped for." Ramahd tipped his head toward the hatch. "Is she awake?"

"Aye. She woke not long ago, and if you'll forgive me for saying it, she's in a foul mood."

"Is she ever *not* in a foul mood?"

"I wouldn't like to say, my Lord."

"Then you are wise, Dana'il. Wiser than I, have I ever told you that?"

"I wouldn't like to say, my Lord."

Ramahd clapped Dana'il on the shoulder. "Well, you are, but don't let it go to your head." He stepped toward the ladder leading belowdecks, pausing at the hatch. "One hour out, south-by-southeast. Sail her as you wish, and then back to Sharakhai."

"Aye, sir," Dana'il said, bowing his head.

As Ramahd made his way into the ship and walked along the narrow passageway toward the forward cabin— the one that had been given to Meryam—he heard the hollow thuds of the crew moving about the ship, then several thumps of sand as three of the men dropped down from the deck. By the gods, it felt strange to be leaving Sharakhai, even for a short while, with Macide an arm's reach away. He couldn't rush his response, though. He merely had news of one of his safe houses, which he'd had three times before. None had led to Macide's capture, and one had led to the death of two of his men, with three more wounded, including Dana'il, who had been saved only by Meryam's careful—not to mention costly—ministrations.

Macide was slippery as a catfish. Had barbs like one, too.

So no, Ramahd would not rush to this tannery. He would sail and report to his King. And then they would take the time they needed to do this properly. Perhaps then, if the gods were just, the man who'd murdered his wife, daughter, and so many others would pay for his crimes.

The ship was nudged from its docked position and began to slip over the harbor's sandy bed. As light as it was

and as fine as the runners were, the *Heron* could be towed
from dock by the crew alone. Soon, the ship was skimming
across the harbor, her sails thrumming as they filled with
cool night wind.

As he neared Meryam's cabin, he swallowed involun-
tarily at the scent wafting into the passageway—a thing
like fermenting apples but much stronger and infinitely
more foul. He would become accustomed to it; he always
did. It would just take time. Within the cabin he heard the
sounds of slurping and the soft moans that often accompanied Meryam's *meals*. He closed his eyes, hand half-raised
to knock on the door, wondering if he ought to leave her in
peace for a time.

"Come," came a gravelly voice from within.

His throat tightened as he swung the door inward and
stepped inside. A red lantern hung from one of the stout
beams crosshatching the ceiling of the small, triangular
cabin. Meryam wore a dark bronze dress with a gold bod-
ice that was tightened to accentuate her dangerously thin
frame. A scarf flowed down over her head and shoulders,
leaving deep shadows over her face from the lamp above,
but the darkness couldn't hide her hollow cheeks, her cavernous eyes. Her lips, once so full, were pulled back into a
near-grimace. It was her hands, however, that always dis-
tressed Ramahd the most. She was holding a chalice, which
she had raised to her mouth. She took a sip as Ramahd
closed the door. Those hands reminded him of a rat's, thin
and long with nails that looked more accustomed to clawing and gouging than the lifting of golden chalices.

When Meryam set the chalice down, a streak of carmine glistened on her lower lip. She licked it away, which
only served to remind Ramahd how much she'd changed.
Meryam used to be beautiful. Used to be genteel. Used to
have a kind heart.

No longer. Now she was a vessel of hatred, of singular
thought: to avenge the deaths of her sister, Yasmine, and
her niece, Rehann. Ramahd had thought *himself* a creature of vengeance. His rage after the deaths of his wife and
daughter had been unquenchable, but it had also been un-
focused, a hammer pounding stones that created little

more than dust and a chorus of raucous sound. In the years since the Bloody Passage, Meryam had honed herself meticulously, silently, and now she was a deadly keen knife, ready to slit the throats of those who had caused her so much pain.

As Ramahd lowered himself into the chair across from her, the stench of her exhalations was enough to make him gag, but as he breathed, slowly and deeply, the urge passed. He thought of telling her about Macide. But if he did, she would insist they stop now, that they go to investigate, and he'd already made his decision, so he said instead, "Once we're underway, I'll have a bit of food brought."

"You know I can't stomach it."

"Meryam, you're wasting away. A small plate if that's all you can manage. Or a little carrot and ginger soup."

"I have all I need."

A common refrain, a phrase she'd been repeating since Yasmine's and Rehann's deaths.

Gods help him, whenever he saw Meryam, he saw Yasmine's bright smile, saw her flowing hair tossed by the wind, heard the laughter that was rare but all the more beautiful when it arrived unannounced. The resemblance had admittedly become more difficult to discern with Meryam's frightful weight loss, but it was there. It would always be there.

By the gods of the bright blue sky, Yasmine, how I miss you.

The visions came again, as they always did when he thought overly much of her—Yasmine running toward Macide, the arrow taking her in the chest, blood dripping onto the golden sand—but he squashed them before they could truly blossom. He'd become good at it, which made him all the more desperate to kill Macide, before his hatred could leak from him any further. Hatred took a lot from a man; when the bright flare of rage exhausted itself, it took work to sustain the heat.

The sound of the yacht's runners skimming over the sand came to them. The shush of the rudder as Dana'il guided them out of the harbor.

When Ramahd spoke again, he put all the authority

into his voice he thought wise. Meryam was touchy, especially after she woke from one of her week-long slumbers, and pushing her too far would make her balk. "At this rate, you'll die before we see the shores of the Austral Sea again."

Meryam chuckled, revealing teeth stained red. "A proclamation you made six months ago."

"And look at you now! You've lost a stone since then! It can't go on, Meryam."

"I have all I need."

"Yes, but your wrath cannot sustain you on its own. Believe me, I know."

"Oh, you do, do you?"

"Don't start, Meryam. Not again." She had never said it outright, but she often hinted that Ramahd hadn't loved her sister as much as she, implying that he wasn't willing to make the sorts of sacrifices she was. "There are ways to achieve our goals that don't involve withering away like a forgotten piece of fruit."

"Is that what I am to you? A forgotten piece of fruit?"

"You are my wife's sister, and I treasure you, which makes your condition all the more painful to see."

"Do we not have more important matters to discuss than my appetite?"

"What if I made fekkas?" he asked. "Just as you like them, with nigella seeds—"

"Tell me what you've come to tell me."

"Not until I have your answer."

She stared at him from within the deep wells of her eyes, anger seething behind them. But she knew, just as Ramahd did, how much Yasmine had loved fekkas. It wasn't something Ramahd or Meryam particularly enjoyed, but they had shared many a plate with Yasmine over tea, especially during her pregnancy, when she'd demanded their obeisance to many of her small rituals. *For the baby*, she'd always say with a wicked smile. *Do it for the baby.* When her bouts of morning sickness had come nearly every day, neither Ramahd nor Meryam had had the heart to refuse her.

Ramahd had grown to hate the small cookies during that time, as had Meryam. They would joke about it whenever Yasmine left the two of them alone, and they'd taken to throwing their cookies over the veranda's marble railing and into the bushes, pretending they'd eaten them when Yasmine returned. Yasmine knew, he thought, or guessed soon after they'd started their furtive little counter-ritual, but she'd never said anything. After Ramahd had given Meryam the tragic news of Yasmine's death in the desert, Meryam had taken to eating them. It was but one of the small and silent paeans to her lost sister, to the point that fekkas were now one of the few things she would eat.

The anger seemed to drain from her. She took another sip from the chalice, licking the mixture of blood and wine from her lips, and said, "I don't like them sweet."

"Then savory they shall be."

"Now tell me . . ."

The ship rode up and over a dune, the lantern swaying, sending the crimson light dancing about the cabin. "As we suspected, Juvaan is lending his support to the Moonless Host, likely at the behest of his queen."

Her eyes narrowed until all he could see were two glistening points of light. "You sound as though you know the sort of support he's lending."

She was always doing this—sensing his heart without his ever saying it. He knew it was to do with the dark rituals she'd fallen into. Blood rituals, a grisly thing indeed. Her decision was no act of desperation. Meryam had always had the aptitude. She'd known it for years and so did her father, King Aldouan of Qaimir, though she hadn't been allowed to undergo the initiation. No one had even considered such a thing. But *after* Yasmine's death, everything had changed. "I managed to find out more, yes."

"Tell me."

Her eyes were becoming heavy. The time was nearing.

"I fought a woman in the pits. She came to me after and admitted that she'd been following Juvaan as well."

"A woman."

"Yes, a woman. She said she'd unlocked a canister, the one sent by Juvaan. It contained a breathstone."

"What was she like?"

Ramahd leaned back. "Are you listening? There was a breathstone inside it. They're hoping to speak to the dead."

"Was she pretty?"

Yes, she was pretty. "She was a pit fighter."

"You took an oath, Ramahd shan Amansir. We both took oaths." The words came slow and slurred. On anyone else it might have sounded comical, but Ramahd wasn't fool enough to think there was anything but deep resentment driving her words.

"I know the oaths we took."

They were oaths to one another, oaths sworn in blood and washed in tears, oaths to make those responsible for Yasmine's and Rehann's deaths suffer tenfold for the agony they'd doled out.

Meryam's eyes were becoming heavier. She licked her lips as though they were irreparably dry. The change was coming upon her.

They were well out from the harbor now. Good. It would make it all the more difficult for the King of Whispers to hear them should he bend his attention their way.

Meryam coughed. Her head drooped, she shivered violently, and when she lifted her head once more, she sat straight and tall—a proud woman, a healthy woman without a hint of the quavering that had hung about her frame like willow leaves when he'd first entered the cabin.

"Two nights," she said, her voice no longer weak. "Two nights you are late." The words poured from her throat like malice.

Ramahd never failed to be amazed by her transformation. Amazed and sickened. It might be Meryam's body sitting before him, but there was no doubt this was the King, his Excellency, Aldouan shan Kalamir, Meryam's father, given voice from thousands of leagues distant by Meryam's particular talents and a special tincture made of his own blood and a rare elderberry wine that preserved it for such rituals for months at a time.

"It couldn't be helped, my King. There was a new trail to follow."

Meryam sat deeper into her chair, which creaked beneath her. "Then tell me of it, this trail of yours."

"I will, but first some news that only came in this night. Macide, My King. We've found him."

"You have?" The surprise that registered on Meryam's face was not as deep as Ramahd had expected.

"We've found one of his safe houses in Sharakhai."

"We've found them before."

"True, which is why we'll be cautious. But we believe he's only just begun to use it, so he may feel safe there for a time, and if we do not find Macide himself, we can learn more from the man who owns the tannery."

Meryam nodded, her expression cautiously optimistic. "Very well. Let's pray to Bakhi that he grants us this boon."

"Of course, My King."

"Your other news?"

"When last we spoke, I said the clues may very well lead to Mirea. We were right. Juvaan Xin-Lei is the one lending support to the Moonless Host. Or perhaps one of several."

"What type of support?"

"Money, certainly. Information. And we believe a breathstone has been delivered to Macide."

Meryam's eyes narrowed. "A breathstone . . ."

"Yes."

"You're sure of it? You saw it with your own eyes? Held it in your hands?"

"No, but—"

"You've been told of it, then. By whom?"

"A woman searching for the same clues we are."

"Very convenient."

Ramahd paused. King Aldouan had been wary of their mission in Sharakhai from the beginning. He wanted vengeance for his daughter and granddaughter, but the thought of upsetting the Kings of Sharakhai made him wary and cautious. *Too* cautious at times. He would never say such things openly—that he *feared* the Kings of Sharakhai—but one could see it in the way his words and actions marched in near lock-step with those of Sharakhai. When viewed up close, the design was difficult to discern, but when viewed from afar, his fears were grand as a temple to the gods.

"You seem to think her word cannot be trusted," Ramahd said, "but she had no reason to lie to me."

"Then by all means, trust her with your life."

"I do not suggest we act on her word alone, My King, only that we investigate further. In the right hands, such a stone might be a powerful weapon to use against us."

And now it was the King's turn to pause. "A powerful weapon indeed."

Ramahd frowned. "Do you know something of this?"

"Of the stone? I know nothing." She lifted her hand and swatted the air, as if chasing away a gnat. "A fanciful worry only."

"If there's anything I need be concerned about, My King . . ."

"Yes, yes. If the time comes, you'll be told."

"Do you know what they plan to do with it?"

"Guesses only, Ramahd. You'll be told." Despite his words, Meryam's face clouded, and she pursed her lips. Several times she opened her mouth to speak, only to clap it shut once more. When Meryam's eyes refocused on Ramahd, they had changed. There was worry in those eyes, a thing he'd never seen before, not since they'd started conversing through this infernal mechanism. "Keep watch on the tannery if you would, but do not attack Macide."

Ramahd stared, stunned. "My Lord King?"

"You heard me, Ramahd."

"I cannot believe my ears."

"You will find the breathstone and, more importantly, the message, if it *can* be found, and only if you cannot find these will we capture Macide and get them from him."

"You cannot be serious."

"I am."

"My Lord King, I am not here to find messages from Juvaan Xin-Lei to the leader of the Moonless Host. I'm here to find Macide and grant justice to those he slew in the desert. My wife and daughter, and many more. I will search for him, and I will kill him as slowly and as painfully as he deserves. That is my right."

"You have that right, but you are in the Shangazi by my will, to *do* my will. And so it shall be. Find the message, Ramahd. Find it, and we'll talk once more of Macide Ishaq'ava." He paused, but only long enough to raise his forefinger as if he were scolding a child. "It is a trivial thing I ask of you, and it does not prevent you from watching Macide, finding the trails he follows to better prepare for the day when you *do* take him. Find the message, Ramahd, and then you may have Macide."

Ramahd could only stare.

"I will hear it from you before we are done."

"I . . ."

"Swear it to me, Ramahd, or I'll order you home."

"I swear it, My King."

"Very well."

No sooner had King Aldouan said these words than Meryam's eyes fluttered and her head tipped back, suddenly listless. The King was gone.

Meryam, the whites of her eyes shining red in the lamplight, took some time to refocus on him. She was always out of sorts after such an episode—for hours or even days. When she focused on him at last, there was a look of burning hatred on her face. She had been privy to the conversation Ramahd had with her father. She would have been unable to do anything about it until the King's spirit faded, but now that it had, she realized that Ramahd had withheld from her the information about Macide. But she was shivering so violently she couldn't speak.

She leaned forward, perhaps attempting to lift herself up, but then Ramahd realized she was tipping over. He shot forward and caught her before she fell. He lifted her gently—light as a lamb, she was—and laid her on her bunk. As he set her scarf aside and pulled the blankets over her, he heard her whisper something.

"Hamzakiir," she said. "Hamzakiir."

A name, but not one that meant anything to Ramahd.

"Who is Hamzakiir?" he asked.

But she only kept whispering, over and over again, "Hamzakiir, Hamzakiir," so he kissed her on the forehead, then headed for the galley to make her fekkas.

Chapter 18

THREE DAYS AFTER THE FIGHT AT THE PITS, Çeda sat in the predawn light, near the window where she kept her plants, sipping coriander tea and reading through a history of Sharakhai, one she'd found in the bazaar only yesterday. It was largely drivel; an idealized version of events, but she flipped through its pages again, hoping it might give her some clue to the riddle in her mother's book. The more she read, though, the angrier she got, and eventually she whipped the book across her room. It thumped against the plaster, then thudded to the floor. Broken plaster pattered around it like rain.

There was more to the tale. She knew it, and she was desperate to learn more. Her mother had found clues that trailed backward in time to the very night of Beht Ihman. Was that why she'd gone to the House of Kings? Was that why she'd been killed?

Çeda was desperate to learn more, to learn the truth behind the legend. But how? Most of what she knew was learned not from her mother—who'd spoken of it only rarely—but from people like Ib'Saim in the bazaar or Ibrahim, who rode about the city on his cart, telling and trading stories. But Çeda knew their tales were a dozen times removed from what really happened. She'd read many of the epic poems and books that recounted the years leading up to the war and the days that followed, but those were the Kings' propaganda, stories written years or even generations after the fact. In some cases, the Kings themselves had penned them.

She would learn little from those. She had to find more reliable sources. But where? The Kings had spent four hundred years retelling the story of those days in any way they wished. Those who had tried to speak against them would have been killed, their voices silenced. There were even rumors in the streets that one of the Kings—Zeheb, the King of Whispers—could hear those who plotted against them. Çeda had no idea if that was true—it might be and it might not—but even if it wasn't, it was a very effective tool of suppression, a deterrent against seditious behavior.

Çeda sat at the edge of the bed and pinched her eyes. The asir's words were linked to her mother, but how? She liked to think she knew a thing or two for a gutter wren, but she was woefully unprepared for this, the uncovering of grand secrets. As she placed the book on the nearest of the three stacks by her bedside, the certainty that had been forming these past few days felt confirmed; she would never unlock the riddle with the texts available on the streets. If she were some desert traveler looking over bones that had been picked clean, at least then she might be able to discern what the animal had once looked like. No, it was as though these stories were a gathering of bones selected from completely different animals, assembled into the approximate shape of what an animal *ought* to look like. Beyond whatever small value the stories held, they were dangerous, for surely they would lead her along the entirely wrong paths. But how to find the right ones?

She needed clues, and it felt as though she had fewer than when she'd started. The thing about Sharakhai, though, was that someone somewhere in this wondrous city would have some secreted away. She just had to find them.

With the sun now well above the horizon, Çeda rose and prepared another cup of tea. She stepped into Emre's room, her tea in one hand, the last of Dardzada's brewed concoction in the other. She sipped from the steaming cup while holding the phial out for him.

He downed half of it in one gulp. "Mule piss, Çeda. Why do you insist on feeding me mule piss every morning and every night?"

She held his gaze evenly. "You'd rather be a feast for worms?"

He raised the phial, his face screwed up in disgust. "If they taste better than this, I might just try it."

"Shut your mouth, you beetle-brained fool, and finish it."

He took one deep breath, downed the last of it, and, afterward, shook his head and lolled his tongue out like a wolf. "Happy?"

"As a babe with a finger full of honey." She snatched the phial away and waved at his shirt. "Off."

He raised his eyebrows. "Is that a proposition?"

She punched his shoulder, hard. When he laughed, she gave him another, harder this time, and he wailed. "For the love of the gods, Çeda, we're not in the pits!"

"Say that word again and I'll give you worse," she hissed at him. He knew she didn't like his talking about the pits, especially not loud enough for their neighbors to hear.

He finally took off his shirt, allowing her to examine his stitches. They were doing much better. Most signs of infection were gone, and the wounds had closed well.

"Good," he said when she'd finished, "because I'm going to Seyhan's today."

Gods, here we go again. "You'll do no such thing!"

"Çeda, if I stay here one more day, I'll drive my head through the wall, if only to dream of being somewhere else."

"You're still healing."

"I'm healed well enough to stand behind a stall and pass muslin bags to the fine Mirean women who happen to frequent it."

"Always the women . . ."

"What can I say? They like me."

She punched him a third time, much harder than the first two.

He howled in pain, but his eyes were smiling. As he sat on the edge of his bed, wrapping the leather cords of his knee-high sandals around his shin, she considered how much stronger he seemed. It was good to see him like this, and it was a far sight better than the haunted look he'd had in the days after the attack.

"If you're going to be mule-headed, then hold on," she said. "I'll go with you."

"And where might *you* be going?"

"Never you mind."

Emre shook his head, starting on the other sandal. "Çeda and her secrets. Why don't you marry them, if you love them so much?"

"They'd make a sight better husband than you ever would."

He smiled at this, but there was something odd in his expression, as if she had pained him. But he said nothing of it, and neither did she.

Soon they were out and headed east toward the bazaar, falling into step beside one another. The sun was bright, but there was a cool northerly breeze, rare in summer but all the more welcome for it. Emre was walking gingerly, but she could already tell he was starting to loosen up. The walk would do him good, she decided, and as long as Seyhan didn't make him lift kegs of spices, all should be well.

"So?" Emre asked as the sounds of the bazaar came to them.

"What?"

"Are you going to talk about it?"

"Talk about what?"

Emre rolled his eyes. "The price of figs. What do you *think*, Çeda? The poem!"

She grew suddenly sober. She'd been so caught up in her worry over him she'd forgotten—at least for the past hour or two. "I think she was killed because of the poem, or something related to it. What I can't figure out is why. The poem may relate to the asirim, or to the Kings, or both, but how? That's the riddle I need to solve, Emre, the truth behind those words."

"I always thought it was because she'd been caught in the blooming fields."

Çeda had thought the same. It was a guess based on the

night before her mother died, when she had returned in a
rush from the night of Beht Zha'ir. Something had happened to make her so fatalistic. She'd said she'd not found
petals that night. Was that because she'd been spotted in
the blooming fields? She'd escaped, but had she thought
her trail would lead the Kings to her, to Dardzada? To
Çeda? That must have been why she'd gone back out, to
lead the Kings away.

She and Emre reached a corner where a line of men
were hauling buckets toward the bazaar—some filled with
water, others with lemons, a few with clutches of green
mint in their hands. Çeda and Emre fell into step behind
the men but not too closely.

"Maybe the Kings knew about her poem," Emre said,
"that she'd unlocked some riddle."

Çeda shook her head. "If they had, they would've come
for the book."

"Maybe they did. Maybe they sent the Maidens hunting
for it but couldn't find it."

"No. Dardzada would've heard about it. The fact that he
gave me the book and never asked about it proves he suspected nothing. If he'd had even a whiff of the Maidens
hunting after her, or suspected the book was anything but
an heirloom, he would've burned it on the spot."

"Dardzada takes care of himself—"

"And only himself," she said, completing the refrain
they used to toss back and forth when running the streets.
The trouble was it wasn't true. Dardzada had taken care of
her—albeit in his own way—for four years. He'd been *over-
protective*, not the reverse.

No, as strict as Dardzada had been, and as cruel, it
wasn't because he didn't care for her.

They reached the edge of the bazaar, where as far as the
eye could see, men and women and children were helping
to set up stalls, laying out wares, putting up awnings for
shade in hopes of stalling their patrons for a few precious
moments longer. Emre stopped and stood there, clearly
trying to order his thoughts before speaking.

"Spit it out," Çeda said.

"Çeda, Ahya died over these riddles, and you'll die too,

if you go too much further." He pointed to Tauriyat, the top half of which could be seen over the stone buildings on the far side of the bazaar. On it stood palace after palace, one for each of the Kings. "They've lived on that hill for four hundred years. Most likely they'll live there another four. This isn't worth chasing."

He was trying to protect her. She knew that. But it still burned, just like it had in the desert when they'd gone together to the blooming fields. "You don't have to help, Emre."

She tried to walk past him but he grabbed her arm and spun her around. "I'll help if it's help you want. You know that. You have only to say the word. But promise me you'll think on it." He looked her over, as if he were truly taking her in for the first time that day. "Where are you going, anyway?"

"Just making sure you're able to walk without pulling open those stitches."

His eyes narrowed. "Well, if you don't want to tell me, just say so, Çeda."

Ahead, Tehla was using her broad wooden peel to pull eight golden biscuits from her brick oven. She slipped the biscuits onto the cooling board, above which was a small brass bell with a red ribbon tied to the striker.

As Tehla struck the bell three times, Çeda took Emre's arm and pointed him toward the stall. "Come on," she said, "my gift."

Emre shook his head at her blatant ploy of changing the subject but allowed himself to be led just the same. When they reached Tehla's stall, Çeda grabbed two goat cheese biscuits and dropped a silver six piece onto the weather-worn board. "No need to ring your bell, Tehla. The entire city can smell them."

Tehla clasped her hands and bowed her head to Çeda. "Welcome," she said politely and with a mischievous smile, and then she turned to Emre, her eyes brightening like the sunrise, "and would you *look* who you've brought with you?" Tehla's smile might be for both of them, but her eyes she saved for Emre. "As often as you come around, you'd think you *hate* my bread."

"Hate *your* bread?" Emre bit into the steaming biscuit. "Now there's a laugh," he said around his mouthful. "A good day to you, my lovely ladies." He turned pointedly to Çeda. "I think I can manage from here." And with that he bowed, grimacing only slightly, and walked away toward the spice market, whose tall mudbrick walls and peaked roof could be seen beyond the stalls of the bazaar.

Çeda waited, taking a bite of her own savory biscuit. After a moment, Tehla caught her smiling and quickly looked down to her peel.

Çeda smiled. "Nothing wrong with looking, Tehla."

Tehla leaned closer and licked her lips, so shamelessly Çeda felt her cheeks redden. "Like a fig, that one. Plump and juicy, am I right?"

"Tehla!" The two of them shared a laugh, though Çeda found herself more jealous of the older woman than she ought to be.

"Don't tell me you've never taken a bite!"

"A gentlewoman never tells."

"Oh ho! A gentlewoman, are you now?"

"Stop it," she said, wolfing down the last of her still-warm biscuit with a smile, "there's something I need."

Tehla's eyes narrowed. "Something you *need?* It wouldn't be Davud, would it?"

"It would, Tehla. It would."

Chapter 19

CEDA RETURNED THE MORNING AFTER the rattlewing attack with water and herbs for Emre. She'd worried over him the entire night and sprinted the last quarter-league, back into the desert, ignoring the pains from the rattlewing bites. She found him lying beneath his blankets in the same position she'd left him. He was still breathing, but shallowly, and he didn't respond when she shook him gently.

He hadn't taken any of the water she'd left him, or very little if he'd had any. She couldn't force him to eat, but she poured water carefully into his mouth, waiting as he swallowed it with painful sluggishness. He moaned from time to time—perhaps from a dream, perhaps from pain—but otherwise was silent as she chewed Sweet Anna leaves and goldenthread roots and packed the poultice into each of his puckered red wounds. She took one of the blankets and cut it into strips, using it to cover the bites, keep the poultice in place and safe from drying prematurely in the arid wind.

By the time the sun was high she was nearly done, and she was exhausted. She drank some water, herself, and looked in the pack for a strip of meat. That's when she realized. She'd left the mouth of the pack open so Emre could reach in and grab whatever he needed, but now there was no food left. None. Emre hadn't eaten it, she was sure. He was too addled.

Lizards, perhaps, or desert mice. Who knew? The point was, the food was gone.

She dropped the pack into her lap and stared at Emre, wishing he could talk to her. "By the gods I've really fucked this one good, Emre."

She might be able to hunt for some food, but she didn't want to leave Emre again unless it was absolutely necessary. It was dangerous enough leaving him like this last night. If he recovered enough during the day to accompany her to the stream, so be it, but for now, they would wait and rest, and she'd let Emre heal. At least, as much as he could. It meant they would be here until morning, and it made her gut churn. It meant they would spend the night in the desert once more. It meant they'd be here, just beside the blooming fields, on the night of Beht Zha'ir.

Everyone knew the asir lived somewhere among the blooming fields. They would rise from their graves and stalk toward Sharakhai, and she and Emre would be in their path.

With the sun high, it seemed like a distant worry. She knew it was anything but, and yet she was so tired she could think of nothing but resting her head awhile. She repositioned the packs to either side of Emre, leaving enough room for her to lie next to him, then pulled the blankets over their heads to shelter them from the sun.

"Emre?"

He didn't respond, but he was breathing somewhat more easily than before, so she drew herself next to him and fell into a deep, deep sleep.

She dreamed. And her dreams were not kind.

———— ⤙●⤚ ————

She woke to the sound of wailing.

It sounded like a child in pain, a child dying from disease. The hair at the nape her neck rose, and she pulled the rumpled blanket off her head and checked Emre.

Tulathan was out, and Rhia was just cresting in the east. Both were bright, giving her more than enough light to check Emre's wounds. They were better, and Emre's breathing sounded deep and restful. He mumbled when she spoke to him but did not wake fully.

It was a blessing, she decided. They couldn't make their way through the desert like this in any case, so perhaps it was better if he could sleep through the worst of the pain. She fed him water as another mournful call came, this one closer than the last. It sounded as though it had come from the blooming field to the north.

Would the asirim in the near field wake? Would they sense the two of them lying there? Would they come for them, as they'd come for the tributes marked by the Reaping King in Sharakhai? She sat up slowly, worried she might be seen but entirely too curious to let that stop her. She moved silently up the gradual slope to the crest and looked toward the wide plateau of rock where the blooming field lay. Points of light were winking slowly into existence. Here and there among the black swath of the adichara, the blooms were opening their petals to the twin moons, bright like lamps across a city grown wary of the night. She could even see wisps of light drifting up from the pale white flowers. Pollen, she realized. Pollen drifting on the breeze.

Of the beetles she could see no signs—a blessing from the gods, surely. No longer did they buzz over the field before her. They'd returned to their hives in the carcasses of the dead, perhaps scared away by the cold of night or the light of the moons or both. Nor did she see what she feared most: dark forms climbing forth from the sand.

Her stomach grumbled as she returned to Emre and poured water down his throat. She gave him enough to keep him for a while, and then drank sparingly from the skin herself. She'd been hungry before, but never *this* hungry—as little as she and her mother had had, Ahya had always made sure Çeda had food in her belly.

Just as she was ready to give Emre more, she heard hoofbeats. She immediately stood and looked to the southeast, toward Sharakhai, where a horse was cresting a distant dune. Who would be coming *here?* Who would brave the night of Beht Zha'ir?

The horse was coming straight toward them.

She and Emre were too high. Too exposed. "Emre!" she rasped. "Emre, we have to go!"

She shook him violently, but he wouldn't wake, so she took him beneath the armpits and dragged him down the dune into the valley. She ran back and grabbed their packs and waterskins and returned just as the horse was nearing. She knelt next to Emre and drew the sand over his body, piling it over his legs and arms and torso before lying on her stomach and covering herself as well as she could.

She rested her head against the sand and stilled herself just as the horse crested the nearest dune. It was a tall horse. Regal. And atop it, limned in silver moonlight, was a man who rode with practiced ease. He was coughing, his entire body wracked by it, but he rode on, heading abreast of the nearby blooming field, blessedly oblivious to Çeda's presence. She thought he might be headed for the fields themselves, but he wasn't. He headed for another landmark entirely: the tamarisk tree, she realized. She remembered the sigil engraved on the stone between the roots and wondered again what meaning it might have.

When the horse had passed by a goodly distance, she stood and ran after, keeping low, ready to drop to the ground if the rider should turn in his saddle. He never did, though. He seemed single-minded, staring determinedly ahead, slapping at the horse's flank to force it onward. She was worried about how well she could keep up, but the horse was clearly winded, and she lost little ground, even as sore as she was. When he came near the tree, the rider slipped over the saddle, dropped down to the sand, and sprinted toward the tamarisk tree, wracking coughs his constant companion.

He stopped before he reached it though. He just stood there, unmoving, body shuddering from his unrelenting coughs. And then something wondrous happened. Dark tendrils were moving, growing up from the ground in a rough circle around the rider.

"Gods be good," Çeda mumbled, numbly realizing how stupid it had been to do so.

These were the roots of the tree, snaking upward like the tines of some twisted crown. Soft popping and cracking sounds accompanied the movement, and soon they had enveloped the rider as if embracing some long-lost love. The roots tightened around him, drew him down, the sand parting like silt. A particularly long and mournful wail came from somewhere to the east as the man, still coughing, was drawn lower and lower, the roots of the tamarisk pulling him down into the desert itself.

Soon he was gone, leaving Çeda to stare at the tree in wonder. By the gods who walk the earth, what had just happened? She waited for something else—for the man to rise once more, for someone to chase after him, for *something* to happen—but she heard only the occasional rattle of branches as the tamarisk swayed back and forth in the nighttime breeze.

The horse stayed for a while, but then wandered southwestward, perhaps toward the stream, making Çeda wonder just how often the horse had taken this journey with its master. She stood, dusted off her clothes, then pulled her knife and stalked warily toward the tree, making sure she stayed well wide of the place where the roots had risen from the ground. She circled the tree for a time, waiting, watching, but nothing happened. The man didn't return.

She returned to the base of the tree and knelt where the sigil lay partially hidden by the roots. The moonlight was well bright enough for her to make it out. Was it the sigil of a King? The very notion made her shiver with fear and excitement: A King? Here? Who else would ride to the blooming fields on an akhala? Who else might command the sort of power she'd just witnessed?

A King, and she'd been only a few dozen paces from him. She stared down at the knife in her hand, and then she laughed. She couldn't help it. How ineffectual she would have been. The mere notion that she might have attacked the King was ludicrous. And yet she hungered for it. For her mother's sake. For her own.

She committed the sigil to memory, drawing it in the sand several times before she was satisfied, then stood and stepped closer to the depression that marked the entrance to the sands. Finding nothing of note, she headed back. She didn't go to Emre, though. She continued past him to the nearest of the blooming fields.

She looked to the blue-white blooms, breathed in their heady scent. She hadn't meant to be out this night. She'd only meant to look upon the trees and return before Beht Zha'ir in anticipation of another, future trip. But here she was now, staring at the flowers everyone in Sharakhai knew about but so few had seen. Her mother had collected these for years, had dried them and given them to Çeda on holy days or days with special meaning.

One of the flowers hung just above her head. It wound this way and that, as if it were lost, as if it were looking for something. She knew the thorns along the branch were dangerous, so she was careful as she reached up and held the flower gently and then cut it free with a snick of her knife. She held it near her nose, breathed deeply of its scent. Dear gods, how it reminded her of her mother.

"I miss you," she said to the cold desert air. "Emre misses you."

She listened, her hearing sharpened by her sudden awareness of all that was around her. Or perhaps it was her loneliness, her yearning to be with her mother once more.

She heard the ticking sounds coming from the adichara, the soft sigh of the wind through the branches, the wails of the asirim far in the distance, but nothing else. Nothing at all.

After tucking the bloom carefully inside her shirt and slipping her knife home, she returned to Emre. She stayed awake the entire night, watching for any sign of the King, listening for anyone else who might be riding here to meet him. She saw nothing, heard nothing, until shortly after sunrise, when a piercing whistle broke the stillness. Soon she heard the plodding of hooves. She watched from over the top of a dune as the same man rode toward the blooming fields. He pulled up near the edge of the twisted trees and slipped from his saddle. He stripped down with a sluggish pace Çeda had seen often in the streets of Sharakhai, men moving gingerly, bodies clenched inward after a night of heavy drink. After removing his khalat and turban and even his small clothes, he stood naked before the rising sun. And then he stepped, hunch-backed, *into* the adichara. The branches spread, then embraced him, as the roots of the tamarisk tree had done the night before.

Tulathan's bright eyes, what was she witnessing? A man, a King, pierced by a thousand thorns. Was he committing suicide? But no. A moment later the adichara branches spread, releasing him. He faced the sun, spread his arms wide, and arched his head back as if he were presenting himself to the new day. While staring at the cloudless blue sky, he drew deep breaths, unencumbered by whatever had been afflicting him before he'd stepped into the trees. Points of red flecked his skin, blood from where the thorns had pierced him, but they didn't appear to hamper his movements in any way. In fact, when he retrieved a bolt of white cloth from the horse's saddlebag and ran it over his body, his skin looked whole, unmarred.

After pulling his clothes back on, he mounted his horse and rode back toward Sharakhai along the same path he'd taken here, and the desert was silent once more.

Çeda had no idea what she'd just witnessed. All she wanted was to return home and be done with the desert for a time. Thank the gods, Emre woke a short while later.

"What's happened?" he asked.

"You attacked a bloody great host of beetles, that's what."

"Did I win?"

"You lost."

He stared at her, bleary-eyed. "Did I?"

"You did," she said as she helped him to sit. Breath of the desert, she was relieved to see him like this.

"How long have we been out here?" he asked after downing half a skin of water.

"A night and a day and a night," she said, sipping from her own skin. Water had never tasted so good. "We should head back. If you're able."

He nodded, and she helped him to stand. He was clearly

in pain from even the simplest of movements, but she didn't wish to stay here any longer than needed. The chance of the King's returning was simply too great.

As she'd suspected—for it had been the same with her—Emre seemed to fare better the more he moved, and by the time they reached the stream, he moved, if not with ease, at least with something akin to it.

"Did anything happen?" he asked as he balanced himself awkwardly over a brace of river stones.

"I fetched water, I made a poultice, I looked after you. What would have happened?"

He shrugged. "How would I know?"

She touched the flower beneath her shirt. "No, Emre. Nothing happened."

Chapter 20

Çeda was late for her meeting with Davud, but she wanted to catch Emre and she was already running through the spice market, so she steered herself past Seyhan's stall. When she arrived, the crowd was thrumming, but Emre wasn't there. Seyhan, a man who often looked old but today seemed surprisingly spry, was scooping peppercorns into a muslin bag for an old man with violently shaking hands. Seyhan's grandson, a waif of a boy with eyes too big for his head, was scooping star anise into small muslin bags, from a burlap sack every bit as large as he was.

"What've you got Emre doing?" Çeda called to Seyhan over the din of the market.

Seyhan glanced her way, eyebrows raised, chin lifted in a questioning gesture.

She cupped her hands and tried again. "Emre . . . You didn't send him to the harbor to pick up barrels, did you? He shouldn't be lifting them for a few weeks yet."

Seyhan's face soured. "Emre," he spat. "He'll be lucky to have a place by my side, assuming he ever returns."

"What?"

Seyhan handed the bag over to the shaking man and

accepted two sylval. As the old patron dropped the peppercorns into a larger muslin bag and shuffled away through the busy market, Seyhan turned to Çeda. "I'm not some pitiless bastard, Çeda. I heard he got jumped, so I was willing to give him a bit of—how do the caravan men say it?—*room to maneuver*, but now I hear he's been running around Sharakhai, healthy as can be."

"But he *isn't* healthy," Çeda shot back. "Not yet. He just needs a bit more time."

"Don't go making excuses for him. Just yesterday, Galovan's daughter saw him along the Trough, moving well enough to sidle up to her and give her a kiss. If he's well enough for that, he's well enough to sell spice."

"A man can walk along the Trough," Çeda replied, more than concerned but unwilling to let Seyhan see it. "The Kannan doesn't prevent him doing *that*."

"Yes, then why did he ask Sahra not to tell her father that she'd seen him? I'll tell you why. So I don't find out. I'm not a cruel man, Çeda, but I'm no fool, either."

No, I'm the fool. Emre was getting himself into trouble. She knew it. She just didn't know the whys or wherefores. "It's my fault," Çeda said as someone bumped past her. "His injuries were bad, and I made him promise to wait just a day or two more so they could heal properly." She shrugged. "I guess he decided to take my advice for once."

Seyhan's face soured even further, but after a moment he softened. "Just tell him to come by and see me."

"I will."

Part of her wanted to go hunting for Emre right then and there, but she had other business to attend to. She found Davud beneath the old fig tree at the edge of the bazaar. He was all smiles and gave Çeda a big hug that surprised her. When she told him what she wanted, however, he grew serious and lowered his voice, nearly to a whisper. "I know little enough of Beht Ihman, Çeda."

"I'm looking for texts, Davud. Texts that were written as close to that night as possible, those that might be untouched by the hand of the Kings."

Davud shrugged. "There might be some, Çeda, but I don't have access to them."

"But Amalos would, wouldn't he?"

Amalos was Davud's master at the collegia, his mentor, whom Davud assisted as he worked his way through his studies.

"He might," Davud allowed.

"Do you trust him?"

"With what?"

And now it was Çeda's turn to lower her voice, waiting for a group of jabbering women to pass by the fig tree. "In the teahouse, you told me he has little love for the Kings."

"I should never have said that."

"Is it true?"

"He feels they are . . . overly strict."

"Can I trust him with a question or two about that night, Davud? Might he let me read some of those ancient works without becoming suspicious? That's what I need to know."

"Forgive me, Çeda, but I must know why."

"No. I won't involve you. Just tell me of Amalos."

Were Davud older, or bolder, he might have demanded more of her, but instead he visibly quieted himself, considering her words, and nodded. "I don't believe he would turn you in for asking a question or two, if that's what you mean."

"Will you take me to him?"

He tried to smile, and made a miserable go of it. "Yes."

"Good." She tugged on his arm. "Let's go."

Davud led her through the winding streets eastward and onto the grounds of the collegia, where more than a dozen redstone buildings were spaced within its walls. Farther east, beyond the walls, loomed the bulk of Tauriyat with the House of Kings crouched along its shoulders. Dozens of students wandered about, most wearing simple flaxen robes with rope belts and woven leather sandals. Some were younger than Çeda, but many were older. Few enough could afford tuition at the collegia, and often the masters ended up teaching as many from Qaimir or Mirea or lands beyond as they did those from Sharakhai, which did little to endear them to the people of the city, or at least not to the part of the city where Çeda lived.

Two men with long beards and the white robes of the

faculty paused their conversation and studied Çeda as she passed, but they didn't stop her. Çeda nodded to them, smiling until they turned away, but Davud sped up until they were well into the cool inner halls of the largest of the buildings, the scriptorium.

"Pay them no mind," Çeda said, her voice echoing inside the massive reading hall.

"Shh," Davud whispered.

Only then, as her eyes adjusted to the relative darkness, did she realize that his face was red beneath his sandy-colored hair. He was *embarrassed* to be with her, she realized.

Her natural inclination was to rib him about it—if only to see his boyish face become even more red—but she knew that he'd had a hard time finding his place here. Despite the prudishness of the masters and her annoyance that Davud had succumbed to it, she didn't wish him to suffer, so she remained silent and let him lead her two levels down into the scriptorium's cool cellars.

She hadn't seen Amalos in years, but when they came at last to his study, she wondered if it had been longer than she thought. He looked decades older. He was hunched over a fresh clay tablet, carefully copying another ancient tablet with a wooden stylus that looked as though it had been cast aside as useless when the first gods fled the world.

"Be a good boy," Amalos said, waving a hand negligently toward the corner of the room, "and mix more clay."

Davud stood there in the center of the room, hoping Amalos would see Çeda, perhaps so he wouldn't have to explain her presence, but when he stayed hunched over his work like a vulture, Davud cleared his throat and said, "I've brought someone to see you, Master Amalos."

How strange, Çeda thought. Such a confident young man elsewhere, but here, before her very eyes, he'd reverted to the untried apprentice.

Amalos still didn't turn, making Davud look positively miserable. "Master Amalos, I've brought someone to see you."

"What?" At last Amalos swung his head around to where Çeda stood. "Who are you?"

With that Davud ducked his head and walked over to

the corner, where a ewer and a bucket of red powder lay, leaving Çeda to fend for herself.

"I'm Çeda," she said. When he continued to stare, his white, bushy eyebrows creeping dangerously toward one another, she clarified, "Çedamihn Ahyanesh'ala? You knew my mother, and you know Dardzada, who was my guardian."

A look of recognition came over his face. "Not your guardian for very long, though, was he?" He turned back to his tablet.

"No, I suppose he wasn't."

When he continued with his work, she could see she was going to have to take the conversation into her own hands. "I've come to ask you of the Kings, and the night of Beht Ihman." He paused for a moment, but then continued with his task, and Çeda went on. "I wonder if there are any texts about that night."

"There are hundreds," he said, his white beard waggling.

"Yes, but I want those that were written in that time," she paused, glancing toward Davud, who was engrossed in his mixing, and lowered her voice, "by those who saw."

"None but the Kings saw. The Kings and the gods themselves."

Çeda spoke more quietly still. "There must have been others."

Amalos's stylus finished the curl it was making through the red clay but then paused, suspended above the tablet, shaking with age, or perhaps a sudden and acute anxiety. He did not turn as he said, "Davud, dear boy. I've completely lost the day. Go and tell Master Nezahum I won't be able to meet her today, won't you? Ask her if we might meet tomorrow over morning meal."

"But you weren't to meet her until midday."

"I've too much to do. Now go on."

"But the clay . . ."

"Forget the clay, Davud."

Davud frowned, but he washed his hands and dried them off with a nearby towel, which he threw on the table before leaving, but not before shooting Çeda a look, one she could only describe as half relief, half resentment.

"Close the door, won't you?" Amalos said, returning to his work.

Çeda did. The old door creaked before the latch rattled home.

At this, Amalos turned in his chair and regarded Çeda. His bushy white brows lowered as he studied her. "You say Ahyanesh was your mother."

"She was."

"And your father?"

Çeda had been asked this a thousand times by the men and women she met—though far less often by women—and usually she would answer with the truth: that she had no father. She couldn't remember a time he'd been in her life, and the few times she recalled asking her mother of him, she had answered with a scowl or a grunt or a pinch on the ear. Only once had she answered, and it struck Çeda like a hammer.

Your father? she'd snapped. *Your father would kill you the moment he learned you were alive.*

Çeda remembered meeting her mother's eyes, seeing her look of shock, as if she deeply regretted what she'd just said, but she never took the words back. She'd been silent, allowing Çeda to absorb them. She cried herself to sleep that night, convinced her father would one day slay her while she slept.

"I never knew my father," Çeda replied.

"But you must know—"

"I don't." Çeda composed herself. "I don't know. I wish I knew more."

The white tufts of his brows quivered as if wrestling with one another. "Tell me why you're asking of Beht Ihman."

Çeda had known he would ask—any one of the masters in the collegia would. She'd been prepared to lie, but there was something about Amalos, about the way he was looking at her, stern yet caring, inquisitive yet deferential. She'd never felt quite so respected, not from Emre, not from Osman. Certainly not from Dardzada. It made her want to tell Amalos the truth, to repay his honest concern, but she couldn't. Not unless it was absolutely necessary.

"I wish to know because I was caught out on Beht Zha'ir

four nights ago. And I saw one of them. One of the asirim. I merely wished to know of their history."

"You?"

"Yes, *me*."

"You've heard the tales."

"I want to know the truth."

Amalos whipped one arm in the air as if he were swatting at one of the rattlewings that swarmed the adichara. "The truth is a mirage, changing with the winds of the desert. The truth is lost, Çedamihn, and you'll not uncover it here."

"Then where *can* the truth be found?"

"Find Saliah for your truth."

Çeda frowned. Many refused to believe that Saliah existed. Others thought she might, but that she would never allow herself to be found, even if one knew where to look. Others believed she *could* be found, but only at a time and place of Saliah's choosing. Whatever the case, it was clear Amalos didn't believe in her, and that Çeda was being dismissed. But if he was so determined to hide the truth of Beht Ihman from her, why had he sent Davud away? Why had he asked her these questions?

"I've come *here*, Amalos. I've come here because Davud trusts you. I've come here because you are learned. I'd rather you help me, because this is a dangerous path I'm walking. I know that. But I'm going to learn the truth of that night whether you help me or not."

Amalos seemed to become smaller at those words, as if he were shrinking away from the danger he saw lying before Çeda. His wrinkled eyes quivered. His lips flushed.

"You know," Çeda said. "You know what happened."

"What I know will do you no good." He turned back to his desk, picked up his stylus, and began making careful marks into the red clay.

"Coward."

He turned his head toward her but did not meet her eyes as he said, "A coward, perhaps, but one who lives."

Çeda waited for him to say more, waited for him to change his mind, but soon enough she realized he wouldn't. Not now. Not ever.

As she opened the door to leave, she was startled to find Davud standing there, his eyes wide as the moons. Gone was the young man she'd had tea with; he'd been replaced by a boy. He straightened himself, running his hands down his robes to smooth out unseen wrinkles. He was plainly asking—pleading—for her not to speak of this to Amalos. Without a word Çeda made her way past him, out and into the cool corridor that would lead her back through the scriptorium and into the heat of Sharakhai. If Davud wished to spy upon that old fool, who was she to stop him?

When she made it back to the streets, the rightful sounds of the city returned. People. Masses of people. Talking, walking, leading horses and carts and wagons and goats. But she also heard a wind chime, a simple wind chime, and it reminded her of something Amalos had said: *Find Saliah for your truth.*

Suddenly, it felt as though a great shroud had been lifted from her mind, and she remembered the chimes. She'd heard that sound out in the desert when she was young. Her mother had taken her on a skiff to see a woman who lived there, alone, far from the cramped bustle of Sharakhai. Saliah. She could remember meeting her when she was a child. Twice. Thrice. Who knew how many times?

By Thaash's golden skin, how could she have forgotten?

And with this, another memory was spurred, of a vision in a tree of chimes. The blade of ebon steel. The hands of a King who granted it to her. It was the memory she'd been struggling to recall when she'd seen Sukru, moments after the asir with the golden crown had kissed her.

Suddenly the chime no longer felt like a random occurrence. It felt like a summons.

Chapter 21

SHARAKHAI'S WESTERN HARBOR was a pale imitation of the great northern and southern harbors. It had a smattering of docks built into a cove filled with sand and standing rocks. It wasn't well suited to ships, but it was the best the west end had to offer, and it had a clear channel out past the bedrock to the great desert beyond. Still, only small ships could dock here, which in some ways was better for those who lived nearby. Low dock fees meant hunters could go out and shoot hare or jackal or even the massive sand skates, which were difficult to catch but whose white meat was rich and exceptionally tasty when roasted over open flame.

No lighthouses stood at this harbor, but if ships were late or feared lost, braziers would be lit and raised onto tall wooden poles to see them home. A few ships were heading out to the dunes already, the tips of their sharp sails cutting through the rays of the rising sun. Çeda went to the ship at the very end of the quay, a two-masted ketch that looked as though the next windstorm would rip it from its runners and scatter its dry remains across the desert.

She knocked on the hull as she walked and then headed

toward one of the three skiffs moored to the other side of the pier. "Djaga, I'm taking a skiff."

Above, footsteps thumped across the deck and a woman with kinky red hair and chocolate skin and a clean scar along her jaw leaned over the gunwales. As always, Çeda was shocked by the beauty of her gray-green eyes, her ebony skin. She might have been a queen, though Djaga herself would sneer at such a notion. She'd been a dirt dog once—*a selhesh,* Djaga always corrected her, *Bakhi's chosen; I was no dog*—but she'd left the pits years ago. She'd forged a brutal path up through the ranks, and then, when her stock was at its highest, she'd agreed to a bout in the killing pits, where fighters fought to the death. Usually twelve dirt dogs entered at once and fought until one remained, but in Djaga's case only two had entered the arena. She'd been pitted against Hathahn, a massive brute, the most efficient and cruelest fighter the pits had ever seen. He'd been victorious in twenty-nine killing bouts before finally retiring, but he'd been lured back for one final match. The chance to take Djaga, a woman who'd won every one of her thirty matches, was simply too great.

He'd left that pit with vacant eyes, blood pouring from the fissure Djaga had cleaved in his skull with a bronze ax. And Djaga, despite Osman's pleadings, had turned her back on the pits. She'd taken the money and bought herself a small but sleek ketch. She'd spent wisely since, and now she had two ships and was one of the more powerful merchants in the western harbor.

Djaga was holding a wooden worm gear in one hand, a grease-filled rag in the other. She set to slathering the grease into the nooks and crannies of the gear. "Only today?" she asked in her rolling Kundhunese accent.

"Only today."

"Don't scrape the runners again, girl."

"I won't."

Djaga rolled her eyes, but then smiled, blew Çeda a kiss, and was gone.

"Djaga?"

She returned a moment later, frowning in that way she

had, half amusement, half annoyance. "What, oh Çeda-of-ceaseless-demands?"

Çeda glanced around the dock and Djaga's ship before speaking. "There's rumor that Macide has come to the harbor."

Djaga stopped what she was doing. "Why you always messing about with things a right-minded girl wouldn't be messing with?"

"Have you seen him, Djaga?"

Djaga's expression became flat and final. She lowered her voice before speaking. "Where it comes to the Al'afwa Khadar, my eyes are closed. Their fight is not mine, Çeda."

"Think nothing of it," Çeda said, stepping back along the dock toward the skiff she meant to take. "It's just something I overheard in the bazaar."

She'd returned to greasing the gear, but at Çeda's words she lowered it and stared straight into Çeda's eyes. "You taking care, girl?"

"I always take care."

Djaga grunted caustically. "No, you don't. But hear my words. Try harder this time."

Çeda nodded and Djaga left.

After untying the skiff, Çeda dropped down to the sand and hauled the craft out from dock. The runners—made from shaped and finely polished skimwood—allowed it to glide like silk over the sand. She hoisted the sail up the lone mast and let the wind fill it before running alongside the skiff and jumping in. The wind was fickle, but it bore her toward the mouth of the small harbor, and soon she was out onto open sand, sailing over the shallow dunes as the heat of the desert began to build. Sharakhai dwindled behind her until she could see only Tauriyat, and all too soon that was gone as well.

As she adjusted her course northward, the desert wind blowing athwart the skiff, her nerves began to build. After the chime in the city, she had begun to remember more and more. Her mother had taken her this way many times when she was young. She recalled the six-pieces memma had paid to the fat man at the harbor, the ride before the sun had fully risen, the tall, handsome woman they'd found far out in the desert. It felt like a dream, so distant it might have never happened.

Off the starboard bow, she saw a red, misshapen feature. Irhüd's Finger, a tall standing stone, notable for the simple fact that there was nothing else near it. It was not as impressive as she remembered, but it was tall and could be seen for leagues around. She pulled at the rudder, changing the direction of the skiff until she was on a bearing aligned directly with the sail's short shadow. She continued for hours more until a swath of land with tufts of withered grass clinging to it appeared along the horizon. She reached the plot of land in little time and misjudged her speed in the strong wind. Before she could lower the sail, sand gave way to rock. She winced as the runners ground over it.

Djaga was going to kill her.

She dropped the anchor anyway and headed for Saliah's home. She could dimly hear the sound of tinkling crystal, and it brought more memories to the surface. She recalled capering around a mudbrick house as her mother spoke with Saliah. She recalled eating a honey sweet. But more than anything she remembered those chimes. How by Tulathan's bright eyes could she have forgotten them?

She had no idea if Saliah might be home, but a tall woman was standing in the open doorway, staring directly at Çeda as she approached. The crook she leaned upon had a head that curled like a snail's shell, and it glinted brightly from small golden gems, or perhaps bits of glass, that had somehow been embedded in the wood. Her rich brown hair was tied into a thick braid behind her back. Her jaw was strong, her eyes sharp as cut stone. Çeda remembered her being tall as the sky when she was young. She thought it might have been the world as viewed through the eyes of an eight-year-old girl that had made Saliah seem so, but even now that Çeda was grown, even now that she'd lived to see thousands upon thousands of women in the Great City, she'd never seen anyone like Saliah. She was a full head taller than Çeda, who was not short for a woman. Surely Saliah's blood was mixed with the first men and women, the ones the old gods made before they left for farther shores.

"May the sun light your way," Çeda said as she approached.

Saliah stared grimly. "I've no use for the sun. Who comes?"

"My name is Çeda. Çedamihn Ahyanesh'ala."

Saliah had been about to speak, but then her mouth closed. "That's a name I've not heard in many years."

Çeda didn't know what to say to that. "My mother died when I was eight," she said lamely.

"Did she?" Saliah asked in a distant way, as if she were seeing the world as it had been long ago.

It was then, as Saliah stared *past* her, that Çeda realized she was blind. Çeda might have realized sooner, but the way her head had turned as Çeda approached, was as if she were watching. Now it was obvious, and she remembered thinking it strange when she'd been here as a child, how easily the woman moved around when she plainly couldn't see.

Yet another memory she should have remembered.

Saliah touched fingers to forehead. "My tears for your loss, child, but why have you come here to the desert?"

"I come because of this." She stepped forward and pressed the book into Saliah's hand.

Saliah frowned. She set her staff against the wall of her home and ran her hands over the book in a tender way. It was as intimate a gesture as Çeda had ever seen, and it made Çeda uncomfortable. She'd been prepared to share the secrets of her book, but this felt as if Saliah were treading on the memory of her mother. Still, she managed to stop herself from reaching out and taking it back.

"I know this book," Saliah said.

"You do?"

"I should. I gave it to your mother."

Çeda paused. She knew her mother had come to Saliah, that they'd had business of some sort, but she'd never suspected any sort of friendship between the two.

"Why?" was all Çeda could think to ask.

"Is that what you wish to know? Why I gave this book to your mother?"

"We can begin there."

Saliah returned the book and took up her staff. She walked not with the tentative steps of the blind but with clear confidence toward the wall of cut stone to Çeda's right. Çeda followed. Just as when she was young, the garden looked much different on the other side of the arched entryway. A stone path threaded its way through a lush display of flowering herbs—valerian and veronica and Sweet Anna. Two small lemon trees bore bright yellow fruit, and fireorange dates hung in three long bunches from a date palm. In one corner, a dozen birds bathed in a pool of clear water, or preened in the branches of a nearby oleander bush. Most were reed warblers, which was strange since they were rarely seen outside the spring rains that brought life to the River Haddah. One, though, was an amberlark, a bird with a long tail, a spotted brown coat, and a golden breast. When Saliah and Çeda approached, most of the birds flew away from the water but remained in the garden. The amberlark, however, released a call—a trilling rise and a mournful coo—and flew out, over the wall and into the desert.

In the center of the space was the strangest manifestation of the garden: an acacia that stood fifty feet tall if it was one. Its branches spread like a canopy, far and wide, but the leaves were small. As a result the sun cast bright and shifting patterns over the garden as the boughs swayed gently in the desert breeze. Pieces of crystal were suspended from the branches with golden thread—hundreds of them, thousands, all of them a different color. They swung as the branches did and chimed, soft as the burble of a mountain stream.

Saliah walked up to the tree, ran her fingers down the bark, perhaps finding her place, and as she did, the sound of the chimes above changed, became more active, as if they were telling a tale. Then she turned to face Çeda. "I gave that book to your mother because she asked for it."

"Where did you come by it?"

"Come by it?" Saliah smiled a wide, genuine smile. "I *wrote* it."

Çeda was taken aback. "But you're . . ."

Saliah frowned. "I'm what? Blind? Do you think it was always so?"

"You seem comfortable enough with it."

"Yes, but we learn, don't we? We change, we learn how to live despite the mistakes we've made."

Saliah's eyes stared over Çeda's shoulder, and it seemed as if she were looking beyond these walls, beyond these days. "I remember coming here with her," Çeda said as the chimes settled.

"You ran about this garden often as a babe."

"What business did my mother have with you?"

Again Saliah frowned, as Çeda often did when her students grew too bold. "The business we had shall remain between the two of us. I would ask instead what business *you* have with *me*."

"We'll start with the book. There was a poem my mother wrote at the back of it."

"A poem."

"*Rest will he 'neath twisted tree 'til death by scion's hand. By Nalamae's tears and godly fears shall kindred reach dark land.*"

Saliah's brow had pinched momentarily when Çeda said *Nalamae's tears*, but beyond that she remained silent, forcing Çeda to prompt her. "I must know what it means."

A tiny red-winged bird flew between them, the buzz of its wings breaking the tension. "And what makes you think I know?"

"Because something as important as this wouldn't have escaped your notice."

"Would it not?"

Çeda pulled herself taller. "It would not."

Saliah's frame seemed to tighten at these words, as if she'd heard the words of an impudent child and was about to send her away, but when she spoke, there was no edge to her words. "Perhaps these are things you should leave alone."

"I can't do that."

"You have no business meddling in the affairs of Kings."

"They killed my mother. They hung her upside down

and left her for all to see with foul carvings cut into her skin."

"All the more reason to leave them on their hill. You are not your mother, Çedamihn, not by half."

Something hard formed in Çeda's throat. Why was Saliah refusing to help? "I will avenge her death, with or without your help."

"Is that why you're here? For revenge?"

"Isn't that reason enough?"

Saliah pursed her lips. "How little you know, child."

Çeda knew she'd disappointed Saliah, but that only made her more angry, more desperate. "Tell me about the poem."

"Tell me what *you* know," the tall woman replied.

"Little enough. The twisted trees are clearly the adichara. Who rests beneath them I don't know. One of the asirim, I presume. Perhaps the one who kissed me." Çeda had withheld this information to gauge Saliah's reaction, but even so, she hadn't expected Saliah to *shiver* at these words.

"What did you say?" she asked softly.

"There is one who wears a crown. The King of the asirim?"

Her brows pinched, and for a moment she seemed as ancient as the desert itself. "Sehid-Alaz . . ."

Çeda waited for her to continue, but when she didn't, said, "Is that his name? Sehid-Alaz?"

Saliah shook her head. "Never mind."

Standing before this woman, Çeda felt eight years old all over again. She collected her thoughts, ordering them like pieces on an aban board, and tried again. "I've been thinking much on the last time I came, the day you turned me and my mother away. I had a vision. A vision I believe you saw." Çeda didn't wait for a response. "There was a rattlewing, a woman dancing along the dunes. A shaikh. And a sword that was handed to me."

"An ebon sword," Saliah said breathlessly.

And there it was. Another secret Çeda needed to unravel. Her lips trembled as she spoke. "How? How can it be so? I'm no Blade Maiden."

"So many paths lie before us."

Somehow Çeda had the impression she was no longer talking about Çeda, but herself. "So help me choose mine!"

"I cannot."

"Why not?"

"There are dangers, Çedamihn, things you're blissfully unaware of. I cannot guide you at the cost of all else."

"Were you my mother's ally or her enemy?"

"You know better than to ask."

"Then be mine as well. I saw myself receiving an ebon sword. Tell me how it can be so."

"I don't know if you're ready for these things. Your mother would have told you in time."

Suddenly Çeda's heart was beating faster. She had no idea why. "My mother is dead. *You* must tell me."

Saliah seemed to come to a decision. Her lips pressed into a thin line, and she nodded once. "Words will mean nothing to you." She stepped aside and motioned to the acacia. "You must see for yourself."

Çeda shook her head. "What shall I do?"

"Make the tree chime."

"How?"

"The how of it is up to you."

Çeda's heart was now racing at full gallop. She stared up to the canopy formed by the clawing branches, to the twinkling crystals. The sound they made was like a daydream, but it was also a sound wholly ignorant of Çeda and her place in the world. She must give the tree a place to begin, but how?

She took in the garden anew. There were heavy stones she might pry up and use to strike the trunk of the acacia, but that seemed crude, as if it would draw the augury Saliah was about to perform too close to Çeda's immediate future. She might climb the tree and shake it from the upper reaches, as she had the last time she'd come, but that felt desperate, childish. She might pray to Thaash to send wind through its branches, but the desert gods would not listen to her—Thaash least of all—and even if he did, she wouldn't want the touch of a god to lay so heavily over her future.

And then her eyes fell upon Saliah's staff, and she thought of the way the chimes had changed after Saliah had run her fingers down the acacia's bark. They'd risen in complexity, like the bustle in Sharakhai in the days that followed the silent observance of Beht Zha'ir.

She walked to the tree and took up Saliah's staff. She thought Saliah might object, but her only reaction was to release it and stand aside.

And now it was left only to determine where to strike. And how hard. There was a knot straight ahead, chest-high. It seemed good enough to her. She hefted the staff like a spear and thrust it forward into the center of the bole as if she were aiming for the acacia's heart. She did not thrust hard, however. She struck it only hard enough for the tree to know of her presence.

As she lowered the staff and listened, Saliah did as well, eyes shut tight, head cocked to one side.

The chiming didn't change at first, but then Çeda heard the sound tilting toward the lower branches, then move further up the tree, like a storm sweeping over the desert. The sound traveled through her. She felt it in her chest, at the tip of her spine, within her very soul. It made her feel as though she were standing at the center of a grand web, and that any move she made would affect the entirety of it—that, or tear it to shreds.

The crystals above glinted in the sun, creating a coruscating pattern, and Çeda found herself mesmerized by it. She saw herself in the lights, holding hands with her mother, saw Emre slipping something into the emaciated mouth of an opulently dressed man, saw a hundred ships sailing over the moonwashed sand.

She saw her mother, much younger than she remembered her, speaking with an older man wearing a richly embroidered thawb. The man had rings in his nose and tattoos around his eyes and a scar that traveled down his neck before it was lost in his thawb. They were angry, the two of them, but then the man took Ahya in a familial embrace and Ahya stepped onto the deck of a small sandship. Soon the ship departed, sailing over the desert with the man watching.

She saw the Amber City rising above the sands as the ship reached Sharakhai. A series of visions followed, her mother walking through the city, watching the Silver Spears and the Blade Maidens, learning their ways. Always in these visions Tauriyat was on display, in the background, ever-present.

She saw her mother wearing rich clothes, seductive without revealing too much. She saw her being smuggled from a horse-drawn araba into a grand palace. She saw her mother walking halls festooned in grand banners with the sign of the Kings: a shield with twelve swords fanned around it. Ahya tread lightly, alone, knowing where she was going and who she would see. She came to a tall set of doors, where two guards holding tall spears pulled them aside, bowing their heads to her as she stepped within the room. The doors shut behind her with an echoing boom.

A brilliant flash of light brought on a change. Ahya was now in Dardzada's apothecary, her belly swollen with child. Dardzada stared at her, an expression of disbelief on his face. *Send word,* Ahya said. *Tell my father the King's child is coming.* The look on her face was one of cold acceptance, as if her news was not glad tidings, but merely a fact to be relayed.

One last vision, of her mother squatting over a birthing mat, dripping in sweat, wailing as she gripped the hands of a woman standing before her. The woman helped Ahya to steady herself while begging her to try harder. As the child came at last, the midwife swathed her in cloths, offered the babe to her mother, but Ahya had lay down on a nearby pallet and looked away, refusing to set eyes on the child.

You must hold her, the woman said.

But Ahya would only stare at the wall, tears streaming down her cheeks, body heaving as she shed tears of bitter regret in place of joy.

"No!" Çeda screamed, breaking the spell. "No! It cannot be!"

She took up the staff and struck the tree again, but this time she struck it as hard as she could. Over and over again she struck it, and she felt the tree shudder.

A high, clear ringing caught her attention. She stared up

through the branches and saw one of the crystals tumbling down. It was close enough to catch, but she let it fall, and it shattered against a rounded stone. The crystalline sound drew her fully back to the here and now. Saliah's head jerked away, her hand flying to her cheek. The tall woman staggered back, but her heel caught on a root, and she fell among the flowering herbs behind her.

Çeda ran to her side and helped her to sit up. Saliah touched her fingers to the cut on her cheek, then rubbed her fingers together as if more curious than pained. She was staring directly at Çeda.

Çeda shivered; she knew Saliah was blind, but it felt as if the woman were staring straight into her, peeling away the layers to unearth her soul beneath.

As the chimes continued to ring in some rhythmic pattern that Çeda neither understood nor cared to, Saliah allowed herself to be helped up. And then, at last, the chaos waned and the chimes resumed their tranquil tones.

"Do you see now?" Saliah asked.

Ahya's words echoed in her mind. *Your father would kill you the moment he learned you were alive.*

"Yes, I see." Çeda stared at the rich growth of the garden. "Which one?" she asked. "Which one is my father?"

"I know as much as the chimes told you."

"Yes," Çeda replied, turning away. "Of course. And Sehid-Alaz? Tell me of him."

"The tree has told you all it can for now."

"I'm not asking the tree. I'm asking you."

Saliah looked profoundly worried. "There is much to consider before I share more with you. Many paths to tread."

"Of course," Çeda repeated numbly. "Games within games."

"These are not games."

But Çeda could hardly hear her. Without another word, she walked from the garden.

"Çeda?" Saliah called. "Çedamihn! These are not games. All I do I do for a reason."

There was a ringing in her ears and it was only growing stronger. She strode from the garden and returned to her skiff. Sailing back toward Sharakhai, she held the rudder and stared at the endless sand. Then she stood and spread her arms wide, tilted her head to the desert sky, and released a primal scream. *"Why?"* she raged, uncaring what gods might hear. "How could you have hidden this from me?"

She balled her hands into fists. Her body shivered as every muscle tightened.

"I cannot be the daughter of a King! I cannot!" And yet she was. She was *one of them*.

She collapsed onto the thwart, numb as she watched the golden dunes pass by. Why would her mother have had a child by one of the Kings? It was no mere chance; she knew this much. Her mother was too careful for it to be otherwise. Had she loved him? She might have given the thought credence if she hadn't seen the meeting between Ahya and her father on the dunes, and heard the way she'd spoken to Dardzada. *Tell my father the King's child is coming.*

Was she just a tool, then? A prop in a grand play her mother had been orchestrating? It was the only thing that made sense. Ahya had seduced a King and given birth to Çeda for some far greater purpose than wanting a child, though what it might be, Çeda had no idea.

Çeda's grandfather might know. She remembered him now, a glimpse only, a remembrance from when she was very young. A man with the same scar had visited Ahya and Çeda when they lived in a bare hovel in the center of the Shallows. Ahya had never revealed that he was her grandfather. She hadn't even revealed his name—not that she could recall, anyway. Çeda asked many times that night to see his scar, and Ahya had always said no, but when she'd went to fetch the man more araq, he'd loosened the strings around the neck of his kaftan and showed her. It went all the way down to the center of his chest. She'd marveled at it, wondering how he could have lived from such a wound, but before she could ask him more of it, her mother had returned and sent her to bed.

He would know what Ahya had planned to do. She was sure of it. But she didn't even know his name. She had no more hope of finding him than she had of sprouting wings and flying from the desert.

She sailed for hours, not knowing whether she was

headed toward Sharakhai or not. The past played through her mind, her days with her mother, the days since her death, and all of it looked different now. It was a different hue, tainted forever. She felt adrift, utterly aimless.

And why not? she thought. *Why shouldn't I be?*

As the sun began to set, she let go of the rudder and lay down in the bottom of the skiff. She stared at the sky, felt the swell of the sands, the twists and turns of the Great Shangazi. She heard the shush of the skis, saw high clouds drifting at an angle that cut across her path like a knife.

"Who am I?" she said to the sky.

I am the daughter of a woman whose final act was to slap her own blood—the thing she claimed was most important in this world—and then abandon her.

I am meant to be a tool, and yet I am utterly unprepared to be one.

I am a means to an end, and a poor one at that.

I am unloved.

Unwanted.

"I am nothing," she said at last, wondering if the gods were watching, laughing at her. "I would speak with you all before I pass to the farther shores. Will you grant me that, at least? One small conversation with the one you played so falsely?"

When the sun had fully set, and the light of dusk burned the western sky bloody, the skiff ran aground. Çeda lay there, uncaring, hoping to simply sleep, but when sleep would not come, she sat up. And gasped.

There, standing like some long-forgotten monolith, was Tauriyat, the mount where the twelve palaces of the Kings stood. She could see no other part of the city, only Tauriyat and the Kings, beckoning to her like a friend, or an enemy tiring of the chase.

Deep within her, Çeda felt a piece of her old hatred cupped and sheltered like an ember in the sand, ready to set the city aflame. Small words, Çeda thought. Weak words. For she was still largely rudderless. Then again, she knew more than she had known before—quite a bit more, in fact. And knowledge was a form of power, an effective lever that might do much, with little applied force, if only the proper fulcrum could be found

As she stepped from the skiff and was reaching for the gunwale to tug it from the rocks, she noticed a mark on the meat of her thumb. It was blood, she realized. Saliah's blood, left when Çeda had helped her up.

The blood of one of the ancients. And she, the blood of Kings. And then she understood. With a clarity she'd never felt before, she knew what she had to do.

After dragging the skiff out and setting the skis on a fresh path, she pushed hard, ran beside it, and jumped in.

Then sailed for Sharakhai.

Chapter 22

ON THE THIRD-STORY ROOFTOP of the Four Arrows, one of the oldest and most famous inns along the Trough, Emre lay flat as a sand skate. He faced not the Trough itself—the myriad sounds of which he could hear billowing up behind him—but a walled estate to the rear. The estate was not overly large, but it was a complicated affair, with a half dozen verandas and balconies situated around it. There was even a limestone gazebo at the center of the tasteful garden.

As had been true for the past three days, no one walked the grounds, no one took tea on the verandas, and the gazebo looked dirty and untended, as though it hadn't been used in years. Few enough had come and gone, at least in the hours Emre had spent watching. A gardener had arrived on the first day and spent four hours watering and trimming the bushes and flowering plants along the garden paths. A water wagon had come the second day to fill a cistern at the rear of the estate. But today, nothing.

Emre lifted his spyglass and peered through it, looking carefully through each of the windows. Curtains billowed in a strangely cool breeze coming from the east. The curtains made it difficult, but he saw no one within. He swung the spyglass to the right, moving it to watch an old water tower that served Ophir's, the oldest standing brewery in Sharakhai. A small walkway surrounded the base of the tank, and lying along this—barely visible in the shade—was Darius, an agent of the Moonless Host.

Darius, like Emre, was watching the estate and had been for the past three days. It was Darius as much as the estate itself that Emre kept an eye on. He had no idea what Darius or the Host were hoping to find, but he would learn if he was patient enough.

Today was Savadi, the busiest day along the Trough, and so, as the sun crept lower in the sky and the time for last meals came, the sounds of the city rose up around him. Men and women gathered in the crowded taverns and teahouses, shisha dens and oud parlors, grabbing tables within or sitting on stools along the Trough to watch the passersby. Behind Emre, from within the well of the Four Arrows' bustling courtyard, poets intoned their lyrical tales. Whistles and the clack of araq glasses on the tables followed each performance, some louder, some softer, depending on the prowess of the poets, who were each given only a short amount of time in which to impress their audience.

Emre worried that this would be another wasted day. From a few carefully placed bribes and by calling in several favors, he knew only that Hamid was looking for something in this part of the city, and Darius had been the one assigned to the task. Even knowing this, he'd practically stumbled upon Darius the first time through the neighborhood. He'd been walking through the streets at dawn, hoping to learn more about who inhabited these homes, when he'd spotted Darius settling himself down on the tower. He'd waited throughout the day, hunkered down in an alley, watching and waiting for Darius to move. But Darius only climbed down after the sun set. Emre had followed him to the Shallows, tracing him back to a smoke house known as The Jackal's Tail, a seedy place Hamid was known to frequent. That had been enough to confirm he was on the right track. Now he simply needed to figure out *what* Darius was looking for, and clearly that wasn't going to happen today.

The idea that had been nagging him for the past several days returned, stronger than before. Go to Hamid. Speak to him directly. They'd grown up together, after all, he and Emre and Çeda and Tariq. For years they'd been inseparable, a covey of four gutter wrens running the streets together until eventually they'd drifted apart, all but Emre and Çeda. But Emre didn't feel right going to Hamid to offer some meek overture. He had to prove himself, or he'd never get anywhere, friendship or not.

On the water tower, Darius was rising to his knees. Emre was just about to do the same when a covered araba drawn by a pair of tall black horses clattered along the lane leading to the estate. The wagon stopped at the gates, and the footman leapt down and unlocked them. With the jingle of tack and harness mixing with the sounds of revelry, the driver whipped the horses, and the araba rattled into the estate proper, pulling around the circle leading to the house's covered porch.

In the back of the araba was a pretty young woman with plaited black hair and a blue pendant that hung over her forehead, glinting in the early evening light. After placing a set of brass stairs in place, the footman ran to the front door, used his set of keys to unlock the front entrance, and hurried inside. As the woman stepped down and spoke softly with the driver, the footman returned with a wheeled chair, which he thumped down the front steps and rolled along the gravel until it was abreast of the araba.

Only then did Emre realize there was someone else in the coach. She'd been sitting so low he hadn't noticed her, a bent old woman swathed in blankets. The younger woman eased her up and helped her to the edge of the araba where, with the attentive footman's help, they lowered her into the waiting chair. As the three of them moved into the house, the driver whipped the horses and drove away, stopping only to leap down and latch the gates closed behind him.

Lamps were lit within the house, but not a soul was visible, suggesting they'd retired to one of the interior or eastward-facing rooms. Emre thought surely Darius would go to investigate, but he didn't; after a few minutes of watching he climbed down the water tower and was gone, surely taking the street south so that no one from the estate would see him.

Emre remained for a time, watching, hoping for some hint as to who the elder woman was. It might give him some clue as to what it was Hamid wanted here, either from her or one of the others. But nothing presented itself. He would have to learn more, and soon, before Darius sprung whatever plan he had. But how could he do that without being seen? Just then the crowd in the street behind him burst into laughter, the poet continuing only when a semblance of quiet had returned. Just as she began reciting the next verse in a liquid-silver voice, the younger woman from the estate came to one of its south-facing windows and was silhouetted by the lamplight behind her.

He watched until she turned and strode away, and he realized something. He *couldn't* do this without Darius seeing him. Nor should he wish to. He'd come to bring himself to the Host's attention, so that's what he'd do.

As he made his way to the trellis at the corner of the roof, whistles pierced the night. Someone in the crowd said something, and the poet shot back a sharp reply, and the crowd roared with laughter.

On a blustery morning four days later, Emre strode along the Trough carrying a simple leather satchel. He was wearing his best clothes, which were still no match for even the worst dressed folk of this quarter. He needn't look like a lord, though, only a passable journeyman.

Reckoning that Darius would be in position by now, Emre headed east and soon came to the estate's gated entrance. The wind was starting to gust, threatening a sandstorm, which might play to Emre's advantage if he managed to get in. He pulled on the thin rope to the right of the gate, and a bell rang on the opposite side. A short while later, the footman he'd seen the other day came jogging out to meet him.

"Good day," he said, eyeing Emre.

"The lady of the house, if you please."

The footman's face pinched in confusion or suspicion or both. "Is your business with Matron Zohra or Lady Enasia?"

Emre's words died on his lips. *Enasia?*

Years ago he had worked for Galadan the stone mason, building a wall around an extension to Tulathan's temple. Over the course of their work, he'd often seen a girl—a *woman*—named Enasia, and he'd made a fool of himself trying to impress her. Once the job had been finished, he'd never seen her again. He'd *wanted* to—she was a rare dove, indeed—but he'd been too shy to approach her without the excuse of the masonry work. She had been an acolyte in Tulathan's temple, after all. She might have giggled at his bumbling attempts to beguile her, but she'd never be seen with a gutter wren like him. After a time, he'd simply forgotten about her. And now, here she was again.

He'd spent the sunlit hours of the past three days—and many of the moonlit—asking around the neighborhood, taking care never to be somewhere Darius could see him. He'd learned that the woman who lived here was the Matron Zohra, and that she'd taken ill in recent months. He'd concocted a plan to speak with the woman he'd seen in the window, the Matron's caregiver, surely, but now the words he'd rehearsed quickly reassembled themselves as the footman's stare grew more and more cross.

"Forgive me," Emre said. "It's Matron Zohra I've come for, but I'd best speak with Lady Enasia."

"What about?"

"Begging your pardon, but the Lady asked me not to say."

"Then our conversation stops here." The footman spun and began walking away.

"Please! There's secrecy, but it's in the name of Matron Zohra's health and privacy."

The footman turned around, but made no move back toward Emre.

Emre patted the satchel at his side. "Lady Enasia was once an acolyte in Tulathan's temple. That's how I know her, but I'm now a member of a caravan that trades in Malasan. I've been to Samaril. The apothecaries there have wondrous things, not the least of which are elixirs that can alleviate and even cure derangements of the mind." Emre had learned little about the Matron's condition, just enough street gossip to know that she was suffering some sort of mental malady. "I'm not at liberty to say what the cure might be, nor its cost, but"—he patted the satchel again—"believe me when I say it could help the Matron."

The footman glanced back at the residence. From the look on his face he was teetering somewhere between barking at Emre to leave and believing Emre's story lest he upset the woman he worked for.

"It makes little difference to me," Emre said. "I don't even *know* the Matron. But Enasia does, and I believe she cares."

A strange mixture of confusion and doubt played over the footman's face, but then he made a decision. "Your name?"

"Tell her Emre's come calling."

"Wait here." The footman returned to the house, and soon Enasia strode from within wearing a peach-colored abaya with orange embroidery that the wind pressed against her body. Her eyes scoured him as she walked, struggling to remember who he was. Clearly there was a spark of remembrance, but full recognition came only when he smiled and said, "Apologies for such an abrupt reunion."

"Emre?"

"The very same," he said, allowing his smile to widen.

"You"—she looked him up and down—"you've grown!"

When last he'd seen her, he'd been sixteen and a full head shorter than he was now, with little enough muscle on his frame. There was a clear glint in her eye as she took him in. He'd seen that look before, on other women. "What brings you here?" she asked. "Why did you tell Rengin that we'd spoken?"

"In truth, *you* brought me here. I was walking the Trough several nights past. Having arrived just the day before, I decided to walk for a bit. I wandered Sharakhai's streets for old times' sake, and who should I see riding along in a wagon but the lovely acolyte I'd met years before!" He waved vaguely southward. "I lost track of the wagon for a bit, but saw it leaving through these gates. It was too late to call on you then, but I promised myself I'd stop by to say hello before I had to leave again."

"And you told Rengin you had a cure for Matron Zohra?"

"Well, yes."

"I don't understand."

"Ah." Emre fumbled a bit, allowing some of his old feelings of awkwardness around this woman to return. "It's a bit embarrassing, but I didn't wish to come to you knowing nothing. So I asked around. I was hoping to learn more about you, but you seem to be somewhat of an unknown around here."

She nodded, the wind blowing her bangs playfully. "I find the neighbors . . . unfriendly."

"Yes, well, when I heard that your Matron was sick, and a little about her malady, it was like a sign from the gods themselves. I told Rengin the truth. I've been to Samaril, many times, and the caravan master I work for plies trade in, among other things, the elixirs that can be found there. I bought some from him in hopes it might help your Matron."

"You *bought some* for a woman you didn't know?"

"But *you* know her. And I know *you*. And, well, it didn't really cost me anything. Burhan owes me a bit in the way of back wages, you see. . . ."

Enasia offered a knowing smile. It wasn't difficult to pretend that it made him even more uncomfortable, but he held her eye and gave her a smile of his own. He didn't want her thinking he was still the callow youth she remembered.

"Sailing on a caravan," she said wistfully. "To Malasan! I've always wondered what that would be like. It's wonderful, isn't it? Tell me it's wonderful!"

"Well, if by wonderful you mean that your deepest desire is to find yourself with hopelessly cracked lips, or to drink of water that tastes of thousand-year-old rain barrels, or to eat mealy biscuits that taste like the first gods themselves had tossed them aside as inedible, then yes, it's wonderful."

Her smile scarcely wavered. "It can't be so bad as that!"

He returned her smile. "No, not so bad as that, but truly"—he looked up to the ancient stone buildings around them—"there are days where I yearn for my old life here in Sharakhai."

"Then come back!"

He chuckled. "If only it were that simple."

She leaned in. "It *is* that simple."

He leaned in as well. "Tell that to the man I still owe a hundred rahl to."

"A hundred rahl! What did you do, kill his favorite horse?"

"Something like that."

"Emre, you *must* tell me."

"Another time, perhaps." He motioned to the residence behind her. "And you? You've left the service of Tulathan?"

She shrugged as the wind blew her hair into her face, and she flicked it out of her eyes, twisting her head until the wind blew it back. "In truth, I was never *in* the service of Tulathan. My father arranged for my place there, but I never loved it." She glanced behind her again. "But I've found a good home now. Matron Zohra is a wonderful mistress, and she's taught me things I never would have learned had I stayed. I might even deliver for the highborn, as she has."

Emre frowned. "Deliver?"

Enasia laughed. "Matron Zohra is a midwife. *Was* a midwife. Her health, as you've learned, has indeed taken a turn for the worse."

"I'm sorry to hear it confirmed. She was a midwife, you say?"

"Yes! For twenty years, to many of the finest Lords and Ladies of Goldenhill. And that after leaving the service of the Maidens."

Emre had to suppress the urge to look for the presence of the deadly women. "She was a Maiden?"

"In her youth, yes. She's led an amazing life."

"I'd love to meet her one day."

"Sadly, she's far too ill for visitors." She glanced back, and then beckoned Emre in. "But do come inside. She's sleeping. You can show me what you've brought."

She led him into the residence, her hand never releasing his, and brought him to a dining room. When they were both seated, he brought out a cloth case, which he untied and lay open on the table. Twelve vials were revealed, each resting in its own snug pocket. He'd bought the lot the day before from an apothecary in the west end who knew how to keep her mouth shut. "There are three types here, strong elixirs, all of them. The first two"—he pointed to the vials tinted red and green—"would likely show signs of improvement immediately if they're going to help her at all, so I suggest you try them first. A spoonful in the morning and another at night. If they don't work, we'll try the third. This one, according to my master, takes longer to show results, which is why we'll save it for last, but it's also the strongest of the three. Gods willing, one of these will help."

In truth, they were simple remedies for cough, itching, and gout. He'd added Malasani spices to all three in case the Matron or Enasia herself recognized any of the unadulterated remedies.

Enasia stared at the set of them, lifting one of the blue vials and swirling the liquid within. "This is a godsend, Emre. What does the Matron owe you for these?"

He raised his hands. "Pay me when we find one that works."

She returned the vial to its sleeve. "Then what do *I* owe you?"

"Well, that's an entirely different question, isn't it?" He stood, ready to take his leave. She stood after a moment, and the two of them walked side by side through the front door and toward the front gates. "You don't *owe* me anything, but I'll admit, when I saw you the other night, I found it intriguing that the gods would cross our paths once more."

Her knowing smile had returned. "There's *nothing* you would ask of me?"

They reached the gate, at which point Emre opened it and turned to face her. "Well. Perhaps a stroll. Perhaps some tea along the Trough."

She reached out and squeezed his hand. "I'd like that."

"Then we'll seal it with a kiss." He lifted her hand to his

lips and kissed her fingers, then released her and stepped back, never once losing eye contact.

She gave a practiced smile, closing the gate with a clank. "Soon, yes?"

"Soon," he agreed.

And then she was gone, waving as she returned to the house, the wind pushing her as if it somehow knew of Emre's ill intent.

Emre, meanwhile, turned and strode slowly away. While doing so, he looked up and nodded at the water tower. He couldn't see Darius, hidden in the shadows as he was, but Emre was sure he was there.

He turned right and walked uphill to the Trough, and then, despite the wind, strolled a short way farther and sat outside a teahouse in plain view of anyone who happened by. There were few enough strolling along the wide thoroughfare. Most were headed for shelter, some going so far as to board up their windows until the storm had passed. Emre was wondering if the teahouse owner would do the same, when Darius walked across the street, strode up to his table, and stared at him with an unreadable expression. Irritation, perhaps. Or maybe jealousy.

"Come with me," he said shortly.

"Why?" Emre asked.

"You know very well why." He turned and began striding away. "Hamid wants to speak with you."

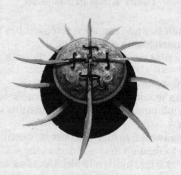

Chapter 23

IT WAS A DAY WHEN King Ihsan would rather be anywhere but out sailing the sands of the Shangazi, and yet here he was on the deck of his own royal clipper, heading southeast over dunes that were just shallow enough to make the ship rock and creak incessantly. He might have stayed in Sharakhai and let King Yusam come on his own, but the Jade-Eyed King had seemed so frightened the other evening when he'd come to Ihsan in a breathless rush, speaking of his mere, the deep well of water that gave Yusam his visions. He'd told Ihsan how strong they'd been, how inscrutable.

Ihsan had seen this sort of fear on Yusam's face before, but only rarely. Only when it was some momentous event that stood not just before Yusam or Ihsan, but before all the Kings. Yusam's visions were often difficult to decipher, but they could be trusted in this much: to know when danger was coming.

The sun glared angrily down as the clipper sailed on, the wind picking up the spindrift and tossing it across the endless sea of sand. Four Blade Maidens stood at the fore of the ship, another three amidships, two aft, and one more sitting in the vulture's nest atop the mainmast. Five asirim escorted them as well. Two galloped on either side, and a fifth ran a quarter-league ahead of the ship, watching for danger. They would sometimes come to a rest at the top of a dune and wail their pitiful wails, but then the Blade Maidens' call would compel them to carry on.

Even Ihsan would admit it was a sizeable force for such a short trip, but it paid to be careful these days. The Moonless Host grew ever bolder, and it wouldn't do to see all his plans unravel from a failure to take a few simple precautions.

Still, he doubted the Host would attack even if they *did* spot his ship. They were flying the colors of Sharakhai—a crimson field with a shield and twelve shamshirs fanned around it—and a strong wind was blowing, carrying the long pennant streaming starboard, snapping as the sails carried them up and over the dunes. The Host would see it; they would know attacking a ship like this would almost certainly mean their death.

Yusam stood at the prow between his Maidens, watching the way ahead. On the horizon, a dark line barred their way. They were the killing fields, where the adichara groves lay. Ihsan went to stand by Yusam's side, waving the Maidens away as he came. "I daresay we'll be well enough without those blades of yours at hand. Stand amidships if you must, but leave us in peace."

The Maidens bowed and left, clearing the foredeck for their Kings.

"Have you felt nothing?" Ihsan asked.

Yusam glanced back, his annoyance clear, but then returned his gaze to the way ahead. He didn't care for interruptions, but Ihsan didn't care for the way he constantly hedged. *And you've been hedging for a hundred years, dear Yusam.*

Yusam's mere revealed paths, paths along which the future might take him, Ihsan, the other Kings, even *Sharakhai*. The mere was both blessing and curse, two edges of the same wicked sword. One need look no further than Yusam himself for the truth of it. Before Beht Ihman he had been a confident man, given to bold proclamations; logic be damned, he would let his emotions control his decisions. Even Ihsan wouldn't have denied that he'd been an inspiring figure. Of all the Kings, he had been the best at breathing life into a tribe that—if they were all being honest—had few enough *other* sources of pride.

In the early years after Beht Ihman, Yusam had used the gift effectively, working out which threats were most dangerous and advising how to avert them—which wasn't to say he made no mistakes along the way. One misinterpretation led to the death of his own daughters, three of them, lost when he'd misjudged the intentions of a rebel tribe. They'd been killed and gutted, their viscera spread across the sand. No matter that the women who'd done it— and *their* daughters—had been found and killed. The damage had been done, and Yusam began to question his own readings, becoming progressively less sure of himself as the decades wore on, always wondering whether what he'd seen was accurate or not, whether it showed the entire picture and, even if it had, whether he was interpreting it in the right way, with the right subtleties and allowances for error.

It was a supremely difficult thing, and in many ways Ihsan was glad he'd been given no such gift by the desert gods. *Yusam can keep his bloody mere. I don't wish to know my future. At least, no more of it than I can discern myself. More than that and the mind goes mad.*

As the adichara groves neared, the captain called orders, and the crew began pulling in sails. The ship slowed, making for an orderly approach. Next to Ihsan, Yusam stiffened as he stared fixedly at the groves—surely something he'd seen in his vision. He pointed two points starboard, and the captain corrected to the more southerly course. Soon they neared the place Yusam had identified—a patch of growth indistinguishable from any other in the leagues upon leagues of twisted trees. The ship curved around to point back toward Sharakhai for their return voyage, and when it finally came to a rest, the two anchors, fore and aft, dropped with the clank of chain and the thud of their dead weight against the sand.

And still Yusam stared over the groves.

Ihsan crossed his arms over his chest. "Come, Yusam, I

have too much to do in Sharakhai to sit about waiting for you."

Only then did Yusam turn to Ihsan. "How many times must I say it? Had I found anything I would have told you, but interrupting my concentration does neither of us any good."

"I thought perhaps you simply didn't wish to speak to me."

"There is that," Yusam said. "For a man known as the Honey-tongued King, you seem to have few enough souls who wish to speak to you of their own accord." He strode proudly past Ihsan toward the starboard side, where the crew were lowering the gangway into place.

Ihsan followed. He couldn't argue. And it was a truth he'd recognized in himself long before now. It wasn't that he didn't like conversation. Far from it. It was that there were too few conversations that piqued his interest.

Together they took the gangway down to the sand. The Maidens followed, but only so far as the sand itself where they remained, their orders to give Ihsan and Yusam their privacy. Yusam walked carefully along a flat plateau of rock, eyes intent, as if he'd been to this place before, as if it held secrets, if only he were clever enough to find them. Ihsan followed silently as the wind played, filling small depressions in the rock with sand, then lifting it out again. Ahead, the adichara trees arched, their branches reaching this way and that, as if grasping for some unseen foe. Açal beetles buzzed through the air, some even landing on Ihsan's shoulder, or his outstretched hand, before flying away. But they avoided Yusam entirely, as if afraid of the Jade-eyed King.

"This is the place," Yusam said.

"Do tell."

Yusam scowled. "Do not mock. This concerns you as well."

"Then get on with it. I've more to do in Sharakhai today."

"We must be careful," Yusam replied easily. "Now more than ever."

"I know very well how careful we must be. Now tell me what you saw."

"Tell me first how the draughts are progressing. Are the experiments of our good King Azad doing as well as we'd hoped?"

Ihsan tipped his head noncommittally. "As well as can be expected. Azad has been helping as well as he's able, and I think their potency has been extended, but it will be years before they're as effective as they once were."

"I am *brimming* with confidence," Yusam said.

"This is no easy thing. We're fortunate enough to have stores of the draughts set aside, so there is still time yet. Why do you ask?"

"Because I saw Azad coming here, to this place. And he faces danger."

"Then perhaps we should not allow it."

Even after eleven years it felt strange to speak of Azad in this way, but there was nothing for it. Ihsan couldn't break the pact they'd all made to hide Azad's true nature.

"There lies the rub," Yusam went on. "Azad comes and is placed in danger, but if he does *not* come, the rest of us face danger in his stead."

"You saw this?"

"Yes."

"What, exactly, did you see?"

"In one vision, I saw Azad dressed as he used to be, crossing swords with a woman. A common girl, here among the twisted trees. I saw a Maiden given an ebon sword. I saw her praised in her defense of the Kings. I saw blood upon one who wears a crown."

"Which?"

"You know I would never be shown such a thing."

It was a peculiarity of the gifts granted to Yusam by the desert gods, and a particularly cruel one at that. He saw much—Ihsan would not deny it—but when it came to the direct fates of the Kings, Yusam had difficulty seeing anything with accuracy. And where it came to his *own* fate, he was blind as a babe.

"And the other vision?"

Yusam had once been an intense man, not given to fear, but the Yusam of old was well and truly gone. When asked this question, terror filled his bright green eyes. He licked his lips, started to speak, and stopped several times, perhaps fearing that to repeat this tale would act as an invocation, bringing that future path into being. "I saw Goezhen standing upon Tauriyat," he finally said, "raging to a stormy sky. I saw Tulathan by his side, trying to calm him. I saw the other gods standing behind them. Thaash and Rhia and Yerinde and Bakhi. All but Nalamae."

"We have witnessed the gods before, Ihsan, you and I and the others."

"True, but in this vision, Sharakhai was gone. Destroyed."

Ihsan pursed his lips, nodding, as if he were giving this the consideration it deserved. But the truth was that the second vision was one that he'd suspected might come. It seemed they were coming to a time when many plans would clash. It would be tricky telling which fork would be the right one, but this decision, he felt, was an easy one to make.

"We'll send Azad. He could use more samples in any case. It seems that when Tulathan is brightest, and Rhia is rising, the draughts take on more potency. We shall see. And we shall see about this vision of yours as well, of the woman who crosses blades with Azad."

Yusam, ignored him, fixated on the adichara again, his eyes scanning them as if he were watching a vision of the days ahead, unfolding before him.

"Did you hear me?"

Yusam turned, waking from his reverie. "What?"

"I said I shall send Azad."

Yusam seemed ill-pleased. Haunted, even. But he nodded just the same. "Very well."

They made their way back toward the ship. "We'll find our way," Ihsan said consolingly. "With your help, we'll find our way."

A proud man, Yusam was never above a bit of flattery. But this seemed to please the Jade-eyed King not at all.

"As you say," was all he said.

And soon they were back on the ship, heading for Sharakhai.

Chapter 24

SEVEN YEARS EARLIER...

ÇEDA AND EMRE had spent two nights in the blooming fields—two harrowing nights that made their return to Sharakhai all the more surreal. Walking through the streets, hearing the sounds of the city, moving with the crowds along the western end of the Spear was very comforting after the silence of the desert. Their first stop was Emre's flat, which he shared with his brother Rafa. Çeda and Emre stood on the doorstep, neither saying a word, and then Emre hugged Çeda, as simple as that, and ducked inside. As she walked away, she thought of losing herself in Sharakhai for a time, but she knew that if she did, it would be avoiding the inevitable. Instead she wound her way through the city to Dardzada's. It was nearly midday when she walked through his peaked doorway and found him working at his table, grating ginger into a wide wooden bowl.

She was tempted to try to slip past him, to run upstairs to her room and hide the swollen evidence of her first encounter with the rattlewings, hide the adichara bloom she'd stolen—it lay within her satchel, heavy as a lodestone—but she decided to face Dardzada and take whatever punishment he chose to mete out. She owed him that much: an admission of what she'd done, against his wishes. Standing before him, though, her gut churned with butterflies and all the confidence she'd talked herself into evaporated like so much water on a sun-baked stone.

Dardzada's hand moved back and forth methodically over the grater, filling the air with the scent of ginger. He was pointedly ignoring her, but Çeda remained where she was, hands clasped, refusing to move, and eventually Dardzada's movements slowed and stopped altogether.

He looked at her, almost as if taking her in for the first time. His face was unreadable, but his eyes looked her up and down quickly, assessing her as he would a client who'd come begging for a cure. It felt as if Dardzada were looking at her for the first time, not as some remnant of Ahya or of the life he'd shared with her. It likely didn't bode well, but Çeda was strangely proud over his reaction.

"Take two teaspoons of the nahcolite," he said. "Mix it vigorously with one tablespoon of vinegar and a half-teaspoon of papain."

"A half-teaspoon of what?"

"Papain." He went back to his ginger with renewed gusto. "It's a powder made from dried papaya. It'll help with those bites."

She pulled out the drawer full of the white nahcolite powder and the bottle of vinegar and looked among the dozens of other drawers in the grand cabinet that covered the walls of his workroom.

"Five to the right of the nahcolite," Dardzada said, "three down."

She found it and mixed the ingredients into a paste, which she then applied to the bites. They were not as swollen as they'd originally been, but they were reddened and painful. As she applied the paste, though, the pain deadened to a dull burn.

When she was done, and when she'd had her fill of water from the urn in the corner, she was feeling a hundredfold better.

Dardzada had moved on to crushing pistachio shells in

a granite mortar. His arm worked, round and round, grinding the contents slowly but methodically, wearing it down like wind against stone. *He's angry, but won't admit it.* Which was not a good thing at all. She'd rather he just say it and be done with it. But all he said was, "Fetch more water," without looking at her. "And then I need milk. Twenty stalks. Not nineteen, this time. Not twenty one. Twenty. Understand?"

"Yes," she said as she retrieved one of the empty urns and went to the well to fetch water. When she returned, she laid out twenty thick stalks of charo and cut the first of them. She used a roller, running tip to stem, forcing the thick white milk out and onto the work board. She finished and tossed the spent stalk into the waste bin beneath the table.

"That stalk has more milk," Dardzada said, still grinding the pistachios. He stood and wiped his forehead with his sleeve. "Finish each one, as I taught you."

She rolled her eyes and dropped the stalk back onto the table, rolling it until she got the last of it out—no more than a teaspoon. It was only charo milk, but to Dardzada it might as well have been the tears of Tulathan herself.

She continued the slow process, expecting Dardzada to demand to know where she'd been, but he never did, and she figured if he didn't care enough to ask her about it, she wasn't about to tell him.

At the end of the day, they each went to bed knowing a large order was finished and ready for pickup in the morning. It was a good day. A day of accomplishment.

Alone in her room, she pulled out the pressed adichara bloom from her leather satchel. She'd put it between two pieces of goat leather that she'd brought out to the desert for that very purpose. On their walk home, Emre had asked about it. Or, rather, he'd expressed disappointment that she hadn't been able to get one.

It's all right, she had replied. *It was a fool's journey in any case.*

Which was true, though it didn't make her feel any better about lying to him. It was just that she felt so terrible about leading him into such danger. And that, in turn, had made her realize she was on a path she needed to walk alone. She'd return to the blooming fields one day, but she wouldn't take Emre with her. She would never take *anyone* with her again.

After checking to make sure the petals were intact, she placed the bloom under her mattress and finally slipped beneath her blanket and tried to fall asleep. She should have been happy—she'd gone to the blooming fields; she'd done something her mother had done and lived to tell the tale—but the silence was stifling. She waited a long while, hoping she'd become tired. She *ought* to be tired. She'd had so little sleep these past few days. But the truth was, she wasn't.

Knowing she wouldn't sleep until they'd spoken, she got up and padded over the creaking floors toward Dardzada's room, only to stop short of knocking on the door.

"What is it?" he said through the door.

"Does my mother remember me?" It was something that had been bothering her since her mother's death, but she hadn't realized how very important it was to her until the moment she'd voiced the question to Dardzada.

"What?"

"In the farther fields. Does she remember me?"

"Why would you ask such a thing?"

"Because you gave her something. Hangman's vine, I'd guess."

"How do you know about hangman's vine?"

"I read about it in your books."

"I told you to stay away from those."

"Does she remember?"

She heard a sigh from beyond the door. "She may. I don't know."

"It's important."

"I don't *know*, child."

Çeda stayed there awhile, screwing up her courage. "I went to the blooming fields."

Dardzada was silent for a long time. Long enough for her to wonder what he was thinking and if he would throw her to the floor as he'd done the last time she'd angered him.

"Dardzada?"

"Go to sleep, Çeda."

"Don't you want to know why?"

"I know why."

He did? "You don't know anything about me."

"I know enough to see your mother in you, Çedamihn Ahyanesh'ala."

How those words stung. How lovely they were to hear. *I know enough to see your mother in you.* He'd meant it as an insult, but to her it was high praise.

"There's much the Kings will answer for one day," she confessed softly. She'd never told Dardzada of her plans. Never even hinted at them.

But when his only reply was to repeat "Go to sleep, Çeda," she realized he'd known all along.

She returned to her bed, unsettled, and sleep was achingly long in coming.

———◆———

The days dragged on, and still Çeda felt Dardzada would snap at any moment and yell at her. Or beat her. Or *something*.

But he didn't. And eventually life returned to normal. She worked in the shop during the day, doing whatever was needed. Grinding, cutting, boiling. Milking the infernal charo. Mixing, fetching water, delivering packages. Whatever Dardzada needed doing, she did.

Her insect bites eventually faded, as did Emre's after she snuck a batch of Dardzada's curative to him. She ran the streets with Emre and Tariq and Hamid whenever her work was done.

One night she brought honeyed almonds home from the bazaar and gave them to Dardzada.

"What's this?"

"Almonds," she said. "You eat them."

He nodded and gave her half a smile, putting the packet of almonds beneath his desk before continuing to tie a set of linen packages for delivery.

"Not hungry?" she asked.

"Not hungry."

Fair enough, Çeda thought, and returned to her chores.

As the days wore on, and the night of the twin moons neared, Dardzada became more and more tight, snapping at her for the least little thing. He made her clean the worktable four or five times until he found it *satisfactory*. He snapped at her when she ate, saying she chewed like a cow. He forced her to brush her hair at night with a hundred strokes before she was allowed to go to bed. "If it's good enough for bright Tulathan, it's good enough for you," he'd say. As if he knew how many times the goddess brushed her hair. As if the goddess even needed such things.

When he asked her to come to the back garden with him, though, two nights before Beht Zha'ir, she knew something was wrong. The sun was setting, and the air was warm if already cooling with the evening's first breeze. He held a blue bottle of wine in one hand with only the smallest amount of dark liquid still left in the bottom. An empty bottle lay among the rows of his lush herb garden.

On the stone bench along the left side of the garden rested a censer. Next to it was a lamp and what looked to be an adichara bloom.

Her shock at finding Dardzada with a bloom from one of the twisted trees was quickly eclipsed by the realization that this wasn't just any bloom: It was hers.

Of course it was hers.

Dardzada had stolen into her room and found it—who knew when?—and was preparing to do something strange with it. With Çeda.

"The adichara are very rare," Dardzada said casually. "Did you know?"

Çeda glanced up at the walls around the garden, walls to other nearby homes. It was not strictly forbidden to speak of the groves or the trees within them—they housed the asirim, the heroes and heroines who had sacrificed themselves on the night of Beht Ihman. But it was sure to arouse the suspicion of their neighbors and of the Silver Spears, too, were their conversation to be reported. Even the Whispering King's attention might be drawn here.

"They have always been rare," he went on, "but the

tribes knew where to find them." He sat on the bench and lifted the bloom with its white petals. "And when they did, they would take a bloom, like this one, and they would burn it."

He held the bloom to the edge of the flames. They did not take quickly, but Dardzada was patient. He waited until the petals were ablaze, then carefully set the burning bloom onto the censer. "They would take the ashes, and they would mark tattoos on one another. Do you know the sorts of tattoos I mean, Çeda?"

"Like the ones the women in the bazaar will lay on your skin?"

He shook his head lazily, his eyelids laden by the touch of wine. "No. Nothing like those. They ink ancient symbols. Symbols that had meaning." He stared at the flames, whose light caressed his face, orange and amber and gold. "The sort that marks the very soul."

"Dardzada," Çeda said slowly. "What are you doing?"

"They would give a child their first when they reached thirteen."

"I'm not thirteen."

"The day is very close, Çeda. The point is that you will be marked, and tonight is the perfect night."

She hadn't realized it before, but there was a tattooing needle on the bench just next to the censer, gleaming like a cruel wink of Bakhi's eye. "I don't *wish* to be marked."

"Don't you understand?" The flames were dying now. When they had fluttered away to nothing, Dardzada poured a little water on the blackened remains and began crushing it with a pestle, mixing it into a thick paste, then he added more water, turning it into a dark pool of ink. "The tribes did not mark a child for them to *become* something. They marked upon them what they already were, their very nature." He looked up to her, surprisingly sober in that moment. "You've already been marked, Çeda. By your mother. By your father, whoever he may be. By the gods. Even by me. And now you are who you are. And *this*"—he held up the censer—"will merely tell the tale."

"I won't let you do it." She backed up a step. "You're

not my mother. You're not my blood. You can't make me do this."

He set the censer down gently on the bench and stood slowly. "Oh, but I can. There's no choice, Çeda."

The moment he took a step toward her, she sprinted for the door. But it didn't open. He'd locked it, somehow.

He came closer but she pulled and pulled until the lock finally gave with a crunch of wood and flying splinters.

He moved quickly now, like a charging bull, and he snatched her wrist. She fought to pull away, but his grip was strong, and when she started to fight he wrapped his other hand around her mouth and nose. He had a piece of cloth in his palm—she could feel it against her lips—which smelled strongly of alcohol and something foul and earthy, like bitumen, and it made her muscles lose their strength. One moment she was fighting him with all her might, the next she fell loose as an eel into his arms.

Yet for all the disregard her body had for her will, her mind still railed, *No! No! Don't do this!*

Dardzada dragged her across the ground and laid her down on the wiry grass near the bench at the edge of the garden. He pulled her dress down enough to expose her upper back.

Please, Dardzada, don't!

He picked up the censer. Tapped the needle into the ink made from her burnt flower, her prize. The very thing that made her feel closer to her mother, Dardzada was using against her.

Merciful goddess, no!

The needle entered her flesh, between her shoulder blades. Piercing her over and over again, the pain untouched by whatever drug Dardzada had given her.

You miserable piece of shit! I'll kill you for this! I'll take up my blade and slip it beneath your ribs! I'll pierce your heart and watch you bleed!

But he didn't even pause. He kept marking her, slowly and methodically, the needle burning her skin, burning *her*. The Kings had marked her mother—not with ink, but with knives, carving into her blood and bone a message for all the world to see. And here was Dardzada doing the

same with ink, a thing he knew would cut Çeda as deeply
as a knife. It was the sort of cruelty she expected from the
Kings, but not from Dardzada, the man her mother had
once referred to as blood of Çeda's blood. Even she could
never have thought he would do something so heartless.

She screamed for him to stop. With her entire being she
screamed. And although she was silent, she knew Dardzada
heard, knew the pain he was causing.

And still the needle bit.

Dardzada carried Çeda from the garden, where he'd finally
finished her tattoo, and deposited her in her room. Aside
from the burning pain between her shoulder blades, she
was numb. She wanted desperately to rise, but her body
would not respond. It took all her effort to move her hand
a mere inch or two.

The night ground slowly past, and the tattoo continued to
burn. It was the pain, she found, that allowed her to crawl
back toward her own body. She concentrated on the pain, on
his betrayal. She was able to move her shoulders first, then
her arms and hands, and finally her torso and legs. But by
the gods she was uncoordinated. Her legs moved like fresh-
cut meat, slapped around on a butcher's block; her arms
were little better, but she managed to roll off her bed, to
prop herself up with her arms and push herself to a shaky
stand. She fell when she tried to reach the door but crawled
along until she could use the handle to pull herself up.

She opened it and staggered out, walked along the hall
to Dardzada's workroom. Somehow, by Rhia's grace, she
reached the worktable without falling on her face, and
once there, she took up one of the knives they used to prepare the dozens of ingredients Dardzada needed for his
curatives, elixirs, and draughts, not to mention the halluci-
nogens he sold to the well-to-do in Sharakhai's east end.

Çeda stared at the keen blade, the edge gleaming in the
moonlight that slipped in from windows in the next room.
Holding it felt wrong, as if her intentions were somehow
tainting the blade.

That wouldn't stop her, though. She would go upstairs and she would fulfill her promise. The way he'd marked her was unforgivable.

She wobbled toward the stairs, the knife in a fist sweaty from the anger at betrayal and from the drug Dardzada had used but more than anything from the way her heart pounded over what she was about to do. She made her way slowly but surely up the steps, then along the hall toward Dardzada's room. She reached it after what felt like an interminable length of time, and when she opened his door, she found him snoring face down on his bed, as *she'd* been in his garden, arms and legs splayed in every direction. She stood over him, her breath coming faster now, sweat beading on her forehead. She tried to swallow the lump in her throat.

She'd never thought of killing someone. Not really. Not someone she knew. She dreamt of killing the Kings, but that was nothing like this. Other than her fleeting view in the desert, she'd never seen one up close, and she certainly didn't *know* them.

Her hands still trembled with rage. "How could you do that to me!"

Dardzada's snoring hitched, then fell into the same languid pattern as before.

She took one step toward him, knife poised, her teeth chattering. But she stopped at the foot of his bed, unable to take another step.

And then the contents of her stomach surged up, and she doubled over, vomiting onto the floor in agonizing waves until there was nothing left. She used the back of her hand to wipe the spittle from her mouth, while staring at the sleeping Dardzada, holding back her tears. Her fingers still gripped the knife, felt the familiar grain of the wood against her skin, and a new wave of anger overtook her. She stepped to his side, raising the knife high, then drove it down with all her might. Into the mattress.

It bit deeply into the slats, where she left it, her final message to Dardzada.

Before she could change her mind, she left his room, navigated the stairs, and stumbled out into the night. The air in his home had been stifling, but the city was little better. She needed to get away. She needed to be anywhere but Sharakhai.

She trudged unsteadily through the streets, the city's tall stone buildings swimming in her vision. The space between her shoulder blades burned. She was fearful of the deep shadows in the darkness, afraid someone would grab her and haul her back to Dardzada's, or worse, into a forgotten alley. She wound her way through the city. She knew she should be mindful of where she was headed, but her mind was too addled, her fear too great, so she simply plodded onward and wove her way into the desert where she could lose herself at last.

A great weight was lifted, then. It felt so freeing to be out and into these open spaces. So she walked, and she *kept* walking, on and on and on. She walked until she could walk no farther, and then she fell to the sand, exhausted and delirious, but more than anything, utterly relieved to be alone.

Chapter 25

Days after Çeda's visit with Saliah, she lay in her bed, watching sunlight leak through the gauzy drapes in the nearby window. She was flipping through her mother's book, the pages brightening momentarily as a breeze blew the curtains inward, making Saliah's beautiful, cursive handwriting seem numinous.

From outside, she heard three short, sharp whistles—a signal in the west end that the Silver Spears had been spotted and were coming this way. The signal was picked up and passed along, further westward. The clack of children dancing at swords, of the two women across the street arguing, of old Hefhi singing a song as he wove his carpets, all died away. Somewhere up the street was the ring of steel-shod horse hooves. The horses clopped closer, their pace slowing as they turned onto Çeda's street. One of the horses snorted, a man called, "Ho, hup!" and then the sound receded. Soon the Silver Spears were gone, the sounds of life in Roseridge resumed, and Çeda began flipping through the pages of her book once more.

The mysteries of the poem had eluded her so far. There were weeks still before Beht Zha'ir returned to Sharakhai, but she was starting to feel nervous. If she was going to put her plan into action, she needed to unlock the riddles of her mother's book. The fact that she was the daughter of one of the Twelve Kings still burned like a dark star inside her. Part of her wanted to shrug the entire thing off as a dream, as a gross misinterpretation of Saliah's wondrous tree. How could Çeda, after all—as far from a desert witch as a mule from a caravan master—be expected to interpret such things?

She knew better than to really doubt it, though. The dream was real.

No matter what she might feel about her mother—and truth be told, she wasn't sure *what* to feel anymore; how *should* she feel toward a woman who despised the child she'd given birth to?—she'd picked up her mother's pragmatic habits. There was no sense avoiding the truth. On the contrary, she would use it to her advantage.

When she'd reached home the previous night, after returning Djaga's skiff, she'd reread the book by lamplight before falling asleep, hoping there might be some clues in the stories—Tulathan's capture, or her escape with the help of her sister, Rhia, or Yerinde's subsequent banishment from the desert for many long years. But there were none. None that *she* could find, in any case.

She flipped to the back of the book and stared at the poem. It felt as though her mother were just there on the other side of the page, trying to speak to her, but Çeda had no way of understanding. How she wished she could speak and have her mother hear.

Did you love me? Ever?

And how she wished she could hear her mother's voice in return, even one last time—not merely to gain answers, but simply to *hear* her. How she missed the timbre of her voice as she'd read stories to Çeda late at night.

Lying there on her bed, she continued to page through the book, though now it was with tears clouding her vision. Sunlight played over the letters. The brown ink of the poem her mother had written was nearly burned into her vision. She examined the tiny marks buried deep in the gutter between the pages, looked to the black ink that

Saliah had used, compared that ancient, looping script with her mother's elegant style.

A huff of wind blew the curtains back. Sunlight shone brightly on the page. And Çeda gasped, blinking to clear her eyes.

She sat up and pulled the curtains back, allowing the full light of the sun to fall on the paper.

One of the words had been inked over. It couldn't be seen in dim light, but in the sunlight it was plain as day. *King*, it read. *King* had been re-penned in brown ink, an exact match for the marks in the gutter.

She turned to the next page. She found no words re-inked but neither did she find any markings in the gutter. She examined each page in the sunlight until she found another: *unsealed*, with three short marks in the margin. And then more: *strength* and *petals* and *loom*. *Draw* and *dunes* and *thorn*.

She searched the entire book, finding forty-five in all. Forty-five pages with forty-five words and forty-five sets of marks. They were linked, she was sure, though how she could fit them together she had no idea.

A soft knock came from out in the street.

Not now!

She snapped the book closed and returned it to its hiding place. Through her open window she could see Davud wearing short linen trousers tied off at the knee and a loose flowing shirt and rope sandals, not the robes of a collegia scholar. He looked so young.

No, she realized. He looked his *age*. His manner when he wore the collegia robes made him seem older.

He caught her looking and smiled, waving nervously.

"Come on up," she said.

He looked around to see if anyone was watching from the shadowed windows that lined both sides of the street, then took the stairs up. She ushered him inside, offering him a seat, an offer he quickly refused with a shake of his head. Finally, after licking his lips, he spoke. "You came to the scriptorium for help."

"I did," Çeda said warily.

"And Amalos refused you."

"Yes, but—"

"Is it important?" Davud asked. "The thing you're looking for?"

"I think it could be very important, Davud. Not just for me, but for Sharakhai."

It seemed Davud had to screw up his courage before asking his next question. "What are you looking for?"

And now it came to it. Davud wanted to know her secrets—some of them, in any case. She was loath to share them, but she knew that if he was going to help her at all, she needed to give him something.

"I want to know more about the night of Beht Ihman," she finally said. "I need to know the truth, not the story the Kings tell."

He nodded. "I gathered that much from the little I overheard. But why?"

"Because I believe the night of Beht Ihman is a story, one written by the Kings for our consumption. In the texts I've read, I've already found dozens of small discrepancies. With the histories available to you, I'm sure you've seen some as well. I believe there are secrets there, Davud, secrets that may reveal the truth behind my mother's death."

"How can you be sure?"

What could she say? There was so much she'd learned that was unclear and yet related in some extraordinary way. She didn't understand it well enough. How could she possibly make it clear enough for Davud to understand?

She couldn't, not here and now, in any case. Nor would she want to, even if she could. As cruel as it was to say, the less Davud knew, the better. So she finally said, "In this you'll just have to trust me."

Davud paused, clearly unconvinced, but finally nodded. "Can we go for a walk?"

Çeda smiled suddenly. "Have you come to court me, Davud Mahzun'ava?"

She'd meant to simply break the tension, but Davud's cheeks burned so brightly she felt she'd been cruel. He looked around a little desperately, with no idea how to reply. He made a half-hearted gesture toward the door, looking like he regretted coming, when Çeda said, "Please," while squeezing his arm, "let's walk."

They strolled through Roseridge together, Çeda falling naturally into the limp she'd been feigning for years. He led her gently, not toward the bazaar, nor toward the center of Sharakhai, but south, and soon she understood why. Ten blocks south of Çeda's home was an ancient well. It was the reason the neighborhood—the same one as Osman's pits— was known as the Well. It had long since run dry, but it was noted for its width, and for having a set of stairs running down into it, as if it were a tower built not upward, but down into the ground. Çeda remembered her mother telling her how children had once swam here to keep cool in the summer heat. It had been a place of joy. But that was decades ago. Since running dry, the well and the houses around it had become a place that many shunned, claiming it was cursed by the gods.

"Davud, what are—?"

Davud held up a hand and began taking the stairs down into the well.

As a donkey brayed and a man *yahed* somewhere in the distance, Çeda followed. The sun cut across open space, bathing much of the westward face in light. Only when they'd circled down to the bottom and were hidden by the shadows did Davud turn to her. "I've something to show you." He glanced nervously up to the rim of the well three stories above, and then squatted to press on one of the stones at its base. "There are many tunnels all throughout the city. Did you know?" He levered the stone outward—it was *hinged*, she realized, and it yawned open like the maw of some great, toothless beast. "One even leads to the scriptorium."

Çeda's heart leapt. This was why Davud had wanted to walk; he was offering her the chance to gain access to the knowledge within that ancient place. She laughed, then clapped a hand over her mouth. "You'll be expelled, lashed, perhaps worse if we're found out."

"You said this was important."

"I did."

"Then let's go."

He was about to duck through the entryway, but before

he could, Çeda stopped him with a hand on his arm and planted a kiss square on his lips.

His cheeks went redder than before, as red as she'd ever seen them, but he didn't flinch away. He held her gaze and nodded, an ally and an equal. And then he kissed her back—a quick thing, and daring. And then he was off into the tunnel.

Çeda entered and pulled the stone back into place behind her. The fit was perfect, and the light leaking in was extinguished, plummeting the tunnel into darkness. As her eyes began to adjust she realized she could see faint shapes. Stones were embedded into the tunnel walls, shaped like the crystals that hung from Saliah's tree, but they were larger and gave off a faint, blue light, not unlike Rhia when she was a sliver in the sky.

Where they were headed in this maze Çeda had no idea. She tried to follow the twists and turns, but she quickly lost her way, relying on Davud to lead her. She saw spots of pure darkness, but also caverns where the glowstones were tightly crowded. There were places where the ground was lumpy, slick, and uneven and others where the stone had been cut by the hand of man.

Or perhaps this place was built by Thaash in the days before the wandering tribes came. Is Sharakhai not favored by the gods, after all?

Çeda guessed they'd walked a quarter-league by the time they came to a tight, winding set of stairs, at the top of which was a thick ironbound door. Davud pulled out a key and unlocked it. After so long with silence as their only companion, the clatter of the mechanism sounded loud as a battering ram. Once it was done, though, the door swung open quiet as a blade slipping from its scabbard.

There was only darkness inside, but Davud used a flint striker to light a lamp, and revealed a circular room with empty shelves and iron pegs near the door.

"They give you keys to the scriptorium?"

"They give Amalos keys," he replied, "and he gives me leave to take them whenever I need. His eyesight is so bad he no longer comes here."

"But others do?"

"Few enough. We'll be safe here if we stick to a certain

schedule." He stepped to the door on the opposite side of the room. "Softly now."

He led her from the bare room, down a short hallway and to another that held a number of bookshelves and a rich carpet of crimson, black, and gold. There was a table in the center of the room, and on it lay a stack of clay tablets in wooden trays.

"I found these, and they should get you started, but if you tell me more about what you're looking for, I can narrow my search."

Çeda shook her head. "Davud, what *is* this place?"

He motioned back the way they'd come. "Amalos is the warden for the door to the tunnels. He used this office years ago, but since I became his apprentice he's stopped coming here. He sends me down once a week, and he stores a few old books here, but otherwise no one else ever bothers to visit. There's an inspection a few times a year by the House of Kings, and the last one was only a few weeks ago. So I can bring things here for you to read." He pointed to the ink and quill sitting next to the tablets, on a stack of mismatched paper, bits and pieces. "Write down whatever you want to learn about and when you can return, and I'll bring what I can." He pointed to a small brass urn on one of the shelves. "Drop the note in that urn, and I'll find it. Otherwise leave everything as you found it."

"Couldn't I just tell you?"

"No! Never speak of it outside this place."

"But the notes might be found."

He glanced back at the urn. "Those I can explain away as research if need be. We can speak from time to time. I'd like that. But not of this. I can't have any of it getting back to Amalos. Or worse, the Kings themselves."

"What, you're worried that the King of Whispers will hear us?"

"You joke, but he hears much in this city. And once his attention is drawn toward you, he homes in, sometimes over the course of weeks, months, until he has you. Men and women have died because they weren't careful enough."

"I'm sorry. You're right." Çeda knew how much he was risking for her. "I understand."

His panic eased, and for a moment he looked like the young boy who used to race through the stalls in the bazaar, his mother shouting after him.

"Thank you, Davud."

"You said it was important." He'd said these words before, but now he said them with great care.

"It is."

He nodded to her. "Then make sure this is all worth it."

And with that he left, leaving the door open just a crack.

She sat down at the table and looked at the first of the tablets. It was difficult to read. Language had changed since it was written. How old were these tablets? A hundred years? More? They could be no more than four hundred years old, since that was when Beht Ihman had taken place, but she doubted it was anywhere near that old. They spoke of the event in a distant way as they recounted the bargain the Twelve Kings had struck with the gods that fateful night.

They had little to teach her, these tablets, but she did find one interesting fact. Whoever had written the fourth account of Beht Ihman spoke of Nalamae. Çeda had always believed that all seven desert gods had been there, but this tablet spoke of Nalamae's absence. *Nalamae's refusal to come was frowned upon by Kiral, supreme among the Twelve Kings, but with the assembled gods untroubled by her absence, the dark ritual had commenced.* She'd have to look for more. In none of the dozens of accounts she'd read so far had Nalamae been mentioned as missing. Some had simply referred to the desert gods as a whole, some had called Nalamae by name, but none had said that the youngest of the gods did not come when called.

When her reading was done, she scribbled on one of the scraps of paper, *recountings of the gods present on Tauriyat,* and *miracles performed by Nalamae,* and, thinking of Saliah's blood left on her thumb, she wrote: *customs of the Blade Maidens.* Below those, she wrote *Savadi.* Today was Hundi—then came Lasdi, followed by Savadi—which gave Davud two days.

She hoped it was enough. She clearly had much to learn and little enough time in which to learn it.

Chapter 26

THE WIND BLEW FIERCELY through the streets as
Emre followed Darius toward The Jackal's Tail, a
shisha den on Tiller's Row, one of the few streets in the
Shallows with any businesses to speak of. The wind was so
thick he could hardly see a dozen paces ahead. All the windows in the city were shuttered closed. A gust of wind blew
his shemagh loose, and he caught a lungful of dust and
sand. He coughed and spat while retying it tighter, leaving
the narrowest of slits for his eyes.

Just before he and Darius reached the Tail's covered
porch, a few young toughs opened the door and stepped
out, their turbans wrapped tightly around their faces. They
stopped just off the porch and watched as Darius stepped
inside. Emre grabbed the door but held it for a moment. He
turned to the two men, who were watching him too intently
to ignore. A month ago he might have been afraid, but
much of the fear that had been with him since his brother
Rafa's death had been burned out of him. Not from the
strange night of Beht Zha'ir, or the asirim that had nearly
ended his life, but from the dual realizations of how long
he'd been running from his past and that he couldn't *keep*
running. He didn't have it in him. Not anymore.

The decision had not felt as liberating as he'd hoped it might. There was too much pain in his past for that. But it had given him a simple, heartfelt confidence that no one could hurt him as much as he'd already hurt himself. Coupled with it was a new *desire* for conflict, as if the years he'd spent avoiding it had stored it up, and now it was coming out in a rush.

The two toughs returned his stare—one even took a step toward him. But when Darius stepped back out and guided Emre into the den with a hand on his shoulder, they turned away and were lost in the storm. Finally free of the biting wind, Emre felt the thundering beat of his heart slowing. He hadn't even realized how bad it had gotten. Darius was unwrapping the veil of his turban and shaking the sand from his clothes. Emre did the same, the sand falling from the them like rain onto the thick horsehair carpet just inside the door. Some in the room turned to eye him, but most merely drew on their shisha tubes, blowing thick, fragrant smoke into the air as they sat on threadbare pillows before low tables.

Emre followed Darius toward the back corner, where a group of young men and women sat at an oval table. A beautiful woman with piercing brown eyes and a trio of golden nose rings was refilling several empty glasses with araq from a tall green bottle. She was leaning far over the table toward a man's glass as he laughed and slid the glass back and forth, making her spill araq on the table.

When the woman sat back down, Emre could finally see the man sitting to her right. Emre almost didn't recognize him: Hamid, his boyhood friend. He'd grown and filled in his lanky frame. And he'd hardened. There was no trace left of the shy, smiling boy he remembered, only the steely eyes of a man who'd seen too much, young as he was. His clothes were darkest green, well made but not too fine. Nothing that would attract attention here in the Shallows. The tattoos on his face and the backs of his hands would attract little attention here, either. The gold bracelets on his wrists, however, and the rings on his fingers and through his nose and ears, were a different matter entirely. They marked him as a man who had no worries in a part of Sharakhai that few trod if they could avoid it.

There were some changes that ran deeper, though.

Much deeper. They were of an age, Emre and Hamid, but he easily looked ten years older.

Emre knew the signs well; of wear, of neglect. As sure as the sun did shine, he'd been taking black lotus. Emre's eldest brother, Brahim, gods protect him, had been addicted to it for years. *And probably still is, assuming the lotus hasn't already taken him into its final embrace.* Hamid had the look of a man who hadn't yet fully succumbed. His skin looked stretched, but you might not notice it if you hadn't grown up with him. His eyes were reddened, though hardly more than might be caused by a hard night's drinking.

Hamid considered Emre with those sleepy eyes of his but said nothing. The others stopped talking, however, noticing the sudden change in the air.

"Hello, Hamid."

"Emre."

For a moment, the two of them merely stared at one another, Emre wondering why he'd been invited, Hamid still silent. Those around them went from ease to wariness as tension filled the air like the scent of a long-dead dog.

"It's been a while," Emre said.

Hamid nodded, grudgingly.

"Perhaps," Emre began, unsure where to go next, "we could have a drink."

Hamid cracked one knuckle. "A drink."

"If you would."

Hamid considered for a long moment, and then reluctantly nodded. The table cleared in moments. "Darius." Darius had made to follow the others, but Hamid shook his head, then motioned to the table.

Emre sat across from Hamid, and Darius sat at the end, a careful distance away from both. Hamid waved for a boy and motioned to the table with two fingers. The boy came with two fresh glasses, and Hamid immediately poured araq from the green goose-necked bottle. Emre opened his mouth to speak, but Hamid shook his head and nodded to another nearby table. The half-dozen men and women sitting there began to chant, a low, throaty thing that Emre could feel in his chest.

"It confuses the King of Whispers," Hamid said to Emre's unspoken question. "Throws him off our scent."

"It's true, then? He can listen for those who speak of him?"

Hamid sipped his araq. "Darius tells me you've found yourself a pretty little wren."

"No," Emre replied. "I've found *you* a pretty little wren."

"You went in there to help *me* . . ."

"You and those you work for."

Hamid's lidded eyes lingered on Emre, uncharitably it seemed to him. "And who is that, Emre? Who do I work for?"

Emre glanced around, wondering why Hamid was being so coy. "For Macide."

"No."

"For Ishaq, then, his father."

"Wrong again."

"Then who?" Emre asked, trying to keep his annoyance from showing.

"For the people, Emre. For you and Çeda and Tariq. For the children who walk through the Shallows not knowing what we're about. For your wren, who walks about that estate as if it were made for her. We fight for her, even though she lives her life on the backs of untold thousands of others." He took a mouthful of his araq, savoring it before swallowing. "Is that who you wish to work for as well, Emre? Is that why you interrupted Darius's work?"

"I know I can find whatever it is you need from that estate, from the old woman."

"We'll come to that. What I asked was who you wished to work for."

"I wish to fight for the people."

For the first time, Hamid's face came alive. "You do? Because it sounded to me like you pulled that stunt for *yourself.*"

"I had to attract your notice."

"We've known one another since we were three, Emre. How could I not notice you?"

"And if I had come to you and asked you to grasp arms in your cause, what would you have done?"

Hamid thought on it, spinning his glass upon the table with idle fingers. "I would have sent you away."

Darius watched this exchange silently, glancing uncomfortably between the two of them. He hadn't realized the history between them.

"I have much to offer," Emre said. "I'm known around Sharakhai. I'm well liked. I've done much in my time. I'm *well rounded*, as Rafa used to say to us."

Hamid shook his head, a distant look in his eyes. "That fucking bravo. My heart still weeps when I think of Rafa."

Emre touched his fingers to his forehead. "Thank you, but those wounds have long since closed."

"Truly. I think of him often."

"Thank you."

"But I will not work with a man who does this only for his dead brother."

"I'm not." Emre was shocked. "I don't."

Hamid went on as if Emre hadn't spoken. "You must do it for those who live, for those who have yet to join us."

"I *do*."

"I see it differently." As Hamid's eyes bored into Emre's, the low, primal chanting continued. "You're a hummingbird, flitting from one thing to another."

"Only because I hadn't found a cause to believe in."

"You knew of the Host, Emre, long before Rafa died. All of us did. And yet it's taken you seven years after his death to take this step."

Because I was a coward. "I didn't know *what* I wanted after Rafa's death. They were . . . difficult days."

"But now you do."

"Yes."

"Convince me."

Emre took a deep breath. How could he explain this without sounding desperate? Emre glanced to Darius before speaking, wondering how much he should share, but there was nothing for it now. "Last week I was out on the night of Beht Zha'ir." Hamid and Darius exchanged a look, but neither said anything. "I was attacked, and I might have died but for Çeda. She found me and saved me, as if I were an infant."

Hamid shrugged. "No man can stand alone against the world, Emre."

"The asirim came while I lay there wounded and bleeding, and I remember thinking what it would be like. I wondered if they would make me one of them. I *hoped* they would. I was desperate for it, so ready that I cried when Çeda came. I felt as though she'd robbed me of the chance to take up the power those creatures hold." Emre toyed with and then drained his glass, feeling the warmth of the sweet liquor make its way down his throat. "When I was back in my right mind, those thoughts seemed foolish. Preposterous."

"You were wounded."

"Yes, but their seeds remained. I yearned for power."

"To harm those who've harmed you?"

"No," Emre replied easily. "To wipe the presence of the Kings from this city. To wipe away the Malasani, and the Qaimiri, and the Kundhunese, and the Mireans. The asirim let me glimpse the Sharakhai that once was, before the Kings. I saw the desert before Sharakhai was made. Then I saw what's become of it, and I wept again." Emre stared deeply into Hamid's eyes. "*That* is why I wish to stand by your side, Hamid. *That* is why I went to the estate and spied upon Darius as he spied upon Matron Zohra. It is a small thing—what I do, what you do—but together we are strong. Together we can stand against the Kings and end their corruption."

"You wish to clear this city then? To level it?"

"I didn't say that. I want to see the city reborn."

"In whose image?"

Emre managed a smile. "Mine? Yours? Who knows, Hamid? I do know that before the gods turn the page on the tale of Sharakhai, many tears will fall and much blood will be spilled. But the Shangazi is thirsty. She'll drink all of it and more."

Hamid was quiet for a time. He poured himself a fresh drink and then one for Emre. He glanced at Darius, and something passed between them. Emre had no idea what, until Hamid raised his glass, motioning for Emre to do the same.

The two of them clinked their glasses together and downed their drinks.

"Now"—baring his teeth from the bite of the liquor, Hamid slapped his glass down on the table—"tell me about this wren of yours."

Chapter 27

IN THE WEEKS FOLLOWING Çeda's first visit to the scriptorium with Davud, she returned many times. Davud always left her tablets, scrolls, or books to read—never more than a dozen, probably so that their absence would go unnoticed. And Davud had a good eye for research; they were always insightful texts that taught her much.

She learned of Tulathan, goddess of law and order, who had spoken to the Kings on the night of Beht Ihman. She learned of Goezhen, god of change and creation, how he'd experimented with foul creatures aeons ago, much as the first gods had done when they created him and the rest of the younger gods. She read of Bakhi, how he came in times of reaping: of harvest, but also of death.

There was one tale of a man called Thebi, who lay dying after a battle in the mountains far to the east. Thebi whispered prayers to the hot desert wind, as did his comrade, a bowman who'd survived the battle unscathed while Thebi lay dying with a spear running through him. Bakhi had come to them and listened intently as both men pleaded for Thebi's life. In the end, Bakhi had pulled the spear from Thebi's gut and run the other man through. Thebi recounted how all that remained of his wound was a simple white scar, while his friend died in moments from the wound given him by the fickle god.

She learned of Thaash, god of hate and vengeance, and his taste for blood. A shaikh's wife recounted in her cramped script how Thaash had saved her desert tribe from the wild men of the northern wastes. They'd camped for the night, ready to take to their ships in the morning, when dozens of men sprang up from the desert like spring grass. The men and women of the tribe had surrounded the children, but their enemies were simply too many. Half their number were already dead, and the other half was soon to follow, when a tall figure strode through the night, swinging a gleaming sword of gold. The wild men had become crazed in their effort to reach the newcomer. They turned on him, their ululations echoing beneath the stars, and the god, for it could be no other than Thaash himself, had dealt cut after cut with low, wicked laughter. Soon Thaash stood alone among the wild men's corpses, breathing hard, blood slicking his bronze skin. The tribesman were grateful, but none dared approach him. None dared speak. And then Thaash turned and strode back into the night from whence he'd come.

She spent many nights reading tales of Nalamae, youngest of all the gods, trying to understand what had happened to her on the night of Beht Ihman. She found no further mention of Nalamae's absence, and in fact many accounts spoke of her presence that night, though few gave any details. She did find one strange tale about the destruction of her temple, though, written at a time when her worshippers had long been in decline. A priest recounted the tale of a blind girl, no older than twelve, who had come to the temple insisting *she* was Nalamae. She said she was being hunted, that she needed the sanctuary the temple could provide. The priest thought of sending her away, but something in her voice, the way she carried herself, even in her desperation, moved him. He took her into the temple, thinking he'd find her a place to stay on the morrow. A few hours later, the temple was shaken on its foundations and voices called from the street.

Come, Nalamae, one voice called.

Come, sister, called another.

The priest walked out onto the steps of the temple and swore he saw, though he knew it to be impossible, a woman with glowing white skin standing in the street. Another woman stepped out from behind the trunk of a large olive tree. She was shorter than the first, but her skin was also pale as the moons above. Both were beautiful beyond description, and the priest stood there, breathless, when a thunderous boom shook the temple. He turned and looked up. On the dome, high above, he saw a dark form with black skin and a crown of thorns. Goezhen, he realized. Goezhen had come. He was ready to run inside, to find Nalamae and guide her to safety, when a streak of lightning flashed down from the darkened sky, and the dome itself caved in.

How he made it through that night alive he did not say, but in the morning he found the temple ruined and Nalamae gone.

As she had bid him, Davud also brought texts that discussed the Maidens and their customs. She hadn't told him specifically what she was looking for, and so found herself reading general accounts of the Maidens' daily life, their birth rituals, their death rituals, what they did each night of Beht Zha'ir and Beht Revahl and Beht Tahlell. She wasn't getting what she needed, and eventually was forced to write *Blade Maidens induction rituals* on one of the notes she left for Davud, hoping he wouldn't piece the puzzle together and confront her about her intentions, or worse, stop bringing her texts altogether. He apparently didn't, because the next time she came, she found several dozen accounts of aspirants—daughters of the Kings, generally between the ages of fourteen and eighteen—being inducted into the House of Maidens. The stories spanned centuries, and almost without fail, the ceremonies were formal affairs, often years in the making, unless of course, a young Maiden was inducted in times of strife or war, which happened on occasion. One account told of a girl who'd fallen to the white plague a week before she was to be inducted. A replacement was found, but the ceremony was delayed three months until after the plague had burned itself out of the city. Another account told of a girl who had been chosen but stepped down so that her twin sister who, according to the girl, had the better sword arm, could take her place. Seeing this selfless act, the Kings granted both an ebon blade.

And one more account that made Çeda sit up straight in her chair as she read it.

A century ago, the Queen of Mirea came to Sharakhai, claiming her daughter was the blood of Kiral, the King of Kings. As part of a sweeping treaty between their two countries, the queen asked that an ebon blade be granted to her daughter. Husamettín, the King of Swords, bristled, but when Kiral himself confirmed the girl's heritage, the girl was brought to the blooming fields, and her blood was confirmed with the prick of an adichara thorn. The girl remained in the Maidens for two decades and returned to her homeland a hero.

Çeda read this story three times before setting it aside. She breathed deeply, the cool air in that place of learning filling her with true hope for the first time since Davud had led her down there.

She wanted to speak to Emre about her plans and tell him what she'd learned of the poem, but she rarely saw him. She spent many days teaching swordplay to her students at the pits and many long nights in the scriptorium reading the tales Davud left for her. A few times she found Emre snoring in his bed when she returned before dawn, but she didn't have the heart to wake him, and by the time she woke, Emre was gone. One night she decided to stay home instead of going to the collegia, but Emre didn't come home that night or the next. After that, her anxiety over the loss of research time grew too great, and she returned to her pattern of nightly readings.

Where are you? she wrote on a note one morning, and left it on his pillow. But then she felt silly and ripped it up into a hundred pieces.

She stopped by Seyhan's stall in the spice market a few times, but these were busy days. Ships were arriving from north and south, the captains trading with merchants of Sharakhai and with one another, until Beht Zha'ir was on them again. Once, when Emre saw her approaching through the crowd, he smiled and waved her closer.

"Glad to see you back here," Çeda said as the din of the market hid their conversation.

"Glad to *be* back. Need anything?"

"What would I need?"

He motioned to the row after row of spices before him. "A bit of galangal. Pine nuts from Qaimir." He raised a bag of bulbous brown tubers and grinned apishly. "Dasheen, fresh from Mirea."

"I don't need *roots* to boil, Emre."

He raised his hands at her tone. "Oh, ho! I didn't mean to offend my lady queen by offering her free goods."

She closed her eyes, took a deep breath, then opened them again. "I miss you."

He shrugged, hands spread, as if to say he missed her too, but what could they do when the world conspired against them.

"Where have you been?"

"No!" This came from Seyhan, who was glowering at Emre and shooing Çeda away from the end of the stall, where five potential customers leaned over, smelling the spices. "No, no!" he said again. "You talk to your wife on your own time."

Emre and Çeda both rolled their eyes.

"We'll speak soon," Emre said.

Çeda nodded, sorry the moment had been missed, then wove her way through the crowd and out of the market.

The days blurred past, with more and more rumors about Emre reaching her. Twice at the pits after her classes and once while chatting with Tehla at the bazaar, she heard he'd been running the streets with Darius, that he'd been spotted with Hamid, that he was quickly rising through the ranks of the Host by some stunt he'd pulled east of the Trough.

Likely they were rumors blown out of proportion, but the thought still made her blood boil, and it did have the ring of truth to it. It would explain where he'd been spending all his time lately. But why now? The night of Beht Zha'ir, she'd wager. Trying to prove himself after almost getting himself killed. *If it's true, Emre, I'll box your ears till they bleed. See if I don't.* He was well aware of her feelings on the Al'Afwa Khadar, which, when she thought about it a moment more, might explain his consistent absence from their home.

It made the desire to wait for him burn even brighter, but her research was too important, and Beht Zha'ir was fast approaching. She was becoming convinced she wouldn't see him before the holy night, which made her uncomfortable given what she was planning. Finally, only a week before Beht Zha'ir, she found herself at home with him at the end of a miserably hot day.

He'd arrived unexpectedly with a small jar of olives in one hand, a bottle of red wine in the other. Even before the door had closed, Çeda was up gathering the lamp, two glasses, and a heel of bread left over from that morning. She joined him on the carpet in the middle of their common room and set the lamp between them. It was a childish ritual they'd been observing for years, pretending the lamp was a campfire, and they were out in the middle of the Shangazi trading stories by firelight as the wandering tribes do.

He sat cross-legged, wearing the wide belt and baggy trousers he favored at the stall. It would occasionally allow him to drive a better bargain from the women who came to Seyhan's stall for spices. She had to admit he looked good in it. He always had, especially with his dark eyes and that black tail of a beard.

"Stop staring," he said, running his hands over the scars where the tribesman's sword had cut him. His tanned skin shone from the sweat and oil of a working day. "They're healing fine."

It wasn't your scars I was admiring. Not for the first time, she wondered what had happened after they'd lain with one another, wondered why he hadn't wanted more. There were days when she wanted to take him into her bed—truth be told the itch was upon her, stronger than it had been in a long, long while. But there was more to worry about just now. "Are you using the salve I gave you?" she asked.

He shrugged and popped one of the rosemary olives into his mouth. "No need."

"The scars will show more."

He smiled and chewed noisily. "I don't know, it gives me a bit of character, don't you think? You've no idea how many times I've been asked about them."

"By tarts, no doubt."

He smiled and winked. "Tarts can be tasty."

She tore off a piece of bread and whipped it at him. "You're disgusting."

He tilted his head, as if to say he couldn't disagree. "Where've you been, Çedamihn?" he asked while pouring the wine into two glasses that looked as if the glassblower had just woken from a three-day drunk. "Have you seen yourself lately? You look a right mess. Your eyes are dark, your step is slow. I've never seen you like this."

"It's nothing."

"You've been skipping classes of late. And the White Wolf has apparently declined to enter the upcoming tourney."

"And how would you know all this?"

He shrugged and downed a healthy swallow of wine. "Asked around a bit."

She hid her surprise behind a swig of her own wine. These past weeks she'd been sure that Emre had everything else on his mind but her, and here he'd been checking up on her.

"Keeping secrets?" he pressed.

"*Uncovering* secrets," she amended.

Emre's wineglass halted halfway to his lips, and he grew more serious. "Ah." He shifted position on the well-worn carpet and sat straighter. He looked as if he was about to say something, probably to warn her away from things she was already doing, so she talked over him.

"I've found something new."

He stared. This was clearly not what he'd been expecting her to say.

"Let me show you." She went and got her book. She lifted the lamp and showed him the words she'd found highlighted in her mother's ink, and the different markings in the gutters.

"And you see," she said, pointing to the marks, "some are slanted and others aren't."

"Why?"

"An excellent question, dear Emre."

She sat back down and let him look through it, glass-shielded lamp held close to the pages so he could discern the different colored inks. She drank her wine and nibbled on the bread, wondering where to start. She wanted to tell him of her time in the desert with Saliah. She wanted to tell him what she'd learned, what she planned.

The words were on the tip of her tongue—*I'm the daughter of a King, Emre, and I'm going to the blooming fields to prove it*—but they never came. Instead, she blurted out, "I don't like that you're running with the Host." She knew immediately it had been the wrong thing to say, but it was already out there, sitting between them on the carpet like a fresh pile of shit. "They're only going to get you in trouble."

He lowered the book, but not the lamp. "Let me understand this. *You* are lecturing *me* on running afoul of the Kings?"

"Don't change the subject."

He raised the book again. "I'm running some packages for them, just like I did for Osman."

"Except Osman doesn't attract any attention. He's careful."

"*I'm* careful. I know what I'm doing, Çeda."

"They're using you, Emre."

"I know very well they're using me, Çeda. They need someone who hasn't been connected to the Moonless Host, someone the Silver Spears won't suspect."

"But they will. They'll figure it out eventually. Or someone will squawk, like they always do. There are enough who hate what the Host bring to the city."

He snorted and flipped the pages. "And what do they bring? A sense of realism? A sense that the Kings are not invincible? That there will come a day when they no longer rule in Sharakhai?"

"Perhaps, but what good is it going to do if you get caught running packages for the Host?"

"I could ask the same of you."

Çeda felt her face heat up. "I'm trying to learn the truth about my mother. You're risking your future for men who would use you every bit as much as the House of Kings would."

Emre went silent. He'd gone terribly still.

"Look," Çeda said. "I know you—"

Emre raised his hand, forestalling her. "Did you see the one without markings?"

"What?"

"Here," he said, motioning with the lamp, *"tomb."*

Çeda felt her fingertips tingle as she took the book from him. He was right. She hadn't noticed it, despite having been through the book hundreds of times, because there were no markings in the gutter. But there it was, *tomb*, highlighted in her mother's ink.

Forty-six words, then—forty-five with markings and one without.

But why? Why would one be different? What makes it special? It was the end of the sequence, she realized. There was no mark, because it was the final word. And suddenly the rest of the puzzle fell into place.

She got up and went for her pen and ink and a fresh piece of paper from her dwindling stack.

"What is it?"

"Shhhh!"

The marks must indicate a number of pages, either backward or forward. Now she only needed to find the one that pointed to the final word and work her way backward.

She found it three pages back—*his*—with three straight marks in the gutter. And then the next, five pages forward— *toward*—with five slanted marks. On the puzzle took her, until she'd reached the very beginning.

It was another poem, she realized, written in the same meter as her mother's.

> *From golden dunes,*
> *And ancient runes,*
> *The King of glittering stone;*
> *By inverted thorn,*

His skin was torn,
And yet his strength did grow.

While far afield,
His love unsealed,
'Til Tulathan does loom;
Then petals' dust,
Like lovers' lust,
Will draw him toward his tomb.

She read it through three times, her fingers shaking and her mind racing. The thorn could mean the adichara thorns, which everyone knew were poison. And petals' dust might mean pollen from the blooms. But the key was the King of Glittering Stone. Who could he be? She knew Azad never slept, and that Cahil went to the blooming fields to tend the adichara. She knew Beşir watched from the shadows, that Husamettín could cleave stone with his great sword, that Ihsan was cruel and Mesut was kind and Kiral led them all. But these were all children's tales. In truth she knew almost nothing about any of them. Nothing that *mattered*, in any case.

"Çeda, what is it?" Emre was worried, more worried than she ever remembered seeing him.

She had to force herself to lift her eyes from the paper. "My mother found something, Emre. She found secrets and hid them in this book." She flipped the poem into his lap. "It's related to the asirim that spoke to me, it's related to the Kings, and it's related to my mother's death."

"How can you be so sure?"

"When she took me to Saliah's, the day before she died, my mother said she had four of their poems. Saliah said *four is not twelve.* I think there might be one poem for each of the Kings. And they contain clues to how they might be harmed."

"That's foolish."

"Is it?" She pointed to the paper. "Read it again."

Emre read it over, looking between paper and book, his face growing dark. "It reads like a riddle."

"It does."

"But who would write such a thing?"

"I've no idea. Nalamae, perhaps? Some accounts say she wasn't on Tauriyat on the night of Beht Ihman. Perhaps she frowned upon the Kings' dark bargain. Perhaps she's left us clues about how the bargain might be unraveled."

"Why not simply tell us?"

Why not, indeed? "That's why they were hunting her," she whispered.

"What?"

"The gods have been hunting Nalamae. There are at least five recorded cases of Nalamae's supposed rebirth."

"The desert is rife with such stories."

"Maybe for good reason, Emre. Perhaps they don't want their secrets revealed."

"Well then"—Emre lifted the paper—"if this is one of their secrets, then what's the answer?"

"I don't know." She picked up the poem and read over the words again. "But you can bet by the gods' own blood I'm going to find out."

Chapter 28

SHE NEVER DID CONFESS her plans to Emre. They got good and drunk that night, and she found her old feelings for him returning. She even thought he might feel the same, but when she unbraided her hair and let it fall about her shoulders, he looked at her as if he were suddenly shocked by the very idea, then mumbled something about being tired. She'd thought about slipping into his bed anyway, but that look on his face, as if she were a disease-ridden whore, doused the flames within her.

In the days that followed she found herself hoping he wouldn't be home so they wouldn't have to discuss it. She needn't have worried. The one morning they saw each other he seemed as eager to avoid talking as she did.

She was desperate to solve this one riddle before Beht Zha'ir, so she arranged for Djaga to come out of retirement and take up her classes at the pits, a thing she did as a favor to Çeda from time to time. Over the following week, Çeda practically lived in Amalos's office in the scriptorium cellars. She brought food and water with her so she could stay longer. She even stayed through the morning one day, but when she heard voices echoing down, she scribbled her next night's subjects for Davud and slipped away.

She wanted to research the parts of the poem she didn't understand. There was the "glittering stone," but she didn't know what *kind* of stone, or which King might wear one. The "golden dunes and ancient runes" was another clue, but again, she had little idea where to begin. So instead she read of the different tribes, hoping she might stumble across something. She read of Tribe Salmük, the Black Veils. Tribe Ebros, the Standing Stones. Tribe Masal, the Red Wind. Tribe Kadri, the Burning Hands. Tribe Kenan and Halarijan and Rafik and all the rest. She searched for any signs or symbols that looked even remotely like the one that had marked her mother's forehead, but there were none. In this, the Kings had done their work well.

At the end of each day, Çeda was swimming in the stories. The names of the shaikhs, the territory where the wandering tribes roamed, the breeds of horses they raised, the types of ships they first sailed onto the desert, and the skimwood forests that were culled for their precious wood. She even learned of their tribal designs, the subtle differences in the tattoos they used. She discovered that the tribesman she'd seen in the Haddah, where Emre had been assaulted, were of Tribe Kadri, the Burning Hands, the only ones who inked the palms of their hands and the soles of their feet. It felt important in some way to know this, but just how, she couldn't say.

As the nights wore on, her desperation grew. She began skimming the material, which made her feel as though she were missing things, and when *that* prompted her to go back and reread, sometimes two or three times, her research went all the slower. She soon felt her resolve beginning to weaken. *I could wait,* she told herself. *I could take my time, go in another six weeks, on the next Holy Night.* But she knew those feelings for what they were—excuses not to do what she'd vowed. No, she would continue as planned, no matter what happened here.

Finally, only one night remained before Beht Zha'ir. She was reading a census of Sharakhai, hoping some of the names might link any one of the Kings to any one of the tribes. She wanted to understand their heritage, because the riddle of the King of Glittering Stone may very well be related to a particular region in the Shangazi, but there was nothing. Nothing. There was nothing on this infernal tablet, nothing in these infernal scrolls, nothing in the dozens upon dozens of books she'd read these past many weeks. This was all useless. She wanted to hurl the tablet across the room, but her mother had instilled in her a love of words that was too strong to break, so she stood and grabbed her chair instead, lifted it high into the air, and brought it crashing down against the floor over and over until it was little better than kindling.

She stood there, breathing heavily, gripping the broken remains of the chair in her white-knuckled fists. Which was the precise moment she realized that someone was watching her.

She turned and found a man wearing the robes of a collegia scholar standing in the doorway. It was Davud, she realized after one breathless moment, staring at her wide-eyed as she'd ever seen him.

"I'm so sorry, Davud."

"You can't *wreck* the place, Çeda!"

"I know. I'm sorry."

"They'll find out! They'll *expel* me! They'll force my family to repay all that Amalos has invested in my education!"

"I'll take care of the chair. I'll take it away and bring another."

"No!" Davud rushed to the wood, grabbing the remnants and tossing them into a loose pile. "*I'll* take care of it."

"I'm sorry, Davud."

As he continued gathering the smaller pieces, even splinters, his movements slowed, then stopped altogether. "You can't come back here, Çeda."

"I know. It was a fool's errand in any case. The Kings were too thorough."

"I can't risk it," he said, as if he hadn't heard her.

"I know, Davud. I wouldn't have come after tomorrow night in any case."

At this, Davud stood straight and looked at her. "What do you mean? Why not?"

She met his gaze, which seemed surprisingly mature. "It doesn't matter, Davud. You've done more than enough for me already." *You needn't be burdened with my fool plans.*

She began walking away, but he grabbed her wrist, releasing her when he saw that it bothered her. "Tomorrow night is Beht Zha'ir."

"Yes."

"What are you planning to do?"

"I won't tell you that, Davud, so stop asking." She stepped in and hugged him. "Be well."

And then she left, feeling strangely free. She'd so hoped that there was something hidden within the collegia, but the Kings had had centuries to alter their history. How could she hope to uncover the truth by pecking through random texts? The failure made her all the more sure that her plans for tomorrow night were the right course.

She returned home with a strong desire to sit with Emre, share more bread, share more wine as well, perhaps enough to summon the courage to tell him. She had to tell him. She had to.

I'm the daughter of a King.

But he didn't return that night. She stayed up until dawn, hoping he would come home. And he didn't return the following day. She slept, hoping she would hear the door open, hear the creak of the floorboards as he made his way to his room. But she never did, and by the time she woke late in the day, it was time to begin her preparations.

She checked her clothes, prepared her small bag with water and provisions. She sharpened then oiled her shamshir, and then her kenshar. She applied a fresh coat of oil to her zilij, a board she'd fashioned from skimwood, the same treated wood she used for the runners of the great sandships. The zilij had rounded edges shaped and polished as much by the desert sands as by the hands of its maker; as tall as her legs were long, a handspan wide, the bottom surface gleaming with paraffin oil that would protect it when she skimmed along the arid dunes of the Shangazi.

All too soon the sun set behind distant clouds. What if Emre didn't come? Perhaps their distance over these past weeks was a not-so-subtle sign from the gods, but if so, what did it indicate? That she shouldn't say farewell? Or that she shouldn't go?

With dusk spreading over the desert, the sounds of the city dwindled in preparation for the holy night. *It's time,* Çeda realized. *I can't wait any longer.* She changed into her black fighting dress and retrieved her jewelry box from its hidden alcove. Placing it on the bed before her, she slid the top off and pushed the velvet tray inside just so while pinching the wooden base. The tray, which contained a few rings and bracelets and anklets that Çeda never wore, lifted free to reveal the hidden compartment beneath.

Three adichara petals lay within. One was shaped like a spearhead, which seemed fitting, so she lifted it carefully and whispered a few quick prayers—to Rhia for guidance and Tulathan for forbearance—then placed it beneath her tongue. As the taste and scent of spices filled her, she took a deep breath and released it as she would a draw from a hookah filled with the rarest of tabbaqs.

Hurry, Emre, please.

Her hands shaking with vigor, she returned the jewelry box to its hiding place and took up her sword harness from the bed. This she pulled around her shoulders and strapped across her chest. She took up her shamshir next and slipped it into the sheath over her left shoulder. She buckled on a belt that held a waterskin and her kenshar and a leather pouch, one she would fill with more petals. If all went as planned, she'd have little need for petals, but one never knew, so the pouch would remain.

Finally she picked up her zilij. A leather cord ran the length of it so she could hang it over her shoulder, which she did now, laying it alongside her shamshir.

She was about to leave when she heard voices in the street. She moved to her bedroom window and peeked through the curtains. By the coppery glow of twilight she could see two men farther up the lane. One, by Rhia's grace, was Emre, wearing sirwal trousers, laced sandals, and his wide leather belt and tooled bracers. The other was a stocky man wearing a long thawb and a brown turban that covered his face.

The other voice . . . She recognized it, but couldn't quite place it.

She couldn't leave without being seen, so she waited, and soon the two of them were hugging, slapping one another's backs, and parting ways. The sturdy man headed toward the bazaar while Emre returned home.

"Who were you talking to?" she asked when he stepped into their sitting room.

He noted her black dress, and seemed to force himself to squat before their small oven, stoking the flames with an iron poker. "A good evening to you as well."

"Answer my question."

"No one . . ." After working the dying coals a little more, he dropped the poker with a clang and stood, as if he couldn't put things off any longer. "Don't go, Çeda. Not tonight."

And suddenly she placed the voice. "Hamid," she said. "That was Hamid, wasn't it?"

"Hamid is our friend."

"He is a thug and a murderer, and you know it." At least Emre had the decency to look embarrassed about it. "Are you taking *orders* from him now?"

"I'm not taking orders."

"You *are*. What's he asked you to do, Emre?"

"Stay and I'll tell you."

Emre looked positively desperate. She could see it in his eyes, in the tightness across his shoulders. Did he know? Had he guessed what she was about to do?

That was impossible. She'd told no one. This was simply his fears coming back to haunt him. She couldn't find the words to tell him the truth—*Emre, I'm leaving tonight, and I may never see you again*—so she gave him a half-truth instead. "I've already taken the petal."

He raised his hands, trying to forestall her arguments. "Davud came to me today."

Çeda felt her face burn. It felt as if she were a child all over again, and she'd been caught stealing figs.

"He's worried you're going to do something rash tonight. Was he right?"

It felt as if a peach stone were caught in her throat, and no amount of swallowing was going to clear it. Why was it so hard to tell him? *Because he'd try to stop me. He'd do something foolish*. No, those were lies. Or, at least, they weren't the real reasons.

The truth was she couldn't bear to say goodbye to Emre. Anyone else, perhaps, but not him. That was why she hadn't said a word in the weeks since her visit to Saliah. That was why she hadn't been able to tell him the other night when she'd had every intention of doing so. That was why the words were so slow in coming now. "I'm going to the blooming fields to poison myself," she finally blurted.

Emre only stared, his mouth gaping open.

"It's the only way to prove it, Emre."

"Prove *what?*"

"That I'm the daughter of a King."

There. She'd said it. It was finally out. And she expected what? For Emre to simply believe what she told him? To accept her fool plan?

"That you're—" Emre fumbled. "That's *mad*, Çeda. You aren't . . ." His words trailed off as he stared at the expression of dire seriousness on her face.

"I saw it in Saliah's chimes," she replied, as if that settled it.

"You saw Saliah again?"

Çeda nodded. "Yes, and the chimes gave me a vision. I know it's true. My mother had me for a purpose, and I'm going to fulfill it, at least in the ways I'm able."

"By doing what? Killing yourself with poison?"

"The Maidens are all tested by the adichara's poison, Emre." To be pricked by the thorns was certain death for those not of royal blood. But the Maidens were different. Their aspirants were sent to the desert on Beht Zha'ir, where they were given to the adichara and poisoned. If they lived, their courage and their blood was proven. And so Çeda would prove that she belonged among them. It was the only way the vision would come true: if she could show the Maidens that she was indisputably the blood of Kings. It was a desperate plan, but she was desperate and had never been more so than when she'd stood before the King in the scent merchants' tower. She'd known for a long time that she had to try something different. She just hadn't known what. Not until she'd gone to Saliah's and the truth had been revealed. "That's how I'll know, once and for all, and if I'm proven the daughter of a King, I can do much."

"Like what?" He lowered his voice to a near whisper. "Kill them all? Is that what this is all about? When are you going to give up on that fool dream of yours, Çeda? It's never going to happen! Your mother was mad, and *you're* mad for following in her footsteps."

Çeda felt struck by a hammer blow. "My mother was not *mad*."

"You can't stop them," Emre went on. "Not on your own. Come with me, and we'll talk with Hamid. They're the only ones who will make a difference, and you can help. Hamid would be glad to have you. So would Macide."

"Gods, Emre, were you *with* me in the scent merchants' fort? Did you see how the Host burned those innocent people? Those innocent *children?*"

"Yes, and did you see what the Kings hung from the walls of Hallowsgate the following morning?"

"I need no reminder that the Kings are both violent and vile."

"Then perhaps you need a reminder of what happened to your mother. They hung her for all the city to see, Çeda, and they'll do the same to you. You cannot make a difference by throwing your life away."

She heard a lonely wail in the distance. Even as far away as the asir was, the hair on her skin rose. The call sounded like one of the desert jackals, but it went on much longer, and sounded too painful, too human, especially in light of what she was about to do.

"There isn't a day that goes by when I don't think of her, Emre. And I'm not throwing my life away." *Dear gods, please let this not be in vain.* "I have to go," she said, heading for the door, but Emre lunged forward and grabbed her wrist.

"Don't," he said.

She stared down at his hand. "Emre, let me go."

"There's so many of them, Çeda. It just doesn't feel right. Wait until the next Holy Night. Wait for a better night."

She'd never seen him so worried over her, and there was

a part of her—the weak part, the fearful part—that wanted to give in to his request. But she couldn't. Wait, and she might never go. "There's never a better night," she said. "Not for something like this." And she wrenched her hand free.

When he tried to grab her again, she slapped his wrist away. "Emre, stop it!"

He tried again, and she fended him off with increasing ferocity. Emre was not as accustomed to fighting as she was, but he was moderately fast and very strong. Even if she weren't fully steeped in the effects of the petal, she could have reached the door, but invigorated as she was, it was child's play to slap his hands away, to skip backward as he lunged.

"I said stop it!"

He knew this was a losing battle so went for the door instead, hoping to bar her way.

She spun low, snapped her heel out and caught an ankle, sending him sprawling to the bare floor while she leapt easily over him.

He came to his knees as she opened the door. His eyes were wide. "*Please*, Çeda."

"I'm sorry, Emre." Another wail, louder this time, sounded over the city. "Don't worry over me. I'll be fine." Before Emre could protest, she shut the door, took the stairs down, and began jogging toward the bazaar.

She could hear him behind her, calling into the night, "Çeda, please!" A foolish, foolish thing.

Thankfully he soon fell silent.

Chapter 29

WIPING AWAY HER TEARS with one hand, Çeda pulled the black veil across her face with the other. The bazaar stalls were torn down, the bright canvas tents folded away for the night. Tulathan was already well above the eastern horizon, her silver face staring down over the desert, watching as the asirim stalked over the sands toward Sharakhai. Her sister, golden Rhia, was bright in the west.

Çeda listened for a moment before choosing her path. The wails were coming from the north, so she jogged southeast along the winding Serpentine and then onto the Trough, heading toward the southern harbor. As she ran, the buildings changed from simple dwellings and shops to stone mansions on either side of the street. As the Trough curved, the buildings shrank once more, but now they were of much older construction. This close to the edge of the city she had to be more careful. The asirim might enter Sharakhai from any direction, and if some had come from the south, they would be nearing the city's edge by now, or they might already be within her borders, wandering, taking those marked by Sukru.

No sooner had she thought this than she heard a heavy

knocking on her left. A more final sound she'd never heard. She cringed as her boots scuffed the dirt and the smell of the asirim came to her, that sickly sweet scent that had wafted from their King just before he'd kissed her. She pressed herself into an alcove in a wheelwright's stables. It had suddenly become difficult to breathe. She could think of nothing but the asir's warm lips pressed against her forehead.

The knock came again, the sound like a skull pounding wood. Çeda dared not move, and yet she found her right hand itching to draw her shamshir, an instinct borne of fighting in the pits, although she knew very well a blade would do her no good.

When the knock came a third time, it was accompanied by the sound of splintering wood. A thumping followed, the heavy tread of feet upon a wooden floor.

Çeda tried to control her breathing, but with the asir only paces from where she stood, she couldn't. It came in deep, rapid gasps. She licked her lips, told herself to remain calm, but a moment later a scream tore through the still of the night.

"No!" A woman pleaded. "Not my son! Take me instead! Take me!"

Her shouts were cut off with a sound like the sledges butchers used to fell cattle. Çeda spun away, refusing to look back. If she did, she might be caught by its gaze. She would not be so lucky as she was last time, King of the asirim or no.

She sprinted down a narrow alley between two houses, flew along the street it led to, listening for sounds of pursuit. She could hear nothing—nothing save the pounding of her heart and the heaving of her breath. The petal's energy carried her on. She made a turn at the old grain mill that always smelled of mule dung and hay, and then again at Kavi the jeweler's.

Ahead, ships' masts stabbed upward from beyond the row of warehouses. The harbor opened up before her. Çeda reached a set of stone stairs that led down to the sand, and there, with practiced ease, she slipped her zilij over her head and tossed it down. As it skimmed over the surface, she jumped upon it, her feet finding the boiled leather straps she'd nailed into the gently hollowed topside. She kicked with her left leg, which sent her sighing across the sand as easily as the sidewinding vipers that nested along the Haddah's riverbed. Leaning this way or that to steer, she moved beyond the borders of the harbor and into a long inlet hemmed in by high stone outcroppings, barely wide enough for two ships to pass one another.

Within minutes she reached the desert proper, the Great Shangazi, where the dunes opened up before her. The dunes changed often, and tonight they were tall. High sands, they were called, the sort that would force ships to wait in harbor to sail, or if they were caught in the desert, to find higher ground or risk being washed under by the shifting sands.

For one lone woman with a zilij, however, they were easy enough to navigate. Çeda used her skimwood board to fly along the slope of a dune, allowing her momentum to carry her up the next one. The moment she slowed she would hop off and hike to the summit, and once there throw the zilij down, leap upon it, and race down, leaning into the curves to keep her balance or to steer away from the occasional outcropping of rock.

Time was already growing short. Tulathan was reaching her apex.

Çeda continued, skimming, climbing, skimming, climbing, for nearly an hour. When the sand became rocky ground at last, she slung the zilij over her back and jogged easily. Rhia stood over the western horizon, a twinkling eye in the distance. Tulathan was directly overhead, surrounded by a host of attendant stars.

The blooming fields soon came into view, the twisted forms of the adichara given definition by the light of the moons. At first they looked like little more than a mass of darkness huddling in patches, but as she came closer, details were revealed: a branch reaching toward the stars, a bough twisting around itself and others. The blooms glowed ever so softly beneath the moon, and when the breeze picked up, Çeda could see trails of shimmering blue pollen carried on the wind. She could smell it now as well, a scent like red wine, like powdered amber, subtle yet deeply powerful, as if these twisted trees somehow fed upon the stories of man throughout all the pages of time.

As she stepped closer, a buzzing filled the air—rattlewings moving drunkenly from bloom to bloom, oblivious to Çeda's presence. Like hummingbirds, they collected nectar from the flowers, but only when the moons were brightest. Çeda approached two trees that looked like lovers entwined in one another's arms. After hunkering down in the shadows, she pulled her slim kenshar from its sheath at her side. This close, the petals of the adichara blooms glowed a pale blue, almost white, not unlike bright Tulathan. The five golden stamen inside seemed to shiver, though perhaps that was merely a trick of the wind. She reached forward and slipped the edge of her knife beneath the flower and cut the stem. She cut a second and finally a third, stashing each in the leather pouch at her belt.

Then, after sliding the knife into its sheath, she stared at the other blooms, at the thorns that graced the length of their stems. In truth, these were what she had come for, not the flowers.

Ever since the sail back from Saliah's, when she'd stared down at that drop of dried blood on her thumb, she'd known she would come to the adichara and taste of their poison. "What say you?" she said softly to the trees.

She held her hand out, saw her hand not merely quivering, but trembling, as if she'd been stricken by palsy. The branches wavered, but made no move toward her. The wind picked up, making the adicharas rattle, and still she waited, hoping it would accept her on its own.

She caught movement from the corner of her eye—a dark form off to her left—and the moment she did, she felt it: a pinprick against the meat of her thumb. Her breath drew in sharply, her heart went wild, not merely for the pain or the implication of what the poison would soon do, but for the sudden expansion of awareness that swept through her. When she took the adichara petals, she often felt as though she could sense the vast ring of trees around Sharakhai. Now she felt not only that, but also a deep, insatiable hunger. She had no idea what it might be, but could only think of the asirim, their anger bleeding through the poison to touch her heart, to infect her like a wound going septic.

A huff filled the cold desert air, the sound of a horse exhaling. She heard the thump of hooves in sand, though it stopped before reaching the rocky ground around the adichara—a clever move if one was wary of an interloper in the field ahead.

Already the poison was spreading. The skin around the thorn prick was going numb. Bakhi's grace, could the poison lay her low before she could return to Sharakhai?

She listened carefully for the horse, or its rider, but heard nothing. Through the boughs of the adichara, though, she saw something: a woman moving with deadly grace. Her dress was cut in the style of the Blade Maidens, but, strangely, it looked a different color, perhaps purple—it was difficult to tell in the moonlight. She must be a Maiden, though, for she held an ebon blade in her right hand. Her face was covered by a veil so that the only skin Çeda could see was around her eyes and the backs of her tattooed hands. A glittering ruby hung on her forehead, just above the bridge of her nose, and she wore a necklace of sleek, finger-length thorns.

The Maiden had fouled everything.

She might kill Çeda outright or take her to the House of Kings to be questioned before being hung or drawn and quartered in the city square. What she might be doing out here, Çeda had no idea, but she knew this: if she didn't leave now, it would mean her death.

The Maiden stalked through the adichara with slow and steady purpose, the ebon blade held easily in her hand. It did not gleam in the moonlight; instead, it shone dully, a wicked, dark smile in the night.

Çeda could already feel the skin along her thumb and the upper part of her wrist going numb. Breath of the desert, how quickly it was happening! As the Maiden tread softly through the twisted trees, the burning anger from the adichara intensified within Çeda, urging her to stand, to attack the maiden and drink of her blood. Çeda smothered the thoughts as well as she was able. She didn't wish

to give the Blade Maiden any sort of edge, but it was difficult; the feelings ran so very deep.

The Blade Maiden stalked closer, listening, hunting.
Çeda hoped she would move toward the bulk of the adichara so Çeda could sprint north, over the dunes toward
Sharakhai, but no. She was headed straight for Çeda's hiding place, and she was no longer scanning the trees to discover who was there.

She knew, Çeda realized. She knew exactly where
Çeda was.

So she ran.

The Blade Maiden called out, *"Lai, lai, lai!"* Both a
warning and a demand for her to stop.

She didn't care. She sprinted faster, pulling her zilij off
her back. But she was still on rocky ground, and the
Maiden—gods she was fast!—was catching up. She shouldn't
have been able to, not with Çeda's petal still giving her inhuman energy, but here she was, pacing Çeda like a maned
wolf—indeed moving *ahead* to cut her off before she could
reach the sands.

While drawing her sword from its sheath on her back,
Çeda slipped her left arm through the straps of the zilij and
held it like a shield. The Blade Maiden lowered into a fighting stance, advancing, dark sword at the ready.

Çeda darted forward, arcing her blade high. The
Maiden blocked her stroke, but as she did Çeda snapped a
kick into her gut. Çeda had only meant it as a warning, to
give this woman pause, and indeed the message seemed to
hit home. The Maiden's kohl-rimmed eyes widened in the
moonlight as she reassessed Çeda. She advanced more
cautiously, while Çeda gave ground, hoping to slow her enemy down; she needed to reach the sands, where the zilij
would be faster than a horse. But the Maiden guessed her
purpose and advanced once more. They traded a flurry of
blows that rang through the cold night air. Çeda blocked
with her zilij, though the ebon blade bit deep into the
wood, and the Maiden ducked one of Çeda's high slashes,
twisted in a blur of motion, and cut from the side.

Çeda barely managed to block it with her sword. It
struck like a hammer, numbing her arm from the elbow

down. She nearly dropped the sword, and she knew, as another blow came for her, that she couldn't hope to win this fight. This woman was too good by far, and Çeda was having more difficulty simply retaining her grip on her sword.

She started to give ground faster after that, feigning weakness. The Maiden took the bait, but didn't overcommit. She was steady and careful, firmly in control of a duel that increasingly favored the Maiden the longer it continued.

Knowing a retreat was hopeless unless she put the Maiden on the defensive, Çeda stopped near the edge of the sand and unleashed a vicious combination of blows, moves that had won her fights in the pits many times before. Never with a numb hand, though. The Blade Maiden blocked her blows and then kicked high, connecting with Çeda's wrist, as if she knew about the poison.

Çeda's shamshir went flying through the midnight air, flashing in the moonlight as it went. And in that moment, Çeda jumped onto the sand, spinning and holding the zilij by only one strap. She brought its tip across the sand, sending a spray up and across the Blade Maiden, who twisted away, raising her arm to fend off the spray. But she was too late and it caught her full in the face. She uttered not a sound, but she stepped back several paces, blade ready, shaking her head to clear her eyes.

It gave Çeda the time she needed. She ran, threw her zilij down against the sand, and leapt on it. In moments she was skimming down the flank toward the trough between the dunes.

She spared a glance behind her. The Maiden had initially given chase, but had already realized her mistake and was running back for her horse.

By the time Çeda reached the crest of the next dune, she saw the Maiden in the saddle, galloping forward. The horse would never catch her, though. It would plod through the sand and tire quickly, while *she* was able to fly down one side of the dune and sprint up the next.

When she'd crested two more, she stopped and looked back, holding her zilij by her good left hand. At the top of a dune, just north of the blooming fields, the Maiden was watching from horseback. Çeda waved, threw her board down, and was gone.

————— ⟨—●—⟩ —————

When Çeda reached the southern harbor, she was forced to rest before climbing the stone steps to the docks. Her throat and lungs burned. Her legs were leaden and white hot with pain. They felt as if she'd been beaten mercilessly with clubs, not only from the run back from the dunes but also because the effects of the petal were beginning to ebb. It was something she was used to, an ache she often enjoyed, but with the effects of the poison still spreading through her body, she had pushed herself harder than ever on her return journey.

Tulathan was low in the sky now, leaving layers of heavy shadows along the streets and alleys. Çeda staggered along the Trough as quickly as her legs would take her, heedless of the sad wheezing sounds she was making. But instead of heading west toward Roseridge she turned east and moved into the merchant district. She listened carefully for signs of the asirim. They were often gone by this time, but some had been known to remain late into the night, leaving only as dawn approached. She heard nothing, however, as she came to a row of two-story stone buildings. The third one had impressive windows filled with thick, wavy glass that gave a distorted view of the shelves of bottles and vials within.

Çeda couldn't knock. She couldn't let anyone know—other than Dardzada himself—that she'd come.

Positioning herself beneath a tall window on the second floor and placing the ball of her left foot against a wide first-floor window pane, she took two deep breaths and launched herself upward. She caught the second-floor windowsill with both hands. Her numb right hand slipped off, but she held on tight with her left until she could swing back and try again. Her hand held this time, and she pulled herself high enough to reach up and grab the ornamental brass sun-and-moons nailed above the window. The simple decoration had been there for so long, she feared it might pull right out, but it held, and she set herself carefully against the window.

Her legs quivered from the exertion, and her wrists began to weaken. But she managed to stay in place long enough to draw her kenshar, wedge it between the window panes, and work it inward, ready to flip the latch. But no sooner had she begun rocking the hilt up and down than the panes swung inward and a meaty hand jerked her into the darkness. She sprawled to the floor as the windows closed behind her. Dardzada's voice was a harsh whisper from the darkness. "What in the name of Nalamae's teats are you *doing* here?"

Only a scant bit of light came in from the edges of the curtains, outlining Dardzada's bulky form. "I need help."

He kicked at her legs, forcing her to slide backward. "That's no worry of mine, Çeda."

"I've been poisoned."

He kicked her again. "It was *you* who sent that note, wasn't it?"

She'd had a messenger deliver it yesterday morning: a note written, supposedly, by a visiting caravan master who requested a meeting here at sunrise, about a large order of Yerinde's Kiss that he planned to bring back with him to Qaimir. It was a very expensive aphrodisiac Dardzada was famed for. The messenger had delivered Dardzada's prompt reply, saying he would be most pleased to meet, first thing, to discuss terms. Her ruse had ensured that Dardzada would be at home over Beht Zha'ir and not somewhere else in the city, but it had also, predictably, enraged him. Not because there was no profit in the offing, but because he'd been fooled, and by none other than Çeda.

"If the Silver Spears saw you come here, we'd both be dead, and let me tell you, you're not worth that. You're not worth *half* that. How could you have been so foolish?"

He tried to kick her a third time, but she slipped away and rolled over one shoulder to her feet. "It was no accident, Dardzada. I poisoned myself."

Dardzada stopped, chest heaving like a winded bull. "You what?"

"I poisoned myself."

"For the love of the gods, *why?*"

"To enter the House of Maidens."

She said it, expecting Dardzada to rail against her. To be confused or tell her she was mad. But instead he stared at her in a silence that was anything but innocent.

"You know I'm the blood of Kings," Çeda accused.

Dardzada looked as though a thousand answers were playing themselves out in his mind.

"You knew and you never told me. Who is he?"

The stocky apothecary closed his eyes, pinching the bridge of his nose for a moment as he shook his head back and forth. "Ahya refused to tell me."

Çeda wanted to spit. "That's a lie."

Dardzada shook his head. "Even in the end, Çeda. She would never tell me."

"She knew she was going to die! Why wouldn't she tell you?"

"Because she was deathly afraid you might be found. She worried that if she told me, that I would pass the tale to you or others, and she wasn't willing to risk the King of Whispers hearing of it."

There had been few times in her life when she felt Dardzada was being completely forthright with her, and strangely, this was one of them. She could see her mother going about it exactly as Dardzada had described, especially since the information had no real bearing on the plans she'd had for Çeda since her birth. Or it might even be deeper than that. She might not have wished for Çeda to harbor any feelings of love toward the Kings, *especially* her own father.

Small chance of that, Çeda thought. "I need to find a way to avenge my mother," she said, "and in order to do that I will enter the Maidens' home."

"They won't have you."

"They will, and you're going to help me."

"I have no control over the Maidens, Çeda."

"Yes, you do. There's a woman inside, you said. An ally. I heard you telling my mother."

"I can't simply reach her at the toss of a coin."

Çeda flexed her right hand. It was numb around the point of the wound, but pain was now spreading along her shoulder. "That puts me in a very precarious position, Dardzada."

"*Why?* Why didn't you *come* to me with this?"

"And what would you have done?" She paused, waiting only long enough for him to open his mouth. "I'll tell you. You would have driven me out of your home, calling me a foolish girl. And if for some reason you thought me serious, you would have moved against me, knowing my plan would put you and your allies in jeopardy."

"It *does* put us in jeopardy."

"I don't care, Dardzada. My mother had a plan. She died before she could share it with me, and you've refused to tell me any of it, so I've made my own. Now, either you take me to the Maidens or I die. The choice is yours."

"You can't just come here and lay this at my feet!"

"I can do *exactly* that. My mother begged you to take me on as your own, and a piss poor job you've done of it."

"You were willful!"

"I was a *child!* But now I'm a woman grown, and you owe me. Do this, and the ledger will be wiped clean."

He stared at her, his heavy breath the only sound in the deadened city.

"Dardzada, my hand is so numb I can't feel any of my fingers. The pain is spreading to my chest even now." She lifted her right hand. He couldn't see details, not in this light, but he could see that it was swollen, he could see the tinge of blue where the thorn had pierced her skin.

"No matter what you may think, I cannot contact her whenever I wish. It takes time."

"Then use the skill the gods gave you. Slow this poison down, and then contact her, with all the haste you can muster."

After one glance toward the window, he motioned to his bed. "Lie down." The stairs groaned as Dardzada headed for his apothecary. "And by Tulathan's bright smile stay still, Çeda. The less you move, the better."

As the sound of tinkling glass rose from the ground floor, Çeda lay down on Dardzada's bed. She'd done so only a handful of times in the past, and only when Dardzada had been away for several days on business. The smell of it—the smell of *him*—took her back to her childhood in an instant, and she found herself wishing she could return to those days, to choose a different life. But that wasn't how it worked. Life chose *you*; it was how you dealt with it that mattered.

She didn't want to die. She was working to avenge her mother's death, and she wouldn't change a thing if she died. Except . . . She would tell Emre she loved him. She cared for him so deeply yet so rarely told him. Their love was an unspoken covenant—they were practically brother and sister; they would do anything to help each other—and yet she thought here, this once, she would voice those unspoken words if he were standing before her.

When the early light of dawn crept around the heavy drapes, her hand was much, much worse. She could see the wound in the meat of her right thumb. The flesh was swollen horribly, and the blue stain beneath her skin had spread to her fingers, the back of her hand and much of her forearm.

"Gods be good," she whispered.

Chapter 30

SEVEN YEARS EARLIER...

"ÇEDA . . ."

Çeda pulled her blanket over her shoulders. She was cold. So cold.

"Çeda, wake up. The rain's about to begin."

Çeda's eyes shot open. She threw off the blanket, heedless of the cold, and sat up in the tent where she'd somehow managed to fall asleep, despite the bitterly chill night. After pulling on her boots, she threw aside the tent's flap and joined her mother on the vast pan of the desert before her. The sun was already up—they'd arrived so deep into the previous evening that Çeda fell asleep the moment they'd finished pitching the tent and laying out their blankets.

An immense lake spread across the landscape before her, so calm that it perfectly reflected the thin morning clouds over the line of dark mountains.

Her mother blew into her hands and rubbed them together. "Ready?"

Çeda nodded, giddy with excitement, and for the first time in a very long while, Ahya took her daughter's hand. Hers was rough and callused and warm—warmer than

Çeda's, in any case. As they walked toward the edge of the lake, their boots crunched over the salty ground. A salt flat, her mother had called it, a vast plain where bright white salt covered the ground like sand. She reached down and pinched some between her fingers, placed it upon her tongue. She spat it out immediately as her mother glanced down and smiled wryly.

"You didn't believe me?"

Çeda shrugged. "I just wanted to taste it for myself."

Ahead, a flurry of bright blue wings rose up from beyond the rightmost edge of the lake where, as far as the eye could see, small salt bushes and wiry tufts of grasses stood. More birds followed the first fluttering wave, and more still, until entire swaths of the shadowed land seemed to lift, as if a great quilt of sapphires had been laid over the earth and was now being lifted by the hand of an elder god.

As Ahya stood by Çeda's side, the immense flock drifted over the center of the lake, parts of the writhing mass coming nearer, parts farther away, the entirety of it holding improbably together as the fast little birds flew over the perfectly calm, crystal clear water.

"Blazing blues, they're called."

"And lapis eyes," Çeda replied, proud of herself for having remembered when they'd spoken months ago about coming here in the heart of winter.

"That's right, for the way their wings beat like eyelids over their breasts."

"I know, memma."

Ahya ran her hand down Çeda's long black hair. "You know so much, do you?"

Çeda stared at the wonder of it. The blues dipped lower, then higher, then inverted and blossomed like a rose with petals of bright cobalt. A more mesmerizing, awe-inspiring, breathtaking sight Çeda had never seen. "They seem *alive*."

"They *are* alive."

"I mean together. All of them."

"I know what you meant. But they *are* alive together. They're a tribe, Çeda. They are each separate, but they are all one."

They walked into the lake, which, even one hundred paces out, even two hundred, was only ankle-deep. There were little creatures in the water—pink ones, no larger than weevils, flitting to and fro along the bottom of the water. These were the brine shrimp her mother had told her about. As Ahya and Çeda walked, kicking up clouds of white salt in the water, and as the billowing mass of blazing blues swooped and wheeled, casting heavy shadows, the tiny pink creatures grew agitated. That's when the birds began diving toward the water.

Hundreds, thousands of them, came low over the lake, dipping their beaks. They hardly made a splash, so quick were they, but it made the mirror surface of the lake dance with movement. Çeda began to laugh. It was happening all around them. They were surrounded on all sides and above by the bright blue birds. The sound of their beaks dipping into the water began to sound like rain.

A rain of blue, her mother had called it several days before, when she'd said they'd be starting their pilgrimage here. *My mother brought me here when I was young,* Ahya had said, *and so I'll bring you.*

Çeda had no idea who her grandmother was—Ahya told so few stories about her—but she was glad to be here now, holding her mother's hand, walking in this magical place.

"Now take a handful of water," Ahya said, reaching down and scooping up some water into the palm of her hand. She lifted it above her, and the birds flew closer, many speeding like javelins over her hand, snatching up the tiny shrimp skipping on her outstretched palm.

Çeda did the same, both excited and afraid. The shrimp wriggled, tickling her skin as she raised her hand and waited, and then she laughed as the blues stormed over her, picking at the shrimp. Their beaks felt like hundreds of beetles crawling across the skin of her palm. But amazingly they touched *only* her hand. Nowhere else was she even brushed, except by the wind of their wings. Still, she cringed away, fearful they'd start pecking at *her,* yet mesmerized in the same breath.

Her mother was smiling, and as she picked up another handful, she too began to laugh. They stood ankle-deep in the water, alive and laughing, as if they were the only two people in all the world.

Çeda let go of her mother's hand. She ran across the lake. Chased the birds as the falcons were doing far above, but just like them, she was much too slow and never so much as touched one.

Suddenly the cloud of them was so thick she lost sight of Ahya. She spun around, wondering where she'd gone and gradually her delight was replaced with worry. She called for her mother, afraid she was going in the wrong direction.

But then Ahya strode through the blue cloud, the birds parting for her as if she were Nalamae herself. "Come, Çeda," she said, holding out her hand. "It's time to go."

"I don't wish to go," she replied.

"And yet we must."

Çeda hesitated, staring up through the haze of birds, the intense blue of their feathers mixing with the pale blue of the sky above them. *They look like the sea. Like waves on the deep blue sea.* With great reluctance, she turned to her mother, who was still standing there, her hand still poised. Çeda didn't want this day to end. She would stay here with her mother forever if she could, but after a moment's pause, she reached out and took her mother's hand.

———— ⟵●⟶ ————

Çeda woke with the sun beating down on her.

"I don't wish to go," she whispered to the dry desert air.

She sat up. Her lips were cracked and bleeding. The memories of her mother and that distant day were so strong she didn't at first remember where she was. Nor could she remember the last time she'd had anything to drink. Yesterday morning, she realized, which wasn't good. Not in the dust-dry heat of summer.

More and more of the horrific night came back to her. Dardzada showing her the adichara bloom. Drugging her. Tattooing her and marking her with something she couldn't even see.

She stood and stared up at the sun, then at the stone and sand around her. None of it looked the least bit familiar.

She tried to gain her bearings but couldn't. She had no idea which direction she'd come from before she'd collapsed to the desert floor. She also had no idea which way she'd gone after leaving Sharakhai. South and east would be a good guess, but that was the best she could come up with. Still, it couldn't be *that* far, could it?

She tried looking for footprints, but it was no good. The ground here was either stone or sand that had shifted a thousand times since she'd fallen asleep. She would wait until the sun started going down to regain her bearings, and then head northwest. She sat up and pulled her shirt over her head. The dried blood pulled painfully at the fresh tattoo, but she desperately needed the shade, so she sat, legs crossed, shirt held over her head like some sorry tent in the bazaar.

She waited for an hour. She would have waited longer, would have waited for the cool hours to arrive before she began walking, but she was already dehydrated, and the risk of desert fever was getting higher by the hour. And, she realized with a shock, tonight was Beht Zha'ir. By Tulathan's bright eyes, the asirim would be roaming the desert tonight.

That was enough to get her back on her feet and heading toward what she judged to be west. She must be quite a sight, plodding along like a boneyard shambler, bare-chested with her shirt wrapped sloppily about her head, a fresh, bloody tattoo on her back.

As she walked, she kept an eye out for Tauriyat, the hill in the center of Sharakhai. It was visible for leagues around the city, but there were places in the desert where tricks of the land—depressions, Dardzada had called them—would hide the city from careless travelers.

She only needed to get to the edge, to the next rise, however slight it might seem from here, and she would see Sharakhai. She knew she would.

That was when a cackle sounded behind her. An animal laugh. A chill ran down her frame. It was the bone crushers' call. Black laughers. Massive hyenas that traveled in packs, taking down horses, gazelle, even unwary travelers and the massive red lizards from the western reaches.

She reached down to her belt. Her knife. Why hadn't she brought a knife?

Stop, Çeda. Think. There might be time to hide from them. There was a rocky ridgeline ahead; it was shallow but might hide her if she was quick, or offer some rocks to fight with, if not.

She set off at a lope, dizzy as she tried to pick up her pace. She'd not gone fifty strides when the sound of the black laughers grew stronger. With a glance back, she saw one of them crest the dune. Massive and broad at the shoulder. Black head and withers and a brown, spotted coat. Round ears and wicked eyes that were locked on her.

It laughed, its head bobbing up and down, as if exceedingly pleased with its find. Another came up beside it, and another after that, both larger than the first. By Goezhen's wicked smile, they were the size of small ponies. Her lope became a run, then an all-out sprint.

The laughers hounded after her, all three of them laughing now that the chase was on. Çeda looked for rocks as she ran for the ridge. She slipped into an uneven wadi that wound up toward it. She slipped, twisting her ankle. The sound of the laughers was closer, and she stood and sprinted on with two fist-sized rocks in her hands. One of the laughers was well ahead of the others. She turned and loosed one of her rocks, catching it against the shoulder. The beast yelped, but kept on running until Çeda caught it square against the skull with another throw.

She ran again, but she was losing hope. The laughers would take her down with little trouble. They'd nip at her heels, then bite, and drop her to the sandy earth. They'd surround her before darting in and clamping their huge jaws on her ankles or throat.

Most of the land below the ridge was bright beneath the sun, but there was a narrow line that sat in the lee. The shadows there were heavy, but Çeda could see something. Forms lying in the shade.

The first of them stood. A wolf with a white pelt. Others stood behind it. One, two, three of them. More.

Çeda kept running, until something heavy hit her from behind. She fell and rolled, kicking sharply, her foot connecting with the laugher's black muzzle. Its yelp turned into a deep growl. It watched, legs spread wide, keg-sized head lowered, beady eyes flicking between her and the maned wolves.

Çeda stood and backed away slowly as the other two laughers joined the first. One was bleeding, red blood matting the rough fur along the top of its head, dripping into its left eye.

The white wolf approached. Even in the weeks since she'd first seen it, it had grown. Its head was now even with hers. It would not be a match for the bone crushers, not even one of them, but its pack padded up behind it, teeth bared, low growls issuing from their throats. Its brothers and sisters were the same size, including the one with the scars along its head and withers that Çeda noticed when she'd first come across them. The white wolf's uncles and aunts were rangy things, their heads higher than Çeda's.

The wounded laugher was a massive brute. It crept toward Çeda while watching the white wolf, making clear that this lost, lonely girl was *its* kill. But as it came, the white wolf came too, and when the laugher darted in, the white wolf charged, growling and barking and snapping for the bone crusher's throat.

The laugher backed away, and then attacked the maned wolf, using its mass to bowl the smaller beast over. The two of them wrestled in the sand for only a moment before the rest of the wolf pack charged in and snapped at the laugher's legs and head and haunches. The scarred wolf was the most vicious of them, the least concerned for its own safety. It bit and growled, its movements a blur.

The bone crushers were violent beasts, but they were not brave and wanted numbers in their favor. The other two laughers darted forward, snapped at the wolves, but only so their fallen brother could rise and sprint away from the pack. Then all three of them galloped away, down the wadi and toward the deeper desert.

The maned wolves watched them go, staring intently until they were lost from sight, and then the adult wolves padded back to the shade and lay down, pleased to relax in the shade once more. The white wolf, though, turned to

Çeda, as did its brothers and sisters. One by one they lost interest and peeled away, leaving only the white, and Çeda standing before it.

"Thank you," Çeda said.

The wolf merely stared, standing tall, its bluish eyes meeting Çeda's. Then it turned and trotted, not toward the pack, but to a path of sorts that led up to the top of the shallow ridge.

Çeda followed, with no idea where the wolf might be leading her but curious all the same. When she came to the top, she saw a dark line in the sand.

The Haddah, she realized. It was the Haddah, and if she followed it back, it would bring her to Sharakhai.

The wolf nipped at her heels until she was in motion and heading down the slope toward the riverbed, then turned and loped back down the path to its pack.

The sun was setting when Çeda knocked on the door, her head pounding, her legs shaking from the walk. She'd stopped when she reached Sharakhai, but only once, to drink her fill of water from a well, before she continued on toward Emre's home, the one he shared with his brother Rafa.

She knocked again. She needed shelter. That was one reason she came. She'd never return to Dardzada's. She knew that much. But there was another driving reason she needed to see Emre.

She was about to knock again when the door opened. Rafa stood there, his curly hair hanging over his face, his eyes bleary, but when he saw her his eyes went wide, and he looked up and down the street, perhaps expecting someone to be following her. But the street was empty, unless you counted the old woman in a billowing yellow jalabiya watering the flowers outside her window a few doors down.

"Gods above, come in, Çeda." He ushered her in, but not before looking along the street one last time. He ran and got her some water, handing it to her with concern in his eyes. His curly hair was a ragged mop around his head. "Now, what *happened* to you?"

"Is Emre here?"

"He's asleep."

"I'm up," Emre said from the darkened doorway on the far side of the narrow room.

"How can you be sleeping now, you bloody great oaf?" Çeda was trying to lighten the tone, but it went over miserably.

"I'm helping Rafa unload a ship tonight," Emre replied while yawning and rubbing his eyes. "Make a few sylval. We can't all find room and board from a fat apothecary." No sooner had he said these words than his eyes widened. "Çeda, what's wrong?" He stepped forward, looking her over with clear concern in his eyes. She might have cried were she not so utterly exhausted.

"Can we talk?" Çeda asked Emre, glancing to Rafa.

Rafa looked between the two of them, nodded and stepped away. "I'll head in early, Emre. Meet me there when you can."

Emre nodded, and soon Rafa was gone, leaving the two of them alone.

"Now tell me." He spotted the bloody back of her shirt. "*Dardzada* did this? I'll kill him, Çeda."

She couldn't summon up the anger. Not now. It had been burned out of her in the desert. "Tell me what he did," Çeda said, wanting desperately to know but fearful just the same.

Without waiting for an answer, she turned around and pulled her shirt up. It tugged her skin painfully in a few spots, but she paid it no mind, and soon it was off, leaving her naked from the waist up.

"It's too bloody," he said. He took the shirt from her, wetted it with water, and cleaned the wound quickly and efficiently, wincing when he saw that it was causing her pain. "I don't . . ."

"Just draw it, here." She shook out her shirt, which made a filthy circle of dust and sand on the floor.

Emre used it to draw and began moving his finger through the accumulated grit, staring at her back, then marking the dust, looking again, embellishing more and more as he went. It was one of the old symbols, a single image with layer upon layer of meaning.

Çeda knew what it was long before he finished, but still she waited, hardly believing what Dardzada had inked upon her back.

"What does it say?" Emre asked, quiet as a mouse.

She reached out and traced a finger along the symbol Emre had drawn. She'd never felt so alone. "He's marked me with the tribes' symbol for a bastard child."

It proved what Dardzada thought of her. It was his way of disowning her, of saying she was no daughter of his. Her mind raced through the times Ahya had spoken with Dardzada, how they'd fought, but they'd laughed, too. She thought how Dardzada had wept when Ahya had died. She thought of many things, and through it all, she was lonely. Alone. Dardzada was her last link to her mother, and now he was gone, too. There was no way she could go back to him, no way she could forgive him.

She didn't know when it started, but she realized she had pulled herself into a ball, her knees against her naked chest, and she was sobbing into her crossed arms.

Emre, gods bless him, was holding her gently to his chest, rocking her slowly back and forth, and when she felt his warm tears falling onto her shoulder, she realized she was not alone. She was not without family. Her mother might be gone; perhaps Dardzada was too. But Emre was her blood. And she was his.

Chapter 31

Emre approached Matron Zohra's estate at twilight. He didn't ring the bell. He simply waited until Enasia opened the door and sprinted across the carriage circle to meet him, her orange dress flowing in her wake.

She opened the gate and drew him by the wrist onto the grounds, then threw him against the interior of the wall with a force that no longer surprised him. She pressed herself against him, kissing his neck passionately, raking fingers through his hair. She pressed her hips against his, grinding as she nipped his ear, then bit him fiercely, but only for a moment. And when her lips met his, they were warm as the Haddah was cool. There was no doubt that her form was soft and inviting. Her scent was like rose and jasmine and the brightness of the desert in spring. But Emre was repulsed by it all, by every aspect of her. Yet his kisses remained fervent. His breath came fast as hers. His hand roamed up along her hip, along the soft valley of her stomach, over one ripe breast, squeezing as he pressed himself against her.

Soon she pulled away and led him along the drive to the carriage circle and into the manor house. The moment she closed the door, he spun her around and pressed her against the door, leaning down to place kisses along her neck, as he grabbed a fistful of her hair.

"Returning favors?" she asked, her breath coming heavily.

"One good turn deserves another."

They kissed for longer this time, his hand now slipping between her thighs, rubbing as she stroked his hardening cock through his trousers. He gripped a clutch of her hair, tilted her head back, and bit her neck. She drew breath sharply and reached to undo his trousers, but stopped when he grabbed her wrists and broke away. "Did you get rid of him?"

"I did better than that!" She tried to step closer, but he held her at bay, a thing she seemed to enjoy, for she fought harder to reach him. "I had my Lady send him away for a week!"

"You didn't!"

"I did! I told Matron Zohra there might be more of your elixir in Ishmantep. Rengin's gone to fetch it."

The elixirs had not, in fact, done a thing to help the Matron's condition—at least, not according to Enasia—but hope had taken root that the third one would have some small effect if given enough time. Emre had hinted that his supply was running low, and that perhaps more could be found in Ishmantep. Enasia had done the rest.

"The Matron won't discover us?" he asked.

She grinned at him, a mischievous twinkle in her eyes. "I've locked her in her room. She won't bother us."

That thought made Emre's stomach turn, but he tried not to let it show. "You are a wicked, wicked woman."

"Isn't that why you like me?"

She squealed as he swept her up in his arms and carried her up the stairs. "I cannot deny it!" When they reached the landing, he frowned and set her down. "What am I thinking? How about a glass of wine?" He took one step down to forestall her from going.

"More than a glass, if you please." She continued up to the second floor, then looked down at him from the railing. "There are dozens of tankards in the cellar. Take any you wish except for those along the far wall." And with that she turned and headed for the parlor, her flame-orange dress sweeping the floor like a painter's brush.

Emre went to the kitchen and took the stairs down to
the cellar. Enasia hadn't lied. There were several hundred
bottles and dozens of small tankards of wine, many of
good vintage from all across the Kingdoms: Mirean, Malasani, even some from the far shores of the Austral Sea. He
selected one of the tankards at random, then returned to
the kitchen and poured the wine into a decanter. He
grabbed two delicate glasses and set them next to it, then
retrieved a folded paper packet from the pouch at his belt.
After unfolding it carefully, he poured the white powder
into Enasia's glass and drowned it in wine. After filling the
other glass, he took them both in one hand, the decanter in
the other, and headed upstairs to the third floor.

He found her in the parlor, naked, lying on her stomach
in the middle of a tiger-skin rug. Her eyes were lost in the
leaping flames of the nearby fireplace, so he moved to the
marble table behind the low couch and set the wine and
glasses down. For a time, he watched the firelight dance
upon her skin. There was no denying it—Enasia was a true
beauty. But he hadn't lied when he'd called her wicked.

For long hours of the day Matron Zohra would sit in her
room and stare at the walls. Zohra had no family to speak
of. They'd been few enough to begin with, and the rest had
apparently died, leaving only Enasia and the generosity of
the House of Kings to care for her. Sadly, though, Enasia
was a woman who cared for the coin that filled her purse,
the advantages that living with a favored Lady conferred,
and precious little else. She was nakedly ambitious.

From what Emre could see, whatever love Enasia might
have harbored for Zohra had evaporated years ago. Enasia
would leave her Lady alone for long stretches at a time,
sometimes not bothering to check on her for a day or more,
especially if Rengin had been called away from the estate
to handle Zohra's business. Enasia stole as well—anything
she thought might go unnoticed. She was head of Zohra's
estate for the time being, but Enasia knew it wouldn't last.
Sooner or later, as she'd told Emre more than once, Zohra
would be gone, and what good would all that money do the
Kings? They would swoop in and gobble up the estate and
any remaining possessions and leave Enasia a beggar on

the street. How could that be considered justice for the time she'd served, she'd asked him more than once.

If they knew what you were doing, Emre had thought, *a different sort of justice entirely would greet you.*

As his days with Enasia had worn on, Emre had forced himself to think of her in other ways, to pretend she was some other woman, lest she sense his disgust and set him aside for another. At first he had tried to imagine she was more like Çeda, but thinking of Çeda and Enasia in the same breath made him uncomfortable, so he began to put different faces on her—of any woman he'd taken a liking to.

The deceptions, to himself and Enasia both, were necessary, for as fate would have it, he was hoping to use Zohra too. His entire purpose here was to find the records which Hamid said would be secreted away somewhere within this house. Searching her home when the woman was already being used gave him pause, but there was little he could do about Zohra's state of mind. As cruel as it was, he had to find what he needed, and the gods could do with her what they would.

"What keeps you, Emre?" Enasia continued to stare into the fire, her calves scissoring lazily as her bottom swayed back and forth.

"The wine. You've a taste for something sweet, I hope."

Before arriving, he'd planned on waiting until they'd finished a glass or two, letting her drink deeply before giving her the soporific. Drink, like so many other vices, was something Enasia wasn't the least bit shy about, but the truth of it was he couldn't stand to be with her any longer. After three weeks with her, the thought of spending another night, even a short one, made him shudder.

She rolled over, baring herself unabashedly. "I've a taste for something salty," she stared down at his crotch, "but the wine will do for now."

He moved to her side, decanter in one hand, glasses cradled in the other. "Then wine it shall be." He set the decanter down and offered her the tainted wine.

He thought she might be difficult, insist on making love before they shared their wine, but true to everything Emre had come to expect from her, she took the glass and downed half of it in one swallow. She stared at the wine

with a puckered expression. "A bit sour, don't you think?"
Then she downed the rest before pouring herself another.
"Drinkable just the same."

Emre glanced at the open doorway. "You're sure Zohra
won't hear us?"

"Why are you so distracted? I told you, she's locked in
her room."

"Even still. I wouldn't like her to know."

"Why not? I may have gentlemen callers."

"You said she was very particular."

"She is. Or was . . ." She drained the last of her wine and
held out the glass for Emre to refill. He did, and she
shrugged. "In any case, you could wage a battle in this
room and no one on the first floor would hear it. And even
if she *did*, she wouldn't care. Not anymore."

"You don't think so?"

"She becomes less like her old hateful self every day. I
tell you, she can already see the swaying of grasses in the
green, farther fields."

"There are days I wish *I* could see them."

"And why, dear Emre, would you wish to pass beyond
this world?"

To beg Rafa for forgiveness. "We'll all be there soon
enough, I suppose. I just wonder what it's like. I wonder if
the old gods are truly there."

"Of course they are. Why wouldn't they be?"

"They passed beyond these shores, who's to say they
wouldn't pass beyond the next?"

Enasia frowned. "I never thought of it that way."

*Of course not. You're too concerned about stealing from
an old, dying woman.*

Her eyes began to droop. She seemed to notice, for she
drew in a sudden breath and leaned over to kiss Emre's
neck. "Why do you still have your clothes on?"

While pulling at the ties to his shirt and tugging the tails
free from his trousers, she pulled his mouth down to hers
and kissed him. One hand slipped beneath his shirt and
raked his skin, then wriggled down into his trousers, stroking him while she stroked herself. He worried that her
thirst for lovemaking would throw off the effects of the

soporific, at least for a time, but he trusted Hamid's promise—a count of two hundred, he'd said, and her eyes will close of their own accord.

He laid her gently down on the tiger skin, laid kisses on her lips, at the hollow where neck met shoulder, on her breasts, and then stitched more of them slowly across her soft belly. As he did, her head lolled to one side, and the hand she'd been running through his hair fell to her side with a thump.

"Enasia?" he called softly.

She didn't respond, and a soft snore mingled with the crackle of the nearby flames.

He rose immediately and found a blanket to lay over her. Then he poured the remaining wine into the base of a decorative fern near the window. He left just enough that she would think they'd nearly finished it. It was a good deal of wine, certainly enough to account for a night of heavy sleep.

After fixing his trousers and shirt, he found a lantern and walked into the hall. He knew much of the house by now, not from walking through it himself, but from talking to Enasia over the past few weeks. He knew where Matron Zohra kept herself most days, where she took her meals, where she might write letters to the Matrons or the Kings or those who lived on Goldenhill; and so, without needing to wander, he already knew the key places to search. He found the study where she kept her writing desk. It looked rarely used—dust upon its surface, a musty smell to the room. He rifled through the desktop and its drawers all the same, looking through the papers. It took longer than he liked. He had come to letters late, and it still took him time to take in what a page was saying. He plodded his way through the pages of each journal, through the few loose papers stored there, eventually realizing there was nothing remotely close to what he was looking for.

He needed names. The names of the babies Matron Zohra had delivered. There was no other way to find the one Hamid wanted.

He found a strongbox in a hidden compartment behind a painting of an oryx standing on a white mountain cliff. It reminded him of his journey to the blooming fields with

Çeda when they'd been young—a dead oryx had been caught in the adichara as the rattlewings buzzed around them. How long ago that seemed. He and Çeda had been so close then, but now . . . Now they were distant, more so than they'd ever been. He missed her. He should tell her, he knew, but she was spending so much time at the pits, with her classes, perhaps, or maybe throwing herself into training for her next bout. She was so evasive about where she spent her time lately. It made him wonder if she'd found a man and was too embarrassed to tell him about it.

The strongbox, oddly, was unlocked, but when he levered the lid open he understood why. It was empty.

He tried another room, a private parlor near the solarium on the ground floor, but found nothing there. He searched other rooms, becoming progressively more worried as he went, not just because he feared he wouldn't find the records, but because he feared they no longer existed. It had been an age since anyone had seen them.

Years ago, an agent of the Moonless Host had worked as an aide to Matron Zohra. She claimed that the Lady kept meticulous records. The Kings would not have approved, for she was documenting the birth records of those she'd personally attended to over the years. Because Zohra had kept it secret, however, they'd had no opportunity to complain; the records were in her own hand, penned after the business of birthing was complete. The aide discovered it purely by accident when she'd stepped into the Matron's offices one day and found her writing in the book. The Matron had closed it as if nothing were amiss, but her aide had seen enough to want to know more. She'd returned to Zohra's office only one other time, to look for the book. She'd found it and was surprised to see that it contained names, dates, notes about the baby's health, hair, eye color, and weight. She'd had only moments alone with it, but managed to write down several names and reported it to the Host that very night. But their sense that they'd found something valuable was short-lived. Three Blade Maidens had come for the Host's agent that very night. She'd been beheaded the next morning.

Hamid doubted Zohra would have stopped the practice.

Likely she'd made up some story about her aide to hide the real reason for having her taken and killed. Emre had agreed, but now he wondered. Perhaps she *had* stopped, or perhaps she'd disposed of her records when she'd taken ill. Or perhaps the Kings had found out and taken them from her.

He searched long into the night, through every room except for those few assigned exclusively to Matron Zohra. But when the soft light of dawn began to brighten in the east, he knew he didn't have much longer. The sleeping agent he'd given Enasia wouldn't last forever.

He might simply wait for Enasia to wake. Come again another night to try again, but he worried she would become suspicious, and Rengin would return at the end of the week. He was already suspicious of Emre, and would only be more so after his fruitless journey to Ishmantep.

So instead of opening the door, he returned to the parlor and found Enasia's belt. He opened the velvet pouch attached to it, and took out a small brass key. With it in hand, he headed for Matron Zohra's rooms. He listened carefully at the door. Hearing nothing, he unlocked it and stepped inside, entering a sour-smelling anteroom filled with dusty tables and a stained carpet. When he moved through the peaked doorway into the next room, the smell of piss and shit struck him like a club.

The Matron Zohra was sitting crookedly in a chair, staring into one corner of the room. He could see little of her from this vantage save her gray hair, which was bundled atop her head, some held in place with ornate gold pins, some straggly locks falling about her face and shoulders.

"Matron?" Emre called as he approached.

She didn't move a muscle. He feared she might be dead until he noticed her quivering.

"Matron?" he said again.

Receiving no response, he moved into the corner and squatted until he was directly in her line of sight. It was all he could do not to let her stench make him gag.

The sun was rising now, and Enasia would wake at any moment.

This was none of his affair. What was one highborn lady to him? Why did he care if she was mistreated by her servants?

He didn't. He needed to get the information he'd come for and leave this place as soon as possible.

"I've come from the House of Kings, Matron." He would never say such a thing to someone in their right mind, but he needed her to think of Külaşan, to think of the sons or daughters of his who she'd delivered. "It's most urgent. The Wandering King is dead. He passed only this morning, and we must find one of true blood, one of *his* blood."

He said it while feeling as small as he'd ever felt. The sight of her like this . . . He had no idea why it was affecting him so, but there were tears in his eyes. They ran down his cheek as he reached out and took one of her frail hands in his. "Grandmother, are you well?" Her head twitched, and her eyes tried to focus, but he guessed it was little more than surprise at being touched, at being spoken to like a human being. He had planned on wheedling out of her the information that Hamid needed. But he couldn't. Not like this.

He returned to the antechamber and poured water from the tall ewer there into a bowl. He rummaged through her wardrobe and found several clean nightdresses. He ripped two of them into rags. The third he left whole.

After placing them on the rug in the center of the bedroom, he moved to Zohra's side and lifted her carefully, then laid her down as gently as he could manage. He pulled her dress slowly up and off her frame, no easy thing, as her night soil had stuck it to her thighs, backside, and hips.

Dear gods, how can anyone be forced to live in such a way?

He began using the strips of cloth to clean her, slowly working along her frame, wiping away the worst of it, exposing the many rashes and sores, moving as gently as he could manage. Then he refilled the water in the bowl and did it again.

She whimpered as he worked, but she didn't try to stop him, nor did she say a word against him. She simply watched, confusion in her eyes—confusion, he imagined, not just over who he was, but who *she* was, why she was here, and what was happening to her.

He was forced to fill the bowl with fresh water a third time, and rip another dress to finish, but when he had, he dressed her in the clean nightdress and carried her to her bed. As he laid her down, she spoke for the first time, her voice a tumble of loose stones. "Who are you?"

"My name is Emre," he said simply.

Her eyes went cloudy for a moment, and when they returned, she managed a smile and patted his wrist. "Where's Enasia?"

"I'm right here."

Emre stood and spun and found Enasia standing in the doorway in her orange dress, eyes bleary, the look on her face a study in rage.

"What do you think you're doing?" She advanced like a captain of the Silver Spears, all cocksure attitude and puffed-up authority. "You will leave this place immediately," she said, pulling herself taller. "You'll leave this place and never return, or I'll have the Maidens come to take you away!"

Cold purpose filled Emre as he strode toward her. He stopped only when the two of them were face-to-face. "And what do you suppose the Maidens will do when they learn how you've treated one of their own?"

"Do you think for a moment they'll believe *you* over *me?*"

Emre smiled easily. "Me? No. But they'll surely believe her." He stepped closer still. "Here's what's going to happen. You will gather your things—*your* things only; you'll show me before you leave—and then you will leave. This very morning. And you'll never return."

She set her chin before speaking again. "And if I don't?"

"When I leave I'm going to the Four Arrows. I'll tell them I heard horrible moaning from within this estate while walking past. Someone will come to investigate. They'll find Matron Zohra, and they'll get her some help. They're good people, and they'll make sure she's well tended until her life can be sorted out. I'll return every day, in the days ahead, and if I find you here, a letter will be delivered to the House of Maidens, detailing the neglect I've found. And when *they* come to investigate, they'll not stop at speaking with you, nor with Rengin. They'll speak with Matron Zohra. And when they do, what are the chances that she'll remain silent?"

Enasia glanced at Zohra. "She doesn't even remember who she is!"

Zohra stared back, a defiant look on her face, but said nothing.

"Are you willing to bet your life on that?" Emre asked. "One recollection of how you've mistreated her is all it will take, and, as I said, we both know how the Maidens deal with those who harm their own."

Enasia licked her lips. Fear had grown in her eyes, but now there was dread. She glanced about the room, to the floor and the shit-stained rags, then to Matron Zohra lying in her bed. And then, without saying another word, she stepped away, spun around, and ran from the room.

As the stairs down the hall creaked with her passage, Emre returned to the bedside. "All will be well," he said, pulling the blankets higher.

Zohra seemed not to care. She had the most determined look on her face, like a child trying to figure out how to speak her mind without all the right words, without all the right concepts. "I remember who I am," she said at last.

"Of course you do."

He was just beginning to turn away when he heard her call, "Veşdi."

He turned around. "I'm sorry?"

"Veşdi," she said, her glistening eyes full of pride. "Veşdi is Külaşan's eldest living son."

"Lord Veşdi, the Master of Coin?"

She nodded triumphantly.

"You're sure?"

"Of course I am."

"Bless you, grandmother." He leaned in and kissed her on the forehead. "You are wise, the pride of Sharakhai." Emre had said these words to give her some comfort, a bit of succor in the storm, but her smile, however bright it was at first, was fleeting, and soon she was staring up at the ceiling, lips quivering, her eyes going glassy once more.

Emre stared at her for a time, hoping her mind had gone to a peaceful place, and then, after one more squeeze of her hand, he gathered up all the rubbish and left the room.

Chapter 32

ĊEDA OPENED HER EYES to see a stone ceiling above her. Dim light came from a lamp hung from a standing iron hook. Five similar, unlit lamps were standing just next to this one along the wall. It smelled dank and the air was humid, with a strange mixture of smells—antiseptic elixirs assailing a mildewy odor. Water dripped in a thin stream in the corner, where the stones were black with mold.

Her head rolled to one side. She was lying on a narrow wooden table, her arms strapped to planks that jutted outward from the table like a cross. Her legs were similarly restricted, and as weak as she was, she couldn't lift her head to see what was binding her. Her bandaged right arm, throbbing like a slowly dying pendulum, flared with pain when she tried to move it. By her left arm were two thick straps that might have been strapped down—one across the elbow, another near her shoulder—but weren't; only the one by her wrist had actually been strapped in place, and for some reason even that had been left loose.

After pulling and working her arm slowly back and forth, her wrist scraped through the thick leather restraint. Her right arm was firmly strapped down in three places, but with her left now free she was able to loosen and finally undo the strap closest to her shoulder. Which was when the contents of the table against the wall finally registered.

Laid out in precise rows were dozens of gleaming saws and knives and pliers and pincers and awls and a host of strange hooked contrivances, the purpose of which Çeda couldn't even begin to guess. A shelf filled with blue bottles and strips of dull brown cloth and pewter bowls stood above the surgeon's instruments. Panic gripped her as she took it in, laying it against the reality of waking in this dank place after going to Dardzada for help.

Dardzada was going to cut off her arm. He'd realized it was too dangerous to take her to the Maidens—or perhaps his agent there was unreachable, or dead, or had refused him—and for some reason he couldn't allow himself to let her die, so he'd brought her here, wherever this was, to cut off her arm and stop the spread of the poison.

No, she thought. *No, no, no. Dardzada would never do such a thing. Not to me.*

But she knew those were the words of the scared little girl inside her. When it came down to it, Dardzada was a pragmatic man. He *would* cut off her arm, with no regrets, if he thought it would save her. But she wasn't willing to accept this fate. Not yet. There was still time to reach the Maidens. She just had to make Dardzada see that.

Fingers shaking, she worked faster at the remaining two straps on her immobilized arm, first with care, then with ever more frantic movements. When she touched the restraint around her wrist, her hand and arm flared with so much pain she mewled like a child while pulling at the leather, but she didn't let it stop her. *I will not lie here and let him take my arm!*

Finally her wrist was free. She managed to pull herself up to a sitting position, cradle her arm, and work at the straps on her legs. Only her ankles were strapped down, and they were both loose enough that she managed to undo them in little time. Even so, she was drenched in sweat by the time it was all done, and her ears had begun to ring.

She was wearing a white thawb with yellow dye worked into the cuffs of the sleeves and hem of the skirt. The right sleeve had been rolled up to expose her arm, but she rolled it gently down to cover the bandages and the sickening blue color of her skin.

There was a metallic clank to her right. As she turned to look, seeing a staircase for the first time, her head swam.

Footsteps scraping over stone. A yellow light shone down, wavering so badly it made her sick to her stomach.

"Hello?" came a gravelly voice.

It certainly wasn't Dardzada. Who the man might be she had no idea, but one thing was certain: No good could come of staying here.

She took up one of the sharpest and longest of the implements on the table. It wasn't a *proper* fighting knife, but it would do. Then she shuffled with drunken steps and flattened herself against the wall near the archway leading to the stairs.

"Hello? Are you awake, girl?"

The light grew brighter, waving over the floor of the room. Çeda leaned more heavily into the wall behind her and fought back the wave of dizziness and nausea threatening to upend her. Into the room, holding a lantern in one hand, walked a crooked old man with a scraggly beard and round spectacles.

Çeda lurched forward waving the knife before her. "Get back!" She swiped it once, twice.

The old man's eyes widened and he stepped away in fright. "Stop it! Stop it!"

"I'm—" She was so bloody dizzy, and the ringing in her ears was growing. She swiped again with the knife. "Stay away from me!"

The man backed further away toward the strange table, his spectacles accentuating his fear-widened eyes. "You mustn't leave."

Çeda backed into the stairway passage.

The man set his lamp down on the table with the gleaming instruments and moved toward her. "You mustn't leave, girl. Dardzada's gone to the speak to the Matron—"

He said more, but Çeda could no longer discern his words. Her ears were ringing so badly all she could hear was her heart pounding and the sound of her constricted throat swallowing over and over.

They were lies in any case. *Dardzada's gone to the speak to the Matron*. He'd done no such thing. And she was proven right when the old man tried to rush her. She swiped the blade viciously across the path of his upraised hands. She felt little resistance, but suddenly blood was cascading down his arms. He gripped one hand tightly, where a deep cut split his palm. She might have seen bone, but couldn't be sure. She was concentrating on backing away, stepping slowly up the stairs.

The light from below dwindled as she climbed, wary of his trying to stop her again, but he never did. She saw only shadows flickering, grasping for her, and thought she might have heard screams of pain mingling with the ringing in her ears. Her mother's screams? She couldn't be sure.

She stumbled from the staircase into a small shop filled with a thousand thousand bottles—green and blue and red, some filled with liquid, some with powders, one massive glass jar teeming with blue leeches.

She staggered through a door and into the city. People watched her with worried glances. She hid the knife up her left sleeve and wandered quickly away, with no real idea where she was. The buildings looked affluent, but she could tell no more than that.

She soon found the Trough, though. Horses and carts clattered along by the dozen, some with crates and amphorae headed to the bazaar, others with strings of animals headed to the slaughterhouses and meat markets, yet more with ivory-skinned barbarians headed to the slave blocks. Most were on foot, however—hundreds, thousands of people, some wearing the thawbs and kaftans of the desert, others wearing the oppressive coats and long trousers of the southern kingdom, others still wearing little more than loincloths and sandals and bright jewelry around their necks and wrists and ankles.

Watching the very lifeblood of Sharakhai pass her by, she wondered where she could go. How had she got here? She failed to recall even the smallest of details. She looked down and found a bloody knife in her left hand, and wondered if she'd cut herself. She didn't recognize the knife, so she dropped it, and it fell with a thump to the street. She headed along the busy street to another she recognized as the Spear.

The Maidens, she realized. She had wanted to reach the Maidens. That was what she'd been trying to do these past weeks, wasn't it?

She walked steadily east along the Spear, cradling her right arm as she walked, watching her path ahead carefully to ensure no one accidentally collided with her. The day had brought rare summer showers, and the humid air reminded her of a dank basement with wicked instruments—perhaps a dream she'd recently had.

Reach the Maidens. Reach the Maidens. It was the only thought that kept her feet moving despite the oppressive heat.

The thought was still circling—*reach the Maidens*—when a strange silence settled over the street, and she looked up and saw them: a troop of Blade Maidens riding along the Spear on horseback.

In one moment she was utterly relieved, and the next the blood was draining from her face. The ringing in her ears faded, and was replaced by a hollow feeling that opened up inside her and yawned wide as the desert's maw. She'd been wrong. She hadn't wanted to go to the Maidens. Not like this. If they found her on their own, they would know what she'd done, and they would kill her.

She'd made a better plan, hadn't she? She was sure she had, but she could no longer remember what it was.

The Maidens rode their black horses at an easy pace, ten of them riding two by two. Traffic stopped. Carts pulled aside. People crowded the edges of the street and bowed their heads as the Maidens passed. Even a pair of city guardsmen in their conical helms and mail hauberks stood to the side and held their spears tight, bowing their heads as low as anyone else.

Çeda wanted to run, but that was just her fear surging up, trying to make her act. This was just like the pits. She could not show her fear. She stepped to the side of the street like everyone else, slipping in ox dung as she did. She was careful to duck behind a cart and then stand behind several other women. Though her bandaged right hand was

swollen grossly and the sleeve of her left arm was marked
with fresh blood, she bowed her head and crossed her arms
over her chest.

The black horses came closer. Two passed, then two
more. Çeda dared not look up, but the urge was so over-
powering she caught herself glancing at the hooves of the
horses, stopping just shy of looking up at the nearest
Maiden.

When men whispered over their wine, they said that the
Maidens moved slowly so they could peer into the minds of
those they passed, but Çeda was doubtful. Had they been
able to peer into *her* mind, they would have known of her
treks into the desert, would have learned of her days shading packages for Osman. Then again, she could count on
one hand the number of times she'd stood beneath their
gaze; maybe she'd simply been beneath their notice, or
been one of so many that they hadn't been able to detect
her sins. Perhaps now that one of them had fought her in
the desert, they'd be able to find her. By the desert's hot
breath, maybe they'd be *drawn* to her.

Gods, she was so infernally dizzy. She raised her good
hand to steady herself on the woman before her, but managed to stop herself, to breathe deeply. More black horses
passed until two remained. They slowed and came to a
halt. The Maidens ahead paused as well, perhaps at some
unseen signal from those at the rear.

There was silence along the Spear. The nearest Maid-
en's horse pulled at its bridle, silver tack jingling. The horse
stamped its forehooves and stepped closer, the sound
against the cobbles like hammers on stone.

Could one of these Maidens be the very same one she'd
crossed blades with?

"You."

Çeda shivered. She couldn't look up. She wouldn't.

"You there!"

No choice now. If the Maiden was looking at *her*, and
she refused to respond, she'd be killed on the spot.

Çeda lifted her head.

The Maiden sat astride her horse, her back straight as a
glaive. She held the horse's reins easily in one hand. Her

sword hung by her side. Henna tattoos marked the backs of her hands, which was the only skin Çeda could see besides her startling, kohl-rimmed eyes.

Çeda's fears waned when she realized the Maiden was staring not at her but at the driver of the nearby cart.

"Follow me," the Maiden said.

The man bowed his head to the Maiden and said, "For the honor of the Kings," the only response now left to him. When the Maiden who'd spoke began heading back up the Spear at a brisk pace, Çeda could see the disheartened look on the merchant's face. He snapped his reins and guided the cart in a half-circle, splashing through a large puddle before following the Maiden toward the House of Kings. The other Blade Maidens continued on, wheeling onto the Trough and heading north.

Çeda began to breathe again. Traffic resumed, and the sound rose until one would never know the Maidens had passed. She continued walking, step after painful step, weaving through the city, skirting the hill on her left where the palaces of the Kings hunched over the city. She walked into someone, and her right arm flared with pain. It felt as if she'd dipped it in gold, so intense was the agony. But then it faded, almost to nothing, which seemed to be a greater cause for concern than the pain.

The sounds of the city faded. Someone was speaking to her, but she couldn't make out the words. The street before her, dark with freshly fallen rain, went white until all she could see were bright outlines of people and buildings, horses and carts; mere hints among the alabaster landscape before her, as if she were looking back on her life while standing in the doorway to the next.

She felt a hand at her back. She was being led somewhere. Where, she had no idea. She had only the vaguest sense of alarm, a sense that she was supposed to be somewhere else, and now she might be too late. Though who she was supposed to see, and why, she couldn't recall.

She thought she saw her mother among the crowd, her face so bright it was nearly blinding. "Memma?" she called, but her mother only stared with a horror-stricken look as she passed.

She was led into a place that was darker than the brightness of the street. She was set in a chair. There were wooden shelves around her, and cabinets with hundreds of tiny drawers. Why anyone would ever need so many drawers, she couldn't guess, and for a moment it struck her as funny. She began to laugh as her arm was placed on a table. Again the dull ache returned.

She had bandages on her arm. Someone was cutting them away to reveal a forearm so swollen it looked like a strange, misshapen fruit. And the color of it! A dark blue, almost black. It reminded her of the very heart of the adichara blooms.

A fat man with heavy jowls sat opposite her. He stared at her hand, eyes wide, mouth slack, a pair of scissors held loosely in one hand. His throat convulsed over and over and over as tears welled in his eyes. In a moment of clarity, she realized that the man was seeing a poison so advanced there was no hope left. She was going to die.

The realization only added to the hilarity, which deepened her laughs. Her body shook from it, forcing the man to take note of her rather than her hand. His reddened eyes shed tears freely. He shook his head vigorously, wiping his tears on one sleeve, then another, apparently lost in his misery. And then he burst into motion. He went to one of the many, many drawers, took out a phial, and tipped out its contents onto a piece of white cloth. He held it beneath her nose, even as she fought to free herself from the acrid smell.

Her eyes rolled up in her head.

━━━━━━━ ◄─●─► ━━━━━━━

The next thing she knew she was lying on something hard and unforgiving, being led through the city on the bed of a dray, the man leading a mule. He was wearing a set of strange silver-and-bronze robes, clothes she'd rarely seen in the limits of Sharakhai, the garb of a monk from distant lands who came from time to time to the Amber City to spread the word of their god. He spoke soft words to her, touching her shoulder or stroking her hair or her cheek,

but she had no idea what he was saying. The city was still
bright, but not so bright as before. She could actually look
upon it without having to shut her eyes. The dray jolted,
and the brightness swept over her.

————— ← ● → —————

When she woke again, she was deeper into the city. She
could tell because Tauriyat now loomed over her. She was
as close as she'd come to it since her mother's death.

Was she being taken to the House of Kings? Did they
wish to speak with her?

Again the brightness swept in.

————— ← ● → —————

She woke a third time, and this time the cart was still. The
mule was there, but the man was gone. To her right, she
could see a high wall. The tall doors set into it were
groaning open, and women strode out and into the street.
There were only a few at first, but then more. One of
them, an old woman with a regal brow, sad eyes, and tattoos on her cheeks and chin and forehead, looked carefully at Çeda's arm.

She spoke—asked questions, perhaps—but she might as
well have been speaking the tongue of the dead, for Çeda
understood not a single word. The woman stared deeply
into Çeda's eyes, and for a fleeting moment it felt as if the
two of them were the same, linked by blood in some unknowable way. And then, like a burial shroud being lifted,
the feeling was gone.

The woman seemed unsure of something, for she looked
from Çeda to the other women several times. But then she
nodded and pointed toward the tall doors. As she was led
inside, Çeda finally recognized these women with their
dark dresses and steely gazes. Blade Maidens.

They were Blade Maidens, and she was being taken into
their house.

Chapter 33

THE SMELL OF THE INFIRMARY was unpleasant. Ihsan the Honey-tongued King had always found them so, even those that had been free of the sick and the dying and the dead for years. He wasn't sure whether it was the taint of the dead he sensed—some lingering remnant of their dark passage from this world to the next. Or the blood and sickness. Perhaps it was everything. *Are the worlds not connected in ways even the gods do not understand?*

The infirmary was empty save for one lone bed halfway along its considerable length. A woman afflicted by the poison of the adichara lay there, sleeping fitfully.

Footsteps echoed behind Ihsan.

Zeheb, King of Whispers, he of heavy tread, came to stand by him. Zeheb had been thin once, almost too thin, but you wouldn't know it to look at him now. He, like all of the Kings, had changed much since Beht Ihman. He had a strained look to him, his eyes shifty and half-lidded, as if he were listening even now to the whispers that plagued him.

"Are you with us?" Ihsan said, snapping his fingers in front of Zeheb's face.

Zeheb swallowed, then seemed to forcibly pull himself to *this place*—the infirmary inside the walls of the Maidens' house. If he was embarrassed by his inability to focus, he made no mention of it.

"This is our little lost dove?" he said, striding forward.

Ihsan fell into step alongside him. "Apparently."

They walked between the two rows of beds and arrived at the young woman's. Her right arm was wrapped, and the stink of a poultice filled the air—one, Ihsan had been told, that would bring the swelling down until the Matrons could work on controlling the poison. Assuming the Kings willed it.

Ihsan had been summoned by Zeheb mere moments before the note came from the House of Maidens, both reporting the same tale—that a woman apparently poisoned by the adichara had been left before the gates of Tauriyat, one would assume in hopes of the Matrons or the Kings saving her. She'd been left on a cart by some priest, a man unknown to those along the Spear who'd been questioned. Normally such a tale would have been met with laughter, followed by a short but sweet interrogation and a quick end to the unfortunate woman's life. But the Matron had apparently seen something in her, and she wanted Ihsan to verify it.

The girl thrashed for a moment, her face flushed. Her fingers looked as though they were rotting from the inside out.

She was very pretty, in a rough and tumble sort of way. And cleaned up, she would be a jewel indeed. Her presence here was no real surprise. Though they had not understood it at the time, this was the outcome of the Jade-eyed King's vision, of their decision in the desert. As Ihsan had agreed, he'd sent Azad out to the blooming fields, and wearing his former skin had indeed crossed blades with this girl. And now here she was, in the very midst of the Kings.

There was something terribly familiar about her, and it took him long moments to remember where he'd seen the like. "In the streets," Ihsan mused, "it is said the King of Whispers never forgets the words he hears, nor the faces he sees. Is it so?"

"You know it is not, and if there's something you wish to ask, stop prancing about and ask it."

"She looks familiar."

"To me as well. The assassin had a child, then."

Ihsan thought back to that day, eleven years ago now, when they'd caught a woman with the blood of Kings upon her hands. She'd been given to their confessor, cruel King Cahil, to learn what she knew, and she'd remained improbably silent. She'd given the Kings' confessor nothing. Nothing whatsoever. She had been little more than a blank slate, brought on, no doubt, from a draught of white acacia, or perhaps even hangman's vine, two rare distillations that could bring on such a state. And there was no doubt this girl bore a resemblance to that woman.

She'd had a child, then. A child of the lost tribe. And if the Matron's intuition was correct, if the things she'd seen reading the girl's palm were true, then she was a child of one of the Kings as well. Ihsan trusted the Matron well enough to believe it. And there was the poison as well. Those of common blood would have died well before now. It wasn't difficult to believe she was a first daughter—the blood of Kings is bound by no walls, as they say. And if it was true, Ihsan certainly didn't know who her father might be. He doubted the King who'd sired her was even aware of her existence. The assassin had been very careful, very good at keeping secrets, as evidenced by how little they'd managed to learn about her. And her identity was a piece of information upon which she would certainly have placed importance.

"Shall we keep her?" the King of Whispers said.

"I believe we shall," Ihsan replied.

"There is risk in doing so."

Which was true.

If any of the others noted her resemblance to the assassin—a woman from whom Cahil hadn't even managed to extract a name—it might come back to haunt Ihsan, but the resemblance was not so great as to leap to it immediately, and even if one of the other Kings *did* make the connection, Ihsan could easily deny that *he'd* seen it. Besides, there would be more than a little mystery over which King had fathered the girl. It certainly wasn't Ihsan himself—he knew *that* much—and whoever it was would have a good deal more explaining to do than Ihsan would. So he was confident he could use this to his advantage no matter which way it went.

And there was more to consider when balancing the ledger. The instrument this young woman might become was not something easily ignored. Given the right guidance, she could prove invaluable. And if there ever came a time when she disappointed, or the risks became too high, well, there would be little difficulty arranging for her demise, protections of the Blade Maidens or not.

"Let me worry about the dangers," Ihsan said. "Just tell me what you've found."

His eyes went heavy and fluttered for a moment. Then he shook his head, took a deep breath, and stared down at the poisoned creature before them. "Little enough so far. She comes from the West End. She fights in the pits. They call her the White Wolf."

Ihsan's eyebrows rose of their own accord. "*This* girl is the White Wolf?"

Zeheb laughed. "I didn't know you watched the dirt dogs scrap, Ihsan. I rather thought you above that."

Ihsan smiled easily. "I've been known to watch the dogs bark from time to time. Besides, even *I've* heard of the White Wolf." Ihsan stared down, wondering how many more mysteries there were to this girl. "A legend nearly as large as the Black Lion of Kundhun, is she not?"

"Just so!" The stocky King grinned. "I am impressed. We'll have to attend a bout one day."

But to this, Ihsan merely shook his head. "I don't care for your killing pits, Zeheb."

Zeheb's grin widened. "Can't stomach the blood?"

Ihsan couldn't help himself. A bark of a laugh escaped him. "I can stomach much. I simply don't like to see lives tossed into the dirt like a handful of copper khet. As well watch the dunes roll past."

"The dunes don't fight back, Ihsan."

"Do they not? What of the Moonless Host? What of the lost tribe?"

At this, Zeheb merely grunted.

At a sound from outside the room, Ihsan looked up. "Well, unless you've any objections, we'd best let the Matrons attend to her, or our decision will be made for us."

"Well enough." But Zeheb remained as Ihsan began to walk away. Then Ihsan stopped, and the King of Whispers said with utter sincerity, "Are you sure it's time?"

Ihsan had gone as far as the foot of the bed, and was facing the doorway through which they'd entered, but upon hearing these words he squared up against Zeheb, pulled himself taller, and put all of himself into his next words. "My dear Zeheb, it is far *past* time."

Zeheb blinked. His eyelids fluttered for a time, but then he nodded.

And the two Kings walked together from the room.

Chapter 34

WHEN ÇEDA WOKE, she was surrounded by cool, clear water. The current carried her, and she was content to allow it to take her where it would. *It must be the Haddah, but the river is rarely so calm.*

Small fish nipped at her toes and fingers. As the current began to rock her, she tried to move but found that she couldn't. Her body refused her, preferring the easy contentment of drifting onward, downward. The current began to carry her faster. The water became more violent, more turbid. She tried again and again to move her arms, to lift her head, to simply *breathe*, but no matter what she did, her body refused to respond. The water pulled her down beneath the surface. It tossed her about. She crashed into something—a rock, or the riverbed below.

Until now she hadn't been too concerned with the simple act of breathing, but as she realized how desperate her situation truly was, it became the only thing that filled her mind. Struggle as she might, though, the surface remained well out of reach. It wouldn't be long before the water took her completely.

Perhaps she should let it. Perhaps she should sink down,

as her mother had so many years ago, and give herself to the river.

But no. She refused to do that. She would fight for life, whatever the world pitted against her.

She pulled at the river, struggling with everything still in her. At last her body responded, and the more she fought, the easier it became. She stroked her arms like a heron taking flight, she kicked her legs and slowly swam for the shore.

Below her, the riverbed was choked with bones. Skulls smiling, arms and legs tangled in a grim yet lovely dance. From time to time the current swept her body against them. Each time it happened, it sent a terrible chill through her, as if by touching them she might wake the dead, might make them aware of her. She tried to avoid them, but the water was so shallow here it was impossible.

A skeletal hand reached up and gripped her wrist. The tip of its bony thumb pressed into the meat of her thumb, harder and harder, hurt becoming pain becoming agony, and yet it did not pierce her skin. It did not draw blood. It fouled the place it had touched, though, made her skin blacken and swell with disease or poison.

More hands grabbed for her and pulled her close while grinning mouths gave macabre smiles, hoping to share one last kiss.

But then she was pulled up through the water, away from the empty eyes and grasping hands. She broke the water's surface, coughing, sputtering, limbs flailing uselessly. She was dragged up and onto green grasses. She fell heavily into them, a lovely feeling, this sense of solidity, of form. Even the pain was almost unbearably beautiful, for it gave her the sense that she was alive. And for now that was enough.

At last, when her coughing expelled the last of the water from her lungs, she sat up and looked for her savior.

Kneeling there in the grass, running her hands over the stiff, sharp blades, was Ahya. The Kings' foul words were carved on the backs of her hands, *whore*, and on her feet, *false witness*, and on her forehead the sign that Çeda still did not understand. A fount of water beneath a field of stars. It was difficult to meet her eyes with such things done to her, but Çeda forced herself to.

By the gods' sweet breath, she was beautiful, even with the carvings. Or perhaps because of them.

"You're dead," she said to her mother, unsure where to begin.

"Have you found them, Çedamihn?"

"Found who?"

She traced a fingertip along the furrows in her skin, making it hopelessly bloody. "Those who killed me." The strokes of her finger were applied with morbid tenderness, as if she were penning verse and rhyme, as if *she* had made those cruel marks, not the Kings of Sharakhai.

"The *Kings* killed you."

"Ah, but which? Which Kings, Çeda? That is the question."

"I don't know. Was it my father?"

Ahya stood and walked away.

Çeda followed, shaking, little better than a newborn foal, but gradually she gained strength until she was able to walk side-by-side with her mother.

Tall grasses gave way to shorter, then to hard-packed earth, then windblown sand. Horizon to horizon there was nothing but wave upon wave of sand dunes, and when Çeda turned back toward the river, she saw that it was gone, lost to the parched maw of the desert.

She heard fluttering behind her. She turned and saw a flock of birds swooping and swirling around Ahya—blazing blues, just like the ones they'd seen over the salt lake years ago. They eddied around her, billowing then tightening like the dust demons that signaled the coming of greater storms. They were so thick they obscured her mother completely. Then they burst apart, flying outward and upward, revealing a different woman, a taller woman carrying a stout staff in one hand. "Do you remember coming to me when you were young?"

It was Saliah, bearing the same markings as Çeda's mother. It had looked foul on Ahya's skin, but on Saliah's it looked like a travesty, a perversion.

"I remember running through your garden," Çeda replied.

"And climbing the tree."

"That too."

"Few others have done so, Çedamihn Ahyanesh'ala. Did you know that?"

"Because you don't allow them."

"Because they are not brave enough. Few would dare to look into their future. But you. You have done so many times."

"Only because I didn't understand."

"No." Saliah's vacant eyes looked over Çeda's shoulder to the horizon, but her left hand reached out and touched Çeda's forehead, traced a mark there. The same mark that was on Saliah's forehead. "The body understands. The mind follows."

Çeda reached up and touched her forehead, and her fingers came away wet with blood. So much blood.

How much had her mother learned before she'd died at the Kings' hands? "I'm lost," Çeda said, more to herself than Saliah.

"You'll be found, Çeda. You have no choice."

"You can help me. I'll come to you."

"Perhaps." Saliah smiled, and Çeda noticed a cut on her cheek, the same place she'd been wounded when the chime had shattered in Saliah's garden. Çeda looked at her thumb, where Saliah's blood had touched her, the very place the adichara thorn had pierced.

Saliah held her hand to her own cheek. She looked pale and somehow fragile. Her whole body shivered, and she fell to her knees. She used her staff to support herself, but she lost her grip and tumbled back, falling to the desert floor. Çeda rushed to her side, but Saliah's skin was drying, flaking and falling away like sand scoured by the wind. "Please," Çeda said. "Please tell me what to do."

Saliah did not hear her. She was reduced to bones, bleaching in the desert sun.

Çeda's thumb hurt terribly. Like a fire spreading across dry grassland, the pain extended through her fingers and along her wrist and forearm until it had filled her entire being. It was white hot, a blaze, an inferno in which she burned.

She opened her eyes. A dream. It had all been a dream.

By the gods, memma, how I miss you.

A dozen Blade Maidens surrounded her, and one was sitting by her side, stabbing her skin with a needle, over and over and over.

Çeda was bound. By the women, by straps. She didn't know. But she couldn't move. She could scream, though, and once she started, she screamed until her throat was raw. She screamed until it was all she could hear.

The pain of the needle moved about. It was not always in the same place, as she'd thought at first. It moved along the palm of her hand, and across to the back. Along her wrist and then back to her palm. She focused on the distinct pain of the needle. It helped her. It kept her from going mad, allowed her to ignore the other burning pain that ran throughout her arm and shoulder and into her chest, a pain that eclipsed the other if she let it. She tried to sense where the point of the needle was being directed, and over time she could feel it, moving in rhythmic patterns. Telling a story. She was being marked, she realized. Given a tattoo, in the way the peoples of the desert did, to tell their tales.

Did the Blade Maidens do the same? Or did they think her a child of the desert, a woman to be marked, her story told before they killed her?

She struggled to move. She refused to let them touch her. She would not allow it.

Her hand moved as the old woman tapped the needle into the palm of her hand. It moved only a fraction of an inch, but it was enough for the woman to frown, to look at Çeda with a disapproving stare. She pressed harder on Çeda's wrist, and the pain took her.

She opened her eyes.

Above her was the old woman, the one with the regal

brow and sad eyes. Primitive tattoos covered her neck and cheeks and forehead and chin. A crescent moon arched over her brow, making her look like a messenger from Tulathan herself. She was hunched over Çeda, using a flat stick to tap a needle into her hand, working on the area immediately around the adichara wound. Somehow the pain had been made distant, but now that Çeda was aware of it, it grew stronger and stronger until she screamed.

There was a smell like burnt honey in the air. It brought on the memory of Dardzada tattooing her back with the ashes of the adichara bloom—*her* adichara bloom—to such a strong degree that she began to question where she was and who was tapping this new design into her skin.

She forced the reality around her to coalesce. This was not Dardzada's apothecary, and the woman tapping the tattoo into her was certainly *not* Dardzada.

How strange that the Maidens had adopted the same technique as the tribes of old. Or perhaps it wasn't strange. She wasn't sure anymore.

"Sümeya, stop staring and give it to her."

Çeda looked up. There were other women around. Six of them, seven, perhaps more; her eyes wouldn't focus. Each wore the black thawb of the Blade Maidens, but none wore a turban. One of them, a woman with brown eyes and a strong jaw, held a thick strip of leather near Çeda's mouth.

"Take it," she said.

She meant for Çeda to bite down on it, if only to prevent herself from chewing off her own tongue. Çeda accepted it as sweat trickled down her forehead. She was damp with sweat, she could feel now. More and more sensations were returning to her—the heat of her skin, the thick leather straps around her chest and stomach and thighs, the smell of urine, no doubt her own—but more than anything she felt the pain emanating from the poisoned wound on her hand. Despite her fears of losing her arm in that other strange place—the place with the host of surgical instruments—were she given a knife right now, she would gladly saw her hand off, just to be free of the pain. She grunted around the leather between her teeth. She looked to the women standing around her. Some would return her gaze, one or two even with looks of pity or sympathy, but most stared at her dispassionately.

The old woman's needle was circling her injury, and the pain had risen to impossible heights.

The woman who'd given her the length of leather looked at Çeda only once, when her cries grew the most desperate. She was not old, this woman with the striking brown eyes; she was perhaps ten years older than Çeda herself. Not an ounce of sympathy registered on her face. But there *was* emotion: Disappointment. Disgust. It radiated from her. Çeda thought perhaps it was simple displeasure over her weakness, but then it occurred to her that these women would know the poison came from the adichara, would know Çeda had gone to the blooming fields. One of them might even be the Maiden she'd fought on the dunes—and now here was one of their own trying to save *her*, a thief, one who should have been put to death the moment she arrived.

Why the old woman had decided to do this Çeda didn't know, but she knew that the younger woman resented her for it.

How long the tapping of the stick continued Çeda couldn't say. It came in waves. Tapping, then a pause, tapping, then a pause, the old woman acting as artist and healer and historian telling Çeda's story—one small part of it, in any case—with the tattoo she was laying upon Çeda's skin.

When she finally stopped, she pursed her lips and stared down at her handiwork. She turned Çeda's hand this way and that, and nodded once. As she did these things, Çeda felt a wave of relief. It was over. There was still pain, to be sure, but with the sudden lifting of so much of it, Çeda's entire body went limp.

She was completely and utterly spent, and darkness soon claimed her.

<hr />

When she woke it was to no small amount of pain. For some reason, she couldn't open her eyes. The world around her felt distant and dreamlike.

"Leave it alone," came the old woman's voice, "the poison must work its way out."

"Very well." A man's voice, deep and ancient, as though the desert itself were speaking to her. "You'll bring her to me when she's awakened."

"She may relapse. It would be best if I could bring her once she's healed."

"And when will that be?"

Çeda opened her eyes a crack, which was all she could manage. Above her she could see the old woman who'd marked her arm. But the man was out of sight. There was a distinct smell about him, though. Myrrh and amber and sandalwood, the scents one would offer to Bakhi for his favor. This came across not as tribute, however, but hubris, for one would never *wear* those scents, not together, not unless you compared yourself to the god, thought yourself better than him.

It had to be one of the Kings.

The woman was pulling the sheets back over Çeda's arm, which had been pulled out for the King to inspect. As she did so, her hand grazed downward over Çeda's eyelids. The motion had been ever so slight, but Çeda had no doubt it had been done with intent. She wished for Çeda to pretend she was still asleep.

"Such wounds do not heal overnight, Eminence. A week. Perhaps two."

There was a pause as the King considered. "Seven days." A chair creaked. Sandals scraped over the floor. "If she is not presented to me by Savadi next, I will send for her."

"It will be as you say," the old woman replied.

When the shuffling footsteps had died away, the woman turned to gather something near the head of Çeda's bed. The clink of glass and the gurgle of liquid filled the air.

"Who—" Çeda's voice was like a rasp. "Who was that?"

"Never you mind."

"Tell me," Çeda pressed.

The woman brought a cool glass to Çeda's lips. She drank from it, but recognized too late the taste of Night Lily, a telltale sign of a sleeping draught. She tried to spit it out, but she'd already drunk too much.

"Thaash curse you," Çeda said as the soporific began taking effect, drawing her downward into the darkness.

"Save your curses, girl. Sleep is what you need now, not stories of the Jade-eyed King."

Nalamae's teats, which one is the Jade-eyed King? But she had no chance to wonder further, before she had blacked out once more.

Chapter 35

Six years earlier...

CEDA STRODE ALONG THE DRY RIVERBED, the sounds of revelry coming from the bridges and walkways above.

It was Beht Revahl—the night the Kings defeated the last of the wandering tribes and sent them fleeing into the desert once and for all. One of the holy days in which the entire city seemed to take part, from the ship races in the southern harbor, to the horse shows in the north, to the bacchanal in the confines of the western harbor. The Haddah's meandering bed had become a wonder of singing and dancing and tanburs and tambanas that jingled as the drummers struck. And the lights!

On this night four hundred years ago, the surviving Sharakhani had walked the city with tallow candles and oil lamps, searching for the wounded, looking for their lost loved ones that they might be buried deep in the desert, as was proper. The candles were a way of honoring that sober day, but they also celebrated the living.

Tonight, the revelers, Sharakhani and foreigners alike, walked with small candles in their hands, many bought just for the occasion. It was a day for which the city's chandlers prepared the entire year. Lights drifted along the Haddah, along the streets and alleys. They were everywhere, moving about the city like lost souls, casting all in a beautiful amber glow beneath the half-moon light of golden Rhia.

"Little Çeda!" came a voice.

Çeda looked through the crowd. On the opposite side of the Haddah, beneath an arching stone bridge, was Emre's handsome brother Rafa. From his work as a dockman, Rafa brought in the lion's share of the money and paid for the flat he shared with Emre and Çeda. It was a tight space, especially when their eldest brother, Brahim, returned for a day or two. But it would do for now, as she and Emre told one another many times, at least until they could save enough for a place of their own.

Emre leaned against the stone wall of the embankment with a canvas bag slung over one shoulder. His eyes brightened when he spotted Çeda, but before he could say anything, Rafa shook his head to clear his eyes of his curly brown hair and called, "Come on, Little Çeda," waving over the heads of Tariq and Hamid.

She hated when Rafa called her that, but she forced a smile anyway and wove through the crowd, bowing her head when she drew near. "Good eve, Rafa." The words sounded stupid to her ears, a child speaking to a man.

But Rafa didn't seem to notice. He gave her that chiding smile of his and used his knee to nudge her leg. "Where were you off to?"

"I was coming to find these beetle-brained fools," Çeda replied, glancing at Emre and Hamid and Tariq.

Emre smiled at her, as if he had a secret he wanted to share.

"I've no idea why," Rafa told Çeda. "You're too good for them. Gods know you're too *clean* for them." Without even looking, he shot his hand out and tousled Emre's hair.

Emre ducked away, running his fingers through his dark hair, putting it back in place while eyeing the crowd to see if anyone had seen. Always preening, was Emre.

"Well, I'm off to the docks, little brother. The wine the harbormaster is opening won't drink itself, you know." He took Emre by the scruff of the neck and pulled him in for a kiss on the forehead, then ruffled his hair again and ran off, easily dodging Emre's hastily thrown punches.

"He's right, you know," Çeda said. Emre raked his hair back into place and returned to leaning against the wall, clutching his canvas bag as if it might fly away. He and Tariq and Hamid all had the look of gutter wrens about them. Their skin was dirty. Their sirwal trousers were threadbare and dusty beyond all hope of cleaning. "You're filthy, dirty, hopeless wrens. The lot of you."

Tariq puffed himself up. "If we're hopeless, then what are *you?*"

At this Hamid grinned. Quiet Hamid. Shy Hamid. He was always bashful around Çeda, but he would watch her from the corner of his eye, especially when he thought she wasn't looking.

"Me?" Çeda said. "I'm nothing like *you*, that's for certain, Tariq Esad'ava."

"Nothing like me?" Tariq said, his smile wide as he kicked dirt onto her sandaled feet and her own much-cleaner pair of boy's trousers. "I beg to differ, My Lady Çeda." He was always calling her that because she'd lived with Dardzada, east of the Trough. Even though she'd left after Dardzada had given her that vile tattoo, Tariq wouldn't let it go.

Çeda stepped back, trying to dodge the dust and dirt, but it caught her around the ankles and shins, dusting her clothes. "Stop it!"

He didn't, and he chased her when she backed up further, so she shot forward and slapped him across the face.

His eyes went wide with shock. Emre grinned, while Hamid uncharacteristically pointed and laughed out loud, which caused Çeda to laugh too. The slap had been harder than she'd meant, but there was little to do about it now. "Tariq, I'm *sorry!*" she said, still laughing, which only served to further enrage Tariq. He lashed out, trying to even the score, but Çeda blocked his wild and hurried attempts. "Too slow, Tariq. As always."

The crowd nearby gave them wide berth, and an old woman yelling, "This is a *holy* day!"

But Tariq was focused only on Çeda. His face screwed up with rage as he charged her, hoping to wrestle her to the ground where, she admitted, he had an advantage, but she never gave him the chance. She grabbed his shirt with both hands, rolled backward, and used her legs to launch him up and over her body.

The revelers were taking more notice now, including the men and women along the banks of the Haddah above. The old woman was still yelling at them, but many only chuckled at the playing children, which made Tariq all the more furious.

Çeda readied for his next charge, which would probably be more bullish than the last, until Emre called, "For the love of the gods, you two, wait!" and imposed himself between them, holding one palm out toward each in order to still them. Emre turned to Tariq, showing Çeda his back, and said more softly. "I've brought something. I was waiting until we were all here." He motioned to the place they'd been standing earlier. Tariq looked over Emre's shoulder to Çeda, his eyes filled with adolescent rage, but when Emre pulled something from the bag at his side, Tariq's eyes softened and he glanced around with a mischievous grin. The crowd took little notice of him now, most continuing to walk past or drink from polished ox horns.

"Come, my friends." Emre stepped carefully away, eyes still on Tariq and Çeda, waving for them to follow. "Come, for we'll not be left out of the revelry *this* year. Your good servant, Emre, has seen to that."

When they'd returned to their spot beneath the bridge, Emre pulled out a beautiful, etched silver flask from his bag. "Araq! Sweetened, too, my friends. Emre spared no expense."

"Expense . . ." Tariq snorted. "As if a gutter wren like you could afford araq." He snatched the flask away from Emre, pulled the ruby-red glass stopper, and took a long swig from it before shoving it back into Emre's hands. As Emre handed it to Çeda, Tariq coughed and smacked his lips. Hamid laughed again, his eyes wide in anticipation.

Çeda wiped the mouth of the flask with obvious care, receiving a sock on the arm and a reluctant smile from

Tariq. Then she tipped the flask and downed a mouthful of
the sweet lemon-infused liquor. Coughing every bit as
much as Tariq from the alcohol burn, she passed the flask
to Hamid.

Hamid took a short swallow, then one more, then a
third before passing it back to Emre, who looked as proud
as a King, seeing them profit from his bounty. As a group
of young women sang a lively tune on the bridge above, the
four friends loosened up and began to enjoy the holy night.
They drank and danced, trading partners among the other
boys and girls walking along the riverbed, some of whom
they knew, others foreigners they'd probably never see
again. Tariq always seemed to choose a dark-skinned
Kundhunese girl; Çeda had always thought he secretly
wanted to leave Sharakhai and travel to the territories, a
place he derided so often she knew there was more to it
than he was letting on.

Hamid remained by the wall, mostly watching, though
there was one point where a Qaimiri girl pulled him forward and spun him around. They danced together a while,
and you'd never guess there was a shy bone in his body, for
he laughed and joked with her as they spun about. But
when they were done he returned to his place along the
wall, reddened cheeks obvious to any who cared to look,
even in the dim glow of the candlelit night.

Çeda danced with Emre, the two of them spinning, then
lifting their coiled hands high, then rolling, back-to-back,
to grab the other hand and begin the dance anew. It was
wonderful. She was so glad to be free of Dardzada. They
might have to snitch food, they might have to run from the
Silver Spears from time to time, but for now life suited her
just fine.

When the dance came to an end, Emre passed the flask
around once more. All four of them were becoming tipsy
from it, laughing at the smallest of things: An old man who
stopped and clapped in time to the beat of the tambana,
two belled goats that gamboled behind a woman and her
three children, a drunk Sharakhani who tipped over and
fell from the bridge to the riverbed, scattering the stones
and scaring everyone around.

On the riverbank above, a dozen Malasani bravos strode along, speaking in their thick tongue. They wore garish clothes, leather caps, and bright falchions slung through their wide cloth belts.

"Fucking caravan trash," Tariq said, nodding toward them. "Think they can take anything they please from Sharakhai and then sail the sands like it means nothing to them."

Here, Çeda and Tariq were in agreement. She watched them sit on the bank, choosing spots along the stone lip of the street above, some glaring at an old couple until they moved and the bravos could sit next to their brothers. They sat and drank and called to the women walking by.

"They should keep them locked in their ships until they're ready to leave," Çeda said.

"They should sling arrows through their hearts is what they should do." They all turned to Hamid, who looked back at them with steel in his eyes.

"At the very least they should leave with lighter purses," Tariq said.

"They should," Emre said, staring up at them, as if choosing one for his mark even now. Then he looked to Çeda, as if asking her permission. He was drunk, she could see it in his eyes. But not so drunk that there wasn't a little fear in him.

"They should," Çeda agreed, pointing to the biggest among them, thickset and bald, with a scar running along the back of his head as if he'd had his skull cleaved and lived to tell the tale.

"That one?" Emre said, swallowing.

"That one," Çeda challenged.

They all nodded, then Emre dropped the canvas satchel in the dust. He remained in the riverbed while Tariq, Çeda, and Hamid walked down a ways until they could jump and climb up to the street that ran adjacent to the northern side of the riverbank, the side where the bravos gathered. The three then strolled along, somewhat unsteadily, until they were between the Malasani men and the squat stone washhouse.

That was when Tariq pulled her hair a good deal harder

than normally, and Çeda spun on him. "I told you not to touch me!"

"Oh ho!" one of the bravos shouted, slapping the man next to him and pointing at the unfolding spectacle. The bald man glanced at them, but then returned his attention to a Sharakhani girl wearing a loose blouse and long skirt she had pulled up over her knee with one hand.

"I'm only playing," Tariq said.

"You've been playing all day. Play one more time, and you'll find yourself with a foot in your crotch, a fist in your mouth, and your stones and your teeth lying on the street, sharing stories of what a bloody coward you are."

The bravos laughed again, more of them watching now, their smiles lit by the large oil lanterns, spaced along the larger streets of Sharakhai's city center.

There were times when a simple display like this was enough, but Emre's mark was still not paying enough attention, so Tariq shot his hand out and grabbed her hair again, and when he did, Çeda snatched his wrist, lifted it high, and spun behind him. The twist was enough to bring him down to the ground. She let it go before he was hurt, and Tariq, on cue, rose from the ground and tackled her about the waist. Down the two of them went, onto the cobbles and rolling over and over again, shouting and swearing and scratching at one another's faces. They did no real damage, but they did enough to make the bravos watch. All of them.

That's when Emre climbed up the riverbank, slipped his knife beneath the bald man's purse, and cut it carefully away.

He would have been fine if it weren't for the araq. He was normally very good with a purse cutting—but his reflexes weren't as sharp as they should have been.

He got the purse away clean, but the man noticed, and the way his face contorted in rage, she knew at once they'd made a mistake.

The man stood, pushed the girl away, and leaped down into the channel. Revelers parted like water before him, and Emre sprinted along the riverbed faster than she'd ever seen him go.

She and Tariq were up and running as well. Hamid had already turned and was sprinting around the corner into an alley. It had a small hole in a broken board at the end of it where he could easily slip through.

"Oh, no you don't," one of the men said, reaching for Çeda and Tariq. He managed to grab Tariq's shirt, but he wasn't ready for Çeda. Men like him had no idea how quickly she could move. She slipped beneath his grasp and punched him as hard as she could in the stomach.

He doubled over and released Tariq. A long bellow of pain escaped him as he lost his breath; immediately, she and Tariq ran in opposite directions.

The two bravos deepest into their wineskins were just getting up, laughing, one pointing at the bald brute running after Emre, the other at the one coughing on the ground behind Çeda. The rest, though, scattered after Hamid, Tariq, and Çeda, chasing them through the streets, shouting the sorts of imaginative beatings that made it clear they had more than a little experience in such things.

The last she saw of Emre he was leaping at the supports beneath a narrow walking bridge. He used his momentum to swing up the opposite side and pull himself up by the rails, narrowly avoiding the outstretched fingers of the bravo chasing him.

Then Çeda was off, sprinting down a wide street that had a dozen alleys within the next eighth-league, any one of which she could use to climb to the rooftops.

The bravos gave chase, but they were lumbering. She'd be safe enough. Tariq and Hamid, too. Emre, though . . .

Gods, the look on that bravo's face. It kept playing through her mind. There was fury, but also a cold determination. And it was clear from the crispness of his movements that he hadn't poured nearly the amount of drink down his gullet as his fellows had. Perhaps he'd had nothing. Perhaps he got drunk on fighting and was just looking for an excuse.

Please be safe, Emre.

In little time, she lost the bravo chasing her. Then she circled back, looking for Tariq or Hamid so they could go after Emre together. But she never found them.

She should have gone straight home. She should have waited for Emre there, not wasted her time running about Sharakhai, but home should have been the last place he'd go. After running a scam, they always met at one of their haunts, never their homes. But she didn't find him along the river, or in the bazaar, or in the streets of Roseridge. She didn't find Tariq or Hamid, either. Dread began to fill her. She searched all the harder, running from street to street to street. When she finally did return home—just as the sun was rising in the east—she found Tariq and Hamid waiting outside the door. As she came closer, a chill ran through her.

The looks on their faces . . . As though someone had died.

"Emre!"

Tariq put himself in her way. "Çeda, don't!"

Even Hamid tried to stop her, but she bulled past them both and ran into the room.

By the gods who walk the earth, it was Rafa. He lay on the floor, and there was blood *everywhere.*

Emre knelt next to him. Just knelt there. Not crying. Not sobbing. Just staring down at Rafa's serene, handsome face.

"Emre?" He didn't respond as she moved around to Rafa's other side, being careful not to tread in any of the blood. "Emre?" She knelt across from him, Rafa's lifeless body between them, and still Emre didn't respond, didn't take his eyes from his brother. He merely knelt there, eyes vacant, hands clasped as if in prayer to the gods of the desert to undo this.

Tears began to slip down Çeda's cheeks. If Emre would not cry, she would cry enough for the both of them. "Emre, what happened?"

"I came home. And he . . . was like this."

The look on Emre's face. He looked so scared.

"But why? Who could have . . . ?" She didn't have to finish the question. She already knew. It was the Malasani bravo. "How could he have known?"

Emre looked up then. "What does it matter, Çeda? If I hadn't taken his money . . ." He opened his clasped hands, revealing the bravo's stolen purse. He tipped it over, and coins fell to the dull, dusty boards, one clinking against the next, Malasani coins mixing with Sharakhani, all coated in Rafa's blood.

"It wasn't your fault, Emre."

"No?" he asked, staring at her, tears now welling in his eyes. "Whose was it then?"

Mine, Çeda thought. *It was mine.* She stood, her mouth feeling suddenly and inexplicably dry. Emre said nothing as she left and stepped outside. She stopped when she came face to face with Tariq. She hadn't noticed it before, but he'd been beaten. Red welts along his cheek. Bloody scrapes on his hands. He'd been found. He'd been caught by one of the bravos, and they'd beaten the location of Emre's home from him, except they hadn't found Emre, they'd found Rafa and killed him in Emre's place.

Tariq looked uncomfortable. "Why'd you have to pick the biggest bloody one of them?"

Çeda didn't say a thing, because he was voicing her own thoughts. Why *had* she picked that one?

She looked up the empty street. The sun was beginning to rise, and soon many ships would be leaving for farther shores. She starting heading east, toward the Trough, but Tariq grabbed her sleeve and forced her to stop and look him in the eye.

"Don't go after them," he said, his eyes wide with fear.

She ripped her arm from his grasp and started walking, but all too soon she was running, and she didn't stop until she'd reached the vast southern harbor—the most likely place for a Malasani ship to have docked.

She asked and asked. For hours she went from ship to ship to ship, looking for them, her knife ready at her side, and eventually she found word. She ran along the bed of the harbor just as five caravels and three dhows were sailing through the narrow pass, all of them flying the blue pennon of Malasan.

She sprinted until her burning muscles could go no farther. She slowed and heaved her kenshar end over end at the ships. The knife rose and fell, throwing sunlight until it splashed ineffectually against the golden sand.

"Goezhen take you!" she screamed, and fell to her

knees, pounding the fine sand over and over until her skin was raw from it. "Thaash drink your blood!"

Yet the ships sailed on, and soon they'd passed beyond the line of rocks leading out to the easternmost lighthouse.

Çeda stayed there a long while, whispering curses upon those men, upon their ships. Whispering curses upon herself, the one who deserved them most of all.

Chapter 36

ÇEDA DID NOT DREAM, but she was aware of the passage of time. She heard an accumulation of sounds: the whisper of footsteps over ceramic tiles, the clink of glass and the gurgle of liquid, snippets of low conversation between the Maidens and Matrons.

She was given more sleeping draughts—how many, she didn't know, but each time it happened she felt the chill of the glass as it was pressed to her lips and sensed the bitter, floral taint of the Night Lily. One night, however, she woke fully from sleep. It might have been a week after her arrival or it might have been a month, she simply couldn't tell.

Sitting in a rocking chair to the right of her bed was the younger woman from the other night, the one who'd offered Çeda the length of leather to clamp her teeth onto. She was cast in dull silver by Rhia's light, which angled in from the window on the far side of the empty room. This was an infirmary of some sort but not one that saw much use. For the moment, at least.

How much death have these walls seen? She tried to sit up, but the deep pain all along her right arm made her gasp and ease back down again, so she leaned on her left side and pulled herself slowly up until she was sitting at last. And all the while, the woman in the rocking chair next to her bed watched, silent as the forgotten corners of the Great Shangazi.

"Who are you?" Çeda asked when the pain finally faded.

"My name is Sümeya. And that is the last favor I shall grant you in this house. You've no business asking who I am, little wren. The better question is who are *you*." She rocked back and forth, considering Çeda. Outside, far in the distance, a pack of jackals laughed at some cruel joke. "So who are you, little bird? Who are you to come to the Hall of Swords begging succor? Who are you to wander to the killing fields and return home as if nothing were amiss?"

The killing fields . . . Çeda had never heard the blooming fields called that, but it must have been what she meant. Whether or not Çeda had an ally in the Maidens, they would all know that her poison came from the adichara. What they *wouldn't* know was whether she had actually been to the blooming fields or if she'd been pierced by a thorn someone else had brought back to Sharakhai.

The Maidens were no fools, though, and they were fiendish. Çeda would be wise to remember it.

"I didn't know where else to go," Çeda finally said.

A soft chuckle. "You came yourself, then? Alone?"

They knew about Dardzada, then. They'd seen him leave her there, surely, but she guessed they didn't know who he was. She recalled through her haze the strange robes he'd worn, perhaps something he'd secreted away in the apothecary. By now, though, those robes would have been burned, so that no one could tie them back to him. "Someone brought me. I begged for help. I remember a cart but little before that." She paused. "I didn't know where else to go," she repeated.

"So you said." The Maiden paused, as if she were choosing her next words with the care of a jeweler about to cut a facet on a gemstone. She leaned forward, the wood of the rocking chair creaked, and at last Çeda recognized her. The woman with the red-brown eyes who had stared down at Çeda with revulsion while the old woman inked her hand. "I know what you've done," she said. "I know you went to the fields to harvest the adichara. What I don't know is why."

The sign carved into her mother's forehead flashed through Çeda's mind. "Surely the Maidens are aware of the market for adichara petals."

Sümeya's laugh was one of quaint amusement, as if she'd expected so much more. "It's money, then? You harvest for *money?*"

"Don't you?" Çeda asked.

"The Maidens do not *use* the adichara. We gain nothing from it save for the glory of our Kings."

"There is little glory to be found in west end, and few enough Kings."

The Maiden scoffed. "What need have the Kings of visiting Roseridge or the Shallows or Hallowsgate?"

"Indeed, because the Kings find their harvest near the Hill."

Sukru, the Reaping King, who chose the victims for the asirim, nearly always chose tributes near the Hill. It was properly known as Goldenhill, though it was referred to as Sidehill by nearly everyone west of the Trough. It was where the progeny of the Kings lived—those of royal blood, though none of them would rise to take the seat of King. The best they could hope for was that one of their daughters be taken by the Maidens, or their sons taken by the asirim to honor their family, the Kings, and all of Sharakhai.

Sümeya leaned back in her chair, and it occurred to Çeda how strikingly beautiful she was. Her thin eyebrows, her graceful lips, her jaw that narrowed like an arrow's tip. Like one of the ebon blades the Maidens wore, here were the elements of art and edge and sanguine confidence all forged into one perfect weapon. "To be chosen is to be blessed."

These were the words that all spoke in Sharakhai, that to be taken by the asirim was to be the chosen of the gods themselves. Most in Sharakhai accepted that it was an honor, but they would still quake in their homes on the night of Beht Zha'ir, wondering what their fate would be. The Maidens didn't merely take their responsibilities as protectors of the Kings and their interests seriously; it was their life. It was clear that Çeda had been saved for a reason, but if she were to speak against the reaping now, she had little doubt Sümeya might ignore her orders and kill Çeda then and there as a traitor.

"When am I to be taken to the King?"

Sümeya paused, perhaps debating how open to be. "You'll be taken before him at sunset. But before you go, I have a question."

"And what is that?"

"Who is Emre?"

A knife cold as the dead of night slipped into her heart. "Who?"

Sümeya's laugh was biting. "Knowing what I know of you now, I'm not surprised you were brought on a cart and left before our gates, but I thought surely someone would come asking for you. They might not come directly to the Maidens. Oh, no. But they might ask those who saw you taken through the city. They might ask those who saw you lying there, dying from poison before Zaïde decided to grant you sanctuary." Sümeya leaned back in her chair, allowing her momentum to rock her back and forth, the silver moonlight playing across her form. "Five days after your arrival, a man named Emre asked about you along the Spear. He's come every day since for the last two weeks, including just this morning. He is always careful. He has no wish to attract the notice of Tauriyat, as I'm sure you're well aware, but I know of him now."

Sümeya paused, evidently waiting for her words to sink in, for the implications to take root.

They did. As did the fear. Fear for Emre, and for everyone she knew in the west end or the bazaar. Davud and Tehla, Djaga and Osman. Even Tariq. She'd take Tariq over a thousand like Sümeya.

"What do you want?" Çeda asked.

At this Sümeya stood. The rocking chair slid back and came to a rest against the next bed. "Zaïde, the woman who saved you, has it in her head that you might become a

Maiden. It was why you were saved, despite breaking the laws of Sharakhai by touching a blessed thorn."

Sümeya leaned down and pressed her hand over Çeda's bandaged wrist. Çeda sucked breath through her teeth as the pain blossomed, radiating out from the wound to her fingers and up to her elbow. She did not cry out, however, a clear sign her injury had vastly improved. Nor did she give Sümeya the satisfaction of hearing her beg for mercy. She merely bore it, breathing through gritted teeth, and stared into Sümeya's unforgiving eyes.

"She can see far, Zaïde. She is gifted in many ways. But in this she is wrong. When you have healed enough to stand on your own, you will be taken before Yusam, the Jade-eyed King, and he will judge you in his mere. He will see you for what you are and give you what you deserve, but if he does not, if by chance he asks you into the House of the Maidens, you will decline. It will be a grave insult to do so, but make no mistake, you will do this"—she squeezed Çeda's wounded hand—"for your Emre."

Çeda had fought often in her life. She'd been the youngest woman ever to fight in the pits, the youngest to win as well, man or woman. She'd fought a hundred fights since, and in each she had received beatings. She'd been wounded. She'd broken bones. But none of that compared to this, a feeling as though her hand were burning, as though her skin were ash. Çeda could feel her blood pumping through her wrist, through her still-poisoned flesh, her entire being reduced to searing white pain.

Sümeya squeezed harder, and Çeda cried out, hating herself for it.

"I will! I will decline!"

Rarely had she felt so fragile, so helpless. She wanted to refuse Sümeya's request, if only to spite her, but she couldn't risk Emre's life. She would bide her time. Her gamble had paid off thus far, after all. She was in the House of Maidens, she'd learned the identity of the Jade-eyed King, and more would come. She simply needed to find a way to nullify Sümeya's advantage. Wait and watch and learn. Show your enemy what they want to see. Isn't that what she'd learned from Djaga in the pits?

Sümeya's grip eased. She released Çeda's hand and stepped back to look down on Çeda like a headsman who'd just been told to stay his sword. "Well and good. In all likelihood it will matter little, sweet bird. Most likely the Kings will relieve you of your hand, perhaps both, and then you'll be back in the streets to live out the remains of your useless life. And to think Zaïde sees in *you* the blood of Kings." She sniffed, her gaze roaming over Çeda's form as if she were a rotten fig. "It was Bakhi's grace and Zaïde's skill that saw you through, not kingly blood." Sümeya leaned down until they were eye to eye. "But even if I'm wrong, if perchance a King wandered the dirty streets of the west end to bed your whore of a mother, you'll do well to keep Emre's pretty face at the forefront of your mind. Won't you?"

Çeda's head was swimming, but she managed a nod. "I will," she said.

Sümeya seemed satisfied, with her own callousness if nothing else, and after a sharp nod she spun and left, her footsteps all but silent, her form a darkening shadow, until Çeda was alone with her thoughts in the cavernous, moon-lit room.

Chapter 37

THE INFIRMARY DOOR OPENED with a clatter. A sharp, if hushed, conversation followed as a group of Maidens helped three wounded women into the room. Two of the wounded were limping, each helped along by another Maiden. But the last was unconscious and lying on a stretcher. She was laid down gently as the other two were helped onto beds, grimacing as they went.

Zaïde swept into the room shortly after. The cowl of her white dress was pulled back to reveal not only her long gray hair but the tattoos along her neck and forehead. Zaïde asked many questions, not all of which Çeda could hear, but she heard the words *we were ambushed,* and the name *Macide Ishaq'ava* was uttered several times. The Maidens had been attacked in the southern quarter while escorting some*thing* or some*one* to Tauriyat. Çeda had no idea what that might be, but she thought it strange that the Maidens were escorting anything or anyone from the harbor this early. It implied that a ship had sailed under dark of night, a dangerous thing in itself. Why not wait until full sun?

When one of the Maidens saw Çeda watching, she spoke to the others, and they all fell silent.

With the Maidens providing any help needed, Zaïde tended to the unconscious woman, focusing first on her right leg, which was gone below the knee. She checked the belt that had been cinched around her leg to stop the blood flow, then cleaned the terrible wound and sewed as much of the skin together as she could manage. Çeda couldn't see clearly, but it seemed to be bleeding terribly. Most likely she'd die—few survived the blood loss from wounds as bad as that—but she had yet to cross to the farther fields. When Zaïde was done, she unwound the bandage around the woman's midsection, cleaned it, and rebandaged it with confident efficiency.

While Zaïde and the Maidens worked, the memories of Sümeya's visit in the night came rushing back. Emre . . .

Çeda had no doubt Sümeya would follow through on her threats. Why hadn't she told Emre more? She should have. She should have warned him away so that he wouldn't do something foolish like this. *We are two fools, Emre, you and I.*

She'd been a coward, she saw now. She could tell herself all she wanted that it was because Emre might protest, that he might do something foolish or desperate to stop her, but the truth was she'd thought that by saying a final farewell it would indeed divide them forever. Part of her had wanted to pretend that things could still be like they used to, the two of them running the streets of Sharakhai, poor but free, with the specter of her mother present but distant.

She wondered why Sümeya was so determined to scare her away. Did she know how much Çeda hated the Maidens? The long-whispered rumors of their talents came back to her—their ability to read their enemies' minds, to see into their hearts. Sümeya had been sitting in that rocking chair by Çeda's bed for a long time. Had she peered into Çeda's dreams?

Emre was in such danger, and he didn't even know it. She should have realized the Maidens would look into her past. She should have warned him not to come looking for her. It was a foolish mistake, but it didn't mean she couldn't warn him now and send him into hiding. Once she'd done that, she could return and see what the Maidens and Kings would make of her.

Zaïde finished tending the wounded a short while later. Many of the Maidens would have left the gates already, headed out on patrols. And with the attack on their own, additional patrols would be out, learning what they could about the attack, while others would plan their response.

Through the window across from her, the luster of the coming dawn lit the sky a chalky blue. The three wounded women were silent in their beds. They must have been given a draught of some kind to ease their pain and let them sleep. Perhaps the same drink of Night Lily given to Çeda.

Çeda slipped out from her blanket and set her feet upon the cool ceramic tiles. She cradled her bandaged right arm with her left hand. It was painful, and she would have little use of it, but it was worlds better than it had been. She stood and walked gingerly to the room's central aisle. Her body ached, but this, too, was manageable. Even a simple walk into the open window's cool morning breeze gave Çeda a sense of her old self, a sense that, other than her weakened right arm, she could trust her body.

As she turned down the central aisle, she noticed the full-length mirror at the end of it. She walked numbly toward it, eyes widening in horror as the bright moonlight revealed a woman she hardly knew. She was gaunt, her jaw and cheekbones standing out like a beggar in the Shallows. There were hollowed, blackened wells where her eyes used to be. Her lips were cracked. Her hair was a hopeless, tangled bird's nest. Gods, she looked like a maiden of death, not a Maiden of the Kings.

She shivered and turned away, moved to the nearest window, and stared out at the courtyard below, looking for a way out. She found it in the form of a stone lip that ran between this floor and the one below it. It was narrow, but there were handholds in the stone that would allow her to creep sideways until she reached the corner of the building. From there it was a long but manageable leap to the curtain wall around Tauriyat and the House of Maidens. Her nightdress, thankfully, was overly large, which would give her more freedom of movement, but she would look quite the sight, running through the streets of Sharakhai.

The courtyard—praise to Yerinde herself—was empty. After scanning the windows and doorways of the nearby buildings, she slipped out and onto the stone lip. She was forced to pause and steady herself against the windowsill as a wave of dizziness overcame her. The feeling passed, but when she took more sidelong steps toward the corner of the infirmary, hugging the wall behind her as tightly as she could, the dizziness came on again, stronger than before, and her breath was suddenly coming in great heaves. Her heart began beating like a war drum. It was all she could do to remain in place.

She stared at the curtain wall, a leap she could have made with ease were she in good health. But like this? She'd likely tip over, fall to the courtyard, and break her neck on the stones below.

Gods damn her, she couldn't go. Not now. She'd die in the attempt, or she'd fail and Sümeya would send someone after Emre to tie up loose ends. She couldn't allow either to happen. As much as it grated to be trapped under Sümeya's thumb, she needed to wait until her body would no longer betray her.

With the breeze tugging the hem of her nightdress, she swiveled and looked up to the palaces of the Kings. They looked close enough to touch, and she wondered at the threads that had led her here. How many lives and deaths and decisions of others had led her here? Like streams converging they had created a river that had carried her all her life: her mother's, Emre's, Saliah's, Dardzada's, and surely many, many more that Çeda knew nothing about. Wasn't that what her mother had always said? Ahya had told her to trust that river, to feel for its currents to avoid the rocks and navigate the rapids that lay ahead.

The river is certainly carrying me now.

As much as it made her insides churn, she sidled carefully to the window and lowered herself back inside. She'd no sooner set her feet down than a voice spoke from deep in the room. "I'm glad you returned."

Zaïde was seated on a nearby bed, hands in her lap.

"Come," she said, standing and motioning to Çeda's empty bed, "I've something to show you."

Çeda looked about the room, expecting more Maidens to appear, to force her to follow Zaïde's instructions. But there were none but Zaïde and the wounded women at the end of the room.

Zaïde struck a lantern and set it on the table at Çeda's bedside, then sat on the bed and patted the space next to her. Çeda sat beside her, and Zaïde, without a word, took Çeda's right arm and began unwrapping the bandage. As the thin gauze was unwound, and more and more of the skin beneath shone through, Çeda saw there was blood as well, centered around her palm and thumb, and no small amount of dark ink that had bled through the bandage.

When the bandage was free at last, Zaïde stared at Çeda's hand as if she dearly wished to inspect it more closely, and there was a strange respect—almost reverence—in her eyes. She looked to Çeda and then nodded to her own handiwork: the tattoos that covered Çeda's palm, thumb, and the back of her hand. By the light of the nearby lantern, Çeda stared. She'd been so distracted there'd been little time to wonder how Zaïde had marked her skin. The desert tribes used tattoos to tell the story of one's life, applying the markings at different times, sometimes at a parent's behest, sometimes at the threshold from childhood to adulthood, but most often at momentous times in a person's life. This is exactly what Zaïde had done for Çeda. She had saved her life with some combination of ink and magic and technique, and perhaps even the story the ink told. Çeda thought surely it would mark her as a thief, a beggar in the slums of Sharakhai—a mark to match the bastard symbol on her back. But it didn't.

As she turned her hand over and stared, taking in the ancient words and images Zaïde had captured on her hand, she nearly cried.

The ink traveled not much further than her wrist, and her fingers were untouched, but the rest was covered in an intricate indigo tattoo. On the back of her hand was the tale of her life in Sharakhai. A child of the desert. A woman who had touched a thorn and lived to tell the tale.

A woman who'd risen from simple beginnings. On the palm of her hand was the tale of a fighter, one who was no stranger to sword and shield. A woman with fire burning in her heart, for nothing else could explain how she had lived so long when all stood against her. And on her thumb was a tale of revenge. A woman who would stand against those who had done her wrong. Along the top, words were written in the ancient script of the desert. Words embellished with tiny leaves and thorns and twisting vines. The vines converged along the back of her thumb. A tree, of course. An adichara. And among its vines the words proclaimed: *The lost are now found.* And: *Bane of the unrighteous.*

"What is your name, child?"

"Çeda."

Zaïde's mouth cinched like an old leather purse. "I asked for your *name*."

"Çedamihn Ahyanesh'ala."

"Tell me, Çedamihn, daughter of Ahyanesh, was I wrong?"

Çeda could only shake her head. "You were not. But how could you have known?"

Zaïde took Çeda's hands in hers and touched the calluses she found there, traced the lines on her palms. "Lives are not so difficult to read as you might think." She touched the adichara wound and pain flared deep beneath Çeda's skin. "The poison will never leave. This is a battle you will wage for the rest of your life. It may wane like the moons. There may be days when you'll forget it is there. But there will also be other times when it will threaten you again, and then"—she tapped the bold lines around the wound—"these will not protect you." She reached up and touched Çeda's heart. "You will need to fight it here instead. Do you understand?"

"I do," Çeda said.

"No, you don't"—Zaïde laughed, an old woman's chuckle, a heavy millstone turning—"but you will. And do not try to use anything to ease it, as you did before coming here. No poultices. No elixirs or salves. You will only make it stronger." She tapped Çeda's heart again. "You can fight only here. Remember this."

Çeda nodded, very uncertain of herself, which she hated almost as much as she hated being at the mercy of the Kings and their Maidens.

At the far end of the room, one of the women moaned softly and turned over in her bed.

Çeda turned her attention back to Zaïde. Part of her wanted to tell Zaïde about Sümeya's threat, but thoughts of Sümeya hurting Emre out of mere spite stayed her tongue. Another part of her wanted to ask if she knew Dardzada. He'd refused to reveal anything about his contact in the House of Maidens, and later Çeda had been too disoriented to ask. For all she knew, Dardzada had told her the name as she lay on the bed of the dray, but if that were so, she remembered none of it. And she couldn't simply ask. It'd be the height of foolishness to tip her hand before knowing this woman better. She would wait and learn more, give Zaïde time to speak of it of her own accord.

"I'm to be brought to the King soon, am I not?"

Zaïde's eyebrows rose as she began rewrapping Çeda's hand with another, shorter bandage, which only covered her thumb and wrist. "I see a bird has been whispering in your ear."

"It's true, then?"

"Yes, it's true, though we'll wait until you're stronger, but when you go, he'll decide if you are worthy for this House."

"I thought *you* already had."

Zaïde grunted noncommittally as she bound the bandage snugly. "I am among many who may choose a candidate, including the Kings themselves, but it is Yusam who judges an aspirant's fitness for service."

"I was told something more," Çeda said, taking her hand back at last.

"Go on."

"The blood of Kings runs through my veins, does it not?"

Zaïde nodded. "I saw this on your palms, yes."

Strangely, the confirmation lifted Çeda's heart, not because she wished to be the blood of Kings, but because she'd risked so much on the presumption that it was true.

"Then please," Çeda said, "do you know which King is my father?"

"Did your mother never tell you?"

Çeda shook her head.

Zaïde's eyebrows rose. "But surely she told you that you were the blood of Kings?"

Çeda cast her gaze downward, embarrassed.

"Well, forgive me, child, but how am I to know these things if you do not?"

Çeda displayed her palms. "I only thought . . ."

"I can tell much from a hand, but not that." Throughout the conversation, Zaïde had been calm, but now her face grew hard, her eyes piercing. Her eyes were a beautiful hazel, but there was a dangerous quality to them, like a snake hidden among tall grasses. "Tell me, Çedamihn, who was your mother. Why did she not say you were the daughter of a King?"

"In truth? She cared for me in her own way, but she was a gutter wren. She came to the city from the desert and lived in the western quarter. I don't know why she hid it from me. Perhaps because of her past in the desert. Maybe she wished to protect me from the burden of knowing I was of royal blood while we lived in squalor."

"The King would have made recompense. Seen to your needs."

Çeda shrugged. "My mother was a proud woman."

At this, Zaïde smiled wryly. "I know of pride, young dove." And then a bitter laugh escaped her. "We are the oldest and dearest of friends."

Zaïde retrieved the lantern from the bedside table. She looked up and around her, as if to indicate the whole of the House of Maidens. "I was born here, Çedamihn. I served the Kings for years with my blade, and for many more with my skill and insight. I've grown to recognize the daughters of Tauriyat before I even lay eyes on their palms. You were one such. There was no denying it. The lines of fate the gods have drawn on your palms only verified what I already knew. Believe me when I say King Yusam will see the same. He is far more gifted than I in the Sight. So do not worry. Do not fret. The Jade-eyed King will embrace you and the House of Maidens will take you in. You will serve the Kings themselves. Isn't that better than where you've been?"

"Yes," Çeda said. "There is no higher honor."

"Of course." Zaïde shuffled to the foot of Çeda's bed, the lantern's light sending the shadows to swaying around the room. "Now sleep. Rest your bones and your soul. We have days yet before we take you to King Yusam's palace, and believe me, you'll want to gather your strength before you meet with him."

Chapter 38

*T*HE *BLUE HERON* OF QAIMIR sailed the Shangazi.
The winds were strange this day, the dunes larger
and more rolling than Ramahd had seen in a long while, an
ill portent for the coming eve. He'd said as much to Meryam
as they'd departed Sharakhai, but she'd merely scoffed.

"The dunes are the least of our worries," she'd said.

She'd promised him that they would reach their destination by end of day, but with the sun now hanging over the
western mountains like a burning copper coin, Ramahd
was unconvinced. He called Dana'il to the wheel, handed
over the piloting duties, then headed toward the prow
where Meryam stood. As he strode toward her, he heard a
thumping belowdecks, as of someone stomping on the
floorboards or kicking at the walls. He ignored the sound,
as did the crew, who moved smartly about the ship, preparing her for battle—winding the ballistae, both fore and aft,
stringing bows and readying quivers of arrows, which were
then hung from pegs around the ship. The preparations
were necessary, at least according to Meryam, who had
given Ramahd strict instructions at dawn.

"Now will you tell me where we're headed?" he asked
Meryam. "And why we've brought our captive all this way?"

Meryam's skeletal hands gripped the gunwales to steady herself. She wore a bright yellow dress with an ivory scarf wrapped around her nose and mouth to ward against the windblown sand. She turned to him as the ship tipped and headed down the far side of the dune. She seemed annoyed by his question, but not to any great degree, and suddenly she reminded him of Yasmine so strongly he nearly cried for the anguish it caused. Meryam, though, had long grown weary of comparisons to Yasmine.

She's gone, Meryam would say. *All that remains is taking payment in kind for her and Rehann's deaths.*

"All will become clear soon." She glanced sternward, then swung her gaze back to the horizon ahead, a vista of rolling dunes with a jagged line of mountains in the distance.

He moved to stand by her side. "I trust you, Meryam, but I deserve to know. So do the men."

The ship navigated several more dunes—hull creaking, runners shushing beneath them—before Meryam spoke. "After my father took my form, and the two of you spoke, I whispered a name to you. Do you remember it?"

Of course he remembered it. "Hamzakiir."

"You asked me who he was."

"And you refused to tell me."

"For good reason. I needed to consider our options."

"And what are they, our *options?*"

She tugged her ivory scarf down, revealing her gaunt cheeks, her drawn lips. "May I tell you a story first?"

"Do I have a choice?"

"We always have choices, Ramahd."

Ramahd closed his eyes. There were days, he had to admit, that he wanted to throttle her. "Tell me your bloody tale if you must. Just be quick about it."

"How many times have I told you to value patience? It is a luxury not always afforded by the gods, and when it is available you should savor it, for one never knows when the world will turn."

He stared at her, pleading silently for her to go on, knowing that if he said anything now he might send her off on another infernal sermon.

"Nearly a century ago," Meryam began, "Külaşan, the Wandering King, had a son. His name was Hamzakiir, a clever child who grew into an inquisitive young man. As many of the first-born do, Hamzakiir learned from the other Kings, among them Ihsan, who sent him to neighboring lands to learn of their ways. Hamzakiir visited Qaimir—many times, in fact—and King Beyaz learned Hamzakiir was studying what was then our sole domain."

"Blood magic," Ramahd said.

"Just so," Meryam replied. "He was learning from back-alley magi, picking up the crudest and filthiest uses for blood. King Beyaz invited him to dinner to speak of this, which had been the young mage's plan all along—to bring himself to Beyaz's attention and into his good graces. He did so, and Beyaz, hoping to gain an ally in the House of Kings, trained Hamzakiir in the proper use of blood. Hamzakiir learned well. Very well, in fact. But no one realized, for he was careful to hide his growing abilities. He became stronger than the masters who taught him, stronger than Beyaz, the strongest magi in Qaimir at the time.

"The Wandering King's son returned home some years later, and he continued his experiments there, as his father eventually discovered. The experiments had grown grotesque. Things unseen by the Kings of Sharakhai. He'd killed dozens of men and women, each taken secretly and brought to his manse for slow and careful experimentation. His father, Külaşan, asked that he stop. He did not. Then Kiral, the King of Kings, demanded it. And again, Hamzakiir opposed their will. At last, the Kings held council, and decided the time had come to force the issue. They moved against him in his manse, and Hamzakiir fled, but not before injuring the Kings and Maidens who came for him. He drew the blood of the Kings and killed three Maidens, all unforgivable crimes. So he fled to Qaimir.

"Qaimir and Sharakhai had long been at odds, and King Beyaz saw a rare opportunity in Hamzakiir: the chance to seize the Amber Jewel from the Kings who had ruled it for so long. If he could convince Hamzakiir, and give him the support to lead an attack, he could place the young blood mage on the throne and rule the desert from afar. Hamzakiir agreed, though whether or not he would have stood by this arrangement, we'll never know.

"He raised an army by treating with the man who was then the leader of the Al'Afwa Khadar, Macide's grandfather, Kirhan. Hamzakiir joined his newly bought forces with Qaimir and together they marched on Sharakhai. But the Kings have not ruled for four hundred years without reason. With the asirim and the Maidens and the Silver Spears at their command—not to mention their own considerable might—they crushed the forces of Qaimir and the Al'Afwa Khadar before Hamzakiir could strike. They marched into the heart of our homeland, preparing to take Almadan itself, and would have succeeded had our allies, the Malasan, not marched into the desert and threatened Sharakhai itself."

Ramahd thought back through the tedious history lessons of his youth. "I don't recall Hamzakiir's name ever being mentioned among the texts I've read."

Meryam blinked away dust from a sudden gust of wind, then pointed to a dark patch of land that lay just starboard of their current heading. "One point starboard!" she called to Dana'il, then glanced at Ramahd with an unreadable expression. "I'm not surprised. It isn't a secret, exactly, but it isn't shared widely, either. We are at relative peace with Sharakhai and have been for generations. The last thing we need is for the memory of Hamzakiir to sour our relationship with the Kings, or worse, for the Kings to think we hatched this plot to begin with. You can understand, knowing this, why my father treads so carefully."

"Understanding and accepting are two different things."

"Granted," Meryam replied.

"What happened to Hamzakiir, in the war?"

Meryam shrugged. "We believed he was dead, killed on the battlefield and lost in the desert. But now it's clear that the Kings of Sharakhai had him all along. They spirited him away. Why, I cannot guess. It appears that the Host have found him, and that they want something from Hamzakiir, some secret, else why secure a breathstone?"

Ramahd felt the ship lean into the sand as Dana'il steered them toward the grim-looking place Meryam had indicated. From belowdecks, Ramahd heard the same thumping as before. He gripped the gunwale as the ship heeled along the lee of an uneven dune. "What could Macide want?"

"That's what I hope to discover." Meryam turned and raised her hand to Dana'il. "Take care, now!"

"Aye!" came Dana'il's reply.

The sun was low in the sky now, nearly touching the broken mountain peaks in the distance. Ahead, the dark stain on the horizon resolved itself into a vast plain of dark rock. Black stones as large as houses littered the sand, making it a difficult landscape to navigate, but Dana'il did so with an ease that astounded Ramahd. The ship sailed ever closer to the edge of the plain, but soon they could go no farther, and Dana'il ordered the sails lowered and the anchor dropped.

"Bring him," Meryam said as she strode toward the port gangway.

Before she could go two steps, however, Ramahd grabbed her wrist and spun her around.

Meryam's eyes lit afire as she stared at his hand on hers. "Unhand me! I am not your wife!"

Ramahd did, to the uncomfortable glances of the crew.

Meryam's eyes were afire, but there was something more. Something deeper. She wasn't here any longer. Not completely. She was in another place, as she often was before she performed her magic.

"Tell me why we're here," Ramahd pressed. "Tell me why we've bound one of the Sharakhani and brought him here"—he flung his hand toward the dark landscape—"to this hellish place."

"Do you care for one of the Moonless Host then?"

"I care nothing for them. I care for my crew. I care for you."

Meryam blinked. "We've come for answers, Ramahd."

"Yes, but from *whom* do you hope to get them?"

"You'll see soon enough."

"You'll tell me now, or we'll turn back."

"Bring him," Meryam countered, "and I'll tell you." And with that she strode toward the bulwarks, took a spear from a rack near the portside shroud, and threw it down to the sand. After untying and kicking the rope ladder over the side, she climbed down after it.

Ramahd turned and stared at Dana'il. His first mate stood at the ready, prepared to do whatever Ramahd wished, including hauling Meryam back to deck, but he offered no suggestions other than an impotent shrug.

"Well, go on then, get him," Ramahd spat, frustrated as he turned to follow Meryam.

He leapt down to the sand, and they walked onto the black stone. It was strange, almost glasslike. Ramahd's boots sounded dull against it. Sand skittered over its surface in whorls, revealing the fickle whims of the desert wind. From somewhere, sometimes from all around them, there came haunting sounds, like the moaning of some lost and long-forgotten god.

A short while later, the crew dragged a gagged man to the ship's side and forced him down the rope ladder. In little time the entire crew was following Meryam and Ramahd, spears and swords in hand, their faces steeled for whatever lay ahead. The gagged man walked ahead of them, his eyes darting everywhere, his nostrils flaring as if he knew what was coming.

"There are creatures in this world," Meryam said when they'd walked a good way, "that have lived longer than you or I. There are creatures that see things in other worlds, those linked to ours. There are creatures that will speak with us."

"For a price," Ramahd replied.

"Aye." Meryam chuckled grimly. "For a price."

He had known, of course, what Meryam planned to do with their captive, the owner of the tannery that had sheltered Macide. Macide had moved on quickly, as they'd known he would. They might have taken him had King Aldouan's orders not prevented it. It still burned that he'd been forced to let Macide go—by none other than the father of his murdered wife—but the King had said nothing about sympathizers like the tanner, so when Meryam had demanded a sacrifice for this voyage, Ramahd had known immediately who he would choose.

Ahead, Ramahd saw the spot where Meryam was headed. Lines etched the surface of this otherworldly plateau, radiating outward from a certain point, as if something devastating had happened there long ago. Meryam brought them to a shallow depression in the otherwise smooth stone.

"There," she said, pointing to the hollow with the tip of the spear.

Dana'il laid the tanner down in it. The man was terrified, but he didn't plead for mercy. He lay there, shivering, pressing his bound fists against his forehead with his eyes closed, mumbling words of prayer to Bakhi.

Meryam stood over him like a sentinel, spear at the ready. She lifted it over her head with both hands, intoning something low in the tongue of the magi, words Ramahd was glad he didn't understand. Meryam's hands began to shake. Her words grew louder as she circled the tanner, once, twice, thrice. Then she lifted her head up to the sky and cried out, *"Guhldrathen!"*—and brought the spear down sharply, through the center of the tanner's chest.

The man writhed, an almighty scream escaping him. His legs shivered and his bound hands clutched the spear as if he were trying to pull it free. But he was pinned to the stone below, and soon his head had fallen back, and his body went limp.

Ramahd wondered at Meryam's strength. She'd driven the spear deep. Fully half its length had been swallowed by the stone. There was not a chance, not in a hundred years, that Ramahd could have done the same, even at his most desperate. *None* of his men could have, yet Meryam had done it with ease, with the magic of her own blood.

She stood by the tanner's side and reverently bathed her hands in his blood. She wrote symbols on his forehead, ones Ramahd had rarely seen. Only in the old texts of the libraries of Almadan had he seen the like. The coppery smell of blood was strong as she came to Ramahd. Her eyes were distant again, oblivious to Ramahd and the crew as her slick fingers worked, painting an arcane symbol over his skin. He might as well have been a canvas for all she noticed him. Then she did the same to the rest of the men, giving them each symbols that looked similar but with unique flourishes.

"Guhldrathen!" Meryam called again, facing the mountains and the now-fallen sun. *"Come! You are commanded!"*

Her words sounded small against the backdrop of the Shangazi, but there was power there, magnified by the darkening sky and the moaning wind and the blasted black stone upon which they stood.

"Thrice I call upon you, Guhldrathen! Come! Come, for your servant has need!"

From the shadows, well out into the desert, Ramahd saw movement. Something coming this way, though it was distant enough, and the land so filled with shadow, that he had difficulty telling what it might be. But he heard it. He felt it in his bones. A rhythmic pounding. A scratching like knives against marble.

Ramahd felt his stomach drop as a low gurgling sound reached them. The atavistic growl of a beast twice Ramahd's size. As the thing advanced, darkness came with it, a cloak of midnight, drawing the shadows around and over its shoulders. But Ramahd could see its eyes, twin points of yellowed ivory.

Ehrekh, they were called, creations of Goezhen, god of fell beasts, god of dark ambition. They were fickle creatures. Capricious. Given to anger and revenge for those who sought to manipulate them.

The blood on his forehead felt suddenly foul. He wanted to wipe it from his skin, and from the skin of his men as well. It wasn't that he felt blood magic was unnatural; aeons ago, before the gods had left these shores, they had breathed life into the first of men. They'd shared with man their own blood, that they might live—a gift even the younger gods hadn't been granted, if legends were true. What, then, could be more natural than using what the first gods had given them?

No, it was because Meryam was using her own blood to treat with a perversion of the first gods. Goezhen, who thought himself equal to the first gods, had made the ehrekh, and they hungered, always, for *true* life. It was why they meddled in the affairs of man, why they enjoyed tasting of their blood. Allying themselves with such a creature could bring only sorrow. That was why Meryam hadn't told him what she meant to do. She knew he would have forbidden it.

He'd been foolish to trust her, blinded by his need to fulfill the King's demands so he could concentrate on planting Macide Ishaq'ava's head on the end of a spear.

The ehrekh's midnight skin glistened as it approached. Its muscled chest and arms were like those of a man, but its lower half was more like a bull, with coarse fur covering legs and haunches. A long, forked tail with barbed tips whipped back and forth. Black thorns rose up around its head—a dark crown visible against the dusk, not so different from that of Goezhen's. It walked hunched forward, arms wide, claws flexing as if it were hunting even now. As it came near Meryam, it crouched even lower.

Ramahd readied to draw his sword and protect Meryam should the beast attack. It was a foolish thought, cast aside as useless the moment it came to him. Weapons would not avail them against an ehrekh, not even had they ten times the men. Until the ehrekh was appeased, *Meryam* would be their shield and sword.

The ehrekh paced back and forth, looking toward but apparently not seeing Meryam. It sniffed, scenting the wind as it lowered itself even further until its head was nearly even with Meryam's. She stood before Ramahd and the others, but the ehrekh seemed unconcerned with them. All its focus was bent upon finding her.

"Who comes?" it called, its voice the deep of the earth itself.

"My name is not yours to ask," Meryam replied. "But I know yours."

Guhldrathen smiled, revealing the yellowed teeth of a lion. "Many have come, thinking I could not find their names."

"I have brought you a taste, ancient one."

"I am no *dog* to lap at your command."

"Take it, Guhldrathen. Taste the blood of man, and be glad I've come."

The ehrekh stopped its pacing for a moment. "This?" It

sniffed the air and took two long strides toward Ramahd, stopping just short of him. It hunched down, as it had near Meryam. Its pointed chin jutted forward. Its blackened lips pulled back to reveal sharp teeth, red gums. It sniffed, nostrils flaring. Despite himself, Ramahd cringed from its almighty mass, cringed from the very smell of it, fire and rot and disease. "Thine gift is this?"

The urge to run was almost overwhelming. The only thing that gave him the strength to oppose it was Meryam's sigil, which he could feel on his brow more powerfully than before. He realized then that the sign was no protection from Guhldrathen; it was to grant them the nerve to withstand the ehrekh's presence. The sign was warm and deep, and gave him a sense that he wasn't alone, that Meryam would see them through this.

Meryam walked calmly toward Ramahd and gently took his place so that *she* stood before the ehrekh, not Ramahd. "Nay," she said, "not this one. Your gift lies upon the desert, marked by ash."

Its eyes shot to the ashwood spear, then the tanner lying on the stone. With one long stride it was standing over the dead man, crouching low, lips pulling back as it lifted and lowered its thorned head to sniff at the spear, then the tanner. Legs spread wide, it lowered its head down near the ground. Its forked tongue lapped at the blood.

It bared its teeth in a grim smile like the massive desert hyenas, the black laughers, just before they attacked. "Why hast thou come?"

"I wish to know of Hamzakiir."

The ehrekh swiveled its head toward Meryam. "What use have thee of Hamzakiir?"

"He came to you once, did he not? He used you."

"As thee would use me."

"No. Not as I would use you. I come with gifts freely given. I ask for but a favor, a small enough thing for you to grant."

"Know thee this"—it rose to full height and stared at her like an angry god—"Hamzakiir I cannot find."

"Perhaps not, but you can find those who touch him. He is near us, near *me* and the others who have come to this place. Like threads in a weave, our tales are intertwined. Follow them to a meeting point, and there you will find Hamzakiir.

The ehrekh looked to the crew now, as if it hadn't realized they were there before. It stalked once more, circling them, arms wide, fingers clenching as it paced.

"Thou comest. Thou barters with blood that means nothing to thee. Dost thou think mine interest lies in such?"

"No," Meryam replied easily. "This is but a taste. There will be more."

"Tell me."

"Guhldrathen, can you not guess? Do you think me unprepared?"

The ehrekh flexed its muscles, as if it were barely able to contain its rage. "I would hear it spoken from thine own mouth!"

"Give me what I seek, dark one, and I'll give you your vengeance. I will give you Hamzakiir."

The ehrekh's nostrils flared as it arched back, arms raised, releasing a cry to the moonless sky. Then it crashed its fists against the ground on either side of Meryam. Chips of stone flew in all directions, one cutting Meryam's chin, drawing blood. She ignored the hot trickle slipping along her neck as she met the ehrekh's eyes.

"Hamzakiir?" the ehrekh intoned.

"He is protected from you. I know this. But I swear before the gods themselves that I will strip those protections from him and deliver him to you, or my own life in forfeit."

It leaned forward, huffed a breath so forcefully that Meryam's dress fluttered momentarily, and licked the carmine trail of blood from her neck. Then it nodded once. "So be it."

It rose once more to stare at each man in turn, its gaze not so different from Meryam's when she was taken by her magic. It returned to Ramahd twice, frowning as it gazed into his eyes. It growled, a sound Ramahd could feel in his chest, in the pit of his stomach.

"Hamzakiir is whom thou seek?"

"It is so," Meryam replied.

"Thou canst find him."

"How, Guhldrathen? How?"

"*He* canst find him"—it leaned in close to Ramahd until the two of them were eye-to-eye, though still speaking to Meryam—"if he but follows the White Wolf."

Chapter 39

EMRE STEPPED INTO THE APOTHECARY'S SHOP without knocking. He scanned the front room filled with bowls of small powder-filled bags and shelves of restorative elixirs and crescent-moon charms to hang over a child's bed to keep sickness at bay.

"Dardzada?"

He continued into the workroom, with its thousand-drawer cabinets.

"Dardzada?" he called up the stairs.

When no one answered, he stepped out through the rear door and into the herb garden.

Dardzada was walking the rows with a huge watering can, sprinkling the medicinal herbs he grew there. He was already facing Emre with a placid gaze that made Emre want to rip his throat out.

"What have you done?" Emre asked.

Dardzada set the watering can down and brushed his hands free of dirt. "You'll have to be more specific."

"How could you have taken Çeda to the Maidens?"

"You seem to have me confused with the Silver Spears. Perhaps they caught her reaching into a desert lord's pocket one too many times."

Emre stabbed his finger north, toward Tauriyat. "You *took her* to the House of Maidens!"

"And why would I have done that?"

Emre lowered his voice so that, if there was anyone listening on the other side of the garden walls, only Dardzada could hear. "Because she was *poisoned*. Because you couldn't heal her and could think of nothing else to do with her." Dardzada's expression changed little. Somewhere far away, a goat bleated; its bell clinked. "Don't think of denying it!" Emre shouted. "I went there. I asked along the Spear, and several people saw a fat man dressed as a Qaimiri monk leading a dray with a sick woman aboard. He abandoned her outside the gates. And minutes later, a Matron came to inspect her. They took her in, and she hasn't been seen since. They killed her, Dardzada, and it was all your fault."

Again Dardzada was silent, and it was too much for Emre. He grabbed Dardzada's collar and shook him furiously. *"Why?"*

Dardzada's face grew red, and he broke Emre's grip in a sharp movement, tearing his striped thawb. He tried to throw Emre to the ground, but Emre latched on to him, and they both tumbled over. They wrestled for a while, Dardzada trying to straddle Emre, but Emre was too quick and too strong, and soon *he* was straddling *Dardzada*. He struck Dardzada hard across the face.

Dardzada fought like a cornered lion, scratching and clawing and pummeling Emre with fists that struck like battering rams, but Emre was so angry he didn't care. He fought back just as hard, connecting with a punch to Dardzada's gut and another to his side. They rolled over the garden rows. Dardzada tried to kick him away, but Emre held on, and the two of them grappled, straining mightily, until both were panting like dogs in the heat of summer.

Emre hauled Dardzada to his feet, planning to give him the haymaker of all haymakers, but his anger for Dardzada had drained in their fight, leaving only his own self-loathing. He shoved Dardzada away with a mighty push that sent him tripping over his own watering can. In the process Emre lost his footing on the crushed plants and fell heavily to the ground.

For a long while the two of them lay there in the garden, bruised and bloody, staring at one another.

"Despite everything you did," Emre said, "your sharp tongue, taking your hand to her, inking that bloody tattoo on her back to brand her as a bastard, she still loved you. She trusted you. And you handed her to the Maidens to die."

Dardzada stared with blood on his face and shame in his eyes. *Shame*. From Dardzada.

"At least tell me why you did it," Emre snapped.

"I owe you nothing. You *least* of all, who led her away from a proper life every chance you could."

He wanted to punch the fat apothecary again, make him feel the same pain *he* was feeling, but the urge soon waned, and he found himself standing and extending an arm to Dardzada.

After a moment's pause, Dardzada took his offered hand, and Emre hauled him up.

"Please, tell me. I have to know what happened to her."

Dardzada cast his gaze about, but just then he seemed to be fresh out of biting replies. His lips began to quiver, and he blinked away fresh tears. "She came to me touched by adichara poison. She'd planned on going to them. I couldn't heal it, and Çeda knew. No one but the Maidens can heal such a wound. They were her only chance."

Emre walked past him. "Then she had no chance at all." He stopped at the door leading from the garden and looked back. "You should have sent word to me. Better she had died in a place of peace, surrounded by friends. Even your home would have been better than the house of her enemies."

Dardzada said nothing. He stared at the wreckage of his prized garden and began ordering the trampled leaves, trying to salvage as much as he could. Emre left him like that, tending to the plants that provided for his livelihood. He could choke on them for all Emre cared.

As he stepped back onto Floret Row, the street outside Dardzada's apothecary, a dozen small girls and a few boys trailing behind sprinted along, chasing barrel rings with sticks. When they'd passed, Emre realized someone was watching him from the shadows across the street. He walked to the arched alleyway. "Hello, Hamid."

Hamid didn't smile. Nor did he frown. He merely took Emre in, his sleepy eyes noting the fresh scrapes and welts on his arms and neck and face. "Business?"

"Of a sort."

Hamid's only reply was a nod, as if he'd conducted the same sort of business himself from time to time. "We've more business to attend to, if you're ready."

"Of course I'm ready," Emre snapped.

"Easy," Hamid said. "Stop trying to prove yourself every moment of the day. You did well the other week. Zohra told you the truth. We've confirmed that Veşdi is indeed Külaşan's son."

Emre hoped Lady Zohra was in better hands. He'd done as he'd promised: sent word to the Four Arrows. It felt strange to have any sympathy for those who aided the Kings, but there it was, and what crime had Lady Zohra committed anyway, other than bringing babes into the world?

Hamid had been furious with Emre after he'd heard the story. He'd been convinced the information was wrong, that the records still existed and he'd simply not searched thoroughly enough, but, having nothing else to go on, they'd sent men to watch Veşdi, to see if their one lead might work out.

"You're sure?" Emre asked him.

Hamid pushed himself off the wall. "Come with me."

Emre fell into step alongside him, and together they traveled northeast, deeper into the heart of the most affluent section of the city. The ground rose gradually as they entered Goldenhill, where the tight buildings of Old Sharakhai gave way to newer estates with tall walls. It was an area where the rich hired private guards to patrol the streets. They passed a few with bright swords at their belts, steel breastplates and half-helms, but Hamid merely bowed his head to them and kept on walking. Emre did the same, trying to appear as nonchalant as Hamid, but he felt the fool. Not just a fool, but an interloper; he always did when he found himself walking these streets. "Why are we here?"

"All in good time . . ." He glanced sidelong at Emre with a wry smile on his face. "You always were anxious."

"And you were always shy."

"I'm not shy anymore, Emre."

"I know," Emre replied.

It was true. Hamid had changed deeply. He was still quiet, but not because he was afraid to speak. It came from a confidence that radiated from him like warmth from sun-baked stones in the cool hours of the night.

They came to an open space, a square where a stone-lined well sat beneath the reaching boughs of an ancient fig tree. The tree's blade-like roots were twisted and gnarled, some of them raising the cobbles surrounding the tree. From somewhere nearby came the sounds of industry—hammers and saws and men calling to one another. Hamid plucked a fig from one of the low-hanging branches. He took a bite from it as he sat on the stones circling the mouth of the well. Fig in hand, he pointed to an estate on a hill in the distance. "There."

Emre looked up at it. He'd seen it before, but had no idea who it belonged to. It was one of the largest in Shara-khai, practically a palace in its own right. "That's his?"

Without taking his eyes from it, Hamid nodded. "His men are good. Attentive and well trained. Everyone, inside and out, is chosen by his captain of the guard. He's very careful. It won't be easy to take him."

"What do you want with Veşdi?"

Hamid took another bite, and looked Emre up and down before swinging his gaze back to the sprawling estate. "The Kings hide their children's identities from the world. This you know. They also bestow gifts. All one need do is find them."

"And Veşdi's? What was his?"

"Two nights ago we sent a woman into his home. She's a wonder, is Irem. I swear to you, Emre, she could steal the hooves from a goat. She reached his study on the topmost floor, and found this in a safe hidden in the wall."

With his free hand he reached into his thawb and pulled out a gold medallion.

"What is it?"

"A seal." He tossed it to Emre. "Few in Sharakhai know of them. There are twelve, and twelve only, and they are given to the first-born of each of the Kings. If a King dies, the lone bearer of this seal will come forth to take the father's throne."

"So a woman could rise to the rank of queen?"

Hamid shrugged. "The Kannan ranks men and woman equally, so yes, but in the history of the Kings it's been a distinction without a difference. The Kings still live. Men still sit the thrones of Sharakhai."

Emre inspected the golden seal. It was beautiful and intricate, with tiny gemstones embedded in its surface. "Can it be forged?"

Hamid shrugged. "Who knows? Doubtful, though. Macide suspects the seal would be verified somehow. Those gemstones are set oddly. Perhaps they reflect light just so, in a pattern known only to its maker and to the Kings themselves. Set them improperly, and it would be obvious that it was forged."

Emre ran his fingers over the design—which looked like one of the ancient tattoos from the wandering tribes—then handed it back to Hamid, who returned it to its pocket.

"Won't Veşdi miss it?" Emre asked.

"Doubtful." Hamid tossed the remains of the fig to the base of the tree. "He likely received it the day he was born. I doubt he's looked at it more than a handful of times in his life."

The clop of hooves mixed with the sound of hammering, and soon two guardsmen riding akhala horses with bright, almost metallic ivory coats approached them from across the square. The horsetails on the top of their helms flowed as they rode. Each bore shamshirs and placed their hands on the hilts as they rode near.

"What business?" the nearest of them asked while the other guided his horse to the other side of them.

"None of yours," Hamid said.

"Ah, but yours *is* my business when you walk the streets

of Goldenhill." The guardsman drew his sword. "So tell me, or we'll have more than words."

"He's a tough one," Hamid said to Emre. "Thinks with a horse and a blade he's better than us."

The guardsman spurred his horse closer. Then he dug his heels against the horse's barrel sides and tugged sharply on the reins, calling, "Hup!" The horse reared, its front hooves clawing the air like a desert cat.

Hamid was forced to back away, but the other guardsman cut off his retreat.

"On your way, river trash," the second one said.

Hamid looked up at them with a deadly smile. "Well enough," he said, and jutted his chin to the street he and Emre had come from.

The guardsmen followed them until they were near the center of the city, at which point they peeled away and headed back toward Goldenhill.

"We'll need a diversion," Hamid said as though nothing had happened. When they reached the Trough and turned right, following the flow of traffic heading north, the sounds of the city enveloped them, a welcome change from the strange silence in Goldenhill.

"What sort of diversion?" Emre asked.

"One so large even the gods couldn't ignore it."

"Can I help?"

Hamid said nothing as they came to the Wheel, the massive circle where not only the Spear and the Trough met, but Coffer Street and Hazghad Road as well. Hundreds of people moved through here with carts, horses, drays, arabas, and wagons of all description, singly and in lines as long as the caravans of old, bringing goods to and from the ships at the harbors, or ferrying them across the city. As Hamid guided them east, the roar of the city washed over them—the braying and shouts and laughter audible above it all. He stopped the moment the Spear brought them within view of the wall surrounding Tauriyat and the House of Maidens. He looked at it pointedly, fixing his gaze on the walls as if he could tear them down with thought alone. Pulling Emre closer, he leaned in close and said, "I don't know, Emre. Can you?"

The diversion. They meant to do something here, to target the House of Maidens.

Emre's first thought was of Çeda. She might still be inside. She might be harmed by any attack.

But it was, at best, a fleeting hope. He knew he was fooling himself with such thoughts. She was gone; either killed by the Maidens for trespassing on holy ground, or fallen from the touch of the poison. There was no way she had survived both.

As he stared at those walls, a burning desire to harm the Maidens, to inflict pain on them, stole over him. "Just tell me what to do."

Hamid turned Emre toward him and stared intently into Emre's eyes. His serious expression faded, and a look of pride lit his face. "There's a man I wish you to speak to, Emre. That'll be the first step."

"What sort of man?"

"An alchemyst."

"And what do we need an alchemyst for?"

"Have you ever heard of demon's fire?"

"No, but if you're planning to use it against the House of Maidens, I'm your man."

A laugh burst from Hamid, as it had when they were young; a spontaneous surge of emotion that once was infectious but now felt wrong, like an old man laughing into an empty teacup. "Very good, Emre." He clapped Emre on the shoulder and turned him back toward the Wheel. "Very good."

Chapter 40

O N Çeda's fourteenth birthday, Emre took her to the pits to see Djaga, the Lion of Kundhun, face a woman who, it was said, was Qaimiri royalty. Indeed, Djaga's opponent was announced as Lady Kialiss of Almadan, which made the crowd all the more eager to see how the fight would play out. They were quite the pair, these two dirt dogs, tall Djaga with her closely cropped, red-tinged hair and crisscross of scars over ebony skin, and Kialiss with her compact frame, honey-colored hair, and bone white skin without a single scar.

"Four sylval on Kialiss," Emre said as the swell of betting rose around them.

"How could a dirty wren like *you* have found four silver coins to rub together?" Çeda asked.

Emre shrugged. "They were in the street, lost without their mother. I thought I'd give them a proper home."

"Well, don't put them on the Qaimiri. Djaga's too good."

"That may be, but I'll only win one sylval if I place them on Djaga, whereas the Qaimiri will gain me ten."

"That's a fool's bet if I ever heard one."

"You know so much, do you? Your bloody Djaga never loses?"

"She hasn't yet," Çeda shot back, "and she won't today."

"Oh ho! Then why don't *we* bet? Even money, the Lady against the Lion."

"Now I *know* you're a fool, but your little lost orphans will be more than glad to join their silver sisters in my purse."

Emre merely smiled and waved to a boy selling bright paper cones filled with sugared almonds. "Two!" he called, and tossed a copper khet. With practiced ease the boy snatched it from the air, dropped it into the thick purse strapped tightly to his belt and lobbed two packets Emre's way. They dropped right into his waiting hands.

Çeda accepted one of the packets and began crunching on the lavender honey almonds while Djaga and Kialiss faced one another in the pit below. Djaga, as she always did before a bout, stared hard into her opponent's eyes, arms akimbo, nostrils flared and lips pulled back like an animal ready to defend its life. This was no act. Çeda had seen Djaga fight often enough to know that in Djaga's mind the fight had already begun. Igniting the will to fight, the hunger to win was but one of the steps in her methodical preparations that allowed her to fight with such wild abandon.

Kialiss ignored Djaga, perhaps hoping to put her off-balance. She looked to the crowd instead, swaying her arms, loosening her muscles. Her braided hair swung as she did so. "Look," Çeda said, tapping Emre on the arm and pointing to Kialiss's blond hair, which glinted like diamonds as it swayed back and forth. "she's woven metal into her hair."

Emre's eyes went wide in wonder. "That's bloody *brilliant!*"

"We'll see how brilliant you think it is when she's eating dirt off Djaga's shoes."

Pelam stepped between them with his gong and rang it to start the bout. It was quickly apparent how good Kialiss was. She was fast and precise, and she used her compact body to good effect, anchoring from her stance, powering each swing with hips and torso, not just her upper body. She rained a series of tight thrusts from her spear into Djaga's center, forcing the Lion to back up.

Emre smiled as the crowd pumped their fists, screaming for Djaga to answer the onslaught, but Djaga, at least for now, was at a disadvantage. And in mere moments it grew worse. In a blurring series of moves, Kialiss stepped in and managed to rip Djaga's shield away, but at least Djaga snuck in a shallow cut along her opponent's side. When the fighters parted, blood streaking the Qaimiri's white skin, the crowd screamed for Djaga to draw more.

Çeda rarely joined in with the crowd. Even now she was silent, despite favoring Djaga, despite almost everyone in the stands willing Djaga to win.

"A fool, am I?" Emre asked, crunching his almonds loudly in her ear.

"Begone, foul beast." She shoved him away with her shoulder, never taking her eyes from the action. She loved watching the fighters' styles, picking up moves they used and trying them when she practiced with Emre or Tariq.

The two fighters were clearly tiring, but they put everything they had into each thrust, each block, each advance, each retreat. She grew more impressed with the Lady with each passing moment. Djaga worked a series of moves meant to goad Kialiss into overextending with her spear, and she nearly did several times. Djaga made the mistake of reaching for the haft at one point, giving an insight into her strategy. She needed to take away the Qaimir's greatest advantage: the greater reach of her weapon.

Çeda wondered if Kialiss really was a lady in her homeland. It wasn't uncommon for nobility to fight, particularly those from Qaimir, who fancied themselves skilled with sword and shield. And they *were* skilled. They'd proven it time and time again.

The Lady swooped in, thrusting, then brought the butt of her spear around, which Djaga blocked with her sword while skipping back along the pit wall. Their chests heaved, sweat and blood slicking their muscled skin. The crowd was on their feet now, and for a few moments, Çeda lost sight of them as the large man sitting in front of her leapt up. Everyone was cheering, some grabbing the ones next to them in their excitement.

Çeda stood on her seat and saw Djaga stagger backward. Kialiss ran forward, thrusting the spearhead toward Djaga's chest, hoping to press the advantage. Djaga barely managed to dodge it, and she reached for the haft again. And then Çeda saw a wondrous thing, a thing that would stay with her through all her days.

The Lady was ready for Djaga. She snapped the spear sideways, hoping to slice Djaga's forearms, but Djaga's countermove was already in motion. She had stopped her retreat just before Kialiss's blinding countermove, so the spear missed its mark, Djaga dropping her arm just as she was charging forward. Kialiss tried to hold her center by bringing the spear back in line, but Djaga beat it away with her sword and drove into Kialiss's midsection. Djaga dropped her sword in the process, lifted Kialiss off the ground and bulled forward, building speed before dropping her opponent against the ground, her body itself like a spear, her shoulder driving down into Kialiss's midsection.

Kialiss tried to fight back, but Djaga was on top of her, slamming her fists down into the Qaimiri's head over and over again.

Pelam, the master of the game, ran forward and struck his brass gong when he saw Kialiss go limp, but Djaga ignored him, continuing to pound the Lady of Almadan until one of the pit's burly enforcers dropped down and forcibly pulled her off.

The crowd roared like lions. They stomped their feet, an ancient desert custom, once done by warriors before battle begins but now used as a way to urge the dirt dogs on. Djaga was not Sharakhani, but she'd been in the city long enough for the people to love her and respect the way she fought. As the pit devolved into a rousing chant—*Djaga, Djaga, Djaga*—Çeda watched the Lion. She stood in the center of the pit, breath still coming in great gasps, her face a mask of fury. She'd baited Kialiss into making that mistake. The pits weren't about fighting. Not really. They were about playing your opponents better than they played you.

Like pieces laid out on an aban board, moves were rarely what they seemed, not if one hid her intent well enough.

And that was it, Çeda realized. That was what she would have to do if she hoped to strike against the Kings. She would have to hide her moves. She would have to plan ahead, for surely they would do the same when they learned of her. She had the luxury of being a faceless child in the midst of the sprawl of Sharakhai, but that wouldn't always be true. She had to be ready.

The following day they would learn that Kialiss had died from her wounds. It was a relative rarity, but not unheard of. Every month, it seemed, someone died, either outright in the pits or days later, succumbing to blood loss, unseen internal damage, or infection.

Çeda turned to Emre and held her palm out. "Four sylval, if you please."

"But you cheated!"

Çeda laughed. "And how, exactly, might I have managed that?"

"I don't know," he said, slapping the coins down onto her palm, "but when I find out, you're going to owe me eight sylval."

"Be sure to let me know when that razor-keen mind of yours figures it out." She pointed him down the aisle, toward the exit. "In the meantime, let's find Tariq."

They left the pits and entered the shadowed afternoon streets. The next bout would begin soon, and they wanted to get back to the Trough so they could run the streets a bit with Tariq before the crowds thinned.

They were just leaving when Çeda noticed a brute of a man with several other dirt dogs she'd seen in the pits at one time or another. She knew she'd seen the big one before, but she couldn't place him in any of the matches she'd witnessed, and she was normally very good at such things.

Only when they were well past him did the memory of a man sprinting along the dry riverbed of the Haddah flash through her mind.

Gods, can it be?

She snapped her head around, bobbing back and forth

to look beyond the passing pit-goers, wondering if she'd been mistaken. Hoping she had been.

Emre, who'd moved a few paces ahead during Çeda's preoccupation, stopped and turned. "Will you hurry?"

She looked back one more time and spotted him. And the scar on the back of his bald head.

"What is it?" Emre asked as they began walking again. "You look like you've seen a bloody shambler."

"It's nothing."

"You're white as a sheet, Çeda."

"I said it's nothing."

He left her alone after that, but he knew something strange had just happened. She didn't mean to hide the truth, but she didn't wish to open old wounds either—especially *these* wounds—not until she could learn more, for the man she'd just seen was Rafa's killer, the Malasani bravo who had broken into Emre's home and killed his brother over a stolen purse.

It had taken Emre months to recover from that. It had been so bad she feared he would kill himself in his grief. He'd taken to holing up at home, never leaving, forcing Çeda to care for him. She'd even contacted his older brother, Brahim, the one addicted to black lotus, to try and help, but Brahim hardly knew Emre. He'd only come by once after Rafa's death, and when he hadn't been able to work through Emre's darkness he'd left, returning to the drug den where Çeda found him.

It had taken her long slow months of talking to Emre, bringing him food, even washing him from time to time, before he'd come back from the edge. But there were times, still—more often than she liked to admit—when his eyes went distant, and she knew the memories were haunting him again.

So, no, she wouldn't tell Emre about the bravo's presence, but as sure as the gods were cruel she would make the Malasani regret returning to Sharakhai.

* * *

"Come."

Çeda heard the call from her spot in the chilly hallway

outside Pelam's office, which sat along the southern end of the pits. She parted the beaded curtain and stepped inside. The sun had just risen and was slanting in through the shutters to fall brightly against one corner of the room.

Pelam was sitting behind a desk, his gaunt form hunkered over a ledger in which he was writing in an impossibly tiny script. He was the master of the game. He was the one you went to if you wanted to fight. He picked the opponents, the types of games, their order in the day, all to maximize the profits for the owner, Osman, a fighter turned businessman.

As Pelam continued to write, Çeda stood before his desk, hands behind her back, a thing she'd seen the pit fighters do when staring up at the crowd or Osman before their matches began. Pelam was engrossed in his ledger, however, and Çeda's attention was caught by the personal effects on his desk—beautiful, delicate glassworks of intricate flowers and spread-wing hummingbirds. She'd seen hummingbirds before, though not in these colors, and she'd never seen the like of the flowers. Their petals were shaped like bells. She wondered if the flowers were real, if one could find such things somewhere out in the world, but the hummingbird was so lifelike she guessed the plant-life was as well.

"Orchids."

Çeda started. "Pardon, Master Pelam?"

"The flowers are called orchids. They grow in the swamps and fens of Mirea." He sat back in his chair and took the narrow spectacles from his nose. "Now, what might I do for you?"

"I've come to enter the pits."

Pelam did not smile, nor did he frown, but his expression made it clear he did not like having his time wasted.

"And," she went on before he could say no, "there's a particular man I wish to fight."

At this Pelam's eyebrows did rise. He sat back in his chair and looked down his nose at her. "Is that so?"

"His name is Saadet ibn Sim, and he came to the pits three months ago."

Pelam interwove his fingers and laid them over his lean belly. "And how do you know Saadet ibn Sim?"

"We have personal business."

"Then conduct it outside the pits. This is no place for personal vendettas."

"I know. This is a business, yes?" Çeda untied a small leather purse from her belt and tossed it in onto his desk. The purse was full and it landed with a very satisfying clink—as it ought to do; it held every last coin she'd saved over the years. "So let's talk business."

He eyed the purse, one eyebrow lifting like a sand dune forming in the Shangazi. With his forefinger he shoved the purse back toward Çeda. "And what, pray tell, is this?"

"Enough coin to buy me a bout with Saadet, I reason."

"Have you *seen* this man?"

"I have."

"Turn around for me, if you would."

She did. She'd worn heavy clothes, but left her arms bare. Pelam saw fighters every day; she knew she could not impress him with her physical form alone, so she put on a face like Djaga in the pits, one filled with barely pent-up rage.

"What did you say your name was?"

"Çedamihn Ahyanesh'ala."

"How old are you?"

"Fourteen."

Pelam's eyebrows rose in surprise. "You"—he waved his hand in a circular motion, somehow capturing her entire physique—"are only fourteen?"

"So my mother told me."

"And where *is* your mother, Çedamihn?"

"Dead."

"Ah . . ." His expression flattened, revealing little, but she had the distinct impression she'd somehow disappointed him. "You're fit enough for fourteen. You might even make a decent fighter in a few years, but not now. And not against Saadet."

"It would make a brilliant match. I promise you that."

"For those who like a slaughter, yes, but for the rest of my audience, I'm afraid they'd be all too disappointed. As would you when the boys scrape you up off the pit floor."

"I can fight. You can test me."

Pelam sighed. "I've been doing this for a very long time. I like to think I can tell after a moment or two whether a prospective *selhesh* will work out. Sometimes I'm wrong, but more often than not, these old eyes are right. And you, Çedamihn Ahyanesh'ala, would not last the passing of a hawk over the desert blue sky against a man like Saadet."

"Saadet deserves a beating, Master Pelam. More than you can know. I will fight him, and I will win."

Pelam stood. "Not in *my* pits, you won't."

"Ask Osman, then. He was a fighter once. He would understand."

"Would understand what? Revenge? *I* understand revenge, girl. Don't think I don't. If that's what you want, find him and kill him when the tourney is done. If you know enough to have found him here, you can surely find his lodgings."

"I don't want to kill him in the dark. I wish for him to know who's come for him. I wish for him to know fear as deeply as he's sown it."

"So that's it, then. You wish to kill him for all to see, including the gods."

"That about sums it up. You don't know what he's done."

"What? What has he done?"

"It isn't my story to tell."

Pelam's snort made her ears burn with embarrassment. "You're wasting my time."

"Please, if you could only—"

"Enough!" Pelam picked up the bag of coins and threw it at Çeda's head. She ducked, the bag bursting through the strings of beads hanging from the doorway and thumping dull as a dead man's purse against the opposite wall. "Take your money and leave. And don't let me catch you haunting the streets around the wells. If I do, I'll have you beaten and thrown in the Haddah's dry bed to rot. Do you understand?"

Çeda could only stare. *What an utter, bloody mess I've made of this.*

"I said, *do you understand?*"

"I do."

"Now, get out!"

She picked up her money and made her way out of the pits and into Sharakhai, feeling a fool but, more than that, feeling as though she'd failed Emre, which she wasn't ready to accept. And yet she had no idea what she could do about it. She couldn't go home. She knew that much.

As she wandered the streets, she realized she was heading toward the west end of Sharakhai. And slowly she realized *why* she was heading toward the west end.

Without even consciously thinking about it, her pace began to pick up, faster and faster, until she was sprinting toward the harbor.

Chapter 41

ÇEDA RODE AN ORNATE, four-wheeled araba up the winding road to Yusam's palace. The setting sun was lost behind the araba's canopy and lit the cloth a burnished gold. The wagon bumped, and Çeda's stomach lurched. She gripped the seat harder with her good left hand. She was not afraid of heights, but the paved road was very narrow, and with only the smallest stone shelf along one side, it felt as though the araba might tip over at every turn.

Zaïde and Sümeya sat across from her, both wearing embroidered cream-colored dresses that were so unorthodox—at least to Çeda's knowledge—that it made her uncomfortable. It was as though they were playing dress-up, and that somehow felt insulting. Both had been silent since they'd left the House of Maidens, but they were a study in contrasts. Where Zaïde leaned her body into the padded bench, Sümeya sat with her back straight, hands and eyes in constant movement. Where Zaïde's breathing was easy, Sümeya's was sharp and erratic. And where Zaïde seemed content to watch the passing landscape, Sümeya stared down at the wagon's floor or at Çeda with a mildly nauseated look on her face.

Çeda wore not a fighting dress, nor the hobnailed

sandals of the pits, but fine slippers, a silk gown of lightest blue and a jeweled headdress with gold medallions, as if she were about to be presented as King Yusam's bride. The mere thought twisted Çeda's guts in knots. It also made her painfully aware of the slim knife she had strapped to the inside of her thigh. Once or twice Çeda caught Sümeya staring, which only made Çeda relive Sümeya's nighttime threat that unless she refuse the Maidens and return to the streets, Emre would pay the price.

Sümeya looked at her again, and Çeda said, "One would think *you* were being presented to Yusam for judgment."

To Çeda's surprise, Sümeya's only reaction was a deep frown, but at least she stopped staring as the wagon continued its steady climb, high above the sprawling city.

When they reached the top they came to a great circle. At its center stood a marble pedestal with a bronze statue of two leopards, teeth bared. It smelled crisp here, and cool, so different from the streets below. The araba swung around the circle and came to a creaking stop. The door was opened immediately by a young footman. A second footman, a few years older than the first, stood ready to help Zaïde down. She waved him away, and Sümeya ignored him. He seemed so eager to please, however, that Çeda allowed him to take her hand as she stepped down.

The moment her feet touched the ground, two more servants opened the tall entrance doors. Somewhere inside, a gong rang. The tone was low, and it went on and on as Zaïde stepped inside the great entrance hall and was met by an older man dressed as a palace steward in a black turban and a fine kaftan of ivory and earthen tones made from a beautiful woven fabric.

As Zaïde stepped aside, the steward scrutinized Çeda. Çeda thought he would search her, that he'd find her hidden knife, but he merely bowed and said, "The honor would be mine if you would follow me."

Çeda gave one last nod to Zaïde and trailed after the steward, heading deeper into the palace. She knew the palaces were large, but even so, it was much larger than she'd guessed. They passed through a hall with tall marble columns and a wide set of stairs, which they followed up four levels into a garden with beautiful flowering plants. It was such a winding section of the palace that Çeda wondered if she'd ever find her way out again. All the while her shoulders pinched tighter and tighter. The vision of her mother that she'd seen in Saliah's garden haunted her: her mother walking the halls of a palace. Had she walked *these* halls? Was the Jade-eyed King her father? Could the responsibility for her mother's death be laid at his feet?

The mere thought enraged her, but Çeda calmed herself. Because the surest way of tipping her hand to a man like King Yusam was to present herself with anger in her heart, she allowed her thoughts to die on the vine. Just as she did in the cool cellars of the pits before a bout, she let the tension fade, allowed the tightness in her shoulders and chest to ease, relaxed her clenched jaw and allowed her eyes to take in and memorize her surroundings instead of searching constantly for threats. By the time the steward led her to another garden, much larger than the first, she was calm itself. She allowed some anxiousness to show, as a young Maiden would, but beyond that, she projected confidence, pride, even eagerness, hoping Yusam would be unable to guess her true intent.

The garden had a burbling stream running along one side of it, and its border was not a wall but the uncut stone of Tauriyat itself. The stream ran into a clear, dark pool of rippling water with a coping of emerald green marble. There were trees here as well, types Çeda had never seen before. They had thick, entwining boughs that created a canopy of dark green leaves over the garden and prevented Çeda from seeing more of the indigo sky than patches and pinholes. She started when she noticed large, lamplike eyes hidden within. She ducked her head, ready to react to whatever it was, and saw a long graceful cat slung over one of the lower boughs—a leopard from the mountains, if she wasn't mistaken. It looked as much a part of this palace as the urns and tapestries Çeda had seen on her way in. There was also a second cat, perched higher than the first, its head resting on one paw. Both of them watched her languidly, golden eyes blinking every so often.

"Beautiful, are they not?"

Çeda spun, realizing the steward had taken his leave and someone new had taken his place.

Standing on the far side of the mere, beneath one reaching branch, was a tall man, sleek as the cats who lazed on the branches above. He ducked his head, abandoning the darkness of the trees for the soft, even light of the garden. He wore a khalat, a long-sleeved robe of black Mirean silk. A squat turban adorned his head, pinned with an emerald brooch of deepest green. He had an aquiline nose and a weak chin, but his eyes were piercing. And their color . . . Jade-eyed King, indeed. Their bright green faded to silvery white at the center, giving him a rapacious look. They made her feel as though she were already caught before she'd even spoken a word.

"Most beautiful, Excellence," she said, her voice catching.

He took slow, deliberate steps toward her, as if she were a doe he might startle. Like his face, his hands were gaunt, accentuating his knuckles and bones. His fingernails, however, were long and thick and yellowed. Like a cat's. The tips of them were stained ochre, the color of dried red wine, as if whatever had touched them had done so so many times that the stain had become indelible.

Blood, she realized. Blood discolored his nails. *From what?* she wondered. *From what flesh?*

In an instant much of the nervousness she'd managed to suppress returned. He was an imposing man, and not from his physical stature, or even from his eyes, but from the depth of his soul, which was somehow palpable.

Perhaps sensing her fear, he motioned to the bandages on her right hand. "The adichara gives an ardent kiss, does it not?"

"It does," Çeda said. "Though it feels much better, with many thanks to Zaïde."

He took another step, a smile stealing over him. "And why were you there, child? How found you among the twisted trees?"

By Rhia's bright face, those eyes . . . "I wanted petals." She was unraveling. She could feel it. She was in danger of telling him anything he wished to know.

"And why did you want petals?"

She swallowed hard, and she was suddenly grateful that a week had passed since her conversation with Sümeya. She'd taken Zaïde's advice. She'd rested herself. She'd drunk Zaïde's brewed concoctions, which tasted more than a little like Dardzada's. She ate, sparingly at first, but as the pain in her right arm faded, her appetite returned, and she ate bread and hummus and even a bit of meat. She felt a different woman, and yet, standing here before Yusam, she felt undone.

Had her mother truly faced these men?

For so long after her mother's death, she'd been angry with her for leaving, angry she had done something so futile. But now, standing before one of them, she understood a part of what her mother had gone through. And she knew there was more to Ahya's actions than Çeda had ever realized. Çeda knew so little of the things her mother had weighed before deciding to go to Tauriyat the night of her death, or of the potential consequences if she hadn't. It was this realization—a link to her mother—that brought Çeda back to herself, to regain a bit of her lost confidence. "The draught from the petals is sold in the secret places of Sharakhai."

"And who would *you* sell your petals to?"

"Why do you need to know?"

His voice grew sharper. "Stealing petals from the twisted trees is forbidden. As is the selling of their distillations."

"There are dozens who do so. Taking one of them will simply create an opening for another, leaving you no better off than when you started."

"I will have his name."

"Forgive me, my King, but you've granted me this audience for a reason, have you not? You wonder if I might join the ranks of the Maidens."

"What of it?" he snapped.

"I understand each Maiden is granted a boon of their choosing, either the day they join or on their naming day. If you accept me then grant me this gift: the name of the one I sold petals to. It's nothing to you and means much to me."

He stared at her more intently then, concentrating, and Çeda could feel her will slipping. But she stood resolute, and Yusam's gaze relaxed. Then he stepped forward and held his hand out to her. "Very well, Çedamihn. But should you prove unworthy"—he motioned toward the mere with his other hand—"I will have the name and your life."

She stepped forward and placed her hand in his. The skin of his palm was rough, like the pads on a cat's paw.

"Who was your mother?" he asked as he led her toward the mere.

She considered lying, but too many in Sharakhai knew her mother's name. "Ahyanesh," she replied.

"And her tribe?"

"Masal," she lied, the very same lie her mother had used when she was young. She knew that her mother had come from somewhere else in the desert—she'd admitted as much to Çeda once—but she had never said which tribe she was truly from. *You're too young,* she would always say. *When you're older, I'll tell you.*

"Ah," Yusam said, sounding disappointed. "I had hoped, little one."

Hoped for what? But then she realized. Yusam had hoped that she might be of his line, related to him in some distant way. She wanted to vomit.

"Apparently not, Excellence."

He shrugged. "The gods will play their games."

"And from which tribe do *you* hail?"

This was hidden knowledge. Still, she thought Yusam might be of the mood to tell her, but he merely smiled and said, "*Not* Masal," and then asked, "And your father?"

"I know not, Eminence, as you're well aware."

"Such a sharp tongue." He smiled a wicked smile. "Take care it doesn't cut your throat."

They came to the edge of the mere, where Çeda looked down, expecting to see its bed, for the water was crystal clear. Instead she saw a bottomless thing that threatened to pull her in. She became dizzy as she stared into it. She leaned forward, caught by its spell.

Yusam grabbed her by the shoulders and steadied her.

"The draw of the mere is strong, especially for one so young." He tugged at her wrist. "Kneel, child."

She did, eyes fixed on the depthless vision before her. The cloth of Yusam's khalat rustled as he moved to the opposite side of the pool and knelt. She saw this from her periphery only, for no matter how she tried she could not withdraw her gaze from the water. Yusam leaned forward. His knuckles whitened as he gripped the coping and brought his face a mere breath away from the surface of the water.

As he stared down into the depths, he murmured in cavernous tones. Çeda could pick out no words among the hills and valleys of his endless, rhythmic utterances. It didn't feel as though he were looking down into a pool of water; it felt as though he were staring into her soul, into her past and into her future. As if he was looking deep within her, pulling her apart to see what she was made of, judging her worthiness for a place in the House of Maidens.

A burst of fear surged through her. He would see her mother's actions, her trips to Saliah, her harvesting of the petals on Beht Zha'ir. He would see all that Çeda had done as well. Her own trips to the blooming fields, her own spying on the Kings. And when he did, all would be lost.

She remained there for a long while, chained by the magic of the mere, or perhaps of the King himself, and the more time that passed, the more her insides churned, the more she wished to be free of the scrutiny. It became so intense she nearly confessed to Yusam, if only to be free of the way he was toying with her.

She heard someone screaming, and finally pulled out of the spell. She'd thought she, herself, was the one screaming, her fears given voice, condemning herself even further before this judgment King. But it wasn't her. It was Yusam.

He still leaned over the water, gripping the coping stones so tightly his tendons looked like crossbow strings. With trembling arms he pushed himself up as though exhausted. His face was white as bone. His eyes stared sightlessly for a long while, until finally he saw Çeda. His lips trembled. His eyes, shrouded within deep sockets, were red. He stared at her with a look of deep regret. And fear.

It gave her a sense of satisfaction knowing that the Kings could fear as Yusam did now, and that *she* might be the cause of it. But then the look faded, and his eyes hardened.

Here it comes. My pronouncement.

"Leave," he said.

"My King?"

"Leave this place!"

Çeda stood, her entire body shaking with nervous excitement. Yusam was ignoring her, assuming that she would obey his order without question. *I should take him now*, she thought. She should take her hidden knife and plunge it into his back. Kill one of the Kings in his own palace; the mere thought filled her with energy. He would probably order her death anyway, so why not take him first? Her death would follow in retribution, but still, it might be enough to honor her mother in the eyes of the gods, to redeem them both in some small way. But then her mother's hidden poem came to her before she could act.

While far afield,
His love unsealed,
'Til Tulathan does loom;
Then petals' dust,
Like lovers' lust,
Will draw him toward his tomb.

The words were burned into her memory. She knew it spelled out how to bring down one of the Kings. She didn't know which, or just how it could be done, but if she were patient, she would eventually tease out the answers. And it wasn't merely this one riddle that transfixed her. It was the certainty that there were more. *I've found four*, Ahya had told Saliah. *Four is not twelve*, Saliah had replied. Where were the other three Ahya had found? And where were the other eight? If there was some small chance that Çeda could stay in the service of the Kings, then there was a chance she could unlock the riddles. Finding those poems had been her mother's life's work, secreting them away so that she or others could use them against the Kings. And if Çeda waited, she could plan better, protect those she loved, or at least give them warning. If she killed Yusam now, they would pay a price for her crime.

Yusam lifted his head, quivering, his eyes aflame in anger, but Çeda spoke before he could. "My King," she said. "I know not what you saw, but know that I will protect you. You and the House of Kings. I was not raised in the House of Maidens, nor Tauriyat, nor Goldenhill. I know not who my father is. But I know that blood is blood." She knelt, bowed her head, and cupped her hands toward him—an offering, plain and simple. "I give to you what little the gods have given me."

When she rose she saw that much of the anger had left his eyes, replaced by a look that said he was weighing her words, weighing *her* against whatever he'd seen, and was clearly having trouble deciding what to do. If she'd learned anything in the pits, it was when to press her advantage and when to retreat. Before the Jade-eyed King could say another word, she stood and left.

He was silent, but as she passed through the garden and into the palace proper, she heard a long growl from one of the great cats.

It sounded like a plea. Or a lament.

She walked blindly through the palace, already doubting herself, until the steward found her and led her back to the entrance. The sun had set, but large braziers lit the carriage circle in its stead, casting wicked shadows against the bronze leopards at its center. Çeda climbed back into the carriage, where Zaïde and Sümeya still sat. The doors of the palace boomed shut. As the driver called "Hup!" and the two horses lurched into motion, Çeda thought surely Zaïde would ask what had happened, or Sümeya would snap at her, but neither said a thing. Meetings with the Kings were clearly sacred, not meant to be shared, and for this she was mightily relieved.

As the araba wheeled around and prepared to head back down the winding road to the base of Tauriyat, the palace doors opened once more, and who but the King himself should step out.

Yusam, looking haggard and troubled, strode down the

steps and across the stones toward the araba. The driver reined the horses to a stop as Sümeya looked at the King, then Çeda, then the King again.

Zaïde stepped down, Sümeya followed, and Çeda came last, all three bowing their heads.

"Rise," Yusam said. He stared into Zaïde's eyes as the firelight glinted off his golden crown. "You may have my answer now if you wish, Matron."

"Of course, O King," Zaïde replied.

"This one pleases me," he said. "You will take her in, our young Çedamihn Ahyanesh'ala. You will train her in the ways of the blade"—those jade eyes glanced sidelong at Çeda's right arm—"though I suspect she may teach *you* as well." And then he turned to Sümeya. "And you, Sümeya, will welcome her into your hand."

At this, Sümeya gasped. She *gasped* at a command from her King.

It was something Çeda would never have expected, not from a woman like Sümeya. It spoke to how dearly she wished Çeda gone, wished her lost once more among the poorest corners of Sharakhai.

The hand was the basic fighting unit of the Blade Maidens, five women who trained together, who knew one another intimately—fighting styles, their strengths, their weaknesses, their loves and dislikes. Yusam had commanded that Sümeya take Çeda into *her* hand, to train her, protect her, and give her everything she needed to benefit the interests of the Kings.

The silence lengthened, Sümeya glowering at Çeda, clearly expecting her to refuse the King's request. Çeda said nothing, however. Her silence put Emre in danger, but she could not turn down this opportunity. Yusam's green eyes hardened, and Sümeya finally seemed to cobble together a handful of words. "Forgive me, O King, but Husamettín grants me my orders."

Yusam smiled, a humorless thing. "In this he will not deny me. You have been without your fifth for too long, and too long from the side of the Kings. It's time you return." He stepped in and kissed Sümeya's forehead, a sight that brought Çeda immediately back to the night of Beht

Zha'ir when the asirim's strangely warm lips had been pressed to her own forehead. He'd been wearing a crown, as Yusam did now.

Sehid-Alaz, Saliah had called him. Had that sad creature once been a King?

"We will speak again," Yusam said to Çeda.

And with that he turned and strode away, his footsteps over the river stones filling the cool night air with a sound like breaking bones.

Chapter 42

WHEN THE ARABA CARRYING ÇEDA, ZAÏDE, and Sümeya returned to the House of Maidens, Sümeya leapt down while it was still moving and strode away, back straight and head held high. Zaïde lowered herself down carefully and led Çeda back to the infirmary. Çeda would eventually be given her own bed with Sümeya and the others from her hand, but for now she would sleep where Zaïde could keep a close eye on her convalescence.

Only one woman was still in the infirmary, the one who'd been badly wounded. She lay there, bandaged and moaning, her eyelids fluttering like butterfly wings under the sedatives she'd been given.

On the way back from Yusam's palace, Çeda had tried and failed to understand why he'd acted as he had. Why assign Çeda to Sümeya's hand? It must have been something he'd seen in the pool. He protected the Kings by detecting those who might mean them harm. She'd thought he had seen something horrible relating to her, but if he had, he wouldn't have hesitated to kill her.

What, then? What could he have seen? Perhaps not a vision of Çeda, but of someone else. Or a memory that haunted him?

"Will I be allowed to leave?" Çeda asked as she sat on the edge of the bed.

Zaïde lowered herself with a grimace and sat facing Çeda from the next bed over. "Not for some time, but eventually, if you please Sümeya, yes."

Çeda was already shaking her head. "I will never please Sümeya."

Zaïde's lips thinned to a dark line. "I won't lie to you. Sümeya is a harsh woman, a grim leader, and she's still angry over the loss of her sister years ago, the woman she replaced as leader of her hand. She's angry that Yusam has put you in the still-vacant position that Nayyan once held. And perhaps she's right about all of these things. It will not be easy for you in the weeks ahead, but Sümeya respects honor. She respects effort. I know not the life you led before you came to my door, but I know a page has turned on that life. There is no going back, and if you try to leave again without permission"—Zaïde jutted her chin toward the window—"you will be brought back to the courtyard and lashed. Leave a second time and you'll be stoned to death. Do you understand?"

Çeda nodded. "I do."

"Do you truly?"

"Yes."

"No, you don't. You are not one of us, not yet. You know little of our ways, only what you've heard in the streets of Sharakhai, which, believe me, is poor education indeed. I knew this when I took you in, but now, after Yusam's decision, I wonder if you'll last the month. Sümeya is First Warden, the commander of the Maidens. She chose the other three in her hand personally. Yusam acted with the guidance of the mere and the best interests of the Kings in mind. But Sümeya will not see it that way. She will see only her lost sister, Nayyan, and you standing in her place. She will see Nayyan's honor replaced with the morals of a thief caught stealing from the sacred groves. And she will use any excuse to punish you. I see you, Çeda. I see your will. I see your desire to leave, perhaps to speak to those who brought you here, or loved ones, or even enemies, but I tell you: Do not do it. I will not be able to protect you if you do."

"Why would you want to?" Çeda shot back.

Zaïde raised her eyebrows, then she stood and looked down on Çeda with something akin to sadness. "Because, though you may not yet recognize it, you are blood of my blood."

No, I'm not. Çeda could only just believe the blood of Kings ran through her veins, but even if that was true, Çeda was not one of these women. Zaïde might have saved Çeda, she might even be Dardzada's hidden ally in this place, but that didn't make them sisters, and Çeda had to remember that. Always.

"Get some sleep," Zaïde said as she moved away. "We'll start early."

"What was she like?" Çeda asked before she'd taken two shuffling steps.

"Who?"

"The lost Maiden. Nayyan."

Zaïde considered this a moment, her back to Çeda. Then she turned, only enough so that Çeda could see the pensive look on her face. "She was a gifted woman. Ambitious. Bright. Beautiful, in her own way. She told stories from the old texts, tales of the Kings before the night of Beht Ihman, but in such a way that they came alive once more. She had a wonderful laugh and a wicked blade. She was First Warden before Sümeya. And she was lost to us."

"Lost how?"

"No one knows. She was here in our House. She was to take a royal clipper to visit her family. But she never reached the ship. We searched the city and the desert for days, but no one ever found her. In the weeks that followed, no one spoke of replacing her in Sümeya's hand." Odd, Çeda thought, since Zaïde had said only yesterday that it was rare for vacancies in the Maidens' ranks to last longer than the traditional seven days of mourning. "So revered was Nayyan that, even after Sümeya rose to First Warden, we honored her by leaving her a place in the hand. Once set, things have a way of remaining in place, and, well, it has been this way for eleven years now."

Eleven years . . . the same length of time since her mother died.

"Why now?" Çeda asked. "Why would Yusam finally choose to replace her when no one has complained for eleven years?"

Zaïde turned and faced Çeda squarely. "Perhaps he saw in you our salvation."

The words sent a chill down Çeda's spine: *our salvation*.

It wasn't until Zaïde left, and Çeda lay down to sleep, that she realized she had no idea whose salvation Zaïde meant. The Kings? The Maidens? Sharakhai? Not knowing left Çeda with the feeling that there were more layers to Zaïde than she might have guessed.

Three nights later, Çeda woke herself from sleep. She'd always been gifted in this way, sleeping easily and waking when she wished. She'd given most in the House of Maidens time to fall asleep.

In the days since her audience with King Yusam, her fear for Emre had only grown. Tomorrow night, a welcoming feast was to be held for Çeda, when she would be presented to any of the Kings who chose to attend. She judged that Sümeya would wait at least until then to follow through with her threats, in case one of the other Kings denied Çeda entrance to the House of Maidens. But Çeda knew that, beyond tomorrow night, the danger only rose, so tonight it must be. Tonight, or the risks for Emre were just too high.

She sat up in her bed and sniffed. The air smelled of henbane, surely from the Maiden sleeping soundly at the far end of the room. She changed as quietly as she could into one of the white dresses she'd been given, then pulled on her slippers and headed for the same window she'd used over a week ago. Outside, only Rhia's half-moon hung in the sky. It made for an especially dark night, but she could see two Maidens walking along the curtain wall that surrounded the House of Maidens. They soon came to another length of wall, the one that intersected the much larger and lengthier wall separating the House of Kings proper from Sharakhai, the one that wrapped around the whole of Tauriyat. The sentry Maidens took stairs up to this common section and strode along the length of it, standing for a while over the main gates to the city.

The punishment for leaving the House of Maidens was still fresh in her mind—a lashing in the courtyard for all to see—but she couldn't remain here without warning Emre. Sümeya's threat had been all too serious. Emre had to know that she was safe and that he must no longer ask for her along the Spear. He had to hide, even if that meant hiding himself among the Moonless Host for a time. Better with them by far than dead by Sümeya's hand.

Çeda watched a third Maiden meet the other two on the curtain wall. They spoke for a time, and Çeda thought she might be able to make a running leap along the ledge to the wall and slip over the other side before they saw her, but the Maidens parted again, two of them walking the walls while the third remained in place, watching the city.

Minutes passed, stretching on and on into the night, while Çeda tried to discern some pattern to the Maidens' patrols, including those who moved through the yard below, but she could see none. And the lone Maiden at the bend in the wall didn't move.

Thoughts of Emre being strung up like her mother, with cruel words cut into his skin, played through Çeda's mind. A part of her, the weak part, the scared part, cautioned her to go back to bed, to try another night, but she tore up those thoughts like weeds before they could take root. She had to go now. Emre needed her.

She stepped out onto the ledge and sidestepped along it, closer and closer to the curtain wall. Her white dress masked her somewhat against the stone of the building, but she was a mere ten paces from the Maiden now. All the Maiden need do was turn, and she would see Çeda plain as day.

Two Maidens rode out from the stables below and into the courtyard. The clopping of the horses' hooves sounded loud as kettledrums. They were headed toward the main gate, surely to head out into the city, but they would pass right by Çeda. She held perfectly still. She even held her breath—sure the women were about to notice her—when a ball of flame flew up and over the wall in a high arc,

twisting like a broken piece of the sun. In the cool of the
night Çeda could feel the heat of its passage. It crashed
onto the far side of the yard. Fire sprayed and spread in the
shape of a spearhead, some of it licking against the stables
wall. The two Maidens wheeled their horses around as a
second ball of flame arced over the walls, then a third. One
struck the center of the yard, making the horses scream.
The other crashed onto the roof of the tallest of the Maidens' seven buildings, the one with the stained glass windows and red clay tiles.

Demon's fire. Çeda had never seen it, but she'd read
about it. Kundhun had alchemysts, and years ago they'd
used demon's fire against Sharakhai, hoping to take the
city before the asirim could be brought to bear. The attack
had been thwarted when King Beşir, the King of Shadows,
had appeared among them, killing their alchemysts one by
one, and Azad, the King of Thorns, had slipped through
their defenses to gut their general, stem to stern, and then
fled, almost too fast for the eye to follow.

A bell began to ring, then another, and another. A section of the wall across the courtyard from Çeda burst into
flame as another projectile crashed against the wall walk
and the battlements. The Maiden who'd been standing there
leapt free just in time, rolling wide as flames licked down the
stone and swelled near the base, bright as a sunrise.

Attacks against the Kings were rare, but they happened,
and with more regularity over these past few years. She
had no idea why this one had been launched, nor why they
would target the House of Maidens, one of the places that
was sure to have the swiftest reprisal. But she knew that if
she were going to leave, it would have to be now.

After one deep breath, she ran and leapt for the wall.
She landed, skidding on the wall walk. She stared across
the fire at the Maiden on the far side, who watched Çeda
with narrowed eyes. Çeda shrugged, an apology of sorts,
then levered herself over the parapet and dropped.

One last ball of fire arced high on the other side of the
Maiden's compound. Where it struck she didn't know, but
she heard a crash and a score or more horses being ridden
through the opened gates. As the sound of galloping

hooves and crisply called orders filled the air, Çeda snaked through the buildings of the old city and into the night.

———————— ‹—●—› ————————

As she neared home, it was strangely quiet. The entire city was. The news must have spread. When things like this happened, the western quarter grew anxious. Few but the boldest went out on such nights, for the Maidens would soon be out, searching the Shallows, drawing blood, cracking skulls, doing whatever it took to find those who'd attacked the House of Maidens.

Çeda heard a babe wailing as she reached the winding lane where she lived, but the babe was hushed quickly. There were no lamps lit in her sitting room, nor behind the curtained windows of hers or Emre's rooms. When she reached the door, however, she checked the latch. Long ago they'd fixed it so that they could lift the latch and it would stick. If the latch was up, they'd know the other was still out. If the latch was down, they'd know either that the other had returned home, or that some other party had tried the door.

The latch was down.

Part of her wanted to believe that Emre was up there, but something told her he wasn't. She opened the door and crept slowly up the stairs. Emre had fixed the steps so they made only the barest of creaks as one crept toward the landing above. She saw a flicker of light above—a candle perhaps, the light stabbing out from beneath the door. There was a pungent smell of smoke in the air, like burning leaves and freshly turned earth in a forest a thousand leagues from the desert.

Someone was waiting for her, and they wanted her to know it. Which meant she was wasting her time sneaking up on him. Or *her*. Sümeya might have beaten her here. The Maiden might, in fact, be waiting on the other side of the door, ready to run Çeda through with her ebon sword. She'd do it with pleasure and spit on Çeda's dying body as she left, glad to be rid of the gutter wren from Roseridge once and for all.

Çeda steeled herself and opened the door and found a

man sitting against the wall, smoking a pipe, studying her with a surprised glint in his eyes.

"Who are you?" Çeda asked warily.

"How quickly they forget."

She recognized the voice first, the man second. His features had been obscured by the deep shadows thrown by the lone candle in the center of the rug, but when he leaned forward he was easy to recognize. It was Ramahd, the Qaimiri nobleman who'd lost his wife and daughter to Macide.

Çeda stepped into the room, closing the door behind her. "What are you doing here?"

He stared at the bandages over her right wrist, but then his eyes noted what she was wearing: the simple white dress given her by Zaïde. From the narrowed waist to the square-cut neck, anyone familiar with Sharakhai would know what it was. "The Maidens got quite a display tonight, didn't they?"

"The Maidens have no shortage of enemies," she replied.

His knowing smile widened. He puffed on his pipe, taking a full, deep breath. He released a large smoke ring with an expert puff, then a smaller one that ran straight through the larger before the two of them dissipated into the haze hanging below the ceiling. "No shortage of allies, either, it seems."

"I asked you why you've come here." And she realized then why he'd been surprised when she'd entered. He hadn't been waiting for *her*. He'd been waiting for Emre. She said nothing of it, though, not wanting to tip her hand, not until she knew more.

"I'll tell you if you answer a question of mine."

"I don't bargain with men who steal into my home."

He pursed his lips and nodded. "So this *is* your home. I wasn't sure. And Emre is . . . what? Your husband? Your brother?"

"That's what you wish to ask?" She scoffed. "A few questions of the locals would answer that."

He took in her dress anew and used the mouthpiece of his pipe to point at her, emphasizing his words. "Did you take part in the attack?"

"I *witnessed* it."

He stood, a thing that seemed nonchalant but was all

the more threatening for it. She took a half-step toward the table on the far side of the room, where the kitchen knife lay.

"That's not what I asked," he said.

"My business is my own."

He took in a deep breath and released it in a huff. "Do I have to spell this out for you?"

She took another half-step. "Yes, you may very well have to."

"You know why I've come to Sharakhai. You know, or at least suspect, that Macide was behind the attack on the House of Maidens. Knowing these two things you'll understand why I might wonder if you're in league with him and why, if you were, I'd need to ask more pointed questions."

"I wasn't part of it, Ramahd. Now take the rest of your questions to the gods, for I'll not answer them. Not upon the point of a knife."

This time when she moved, he took a half-step of his own.

She made a move for the knife, sending him in that direction, then pulled out the slim knife she'd hidden along her thigh. As he approached, she flicked it toward his arm, hoping to nick him and get him to back away, but his reflexes were viper quick. He grabbed her poisoned wrist, all but ignoring the strike from the palm of her left hand, though it connected with his chin.

Pain ran through her, not just in her wrist and hand, but up her arm, through her shoulder, and into the hollow of her chest. It felt as if the poison were running rampant once more, eating her from within. The agony started strong and then built and built until her entire world went a brilliant and blinding white.

⊱─●─⊰

Çeda stands in Saliah's garden, Saliah herself nowhere to be seen. Above her the crystals are ringing. They're aglow among the acacia branches, splinters fallen from a broken autumn moon.

The sound of it . . . Dear gods, why has she never heard it before?

There are *voices* among those melodic sounds. Perhaps the voices of the dead, whispering of the lives they once led. Or the echoes of the future, passed back through the doorways of time. Whatever the case, it's suddenly clear that the chimes are not just connected to the garden, but to the Shangazi itself, from the great mountain ranges that surround it to the caravanserais that stitch the desert's fabric. They are the strings by which Saliah touches the lives of every man, woman, and child who treads the amber sands. That was what she had done when Çeda struck the tree with Saliah's staff, what she had done when Çeda came here as a child with her mother and climbed the tree: Saliah had listened, hearing the tale of what might yet be.

As Çeda watches, a child steps into the garden. *Me*, Çeda says in awe. *That girl is me*.

The young Çedamihn moves to the tall acacia. Walks slowly around it, glancing every so often toward the entrance to the garden, listening, Çeda knew, for her mother as she bargains with the desert witch. Young Çedamihn steps around the tree, staring up through its branches, much as grown Çeda had done mere moments ago. Then the child runs and leaps. She climbs through the tree's branches with a smile wide as the bright blue sky.

Çeda envies that child, who doesn't yet know that her mother is going to die. It is still only a small fear hidden somewhere inside her, distant enough that she can pretend it won't happen.

Mere hours from now, Ahya will be found hanging from the gallows, foul words cut into her skin: *Whore. False witness.* And the strange symbol that has haunted Çeda ever since.

The sounds from the chimes change. They become deeper, the voices within them clearer. Çeda tries to comprehend, but they are confusing—strands of a spiderweb she has no hope of untangling.

Saliah, however, understands them well; of this Çeda is sure. The regal woman stands at the garden's entrance, staring sightlessly toward young Çedamihn. But more importantly, she listens. She hears. She knows what the chimes are saying—it is, after all, why she allowed

Çedamihn into the garden in the first place. She might have pretended to listen to Ahya's words, pretended to listen to her pleas to take Çeda in, but she had been waiting all along for the chimes to tell her what to do.

Does she *need* others to ring the chimes, Çeda wonders, or is it simply the first step to seeing one's future? Saliah stands tall, eyes closed, listening to the chimes, listening to the voices, and then she turns her back on Ahya.

Çeda sees it all play out, so similar to and yet so very different from what she remembers. As Saliah walks toward her home, Çeda sees the look on her mother's face. How dearly she hoped that Saliah would take Çeda in. How dearly she hoped that *someone* would protect her daughter. Çeda hadn't been able to see it at the time, but now she does: the instincts of a mother rising above the strict rules and harsh lessons she'd set for her daughter. What Çeda sees now is the very core of motherhood. Love, when all else is pain and confusion and worry.

Çeda feels foolish for not having recognized it, for not having acknowledged it in some way, but she also wonders why her mother so rarely showed that side of herself. Perhaps because her mind was ever on her journey, her hidden war against the Kings. *And surely in me she saw the face of my father, one of those very same Kings. No easy thing to reconcile for a mother obsessed with their downfall.*

Ahya recovers from her reverie and snatches Çedamihn's hand, and off they go, into the skiff to sail over the desert sands, where their forms diminish until all Çeda sees is a swiftly moving ship on the horizon. Dark hull. White sail.

And then they are gone.

And Çeda is left feeling utterly, helplessly alone.

Chapter 43

CEDA BLINKED and found the man from Qaimir poised above her.

By the gods, what was his name? Her mind was so muddled.

Ramahd. His name was Ramahd.

He was above her, straddling her waist and pinning her good hand down while leaving her wounded one free. He slapped her cheek, worry clear on his face. She got the impression he'd been doing so for a while. "Wake up!" he hissed.

She stared at him as sweat trickled down her temples. Her skin was still alive with pain, but it was manageable now. The memories of Saliah's garden were oh so vivid. The garden, the acacia tree, the chimes . . . dear gods, how beautiful the sound.

Ramahd was staring at her as if she were mad. No. His face was a mask of *worry*, not caution. It was *concern* that filled his eyes. How strange that she would fail to recognize it as such when it was directed at her. She'd nearly forgotten him in the weeks since she'd last seen him. His strong jaw, arched brows, and rough-shaven skin gave him a rakish look. And his scent was redolent of faraway places. As much as Sharakhai ran through Çeda's veins, she couldn't deny the lure of lands different from the sands of the Great Shangazi.

"Feeling better?" he asked.

She nodded, not quite able to speak.

He lifted himself up and carefully released her left hand, glancing at it as if he expected her to strike him. He slid farther away on the floor and worked his jaw back and forth, then opened his mouth like a yawning hyena, all while continuing to eye her warily.

"You were speaking to someone," he said, "pleading with her."

"I was dreaming of a woman I saw in the desert."

"Ahyanesh?"

A shiver ran along her frame.

Part of her wished she hadn't spoken her mother's name aloud, but another part was glad to share it, so someone *other* than herself and Emre would know of Ahyanesh Al-lad'ava.

"My mother's name." Çeda sat up and slid back until her back was against the shelves separating the open room from the simple kitchen. "Ahya to those who loved her."

He pulled one leg easily over the other until he was sitting cross-legged, the position Qaimiri used when praying. He stared at her, chewing on his words for a while before speaking again. "You were begging her not to leave."

She pictured Ahya hanging by the ankles from the end of a rope.

Çeda swallowed the knot in her throat. To have seen her again so vividly, even in a dream, was a gift from the gods—truly it was. But it had brought her face-to-face with Ahya's death once again, which was infinitely more difficult to cope with than she thought it would be. "My mother died when I was young."

"I see," Ramahd said.

"No, you don't," she replied, more harshly than she'd meant to.

"No," he said, "of course I don't."

She wanted to apologize, but didn't.

Thankfully, he stepped into the uncomfortable silence.

"What happened?" he asked, nodding toward her bandaged hand.

It felt less painful now. In fact, it felt better than it had at any time since she'd been poisoned. She began to unwind the bandage, curious beyond reason to see the wound again, to see the tattoos surrounding it. When she unwrapped it at last, she stared at the puckered white crater where the thorn had pierced her skin. "A kiss from an adichara," she said, holding it up for Ramahd to see. The tattoo circled the wound, but did not touch the wound itself. It crawled to the back of her thumb, covering it to just short of the nail. It was beautiful in this dim light. Hypnotic.

She read again the words Zaïde had hidden among the tattooed vines of the adichara: *The lost are now found* and *Bane of the unrighteous*, and she realized that they might be taken several different ways. It all depended on whose point of view you had. They were important, Zaïde's words. One day Çeda would have to ask the Matron about them, though she would need to do so with the utmost care.

As he stared, Ramahd's eyebrows rose. He glanced to her wrist, then her dress, then his piercing eyes met hers as the implications of her words played themselves through. "The Maidens *healed* you?"

Çeda nodded.

"Then let you go?"

She shook her head. "I wouldn't put it so."

"Then how *would* you put it?"

"I'm to join their ranks. They're taking me in."

He frowned at her wrist. "Because of that?"

"In spite of it."

"Then by the gods why? What could they want from you?"

She chose her words with care; Ramahd was too sharp of mind to do otherwise. "They feel that I'm made from the right stock."

"But—"

"Enough," Çeda interrupted. "I've given you plenty of answers already. We trade in the desert, yes?"

Ramahd was still confused, but he allowed her the

point, and his attempts at hiding his confusion in a smile were miserable. "As you say."

"What are you doing here?" Çeda asked.

"I'm waiting for Emre."

"Why?"

"Because he knows Macide. He's been working for him."

"How do you know?"

"My men have been following him. In the past two weeks he was seen with Hamid Malahin'ava three different times. There may have been many more meetings between the two." Ramahd paused. "Do you remember the albino? Ambassador Juvaan of Qaimir?"

"How could I forget?"

"There's a half-Sharakhani man," he went on, ignoring her gibe, "who works for Juvaan. His name is Ruan, and he visits a woman in the southern quarter from time to time."

"*Visits a woman?* You can just say she's a whore."

Ramahd waggled his head. "She is, but she trades in more than the arts of the flesh. She provides safe places for men to meet. She transfers money and goods, not so different from Osman, but for a different clientele."

"And?"

"And Ruan was seen leaving her home an hour before Emre arrived."

She tried not to let her discomfort show. "Emre's friendly with many in Sharakhai. That doesn't mean that Macide's pulling his strings."

"After he left the woman's home, he went to see a man named Samael. Do you know him?"

"I thought Samael fled Sharakhai years ago."

"So did we," he replied. "Apparently he's returned. So, three weeks ago, an alchemyst capable of creating demon's fire returns to the city. Emre met with him not three days ago, and tonight pots of demon fire were launched against the House of Maidens."

"Get to your point, Ramahd."

"Patience," he countered. "There's one last piece of the puzzle. Do you know the name of Hamzakiir?"

Çeda's heart went cold. "Every Sharakhani has heard of Hamzakiir, though most don't believe him to be real."

"Do *you* believe him to be real?"

"I do," Çeda admitted.

"And who do the people of Sharakhai think he was?"

Çeda swallowed, not really wanting to share street rumors with Ramahd. "He was a blood mage," she said, "but he died generations ago."

Ramahd nodded. "We believe the Kings killed him nearly eighty years ago. His grave was never located—and believe me, we tried—but now we're convinced that Juvaan has given the location to the Moonless Host."

Çeda's mind was racing. "The message I delivered . . . That canister went directly to Macide."

"As did the breathstone that Emre carried."

"And breathstones are used to speak with the dead." *By Thaash's bright blade, what have you gotten yourself into, Emre?* "You think they want some secret from Hamzakiir, some secret that was lost with his passing."

Ramahd had a grim expression. "I believe so."

Suddenly Çeda wished she had kept the breathstone, wished she could find her mother's remains to ask *her* questions: *Who is my father? Where are the other poems? Why did you leave me?*

"But why?" Çeda asked. "What does Hamzakiir know?"

"That is the question, isn't it? That's why I'm here to speak with Emre. He was as much a part of the attack on the House of Maidens tonight as Macide or Hamid. As much a part of it as Juvaan, who is funneling coin, information, and more, to the Moonless Host."

She could see the anger building in his eyes now. To him, Emre was just as bad as Macide. "But why launch such a pointless attack against the House of Maidens?" she asked. "It set some walls on fire and scared the horses, but otherwise did little but rile them up like a swarm of bees. They'll be buzzing about the city for months now."

"Perhaps that was the point."

"To what end?"

"That's what I'd like to ask Emre. Do you know where he is?"

Even if I knew, there isn't a beggar's chance at the gates of Tauriyat I'd tell you. "You know," she said easily, "that I've only just returned."

He studied her carefully as she said these words. His eyes searched her face. He even glanced at her hands. He was *reading* her, she realized, weighing her every move to assess if she was lying. Yet another thing she would have to be careful of in the future.

"I'm telling you the truth." She lifted her wounded hand. "Is this not evidence enough?"

He sighed, and much of the suspicion in his eyes faded with that simple gesture. "Some days I no longer know what to believe. My life is filled with distrust, Çeda."

"Wait a moment," Çeda said, realizing something, "if you've been watching him so closely, why don't you know where he is now?"

"He became suspicious. We lost him two days ago."

"And you think he'll be back tonight?"

He shrugged. "Who can tell? I thought after the attack he might return to a show of normality, if only to keep suspicions from landing on him. After tonight, the Maidens will be asking questions across every threshold in the city."

Çeda nodded. "True, but that could just as easily drive Emre into hiding. He's run afoul of those in power before."

"Caught stealing?"

"No." She shrugged. "Well, occasionally. He's stolen enough in his life. But when he was young, he lost his brother to a caravan tough." Çeda could still see Emre running down the Haddah, Saadet chasing him. "Emre went to the Silver Spears after, and they laughed at him. They *laughed*. Said to him, what did he expect? It just so happens that caravan was one of the richest from Malasan, and they'd paid the Silver Spears for a bit of freedom from local troubles. It might have been why the bravo was so angry to be stolen from. He felt entitled here, as if he owned the city. And he *surely* felt entitled when he went looking for retribution."

Ramahd was silent for a time. "My tears for his loss. I know what it's like."

"You know what it's like to lose the ones you love," Çeda allowed, "but you have no idea what it's like to live on the streets of Sharakhai, especially as a child. Emre saved me when I was young. When my mother died, he kept me from throwing myself at the walls of Tauriyat and getting myself killed for it. He put food in our bellies. He made me laugh when my heart was filled with salt. I owe him much, and I tell you this: he is a good man. He deserves more than to have some lord from Qaimir steal into his home and question his honor."

"So what would you have me do?"

"Leave Emre to me. Let me speak with him. I'll find out what's happening, and I'll share with you what I learn." It was all she could think of to save Emre from a beating, or worse.

"And if he's with Macide?"

Çeda swallowed. "I'll tell you that as well. I swear it, Ramahd."

He looked into her eyes, then glanced to the door, the shuttered window. A great clattering of horse hooves could be heard in the distance, riders throughout the city streets. Somewhere a woman cried out, followed by the shout of a man, a short clash of steel. The Maidens were not close yet, but who knew where they might be headed? "Very well," Ramahd finally said. "I'll wait, if you'll do for me one thing."

"And what might that be?"

"You'll be presented to the Kings soon, will you not?"

"I will," she admitted.

"It will be a formal affair, so that the Kings can get a good look at you, so they can choose you for their service if they wish."

"But I've already *been* chosen."

Ramahd's head jerked back, his shock clear. "By whom?"

"The Jade-eyed King."

He stared at her, clearly waiting for some stronger reaction. "Do you really not know?"

"Know what?"

"King Yusam chooses very few Maidens, Çeda, none in

the years I've been coming to Sharakhai as my Lord King's emissary."

"And how long is that?"

"Seven years now. And he's chosen none for many years before, if what I've heard is true. He doesn't like people getting close to him. So why now? Why you?"

She felt so woefully unprepared to return to the House of Maidens, and this was only more proof of it. She knew so little about life inside those walls. "I have no idea," she finally said.

The look of shock on his face faded, but there was still a curious look in his eyes, as if Çeda were some Kundhuni puzzle box to be solved. "No matter." He seemed to come to some decision, for he took in a sharp breath and smiled at her. "There's a good chance Juvaan will be invited to the feast being held in your honor. There's a good chance I will as well. If we are, would you join me in a conversation with him?"

"That's all? A conversation with Juvaan?"

"Don't you wish to know more about him?"

"Yes."

"Well, so do I. I've never met him. Well, beyond a quick introduction here or there. We've never spoken in depth, and I'd like to rectify that."

"So meet him and talk to him yourself. It's called conversation, Ramahd. It happens at parties."

"I could, but he's a particular man, and Mirea and Qaimir have never been fast friends. But he's an avid admirer of the pits." Ramahd paused. "*Admirer* isn't nearly a strong enough word. He's a devotee. If he knew *you* were the one I fought. . ."

Çeda stared. "You want me to reveal that I'm the White Wolf?"

Ramahd shrugged. "It's a small token that could gain you much."

"That's no small token! And you and your king stand to gain as much as I, or more."

"True, we stand to gain, but don't tell me you aren't curious. Besides, is the White Wolf likely ever to make another appearance in the pits? Her identity is a currency in high regard right now, but that will change when she disappears. Memory of her will fade, and you will have wasted your chance."

It was true. She wanted very much to know more about Juvaan than she did at present. Anyone supplying the Moonless Host was someone she wanted to know more of. And Juvaan was no man of modest means. His connection to the Queen of Mirea gave hint to a much deeper story. But to give up the identity she'd worked so hard to keep secret? "I'll think on it."

"A fair enough response." In one fluid motion he rose to his feet. "Be well Çedamihn Ahyanesh'ala."

"Goodbye," she replied, though some small part of her wished he would stay.

Perhaps he sensed that desire, for he moved to the door with a pace that spoke of reluctance. His hand strayed toward the handle, stopping just short of touching it. He turned his head toward her, looking as though he were about to say something, but then his eyes wandered to the doorway to Emre's room, and everything changed. The diffident look on his face vanished, and he opened the door without another word.

He was gone, while deeper in the city, horse's hooves and the cries of the accused filled the night.

Chapter 44

"**U**P."

Emre opened his eyes. "What?"

"Get up."

He sat up on the small pallet, rubbing the sleep from his eyes. He had no idea who'd spoken. He thought it might have been Çeda. The room was packed with other sleeping men and women, and a woman stood not far away. She looked like Çeda.

But no, it wasn't her. Of course it wasn't. Çeda was dead, killed by the Maidens or by Dardzada. Or perhaps he, himself, was to blame. He'd let her go when he knew very well he should have fought harder to keep her home.

"Time for food," the woman said.

She was Nirendra, he finally realized, the woman who owned this shit room on this shit alley on the backside of the Shallows. Around the room were a dozen more narrow pallets and reed mats with men and women snoring upon them. It *smelled* in this place. Of unwashed bodies. Of piss and shit. It was late in the day. Orange sunlight spilled in through the blanket-covered window and around the ill-fitting door. The noise of the cramped Shallows was forcing its way in like an unwelcome guest. Most in the slums were preparing their final meal, a bit of song or a bit of talk before readying for bed, but not in the house where Emre had been hidden away. It was not filled with daytime laborers; this was a crew that plied their trade by moonlight.

Nirendra was a drawn old woman who Emre suspected was once much larger from the way the skin sagged along her neck and arms. She was bent over an iron pot set into the embers of a cook fire. She looked nothing like Çeda. Why had he even thought that? After scooping a helping of rice and peas into a wooden bowl, she limped over to Emre and held it out with a shaking hand.

Emre was hungry—ravenous, in fact—but he shook his head. "You take it."

She shook it at him, staring with those haunted eyes of hers. "I've had mine."

"I'm not hungry."

Her face hardened. "Fuck your mother and fuck your pity." She tossed the bowl into his lap, rice and peas and parsley spraying over his blanket. "You've a long night ahead. Eat."

Emre collected it back into the bowl and began shoveling it into his mouth with his fingers.

"When will they come?"

She seemed to measure the light as she glanced toward the window. "Shortly, I expect."

Indeed, as Emre was finishing his rice—a meal that tasted much better than it had any right to—Darius entered without knocking. As his eyes adjusted, he spotted Emre. "Ready?"

"As I will be." Emre stood and headed for the door, handing the bowl to Nirendra on the way. "Thanks," he said. Her only reply was to grunt and set the bowl on a stack of others near the pot.

With deep shadows darkening the alleys, Darius led Emre east through the Shallows. After several turns they came to an intersection where six narrow streets met. Darius whistled, and a few moments later, Hamid appeared from one of them. He nodded to Darius and Emre, and the three of them wound their way toward the heart of Sharakhai, where they walked in silence to the rear of a tiny teahouse near the Trough and, without announcing themselves, entered a small kitchen.

A Mirean man with a paunch and a mustache that hung like damp moss looked up from the platter of tea cups he was preparing. He nodded to the three of them. Emre nodded back, but he'd already returned his attention to the tea. Darius led the way down a cramped set of stairs into a cellar while the sounds from above—the beat from a pair of tambours, a group of old women laughing and hooting, the clatter of teacups—dwindled.

Hamid and Darius pulled a stack of tea crates away from the wall, revealing a cleverly designed stone door that hinged inward when Hamid pushed at it. It was a tight fit, but Hamid, then Emre, then Darius, made their way through it and into a narrow tunnel, even tighter than the cellar stairs. Their footsteps made an odd, shuffling chorus as their shadows danced in the light of Hamid's swinging lantern. Beetles skittered along a damp section of wall, but the air was bone dry and chill as they navigated connecting tunnels, climbed down stairs, and treaded along slow declines.

"You suppose it's safe to tell him now?" Hamid asked Darius.

"Might be better to wait until after," Darius replied. "We don't want him all moon-eyed before he speaks to Macide."

"Perhaps that's exactly what we want," Hamid shot back.

Emre looked between them. "Tell me what?"

"Three nights past, a certain young woman was spotted returning to your home a mere half turn after the attack on the House of Maidens began."

A certain young woman? A thousand thoughts fought to be spoken, but what came out of his mouth was, "Çeda's *alive?*"

"Apparently," Hamid replied, "though she returned to the House of Maidens the morning after."

Emre hardly heard his reply. His whole body was tingling with a strange mixture of joy and the desire to rein his hopes in. He'd been so certain she was dead. He felt a pang of regret immediately after—he'd helped in the attack on the House of Maidens; what if she'd been hurt? But whatever small regret he might be feeling was soon overcome by the relief that filled him at the thought of her living and breathing.

Eventually Hamid's words registered, though, and it made him wonder. "Why would she have returned?"

"One of the many mysteries of that night." Hamid glanced at Emre in the lantern light before returning his attention to the path ahead. "As curious as her reason for staying with the Qaimiri lordling who had been waiting for you, and what they spoke of."

A Qaimiri lordling? "Who?"

"Ramahd shan Amansir. He was a minor noble until he married the daughter of their King, Princess Yasmine. His wife and child were later killed by Macide. He's been the voice of King Aldouan in Sharakhai and hunting the Moonless Host for revenge, ever since." Hamid paused as they ducked beneath a stone overhang then continued. "Did she ever mention him?"

"No. Never." A Qaimiri lordling? Why wouldn't Çeda have mentioned him? The answer was obvious, of course. She'd warned him away from the Host, and he'd practically laughed at her for it. Why would she breathe a word to him of someone bent on revenge against Macide, especially someone she was friendly with?

"You're sure, Emre? It's important."

"I'm sure, Hamid. I wouldn't protect some mouthpiece of King Aldouan."

"No, but you'd protect Çeda."

"She never mentioned him."

Hamid walked in silence for a time before replying, "Well enough, Emre."

They continued through the tunnel, and eventually heard distant voices, but before they reached them, a darker shadow slid into the tunnel ahead. Hamid held the lantern high, shedding light on two women clad in leather armor. Each bore a long, slim knife useful for fighting in tight quarters.

"Who comes?" the woman at the rear called.

"You know who comes," Hamid shot back.

"Then best you hurry," the nearest of them said. "Macide arrived an hour ago."

"I know my business," Hamid said. He leaned in to kiss the one who'd spoken. "Unless you'd like the Spears running along these halls with us."

She pressed the tip of the knife into his ribs. "They do, and they'd get a surprise or two for their trouble."

As they kissed again, Emre saw Darius giving Hamid a strange look, but it was gone in a moment, and soon they were heading down a gap in the tunnel so narrow they had to sidestep along it to reach the end. It opened into a natural cavern filled with glistening formations. A low fire burned in a brazier at the far end of the cavern, its orange light glistening off slick walls and columns and a forest of mineral skewers, stakes, and thorns piercing floor and ceiling. The sound of echoing drips mixed with the soft murmur of voices.

When Emre finally reached the far end of the cavern, he found several dozen gathered there. Many wore the thawbs of the desert, but others wore clothes that were fashionable in the city—fine khalats for the men, jalabiyas for the women.

"You said this would be a small gathering of the Host," Emre whispered to Hamid as they walked along a path between the stalagmites.

"Is this not small?" Hamid replied with an easy smile.

"It is not, you miserable shit," Emre shot back. "Not by a long stretch." He'd never liked crowds, not when it felt like he couldn't escape them.

Many of those gathered looked his way, exchanging words as they stole glances, but one man broke from the crowd and strode to meet them. He was tall and broad. His beard was forked and braided into two long tails. The viper tattoos on his forearms marked him as much as anything else, but Macide was recognizable from his mere presence as well. He was a man Emre had both hoped and feared to meet.

He hugged Hamid, and then Darius, and finally stood before Emre, staring down his nose with a mischievous glint in his eye. "And here is Emre Aykan'ava."

A statement, not a question, but Emre nodded and held out his hand. Macide offered his in return and the two of them gripped forearms.

"You did well at Matron Zohra's."

From the far end of the cavern, in an area hidden by a bend, came a muffled sound. Emre tried to see who or what had made it but couldn't from his present vantage. "It was nothing," Emre said.

"You'll forgive me if I disagree. It was something we needed, and we are in your debt." Macide put his arms behind his back, looking for all the world like one of the masters in the collegia. "So I say again: you've done well, but there are further things to do if you wish to join us in earnest."

"I'm aware."

"Are you? Because from what I hear from Hamid and others around Roseridge, you're not." He said this with a casual air, but Emre knew his words were deadly serious.

"This is nothing I enter into lightly." Emre knew he was treading on very dangerous ground.

"No?" As the light from the brazier cast flickering shadows throughout the cavern, Macide stared deeply into Emre's eyes, and seemed to come to some conclusion. "No, you don't enter it lightly. But I wonder how long you'll stay when things get difficult. And they will, Emre, sooner than later."

"I have many talents."

"*We* have many talents. What we need are men and women with loyal hearts." He stepped forward until he was almost chest-to-chest with Emre, who resisted the urge to back away as he met those piercing eyes. "What do you care if the Kings sit in their palaces? What do you care if the Host works to tear them down?"

"Because while the Kings sit their thrones in their high palaces, we are reduced to prey. On each of their holy nights, we are their prey. When the Blade Maidens strut about the city, we are their prey. When the Silver Spears choose to protect Goldenhill and the east end and their precious harbors and nothing else, we are their prey. How many souls have perished at their hands? How many from their neglect?"

"Many," Macide replied.

"Too many. It's for them I wish to join the Host."

Macide looked to Hamid, then Darius. What their expressions told Macide, Emre had no idea, but a moment later, Macide nodded and led Emre toward the far end of the cavern.

As the crowd parted for them, a portion of the cavern previously hidden was revealed, and Emre saw a man hanging upside down from a rope tied to a hook in the cavern's ceiling. The man was naked save for a loincloth. Except for the raw abrasions around his ankles where the rope was cinched, his skin was surprisingly clean and unblemished. Emre didn't have to ask who the man was. This was Lord Veşdi, the man Emre had identified as King Külaşan's son. The Host had taken him three nights ago, using the attack on the House of Maidens as a diversion.

The crowd closed in, staring at Veşdi, at the wide brass censer beneath him, at the cloudy white stone sitting in its exact center. The breathstone, Emre realized, the very one Çeda had discovered in the canister Emre had been delivering for Osman.

As the crowd squeezed closer, making Emre feel like a pressed grape, Macide pulled a curved knife from his belt, flipped it easily, and handed it hilt-first to Emre. Emre stared at the knife, then looked up to Veşdi, who was staring at him with eyes crazed with fear. Macide put his hand on Emre's shoulder and nodded to him, an offering of support as Emre was reforged into something altogether different than what he'd been before: a murderer.

He had known this time would come, but that made it no easier. To enter the Al'afwa Khadar was to step over a threshold that could never be crossed again.

Emre took up the knife. It felt obscene, but he had to admit it felt freeing as well. It made him feel powerful in a way he hadn't experienced since Rafa's death. When Rafa was alive, Emre felt as if the world were in his hands, but only through naiveté. Now he *understood* the world. He knew it was insufficient to merely defend. Do that and life nibbles at you like a rat until there's nothing left. No, one had to sally forth lest the world around you crumble and fall.

He strode toward Veşdi, this Lord from Goldenhill, this Prince who wriggled and squirmed, a man who knew his fate had come. The handle of Emre's knife felt suddenly slick in his hand. *Cold blood*, he thought. *Cold blood. By the gods, I'm readying to kill a man in cold blood.*

He licked his lips and tried to ignore the weighty stares of those gathered. Tried not to care what they thought of him, wondering if he were forged from the proper elements.

He was. Absolutely he was. He was no brittle blade. Not any longer. The pain he'd endured following his brother's death had nearly killed him. But he stood here now a different man. He'd found himself through the simple act of standing before a mirror and seeing his true nature for the first time. He wasn't reborn, but stripped bare, his weak outer shell removed at last. It was as if he'd been lifted from an oubliette after years of seclusion, to see the world once more. And the light had burned away all the fear, all the worry, all the self pity that had festered within him. He refused to go back to his old self. He wouldn't go back in that hole again. Not ever.

As he considered Veşdi, he didn't see the face of a Lord of Sharakhai—he saw the face of a Malasani bravo who deserved to die. As he drew the knife across his throat, he saw Rafa's eyes staring back at him. Saw Rafa dying. Saw Rafa dead.

He heard the patter of liquid, and when he looked down, he found the blade blood-slicked. His hands and arms were covered in red. It dripped down his face, warm but already cooling. He wiped it from his eyes, from his face, and saw the censer, below the still-wriggling man, full of blood. It overflowed onto the stones and ran in rivulets to a once-clear pool of water, staining it scarlet.

As cries of joy and fury rose up around him, footsteps approached. Whose, he wasn't sure, but when he felt a hand on his shoulder he turned and saw Macide—not smiling, not proud, but intent. "Pick it up," he said to Emre.

Emre crouched down and lifted the surprisingly heavy stone from the warm pool of blood. The stone was no longer white. It was red. Red as death. And not merely on its surface. He wiped the blood with his thumb and found it was red through and through. It had *drawn* the blood into itself, absorbed it, as if a man's life were no different from broth waiting to be sopped.

"You've done well," Macide said. "On the holy night, we'll go to Külaşan's desert palace. And then, my friend, we shall see who is the hunter and who the prey."

Chapter 45

Çeda's meeting with Pelam in the pits still burned as she ran for the western harbor. But she had hope now. A small hope, but a hope all the same.

By the time she reached the harbor, her muscles felt like forge-brightened metal. She wandered along the quay, checking the ships moored there, looking among the warehouses standing opposite the piers. Some noticed her, wondering why a girl was poking her nose into things in the harbor, but most ignored her. What was one more gutter wren in the cramped west end of this overcrowded city?

"May I help, dear girl?"

Çeda turned and sighed with relief. It was Ibrahim, and Ibrahim knew everyone. He was standing beside his mule wearing sandals and sirwal trousers and that wide-brimmed hat of his, while a short, thickset man unloaded rolls of carpet from the bed of his dray.

"Where can I find Djaga?" Çeda asked.

"Oh," he laughed, "it's *Djaga* you wish to see. The Black Lion. And why might you be needing her?"

"My business is my own, Ibrahim."

Ibrahim grunted, allowing her the point, while the man at the back of the cart gave her a sour look, the sort of look one gave to a gutter wren when you thought they might be planning to nick something. "And what do you have for *me*, little Çedamihn? What do you have that *I* want?"

"I'm only looking for the pier where she works, Ibrahim. Anyone here could give it to me."

"A small thing, then. So give Ibrahim something small in return."

Çeda thought about simply leaving, but she was in a hurry, and in truth, there was a part of her that liked trades like this. "There are birds in the desert that fly like a cloud given life by Bakhi himself."

"Blazing blues, Çedamihn. Lapis eyes. Tell me something I don't know."

"They eat tiny shrimp in the salt lakes in the dead of winter."

Ibrahim's eyebrows rose. "And?"

"You can hold the shrimp in your hand and the birds will peck them off your palm without touching you with their wings or scratching your skin with their hungry beaks."

Ibrahim stared at her. He blinked. And then he reared back and laughed harder than before. "Do they really?"

"I wouldn't lie, Ibrahim."

"That's *wonderful*. I never knew, and I believe, if I'm being honest—and Ibrahim is always honest—that *I'll* owe *you* after this. You come find me again, won't you? We'll trade again?"

"I'd rather have two things now."

Ibrahim scratched his stubbly chin and smoothed his mustache down. "Two now, is it?"

"Neither would be difficult for someone like you to answer."

Ibrahim goggled his eyes. "*I'll* be the judge of that, Çedamihn."

She nodded, suppressing a smile. "First, do you remember this life when you pass to the next?"

"Of course you do!"

"Even if you couldn't remember your life at the moment you passed beyond?"

Ibrahim frowned. "What do you mean?"

Çeda shrugged. "What if you were so drunk you couldn't remember your own wife?"

Ibrahim laughed. "Would that I could!"

"Would you, though? Would you remember?"

He grew more serious, stretching his neck as his face screwed up in thought. "We are granted a new life when we pass, but one of the gifts, or curses, are the memories from this one. This is a covenant that cannot be broken by mere drink, I judge."

What about a drug? Çeda wondered. *What about hangman's vine?* But she couldn't press further than she already had. Ibrahim might connect her questions to Ahya, and she was wary of that, especially with a man who told stories for money.

"Well enough?" Ibrahim asked.

She nodded.

"Good," he said. "Now to the second." He pointed with a long, crooked arm toward a pier with a mid-sized cutter berthed at it. "Djaga works the *Willow Wind* most often."

"The *Willow Wind*?"

"Are we trading again already?"

"Never mind," Çeda said as she set off down the wooden boardwalk toward the pier.

In her wake, Ibrahim cackled. "The owner hails from Mirea, where the willow is sacred. That one's for free, Çeda!" As Çeda ran, she heard Ibrahim call behind her, "Come see me, girl! I like your stories!"

She found Djaga polishing the skimwood runners of the cutter, which stood on two stout boat stands that lifted the entire ship up off the sand. Djaga was dipping a horsehair brush into a large bucket filled with a viscous golden liquid, which she slathered over the runners.

"Djaga Akoyo?"

Djaga looked up to the dock, shading her eyes from the sun beating down over Çeda's shoulder. "Who are you?" she asked, and then went back to her work, moving slowly down the runner, making sure to get underneath and on either side of the round-bottomed wood. The smell of it was sharp like pitch and sweet like amber.

"My name is Çeda." She jumped down to the sand, and stood, awkward, unsure where to begin. "I've just come from the pits."

Djaga ignored her. "Have you, girl?"

"I've seen you fight. You're very good."

"Am I?"

"I'd like to enter the pits as well."

Djaga stood, making Çeda realize just how tall this woman was, how sleekly muscled. *"You?"* She pointed to Çeda with her brush, which was dripping beads of gold onto the sand. *"You* would fight in the pits?"

"I would, and I'm hoping you'll train me."

Djaga barked out a single laugh. "I wouldn't if I were you. The pits are nasty business, girl, not made for the likes of you."

"I'm made for the pits."

"You aren't, either."

"I am. And I'll prove it one day, with or without you."

"Then do it without. I have work to do." And she bent her back and returned to swabbing the port runner with dripping wax. She moved to the rudder next, the smaller ski at the aft of the ship, used to steer it over the sands.

Çeda trailed her. "There's a man I wish dead." The Kundhunese took such things seriously, but Djaga would probably doubt whether Çeda—a young woman and a Sharakhani—would feel the same.

"Then kill him. You don't need the pits for that."

"He's entered the tourney. He's protected until he leaves."

"Then wait 'til he leaves."

"He may leave on a ship again, like he did after he killed my *alangual's* brother."

Djaga stood tall once more. *"Alangual . . ."*

"Yes. His name is Emre, and he's been my closest friend since I was a girl."

"Do you know the word you're using?"

"I know what it means. I would die for Emre. And he would die for me."

"You're sure?"

"Of course I'm sure."

"There is more to it."

"I believe that we are two halves of a whole, that we will hold hands in the farther fields." In truth she hadn't believed anything of the kind. As the words had came out, though, they'd felt truer than anything she'd ever said, and she was somehow glad that her paths had crossed Djaga's, if only for this.

Djaga stared at her with doubtful eyes, but there was some grudging approval there as well. "Are you smitten with this boy?"

"Smitten?" Çeda laughed. "Of course not!" The mere thought of it was ridiculous.

Djaga finished slathering the wax over the rudder. That done, she hoisted the bucket and set it down in the shade under the pier, and from another bucket chose two bolts of stained cloth from the crumpled pile within it. She threw one of them to Çeda, who snatched it from the air.

"Come," she said, and moved to the starboard runner. While wiping the cloth along the skimwood, buffing the dried wax she'd applied earlier, she nodded to Çeda, an indication for her to do the same. Çeda liked making the cloudy surface glow under the brightness of the sun.

"Not so hard that the cloth skips. Run it smoothly but with power. You see?" The muscles along Djaga's shoulders and arms rippled as she worked.

Çeda did as Djaga said, and felt the smoothness of the wood, but also the nicks the sand and stone of the Shangazi had taken as its price of passage.

"Now, what did this man do to your Emre's brother?"

They worked the runner, making it shine, before moving portside and doing the same, and all the while Çeda told her story. Djaga interrupted to ask a few questions about where the man had come from, how she knew he hailed from Malasan. Her smooth motions continued without pause, but the look on her face changed. It went from one of doubt and curiosity to concern and then restrained anger. More than once Çeda caught the tall Kundhunese woman staring at *her* arms, *her* shoulders.

"This Saadet ibn Sim did this to a man he'd never met over a purse stolen by a boy on a festival night?"

"He did. I swear it beneath Rhia and Tulathan."

Djaga turned and spit onto the sand. The spit sat there on the sandy surface of the harbor, and then was drawn down, leaving only a dark stain. "And you wish me to do what? Train you to beat him?"

"Train me enough to get me into the tourney."

"There's not enough time. It starts in three days."

"My mother taught me to dance. And she taught me well."

"Dancing with swords and fighting dirt dogs in the pits are two different things."

"I can pay you."

Djaga snorted. "I don't want your money."

Çeda was ready to protest, but Djaga held her hand up. "You'll need your money, Çeda, for there are three things I will do for you, three things in payment for this crime within our borders." Djaga was not born here, but she was Sharakhani, through and through. "First, you will take your money, everything that was stolen from this Malasani dog, and you will return it to him."

"What?"

"Emre stole it, and you had a part in it. You will return it so that your debt is paid."

"I can't do that. He killed Rafa!"

"You will do it if you want me to help, girl."

Çeda seethed at the thought, but she knew there was more to come. "I will do it, if that is what you require."

"It isn't what *I* require, Çedamihn. It is the *gods*. The scales must be righted before you begin the second part of your journey."

"Which is?"

"Once this is set right, I will enter you into the tourney."

"But Pelam won't allow it! He'll kick me out as soon as he sees me. And even if he didn't I'll have no money left to buy my way in!"

"You will come as an honored guest to Sharakhai, a Qaimiri noblewoman who demands anonymity and is willing to pay extra for it."

"A Qaimiri?"

Djaga shrugged. "It happens often enough, and Pelam will never see your face."

"Very well, but I can't be Qaimiri. I'll be a Sharakhani noble who doesn't wish to be known."

"That's more rare."

"The Qaimiri do it, you said. Is there not a single noblewoman in Sharakhai who doesn't wish to test herself in the pits?"

Djaga nodded, allowing her the point. "Well enough. *I* will broker the arrangement. *I'll* vouch for you, and *I'll* pay your way in."

Çeda's head jerked back. "You would do this?"

Djaga smiled fiercely, not so differently from her smile in the match several days before. "I do not do this all out of love."

"Then what?"

"Consider it an investment. If you win, Çeda. If you beat this man and have your revenge, you will come to me, and I will train you. And when you win again—and you will, the gods as my witness—I will take back three times what I'm paying for you now. Understood?"

"*You* will train me?"

Djaga folded her cloth over, exposing an unblemished patch. "Unless you consider the price too steep, or the thought of training under me distasteful."

"No! I don't!"

"Then it is done. Come back to me once you've returned the money."

"My heart is yours," Çeda said as she dropped the cloth onto the rudder and began backing away.

"Keep your heart." She went back to her waxing. "And you'll need a disguise," she called as Çeda took the ladder up to the pier. "Best it be one that means something to you!"

Çeda's heart lifted as she ran through the west end of Sharakhai. There was worry, too. She was no fool to think the tree of Malasan would fall easily, but she was now walking along the path she'd been so desperate to find.

A disguise, Djaga had said. *Best it be one that means something to you.*

She thought all the way home, thought long into the night for something that would suit her. She had no idea what it might be. None. Not until the sun went down and the maned wolves began howling in the desert.

And then she knew *exactly* what it would be.

———— ⊷●⊶ ————

Beneath the pits, Çeda's heart beat so madly she thought it might rattle up her throat and fall to the cool tiled floor for all the other dirt dogs to see. Saadet was across the room from her, sitting easily, his back against the wall, staring into the distance, glancing occasionally at the other fighters but otherwise keeping to himself. Fourteen others wandered the long, narrow room. The sixteen of them comprised all the morning's contests, the first of the tourney—a bit of luck granted by Nalamae for which Çeda was immensely relieved, for if she'd had to wait another day to begin fighting, she would surely have gone mad.

She wore a pieced-together set of ragged leather armor she'd found in the bazaar after a full day's search. It was little more than a breastplate with pauldrons and a battle skirt, with greaves and bracers to match. She had a bit of growing to do before her body would fill the armor properly, but it didn't hamper her movements. It was old as well, but the boiled leather was in good shape, and Djaga had given it a gruff nod of approval after looking it over.

Çeda had dyed the armor white and fixed a wolf pelt to the top of the helm to look like the white wolf that had saved her out in the desert. The helm she'd found in the bazaar after rummaging through nearly every stall, and she'd paid nearly her last copper khet for it. The hinged visor of the helm had been shaped by a gifted artisan into a woman's face. The steel was nicked here and there, but it was well kept—not a speck of rust and few enough dents.

"It's of Nalamae," the old woman had said as Çeda was looking it over.

"What?" Çeda had asked.

"The face," the woman repeated while smacking her toothless gums, "it's Nalamae's."

That didn't quite sit right with Çeda—Nalamae seemed eternally blind to her pleas—but she'd bought it just the same. The rest of her money had gone to Saadet, to repay all that Emre had stolen, and then some. She'd given it to Hamid and asked him to drop it at Saadet's feet when he stepped from the pits. Saadet had frowned as Hamid stepped shyly up to him, threw the purse down, and sprinted away through the crowd. But he had still picked it up, examined its contents, and dropped the small purse into the larger one at his belt, as if such things happened to him every day.

When she had watched him do it from the shadows of a nearby alley, a niqab making her faceless to any who might see her, she'd felt strong, almost invincible. But here, sitting in the room with the other *selhesh*, she was not nearly so sure of herself. And yet the moment was growing near, and she knew she had to act, so she stood and marched over to Saadet, who eyed her with something akin to amusement. Çeda stopped before him, her heart beating so hard she thought the Malasani might hear. He was a burly man, but he'd grown fatter since that fateful night of Beht Revahl.

"You are Saadet ibn Sim," she stated simply.

Saadet's eyes narrowed as he took her in anew. "You don't sound like a bitch from Goldenhill to me."

"You came to Sharakhai two years ago." She said it loud enough for everyone in the room to hear.

"I come to Sharakhai often. What does a girl barely into her woman's blood care of my comings and goings?"

"On that visit, a purse was stolen from you."

Until this point, Saadet had seemed amused, but now all trace of humor fled, replaced by a severe expression. He sat up straighter. "Who are you?"

"You found the thief's home, and you killed his brother in cold blood."

Some few of the men and women in the room had been talking with one another, others hummed or sang softly to themselves. Still others lounged easily while waiting. But when Çeda said these words, everyone went silent, every ear turned her way.

Saadet stood. He stared down at Çeda. She was tall for a girl of fourteen, but she still only came up to his nose. She gave up seven stone to him at least.

Çeda hadn't known what to expect from him. She'd imagined him saying all sorts of things. Denials. Diversions. Even an admission. But she hadn't expected him to smile. By the gods she nearly went for his throat then and there. "What of it?" he asked.

"I've come to right the scales."

Saadet laughed and took a step forward until they were chest-to-chest. "You have, have you?"

"I have," she said, looking up at him. "Blood is owed."

"And you're the one to take it from me?"

"You will beg for my mercy before this is done."

There was a pregnant pause as the other dirt dogs watched this exchange, and then Saadet tried to snatch her helm. He was fast, but she'd been expecting something like this. She leaned back and slapped his hand away. He tried again, and she leaned away once more, this time slapping his neck with the heel of her palm. Hard. Saadet coughed. His face went red. When he rushed her, she dodged to one side, rolling and coming to a stand before he could so much as lay a hand on her.

Two of the pit's enforcers stepped into the room, each holding a thick, nail-studded cudgel. The one who'd come in first banged his against an empty bench three times. "None of this, now! You all know the rules! Blood spills when the gong is struck, and not a moment before."

Saadet frowned, and then he looked around to all the other fighters, one by one. "None of you touch her." Then he turned his eyes on Çeda. "None of you."

The others sneered at his words, and yet when they were led up, and Pelam released the viper, allowing it to decide who would choose their opponent for the next match, none of them chose Çeda. Bout after bout Çeda and Saadet were left, until there were only six.

Çeda was standing in the center of the circular pit, waiting for Pelam to drop the viper onto the dusty floor. Osman himself had come to watch the bout. He was sitting in his private box overlooking this, the central pit. He watched with interest as Pelam dropped the snake, and when Saadet was chosen, and selected Çeda as his opponent, Osman's brows rose. He sat higher in his chair as the spectators began to rumble in their seats, wondering what sort of strange match this might turn out to be.

That Osman was interested made some sense, but it made her all the more nervous. She wondered if Pelam had told him about his encounter with her. But even if that were true, surely Osman wouldn't guess that the slight woman in the pit was the same girl.

She shook these thoughts away, knowing she must concentrate or lose; and if she lost, all would have been for naught. Worse, Saadet was angry enough that he might try to kill her.

Which is fair enough, she decided. *I'm trying to do the same to him.*

As the four remaining fighters left the pits, Pelam gave a flourish and a bow to Saadet. "Saadet ibn Sim of Malasan," he said in a resonant voice, repeating the motions for Çeda, "chooses the White Wolf of Sharakhai!"

The crowd had never heard of the White Wolf, but they began to cheer when they realized she was Sharakhani and her opponent from Malasan. Such matches always made for a higher volume of betting. Rarely, however, were two opponents so unevenly matched. Under normal circumstances Pelam wouldn't allow such a thing, but in the tourneys, any of the sixty-four fighters who'd entered might face any other, and so, seemingly one-sided bouts such as these, while not commonplace, were certainly drawn from time to time. It made the day more interesting, and the oddsmakers began calling out the odds, weighing the match heavily toward Saadet. So heavily, in fact, that it made Çeda angry. And that made her all the more eager for the bout to begin.

Before coming up from the cool lower levels of the pits, Çeda had set two dried adichara petals between her lips. She hadn't wanted to ingest them until she knew she and Saadet would face each other, but she couldn't be seen taking them, either, so holding them in wait in some way had been her only option. As the pit boys ran out, laden with weapons that she, as the challenged, could choose from, she slipped the petals beneath her tongue.

Two petals.

She'd never taken more than one before, neither before

her mother's death nor after, and it was already filling her with verve. She'd expected it to come on strong, but she'd had no idea it would come on so quickly. As she stepped toward the pit boys and examined the spears and nets and swords and fetters, she felt her fingers tingling, her lips trembling. She swallowed again and again as spit filled her mouth. The floral taste of it filled her, overrode the smell of sweat and blood and the faint whiff of decay that was ever present in the pits.

The petals brought her back to the blooming fields where she'd harvested them last month. The twin moons had been so bright, so large, she'd thought they might swallow her whole and never let her go.

"If you do not choose," Pelam said calmly above the growing muttering among the crowd, "your opponent will choose for you, a thing I doubt you would like."

Osman watched her closely now. He had risen from his seat and was staring, not at her, exactly, she realized, but at her hands. They were shaking terribly. She gritted her jaw and blinked hard, chasing away the memories. She looked over the weapons with care, taking her time to allow the vitality of the petals to smooth out, and also to annoy Saadet.

In the end, she chose fighting sticks, a pair of wooden bars as long as her calves, weapons she and Djaga had drilled with often over the past few days. It often made the match more brutal, as the weapons gave out less punishment than a sword, so the fights took longer, but it also gave the edge to the quicker opponent, which was something she desperately needed.

As she took the sticks to her starting position, some of the Sharakhani in the crowd cheered, but others seemed only amused. Some few even howled—Malasanis, mostly, mocking her armor and namesake.

Saadet walked to the weapons, picked up his own sticks and placed himself opposite Çeda. The two of them stared at one another, her entire body shivering and Saadet smiling, not with murderous eyes, or even rage, but with cool confidence, and an assurance that this would be an immensely satisfying fight.

All too soon, Pelam stood between them with his gong. He struck it and stepped back. Çeda strode forward to meet Saadet, making sure to give herself enough room to retreat, for she knew what was coming.

Saadet came on strong, beating the air with powerful swings. But she dodged backward, sending a few strikes in return, enough to slow him down. Again and again he came at her, but she refused to engage. She would step away, and as she came close to a wall she would dart to one side or the other and set up her defense once more.

Saadet came faster after that, trying to catch her, and there were times when he connected with glancing blows against her pauldrons or helm.

Like waves upon a storm-swept sea, the effects of the petals were strong, almost overwhelmingly so. They drove her against the cliffs, granting no subtlety to her movements. Like this she was little better than Saadet, but the longer she fought, the more the effects of the adichara began to sweeten, the waves calming, giving her an energy she could manage.

Soon, as she knew would eventually happen, Saadet's lips pulled back in rage, and he charged toward her. She blocked several tight swings and rolled away, but not before cracking one stick hard against his ankle. His thick leather sandals absorbed much of it, but she could tell it had an effect. As he limped away, she could think of nothing but Emre's look as he knelt over Rafa's dead form, the feelings of guilt coursing through him. It lit a rage within her that she'd suppressed during all the uncertainty of these past few days. As she maneuvered herself into position, she held the memory to her like a skin of water in the deep of the desert. But she should have waited.

He was getting tired. She could see it in the way he was overreaching, in the way he overextended his swings. She could hear his breathing becoming labored. But the memory of Emre so maddened her that instead of retreating and waiting for Saadet to slow from exhaustion, she pressed and met him head-on as he came at her once more.

She was not nearly as strong as Saadet, even with the

petals, but she was stronger than he guessed, and she used his ignorance to her advantage.

She beat away his first few blows, holding her ground, striking at his head or knees when he came too close. And when he struck at her, she would sidestep and crack his knuckles or his wrist with the end of her fighting sticks. They were not hard blows—she couldn't afford to put her whole body into it lest he catch her off balance—but they took their toll. Slowly but surely, she saw him wincing each time she connected with his joints. He began grunting as well, and his breath became more labored from pain and exhaustion and perhaps fear. To be bested by a girl like her. It must be wearing on him.

When she came at him again, however, he was ready. He blocked a strike from her cleanly, and when she aimed a blow at his wrist, his hand shot forward, dropping his weapon and grabbing hers with his free hand. She tried to wrest it free, but with two strong tugs, he had it. He tried to grab for the other, but it was a ruse. When she drew it back he stepped on her foot, preventing her from backing away, and grabbed her neck. She tried to slip free, but he dropped his one remaining stick and brought both hands around her throat. She brought her stick down with all the strength she could muster, but she couldn't put her body into it. He let the blow fall against his helm, no matter the pain, for his hands were now squeezing hard.

The crowd was on their feet, shouting, screaming, stomping their feet and whistling. It all became a single shrill note in Çeda's ears as Saadet's hands tightened. He lifted her, slamming her against the wall of the pit.

Pinpricks of white appeared in her vision and began to dance. For a bare moment she felt a greater presence around her—not those in the pit, nor those in the Well, nor even in Sharakhai. It was a presence outside, ringing the city. The adichara, she realized. The asirim. She could *feel* them, though she didn't know how. Her anger at Saadet was great, but it was nothing—a grain of sand in an endless desert compared to the anger in the minds of those sad creatures.

She used their anger—or it used her, she wasn't sure.

With her free hand, she reached over Saadet's forearms, grabbed a fistful of his fingers, and wrenched them up, twisting as she went. She heard and felt a crunch as one of them gave way.

Saadet screamed and released her, trying to twist away and free his hand from her grasp, but she controlled him down to the ground until his face was in the dirt.

Lest he pound the pit floor and give up the match, she let his hand go, but as she did she slipped the fighting stick she still held under his neck, then wrapped one knee around the end of it and pressed a forearm against the back of his head. Before Saadet knew what was happening, she levered the end of the fighting stick sharply. The haft of the weapon pressed ever harder against his windpipe, until she felt it give way with an audible pop.

The gong was ringing over and over again. When it had started she had no idea. Hands pulled at her, and still she heaved over and over, wrenching the length of wood against his neck, listening to the wet gurgling in Saadet's shattered throat. With a sound like stone breaking, something hard struck the back of her head. She lost track of which way was up as sky and ground and roaring crowd spun in her vision.

She was pulled to her feet as the fat man on the pit floor clawed at his throat and writhed and arched his back, legs making furrows in the dirt, all in the hopes of regaining breath that even the gods would no longer grant him. He was dying, and there was nothing Pelam or Osman or Saadet or anyone else could do about it.

Chest heaving, breath coming in ragged gasps, Çeda stared up at the crowd, many of whom were howling now—not the Malasanis but the Sharakhani, in honor of the skill she'd shown, and the viciousness. But there was one in the crowd, one near the very edge of the pit wall, who did not shout. Nor raise his hands to the sun. He merely stared at Çeda, eyes wide, mouth open.

Emre. It was Emre, his eyes taking her in as she stood over Rafa's killer like an avatar of Bakhi himself. By the gods, the look on him, as if *she* had killed Rafa.

She should have told him, she saw now. She should have

said she was coming to kill Saadet in revenge. But if she had told Emre, he would have come for revenge himself. And he would have died trying.

She'd kept silent to protect him, but right then, in front of the cheering crowd, it didn't feel that way.

It felt as if she had utterly betrayed him, and it seemed that Emre felt the same, for the moment Saadet's body fell still, even as Pelam tried to revive him, Emre turned and climbed up through the crowd. Tariq and Hamid had been standing next to Emre, Çeda realized. Hamid stared with a look of apology, then turned to follow Emre. Tariq, however, stared at Çeda with a look of annoyance, as if Çeda had betrayed not only Emre, but him as well, and then he, too, turned and followed Emre toward the pit exit.

And then Çeda was alone in the pit, with the crowd cheering her.

Chapter 46

A SHORT WHILE AFTER her candlelit encounter with Ramahd, Çeda took the stairs up to the roof of her mudbrick home. She sat on its edge, just as she had done weeks before, on Beht Zha'ir, when Emre hadn't returned from delivering his canister across the city. She would have searched for Emre if she could, but unlike the last time, she had no idea where he might be.

So she waited.

As Rhia crawled across the sky, as true night fell, she waited and prayed that Emre would return. But he didn't, and when the first signs of light began to brighten the eastern horizon, she wrote a note and left it under his pillow.

Leave and do not return. I'll find you when I can.

Then she went to her room and retrieved the wooden box in which she hid her petals from the nook above her bed. She took out the two remaining petals and crushed them into dust, then threw them to the night wind from her window. Then she pulled out her mother's book and carefully ripped out the page with the poem that had started her down this path.

Rest will he,
'Neath twisted tree,
'Til death by scion's hand.
By Nalamae's tears,
And godly fears,
Shall kindred reach dark land.

She held the page over the candle, which had nearly burned down to the nub. It pained her to do so—it felt as if she were burning her memories of her mother—but she imagined that Ahya, wherever she might be, could see the flames licking along the page, the two of them staring at it from opposite sides of the great divide, imagined that by the light Ahya could see the words and remember her past life, remember the daughter she'd had. The flames brightened, illuminating this room that was no longer her home. For a moment it looked like the place she remembered, a place of relative peace she'd shared with Emre for so many years, but when the flames dimmed, and she dropped the page's burning remnant into the wax pooled around the candle's base, the darkness of the days ahead returned, and this home again looked like some echo from her past she'd be a fool to revisit.

"I'm sorry, memma," she whispered.

After tucking the book into a small bag at her belt, she left and ran through the city toward Tauriyat. The streets were empty. The Maidens might still be out, but if they were, she could no longer hear the clatter of their horses. The wall that housed the gates looked impossibly tall. Black soot marred the crenellations, and in one place a great swath of it discolored the wall from the base nearly all the way to the top. A dozen Maidens stood guard. Çeda watched them for a time, but they were more vigilant than she'd ever seen them.

There'll be no sneaking in, not with the place looking busy as a beehive.

Deciding it would be better to have them aware of her approach, she stepped out from behind the corner of the building and strode purposefully toward the door. The

Maidens watched her. She knocked upon the doors with her the heel of her hand, the dull thuds pathetic as a beggar calling for coppers.

"Who comes?" called one of the Maidens from atop the wall.

Çeda backed up so that she could see the one who spoke. "It is I, Çedamihn Ahyanesh'ala."

"Where have you been, little dove?"

"I returned home, to check on my family."

"Are we not your family?" called another Maiden.

"I know you not at all," Çeda replied.

There was a silence, a silence in which the whole of Sharakhai seemed to pause.

And then one of the tall doors before her groaned open.

Sümeya marched forward, her veil gone but wearing her black Maiden dress, her ebon blade at her side, her eyes afire. She grabbed a fistful of Çeda's hair at the back of her head and forced her roughly through the doors, into the courtyard of the House of Maidens. Çeda tried to wrest herself free, but Sümeya's grip was strong, and Çeda was off balance. She stumbled several times, but Sümeya used her grip on Çeda's hair and arm to keep her upright and moving.

As the gate closed with a clank of metal, Sümeya threw Çeda to the ground. "You'll not speak your name like some urchin at our door. Your name is now sacrosanct, not to be spoken outside these walls while you wear our garb."

Çeda stared up at the wall, realizing the Maidens who had called to her from atop it had done so to embarrass her. "I didn't know."

"Of course you didn't. Because you know nothing. You're a sneakthief who's stumbled into the luck of having the blood of Kings running through her veins, and believe me, that's all that's saved you."

Çeda tried to rise, but Sümeya stepped forward and knocked Çeda over with a shove from her sandaled foot. Çeda tried again, faster this time, and again Sümeya darted forward and knocked her over.

The third time, Çeda blocked Sümeya's leg with a slap of her palm, then she spun about, sweeping her leg out wide and catching Sümeya's ankle.

Sümeya, however, would not be caught so easily. She rolled over one shoulder and was back on her feet in a flash, drawing her ebon blade as she stood. She gripped the sword easily while advancing on Çeda.

The sword . . . Çeda had never seen one so close in daylight. It looked like a sliver of night, a thing hidden from the sun's eye.

Çeda prepared to dodge, to retreat, but she knew it wouldn't stave Sümeya off for long. Çeda had an eye for such things, an instinct honed over the course of dozens of bouts in the pits and thousands of hours of practice. Here was a woman at the peak of physical condition, and as gifted a swordswoman as Çeda had ever seen. Çeda retreated until the wall met her back. Sümeya smiled, mirroring Çeda's movements as Çeda tried to slide left. "Where were you last night, thief?"

Çeda had thought long about this on her way back, what she would say. The truth, she'd decided, was the only way to answer. "I went home to warn Emre about you."

Sümeya's eyes went wide, a look of amusement now mixing with the anger. "Do you think him now safe?"

"You won't find him," Çeda said, "not if he doesn't wish to be found."

"You underestimate me, child. You know me as little as you knew your own father. Believe me when I tell you I am steadfast. If I wish your Emre found, then find him I will, and then—"

"Lower your sword!"

Sümeya, to Çeda's utter surprise, immediately complied while turning toward the voice. In that moment, Çeda had seen a flash of embarrassment play out on her face—*embarrassment* from the First Warden of the Maidens. There were only a handful of souls, Çeda was sure, who could command such respect from her.

Çeda turned toward the voice and was struck by a vision, a rich and powerful painting brought to life. A tall and imposing man strode toward them. His black turban and thawb wrapped a well-proportioned frame. He wore no adornments, none save the tattoos that marked the backs of his hands and the corners of his eyes. The ink on the back of his hands covered the skin completely, obscuring whatever tattoo had once been visible, as if it had been too dangerous or too sensitive to remain. The small tattoos on his eyes, however, appeared to be intact. They were in the shapes of spearheads—six on each side, one for each of the twelve tribes. They looked old and faded, but his eyes did not. They were rimmed heavily in kohl, as the men and women of old once did. They were such a light blue they almost appeared white. They pierced her, those eyes. Pierced her and made her want to retreat, to run and hide in a place where he wouldn't find her.

This had to be Husamettín, King of Swords, the one who commanded the Blade Maidens and saw to their preparedness, who even took a hand in the training of new Maidens. Or so it was told.

"My King," Sümeya said, lowering her blade and bowing her head as the King came to a stop before her.

When he spoke, his voice was low and primal, like the back-of-the-throat growl a cat makes as its enemies near. "You've drawn a sword against a sister Maiden, Sümeya."

"*Siyaf,*" Sümeya replied, using the term for a master swordsman, "I was set to teach her a lesson."

"And what lesson might that be?"

"That she cannot leave this House, she cannot spit upon it and return, expecting to go unpunished."

"She has been claimed," Husamettín countered easily.

"*Siyaf,* she *left!* On the eve of her naming, she turned her back on this house. She doesn't deserve a place among us."

The entire focus of the House of Maidens was now centered here. More Maidens had come and were gathered in a circle. Many Matrons had come as well, Zaïde among them, wearing their white dresses, cowls wrapped around their heads or gathered around their necks. None seemed sure what to do or what to say.

The King turned toward Çeda, but when he spoke, he spoke to Sümeya. "Did she tell the truth? Did you threaten her family?"

Before Çeda could respond, Sümeya cut in. "The boy she refers to is not her family."

"Yes, he is," Çeda said.

"No, he isn't," Sümeya countered. "He's just another gutter wren."

Husamettín, his gaze unwavering, jutted his chin toward Çeda. "Is he your brother?"

"More than anyone, Emre is my brother, the only family I have left."

A weight seemed to lift from Çeda's shoulders as Husamettín returned his attention to Sümeya. "We do not harm the blood of our blood, Sümeya. Not without cause, and she has named him her brother."

Sümeya scoffed, the tip of her sword lifting toward Çeda's neck. "We do not harm the family of our *sisters*. She is not one of us."

"Is she not?" He waved to one side. "Zaïde has seen it, Yusam has said it is so . . ."

"My Lord King, this piece of dung deserves only the sword, not *shelter*. I would sooner see my grave than have one such as her at my side."

"You will teach her," Husamettín said calmly, "and you will take her into your hand, as Yusam bade you."

"No," Sümeya replied, "I will not."

Before Çeda could blink, Sümeya had lifted her sword and swung it sharply toward Çeda's neck. There was a blur of dark movement. A clatter of steel a hair's breadth from Çeda's neck.

Husamettín's blade had blocked Sümeya's killing stroke.

The King stepped in while Sümeya and Çeda were both in shock and kicked Sümeya away. She flew backward through the air, landing hard, but she was up in a moment, facing the King, ebon blade in hand. She approached Husamettín, not with anger, but with an expression that Çeda could only interpret as deep and utter resignation. She meant exactly what she'd said about preferring the grave, and now she meant to force the King to take her life.

Husamettín stood tall, one arm behind his back, his own sword at the ready. It was a strange pose for a swordsman, but somehow he made it look both elegant and deadly. "When the desert was young," he said, "there was a tribe of wanderers who lived in the Vandraama Mountains."

If Sümeya's ebon blade could be said to be made of night, Husamettín's was deeper still. And it was not merely black; it *drew* light from anything that surrounded it. Everyone in the Shangazi knew of Night's Kiss, the blade the dark god, Goezhen, had granted to Husamettín on Beht Ihman four hundred years ago. It was said to thirst for blood. It was rumored to feast upon those the King slew, and if it had no feast, it weighed on his mind, calling upon him to take another so the dark sword might slake its thirst.

Sümeya seemed angry at the King's cavalier attitude, for she closed and swung at him. The King blocked, and retreated three steps as Sümeya launched a flurry of blows. Çeda couldn't take her eyes from them. The ringing of their swords sounded clear and high and hypnotic, as if this were some echo of a duel waged centuries ago.

Husamettín continued his tale between blows. "The tribe wandered the mountains, looking for food. They were starving, for there had been a drought the likes of which the mountains had never seen."

As Sümeya continued to seek an opening in Husamettín's defenses, it became clear that he had chosen to deny her wish. He would block a strike and retreat, block and retreat, never advancing, though it would have provided an advantage to do so. He was wearing her out, Çeda realized, pressing Sümeya to the edge of her abilities but no further.

"One day a boy of the tribe was beaten by two elder boys for trying to steal their water. Late that night he prayed for Goezhen to come for them, to take them into the desert and to turn them into slivers, pale and cruel imitations of men that steal souls when the twin moons are darkest."

Sümeya's face reddened as she pushed harder. Husamettín's sword flashed, darkening the space between the King and Sümeya. Their swords rang louder and louder, as every woman in the courtyard stood transfixed. Even Zaïde, who always seemed so calm, seemed fearful of how this would end.

"A god came to the boy that night, but it was not Goezhen. It was Thaash, and he frowned upon the boy, asking him why he would wish ill upon his brothers." The King sidestepped a charge from Sümeya. He fended off her blows with an ease that Çeda had never seen before. "'Because they beat me,' the boy said, 'and because they're hiding water from the tribe.' 'Are they?' Thaash asked. 'Then if you wish it, I will kill them.'"

Sümeya's breathing was becoming labored, her swings and footwork slower. That was when Husamettín slipped his sword inside her defenses and cut her arm, just below the shoulder. It was a light cut only, but enough to draw blood. Sümeya merely grunted and redoubled her efforts.

"The boy agreed, and in the morning four were dead. The two boys and their two sisters. The boy had loved those girls, and he had not truly hated the older boys. He grieved over his choice and prayed for Thaash to return, to explain why he'd taken more than he said he would, more than was necessary, but the god never visited the boy again."

Husamettín blocked a blinding succession of strokes and then slipped his sword inside Sümeya's defenses again, cutting her other arm in the same place as the first. Then he stepped in and kicked Sümeya in the chest, launching her backward.

Before Sümeya even came to a rest, he had sheathed his sword in one easy motion. He paced forward, hands behind his back, never taking his eyes from Sümeya, who was staring up at him not with hatred, but awe.

"We never know the consequences of our actions," he said. "Be careful you consider them before you call for blood again." With deliberate care, the King turned to Çeda. "You have a tattoo on your back, do you not?"

Çeda swallowed. Of course they would have seen it when they'd changed her out of her dirty, bloody clothes. Dardzada's tattoo. The one that marked her as a bastard. She could feel her face redden as she replied, "I do, my King."

"Show it to Sümeya."

"My Lord King?"

"Your tattoo. Show it to your sister Maiden."

Çeda stared at the King, then at Sümeya, who seemed utterly lost. It was a request she couldn't deny. They'd find out soon enough anyway, so she turned away and pulled her dress off her shoulders, holding it down around her waist. Sümeya drew in breath.

The King's voice filled the courtyard. "Who marked you, Çedamihn?"

"My mother," she lied.

"Do you know what it means?"

Çeda nodded slowly. "It means bastard."

"No. Your mother would never have marked you so. *Bastard* is what it has come to mean, but it once meant, *one of many* and *many in one*. It means you are not alone, Çeda. Your mother knew this, and it is a lesson you have yet to learn, Sümeya Husamettín'ava."

Çeda pulled her dress back up, staring in wonder at Husamettín. Had Dardzada known? Of course he had. He was too learned a man, too careful. Why hadn't he told her?

And then the name Husamettín had spoken registered: Sümeya Husamettín'ava. By the gods' sweet breath, Sümeya was Husamettín's *daughter*. Husamettín's refusal to do her harm suddenly made sense, but Sümeya had been trying to goad her own father into killing her.

Husamettín turned and strode toward Çeda. He came to a stop before her, and his hand shot out, quick as a striking asp, to grip her about the throat. Her first instinct was to wriggle free, but his grip was like stone. Besides, this was clearly a test, so she let him have his way and met his gaze with as much resolve as she could muster.

The King's gray-blue eyes stared into hers, and for a moment, she felt as if he were peeling away her memories, stealing them from her like copper khets from a child. But she refused to let her fears show. She met his eyes, and for a moment it felt as if *he* were the boy his story had spoken of, the boy who had ordered the death of his tribal brothers. But then the moment was gone, and the King was as fearsome as he'd been moments ago.

"She is a Maiden now," Husamettín said loud enough for all to hear, then he shoved her away. Çeda staggered backward, catching herself against the nearby wall, as the King made his way calmly toward the prayer hall on the far side of the courtyard.

Sümeya lay on the ground, wounds bleeding, eyes wide. Çeda thought she would be furious, but she looked more confused than anything else. On his way across the courtyard he came abreast of his daughter and stopped. He stared straight ahead, as if he were too disappointed to look at her, but he spoke in an unhurried and tolerant tone. "She is but a child, a girl who has not had the gifts of Tauriyat to lift her. And she is not Nayyan, nor does she pretend to be. Place not that heavy mantle upon her shoulders. Trust in Yusam's judgment. Teach her"—the King resumed his measured pace toward the prayer hall—"for in the days ahead, we will have need of all we can find."

Chapter 47

SÜMEYA WATCHED HUSAMETTÍN leave with shock fresh in her eyes. Only after he'd retreated into the prayer hall did she pick herself up off the ground, recover her sword, and clean it with the length of her sleeve. As she sheathed it at her side with all the deft efficiency of a seamstress threading a needle, her eyes stared sightlessly at the courtyard's paving stones. "Melis, take her. Clean the refectory walls." And with that she strode the other way, careless of her wounds, to lose herself in the shadows of the barracks.

For long moments, no one in the courtyard moved. A few stared after the King of Swords, or Sümeya, their first warden, but many looked at Çeda. They weighed her, some with looks that wished they were standing on the gallows, reading her crimes to her before slipping the noose around her neck; others with cold assessment, as if they'd not yet made up their minds about her; still others with regret, as if they dearly wished Çeda had never turned up. Then, in ones and twos, they recovered and began to set about the business of cleaning up after the attack. A Maiden of thirty summers at the least, with hardly an ounce of fat on her, came and stood before Çeda. "Come," she said, and walked toward the refectory on the far side of the courtyard.

Çeda was exhausted, and what followed was a blur. She wanted nothing more than to sleep, but Melis took her to get brushes and buckets and soap and a degreasing solution she said would help remove the stains. She was not a beautiful woman, Melis. Her curly brown hair was tied in a knot behind her head. Freckles and blemishes marred her cheeks and forehead. But she was handsome, and she had an intensity about her, a look that said she would do anything she set her mind to.

They went to the refectory, a long building that sat along the inner wall. It had been scorched in two places by the attack the night before. The ground near the walls was scorched as well, and there were still some fragments of clay and a viscous substance on the stones.

"Start with the walls," Melis said, pointing to one of the stains before scrubbing at one of her own.

Çeda mirrored Melis's movements, feeling awkward with this woman she didn't know, performing a mundane chore after such an emotional night.

"Sümeya is stern," Melis said after a time, "and fiercely protective of the things she holds most dear. The Kings. Our House. Her honor. She is hardened steel, but she will warm to you if you show her your heart."

If I show her my heart she will kill me. "Was anyone burned?" Çeda asked, hoping to change the subject.

"Three, though none badly. That was never their goal in any case."

"What do you mean?"

"It was a diversion. It's why Sümeya is so angry."

"A diversion for what?"

"This morning we discovered another attack had been waged mere moments after the attack here began." Melis spit on the ground. "Thirty rebels broke into a manse near Blackfire Gate." Blackfire Gate was one of the largest gates into the old city, and near it, inside the ancient walls of Sharakhai, lay one of the wealthiest sections of Golden-hill. The elder families lived there, children of the Kings, and others who had survived Beht Ihman. "Eight were killed, and a score or more wounded, but worse, they took Lord Veşdi, a first son."

"First son?"

Melis rolled her eyes. "You really are a moon-eyed calf, aren't you? It means he is first blood of the Kings themselves—a son, not a grandson or some more distant heir."

"Why would they take a lord?"

"Do the Al'Afwa Khadar need a reason?"

Çeda shrugged. "It's an expensive endeavor, is it not? The time and money to wage such a campaign against the House of Kings. The cost in lives. Why do all that to steal away a single lord? There must be a purpose, but what? Ransom?"

"I doubt it. The Al'Afwa Khadar have only rarely ransomed their prisoners in the past, and none since Ishaq retreated to the desert and ceded control of the rebels to his son, Macide."

"Why, then? Why steal into a manse and kidnap a lord?"

"That is the question that plagues Sümeya. No doubt it plagues the Kings as well, though none of them would admit it."

"Well, I'm sorry to hear this news," Çeda said, but she was really thinking of Emre. Had Ramahd been right? Had Emre arranged all of this? Even if he'd only played small part in it, he must have known what he was doing. The Emre she knew bore no love for the House of Kings, but neither did he harbor much resentment. He wouldn't go out of his way to do them harm.

So why?

Why now?

She had no answers and no idea how she was going to find Emre to ask him.

"Don't scrub so hard," Melis said, pointing to Çeda's patch of stone. "Give the bristles a chance to work."

Çeda did, and the soot began to fade with more ease. "It will never come out," Çeda said. "Not fully."

"We don't mind scars in this house, but neither do we leave our wounds untended." Melis swiveled Çeda's direction and examined the skin along Çeda's hands and face and neck like a collegia scholar would a newfound tablet, then set back to work, hiking up her black dress so she could move more easily. "You have a fair few scars of your own. Who gave them to you?"

"Mostly men I didn't see eye to eye with."

Melis scrubbed viciously for a moment as a reluctant smile overcame her. And then she laughed. "Let all men quake who stand before Çedamihn of the Endless Scars." She laughed again, and this time Çeda joined her.

Melis talked more easily after that, opening up more than Çeda would have guessed. She told stories of her childhood in Tauriyat. She'd been born here. Her father was Kiral, the King of Kings.

"Do you have brothers and sisters?" Çeda said.

"I had two sisters, but both died when I was young. I have dozens of half-brothers and half-sisters, though. The Kings rarely stay with one woman—or man, for that matter—for long."

"Do they have so much trouble finding love?"

Melis shook her head while shuffling to her right. "It's love they're guarding *against*. Wouldn't you if you lived so long as they?"

Çeda had thought about this before. Who in Sharakhai hadn't? It would be a curse, the way they lived, to watch all those you loved die.

Çeda asked Melis more about her father. Kiral did not rule over the other Kings, she learned, but most bowed to his wisdom, and his word carried much weight when there was something he wished to have done. To Çeda's great surprise, Melis had spoken to him only three times in her life. Once when she had become a woman, once when she had become a Maiden, and once when she had struck the head from the leader of a desert band during a vicious fight in the eastern passes.

"And how did you find him?" Çeda asked.

Melis stopped scrubbing a tenacious patch of soot. "How do you mean?"

"Was he kind?"

Melis shrugged and resumed. "He barely acknowledged my presence. He has many daughters among the Maidens,

more who have left this House, and more still who live elsewhere in the city and in the desert. In truth, though, I see
them rarely. My sisters in the House of Maidens are my
family now, as will soon be true for you, I suspect."

It felt so bizarre to hear the word *sister* as it applied to
Çeda and the Maidens. She was sure she'd never become
accustomed to it, but she had to try. "I doubt Sümeya will
ever consider me a sister."

"You'll forgive Sümeya in time. And she'll come to respect you, if not love you. You may find her hard now, but
in time you'll thank her for it."

"And you? Why don't you spit on me the way she does?"

The smile on Melis's broad face returned, and Çeda realized how wrong she'd been before. There *was* a raw
beauty to Melis, and it blossomed when she smiled. "Would
you rather I did?"

"The gods care little for my prayers, Melis."

Melis stopped her scrubbing for a moment, and regarded
Çeda with a mischievous smile. "The gods care for all our
prayers. They merely care for their own more." Then she
shrugged and went back to work. "My mother's father came
from the Shallows, and his father came from the desert. We
are all connected in the Shangazi, are we not?"

"I suppose we are," Çeda replied.

"Sometimes Sümeya forgets that. Too often she looks at
you and other innocents as the enemy. She forgets our history, how we ourselves broke from the desert tribes for
mutual protection, how the gods favored the Kings of
Sharakhai and the people they vowed to protect." She
stopped for a moment and stared into Çeda's eyes. "She
also forgets how far Yusam sees. When I was a girl, years
before my naming day, Yusam told me I would come to
him again."

"That's hardly prophetic," Çeda countered. "Were you
not meant for the House of Maidens?"

Melis shook her head. "I was the third daughter. My
eldest sister, Hajesh, was meant to take up the blade. She
died when I was seven. She slipped from a wagon and
struck her head on a blunt stone near Bent Man Bridge.
Phelia died less than a year later. She was swept away by

the Haddah when a storm washed through the desert. And that left me. When I went to him on my thirteenth birthday, he told me more, and all of it has come true, all save one."

"And what is that?"

"That one day I would stand beside a queen. That I would protect her above all things."

"A *queen?* Queen Alansal of Mirea?"

Melis's expression made it clear she didn't understand it either. "Who can say? Yusam sees far, and if he says it will be, then it will. I don't know when, or how, but it will happen one day. So I believe he has seen true to your heart, too. If he wishes you to be among the maidens, it is for good reason, and Sümeya would do well to recognize that."

"Sümeya has no say in the decision?"

Melis smiled. "Do you wish her to?"

"No. It's only—"

"I know what you mean, and if things had gone differently, if you'd been brought up near the Hill, perhaps Sümeya might have held some sway over which daughters were chosen. But now it is out of her hands. In some ways it is out of Yusam's and the Kings' as well."

"But Yusam already chose me. Husamettín approves of having me in his house."

"There is tonight to consider as well," Melis allowed, "when you'll be presented to the Kings. But none of these are the true test of the Maiden."

"Then what is?"

"Assuming nothing amiss happens tonight, then you will be taken to the desert in two weeks, and the asirim will judge you for themselves. *That* is the true test, so enjoy tonight. Be proud. That is why you are being taken to the Sun Palace, after all."

Çeda had known about the aspirant's vigil from her research in the scriptorium cellars, but it had seemed distant until now. The thought of being left alone among the asirim for a night struck fear into her heart.

Melis chuckled at Çeda's look and said, "Fear not, little wren. The holy ones will treat you well if your heart is true."

Çeda could only think of the asir that had kissed her,

the warmth of its lips. She tried to get Melis to tell her more of what to expect that night, but no matter how slyly she thought she was asking the question, Melis refused to take the bait, so she changed tack. "How many Maidens are there?"

Melis frowned as she scooted to her right, the muscles along her arms cording as she worked. "Have you not heard the song?"

"What song?"

"Twelve Tribes with Twelve Daughters?"

"That's a children's rhyme."

"Written about the Maidens a century and a half ago. Do they teach children nothing outside the walls?" She meant outside the old city walls, where Roseridge lay, and the Shallows, the Well, and other poorer sections of the city. "That is our number, oh Çedamihn Leather-headed. One hundred and forty-four blades of black, one hundred and forty-four black-clothed maidens, and Husamettín, the King of Swords, to lead us all."

"But the barracks are huge. Surely there are beds for many more than that."

"There are," Melis allowed. "Some are for the Matrons, and there are Maidens who remain for a time with us after they've laid down their blades due to age or infirmity. Instead of the usual five, our hands can number nine or ten for convenience, such as those hands assigned to watch over the caravanserais. At other times they will number only three or four. Some Maidens are assigned singly to the Kings and never enter a hand at all." Çeda had heard rumors of such women, assassins and spies and other agents who answered directly to Zeheb, the King of Whispers. "And beyond that," Melis went on, "our total can fluctuate. At times we have been as few as seventy and as many as three hundred. Some have only just entered our ranks and are not yet true and proper Maidens. Others may be wounded and unable to fight. Some may die, leaving ebon blades orphaned."

"And some may go missing." Çeda left the thought to hang between them like a thread ready to unravel.

Melis swung her head around and leveled a most

uncharitable look at Çeda. "If there's a question you wish to ask, then ask it."

Çeda liked Melis's forthrightness, and saw no reason to dance around the point. "Zaïde spoke of Nayyan. Sümeya hates me for many reasons, but most of all because of her sister. If I am to take her place in the hand, I would know who she was."

At this Melis bristled. "You will never *take her place*."

"Nor do I mean to, but that's how Sümeya sees it, as if I'm trying to take up her thawb and turban and sword."

For a time, Melis scrubbed the stone with broad, circular strokes, assiduously avoiding Çeda's gaze. But then her motions slowed, and she took a deep breath. "Nayyan was the fifth in Sümeya's hand. There were Jalize and Kameyl and me. And there were Sümeya and Nayyan. We were close, all of us, but the love between Sümeya and Nayyan was strong. They came into the sisterhood in the same year, but Nayyan was always one step ahead. In her bladecraft, in the way she took to the blooms, even in the way she carried herself. Sümeya looked up to her, and well she should have. Nayyan rose through the ranks and took the post of first warden the day she tried to save our former first warden from an ehrekh attack, deep in the southern passes of the desert. She killed the ebon beast and took the thorns from his bristled head for a necklace."

Çeda thought immediately of the Maiden in the desert. She'd worn a necklace of thorns. They could have been the thorns of an ehrekh. Could that have been Nayyan? Doubtful, for if it had been, everyone would know she still lived. Unless Nayyan was hiding from the others for some reason. She *had* come to the blooming fields alone.

Melis said, "We voted her to first warden upon our return to Sharakhai, a position she kept for years until she went out one night eleven years ago. It was the night after Beht Zha'ir. She was to visit her family. She left King Azad's palace in the early hours, but the next morning the captain of the ship she was to have taken said she never boarded."

Çeda knew in her bones that this had something to do with her mother. A thousand questions were ready to tumble from her lips, but she managed to still her tongue long enough to gather her thoughts. "And what did the King say? Did he have no news of Nayyan?"

"Beyond saying she left the palace in good health and good spirits," Melis replied, "nothing."

"And the search produced no clues?"

"None." Melis bent down and rinsed her brush out before attacking the wall once more. "King Ihsan undertook the investigation himself. It was as if the gods had plucked her from the earth and sent her on to her next life."

"Did you ever wonder if Ihsan was telling you the truth?"

Melis's circular motions against the stones slowed. "If Ihsan wishes to hide what happened that night, if the other Kings have chosen not to reveal anything to us, then what are we to do?"

"Press him."

Melis turned, angry. "It isn't our place to press the Kings." She thumped the end of the soot-stained brush hard against Çeda's chest. "Nor is it yours. You haven't learned our ways, so I'll let your words lie as the foolish thoughts of a child who knows nothing. But I won't do so again. They are our Kings, and you will treat them as such. Never let me hear you question them again. Do you understand?"

Çeda nodded numbly. She'd had no idea how angry Melis would become, but still, it was good to have a reminder that these women—every last one of them—were her enemy.

Melis threw the brush into the bucket, splashing water everywhere. "Bring the buckets. It's time to get you ready for tonight."

Chapter 48

Ç EDA WAITED in a beautiful, mosaic-covered hall. She stood beneath a scalloped arch with a thick set of carmine curtains before her, through which came a tumult of conversation punctuated by laughter and the sound of milling footsteps.

Zaïde and several of the palace's servant boys had led her here, positioned her beneath the arch and told her to wait until the curtains parted. She had the urge to reach out and part them herself, to see what lay beyond, but she knew she must wait. Today was no day for missteps.

Hours ago, Melis had brought Çeda to Zaïde. All warmth had vanished from Melis, replaced with a sufferance that made Çeda wonder when these women would see through her guise. Surely they would; it was only a question of time. For the next several hours, Zaïde had helped Çeda to wash and brush her long hair, to carefully braid it and pin it at the back of her head. Zaïde had presented her with a bistre silk dress with beautiful panels running down the front and the back. The skirt was slitted up to her knees.

"It's to allow you to dance with the sword."

"I have no sword."

Zaïde had merely smiled. "When the sun sets, you're to

be granted your ebon blade"—she smoothed the cloth along Çeda's shoulder—"by the King of Swords himself."

Çeda had known it would happen, but she was still caught off guard. To be granted an ebon blade, a symbol of the oppression of the Kings . . . She had spat upon the ground so many times, picturing Maidens holding those blades. They were used to make the men and women of Sharakhai cower. And now she would be given one of her own.

The gods lead us down strange paths.

The red curtains shifted. Outside, the flow of conversation waxed and waned, some coming near the curtains, but never too near.

"A handful of Kings may come," Zaïde had said while working at the ties to Çeda's dress, untying, retying, making them fit Çeda's frame just so. And Çeda had realized in that instant just how *worried* Zaïde was about Çeda's presentation. Like a mother for her own child, Zaïde was fretting over a young woman she hardly knew. "But trouble yourself not if there are only one or two. The Kings rarely attend in mass these days."

One or two . . . Çeda had worried before her presentation to Yusam. Husamettín's arrival in the courtyard had been unexpected, but he was a man who struck fear into one's heart as well. How would she handle it if four or five came?

"What will they ask of me?" Çeda had asked.

"The Kings? Little. They may not even speak to you at all. The rest will speak to you of where you came from, your loves, your mother and your father. What else do people speak of?"

Of betrayal. Of murder. Of war and hangings.

"Stop worrying," Zaïde said. "Today is a formality. No more. Your time in the Maidens begins in earnest two weeks hence, in the desert with the sisters of your hand."

Çeda had nodded silently. This was all moving so swiftly. Part of her wanted to slow it down, but what was there to do but wait and allow the current to take her?

When Zaïde was satisfied, Çeda had been taken to a grand palace near the base of the mountain at the rough center of the other twelve palaces.

"No one King owns the Sun Palace," Zaïde had said, pointing up to its many minarets and the domed building in the center. "It is the thirteenth upon Tauriyat, the one used by all the Kings when they wish to take council. It houses diplomats from other states. It is used to entertain the powerful in Sharakhai. Or, as in this case, to welcome another Maiden."

"How many will come besides the Kings?"

Zaïde shrugged. "That is dictated by the power of the Maiden's family, and the sway of the King who fathered her. In your case, I have no way of knowing, but I suspect you will already have attracted much attention in the halls of Tauriyat."

Çeda had doubted it then, but by the sounds of the crowd in the next hall, it seemed Zaïde had been right. And she was still totally unprepared for the scene that unfolded before her.

The curtains were parted by two young boys, revealing a room as grand as it was massive. Above was a vast dome with dozens of open windows that allowed the afternoon light to filter down over the filigreed walls, painted columns, and brilliant emerald floor. A crowd of hundreds upon hundreds were gathered, most occupying the center of the room, talking and milling about, but many more wandering the hall, drinking from small cups or sitting on pillows gathered around shishas with clutches of smoking tubes snaking outward from each.

Çeda stood at the top of a short set of stairs. As she took the first step down, the conversation hushed. The gathered men and women turned toward her. The men wore fine kaftans and abas and burnooses. Some of the lighter-skinned—those from Qaimir—wore trousers and shirts with ruffled necks, sleeves, and half-cloaks. The Mireans wore muted, tight-fitting clothes with half-collars. And the women . . . Their numbers were surprising. They comprised well over half the audience, and they were dressed in styles as distinctive as the men's, and much more diverse. Sleek silk gowns and patterned kaftans with towering headscarves, and bright jalabiyas with a dizzying array of patterned stitchwork.

In rapt silence, all turned their curious eyes to Çeda as she took the steps down, and the moment her foot touched the cool tiles of the palace floor, they bowed as one. So quiet were they, Çeda could have heard the shift of a foot, the rustle of cloth. But then they rose, and the gathered Sharakhani women released melodic cries of *"Lai, lai, lai,"* while the men whistled and the foreigners clapped and whooped and bowed with a smile and a flourish of the hand.

She recognized so very few among them, but there were two who attracted her notice. One, a tall man with moon-pale skin and bone-white hair pulled into a tail: Juvaan Xin-Lei of Mirea. And, not so distant from him, Ramahd, looking completely different. He was clean shaven. His shoulder-length hair was washed and styled and parted around his face in elegant waves. His clothes were cut from impeccable green and black cloth. Gone was the man she had fought in the pits, whom she had spoken to only last night, replaced by this lord from Qaimir, a lord who knew altogether too much of what was happening in this city. A lord who wanted her to spy for him.

With her next step, the crowd parted like water before the prow of one of the rare river ships that came to Shara-khai in spring. They spread until she could see the far side of the room, where several men stood. They wore fine raiment and golden crowns.

The Kings, Çeda realized. These were Kings of Shara-khai, and they were waiting for her, standing like a tribunal ready to hang her for her crimes, as they had her mother.

Had Ahya seen so many? Had she met all of these Kings before they'd found her out?

Surely not. Surely she'd seen only a few. They would not have gathered in numbers for a common criminal like Ahya. They would not come to cut her skin with some wicked knife. They could not be so cruel, could they?

And then it struck her. Their number. She counted as she walked, doing her best to keep her hands from quivering, her legs from shaking.

There were *twelve* of them. *All twelve Kings* had been drawn here to see her.

Yerinde's dark gaze, *why?* Why would she attract so much attention? Surely there had been other Maidens who had come when they were older. But no, there couldn't have been. Perhaps one or two during the years of their reign, but no more than that. This was a rare event, much rarer than Çeda had initially guessed. Or perhaps it had been Yusam's strange vision, the one that made him scream. Perhaps he'd shared what he'd seen with them, and they'd wanted to see this young woman for themselves.

She'd read so much about them, and now here they were, these Kings with their fine robes and golden crowns and humorless stares. *Carefully, Çeda. Step very carefully indeed.*

Soon she stood alone before the Kings, who waited on a low stone dais shaped like a crescent moon. Husamettín, the King of Swords, stood near their center. He did not carry Kiss of Night, but instead a curved sword with a wooden scabbard lacquered to a dull but beautiful sheen. Jade-eyed Yusam stood next to him, looking pleased. She recognized Sukru as well, the Reaping King—a wizened man, all bone and angles like a spider. And was she wrong, or did Sukru recognize her as well? He looked pained, somehow. They'd met once, a random encounter in the west end of Sharakhai. She wasn't sure if he remembered her or if the look was from some other inscrutable cause.

Azad, the King of Thorns, was said to be the smallest of the Kings. He stood farthest to Çeda's right, staring at her from within a darkened cowl. To the left of Azad stood a King whom she recognized, the one who'd nearly been caught in the attack at the old fort in the spice market, the one who'd been saved by the two Maidens. She'd wondered if he'd been burned during that attack. If he had been, it wasn't obvious. He looked to be a man a few decades Çeda's senior, hearty and hale, his face and hands unmarred by the touch of flame.

She knew from reading the dozens of accounts in Amalos's forgotten office below the scriptorium that this man was Külaşan, the Wandering King. His crown had been mentioned a dozen times, made of rare red gold, with falcon wings worked into the design, just above the temples. What the texts had failed to mention was the symbol at the center of the crown. It was an ancient symbol, and one that Çeda had seen before, but for the life of her she couldn't remember where.

Kiral, the King of Kings, stood next to Husamettín, marking the two of them as equals in a way. But Kiral was a vision, a man with burning eyes and pock-marked skin who had gravitas in the set of his shoulders and in the dark expressiveness of his face, as if the blood of the gods themselves ran through his veins.

Not so different from Saliah, Çeda thought.

She knew the names of the others too. Ihsan, the Honey-tongued King. Zeheb, King of Whispers. The one who appeared to be the youngest among them was Cahil, the Kings' Confessor, the King of Truth. How strange to have a face that looked no older than Çeda's, and yet had seen the passage of centuries. Strange, too, how innocent he seemed when hundreds had died by his cruel hand as he slowly and meticulously tortured them for their secrets.

Did you touch my mother, you cruel dog? Were you the one to mark her skin?

Tall Beşir was the King of Shadows, but most knew him as the Golden King, the King of Coin, for he controlled the city's treasury.

Onur, once known as the King of Spears, was more often referred to as the Feasting King in the west end, or the King of Sloth. If Zeheb was burly, Onur was a mountain of a man who wore black robes, a wicked frown, and enormous jeweled rings upon his fat fingers.

And the last King she recognized was the only other King, besides Külaşan and Sukru, who she'd seen up close before entering the House of Maidens. She hadn't known his name when she'd seen him years ago, but through the many scrolls and books she'd read, she knew it now. King Mesut, the Jackal King, Lord of the Asirim. He had the same intense gaze she remembered, and on his wrist he wore the same band of gold inlaid with jet. If he recognized her he didn't show it, but she remembered him well. He had been visiting young Mala's mother, Sirina, in a small patch of Sharakhai known as the Knot. Sirina and Mesut had been lovers, at least for a time. Mere days after Çeda had stumbled across him, Sukru marked Sirina's home for the asirim. Çeda had never learned whether it had happened by Mesut's leave or not, but it had been a strong reminder of how the Kings toyed with citizens they had sworn to protect, as if Sharakhai were little more than an aban board, its people the pieces.

Çeda bowed to the gathered Kings, turning her body as she did to take them all in, but she did not speak, not wishing to offend. For a long while the Kings merely watched, as if she were some oddity not worth speaking to.

And then came a voice. "We are quite the assemblage, are we not?" She turned to the leftmost King, the one who stood closest to the gathered crowd. The gods had granted them much, these Kings, and to Ihsan they had given smooth skin and white teeth and a melodic voice. "I am Ihsan, and forgive us, for there are times when even we are shocked and surprised."

"Surprised, Your Eminence?" Çeda asked, praying her fears would not be revealed by a tremulous voice.

"Your beauty. Your grace. Your composure before this poor tribunal."

Several of the other Kings bristled at these words, especially young Cahil and fat Onur, who stared with hate-filled eyes and frowned with a mouth that seemed all too familiar with the tearing of flesh.

"Zaïde told us what she saw in you," Ihsan continued. "And Yusam shared the visions within his mere, but it has been many years since one such as you has come to us, one born beyond the walls of Tauriyat, one brought to us in a time of need." Again several of the Kings bristled, one even snorting, as if the mere thought were blasphemous. It was not this that Çeda noticed most, however. It was the utter silence that followed. Every single ear in the room was listening to this conversation. They were rapt, wondering what the Kings would do with this little lost wren. Ihsan stepped down from the dais and strode toward Çeda. As he came, his calm and charming eyes stared down at her right hand, which was unbandaged for the first time since she entered the House of Maidens. "You even came

to us with petals upon your tongue and an adichara's kiss
upon your skin." Then he locked eyes with her, and a sly
mongoose smile came over him. "Is it not so?"

"It is," she admitted.

"As if the gods themselves had prepared you for this
day."

"The gods had no part in it, Your Eminence. My *mother*
prepared me for this day."

Ihsan smiled, intrigued. "Pray tell, child."

"She was a brave woman, who taught me to fight for
what I needed in this world, for if I didn't, no one else
would."

"We may fight, but there is always an arm stronger than
ours, a blade sharper."

"It is so," Çeda allowed, "but one must know *when* to
fight as well."

"And your mother. Where is she today?"

"She died when I was ten." The lie was necessary. The
Kings had never discovered her mother's true name—Çeda
would have been found and killed long ago if they had—
but she mustn't link herself to her mother's death. If she
did, one of them—whichever one had killed Ahya—would
eventually piece the puzzle together.

"Most unfortunate." Ihsan's face took on a look of gentle regret—an act, surely, but it somehow seemed genuine
on his fair features. "How did she die?"

"A spear from a desert tribesman." Çeda made a show
of glancing back toward the crowd, as if they made her
uncomfortable. "They raided the city in winter, while we
were washing our clothes in the Haddah." The raid had
really happened, and Çeda had long since used the story
whenever her mother's cause of death came up.

"A spear? They rode in and found your mother and
drove a spear into her gut?"

"Not quite so simple, my King. They were pirates, driving into Sharakhai after a train of mules bringing grain and
liquor to the western harbor, a train they'd been chasing
for weeks. They came into the city to complete the slaughter they'd started in the sands. When they came across our
path, two of the warriors stopped. They spotted my mother

and rode straight toward her. The first of them threw his spear and missed. The second did not. His spear flew true, and my mother's blood stained the Haddah red until merciful Bakhi led her to the farther fields."

Ihsan made a show of shaking his head sadly. "But why?"

"I never learned. The Maidens and the guard came upon them shortly after and killed them both." Another truth to leaven the lies.

"You must have your suspicions."

Çeda nodded. "I do. Surely those men were of her tribe, the tribe she left when she brought me to Sharakhai to find a new life. I believe they were honor bound to kill her."

It was a rare but not unheard of thing. Those who abandoned their nomadic lifestyles to come to Sharakhai and forge another were sometimes hunted by their tribesmen—sometimes their own family—for the insult. It was a message to those who remained. *Honor the old life,* such murders said. *Never turn your back upon the tribe.*

"And from which tribe did they hail?"

"I can only assume Masal, for that was the tribe my mother came from."

"You cannot recall the marks upon their skin?"

"It all happened so quickly," she replied. "I remember only the sound of charging hooves. The shine of the sun off their spears." It was a well-composed lie. She had avoided contact with anyone who had direct ties to the Masal tribe, so if the Kings ever looked into her past in the pits and in the bazaar, they would detect nothing amiss.

"Ah, well, you were young." Ihsan offered her a comforting smile, and then he waved to the crowd. "Such things we understand." He paused, staring more closely at Çeda's eyes, her lips, her chin. "And your mother, did she ever tell you who your father was?"

"Had I known, my Lord King, I would have come far sooner."

Ihsan's eyes lit up while the crowd around them tittered. "And why do you think that was? Surely you would have asked your mother of your father."

Why indeed? Çeda should have. And Ahya should have

told Çeda so much. Perhaps she meant to. "I did ask, my Lord King, but she refused to speak to me of it. And beat me when I asked too often."

"You must have been a willful child."

A ripple of chuckles.

"That I was, my Lord King, and I fear I have only grown worse."

The laughter rose, and a smile lit Ihsan's beautiful face, where the other Kings were little more than a study in stone. "Well," Ihsan continued, glancing slyly back at his fellow Kings, "of your father, perhaps we'll never know. There are tales only the desert can tell. Is it not so?"

"Of course, Your Majesty."

"Please, there will be time aplenty to discuss your past. For now, let us celebrate the return of one of our own to the fold." Ihsan turned with a flourish and faced the other Kings. He regarded each, and then rested his gaze upon Kiral. "Should we not?"

Çeda had no idea what would happen if any of the Kings denied this request, but there was no dissent, and eventually Kiral nodded.

The Kings remained aloof, but the rest of the gathering welcomed Çeda once more. Ihsan took Çeda's hand and led her into the crowd, which was now closing in, many smiling and nodding their appreciation. Çeda realized that most were moving as couples. They arranged themselves in a pattern on the floor, with Çeda and Ihsan at their center.

Ihsan spun her into position and held her hand high, their bodies now close. Ihsan looked at her as if he knew her well, as if there were more he wished to do with her than dance. His hands were soft. His hair gave off the warm and woody scent of myrrh. "Has Zaïde prepared you?" he asked softly so that only she could hear. "Do you know you will be part of a final dance when the day closes?"

"Zaïde told me, yes." Ihsan's eyes. By the gods, he was beautiful.

The music began. A rebab and a flute and a doudouk played a slow song that touched the roots of Çeda's soul.

"You will be given your blade. Did she tell you that?

And in the dance you'll stand across from one chosen from your new hand?"

"She did."

"I can tell Kameyl to swing the blade more gently if you wish." Çeda knew little of Kameyl, only that she was one of Sümeya's hand, and that Zaïde considered her to have one of the best sword arms the Maidens had to offer. "No one would think poorly of you," Ihsan went on. "There are those who have been gravely wounded. There have even been deaths on the night a young Maiden was given her sword."

"I am no stranger to the dance of blades, Eminence. I'll not disappoint you. Or Kameyl."

Ihsan laughed; a more beautiful sound Çeda had rarely heard. "It isn't me you need to impress. Or Kameyl. As I hear it, the High Blade of the Maidens is ill-pleased with you. It may be time to begin impressing *her,* rather than giving her reasons to dislike you further."

"Dislike puts a rather rosy blush on it. She despises me."

"I didn't wish to be unkind."

Çeda laughed. She *laughed*. What was she *doing* with this King?

"You *are* a rather curious specimen," Ihsan went on. "Dozens have been killed and hung before the gates for crimes such as yours."

And there it was. With those words—*hung before the gates*—Çeda found herself once more. She remained, however, intent on Ihsan's every word. She didn't want him to suspect that anything had changed.

"I wonder what Zaïde saw in you."

"I couldn't say, my Lord King."

Ihsan's brow pinched, and he lifted her right hand to examine the fresh tattoos and the puckered white wound at its center that had all but ceased to cause her pain. He seemed amused by her response, or by the words now written on her hand, or both. "I'll have to ask her one day. *And* Yusam. I expected him to find the heart of a thief in you, but he didn't, did he?"

"I rather think we wouldn't be here talking if he had."

He leaned in conspiratorially. "You may be right." He

held her closer as the pace of the music increased. "You're an unforeseen wonder, Çedamihn Ahyanesh'ala, like the bright jewels found within the dull stones of the glittering fields."

The glittering fields . . . The wording was similar to the poem in her mother's book.

From golden dunes,
And ancient runes,
The King of glittering stone;
By inverted thorn,
His skin was torn,
And yet his strength did grow.

While far afield,
His love unsealed,
'Til Tulathan does loom;
Then petals' dust,
Like lovers' lust,
Will draw him toward his tomb.

Could that be it? The desert tribes all wandered the desert, but each had their ancestral grounds. Could it be as simple as finding the King who came from a place of golden dunes and ancient runes? But who besides the gods and the Kings themselves knew their origins anymore? The Kings had long since hidden the names of their mother tribes.

The music slowed and stopped, and Çeda bowed to Ihsan. "I hope that bodes well," she said.

He smiled and kissed her hand. "We shall see."

And with that he turned and walked away.

There were many more waiting to dance with Çeda. She assented to each with a smile. She saw Ramahd among those dancing, but he never came near her. Perhaps so Juvaan wouldn't suspect anything when she spoke with him.

As she danced with various partners—from the wealthy of Sharakhai to merchants from Mirea and Qaimir, to an impossibly tall jeweler from Kundhun—she couldn't help but think of Emre. She didn't want to be here among these people. She wanted to be at home, eating marinated peppers and dipping bread in oil and telling Emre about her day, and listening to his exaggerated tales in turn. In some ways those days felt like yesterday, but in others they were a thousand years away, buried in the past and never to return.

They'd changed, both of them. They were on a strange course now, two diverging paths, and it made her wonder whether they would ever cross again. Was there room for Emre in her new life? Would Emre want to be a part of it if there were? She supposed it didn't matter. Not anymore. There was nothing she could do about it, and there was no way she would turn back.

She ate sparingly, tasting cumin-spiced flatbread and a spicy bean paste that reminded her of long days in the desert, and a drink of honey and lemons and rosewater that made her mouth water even while she drank it. She marveled at the sheer variety of food, but more than this, at the amount of it. The waste. People on the streets had so little. In the bazaar there were treats and delicacies brought from far and wide, but they cost so much, few in the west end ever sampled them unless they managed to tuck some up a sleeve. But here was antelope and lizard and tortoise from the far reaches of the Shangazi, roast boar and venison from the humid forests of Qaimir, quail and pheasant and some massive flightless bird—if the tales were to be believed—from the plains of Mirea. Dozens more meats and vegetables cooked in a hundred combinations. There was so much it could never be eaten, not even by the host that was gathered here this night. Such a sickening waste.

The light through the windows above was turning a deeper shade of orange. Sunset neared, and soon she would receive her sword and dance with Kameyl. She looked for Ramahd again, thinking she might need to go to *him* if he wouldn't come to her, but he was gone. She strode easily through each of the four patios around the great hall, talking lightly with those who approached, but she never saw him.

She bided her time in the great hall because it gave her a chance to wander and watch for Juvaan Xin-Lei. She hoped he would come to her, and she sent him glances from time to time, inviting him to do so. Their eyes met once or twice, but he never approached, and when sunset arrived her chance would be lost. When it was clear Ramahd would not return, and that Juvaan apparently had little interest in speaking to her on his own, she walked straight for him. He and several other richly dressed men were in conversation, but they stopped and turned to face her when she drew close. Juvaan had the same soft features of the other men, but with his bone-white skin he stood apart. Next to his countrymen he looked thin, though she wouldn't go so far as to call him sickly, and there was a confidence in the set of his chin and shoulders that gave her pause, as might a wild dog, no matter how sleek its coat.

Çeda bowed. "I wonder whether the envoy of Queen Alansal has time for a dance."

Juvaan's eyes were of the palest blue, like the glacial ice Çeda had once seen packed in hay in the bazaar. He looked at her with something akin to amusement, but there was more—annoyance that he'd been interrupted, or at her presumption. He was a man used to setting rules that others followed.

He looked as though he were about to give his regrets, so she spoke over him. "Did you know, my Lord, that we've seen one another before?"

Juvaan bowed his head, granting her the statement, but doing so with a quizzical look on his face. "I regret to say that we have not."

"We have," Çeda replied, smiling coyly, "but I forgive you your forgetfulness."

Juvaan looked perturbed, but also curious. "I would certainly remember *you*."

"I'm making light, my Lord." Çeda's smile was just the right blend of humor and deference. "Of course you would remember"—she made a flourish with the skirt of her dress—"had I been dressed like this." She leaned in and spoke softly. "But I wasn't. That day, I wore a white battle skirt, with an iron mask across my face."

Juvaan's eyes narrowed. He glanced at the men standing next to him, and then, without another word, took Çeda by the arm and strode away. He released her when they were distant enough that their words would be lost in the din of the great hall. "*You* are the White Wolf?"

She stepped back and bowed, but kept his eye, as she might with an opponent before the start of a bout. It felt strange to make this confession, especially to a complete stranger, but she'd thought long and hard about what Ramahd had said, and she'd decided he was right. She *would* never enter the pits again, so why not use this opportunity to get into Juvaan's good graces?

Juvaan shook his head ruefully. "A pit fighter turned Maiden. In all her years, has Sharakhai ever seen such a thing?"

"I believe I am the first."

"I would think so," Juvaan replied. "And it makes me wonder what you were doing in that pit, and why you've sought me out now."

And now it came to it. Çeda hadn't been sure how she was going to convince Juvaan to tell her anything. She knew Ramahd wanted something from him. She just had no idea what. But Çeda wanted something from Juvaan too, and the only way to get it, barring violence, was to give him something he wanted.

"I went to that pit looking for you."

"And why would you have done that?"

"Because the man who was to deliver your canister to Macide on the night of Beht Zha'ir was waylaid. I found him, and saved your precious package."

Juvaan's eyes had held a touch of sly amusement a moment ago, but now they hardened to such a degree that Çeda tensed, ready to dodge if he thought to strike her. Two of the courtiers he had been speaking with approached. They looked perturbed, surely due to whatever business Çeda had interrupted, but they stopped when they saw Juvaan's look and then walked away at a dismissive wave from him. As Juvaan turned back to Çeda, his eyes passed over the seven remaining Kings on the dais, along the far side of the room. He was worried. Very worried.

"No one knows except me. Not even the messenger," Çeda went on. "You've covered your tracks well, but I've made out your scent in Sharakhai since, in the attack on the House of Maidens, for example."

"I don't know where you've come by these fool notions, but I tell you this. It would be best if you forgot about them, and this conversation, immediately."

He tried to turn away, but Çeda grabbed his arm. "I tell you these things because I want to help."

Juvaan stared at her hand upon his wrist. "I've no idea what you're talking about."

"Then perhaps I am wrong, but this I tell you true, if I *were* right, then what sort of ally might I be?"

Before Juvaan could respond, the crowd began to murmur, many of them looking Çeda's way. Then they parted, stepping away from a ray of light that shone down from the top of the dome above. Sunset was upon them. Some contrivance set into the top of the dome was capturing the light, sending it down upon the floor. It was time for Çeda to dance.

"Think on it," she said as she released Juvaan. And with that she walked away, for the King of Swords was standing ready at one end of the makeshift arena.

Chapter 49

THOSE IN THE CROWD nearest Çeda clapped. Others whistled. But they all retreated, giving her space to walk to the center of the room where the column of light shone upon a mosaic of two moons, split by a spear head.

As Çeda neared the center of the open space, Husamettín pulled the ebon sword from his belt, scabbard and all. When Çeda came within a few paces of the King, he nodded to her and said, "Are you prepared to enter the service of the Kings?"

"I am, my Lord King."

"Then come. Take your blade." As Çeda stepped forward, he pulled the sword from its scabbard and held it high. Near the base of the blade, etched into the dark steel just above the guard, was a pattern of reeds along the banks of a river. The steel itself was a sight to behold. It was very dark, nearly black, with a wavy pattern running along its length. The blade held a sheen that turned dull at its sharpened edge. The hilt was wrapped in the finest leather, and held the pattern of a vine with thorns running along it. The pommel was shaped like the closed bud of one of the adichara blooms.

"Her name is River's Daughter," Husamettín said. "She was worn by seven others before you, among them Rasel, Scourge of the Black Veils, and Gelasira, the Savior of Ishmantep. May she bring you calm in the face of battle." With a speed and ease that showed just how comfortable the King of Swords was with a weapon in his hands, he sheathed River's Daughter and held it out for Çeda.

She accepted it, noticing the pulsing in the meat of her thumb, where the adichara poison still resided. She also saw the beating of Husamettín's heart in the veins of his neck. The two of them matched, she realized. Matched exactly, as if the gods had linked them in some way. He took her head with both hands and kissed her forehead with warm lips—an act infinitely more sickening than the kiss from the asir. She could feel the rush of his blood, the pulsing warmth within him, and all she wanted to do was pull the ebon blade from its scabbard and draw it across his throat. She wanted to see his lifeblood spilled, as her mother's had been.

Her right hand squeezed the fine leather straps along the sword's grip. She felt the muscles of her arm drawing on the blade. She could do it. She could kill him. And perhaps one other if she were fast enough.

But then Husamettín looked more closely at her, seeing something in her eyes. He held her shoulders at arm's length. "Calm yourself, child. The dance will be over soon enough." As if she were an untested child to be cowed by the mere crossing of blades.

A Blade Maiden in a black dress stepped to his side. A veil covered her face, but Çeda knew this was Kameyl. Husamettín stepped away and motioned for Kameyl to take her place. Then he returned to the dais and sat on his throne with the other Kings. All twelve of them now watched closely, their attention rapt.

Kameyl slid into position across from Çeda so that they were three paces apart. Kameyl wore a shemagh that veiled her face, but not a fighting dress. Her dress was more like Çeda's, black cloth with bright, festive designs that had once been fashionable in the early days of the Amber City. Çeda had no veil. She was not yet a Maiden, so she

would come to this dance as an outsider, asking for entry
to their House, to their inner circle. Kameyl played the role
of warden, ensuring that Çeda was ready. To do this they
would cross blades.

Using her left arm, the sword held halfway along the
scabbard's length, Çeda presented River's Daughter, hilt
upward, a request to pass. Kameyl held her sword by the
scabbard as well, but held it crosswise, barring Çeda's way.
Motes of dust danced in the beam of light equidistant from
them both. Çeda took one step forward and pulled her
blade so that an inch of dark steel was bared, an indication
that she held no fear in her heart.

In an elegant flash of movement, Kameyl raised the
scabbard above her head and pulled the blade free. She
took precise steps forward while holding her scabbard at
the ready, as a shield, in effect. Her sword was not in the en
garde position but mirrored the scabbard, as if she had
nothing to fear from Çeda.

Çeda retreated, drawing her sword as well.

This dance, the song of blades, the *tahl selheshal*, had
been old well before the Kings had come to Sharakhai,
well before the city itself had risen from the sands of the
Shangazi. The women, the protectors of the tribe, had created it to hone their craft and to teach their children the art
of the sword. When war came, it was often the men who
went to fight, but that didn't mean the tribe was safe. It was
left to the warrior women to protect the tribe if an enemy
war party found them.

Children used sticks to dance the *tahl selheshal* until
they reached a certain age, a certain level of ability.
Then they used real swords, as Çeda and Kameyl were
doing now.

The opening moves were scripted. Kameyl took one
long stride forward, holding the pose until Çeda did the
same. In that moment the two of them were opposites, two
halves of an image split perfectly by a flawless mirror. Then
Kameyl rose, bringing sword and scabbard high, and spun,
slashing toward Çeda's left side.

Çeda blocked with her scabbard, which created a sharp
clack, and then she rose up, locking her sword and

scabbard together before performing the same spin and cutting at Kameyl's ribs.

Kameyl blocked and dropped low, spinning and sweeping her leg. Çeda leapt into the air, spinning as well, slashing her sword above Kameyl's head.

The foreigners among the crowd gasped, for the moves had been performed with both speed and power. The Sharakhani were silent, but their eyes were bright. They knew they were in for something not seen in generations. Even the Kings seemed to be sitting higher in their chairs, some even leaning forward.

The dance continued, moving through the thirty and nine scripted positions required from both challenger and challenged. When it was sword or scabbard against only scabbard, the hardened wood created a chatter as a flurry of blows landed. When it was sword against sword, the sound of ringing steel filled the massive space and echoed in the relative silence. Shouts of surprise came as they moved through the middle act, with its series of spins and silent swings coming near but not quite touching the opponent. They wove in and out of the reflected sunset, the light flashing dully against their ebon blades and dark clothes.

Kameyl was very good. But so was Çeda. It was a rare thing to find two so able to trust one another that they could unchain themselves, but they were, and they did, their bodies spinning, blades flashing. Çeda could feel her right hand, her poisoned wound. It was becoming painful once more, perhaps from the sudden exertion. But what she noticed more than pain was that, despite it, her hand and arm were more steady than she could ever remember. It was almost as if she could feel the swing from Kameyl before the blow struck—indeed, before she could even *see* it, if she or Kameyl were turned away.

At last the final blows of the prelude came to an end. Their swords crossed and remained in place as the two circled one another. Now they would show what they were truly made of. Often it was the younger who waged an offensive against the elder, but Kameyl gave Çeda no rest. She lunged for Çeda's chest.

Çeda blocked and stepped back, and again Kameyl

advanced, using her scabbard to block and swing low at Çeda's legs. Çeda narrowly beat the strike away before Kameyl's scabbard flashed in and struck the side of her head.

The faces in the crowd were either utterly entranced or horrified. There were no expressions between these two extremes. The blows were coming so quickly, Çeda could barely keep up. Again and again she was struck by Kameyl's scabbard. She tried to find openings to return the blows, but Kameyl was too good. Too fast.

One strike came in so hard it sent Çeda staggering backward, but the crowd caught her and threw her back into the mêlée. Çeda prepared to defend herself, but Kameyl had retreated. She was standing tall, her sword hanging low at her side.

The crowd murmured. The Kings, especially Husamettín, seemed concerned.

This was a point in the battle in which she should have saluted Çeda for her bravery, for her skill. But she did not. Hanging her sword low was an insult. Leaving her defenses down showed she had no respect for Çeda's skills.

Çeda held her sword up, the hilt at chest level, the tip pointed skyward, a sign of honor for her opponent. She did it because she truly did respect Kameyl's skill, but also to provoke her. Kameyl was toying with her, and she was determined not to do anything Kameyl expected.

The light from the setting sun had almost completely faded, but there was still a burnt orange glow on the floor. The Sharakhani in the crowd knew the end was near. They began to whoop, to release a collective ululation.

Kameyl began to spin. She moved swiftly toward Çeda, sword flashing, dress flaring, until she'd reached the halfway point between them.

Çeda did the same, twisting about as fast as she was able. The frenzy of the crowd rose to new heights as she came to a stop, whipping her sword in the air mere inches from Kameyl's chest. She raised her sword and held it above her head while Kameyl spun and did the same, slashing at the air.

In this final act, the two women, now sure that neither

would relent, that neither had an edge over the other, would cut one another in a prescribed move with precise swings of their swords. They did this so neither would lose face, but also in remembrance of the brilliant battle they had just waged. Most often this was symbolic. Çeda had expected to hold out her arm to take a precise, shallow cut from Kameyl on the palm or the inside of her forearm, but Kameyl continued as did the women warriors of old, when each would slash through the air, closer and closer to the other woman, until blood had been drawn.

It was an unspoken challenge, and she expected Çeda to back down.

But Çeda wouldn't. She would take a cut if it meant acceptance into the Maidens. She spun and swung at Kameyl's thighs, the tip of the blade coming within a finger's breadth.

Kameyl twisted and slashed her blade at Çeda's throat. Çeda could feel the rush of air in its wake as it licked her skin.

Çeda spun again, this time cutting a razor-thin line through the cloth of Kameyl's dress and into her skin. It was perfect. Exactly what she should have done, something memorable, but not deep, a mark of her skill with the sword.

Kameyl did not move. She did not react at all. Her eyes were calm itself. She had positioned herself so that Husamettín could no longer see Çeda, at least not clearly. As Kameyl stared into Çeda's eyes, she inched her stance forward. She spun, bringing the sword up and into the ready position. And then she swung it across her body, toward Çeda's neck.

Too close, Çeda realized. It was going to be too close. She was going to cut deep enough to sever the artery that pulsed beneath her skin. Her lifeblood would spill across the cool floor of the Sun Palace for all to see.

Çeda might have stepped away, but she was so enraged she lifted her sword and blocked Kameyl's ebon blade with her own. As she did she felt white hot pain coming from the poisoned wound in her right hand. So quick and fierce was the blow that it shattered Kameyl's blade. The tip of it flew to Çeda's right, spinning end over end and slicing into the forearm of an observer, a frightened, dark-skinned woman in a blue gown.

Kameyl stood in the center of this grand space staring not at Çeda, but at her own broken blade, then at the bleeding woman, as if she couldn't quite believe what had just happened. Kameyl hadn't meant to have her blade shattered. She'd meant to kill Çeda. She'd meant to slice her neck open and watch her bleed, and then claim that Çeda had moved at the last moment, or that it had been a mistake. It would have been a stain upon Kameyl's honor, but it would have been worth it to remove a deeper, darker stain from the House of Maidens. This was how strongly the Maidens would fight to rid themselves of her. They would not be above deviousness, which Çeda should already have known.

The woman in the blue gown howled with pain, staring in horror at the deep gash along her arm while blood gushed down her arm, over her dress, and onto the floor. The piece of blade that cut her had caught in her dress, but as many rushed to help her, it clattered to the floor, its sound rising above the woman's cries. One man used a cloth belt to wrap the wound tightly, but the rest of the vast crowd were simply staring at Çeda, aghast, especially the Sharakhani, who knew how grave Çeda's actions were.

The entire purpose of this dance was to prepare for the symbolic cut she would receive at the end. Small children would thump one another clumsily with sticks, hoping to make the other flinch, but as they grew older they would practice coming close with the blunt end, barely grazing their opponent. And when children were preparing to take the blade at last, they were slowly prepared by their mentors until they were ready for the cuts they would be given. For Çeda to block Kameyl's swing proved she was unprepared for the Maidens, that either she would not or could not trust her warrior sister, that she wasn't brave enough. For young women on the cusp of adulthood, such a thing would be frowned upon, but for Çeda, a woman grown, it was a deeply shameful moment.

She could see the disappointment in Husamettín's eyes.

He'd come to his feet, as had the rest of the Kings. Husamettín strode toward. "Clear the room," he barked to the servants. As the crowd was ushered from the hall, the woman's wails of pain going with them, Husamettín stared at Kameyl with a deep frown. "Tell me what happened."

"You saw yourself, my King. She is a coward. She did what cowards do." Except that the King *hadn't* seen. Kameyl had blocked his view before her final stroke.

"No," Çeda said before the King had finished with Kameyl, "I swear by the gods, had I not blocked her swing, a red smile would have blossomed across my neck." The other Kings had been in a position to see, but who among them might have recognized the move as one that was meant to kill? Çeda looked to them, hoping they would say something, but they all remained silent, judging.

"A lie to hide the truth," Kameyl replied easily. "You can see it on her face."

Despite what Çeda thought—that Husamettín would defend Kameyl's version of events without question—he appeared uncertain. "Is that true?" he said to Çeda.

"Kameyl wished me dead. She never thought I would be *able* to block her blade, or that I wouldn't recognize her killing stroke."

Husamettín waved one hand to Kameyl's broken blade. "You have proof of this?"

"Only what I saw in the heat of the dance. Her blade swung not to scratch, but to kill."

Husamettín held his hand out toward Çeda's ebon blade. Çeda sheathed it and held it out to him. Taking it, the King said, "Is there any reason to give you this blade?"

"I'm a poor judge of that, my Lord. I asked for no place among the Maidens, and yet one was found for me."

The light from the braziers glinted in Husamettín's dark eyes. His face was becoming angrier by the second.

"I can only say that the gods led me," Çeda went on quickly, "that they led me to you, and that I take such things most gravely, my Lord King. I am humbled by the honor you and the Kings have shown me."

"Give her a place in the Maiden's House." These words had come from Onur, the King of Sloth. He waddled as he walked toward them, the grimaces on his face making it clear just how much each step pained him. "But grant her no blade. There is no place in the Maidens for one such as she."

Husamettín's hard expression softened, as the other Kings gathered around.

"The decision does not fall to you, Onur," the Jade-eyed King said, his piercing green eyes studying his brother King carefully. "*I* have chosen her, and in *my* employ shall she remain."

"Then take her as a servant," Onur said with a gallows grin as he came to a stop a few paces from Çeda. He stared up and down at her, lips pursing, breath coming coney-quick, as if he could hardly breathe. "Clearly she isn't fit for such things."

"The choice is not yours," Yusam said again.

Husamettín pulled himself higher. "Nor is it yours where it comes to the Maidens."

"Her sword has already been given." This was from Ihsan, who stepped carefully, as if he didn't wish to upset the delicate balance of the conversation. "Only death may take it back."

Husamettín was surely annoyed by this intrusion into something he deemed his territory. His entire body was rigid, and yet he considered the blade in his hand soberly, as if what Ihsan had said was an inviolate truth. He pulled the blade out and regarded its length, as if examining each and every minute nick Çeda and Kameyl had just etched would somehow give him his answer.

"We will see if she's ready." He pointed to an open space on the floor, away from the others. "Stand there," he said.

Çeda did. She moved into position, taking a deep breath and releasing it slowly, for she knew what the King of Swords was about to do.

Husamettín held the scabbard loosely in one hand, the sword in the other. He took a few tentative swings, and then turned with an elegant sweep of the blade, bringing it high above his head. The tip pointed unerringly toward the center of the dome high above. The King stared deeply

into Çeda's eyes, and in that moment, she saw pain within
him, something as deep and old as the dried bones of the
desert. She could see in his eyes that he wished he could
speak of it but would not. Or could not. Then the look was
gone and the sword was spinning in a series of arcs and
twists and turns that brought it ever closer to Çeda. He
spun his entire body, once, twice, thrice, the sword arcing
high. Ever closer he came, the sword's tip inching closer
and closer to Çeda's neck, just as Kameyl's final swing had
done.

Husamettín was preparing her, letting her know that he
would do the same. But in allowing her to see it, he was
letting the fear build. If she had any doubts, any worries
that he would not wield his sword as a master could, those
fears would fester and grow, so that by the time he came for
the final swing, she would flinch. He would see. They would
all see. And if she did, they would never trust her again.
There was fear in Çeda's heart. Fear that Husamettín
might believe he had made a mistake. But she suppressed
it. Made herself breathe easily. She *trusted* Husamettín's
skill.

When the sword blurred across her field of vision and
nicked her neck, she didn't flinch. Not in the slightest.
Husamettín followed the motion through and returned to
the position from which he'd begun, with his sword aimed
high. But his eyes now bored into Çeda, assessing her.
Without ever taking his eyes from Çeda, he slipped the
blade into its scabbard. He strode toward her, put his hand
against the side of her neck. Using his thumb, he swiped
across the shallow cut, which was only now beginning to
burn. He showed her his thumb, with the streak of carmine
marking his sun-aged skin. Then turned to Kameyl, allowing her to see it as well, and finally he showed the rest of
the gathered Kings.

"She will remain in the Maidens. Kameyl, you will teach
her. And that is the last we will speak of it."

Kameyl still wore her veil, but Çeda could see the hint
of color upon her cheeks. She did not reply. She merely
bowed and left the room.

Husamettín gripped the sword by the scabbard, laying

it across his free arm, hilt first, for Çeda to take. "Go with her," he said. "She'll not attempt such a thing again. This I promise."

She took the sword and nodded, then strode after her sister Maiden, recognizing how wrong he was. This had only been the first attempt. Kameyl might decide to obey and leave Çeda alone. She might even teach Çeda a thing or two, as might some of the others, but many among the Maidens would not. They would continue in their attempts to see Çeda dead until they succeeded, the word of their King or not. But Çeda would no longer consider leaving. Her mother had left her much, among them clues to the downfall of these Kings. So she would remain, and she would find the King of Glittering Stone.

And she would drain him of his blood.

Chapter 50

Five years earlier...

ÇEDA SAT WITHIN A LARGE and richly appointed room. Upon stone pedestals stood marble pitchers limned in white gold. Beautiful brass plates hung on the wall. It smelled of sandalwood and lavender, while she smelled of sweat and blood, fresh as she was from defeating Saadet in the pits, a mere minute's walk from where she sat.

She still wore her armor, but not her helm. That had been taken by Osman's men after she was led to this room. Strangely, the bout had drawn to a close as if nothing unusual had happened, with one exception. Pelam announced her the winner, and the crowd had cheered her victory, but the Master of the Games had gone no further than that. He would normally have announced where and when she would fight next, so those who wished to see her next match could do so, but in her case, he'd merely ushered her from the pit, accompanied by the two toughs who had wrestled her off Saadet's dying form. They'd brought her here, to the room she could only assume was in Osman's own apartments. It was the highest room in the pits, four stories up, and gave a good view of four of the seven pits below.

She wished she could have gone to speak to Emre right away—gods, the look on his face—but there was nothing for it. She had to finish what she'd started, and then she would go to him and try to apologize.

Voices came from outside the room. They grew louder, and Çeda could hear Osman speaking with someone, perhaps Pelam. Unfortunately they were quiet enough that Çeda couldn't make out their conversation. Eventually Pelam's footsteps receded, and Osman strode into the room and walked behind the rich walnut desk in front of Çeda.

Osman's black beard hung down the green silk kaftan he wore. His hair was tied into a tail, the loose curls falling down to his shoulders. He did not sit, however. He stared at Çeda with his bright, expressive eyes—eyes she'd been sure would be full of anger but were not. He looked at her with something akin to amusement. That, and—dare she say it?—pride. He motioned to the patio behind him. "Come," he said with that low timbre of his, and strode through the peaked archway ahead of her.

She followed and joined him at an ironwork railing with filigreed balusters. He made no move to face her. He merely stared down upon the pits, so Çeda moved next to him and did the same. Together they watched one of the matches as the crowd cheered. It felt strange to be standing there with him, as if they were equals. She knew they weren't, but the gesture felt like a small nod of appreciation for what she'd done in the pits.

"Pelam is furious," Osman said calmly, as if he were commenting on the cloudless sky.

"I imagined he would be."

"I can't let you continue in the tourney."

She was surprised to find herself disappointed by those words. She had killed a man today, and in some ways that made her feel more mortal than she had since the days and weeks following her mother's death, but there was no denying how freeing it had been to fight in the pit, just her and the man upon whom she'd sworn to gain revenge. "But I beat him. Neither you nor Pelam can deny that."

"Yes, we'll get to that. In the meantime, do you know why I've brought you here?"

"I've a few good guesses."

"Then tell me."

"Why do you need me to tell them to you?"

"Because if you haven't guessed, I'd like to know your perceptions of the situation, and by extension, how perceptive you are. Humor me."

"You're concerned that I went behind Pelam's back and snuck into the tourney."

"I am, yes, though I don't know that I'd use the word *concerned*. Go on."

"You feel betrayed by Djaga for helping me."

"Yes."

"You're upset that I killed that Malasani dog."

"I am that as well, yes. Anything else?"

"Isn't that enough?"

"It's quite enough, but that doesn't mean there isn't more."

She paused, hoping to get him off track, for she was starting to suspect the real reason he was questioning her this way. "I'm too young to have entered the tourney."

She watched Osman from the corner of her eye, but Osman continued to stare down at the pit. The crowd had risen to their feet as the two combatants locked shields and fought for the upper hand, turning and shoving and trying to sneak in a blow from their heavy-headed flails. A collective groan followed when they broke apart and began circling one another warily once more.

"Do you know how often those of royal blood come to the pits?"

"Often enough. I see them from time to time."

"Then you know that some follow the dirt dogs quite closely. Most are not as keen as you, but there are a good many who know their way around a brawl in the pits. There's something else about the nobility that we can say with certainty as well. Do you know what it is?"

"They eat antelope while we scrap over goat? They sip wine from chilled glasses while we drink from dirty wells?"

He laughed ruefully, but chose that moment to turn toward her. She faced him squarely, willing the hummingbirds fluttering inside her chest to quiet themselves. Almost to spite her, they grew worse, partly from the fading effects of the petals, which always made her jumpy, but more so from the hungry glint in his eyes, the subtle smile, as if he were about to enter the pits himself.

"A bit melodramatic," he said, "but in essence, you're right. There are different rules for royalty and those like you and me." She could hardly believe her ears. To her, Osman *was* nobility, no matter that he used to fight in these very pits. "They might have wine, but they'll begrudge you yours. They might eat venison, but they'll snatch away your plate should you manage to find some of your own, or grant you that one small boon and act as if it were the greatest gift in all the world. But there are certain things, certain laws, over which they are particularly vigilant. You and I might not see the reasons for every verse in the Kannan, but *they do*, for they are the eyes and ears of the Kings in Sharakhai. They watch for those who wander the streets on the holy night. They watch for those who take forbidden fruit from their gardens."

Çeda swallowed before speaking again. "What does this have to do with me?" she asked, perhaps too calmly.

"They know the signs of the adichara, Çedamihn Ahyanesh'ala. Some know them very well, and you won't always be able to tell when someone is nobility and another is not, and you certainly won't be able to tell those who go through the city looking for the sort of infractions you committed today. Believe me, if I can see the signs, so can they."

Çeda swallowed, hoping it wasn't obvious how nervous she suddenly was. "Why are you telling me this?"

"Because if you wish to fight in the pits again, you'll promise right now that petals will never be a part of it."

Çeda blinked. "I can fight again?"

"Isn't that the arrangement you have with Djaga? She pays your way in, you scrap to pay her back?"

But how did he know? The crowd below roared. Çeda glanced down as one of the fighters fell from a heavy blow, then pulled her gaze back to Osman. "I didn't think . . ."

"No. But even you must see that your legend will now grow. The White Wolf of Sharakhai defeating a Malasani

brute three times her size? What sort of fool would I be to
keep you from the pits?"

Osman was more than twice her age, but he didn't seem
so old to her just then. There were the marks of the pit
about him—small scars, a bend in his nose where it had
been broken, a chipped tooth. It all served to make him
more striking, like a ram who'd survived the black laughers
and the jackals, who'd been wounded once, but was all the
wiser for it, all the stronger.

"I mean what I say, Çeda. I'll not risk my interests—the
pits or anything else that's mine—over a girl who doesn't
know when and where to draw the lines."

She nodded to him.

"I must hear it from you."

"I'll not use them again."

"Use what?"

She took a deep breath. It felt like a betrayal to say it
aloud, but he'd already guessed, so what did it matter now?
"I'll not use the petals in the pits again."

"Ever," he said.

"Ever."

A change overcame Osman then. *He* became the black
laugher, transforming from the regal ram with a knowing
wink and a wicked grin. "We wouldn't want your friends to
find you face down in the Haddah, now would we?" He
said these words with nonchalance, but the look in his eyes
was so fierce and untamed that Çeda's stomach churned at
the thought of crossing him.

"No," she said at last. "We wouldn't."

"Good," he said, slapping her on the back and returning
his attention to the pits, where one fighter was now mercilessly beating at the other's upraised shield with a two-
headed flail. "Djaga was serious, you know, about getting
her money back before you can start making your own."

Gods, he must have spoken to her before coming here.
"What of it?"

"Unless I've missed my mark, you'll need something to
tide you over until that happens."

"Djaga will give me some of it, won't she?"

Osman reared back and laughed, an honest laugh, from

the belly, as if she'd truly surprised him. "Let me tell you something about Djaga. She grips her money so tightly it cries at night. She can stretch a sylval from here to Kundhun. Her purse strings are cinched tighter than mine ever were, and believe me, my life is not an extravagant one, even now. If she says she'll keep your earnings until she's been paid three times over, then that's exactly what she'll do."

"What would you have me do, then, work in the pits?"

"Nothing so mundane." He paused for a moment as the fight below came to a thrilling conclusion, the man with the flail breaking his opponent's shield, forcing him to concede or have his head caved in by the next swing. "Have you heard of shading, Çeda?"

She *had* heard of shading. She had indeed.

———————— ‹—●—›› ————————

Osman was true to his word, and Djaga was true to hers. In the weeks that followed, Çeda began running packages for Osman. Collecting a box from Roseridge and taking it to the foot of Blackfire Gate. Delivering a short message from a man as old as the desert to a Malasani caravan master with a wicked tongue and a penchant for pinching Çeda's backside. Taking a ring—nothing at all remarkable about it—from a reed-thin woman in the bazaar to a certain captain of the Silver Spears. Çeda earned a few copper khet for each delivery, and she didn't mind doing it, but she had the distinct impression that Osman was merely testing her. Giving her simple assignments to see how she handled herself before he gave her anything challenging.

She also learned that Tariq had joined Osman's group of shades. Tariq intimated as much when she and Hamid were out running the Trough one day, and then she began to notice him hanging around the pits more often. He acted oddly around her now. They still ran the streets from time to time, but he'd become territorial, asking her when she'd shaded last, what she'd run, how much Osman paid her. When, in return, she asked what he'd done, he offered few details, waving her questions away and changing the

subject. So she stopped sharing anything related to shading.

Djaga continued to train Çeda in the western harbor
where Djaga lived and worked. They drilled beneath the
piers, partly to avoid the sun, but also to avoid too many
observers. Djaga was as skilled a fighter as Çeda had ever
seen, but she knew how to teach as well. She was strict and
never let Çeda go beyond what she thought she could handle, but she pressed Çeda at times too, in order to bring her
along quicker, to expose her weaknesses. She taught Çeda
not just how weapons might be used, but how they could
debilitate, slow her opponents, how she might fool them
into thinking she was unskilled in a particular weapon
when in fact she was preparing a finishing move.

"Your size," Djaga said, "will work to your advantage
for a time. People will think Saadet was a fool to let you
beat him. We'll play to those expectations. You'll not win
bouts handily, girl, even if you might. You'll show yourself
skilled, but not overly so. You'll fight to the level of your
opponent right up until you're ready to end it."

"Why wouldn't I finish them as soon as I can?"

Djaga pointed her shinai, a slatted bamboo practice
sword, eastward toward the heart of Sharakhai. "If you
merely wish to win you can find that sort of bout any day.
If you want to rise in the ranks, then there are more games
to play than the ones you wage with these." She waved her
shinai, then came at Çeda with a furious sequence of blows
that Çeda barely managed to fend off.

When the tourney ended, Çeda was entered into her
first arranged bout. Pelam scheduled her for early in the
morning—the first bout of the day—against a woman
who'd been fighting in the pits for so long it was child's play
for Çeda to beat her. It was a message from Pelam. He was
still annoyed at what she'd done. Her next bout a few
months later, however, was much more challenging. An ac-
claimed swordsman from Mirea had returned to Sharakhai
and wanted a bout before returning home. With the flip of
a coin, Çeda had been allowed to choose the weapons, so
she chose a three-sectioned staff, something rare in Mirea,
but that Djaga was particularly gifted with. They'd spent

days training with it. Çeda could have beat him easily, but as Djaga had instructed her, she'd held back until Djaga gave a short nod from the stands.

The crowds grew for Çeda's bouts. More and more began to howl when they saw her in her white armor and wolf-pelt helm, both of which she was starting to fill in as she grew and gained muscle from Djaga's merciless regimen—running in the mornings, swords before high sun, lifting stones after a short lunch, and more weapon sparring with anything under the sun *except* swords before finishing a few hours before the sun went down.

She was given every Savadi to herself, and more time if Osman needed her, but even her free day she spent walking around Sharakhai, learning more of its ins and outs, for there was no telling where she might pick up or drop off one of Osman's packages. She was gone from home so often, in fact, that she rarely saw Emre.

She did from time to time, though. She made sure of it. She'd thought he would be angry that she killed Saadet, for taking his revenge into her own hands. She wanted to apologize and practiced a speech for days at a time. But whenever she found herself in the same place with him, whether in their home or in the bazaar or in the streets, the words all fled, leaving her speechless until Emre started talking about how Tehla the bread baker had made moon eyes at him again, or the things Hamid had pilfered from a caravan wagon, or anything besides the thing they needed to talk about most.

It was like a wound between them, festering. It needed to be lanced, but Çeda didn't have the right words, and Emre never brought it up, so she assumed he simply didn't wish to speak of it.

Osman drew more of her friends into his shadow empire. He gave Hamid a proper knife and sent him to act as a lookout for Brama, a second story man. Tariq and Hamid could do whatever they wished, but she worried when Emre started to run packages, too.

Thankfully, though, Emre didn't stick with it. He began picking up odds and ends to make a bit of coin—a breaker in the quarry to the northwest, a stevedore lading and unlading ships in the northern harbor, shaping wheels for a wheelwright near the Trough. Anything to keep his body busy, he'd said. That's what he needed.

She followed him one morning when he headed off to his latest job, wandering the desert with a craftsman named Halond, looking for lightning strikes. He would dig up the root-like structures from the sand and sell them as art. Rhia's trees, he called them, though what they had to do with the lesser of the two moon goddesses Çeda had no idea. They were haunting, treelike shapes the lightning made of the sand, more like something Goezhen would make than Rhia. But she supposed that idea was bad for business—one didn't want a totem above their hearth from the god of twisted creatures. But a sculpture touched by the goddess of dreams and ambition? Now there was something to treasure.

"Are you well?" Çeda asked Emre as they shared a pear, a luxury she'd bought in the bazaar yesterday.

He crunched into it and chewed noisily, his breath misting momentarily in the chill morning air. "Of course I'm well. Why wouldn't I be?"

She really should have asked him months ago. They were growing apart. She could feel it. And she knew this was the reason why. "I want to talk to you about Saadet."

He handed her the pear. "What of him?"

She wanted to slap the pear away, but she didn't want him to know she was upset, so she took a bite and handed it back. "I should have told you."

He shrugged. "But you didn't. And it's over now. What need is there to dredge up the past?"

"It's only . . . the look on your face, Emre."

"What? I was shocked, Çeda. Wouldn't you have been?"

"It wasn't just shock I saw on your face. It was anger."

Emre stopped walking, forcing Çeda to do the same. "What do you want me to say? The world is a better place without Saadet ibn Sim? You did Sharakhai, and me, a favor that day. I probably should have thanked you for it before now." He bowed formally. "Thank you, Çedamihn, oh White Wolf of Sharakhai, for saving me. Is that what you're looking for?"

"No, I—"

"Then please, for the love of all that's holy, leave it alone." He turned and strode away, leaving Çeda standing there.

She let him go. He was still angry, and if she pushed him, it was only going to force him into further silence. She could only hope that one day he'd tell her. Except he didn't, and eventually her hope withered, and she wondered if she would ever know his true feelings that day of her first bout.

Emre's flightiness continued. The next year saw him move from cobbler's apprentice to a delivery boy for a west end cooper to a butcher in an open-air abattoir—a *shambles*, he corrected her once when she asked him how long he would stay there. He brought home fresh meat from this job, but there was something in his eyes when he returned home at night, a sickening gleam that sometimes lasted for hours. His work in the shambles lasted surprisingly long, nearly a year, but he eventually moved on, this time to a florist who had him fetching bunches of wildflowers from the banks of the swollen Haddah.

Emre's income was unsteady, but Çeda eventually paid off Djaga's investment, and then began earning good money. Some came from the pits, some from Osman, some from teaching children at the pits, a ruse Osman had come up with to hide her identity and give her reason to be near the pits at all, so that no one would suspect she was the White Wolf. Eventually they moved to a flat in Roseridge, close to the bazaar and the spice market. It surprised her that, initially, Emre didn't wish to go. It was too expensive, he said. They'd be better staying where they were. But she suspected it was only so he could be near the place he'd once shared with Rafa. Although they'd moved after Rafa had been killed, they could afford very little at that time, and they'd ended up not far away.

Çeda pressed him to move, and Emre had finally relented, though she had the feeling he resented her for it. His resentment eventually passed, but she wondered how much Emre kept inside him. Was it slowly building up, all his anger and resentment and loathing? He could only mask it for so long, she thought, and one day, it would all come pouring out.

One day, while shading a note in a small ivory box,
Çeda cut through the Shallows, and three boys began following her. A fourth soon joined them, and Çeda ran as the
boys gave chase. She had no idea if they knew about the
box or not—in all likelihood they didn't—but she wasn't
about to take chances. She hurtled through back alleys and
byways and leapt over fences.

What the boys wanted from her she never found out, for
after several more turns, they skidded to a stop and ran the
other way. Çeda saw why a moment later. Ahead of her were
two women standing outside a door. She was in a neighborhood known as the Knot. The homes in this cramped and
winding set of streets created a veritable maze of mudbrick.
Many of the homes spanned the street itself, creating impro-
vised tunnels; others leaned this way and that as if they'd
drunk too much araq and needed the support of their brothers. Often the windows of the homes in the Knot were open,
the residents chatting with one another or watching those
below pass by. But not today. Today the windows were shuttered, the doors closed. And Çeda knew why.

These women were as out of place as a kettle of golden
rahl sitting in the middle of the street. It was not merely
their assured stances, nor their steely gazes, but their
swords that gave them away. The sheaths were made of lacquered wood with a beautiful black grain. Ebon swords.
These were Blade Maidens.

What under the bright desert sun were they doing in the
Knot?

The two of them stared at Çeda, sizing her up. Without
a word, the one closest to Çeda paced toward her. The
Maiden had not gone two steps, however, before the door
behind her opened, and a man stepped out. He was a tall
man with clothes of the finest quality—a khalat of rich
green silk, patterned with the branches of a springtime
tree with tiny pearls for buds; boots of supple leather,
barely dusty from the streets of the city; his turban, the
beautiful amber of the desert with bright red piping along
the edges. And a golden band on his wrist, set with a dark
stone, a stone that seemed somehow darker than a stone
should be, and deeper, if stones could be deep.

This was a King of Sharakhai or Çeda was a beetle scuttling along the sand. He saw her staring at the golden band and the impossibly black stone. He might have covered it with the sleeve of his khalat, but he didn't. He considered Çeda instead, as if he were coming to some decision.

Çeda immediately averted her gaze. She bowed and moved to the edge of the street, kneeling, as was required in the presence of either Maiden or King. And here were both!

Believing each shuddering breath would be her last, Çeda waited in the relative silence. Even the sounds of the city seemed to fade around them, as if Sharakhai itself were waiting to see what would become of Çedamihn, daughter of Ahyanesh. *Please, Nalamae, grant me your favor.*

The footsteps of the Blade Maiden approached. She could hear the sand and dust grind beneath her well-worn boots. They stopped just short of Çeda, and then there was a pregnant pause. Utter silence.

I'm not ready yet. I'm not ready to face them.

Somewhere, a child began to cry. On and on it went, a primal wail, as the Maiden stood before Çeda, perhaps drawing her blade, perhaps preparing to bring it down across Çeda's neck and be done with her.

Closer to the door, the King's footsteps picked up, the other two sets followed, and Çeda was soon alone in the street, sweat across her brow, ready to collapse with relief.

Chapter 51

AFTER THE RITUAL AT THE SUN PALACE, Çeda was taken to the barracks in the House of Maidens. It was a massive building built four stories high with a large central courtyard where the Maidens trained at swordplay. Each hand of five Maidens was given an apartment with five bedrooms and a common room between them. Not so different from the home Çeda had shared with Emre.

Zaïde led her there, knocked softly on the door, and ushered Çeda into the central room where Sümeya, Melis, and Jalize were sitting, drinking watered wine from earthenware mugs.

If Sümeya was displeased that Çeda had returned, she didn't show it. Jalize, an intensely beautiful woman with delicate features and curling brown hair, merely stared as if it meant little to her, but Melis smiled. It was a small thing, but it lifted Çeda's spirits.

"Where is Kameyl?" Çeda asked.

It was Zaïde who answered. "She's gone to Husamettín's palace so that another sword can be chosen for her."

The other three Maidens all stiffened at this.

"It was shattered," Zaïde told them, "by Çeda's own blade." Sümeya opened her mouth to speak, but Zaïde spoke over her. "A story for another day. Welcome your sister, then let her sleep."

Sümeya stared at Çeda, then Zaïde, and then stood and strode to her bedroom, the beads across her door clacking in her wake. Jalize, however, crossed the room to stand before Çeda. "Welcome," she said, and took Çeda in a full embrace. She kissed Çeda's cheeks and then stepped aside. Melis did the same, but it was a stiffer gesture than Jalize's.

"Sit," Zaïde said in the doorway, "take wine, and we'll speak again in the morning. Tell me then who you wish to visit on the night before Beht Zha'ir."

Çeda could only stare. "Visit?" She had read much about the customs of the Maidens, but she hadn't read this.

Zaïde smiled like a cat with a particularly fat mouse, and suddenly she seemed much younger than the gray-haired Matron Çeda was growing used to. "You'll be given a night to yourself, to visit with whomever you wish. You have only to tell me their name and a message will be sent."

Emre. I want to see Emre. But she couldn't. He was too wrapped up with the Moonless Host. And besides, she had no idea how to reach him. But there was one person, a certain lord from Qaimir, that she might not mind seeing once more, especially if her night in the blooming fields was to be her last.

"I can tell you now," Çeda said.

"As you wish."

"Lord Amansir of Qaimir."

Jalize and Melis exchanged a look, while Zaïde smiled a knowing smile. "You could do worse, my dear." And then she left.

"A *lord*," Jalize said, leading Çeda to one of the low couches and setting her on a lush pillow. "Tell us."

Çeda merely waved her hand. "I met him tonight. He's a handsome man."

Jalize's eyes flashed. "A good enough start, and the Qaimiri are deft when the clothes come off." She glanced at Melis. "Or so I've heard."

Melis rolled her eyes as if she'd heard this a thousand times before. "Do as they say," she said to Çeda, "spend time with your lord. But then strike it from your mind.

Your night in the killing fields will not be an easy one, and you should be pure of heart, pure of mind. Think of your Kings. Think of Sharakhai and those you will protect. Don't dream of Qaimiri noblemen, and all will be well."

Think of your Kings. As if Çeda could do otherwise.

She wondered what the asirim would sense, what they would learn of her, whether they would tear her limb from limb when they saw her true heart. Sehid-Alaz, their King, may have kissed her, but would anyone other than the King himself know what that meant? If the asirim squabbled, as men did, it might mean nothing. Or if their King had enemies among their number, they might be all too glad to kill some lonely girl who had been marked by their lord.

If it was so, Çeda decided, then it was so. She was exhausted, so she took up the bottle of wine, poured until her mug was nearly overflowing, and drank deeply.

She and the others talked long into the night. She learned of their childhoods, their parents, their lives of luxury in Goldenhill before coming into the service of the Maidens. When Çeda retired to her room at last, it was with a self-loathing she hadn't felt in a long, long while. By the gods, she *liked* Melis. She liked Jalize, too, though she had a foul mouth and a wicked mind.

She set her ebon sword carefully in one corner. As she undressed and lay down, staring at it, she wondered at all that had happened to her.

Prepare, she thought. *Prepare, and the gods will see to the rest.*

She fell asleep and dreamed of shifting sands and foul creatures and twisted trees. She dreamed of someone standing by her side. A man, though she wasn't sure if it was Emre or Ramahd or someone else.

———— ⟝•⟞ ————

Çeda woke well before dawn. She dressed quickly and quietly, in one of the black Maiden's dresses she'd been given, then took up River's Daughter and strapped the ebon sword to her belt. She went to Kameyl's room. She'd heard her come in late. Kameyl was sleeping lightly, but the moment Çeda tapped her on the shoulder, she woke and fixed her gaze on Çeda. Her eyes drifted immediately to Çeda's sword. Çeda motioned for her to get dressed and to follow, which Kameyl did with a confused frown. Soon the two of them were standing opposite one another in the barracks courtyard.

Kameyl put her left hand on the hilt of her sword—her *new* sword, granted to her by Husamettín. "Is it forms you wish?" She looked down at Çeda's sword, which Çeda had made no move to touch. "No?" she asked. "It was just a bit of swordplay, little wren. If it upsets your tender heart, then get you back to the west end."

Çeda still refused to touch her sword. She stared hard at Kameyl and walked forward until the two of them were a hand's breadth apart. Kameyl was a half-head taller than Çeda. She was imposing, not merely in physical form and in her swordplay, but because of the crazed glint in her eyes, the one that said she would do anything, suffer any pain, to protect her sisters and the Kings from harm.

Çeda didn't care. She couldn't live with the fear that Kameyl might be waiting around every corner, hoping to do her in. "Where I was raised, what you did in the Sun Palace would demand a duel to the death."

Kameyl had been amused up to this point, but now she faced Çeda squarely, grim-faced and ready. "Is that what you wish? A duel?"

"I don't," Çeda admitted, "but if you ever do something like that again, so it will be, and this time, there'll be no King at your side to save you."

Kameyl stared into Çeda's eyes, searching her face for the truth of it, the depth of her sincerity. Çeda had never been more serious about anything in her life; she might die, but she wouldn't lay down for Kameyl or any of the Maidens. And then Kameyl barked a laugh. She laughed long and hard, more surprised by Çeda's bravado than anything else. Still smiling, she drew her sword, almost as fast as the eye could follow. But she didn't attack. She merely held it by the hilt, blade pointed upward, showing Çeda the mark that had been etched into it. "Her name is Brushing Wing. Husamettín chose it himself."

It was an amberlark. A sign of peace.

Çeda couldn't help it. All her nervous tension came out in a laugh that filled every corner of the Maidens' courtyard.

"The first sword I was given, the one you broke, had a viper on its blade." Kameyl lifted the sword higher. "Although this may be a sign of peace, the viper remains, you understand?"

"I understand," Çeda said. As much as she might dislike her, there was something about Kameyl's loyalty she couldn't help but respect.

With a nod, Kameyl sheathed her sword and slapped Çeda's shoulder with enough force to knock her off balance. "Where *I* come from they'd call our exchange a bargain well struck." She held out her hand to Çeda. "A *dark* bargain, to be sure, but a bargain just the same."

Çeda couldn't tell whether she was serious or not, but there was a level of sincerity in Kameyl that was difficult to doubt, so Çeda gripped her forearm and shook it. Then, without another word, the two of them stepped into position and began moving through forms, warming up to the point that they could cross blades.

And cross them they did, moving through the same scripted set of moves as in the Sun Palace the night before, though with little of the grave mood. When they reached the point where they could improvise, they let loose, though there were several times that Çeda could tell Kameyl held back rather than inflict a wound. And once or twice, Çeda did the same.

The Maidens came out when they heard the ring of swordplay. A few at first, then dozens. Some were Çeda's age, but many were years older. They watched the two of them trade blows with speed, some even whistling shrilly after a sharp exchange.

Kameyl and Çeda finished, after which the watching Maidens snapped their fingers, some calling, "Don't go easy on our young dove, Kameyl. It will do her no good in the end."

Kameyl ignored them. She stared at Çeda, then Çeda's blade, which was held easily in one hand. "It's a start, little wren."

"Kameyl!" Above them, Sümeya was standing at the railing, staring down with flinty eyes. "Come."

Kameyl nodded to Sümeya, then turned to Çeda. "Careful steps, Çedamihn Ahyanesh'ala, and we shall see what we shall see." She walked past Çeda and took the stairs up, and then she and Sümeya were gone. Jalize followed immediately, but Melis gave Çeda an encouraging nod before she left.

The following weeks went quickly. Çeda received several sets of black dresses. She took part in morning prayers, kneeling with the Maidens, intoning thanks to each of the gods who had stood atop Tauriyat and saved the Kings on Beht Ihman. Husamettín led them in song afterward. He had a rich baritone that could be heard above the gathered Maidens, though they outnumbered him a hundredfold.

Their numbers changed constantly. She would count one hundred and eight Maidens one morning, eighty-three the next. Some Maidens would be on patrols in ships, or stationed in caravanserai, or out on special assignment in the streets of Sharakhai. Or wounded, Çeda thought, thinking of the Maiden in the infirmary, her leg missing from the knee down.

After prayers, Çeda went through forms with the assembled Maidens in the courtyard. She saw with her own eyes how graceful they were, how disciplined. Several dozen children—mostly girls, but some boys—joined in with wooden shinai. Many of the Matrons took part as well, including Zaïde and an old crone named Sayabim, who at eighty-three was still every bit as fluid as the other women. She and Zaïde wore white dresses and hijabs, a stark contrast to the black dresses and turbans of the Maidens.

When they were finished, Sayabim worked for an hour with Çeda, using a shinai, a slatted bamboo practice sword, to tap Çeda's wrists and knees and ankles when they were out of alignment. "I've no idea how I'm going to unlearn you your ridiculous habits."

Çeda had worked with many gifted instructors, her mother and Djaga foremost among them, but Sayabim was a wonder. She might not have the speed she surely had when she was young, but her grace and precision, qualities she demanded from Çeda as well, were refreshing.

After the morning meal, Çeda was shown the various buildings in the House of Maidens: barracks, refectory, stables, and the archives, where many Matrons lived and had offices to administer to the needs of the Maidens and the Kings. Çeda was set to dusting and then mopping the infirmary floor. She saw the woman there, the Maiden who'd been ambushed by the Moonless Host and had lost her right leg below the knee. She looked haggard, but she was sitting up in bed, reading a book with weathered wooden covers. She was holding it up with one hand while her other hand dug and scratched at the bulky white bandages around her knee.

When she realized she wasn't alone, she immediately stopped scratching and closed the book. "What do you want?"

"I'm here to wash the floors," Çeda said.

"Then get to it."

Çeda did, moving as fast as she was able. Every time she looked up, the woman was watching her.

The days that followed fell into a routine. Prayers in the morning, then forms, then Çeda was sent to clean the stables. One day, however, Zaïde came to her and said it was time.

"Time for what?"

"For your visit with your Qaimiri nobleman."

Çeda had known it would come, of course, but the days had been passing so quickly it surprised her.

Zaïde led the way to her own apartments in the archives. Once there, she opened a wardrobe by an open window to reveal dozens of dresses hung within, each of the highest quality. "I thought you might not have one of your own."

Çeda could only stare as Zaïde considered them, lifting one, then another, holding some up against Çeda's frame. "We're close enough in size that I think these might fit." She pulled out an ivory dress with carmine accents, a pale violet dress that tightened nicely at the waist, and a brown, ankle-length dress with tiny golden beads that looked like it might have been sewn by Tulathan herself. "Anything of interest?"

Çeda reached for the brown dress. "May I?"

Zaïde smiled and held it out to her.

Çeda laid it across her shoulders and stared down its length. It was beautiful and elegant and rich, like nothing she'd ever worn.

"Come," Zaïde said. "Let's get you bathed, and then we'll worry about that bird's nest you call your hair."

Çeda ignored the insult. She was too busy thinking what it would be like to be with Ramahd, wearing that dress.

After a steaming hot bath in the bath house, Zaïde and Sayabim worked on her hair, braiding it carefully and threading rare red pearls through it. They gave her a mirror when they were done, and Çeda could only stare. She hardly recognized herself. She wondered at how this had all come to be. It frightened her how quickly it was happening, but for now she would welcome it, because tomorrow she went to the blooming fields to face the asirim.

One of the stable girls took her down the hill in a covered araba to the estates set aside for dignitaries and emissaries from distant lands. Qaimir had one manse of its own. A servant led her to a rich sitting room on the first floor, appointed with granite pedestals, fresh flowers in pewter vases, and a marble-lined fire pit with a beautiful arrangement of pillows surrounding it. She couldn't sit, however. She was too nervous. She wished to see Ramahd again, though what she would say, or what he might say in return, she had no idea.

She heard footsteps behind her. The doors opened, and Ramahd stepped in wearing a silk brocade coat opened to reveal a white shirt. He wore black boots and trousers that matched his bronze coat. He looked every bit the lord her fellow Maidens imagined him to be. But for some reason he looked supremely uncomfortable. And he wasn't alone. Another man stood behind him.

It took her a moment to recognize him, dressed in fine Qaimiran clothes, his face bloody, cuts and scrapes marring his cheeks, lips, and jaw. His left eye was badly bruised, and there were red gouges in the knuckles of his hands.

She recognized him only when he'd lifted his head. By the gods who shine in the night, it was Emre.

Chapter 52

RAMAHD SAT ON THE THIRD-FLOOR BALCONY of his apartments in the Qaimiri emissary house. Above him loomed Tauriyat and its thirteen palaces—twelve for the Kings themselves and the thirteenth, the Sun Palace, near the base of the mountain. They were an imposing sight, not merely for their grandeur, but also for the power they represented—the Kings, the Maidens, the asirim; even the gods who seemed to favor them.

He wondered, as he sipped his glass of sweet Malasani wine, whether he and Meryam were playing with fire so hot that they would not only burn themselves, but everyone around them, people they'd never meant to burn. The Kingdom of Qaimir itself might pay the price for what they were about to do. Part of him wished to go to the Kings and give them the evidence they'd collected so far—that Macide was searching for the blood mage, Hamzakiir, the long-dead son of Külaşan the Wandering King; that they'd secured a breathstone in order to speak to him; that Juvaan Xin-Lei was lending information, money, and resources to help in the effort. But it would be hard to prove, and he was loath to bring up the subject of Hamzakiir with the Kings. Hamzakiir's ties to Ramahd's homeland were simply too strong, which surely pleased Juvaan greatly. It might even have been Juvaan or his queen who had suggested it to the Host, not the reverse. Hamzakiir's position in this grand equation made it all the easier for Mirea's Queen Alansal to deny Mirea had anything to do with it. What, she would ask, would we stand to gain?

And there was Macide to consider. Ramahd's thirst to find him was no less strong than it had been when Yasmine had died. And now it felt as though he was close. Truly close. *Follow the White Wolf*, the fork-tailed ehrekh had said.

And so he had, tracking her as well as he could. He'd heard the rumors flooding Sharakhai, that a woman had been taken to the gates of the House of Maidens and abandoned by a foreign priest. He'd spoken to enough witnesses who had seen it firsthand that he was convinced the story was true, and, from their descriptions, that the woman was Çeda. He'd waited for her in her home for many nights, hoping to find her on her return, or perhaps her lover, Emre. She'd come at last, just as Meryam had said she would.

That same night, Dana'il had stumbled upon news of Emre, and Ramahd wondered if he'd made a mistake by letting Çeda leave, or worse, by giving her his word that he'd wait to let her speak with Emre. But the ehrekh's words . . . Meryam had made it clear that they should let this play out. So he'd waited and worried.

Whatever was going to happen would happen soon. King Aldouan paid informants dearly for news of Sharakhai, and they reported that the Host was planning something. It seemed likely to happen two nights hence, on Beht Zha'ir.

As the wind played among the potted palms on the balcony, Ramahd sipped more of his wine. It was fine enough, but the sweetness was cloying.

There was a knock at his door.

"Come."

The knock came again.

"I said, come!"

Mykal, his nephew and pageboy, stepped into his rooms bearing a silver tray with a note on it. He walked with a motion that made him look as though he had something lodged firmly up his bum.

"For the love of all that's good, *patience*, Mykal." Ra-mahd took the note from the tray. "One can rush without making it look like you're late to your own birthing."

Mykal's cheeks flushed. He glanced to the note, then to Ramahd, then to the tray and the note again.

"Do you understand?" Ramahd pressed.

"Yes, my Lord."

"No, you clearly don't, but think on it, and one day you might. Now go."

"Of course, my Lord." And he left, moving even faster and looking more awkward than when he'd come in.

Chuckling at how blissfully blind the boy was, the wax seal upon the note registered at last. It was the seal of the House of Maidens—twelve shamshirs fanned out in a circle around a shield, sword points outward. He cracked the seal, opened the letter, and read it carefully. Then he folded it back the way it had come and made his way from his apart-ments to Meryam's across the hall. He knocked loudly and entered, not waiting for an answer. She was sitting with her handmaid on the south-facing balcony, both of them paint-ing on canvases the amber cityscape of Sharakhai.

"What if I'd been naked?" Meryam asked without turning.

"You're not."

"I might have been."

Ramahd held the note out to her, shaking it when she made no move to take it.

"A note does not concern me when I'm halfway through a painting," she said.

"It's from the House of Maidens."

Meryam's hand went still. She turned, setting her brush down on the nearby table, and snatched it from his hand. She read it over once, then snapped her fingers for her handmaid to leave the room.

The girl began cleaning their brushes until Meryam snapped her fingers again—"Leave them"—at which point the golden-haired girl bowed to them both and left the room.

Meryam read the note a second time. "It seems you've made an impression."

The note was from a Matron named Zaïde, who

explained that a young aspirant named Çedamihn Ahya-nesh'ala was about to take her final test before entering the service of the Maidens. She was to be granted one night for herself before this happened, and she would enjoy the company of one Ramahd shan Amansir of Almadan.

Ramahd wondered at all that had happened since he faced Çeda in the pits. Chasing Macide, speaking with the King, the visit with the ehrekh, and then finding Çeda in her home while waiting for Emre. It was a dizzying series of events that made him feel as though the gods were toying with him—toying with all of them—as if they'd *meant* Ramahd and Çeda to meet for a purpose known only to themselves.

"You'll see her, of course," Meryam said.

Ramahd was glad she didn't mention the ehrekh. She trusted far more in that creature than he did. Even if everything happened as the ehrekh had predicted, even if they found Hamzakiir and Macide and took them both, it still felt as though they'd given away too much in the bargain made out there in the desert. Bargains with Goezhen's children never ended well. "She may come, but she knew little enough the last time we spoke, and as far as I know, she's been in the House of Maidens since last I saw her."

"You still believe she was telling the truth? That she knew nothing of the Host's plans?"

"She didn't say that exactly, but yes, I think she knew little enough. She doesn't believe in their methods. She thinks them too harsh."

"To deal with change is to deal with harsh realities, and sometimes, harsh methods," Meryam countered, in a tone not unlike the one Ramahd had used with his nephew mere moments ago. Setting the note aside, she took up a paint-stained rag and rubbed at the cerulean paint on her hands. "She might have been trying to protect this Emre of hers."

"Perhaps, but I don't think so. She seemed surprised at what I told her of him, his dealings with Macide and his ties to the attack on the House of Maidens."

She stared at him from the hollows of her eyes. "You made her a promise."

"I promised her she could speak to Emre before I did. I didn't promise not to arrange for her to meet him."

"I only wonder whether you're seeing things clearly."

"I won't have this argument again, Meryam."

"She asks for *you*, of all people, on the one night she has before she's put on trial by the foul asirim. Does she have no one else in this city?"

"The ehrekh saw this, and now you're surprised?"

"Like the gods, the ehrekh see into the hearts of man. Strange that he stopped before *you*, of all of us, and gave word to sniff along the White Wolf's trail."

"Well, she might have asked for Emre before me, but he's gone, isn't he?"

"She has her Emre, true." Her voice trailed off, none too subtly. "But now there's you as well. It *has* been some time since you . . ."

"What are you saying, Meryam?"

"I'm saying there would be no harm in toying with her affections. It might even bring her closer to us."

"She's using me. And we're using her. There's nothing more to it than that."

Meryam tilted her head, raising her brows with an expression that supposed none of this meant anything to her. "As you say."

Ramahd stifled a sigh. "It *is* as I say. Now are we done? There's much to do before I meet with her."

Meryam had already returned to looking out across the city. "Then by all means, go."

Ramahd thought of trying to talk her out of this mood, but he was sick of her games. She could judge him if she wished.

He had work to do.

The following day, Ramahd stood before his mirror, adjusting his shirt, adjusting his coat. By the gods, he was even checking his hair to make sure it didn't look too disheveled.

It's only for appearance's sake. The servants, and the

Matron, Zaïde, if she happens to come, must think I'm taking this seriously.

But as time wore on, he found himself thinking more and more of that night with Çeda in her home. She'd looked so confident, so *angry*, when she came in. He couldn't deny he was attracted to that sort of woman. Yasmine had been like that—fiery in her own way. He thought of the ceremony in the Sun Palace as well, where he'd planned on introducing Çeda to Juvaan. When he'd mentioned it in Çeda's home, he'd merely hoped to learn more of Queen Alansal's ambassador, but he'd spotted Juvaan speaking with one of the ladies of Goldenhill, a woman who was said to be a close confidant of King Ihsan. Of all the Kings, he was the one Ramahd trusted least—he hadn't been named the Honey-tongued King for no reason—so Ramahd thought it best to steer clear of that conversation, and even avoid being seen with Çeda, at least until he saw how Çeda's presence changed the lay of the land, if at all.

He'd seen Çeda looking for him and the disappointment on her face, but it couldn't be helped. Navigate the intricate weave of Sharakhai's politics recklessly and the wrong thread might be cut, and then everything might unravel.

Just before he'd left the Sun Palace, he'd seen her speaking with Juvaan, taking things into her own hands. She was bold, that one. He'd be lying if he said it didn't send a bit of a thrill through him just to be near her, but it was also a thing he'd have to be careful of in the future. He was not so blind that he couldn't see how much of a liability she might become, if not handled properly.

He shook his head and smoothed down the front of his coat. He'd promised himself he wouldn't begin a relationship with another woman, not even an affair, until his debt to Yasmine and Rehann had been paid in full, but he had to admit he'd been sorely tempted that night in her home. Still, there was too much happening to consider such a thing. There was Emre, a man she lived with, and certainly seemed to love, not to mention the mess they were all embroiled in—the Moonless Host, the Kings, Mirea.

From the window came the sound of horse hooves and wagon wheels grinding through loose gravel. Ramahd turned and walked out and down to the ground floor. When he stepped out, Dana'il leapt down from the driver's bench, holding his hands up, trying to prevent Ramahd from approaching. When Ramahd kept his pace, Dana'il placed himself in Ramahd's path.

"What happened?" Ramahd asked, peering into the darkness of the wagon. "Do you have him?"

"We have him. But he . . . My Lord, he refused to play nicely."

"What does *that* mean?" Ramahd pushed past Dana'il.

"My Lord!"

Ignoring him, Ramahd opened the door and found Alamante, Ramahd's second after Dana'il, sitting across from a man who was slouched on the padded bench, wrists bound, blood marking his ripped shirt and sirwal trousers. Emre, his face bloody and swollen and bruised.

Ramahd spun to face Dana'il. "And just what does the word *unharmed* mean to you?"

Dana'il shrugged. "He refused to come with us."

"So you *subdue* him!"

"We tried! He's a scrapper, that one."

"Well, he looks like a gods-damned side of meat, now!" Ramahd closed his eyes, imagining presenting *that* to Çeda, imagining what she would do, what she would think! There was nothing for it now, though. "Bring the wagon around the back," he said. "Sneak him in, and see if you can avoid dropping him down any flights of stairs. Do you think you can manage that?"

Dana'il bowed. "Of course, my Lord."

"Clean him up. Get him changed. Take anything from my wardrobe that will fit him and make him look presentable. And by the gods, cover up those bloody wounds!"

"Of course," Dana'il replied, and then hopped up to the bench.

As the wagon rattled away, Ramahd knew it was useless. There was no covering up this bloody great mess, no explaining it away.

He thought of confronting Emre over his involvement with the Host and what part he'd played in the attack on the House of Maidens and the abduction of Lord Veşdi, but he'd gone to the effort of finding him with the express purpose of having him speak to Çeda first, and he refused to break that promise now. Çeda would get that much out of him at least.

Besides, what might he get out of Çeda *without* Emre? He truly believed she knew nothing of the Host's plans, and if that were so, there was no sense in questioning her again. He had to give Çeda a chance to speak with Emre. It was the only way he and Meryam would get what they needed.

After the noon hour, he had Emre brought to his room. Emre's hands were no longer bound, and he was dressed in Ramahd's clothes, looking for all the world like a goat in horse's tack. He was a fine enough looking man, but he was Sharakhani, through and through, with his long beard and dark skin and darker eyes. His face looked horrible, even cleaned of the excess blood.

"Do you know why you're here?"

Emre stood tall, looking down on Ramahd as best he could. "Your man claimed it was to speak to Çeda."

"And don't you wish to speak to her?"

He hawked and spat blood-tinged spittle onto the carpet between them. "I'll speak to her when and where I please. I need no meeting arranged by some piece of Qaimiri trash."

"She's been taken in by the Maidens. You must know this by now."

Emre didn't respond, confirming Ramahd's suspicions.

"You think you can steal into their House?" Ramahd went on. "The Maidens look upon you with that sort of favor? They would allow you to—how did you say it?—speak to her when and where you please?"

Again, Emre chose only to stare, to blink slowly. Through Ramahd's window came the sound of another wagon—a lighter one—entering the circle out front. Emre glanced in that direction but made no mention of it.

"She's about to go to the blooming fields, did you know? As part of her initiation to become a Blade Maiden?"

The edge in Emre's hardened look softened.

"Are you so confident the asirim will look into her eyes and judge her worthy to join them?"

It took Emre a long time to respond, but eventually he said, "There's nothing I can do about that anymore."

Outside, a wagon door opened and closed. Soft words came, a welcome for a new guest.

Ramahd pointed his chin toward the window. "That will be her. Speak to her, Emre. That's all I ask."

"*Speak* to her?"

"Yes."

"About what?"

"Whatever it is she wishes to speak to *you* about."

Emre's eyes narrowed. "You expect me to believe that you've brought me here—that you had me beaten and stuffed in a wagon—so that I could *talk* with Çeda?"

"Just so."

Emre, his eyes full of mistrust, considered Ramahd for a time, but then his look softened. "You're after the Host, aren't you?"

The young man was smarter than he looked. "I'm after many things."

"You won't get them. I won't tell you about them. You'll kill me before that happens."

His eyes were so fierce that Ramahd nodded and said, "You know, I believe you." They could hear the entry door downstairs open and close, and Ramahd stood. "But I doubt that will be necessary." He strode forward and squeezed Emre's shoulder. Emre winced and knocked Ramahd's hand away.

"Just speak to her."

Emre stared into Ramahd's eyes, weighing his options, and then nodded.

Ramahd nodded back and led Emre out to the stairs and down to the ground floor.

Chapter 53

ÇEDA STARED AT EMRE'S WOUNDS, his fine clothes, and wondered what in the wide, bright world had happened to him. But of course she knew. Ramahd. His men. They'd brought him here. They'd made *sure* he had come. She was about to give Ramahd her thoughts on the subject when he backed out of the room, refusing to meet her eye. He closed the doors behind him, the crisp sound of his footsteps fading as he strode away.

When the doors closed, Emre looked as though a hundred pounds had been lifted from his shoulders. He moved toward Çeda, Çeda met him halfway, and they fell into one another's arms. Emre held her so tightly it surprised her. She felt his cheek against hers, and slowly her anger was replaced with the simple desire to live within Emre's arms and forget the world for a moment or two.

"I thought you were dead," he whispered to her.

"I thought I was too," she whispered back.

After a long while, they separated, and it felt as if she were losing him all over again, as if she were being drawn back into the House of Maidens even now. "You look terrible," she said, wincing as she examined the wounds on his face and on his hands, which she still held in hers.

He shrugged, wincing immediately after. "I had a rather unfortunate disagreement with a set of stairs." He smiled, copying the face Çeda had made when she'd once used the same beetle-brained joke. "It didn't go so well."

She smiled, and then gave his jaw a mock punch. He moved with the blow in slow motion, coming back with a honey-slow punch of his own. She couldn't help it. She laughed. He looked such a fool, but that was what she remembered most about him. And the times they'd laughed together. Nalamae's sweet tears, how she would miss them.

Emre lifted her right hand and examined the tattoo that now marked the front and back of it. He ran a finger over the puckered white scar that didn't quite look healed—a wound that would *never* heal, if Zaïde had spoken truth. "By the gods, Çeda, what happened?"

She stammered for a moment. "There's a lot to tell."

Emre looked around, eyes wide, as if he were peering into corners for hidden spies. "It appears we are alone." He moved to a cart with delicate glasses and a large decanter of deep red wine—the only thing in the room to drink—and poured two glasses. "And we have time."

She took one from him and waved to the pillows that surrounded the grand fire pit at the center of the room. They sat next to one another, drinking their wine. It had rich currant and pepper overtones, and something Çeda couldn't quite put her finger on. Something almost metallic. Çeda took Emre's bruised hand, kissed it once, then launched into her tale, her night at the blooming fields, going to Dardzada for help, waking in that strange physic's cellar and cutting him before she escaped. She now suspected it was a place she'd been taken for healing and for safekeeping, not for Dardzada to cut her arm off to save her from the poison. Wounding him was a thing she felt acutely ashamed of, but at the time she'd had no way to distinguish reality from her fears.

She told him how she'd wandered through the city, how the poison nearly destroyed her; how Dardzada disguised himself and brought her to the House of Maidens. She told him of the days of pain, and how Zaïde had tattooed her hand and hemmed in the poison. She told him about her visit with the Jade-eyed King, his grand palace, and of Nayyan, the woman whose place Çeda had taken in Sümeya's hand.

When she told him about the attack on the Maidens' compound, she watched him closely and saw exactly what she expected to see: a note of embarrassment, a touch of chagrin. She'd guessed that he had been involved with it in some way, and this was cold confirmation of it, but she said nothing and moved on to the fight between Husamettín and Sümeya, finishing with her presentation to the Kings in the Sun Palace and her ill-fated dance with Kameyl.

By the gods, can it be that so little time has passed? It's a lifetime wrapped into a handful of weeks.

Emre finished his glass and poured them both another as Çeda told him about her sword, River's Daughter, a thing that made his jaw fall slack. "You with an ebon sword . . . The gods play strange games, Çeda."

"They do," she replied. "And tomorrow I'm to go out to the blooming fields so the asirim may judge me."

"But you're not going to stay with them, are you? You can leave now. We can hide. The city will protect us."

"You know I can't. They'd come for me. They'd find me."

"Then we'll go to the desert. We've always talked about sailing the sands."

"I don't want to, Emre. I've been given an opportunity, a gift, and I'll not waste it."

"But the asirim may kill you, Çeda."

"They may," she allowed, "but the one who kissed me? I wish to find him again."

"Are you listening to yourself? You might live out the rest of your days and never see the crowned asir again, and there's no telling what the others might do to you."

"I know. Believe me, I've thought of little else these past few days, but our lives are fleeting anyway. The Silver Spears might find you tomorrow and kill *you*, Emre."

"That's different."

"How is that different?"

Emre frowned, as though he didn't want to answer. "What can you hope to do, even *if* the asirim somehow approve of you? Will you kill the Kings as a Maiden? Don't you think they might object? That someone might notice?"

"Know thine enemy. Isn't that what the Al'Ambra says?"

"*Know* them. Don't sleep in their halls. Don't raise your glass in their honor. It's too *dangerous*, Çeda."

Çeda laughed. "Don't speak to me of danger, Emre. Don't think I don't know what's become of you."

"What? What has become of me?"

She lowered her voice. "You were involved in the attack on the House of Maidens, weren't you? Or in the attack on Lord Veşdi. Or both!"

Emre paused, gathering the right words. "I wasn't there, if that's what you're asking, and I thought you were dead. You weren't harmed, were you?"

"No. But others were."

"What do you care about the Maidens?"

"I don't, but I would never have guessed you would do such a thing." She stared into his deep brown eyes, wondering at the Emre she used to know. "You've changed, Emre."

"My eyes have been opened. There's a difference."

"No, it's more than that. You would never have done these things a year ago."

"That Emre disgusts me. That Emre doesn't exist anymore."

She knew where this had all started, knew to the very night. "What happened that night, when I found you in the Haddah?"

He was staring into the cold ashes in the fire pit, a hard expression on his face, until Çeda took his hand and squeezed it.

"Tell me."

"You don't want to know."

"Yes, I do."

As she watched him, his eyes lost their hard look, and the expression she remembered so well—the fearful look that had been with him so often after Rafa's death—returned. He was silent for a long time, his mouth opening and closing, his eyes searching the fire's flickering fabric for answers. When he spoke again, his tone was as distant as the winds of winter. "What happened that night in the Haddah . . . It was the same thing that happened with Saadet the night he killed Rafa."

She squeezed his hand again. "There was nothing you could have done. You weren't even there."

Emre ripped his hand away. "I *was* there!" Tears formed in his eyes. "I lied to you, Çeda! I've lied to you all along!"

A shiver ran down Çeda's frame, and with a sudden clarity she understood exactly what he meant. "The bravo. You saw what he did."

"I wasn't half as smart as I thought," Emre said, "and that Malasani pig not nearly so dumb. When I got home, he bulled his way into the house, just as I was opening the door. Rafa was home, and he came running out to see what was the matter, but Saadet," Emre shook his head, jaw rigid, perhaps reliving the events of that night, "he was too large, too strong. He cuffed me and I fell, hit my head and crumpled to the floor like a pup. He held Rafa down, and he pulled out that long knife of his. Do you remember it? The blade was straight. And the edge was keen. It had an ivory handle with little nicks along it. *See these, boy?* he said in that thick fucking accent of his. He was holding Rafa's throat and showing me the nicks in that foul knife, like he was *proud* of them. Every single one of them. *These are men I killed,* he told me, *men who do less to me than you. But you are young still. I give you that. Maybe young enough to learn that stealing from a man of Malasan is a dire mistake.* And then he smiled, he *smiled,* and offered me a choice. *You tell me who you want to die, you or this one?* And he pointed to Rafa with the tip of that knife."

Emre sniffed. Tears streaked down his cheeks and fell to the lush pillows. She had never seen him look so grief-stricken. She wanted to take him in her arms, but she was certain that would be a terrible mistake. "You were *fourteen,* Emre. I remember how huge he was. There was nothing you could have done."

He pinched his eyes tight and shook his head, more violently than before. "Nothing? I had my knife Çeda. He smiled and watched as I pulled my knife and held it against my chest like a useless little talisman. That dog turned away from me, turned his *back* to me. *No choice*, he said, *means I choose*. Rafa was dying before my eyes. His eyes bulging. His face going red." Emre's hands tightened, as if he were still holding that slim fisherman's knife he'd found along the river the year before Rafa's death. "I could have done it. I *should* have done it. Saadet practically dared me to. But I sat there. I sat there as he held my brother down and slipped that knife between his ribs. I stayed there all night, holding Rafa's hand, hoping he'd wake. I waited until the sun came up." He blinked away his tears and drew in a deep, stuttering breath. "And then I told everyone I'd just come home and found Rafa dead."

Çeda had never seen Emre look more devastated, not even right after Rafa's death. "Emre," she said with care, "you were *fourteen*."

"You killed him at fourteen!"

"I had help from the petals."

Emre threw up his hands, looking around this rich room, to the windows bright with sunlight, then back to Çeda. "Are you listening to me? I was a *coward*," he said. "I was a coward then, and I was a coward that night you came and found me on the Haddah."

"You were unconscious when I found you."

His hands balled into fists and he shook from head to toe. "Just *listen*. I'd already picked up the case from my contact at the southern harbor. He said to be careful, as there was word tribesmen were about, men sympathetic to the Kings, men who knew about Macide and the Moonless Host and even of the agreement Macide had forged with Juvaan, and thought ill of it. They were on us only moments after his warning. Juvaan's man pulled his sword and attacked." Emre shivered, as if the very thought of that night left him feeling cold and useless. "They attacked him, and he looked to me for help, but I couldn't. I froze. Like a cold, gutless lizard. And then I ran. They killed him. They must have done. I don't know. But when we'd made it back home—after you'd saved me *again*, Çeda—I swore on Thaash's bright blade I'd never let myself be like that again."

"Emre . . ." Dear gods, she'd made so many mistakes.

"What?"

"I should never have fought Saadet without your permission."

Emre shook his head. "You were only trying to protect me."

"Yes, but I killed him. Without warning you."

"It doesn't matter. That was lives ago."

"And now it's led you to the Host."

"Çeda, *I knew* he was in Sharakhai."

Çeda sat there, stunned. "What?"

"Tariq told me. He'd seen Saadet, and he told me about it, asked if I wanted him to help avenge Rafa. I told him I needed to think about it." Emre laughed and threw up his arms. "I told him I needed to *think* about it. I would never have gone after him. Never. And when you did, it showed me just how great a coward I truly was. When you killed him in that pit, it freed me, Çeda."

"What do you mean it *freed* you?"

"It was the first step toward rising above my fear." Emre's face had taken on a completely different quality. The change was startling. No longer did he look like a lost little boy. He was confident, bordering on fearless, and she could tell it wasn't mere bravado. It was a look she'd seen in the pits, in hardened warriors who no longer cared what happened to themselves or to their bodies. It was also something wholly alien on Emre, a thing she would wipe from him if she could. It looked unnatural on him, but more than that, she knew it had been born in deep, indescribable pain. "I was there when they brought Lord Veşdi."

He said the words with pride, and it chilled her. This wasn't the Emre she knew. Remembering what Davud had said about preparing the breathstone and what it needed, it took her only a few moments longer to reason what had come next. "They used Veşdi's blood to feed the stone, didn't they?"

"You *know?*"

"Enough of it, but not *why*. Or where they hope to find Hamzakiir." She took a deep breath, committing herself to the next step. "Don't you see, Emre? I might be able to

help." There was a part of her that didn't want to usher him
into danger, but she could no longer protect him, not to the
detriment of all else. Besides, the longer she stared into his
eyes, the more convinced she was that he wasn't going to
change his mind, and neither was she, so why not try to
help one another?

"They trust me to a degree, Çeda, but not enough to tell
me that."

Çeda glanced at the doors, wondering how long Ramahd would give them. "Are you to go with them?"

"Yes."

"And they told you nothing of it?"

"Only that it would be another week before we left, and
that the target was one of the palaces."

"They said that? One of the Kings' palaces?"

"Külaşan's desert palace, Macide said."

Çeda froze. "By the gods who shine above . . ."

"What?" Emre asked. "What is it?"

She rose to her feet, her mind working feverishly. At her
presentation in the Sun Palace, Külaşan had been the King
wearing the crown made of red gold. The medallion in the
center of the crown had tickled a memory, but she hadn't
been able to suss it out then. The moment Emre had said
those words, though—*Külaşan's desert palace*—it had all
came back in a rush. "Do you remember the night we went
out to the blooming fields?"

Emre stood as well. "I nearly died. I'm not likely to forget."

"When you were unconscious from the rattlewing bites,
someone rode a horse—an *akhala*—out into the desert as
if Goezhen himself were on his tail. He rode to the tree I
climbed. You remember? The one with the stone wedged
between the roots."

"It had a symbol on it."

"The same symbol that's on his crown."

Emre frowned. "You're sure? That was a long time ago,
Çeda."

"I remember it like it was yesterday, and I saw it again
two weeks ago, Emre. I'm sure of it. Külaşan was wearing
it. When he reached the tree, out in the desert, the roots

reached up for him. They *embraced* him and drew him down into the sands. I'm sure it was Külaşan, and he was being taken to his palace."

"How can you be so certain?"

"He's known as the Wandering King. The Lost King. This must be why. He goes to a place in the desert, hidden away from Sharakhai."

Emre's eyes went distant. "That was on Beht Zha'ir, right? Why hide himself in a palace, if that's where he went?"

"The poem: *While far afield, his love unsealed, 'til Tulathan does loom. Then petals' dust, like lovers' lust, will draw him toward his tomb.*"

"Petals' dust . . ."

"The pollen." Çeda began pacing back and forth near the windows. "He's hiding to escape the pollen from the adichara blooms."

"But he's practically *in* the blooming fields, maybe right underneath them. Wouldn't that make it worse?"

"The roots may have delivered him to a place deep underground, some chamber he had built for the purpose. Perhaps it's been enchanted in some way, I don't know, but after he'd risen from the desert, in the morning, he stepped into the adichara. The trees embraced him, and all his ills seemed to vanish. He stepped from those trees unharmed, a new man."

"By inverted thorn his skin was torn . . ."

"And yet his strength did grow," Çeda said, completing the verse.

"But an entire *palace* out in the desert?"

"We don't know how large it is," Çeda replied. "And don't forget. Beht Ihman was four hundred years ago. How long would you wait to have a place to hide from the thing that threatens to lay you low every holy night?"

Emre's face screwed up, trying to remember something. "What was the first part?"

"*From golden dunes and ancient runes, the King of glittering stone.* There was something King Ihsan let slip in the Sun Palace about glittering stones. I knew I'd read about them, but it took me a few days to remember: to the

southwest of the Shangazi, the ancestral homeland of Tribe
Rafik has dull stones that can be found littering the ground
in places. They look like eggs, and when you break them
open, the insides are thick with gemstones. And there are
dunes there tinged gold, especially when the wind gusts
and the blowing sand reflects the sunlight."

"Which accounts for the King of glittering stone and
golden dunes, but what about ancient runes?"

Çeda recalled her readings night after night in the collegia cellars. "On the low plains before the mountains,
there are massive runes cut there, each symbol as large as
a palace, and in a language that's no longer in use. Many
believe they were written by the first gods or their disciples,
in the days before they fled this place. It all fits."

Emre considered her with a calculating look on his face.
"And Hamzakiir is Külaşan's son."

Çeda walked over to a nearby window and pulled the
curtain aside to stare up at the House of Kings, wondering
where Külaşan was right then. "We couldn't ask for a better chance. If we went at the same time, we could divide
Külaşan's attention."

"But how will you get away from the Maidens?"

"It's a vigil, Emre, and aspirants are granted the right to
choose the location of their vigil, so I'll be near."

"How will you get into Külaşan's palace?"

"I'll find a way."

Emre shook his head. "This is madness."

"Yes, it's all bloody mad, but here we are."

He paced, lost in his own thoughts. "Macide wasn't
planning on going for another week, but I'll make him go
early."

And here, she thought, was a flaw in their plan. "He's a
careful man, Emre. I don't know that he will."

"He'll do it if he thinks there's a chance you can kill
Külaşan."

"Emre, Macide doesn't even know me."

"I'll make him," Emre said. She tried to speak again,
but he raised his hand. "I'll make him, Çeda."

Çeda nodded. "I'll find a way into the palace as soon as
I'm able." Further planning would have to wait for their

arrival, for neither of them knew the layout of Külaşan's desert palace.

The two of them stared at one another for a time. Çeda felt as though she were losing him already.

Emre glanced toward the window.

It was getting darker.

"I should go," he said. "Hamid will want to know what's become of me."

"I need to leave as well," Çeda lied. She was allowed the night here, but she refused to spend any more time in this place.

First, though, Ramahd was owed a reckoning for what he'd done to Emre.

Chapter 54

RAMAHD SAT IN THE STUDY across from the sitting room where Çeda and Emre were speaking. They'd been in there a long while. Which was natural, he supposed. The two of them had much to discuss. When he heard the doors open at last, he moved to the study door and found Çeda stepping into the foyer, followed by Emre.

Emre looked to Ramahd. "I'm leaving."

"Very well. I'll have the wagon take you anywhere you wish."

Emre gave him a flat stare. "I'll drive a spear through my own foot before I take another ride in one of your wagons."

"As you like, though you may have trouble at the gates."

Emre's gaze shot between Çeda and Ramahd, an uncertain look in his eyes. He knew every bit as well as Ramahd how particular the Silver Spears could be at the gates of Tauriyat, even for those leaving. Emre exhaled noisily. "Fetch it then, you bloody Qaimiri bastard."

"It's waiting outside. Dana'il will take you wherever you wish."

"Not without Çeda."

"No. I would speak with her."

Emre looked to Çeda, who immediately squeezed his hand. "All is well," she said. Emre nodded and left, but not before shooting Ramahd one last look, as if he were measuring Ramahd's coffin.

When the wagon outside clattered away, Çeda turned on Ramahd, her face a study in rage. She strode purposefully toward him, her hand swinging out to slap him.

He grabbed her wrist before she could connect. "I never meant for him to be hurt. I told my men not to harm him."

"You *beat* him."

"I was merely fulfilling my promise to you."

"Your *promise?*"

"I said I would allow you to speak with him first. How did you suppose that was going to happen without my involvement? I needed to know where the Host is going. I *still* need to know."

"Well, you'll not have that now."

"You gave me your word."

When she struggled to pull her hand away, he kept his grip strong. She went through a change, then. Her gaze softened but was also very intense, as if she'd come to a decision. "I said I would tell you if Emre was in the Host or not."

"And is he?"

"Yes. But he didn't kill your wife. So you'll leave him be, or I'll hunt *you*, Ramahd Amansir. I'll hunt you down the way you hunt Macide. Now let go of my wrist."

She didn't struggle as she said this; she didn't try to make him loose his grip, but he kept it firm just the same. "You promised to tell me the rest as well. Where is he going? Where are *you* going?"

In a blink her arm was high and she twisted—body and hip and shoulder and arm—torquing his wrist as she went. He was forced to release her, but she grabbed and continued to twist his arm, angling him forward and down with a sharp, precise motion that sent him falling. He rolled with it lest his wrist break. She could have held on to him, pulled his arm from the socket, but she let him go.

He rolled to his feet, but Çeda was right there stabbing her finger at him like a scolding mother. "A real man would have taken the slap and been pleased with the bargain. I don't owe you anything else. Not anymore. You lost that privilege when your men decided to put their hands on Emre." She turned and strode toward the door like the goddess of anger incarnate.

"Çeda, please!" He ran after her, but the moment he came close, she spun, slapped his hand away, and struck him across the jaw.

He lost where he was for a moment. He tried to call her name, but she was already stepping in. She lowered her body, powering her right palm into his chest and sending him flying to the floor. Before his slide along the white tiles had stopped, she was on top of him, a swift punch landing on his right cheek.

"That's for Emre."

Then another above his left eye.

"And that's for me."

Then she stood, shaking out the fingers of her right hand while striding toward the door.

"Leave us alone, Ramahd. I meant what I said."

And then she was gone, the door thundering shut behind her.

As her footsteps faded, he made it slowly to his feet, grimacing from the pain in his shoulder where it had crashed against the tiled floor, wincing from the cuts inside his cheeks and lips as well as the bruises along his face and the back of his head. He stared at the door, realizing what an utter mess he'd made of things.

"Well, brother?" came a voice from behind him and somewhere above. He turned and found Meryam standing at the top of the stairs. "Did she give you all you'd hoped for?"

"Humor isn't your strong suit, Meryam."

"You don't think so?" Meryam began taking the stairs down, laughing as she came. "I think I'm rather gifted at it for a noblewoman." She caught his look and frowned. "Tut, tut, Ramahd. She was never an ally of ours, and she never will be."

She might've been had I handled this differently. But you're right. She never will be now.

When Meryam reached the base of the stairs, she didn't

stop to speak with Ramahd or see if he was well. She headed straight for the sitting room where Çeda and Emre had been. When she reached for the door latch, the sleeve of her dress pulled back to reveal a blood-stained bandage wrapped around her left wrist. Ramahd followed, wondering whether Meryam's plan had worked. Once inside the room, she moved to the wine cart, where she lifted the wine decanter and sniffed at the mouth.

In the span of time it took her to draw in one deep breath, her eyes went distant, as they did when she slipped into her place of dark magic. She remained that way for a long while, her expression unchanging, her mind's eye seeing something unknowable for someone like him, a man who had never touched blood in an arcane manner.

"Enough, Meryam. Tell me. Did it work?"

A smile stole over her then, like the cheetah from the children's tales that had finally caught the vulture after years of disappointment. "Yes, it worked."

Blood. Her own blood. She'd added it to the wine, and from what little was left in the decanter, and the dregs sitting at the bottom of two glasses, he knew Çeda and Emre had both drunk some of it.

"What now?" he asked.

"Now?" Meryam strode toward him, her eyes no less fierce than the ehrekh's had been in the desert—a thing that had been happening more and more of late. "Now, dear brother, you and I will have Macide."

Ramahd nodded, the long-burning flame within him rekindling. He was not pleased by his encounter with Çeda, but this was something. To have Macide within his grasp—after waiting so long, after being denied by his own King, his wife's own father!—was pleasing in a way he couldn't describe.

Yes, this was something, indeed.

Chapter 55

TWO DAYS AFTER SEEING THE KING in the streets of the Knot, Çeda learned his identity. He was Mesut, the Jackal King, Lord of the Asirim. What the Lord of the Asirim did, or why he was called the Jackal King, no one seemed to know. Or rather, those who had any opinion at all presented differing accounts. He'd been the King to grant immortality to the asirim on the night of Beht Ihman long ago. He went to the blooming fields on Beht Zha'ir and called on them, sending them to Sukru, the Reaping King, to begin the tithe for the glory of Sharakhai and the gods. He chose a precious few from those taken by the asirim and created more of the holy defenders. One old woman in the bazaar even said he changed to a jackal on the night of Beht Zha'ir, and if he locked eyes with you, you would be turned to stone by his gaze.

They were wondrous tales, to be sure, but Çeda had no way of telling which of them, or more to the point, which *parts* of them, were true. The best stories thrived when they contained a kernel of truth. One just needed to know how to prune the falsities and deceits to find the truth lying at their shared center.

But how could she weigh stories hundreds of years old? That was the key, she knew, for the more she learned of Beht Ihman, the more she realized that exhuming the real story of what had happened that night would be the key not only to avenging her mother's death, but finishing what her mother had started.

She didn't tell Emre she'd seen the Jackal King in the Knot. He'd only worry, and there was little enough to tell in any case. And yet, despite her silence, he said to her one day, "You're acting strangely."

Which was rich, coming from Emre.

They were hauling on a rope together, lifting a stone that Galadan, the old stone mason, was guiding into position. Emre worked for him, and they were helping to build a stone wall around a new garden in Tulathan's temple grounds, just east of the Trough. Çeda had joined him because Djaga was in the final days of training before a new bout and said she needed to work with her regular sparring partners.

"Emre, what do you mean, I'm acting *strangely?*"

"You're skittish. You keep watching the road like Bakhi himself is coming to collect you."

"I am not."

"You are!"

"Higher!" Galadan called, tugging at the stone, which hung from the stout wooden crane.

They hauled on the rope again, lifting the cubit stone high enough for Galadan to swing the crane over it, and then they lowered it down. With practiced ease, and no small amount of wiry brawn, Galadan tilted the stone up, unhooked and unwrapped the rope, and then dropped it back down so Emre and Çeda could prepare another from the dozens that lay along the base of the wall.

As Emre lifted the next stone, she could see how his frame was filling out. Not all of the jobs he'd taken on were physical, but many were, and he had the muscle to show for it. He tilted the stone up, and Çeda slipped the rope under once, twice, then hooked it together on top. Then the two of them waited as Galadan tapped the first stone into position with a massive wooden mallet.

"Good day to you, Emre."

Çeda turned and saw a lithe young woman who'd managed to catch Emre's eye—not a difficult thing these days—carrying a clay ewer toward the well near the garden. Emre turned as well. His face positively lit when he saw her. "And you, Enasia." He waved to her, and then turned back to Çeda, his cheeks reddening.

"'And *you*, Enasia.'" Çeda gripped her stomach and pretended to retch up her breakfast. "I feel sick."

"She's nice."

"Nice . . . She's a dainty little *girl*, Emre."

"She's three years older than we are."

"And all the more frail for it. Just look at her." Enasia was struggling with the well's wooden crank handle. "She can hardly lift a bucket."

"Just because you look like a man . . ."

Çeda stared at Emre, feeling as though she'd been dropped into a pool of ice water. Did she look like a *man* to Emre? To other men?

Emre's joking smile vanished as he stared back at her. Perhaps he was embarrassed by what he'd said, or perhaps just embarrassed the truth had slipped out; either way, he made no apology and went back to work, infinitely more focused on the mundane lifting of stones than he'd been minutes before.

Soon Enasia walked back toward the temple. She looked toward the half-built wall, but Emre pointedly did *not* look at her, which made Çeda feel acutely uncomfortable. Far be it for her to stand between Emre and someone he wanted to know. But, why *her*?

When they'd finished laying several more stones, Galadan called for a short break and went to check on the work of his son's crew. Çeda wiped her brow and sat on a stack of the ivory-colored stones, her breath coming fast. "It's just that it's so near," she said when Galadan was out of earshot, hoping to guide the conversation away from embarrassing things.

When Emre looked up at her, she jutted her chin across

the lush green garden toward Tauriyat, which loomed over them. Emre knew what she meant. The Kings. The Maidens. Çeda's mother, Ahya. "Seems to me you were acting strangely before we got here," he said.

"You told me about this job three days ago, Emre. You don't think I know where Tulathan's temple sits?"

He stepped closer and peered at her, as if he were hoping to use his gaze alone to bore a hole in her skull and steal her secrets, but just then Galadan returned and waved to the crane. "Stop it, you love birds, and start hoisting."

Emre's face flushed again, even more deeply than before. She could feel hers doing the same as the two of them returned to the rope. For the rest of the day, she tried not to notice how the muscles along his shoulders and arms gleamed under the sun and bunched as he pulled at the rope. A few times, from the corner of her eye, she caught Emre watching her as well, but he would quickly look away.

She made no mention of it, and neither did he.

———◦●◦———

Over the next few days, Çeda couldn't get out of her mind the image of King Mesut stepping out from that ramshackle home in the Knot. By Goezhen's wicked grin, why would he have been there? She needed to know more.

So that night, one night before Beht Zha'ir would come to Sharakhai once more, she snuck from their home in a dirty, threadbare thawb with a niqab to cover her face, and walked south along the streets of Roseridge. Only a few were about, as most in the city had sat down for their evening meal.

As she neared the edge of the Knot, a tanbur was playing somewhere to the north, a doudouk somewhere east. They were nowhere near one another, but they were playing the same song, a mournful threnody to souls lost in the desert. It was not uncommon in Sharakhai for a musician to begin a song and for others to join in. There were nights when whole sections of the city came alive with it. But tonight, it was only these two, others perhaps as moved as

Çeda was now, unwilling to join in and ruin the perfect sorrow being woven like threads in a grand tapestry. The song was just coming to a close when Çeda reached the street where she'd seen the Maidens and the King. A long pause followed, one filled with whistles of appreciation from all around, and then a drum picked up a lively beat, and the tanbur and doudouk joined in, followed quickly by a melodic qanun and a Kundhunese rattle. It lifted Çeda's spirits, especially as darkness came on, for she'd been thinking too much about her mother these past few days.

Those thoughts all vanished, however, when she realized someone was standing near the door, the very door the King had stepped through before he passed by Çeda as she cowered in the dirt.

She stopped in her tracks. The sound of her boots grinding against the street was loud in her ears, and yet the man didn't turn around. He was tall and thin, and wore a green turban in an ancient style. Only those of noble blood, or those who wished to pretend to noble blood, wore their turbans tall with the crown overflowing. His dark clothes, and the shadows in the lane, nearly hid the coiled whip at his side. He stood with a kenshar in one hand, the tip of the blade against the palm of his right hand. He pressed the point deeply into his palm, drawing blood. As the wound bled, he put the knife in his mouth, sucked the blood from it, and slipped it home into the sheath at his wide cloth belt.

He moved his hand in a circular motion, allowing the dripping blood to cover much of his palm, and then he squeezed his hand into a fist. With care, he opened his hand, inspected it, and then pressed it against the face of the wooden door. When he pulled his hand away, a bloody handprint remained, glistening in the fading light of dusk. But as he leaned forward and blew upon it, it faded entirely, as if it were little more than water drying on a sunbaked slab of limestone.

The whip, she realized, was the sign of Sukru, the Reaping King, the one who wandered the city, choosing those who would be taken by the asirim. Surely he had just marked someone who lived behind that door.

He turned to her and looked straight at her as if he'd

known all along she was standing there and had allowed it. As the lively song continued to play, he strode her way, every bit as calm as the other King had been. And why not? This was his city. He had little to fear from a lone girl in the streets of Sharakhai. He stopped and looked into her eyes, which was all that her niqab revealed, but then he pulled her veil away and stared at her face. He inspected her as if he were reading some ancient scroll, learning her every secret.

She blinked, the impotent rage for her mother's death bringing her back to herself. She should have knelt long before now. She should be prostrate before him. But this, at least, she could do: stand before one of those responsible for her mother's death and face him without flinching.

Sukru held up his right hand, still bloody, still wet. "The mark of the chosen," he said in a throaty voice. "They are blessed, are they not?"

"They are, my King."

"And what of you?" he asked, glancing at his bloody hand. "Do you wish to be marked as well? Do you wish to walk among the farther fields, glowing from the kiss of the gods?"

I would pay anything to walk hand-in-hand with my mother. But not yet. Now is not the time.

The song reached its frantic conclusion, the drumbeat thrumming in time to Çeda's heartbeat. She looked to his hand, to the King's twinkling eyes. "There are paths I have yet to walk, my King. Streets I have yet to tread."

He seemed amused by her words. "This is a gift I bestow upon few."

"Then perhaps one day you might ask me again. Maybe I'll have changed my mind."

He stared at her, perhaps shocked, but then he tilted his head to her, as much of a bow as someone like her would ever receive from one of the Kings. "Perhaps I will, little wren. Perhaps I will." He pointed over her shoulder. "Now go. Return home and leave this street in peace."

She did as the King commanded, as around her, the music came to a rousing finale and then fell silent. As piercing whistles played over the Knot and the surrounding neighborhoods, Çeda glanced back and found the King gone.

Çeda knew that Sukru's appearance at that door had something to do with the other King's interests. It seemed likely that he was working behind Mesut's back. Why else go to a place clearly favored by the Jackal King? Or if not that, was it some inconvenience the other King was forcing Sukru to deal with? Or perhaps they shared common interests? Whatever the case, Çeda knew she had to return. She had to know why the Kings were so interested in that place.

She left home just before dusk on the night of Beht Zha'ir. She padded along the streets, moving steadily toward the Knot. The city was hidden behind closed doors, giving her all the cover she needed, but she felt terribly exposed. She'd been out on Beht Zha'ir often to collect petals from the adichara, but she always left before nightfall so she was well clear of the city before the asirim arrived. Now, she felt hemmed in, as if she were running a maze that could only lead to Sukru. Then the King *would* mark her with his bloody hand, and the asirim would find her and take her to the desert to do whatever it was they did with the sad souls they collected.

But the streets were empty as she reached the Knot, empty as she came to the marked door. She crept closer and stood before it. Tulathan had already risen in the east, and its light shone on the wood. Ever so faintly, she could see Sukru's mark glinting in the moonlight.

After glancing up and down the street, she tried the door, and found it unlocked. She stepped inside and saw a woman lying in a bed on the far side of the one-room home. She sat up immediately, and Çeda saw a girl in the bed with her, perhaps three years old. Çeda could see, even in the moonlight, how beautiful this woman was. Beautiful enough, perhaps, to attract the notice of Kings. Beautiful enough to draw them away from Tauriyat and into the streets. Were there not numberless stories about the Kings doing exactly this, wandering in disguise or even in the open, having dalliances among those of lesser blood?

Çeda put her finger to her lips and closed the door.

"Who are you?" the woman whispered, standing,

grabbing a knife from the bedside table and unsheathing it. The blade gleamed in the dull moonlight coming in through the shaded window to Çeda's right. "Get out of my home!"

"Please, I'm not here to harm you. You and your daughter are in grave danger."

The girl sat up, and shrunk back into the bed, pulling the covers up to her eyes. Çeda was about to answer when she realized the woman was holding her stomach with her free hand. Kenshar in one hand; the other over her belly, protectively.

"Gods—" Çeda's mind was racing. "Are you *pregnant?*"

Of course she was. But why would Sukru do such a thing? Mark a woman carrying the child of another King?

"I'll answer no questions of yours!" The woman was still whispering, but loudly now, in a rasp. She stepped forward, brandishing the knife, though it was with rushed, exaggerated movements.

"I was here the other day"—she lowered her voice—"when the King was leaving."

The woman's eyes narrowed, and then she stepped forward, slicing the air between them with her knife. "What of it? What is that to you?"

Çeda dodged the swing easily, stepping back toward the door, and as she did, a long wail settled over the city, sending a shiver crawling along Çeda's skin. The woman looked to the window.

"Memma!" the girl cried from the bed.

"Quiet, Mala. And you, get out! Now! The Holy Night is upon us!"

"Just listen to me," Çeda said, holding her hands up as the woman swung again. Her mind was reeling, piecing together the pieces of this very strange puzzle. "They're coming. They're coming here, to *your* home."

This caught the woman so off-guard she stopped advancing. "What?"

"The asirim," Çeda said as another tormented cry came, closer than the last, and more pained, as if the one who had released it was being whipped by Sukru's black scourge. "They're coming *here*. Sukru marked your door.

Don't you see? You and your daughter and your unborn child have been chosen!"

"You're talking nonsense!"

Çeda stepped aside and motioned to the door. "See for yourself, but for your children's sake, hurry!"

In the dim light, the woman looked to Mala in their shared bed, then down to her hand, which was still resting on her stomach, then to the door as a third wail came, a primal howl filled not with anguish, or even agony, but with rage. "Get in the corner," the woman said, pointing to a wooden cabinet, "behind that table."

Çeda complied, stepping behind a low eating table and a stack of pillows. The woman moved to the door and opened it with great care, so as not to make a sound. She stared at it and whipped her head back to Çeda. "Nothing!"

"Look *carefully*, in the moonlight."

She turned back. Peered at the door. She swallowed hard. Then squinted, moving even closer to the wood, glancing up at the moon then back to the handprint, which she had evidently seen. The hand that held the knife quivered in fear or confusion or both.

"Rhia's grace," she said. *"Why?"*

More wails came. They were spread across the south-eastern section of the city. How they might sense the blood that Sukru left—its odor perhaps, or some arcane faculty granted by the gods—Çeda didn't know, but she knew they would be here quickly. "I don't know," Çeda answered, "but I know this: the asirim move quickly. And when they have their prey in sight, there is no escape. So I leave it to you. Do you wish to be taken by the asirim? Do you consider it an honor? If so, I'll leave. But if not, we must go now."

Mala was crying into her blanket now. The sound was muffled but desperate. The woman cried as well, the moon-lit trails of her tears giving light to how deeply terrified she was.

"Mala, get dressed," she said and moved to the cabinet, rummaging through its lower shelves.

"No time!" Çeda said. "Get your sandals on, girl, and follow your mother."

Çeda made to grab the woman's shoulder, to get her to rise. The sound of the asirim filled the streets now, and she heard a shout somewhere in the distance, a man screaming until his cries were cut suddenly short.

The woman rose with a small wooden box clutched in her hands. "Come, now, Mala."

They ran out and into the night, weaving through the streets as quickly and quietly as they could manage. As they were leaving the Knot, Çeda turned and saw a dark form bounding along the street toward them. She shoved the woman down an alley and turned, preparing to draw her pitiful shamshir, hoping to the gods she wouldn't need to.

The asirim galloped toward her, dark arms and legs eating up the distance between them at an alarming rate. Çeda breathed out. Drew her sword. Held it before her with both of her quavering arms.

But at the last moment, the asirim turned, heading along the street they'd just come from, perhaps toward the empty home they'd just fled, or to another. Çeda didn't know, she was simply glad to be alive.

She fled, leading Mala and her mother deeper into Sharakhai. When they came to the Serpentine, the woman grabbed her arm with a desperation that surprised Çeda, then leaned in and whispered, "Sirina. My name is Sirina Jalih'ala al Kenan. I would have you know it if we die this night, so I might find you in the farther fields and thank you there."

In the distance, the wailing rose as a strangled cry was cut short. Several jackal bays followed, as if the asirim were pleased with their kill.

"You won't die tonight, Sirina. Not you. Not Mala. And not your unborn child."

Before Çeda could take them any further, Sirina pulled her in and kissed her forehead. "My heart is yours."

It was a very old expression of gratitude, and a very serious one.

Çeda gripped Sirina's arm, then did the same to young

Mala, lending them what strength she could. And then they were off once more, wending their way toward Roseridge.

——————◆——————

Çeda laid an extra blanket over Sirina and Mala, who, while not yet fully asleep, were resting quietly in Çeda's bed. Emre stood at her door, looking for all the world like a useless man. But he was only trying to help, and she loved him for it. She kissed him on the cheek.

"What was that for?" he asked as she walked past him.

"For trying."

He frowned but said nothing as they entered his room. Wordlessly they slipped into his bed and pulled the covers up. Now that the excitement of the chase had worn off, she felt cold, colder than she'd felt in years.

The city was quiet now. The moons were high and bright, but they would be setting soon, and then it would be a few hours of pitch darkness before the sun rose. It would feel good to have a bit of darkness, Çeda decided. The brightness of the moons as she and Sirina and Mala had run through the city was harrowing. It had felt as if they'd be caught at any moment, that the alarm would be sounded. But no one had seen them.

"What will we do with them?" Emre asked her.

He was warm against her back, and his arms around her felt like the home she'd never had. She turned in the bed until the two of them were face-to-face. "We find them a new life."

"Won't the Kings come for her?"

She shook her head. "I don't think so. Sukru marked her door, and she won't go back there. I doubt they'll think at all of a dead mistress and her bastard child." Emre's gaze flicked to her shoulders, and she knew why: the tattoo on her back, the one Dardzada had forced upon her, the symbol for a bastard child.

"It's all right," she said. "It doesn't bother me anymore."

"It doesn't?"

And to this she merely leaned in and kissed him.

He leaned into the kiss and soon it became more

passionate, the two of them running their hands along each other's hips, then waists, then Emre slipped his hand beneath her night shirt. His fingers were warm, and it felt good against the cold skin of her stomach and hip and back.

She'd not lain with a man yet. She'd come close. She and Tariq had gotten drunk on cheap wine he'd bought— *bought*, he'd said, swearing he hadn't stolen it. They'd wound up below Bent Man along the Trough, kissing one another roughly, inexpertly. But Tariq had drunk too much wine. That or he was intimidated by her—Tehla the baker had told her more than once that it might happen with men.

This was different, though. There were times when she'd looked at Emre that way, and times when she'd seen *him* looking at *her*. Many times, in fact. But the two of them had so much history. He'd been there when her mother had died. He'd been there after Dardzada marked her. He'd been there the first time she'd ventured out to the killing fields. And she'd been there when Rafa died. She'd been there to console him, however much good *that* had done. She'd seen him grow from a gangly boy into a well-muscled man. And more than that, a kind man, even if there was a part of him that always seemed scared.

As she ran the backs of her fingers along his jaw, slipped them around his neck and pulled him deeper into the kiss, it felt . . . not wrong, but risky. Their relationship was so much deeper than tumbling between the sheets, and she didn't want to ruin that.

Perhaps Emre felt the same, for though he crawled on top of her, though he kissed her neck and spread her legs apart with his hips, his movements slowed. He rose up and stared at her, and for a time the two of them merely gazed into one another's eyes.

With a tenderness she felt in her heart, she reached up and pulled him close. With one hand she reached down and felt his manhood, stroked him for a time before guiding him inside her. She used her legs to pull his hips close, gasping for the pain that it brought. Emre recoiled, but she held him tight. This was a sweet pain, one she had been hoping to share with Emre for so long.

When Emre saw her smile, his own smile returned, if

slowly, and then he began to lose himself in the motions, rocking back and forth, his eyes closing as the two of them grasped one another tightly and he thrust himself into her with increasing ardor.

When he released, he cried out, and Çeda pulled him into her, arching her back as she was sent over the edge. She never thought she'd experience anything else like the petals. The energy they granted was like nothing else. But *this* . . . It wasn't the same, exactly, but it was every bit as grand, every bit as wonderful, like two symphonies playing out over the desert.

And she swore to the gods she'd drop a handful of sylval onto Yerinde's offering plate if it didn't give her the same sort of hangovers. Then she laughed at the very thought.

"What?" Emre asked.

"It's nothing."

"You just laughed. While we were making love."

She reached up and stroked his cheek. "If you were feeling what I'm feeling, you'd be laughing too."

And then he did laugh, a short, beautiful thing, and they kissed again.

Slowly, they came down from their heights, and the two of them lay side by side, their breathing in sync.

As Emre stared at her, running his hand over her cheek, his brow furrowed.

"What?" she asked.

"There are days when I wish we could go back and start again."

"What do you mean?"

"I wish we had run away, before any of this had happened."

"Before what had happened?"

Emre shrugged. "Your mother. The Kings finding her."

"And Rafa."

He nodded tentatively. "And Rafa. I'd wipe all of it away, and our life would be grand."

With dawn on the horizon, they kissed one last time. She nestled into the crook of his shoulder and held him close. "Where would we have gone had we run away?"

"To the desert. We'd take a ship and travel the sands.

We'd visit all the twelve tribes, then find a place of our own among them, or live in a home like Saliah."

There were days she wished she could change things as well, but what good did it do to wish for things you could never have? "We can't go back, Emre."

"I know," he said.

"And life is never grand."

"I know."

Chapter 56

THERE WAS A STONE LIP beneath Bent Man Bridge where one could sit and watch the riverbed. It was dusty and dirty, and there were massive spiders that hid in the dusty recesses of Bent Man's undercarriage, yet it was still a favorite of the gutter wrens in spring, when the river was strong and flowed bright and clear and cool. At other times of the year, it was rarely used. Those were the times when the Haddah became little more than a reminder of how harsh life was in the Shangazi.

Even so, Emre had liked coming here with Çeda. They'd sit and eat stolen honeymeats, licking their fingers and smacking their lips after. They'd rest from the heat with Tariq and Hamid. Sometimes Rafa would come by and tell them jokes, or Hamid's uncle would come and toss them a few lemons to suck on. Often it would just be the two of them, and they'd sit and talk about what they'd do when they grew older, things neither of them thought they would ever *actually* do—sail the Shangazi from one end to the other, dine in the halls of the long-dead Kings, visit the tribes and hear their stories over an open fire and tell stories of their own.

Sometimes they'd sit and kiss, hands roaming, groping

one another, though it never lasted long. He would have liked it to, but Çeda would tense up. He always had the impression it was because of her mother, yet strangely enough, the one time they *had* lain together, he was the one who'd thought about Ahya. There were times when he wished someone else could have told Çeda that fateful morning, so she wouldn't always think of him when she thought of her mother's death. But then, like now, he rejected the notions quickly. He was glad he was the one who'd told her; he just hoped it didn't stand between them.

This stone lip, this place filled with so many memories, was where Emre sat the day after being taken to the Qaimiran Lord's manse to speak with Çeda.

His knees were drawn up against his chest. He listened to the wind whistle, watched the swirls of sand whip past, looking like waves in the sea, crashing against the shore. But what did he know? He'd never been to the sea and was sure he never would. Not in this life. He was a gutter wren. Always had been. Always would be.

He waited as the day grew dimmer. He was starting to think he shouldn't have gone to Hamid after all. Hamid had been ill-pleased by Emre's request, but Emre had insisted it was necessary. It was information Macide would want to know.

"Then tell me," Hamid had said.

"No," Emre had replied. "I can only tell Macide."

Hamid, with deceptive casualness, had pointed with his chin to Emre's wounds. "What happened to you?"

"That's what I need to talk to him about."

"I don't like it, Emre."

"Even so," Emre had said, refusing to back down.

In the end, Hamid had nodded and sent him away, pausing only to ask where, assuming he assented, Macide could find him.

"Bent Man," Emre had replied.

Hamid had stared at him, perhaps wondering if he was serious, and then he'd laughed and nodded. "Very well, Emre. It's your grave."

Emre saw forms walking through the sand, which blew even harder now. They darkened and formed into a group of older wrens, seven of them—five boys, two girls. They pulled the veils and scarves from their faces and headed for the incline that would take them up toward Emre, but they stopped upon realizing someone was there.

One of the girls broke away, taking a few steps closer to Emre. "This is our place." She and the boy who came to stand just behind her were both nearly Emre's age.

"Not today it isn't," Emre replied.

Two more of them fanned out beside the other two, their faces intent. "You heard her. Move on."

Emre didn't. Instead, he pulled his knife and held it, blade against forearm, and stared into the girl's eyes. He'd seen her look before. False bravado. He knew it well. He'd used it nearly every day for the past six years. Not anymore, though. He'd changed. He didn't quite know how, but he had, and in some fundamental way.

He stared into the girl's eyes and held his knife, part of him hoping they *would* attack, if only so he could release some small amount of the endless store of rage that had been building within him for years.

He didn't know what the girl saw in him—perhaps a place she was afraid to touch within her own soul—but in the end she looked to the others and said, "Come on. I'm hungry." And off she went, back into the sandstorm.

The others looked from her to Emre, but then followed her, and Emre was alone once more. Though not for long. Only a few moments later, another form resolved from the amber-streaked winds. A tall man with a forked beard and a turban with a veil pulled tight across his face. When he saw Emre, he pulled the veil free. It fluttered in the wind like a child playing snap the snake.

He nodded to Emre as he approached, his smile a shallow one, a knowing one. He didn't say anything, though, not until he was sitting next to Emre and the two of them were looking out over the riverbed. "I used to come here as a child."

Emre was surprised. "I thought you were raised in the desert."

"I was, but my father brought me to Sharakhai from time to time."

"Why?"

"Why what?" Macide asked.

"Why did he come to Sharakhai?"

Macide shrugged, an unexpectedly childlike gesture from such an imposing man. "For many reasons. He tells me he hates Sharakhai, that he would burn it to the ground if he could, but all men who see Sharakhai cannot help but be impressed, cannot help but be drawn to some part of it. I think that was why he came, to experience the thing he hated, like pressing your tongue against a canker."

The wind blew fiercely for a time, the sound of it like a lost soul, shrieking its pain to an uncaring world.

"Why did you ask me here, Emre?"

"So that you could help me."

"You are newly beneath my wing, and you summon *me* to ask for favors?"

"It will help you as well."

"So much mystery, young falcon. I'm intrigued."

"You wish to capture Hamzakiir, and you hope to find him unguarded in Külaşan's palace. Is it not so?"

Emre tried to read Macide's expression, but Macide simply watched the riverbed and nodded. "It is so."

"There is one who will go there tomorrow on Beht Zha'ir. She goes to kill Külaşan."

Macide frowned, his eyes blinking away a bit of gathered sand. "Killing a King is no simple matter."

"Even so, that's what she plans to do. And I would help her if I could."

"How?"

"By drawing the King's attention away. Or his guards. Or both."

"Drawing them toward *us*."

"Yes."

"You know that my father has plans for us beyond Beht Zha'ir. You know there is much to do if our mission in Külaşan's palace is successful."

"Of course, but how often might we have a chance to kill one of the Kings?"

"How? How can she hope to kill one of the Kings when so many others have failed?"

"Using the secrets she found."

"Secrets?"

"Secrets from the night of Beht Ihman, long thought buried or forgotten."

"She has some trove of information that no one else has? Some scroll? Some placid mere to grant her such foresight?"

Emre considered lying, but there was power in Çeda's story, power that a man like Macide would recognize. "There were riddles, hidden in a book of her mother's. Riddles passed to her even after her mother's death, as if the gods themselves wanted her to have them."

"And who is this woman? What is her name?"

"Çeda." He'd thought of lying, but surely he knew of Çeda already from Hamid.

"Çedamihn Ahyanesh'ala."

"Yes," he said, surprised that he would know her full name.

Macide was quiet for a time. He stared out, arms crossed and laid across his knees like a bridge. There was a glint in his eye. A tug at the corner of his lips. "Very well, Emre. We will go. We will go on Beht Zha'ir, and we will see if your Çeda can do what she hopes to do."

"And we'll have what *we* want as well."

"Yes," he said, patting Emre's knee. "We will."

With that he stood and began taking measured steps down the stone slope, but he stopped when Emre called out to him.

"Wait!" The way this had gone . . . It had all been so easy. "Do you know Çeda? Did you know her mother?"

At this, Macide turned to face Emre. There was a look in his eye—a wry look, a knowing look, a tricky look as well, one that gave a small glimpse into the emotions roiling inside him. "I very well may have, Emre." He turned and resumed his trek down to the riverbed. "I very well may have."

The wind howling around him, Macide strode along the Haddah as if he had not a care in the world. And the blowing sands seemed to lift him away.

Chapter 57

AT NOON ON THE EVE of Beht Zha'ir, a message arrived for King Ihsan, summoning him to Eventide, the palace of Kiral, the King of Kings. He went as bid, traveling up to the highest of the palaces on Tauriyat, reaching its central courtyard as Kiral himself paced at its center with his greatsword Sunshearer sheathed at his side. Navakahm, the Lord Commander of the Silver Spears, a veteran with three decades of service to the Kings, stood facing him.

Standing might be too generous a word for the Lord of the Guard, Ihsan decided. Swaying was more like it. Shuddering. He was a bloody mess from the attentions of King Cahil, their self-elected, baby-faced confessor, who stood behind Kiral with a bored-looking expression and hands clasped behind his back. The man hadn't even bothered to wash before coming here. His hands were still bloody from his time with Navakahm. He enjoyed his work altogether too much, and it was often a waste, the things Cahil did, electing to torture their prisoners as a first option, rather than giving Zeheb and Ihsan time to wheedle the information from them and their allies. Too often Cahil's eagerness tipped their hand to their enemies, but try telling that to Cahil, or Kiral—a man quick to anger, quicker to act, rarely sifting through the implications to see what might lie beneath the surface.

King Onur might have come—the Spears were his to command, after all—but the King of Sloth had long since given up caring what happened outside of his own palace, and Kiral had long since given up caring what Onur thought of anything.

Cahil had apparently finished with Navakahm, using whatever methods he felt necessary to determine whether the man was telling the truth when he said he'd had no idea that Külaşan's first son, Lord Veşdi, had been targeted by the Moonless Host, and, further, that he'd uncovered few clues to where Lord Veşdi had been taken since his abduction two weeks ago—or, more importantly, *why* he'd been taken. Making matters worse, Navakahm also had no leads regarding the attack on the House of Maidens.

None of this came as any particular surprise. Zeheb himself had little to report. The Host were becoming particularly adept at foiling his abilities, and he wasn't a man who could claim to be infallible in any case—even the King of Whispers could not bend his ear to all that was whispered in every corner of Sharakhai.

Still, whatever limitations he might have, Zeheb was an indispensable ally. It was why Ihsan had chosen him decades ago and eventually told him of his plans. There was some risk in this but, unlike Kiral, Ihsan recognized that he could do none of what he wished alone. And besides, Ihsan had known Zeheb's answer long before he'd broached the subject. He might be good at keeping secrets, but there wasn't a man or woman in the Great Shangazi who Ihsan couldn't read or turn to his own purposes given enough time. It was a thing he was particularly proud of, especially with a specimen like Zeheb, who had once been the most faithful to the Twelve Kings and their common cause.

No longer, though.

Time deals all wounds, as they say.

Zeheb's slow change of heart was all the more satisfying for the decades of care it had taken—the subtle lies, the reveal of betrayals, however small, the revelation that the house they had built would not last forever. Bit by bit Zeheb had come to see things as Ihsan wanted him to.

And make no mistake, having Zeheb by his side was essential, as was remaining a confidant to Yusam so that he could guide the Jade-eyed King in his readings, an objective as necessary as remaining in Kiral's good graces. To move forward without these three Kings—Kiral, Yusam, and Zeheb—would mean a quick end, not merely to Ihsan's plans, but to Ihsan himself. And he had no desire, the gods of the desert as his witnesses, to submit himself to Cahil's attentions.

In the courtyard, Kiral glanced back at Ihsan and Zeheb, then drew Sunshearer, his massive two-handed shamshir, and regarded the bloody, beaten man before him. As dissatisfied as he might be with Zeheb and Ihsan for their lack of answers, he had no opportunity to vent his frustration on them. Navakahm, on the other hand, was a different matter.

Kiral stared intently at the heavily jowled man, his jaw working so hard his pockmarked skin rolled like the dunes. Sunshearer swung lazily back and forth, as if the King of Kings was itching to use it. "Do you have any last words?"

"Only that I know I have failed, and that I swear to take up the sword for you once more in the farther fields."

A fool's oath, Ihsan thought. *Who knows what the farther fields will bring?* It might have been that Navakahm, having crossed to the other world first, would have reign over Kiral, but no longer, not after a pledge like that. *The gods have ears, my friend, even the first gods*—especially *the first gods—and they might just hold you to your oath.*

Kiral seemed to care little for Navakahm's oath. He'd heard much the same over the centuries, from men and women more loyal to him, and considerably more gifted, than Navakahm. Little chance that Kiral would give him a place of honor once he'd reached the other side.

But Kiral still followed custom. With his free hand he grasped the back of Navakahm's neck and pulled him forward to place a kiss upon the crown of his head. Then he stepped back and lifted Sunshearer, the sword glinting in the sunlight, and with a mighty swing of both hands drew it swiftly across Navakahm's neck.

Like a vase spilled from a pedestal, the Lord of the Guard's head tipped from his body, rolling down along his frame before his headless corpse fell like a drunken reveler.

Kiral turned to Ihsan and Zeheb and strode toward them. He took up the bolt of white cloth Cahil handed him and wiped his sword clean of the bright scarlet smear along its length. He may have meant it as a message to Zeheb and Ihsan—this dark theater with Cahil and Navakahm—but if so, it was ineffective at best and at worst cemented Ihsan's feelings that things could not remain as they were. Ihsan cared little for Kiral's innuendos. He only wished to stay close enough to know what Kiral would do, which way he would turn. Kiral held much sway, the most of any one King, so Ihsan pasted on a face that would look as properly chagrined as the King would expect and then waited for the King of Kings to speak.

"What news?" Kiral asked. "Have you found Külaşan's son?"

"I bear dark tidings," Zeheb said before Ihsan could say a word. "We've found Veşdi. He was discovered by one of our patrol ships a league out of Sharakhai, in the center of the Haddah's riverbed."

Zeheb had told him nothing of this, so Ihsan didn't have to feign surprise. He hated surprises, but they hadn't spoken since the day before, and he trusted it was merely timing that had prevented Zeheb from warning him.

"It's a ford the royal patrol ships cross often," Zeheb continued, "so easy enough to spot."

Kiral's jaw worked, his eyes calculating. "They wanted us to find him."

Zeheb nodded. "Adichara vines were braided like a rope and wrapped around his feet, and the mark of the lost tribe was carved into his forehead."

Kiral's eyes widened. His head jerked back. It took much to surprise Kiral, but this did, and it surprised Ihsan as well. The assassin, the mother of their young new Maiden, had been marked in the very same way, by Cahil himself. It had been a foolish thing; *a warning to those who would oppose us*, Cahil had said after he'd hung her before the gates of Tauriyat. But such things had a way of coming home to roost.

Kiral turned to Ihsan. "A reprisal?"

"Of course," Ihsan replied, bowing his head. "But why warn us?"

Kiral's broad chin jutted forward. "And why now, so many years later, on the eve of Beht Zha'ir?"

Zeheb shrugged, a ponderous and awkward figure next to well-muscled Kiral. "I cannot say, other than to note that the Moonless Host have proven themselves patient."

Ihsan found himself more intrigued than he'd been in a long while. This had something to do with their new Maiden or he was a beggar's son. And surely it had something to do with Külaşan too, else why take *his* son? He thought on it for a moment, and came to one conclusion. If he was right, it wouldn't do to have Kiral worrying for Külaşan overly much, especially tonight and perhaps not for the next few nights. "The woman who last wore that sign," he said, echoing what the others were surely thinking, "stole into Tauriyat to attack one of our own. Who's to say it won't happen again?"

Kiral frowned. "What, an attack where we're strongest?"

"Had this happened any other night, what would we have done? We would have scoured the city for answers. We would spread ourselves thin looking for clues. Were we to do that tonight—as I suspect the Moonless Host hope we will—it would give them exactly what they're looking for. We draw our attention to the city when their true goal lies within the House of Kings."

Kiral looked to Zeheb, who played it well. He nodded noncommittally, as if what Ihsan had said sounded plausible but he hadn't yet had time to digest it. "They are becoming more bold. They may have done this to bait us."

"Where is Külaşan?" Kiral asked.

"By now, he'll be taking Veşdi to the tombs beneath his palace, to grieve in peace."

Were it any but Külaşan, a King would have waited in

Sharakhai and grieved properly, but Külaşan's particular sensitivities made him shun Sharakhai, especially around the Holy Night. He would have done exactly what Zeheb said: taken his son with him to wait out the night and grieve as he chose, well away from the other Kings.

"It is a safe enough place for him, Kiral," Ihsan said.

"We'll send him more men."

"As you wish, but we have work of our own to do."

Kiral bristled. "Will you cower in your palace, Ihsan?"

"Cower? No. But I'll prepare a proper welcome for those who might come. As should we all."

This had the desired effect. Kiral, as did all of the Kings, including Ihsan himself, wanted to strike back at the Moonless Host. The only difference was Ihsan could wait. The time to deal with the Host would come, but today, there were others he needed to focus his attention on.

Kiral gave Ihsan a half-lidded expression that bordered on disappointment. "Best you get to it, then."

No one could fail to recognize this as the insult it was, but Ihsan merely bowed his head and smiled. "And so I shall."

Chapter 58

$\mathcal{T}$HE SUN HAD ONLY RECENTLY SET, but the moons had risen full and bright as Çeda rode at the rear of a line of six tall horses. Zaïde rode at the lead, then Sümeya and Kameyl, followed by Melis, Jalize, and finally Çeda. Zaïde wore her white Matron's dress, while the rest, including Çeda, wore the black dresses of the Maidens.

Çeda's horse, a black gelding that fought the reins with every plodding step it took, shook its head and whinnied until Çeda tightened the reins once more. "Foul beast," Çeda muttered under her breath. She'd never liked horses, and they'd never liked her. She'd much rather be riding her zilij over the sands than a willful creature who could throw her the moment she wasn't looking.

They were headed for the blooming fields—the killing fields, as the Maidens sometimes referred to them, a reference to the death sown by the asirim after the gods had transformed them into the vengeful creatures all in Sharakhai knew. Legend had it that the bodies of their enemies had been lain in a great circle around Sharakhai, forming the beds of the blooming fields that gave life to the twisted trees.

When they'd left Tauriyat at sundown, Çeda had been allowed to choose her path, so she'd chosen to head toward

the place where she and Emre had been attacked by the
rattlewings, where she'd seen Külaşan slip down into the
sands. They'd ridden three leagues at least, and Çeda knew
they were near. Indeed, when they crested the next dune,
Çeda could see the light of their blooms and the telltale
shadows of the twisted trees, dark shadows over ochre sand.
They continued without a word, the only sound the jingle of
tack and the soft thump of hooves plodding through sand.
As they rode down the sandy slope and started up the next
rise, however, Çeda could hear the drone of the rattlewings as they flitted from flower to flower. Some landed
among the branches or on the sandy floor below and made
their piercing buzzing sound, a thing that made Çeda's
teeth itch.

   Zaïde led them to a clearing among the adichara. All
around them the blue-white blooms were open to the chill
desert air. They gave off the faintest glow, a panoply of
moons hanging low beneath the stars, the countless children of Rhia and Tulathan. Running beneath them, around
them, through them, were the adicharas' thorny vines,
twisting slowly in the breeze.

   "Here," Zaïde called as she pulled her horse's reins and
dismounted. The others did so as well, with Çeda coming
last. The horses, all well trained, remained where they
were as the six women stepped onto a plateau of stone and
held hands. Melis stood on Çeda's left, tall Jalize on her
right. Sümeya and Kameyl held their hands in turn, and
Zaïde, as their Matron, their spiritual guide this night,
stood opposite Çeda.

   "Our custom," Zaïde began, "is for an aspirant to be
poisoned and then to choose her adichara bloom, but as
you've already passed that first test, you will simply go and
choose one of the flowers." She paused as a rattlewing hov-
ered between them and then flew up and over the adichara.
"Are you prepared for your vigil?"

   "I am."

   "Then go. Choose wisely."

   Çeda looked about the clearing. There were many adichara blooms. With the moons so full and the petals so
bright, the subtle movement of the vines made them

hypnotic, a fleet upon a stormy sea. Most of the flowers faced the moons, making it difficult to choose, but she found one so full the petals seemed ready to burst from it, as if it were shouting at the gods that it was not afraid.

You are the one, Çeda decided.

The bloom was high, up, unreachable, and she didn't wish to brave the thorns again by trying to maneuver its branch closer, so she pulled her sword from its scabbard and sliced the flower neatly near the top of its stalk. It floated downward and would have been lost among the branches had Çeda not caught it on the flat of her blade and carried it neatly to her waiting hand.

How strong its scent! It reminded her of nothing so much as her mother placing that last petal beneath her tongue. And for that she was glad. This night of all nights she wanted her mother by her side.

She carried the flower to Zaïde.

The old matron nodded—was there a smile on her lips?—and waved for all six of them to kneel. They did, Çeda holding the flower in her lap with both hands, the Maidens' hands in their laps as well.

"We bring our sister to this place," Zaïde intoned.

And then all five of them, all except Çeda, spoke together. "We leave you in body, but not in spirit."

Zaïde reached forward and gathered a fistful of sand. As she allowed it to pour in a thin stream, she spoke loudly and clearly. "Goezhen grant you strength, that you may endure."

Then Sümeya gathered sand. It whispered against the stone at her knees as she spoke her own prayer. "Thaash grant you courage, that you may strike at our enemies."

Melis approached the ritual with a reverence that Çeda had rarely seen in anyone—whether from Tauriyat or the west end or in the temples. She looked taken by the spirit of the gods, as if she were kneeling before them. "Tulathan grant you insight, that you may judge right from wrong."

It took Kameyl several moments before she followed with a devotion of her own. "Yerinde grant you foresight, even in times of darkness, for only with this will you see the true path."

And last came Jalize. "Bakhi grant you joy in this call-ing, for in it there is righteousness."

Çeda would have expected them to perform this cere-mony half-heartedly at best, but all of them spoke their prayers with reverence, even Kameyl and Sümeya, which Çeda could only assume meant that they placed more weight on the ceremony than they did on their disdain for Çeda.

It was Çeda's turn. She knew the words but had diffi-culty speaking them. She reached down and gathered a handful of sand, mindful of the pledge she'd made so long ago to the Kings: to come for them, to kill them all. "Rhia grant me the will to act, for only in this will I protect Shara-khai from those who would harm her." The words tasted bitter, because of the Kings but also because she felt the gods had abandoned her long ago.

"May the gods will it," Zaïde said.

"May the gods will it," Çeda and the other Maidens re-peated.

Çeda remained on her knees while the others stood, one by one, each of them in turn kissing the crown of her head and walking back to the horses. Zaïde came last. She squatted down and held Çeda by the shoulders. "No matter what you may think, you've done well. Husamettín believes in you. Yusam and Ihsan as well. The others will watch you closely, for you are a jewel freshly plucked from the sand, but they will come to trust you in time."

"And the other Maidens?"

Zaïde shrugged. "After this last test, they will accept you."

"Yet they will never love me."

"Love is an overvalued thing. Gain their respect and be satisfied with that. It will carry you much farther than love."

Çeda wasn't so sure, but she nodded.

"Take all of the petals, but pace yourself—not too many at once—and make your way back to Sharakhai when you're ready."

No sooner had she said those words than a wailing spread across the desert.

Zaïde turned toward the sound. "They've awakened late." She stood and kissed Çeda's head. "It's a good sign, Çeda. Surely they waited for your arrival, so they can greet you properly." As she walked away, Çeda thought she heard another whispered prayer. It was difficult to make out, so soft were her words, but Çeda would swear she'd said, *Please, Nalamae, guide her.*

They rode away single file over the sand, down the slope and up to the next dune. As they crested the ridge, another wail came, nearer this time. And then the Maidens were gone, and Çeda was left alone with the vibrant flower still cupped in her hands.

She plucked the first of the petals and, instead of placing it beneath her tongue, chewed and swallowed it. The scent of the adichara filled her lungs as the taste of the bloom infused her with an energy that felt like the first time she'd ever been given a petal. Surely it was only her nerves. She was not nearly so confident about the asirim accepting her as she had been while speaking with Emre in the relative safety of Tauriyat, far from the blooming fields.

She swallowed and took another petal as more wails filled the night. Zaïde had said to pace herself, but she didn't want to. Why should she? If these somehow summoned the asirim, then she would summon more of them. She refused to allow fear into her heart. She would look upon them and learn from them, perhaps even summon the very one who had kissed her, the King of these twisted creatures. She ate three petals. Four.

She could feel every part of her body now, both inside and out. Five petals, then six.

A high-pitched ringing filled her ears, but she could still hear the asirim trudging through the night.

The adichara began to move and shift. The branches twisted, pulling back as dark forms crawled up from beneath them. The asirim, she realized with shock. The trees' spiny limbs lifted them, the poisoned thorns digging deep into their skin before setting them on their feet. Many of the asirim seemed weak, unable to easily support themselves, like diseased dogs about to collapse under their own weight. And by the gods she could *feel* them.

Zaïde said this would happen. And this was why she'd been brought here, to the blooming fields, so that she would be *imprinted* upon the asirim and on the adichara as well. Indeed, as the adichara waved, she felt their movement. Like a nervous churning in her gut, the asirim made themselves known to her. She could feel not only the ones that were near, but the others in the blooming fields to the south and north, and beyond.

As she swallowed the seventh petal, then the eighth, the first of the asirim approached. Their presence filled her like strong drink, making her swoon, threatening to overwhelm her. When she shook her head from side to side, the light from the moons, stars, and blooms trailed across her vision like children's streamers, making her dizzier still. But she continued to do the one thing—the only thing—that was necessary. The petals. She ate the petals, one by one, until they were gone. Thirteen in all.

The asirim stood more upright now. They shambled less, took on a more feral gait, as if they'd thrown off the effects of their slumber and had remembered their true nature. Or their hunger.

Some shuffled off into the desert toward Sharakhai, perhaps called to perform their duty by Sukru. But many more remained, and in silent concert they closed in around Çeda.

She felt the familiar fear she'd always felt for the asirim—a child's fear of the dark, of the unknown and the unknowable. But seeing them like this, these poor creatures crawling up from the sand like a host of beetles, she felt more pity than fear. Pity, and a curiosity that had been born long ago, from somewhere deep inside her. Her jaw chattered, as if she were cold. But she *wasn't* cold. She was a furnace.

"Come," she told them. "I wish to look upon you."

Were the tales of the Kings true? That these were the men, women, and children who had sacrificed themselves on Beht Ihman. The whispers—whispers hidden between and among the many, many stories Davud had given her—spoke of betrayal, spoke of these men and women being chosen because they had been the weakest of the twelve tribes.

The asirim gathered around, more and more of them coming close, until Çeda was totally surrounded. If they wished to kill her, to rend her flesh and devour her, well, there was little she could do about it now. They were so close she could see the wrinkles in their blackened skin, the stains upon their yellowed teeth. Their bodies were so emaciated their tendons stood out like rigging in a sandstorm. They cowered as if they expected her to strike them, yet they unfolded their cadaverous arms and probed her shoulders, her cheeks through her black veil, even her head through her black turban.

"Who are you?" she asked.

One of them—a tall man once, but now a bent and broken thing with a hunched back and a twisted neck—touched her sword hand and turned it over to examine her palm. He pressed the meat of her thumb, tracing the words and designs that Zaïde had imprinted there. There was pain from the poisoned wound, but the effect of the petals was so strong she hardly felt it. And then the asir began to whisper, though the words were too soft for her to understand. The whispering spread, the others picking up the sound, and soon she was surrounded by a susurrus that blended hypnotically with the muffled clatter of the swaying branches and the hum of the rattlewings. It made the night dreamlike. She even thought she heard Saliah's chimes among the sounds.

The current of the petals was taking her, she realized, a thing she had to stop. "Speak to me!" she called to them, to any who might respond. "Tell me what you're saying!"

The nearest of them cringed at her words, but they otherwise ignored her. The lone asir continued his inspection of her tattoo. He ran one finger directly over the wound, bringing a stronger pain that sharpened the world around her in a more effective way than anything she had managed so far.

"I saw your King once," Çeda said to him, breathing sharply as he pressed the wound harder. It was a sweet pain, a grounding pain. "He spoke to me. *Rest will he 'neath twisted tree . . .*"

The asir looked up at her then, his eyes going wide, his expression, his very manner, filled with sorrow and fright.

"You know those words, don't you?" Çeda said. "*Rest will he 'neath twisted tree 'til death by scion's hand. By Nalamae's tears, and godly fears, shall kindred reach dark land.* That's you, isn't it? The kindred."

And then he said a word she could understand. It came out breathy, raspy, from an instrument that saw little use, she was sure. It was barely a word at all, but she recognized it, for she had just spoken it herself. "*Kiiinnndred,*" he said.

"Do you wish for release? Is that what the poem means?"

"*Releeeeaaaaasssse . . .*"

"From whom? The Kings of Sharakhai?"

At this many of the asirim wailed. They reared back and released their anguish up and into the uncaring skies. Çeda felt their call along her skin, felt it in her bones and in the beating of her heart.

"Tell me," Çeda urged them. "Tell me what they did."

But they would not, they would only wail, longer and harder.

The one who held her hand, however, was silent. He trailed a thick, blackened nail over the designs enwrought within the tattoo. He was doing so in several spots over and over. Still holding her wrist, he knelt and began to trace bits of the design into the sand before her. As the mark filled in, it seemed to draw the world in around it. Like a form resolving from the dark, the mark became known to her, and she gasped, her free hand moving unbidden to her throat.

By the gods who walk the earth, the asir was drawing the very mark that had been carved into the skin of her mother's forehead, the sign whose meaning had escaped her these many years.

But how could they have known?

The asir stopped partway through and flexed his hand as if the mere act of drawing the sign pained him, but then he continued and finished it at last, whereupon he released her and bowed to the symbol, as did all of the others.

A low moan escaped her as sorrow filled her heart. To look upon that sign again . . . It had caused so much pain, and yet the asirim treated it with reverence. She was just about to ask them why when she heard movement, and a fresh whispering among the asirim. Off to her right, they were parting, making way for another. For one who wore a crown.

"Sehid-Alaz," Çeda whispered, voicing the name Saliah had given when she described this poor creature.

He strode beneath the dual moons like a wounded man, perhaps, but a man still filled with pride, a man who refused to bend to the will of the Kings, or even the will of the gods. But the effort wore on him; she could see it in the tremor in his shoulders, the way he strained to keep his head high.

When he came to stand before her at last, the others stepped away, giving them space. As one, the asirim bowed to him.

The King held his hand out to Çeda. She understood that he too wished to look at the design, so she gave her hand to him and stood. But instead of examining her tattoo, he took several deep breaths, as if he were preparing himself for something. *"Give me thine name,"* he said in a voice as old as the desert itself.

"I am Çedamihn Ahyanesh'ala."

Then he turned her with unyielding strength and grabbed the hilt of her sword. He pulled it free, lifting the ebon blade to the night sky as the asirim wailed.

Using the sword, he drew another sign in the sand, several feet away from the first. It was the ancient sign for shaikh. In a circle around it, he drew twelve marks in the sand.

"Twelve shaikhs," Çeda said. "The leaders of the tribes."

The King shook his head and drew another sign beneath the first, the ancient symbol for Sharakhai.

"The Twelve Kings."

The King put his finger over Çeda's mouth and shook his head, pointing up to the twin moons.

They would hear, he was saying. *The gods would hear,*

and perhaps warn the Kings, so keep this conversation in secret. He drew a thirteenth mark near the signs around the Kings. A thirteenth King. He pressed his palm to his chest. And finally he drew a line from the mark of the last King to the sign that had been left on her mother's forehead as a warning.

There had been *thirteen tribes.* And these gathered souls were what remained. The lost tribe. The asirim were all that was left of the thirteenth tribe.

Suddenly the term killing fields took on a whole new meaning, for as surely as the desert was dry, the Twelve Kings had condemned the lost tribe to this fate. Çeda didn't know how, or why, but that much was clear.

She also knew that her mother was one of them. *And so am I. I am my mother's daughter, and these are my people.*

The Kings carved the sign into Ahya's skin as a warning to others of the tribe who hoped to come for them. She stared at the tattoo, at the hidden symbols the asir had traced with the yellowed nail of his forefinger. They were plain as day now. How had she not noticed them before? She knelt and traced her finger lovingly over every line the asir had made, making it stand out even more. It reminded her so much of her mother that tears came unbidden. But as they slipped down her cheeks, she realized there was an undeniable feeling of release as well. She'd buried this for so long—her mother's death, her search for vengeance, her will to put an end to the cruelty of the Kings. To now share it, even in this one small way, this terrible, strange, unexpected way, made her feel as though she wasn't alone.

She'd been fighting on her own for so long but had been doing so blindly.

Did she have *allies* now? Did she have *kin?* The King of the asirim had started her on this new path. She'd been sheltered by Zaïde, a woman who hid the design of the asirim in this very tattoo. It was clear she was allied with the asirim in some way. But how? And what did she hope to do? There was no longer any doubt in Çeda's mind that she was Dardzada's contact in the House of Maidens, a thing Çeda must speak to her about soon, assuming she lived to see the sunrise.

Beneath the light of the twin moons, she saw these wretched creatures anew. No longer were they faceless things, separate from her. She was a part of them, and they were a part of her.

"What happened that night?" Çeda asked around the lump forming in her throat. "What happened on Beht Ihman?"

The King's eyes met Çeda's with deep emotion, as if the events of that night were playing through his mind even then. He opened his mouth to speak but his eyes teared and his throat convulsed. He levered his jaw open but shook his head violently, as if he dearly wished to rid himself of his memories if only he could speak them aloud. But nothing came out. He was compelled to silence, perhaps by the Kings, perhaps by the gods themselves.

He turned his head, then, to Çeda's right. He lowered in his stance, devolving into a feral beast once more. The others around him did the same, as one, turning in the same direction. Çeda looked and listened, but could detect nothing untoward in the dunes or the blooming fields, and yet the hairs rose on the back of her neck.

She watched the night carefully, until there came from the opposite direction the rhythmic hiss of footfalls against the sand. Someone was sprinting toward them.

"Go," said a voice in the night, barely loud enough to hear. "Go, my children."

The asirim scattered, all but the King and two other asir, including the one who had traced the designs in Çeda's tattoo. Out of the darkness came a tall woman bearing a staff.

"Saliah," Çeda whispered.

By all that was good, the desert witch had come.

Chapter 59

Ç EDA HAD NO TIME TO WONDER at Saliah's arrival, for as the tall woman approached, she whipped the head of her staff against the sand, sending it spraying up and into the night sky. As the sand drifted downward, glittering beneath the light of the moons, Sehid-Alaz and the two other asirim used their hands and feet to wipe away the signs they'd made in the sand. And then they, too, fled toward Sharakhai.

"Quickly!" Saliah hissed as she took Çeda by the arm. "Quickly now!"

She took Çeda to the wall of adichara. The adichara rose and twisted away, creating a path into the heart of the twisted trees. When they were five paces in, the branches moved back into place, coming to rest as if they'd never moved in the first place, except that the branches around Çeda were now well clear of her, and they twisted away if she came too close, lest the thorns prick her.

"*Shhhhh,*" Saliah whispered as she held her staff in both hands before her. Çeda wasn't sure if she was talking to Çeda or herself or to the adichara, but she knew enough to be quiet. She knew enough to be still.

They waited a long while, but that only heightened the

sense that there was something treacherous in the air. Saliah didn't move, nor speak, but Çeda could see her lips moving, as if she were whispering prayers.

At last there came a sound. A scraping, as of claw against stone. Forms darkened the way ahead. Çeda could see them dimly through the adichara, two creatures with massive withers and sawtooth fur and backs that sloped down toward their shortened hindquarters. They were followed by another, and another, then one more.

Black laughers. Bone crushers, like the ones that had chased her in the desert. They were easily as tall as Çeda at the shoulder. One of them opened its mouth wide, revealing long canines and shovel-shaped incisors.

They snuffed over the sand, especially around the spot where Çeda had been standing. In the air, however, Çeda could see the barest glint, the suspended remnants of the sand Saliah had struck into the sky.

One of the laughers sneezed, a thing that sounded more like a breathy grunt.

At this, the others let out a bestial call that sounded like the lowing of a bull, but more primal, somehow, as if they were calling to the earth itself. Çeda could feel it deep within her. It made her skin itch, made her stomach tighten and her mouth go dry. On and on it went. Çeda's hands moved toward her ears, but Saliah grabbed her wrist, warning her to remain exactly as she was.

One of the beasts swiveled ears the size of a man's hands back and forth. Then it swung its great head toward Çeda's position. It snuffed closer. The others turned and watched, perhaps unsure what their brother had heard or smelt. They neared, crowding around the place where Çeda and Saliah were hiding, until one of the adichara branches swung outward and waved before them.

The nearest of the black laughers retreated, whining as it went. The rest of the pack giggled, a pitiable and fearsome sound, and backed away as well, some bowing their heads.

Footsteps could be heard trudging across the sand, and Çeda felt Saliah's hand tighten on her wrist.

No longer was the witch whispering. She was deadly

silent now, as a smell like bitter, burnt myrrh filled the air,
and a masculine form appeared. He was tall. His legs bent
at strange angles, as if he were half-man, half-beast. His
skin was black as night, a void against the blanket of stars
on the horizon behind him, and on his head he wore a
crown of thorns. The very stone and sand around him
seemed to bend inward, as if his gravitas were too much for
the desert to bear.

Çeda's knees went weak. Her breath came in quick
gasps, her ribs and stomach tightening to the point of pain.
The little girl inside her wanted to weep, to cry out, but she
knew that doing so would mean her death.

For this was Goezhen himself. The god who'd created
many of the twisted creatures that filled the desert, these
bone crushers among them. He squatted down in the exact
place where Çeda had stood mere minutes ago. He ran his
hands over the sand where the symbol of the thirteenth
tribe had been. After gathering up a handful of that very
same sand, he allowed it to trickle between his fingers to
the desert floor.

He stood tall and looked over the adichara, his gaze
sweeping over Çeda's position. Çeda thought surely they'd
been found, that he would walk toward them and pluck
them from the twisted trees, but instead the god of fell
beasts turned away, toward Sharakhai. For a while, he considered the city. He looked hungry, somehow, bent as he
was, breath huffing in and out, arms spread at his sides as
if he wished to destroy something. Anything. Perhaps
Sharakhai itself.

The black laughers approached. One rubbed its head
along his hip. Another rubbed its shoulder along Goezhen's thigh. He ran his hands absently over their muscular
withers.

He said something to them, the sound of it low, like a
war drum pounding in the distance. She could not make
out his words, but a moment later, the bone crushers
laughed and were off, loping into the desert with long
strides, sand kicking up behind them. Goezhen followed,
his dark form quickly lost behind the dunes.

Then all was silence once more, all save the faint rattle

of the adichara branches, the thorns rubbing against one another.

Saliah released her grip on Çeda's hand. The adichara slowly unraveled behind them until they could walk to the other side, to fresh land. Like Çeda, Saliah surely felt the stone where they'd been standing had been trod upon enough this night.

Çeda opened her mouth to speak, but Saliah raised her hand. "Enough words have been spilled this night." She looked up, though Çeda was sure that Saliah was blind. The moons had continued their westward trek and were nearing the horizon. "The God of Thorns has heard us," Saliah said. "He does not yet know you, but he may if we don't take care." Çeda was about to speak, but Saliah spoke over her. "Utter not his name. Not when the moons are out. Speak of him only in the daylight, Ahya's daughter, and then only to those you trust most. The days are coming near when we must all act, but I think there is time yet."

"Time for what?"

"To prepare."

"But how?" Çeda asked.

Saliah touched the tip of her staff to Çeda's hand. She pressed it to the wound, which flared with pain. "It has already begun. You are an arrow, Çedamihn. A spear pointed at the heart of Sharakhai. And we will work together to unravel what the Kings have done in the name of their gods."

Çeda's thoughts were brought back to the stories of the gods chasing one of their own through the desert. Of Goezhen and Bakhi and Tulathan tearing down a temple built to honor their sister goddess. What Saliah had just done no desert witch could do. Not even one of godsblood, the old folk. There was only one explanation.

"You're—"

But Saliah clapped her hand over Çeda's mouth. "Do not say it!"

You're Nalamae. As sure as the desert winds blow, you are Nalamae. "Why?" Çeda asked. "Why can't I say your name?"

Her only answer was to take Çeda's hand and lead her along the sand to a lower place. "Come," she said. "Come, for it is time you see what the Kings have wrought."

Saliah turned toward Sharakhai. The moons were bright. The wind was cool. The goddess looked over the landscape. She lifted her hand and made a motion like the plucking of a harpstring. And in that moment, the wails of the asirim sounded in the distance. They came, nearer and nearer to the place where she and Saliah stood, and eventually Çeda saw them trudging over the dunes with bodies in tow.

A dozen of them came, four dragging bodies across the sand, leaving deep furrows in their passing. Furrows that would soon be lost to the wind. The nearest of the sacrifices was a woman. She woke groggily as she was being dragged by the arms toward the adichara.

"Tulathan protect me!" she cried. "Tulathan protect me!"

She was not trying to escape. Her words were a desperate attempt to bolster her spirits, to smother her fear. She was trying to be brave. Many taken by the asirim had prayed for the honor, but now that it had come she was having doubts. As she was dragged ever forward, she stared at Çeda.

"Peace be upon you," Çeda said, for she had no other words.

The woman didn't respond. She looked to the adichara again, then ripped her arms away and tried to run. The asir was on her in a moment, grabbing her legs. The woman scratched and clawed at the sand. The asir dragging her, a shriveled crone, paid her little mind. With no preamble whatsoever, no words whispered to the gods for this sacrifice, she picked the woman up and tossed her into the center of the thorns. The white blooms were still wide and staring at the twin moons, but the limbs of the adichara were much more active than they'd been earlier. Those nearest reached up and snatched the woman from the air as she screamed.

Her screams pitched higher as her body was torn limb from limb. Her blood showed a shining black against the bark of the twisted trees. Other bodies followed—one, two, three—each of them tossed to a different section of the field like meat to starving hounds. Thankfully none of the others awakened, but their blood spilled every bit as easily as the woman's.

By the gods above, they feed the trees. They take people from Sharakhai and feed them to the adichara.

One of the asirim stopped near Çeda, a man with long limbs and lost eyes. He bowed his head to her, a thing that made Çeda wholly uncomfortable. It struck her then why he had done so, what had changed: They had *accepted* her.

The mere thought of accepting them in return, thereby accepting what happened each Beht Zha'ir, sickened her, but she didn't know what else to do. She bowed her head in return, and the asir moved on.

One by one, the asirim trudged into the adichara, and one by one, the trees accepted them. They folded their thorny boughs around those lost souls and pulled them deep into the sand until they were lost from sight.

When they were all gone, when the desert was peaceful once more, the adichara began to sway gently. A beetle lifted into the air, wandering aimlessly over the twisted trees. It was horrifically ordinary. In another few hours, the sun would rise, and the blooming fields would look no different than they did every other night. Yet they hid so much, hid their secrets like thieves spreading their arms over piles of stolen gold.

Çeda and Saliah were alone once more. No dark creatures. No asirim. No screaming sacrifices.

Çeda felt as though she'd lived an entire life this night, and in a way she had. At the very least she had been reborn, and a new world opened up to her, all because of her mother.

It has already begun, Saliah had said. *You are an arrow, a spear pointed at the heart of Sharakhai.*

"The King," Çeda said, remembering her mission this night, remembering Emre and all that he and the Moonless Host were set to do. "I must find his palace."

Saliah merely nodded and walked carefully, one hand stretched before her as if she expected the heat from a fire. She began leading Çeda southwest.

"Wait!" Çeda went to the nearest of the adichara,

pulling her ebon blade as she went. Four quick swipes of
the blade and four blooms were dropped easily down to
her. She stuffed them inside her dress and moved back to
Saliah's side, and together, they moved beyond the blooming fields and over open sand.

Çeda knew where they were headed well before they
reached it: to the tree where Külaşan had been drawn
down into the sands. She could see it—a dark smudge on
the horizon—but Saliah didn't head straight for it. She
seemed to find something that pleased her and pulled
Çeda by the arm, setting her in place, just so.

The sand beneath Çeda began to shift. It parted, a soft
hissing accompanying the movement, swallowing Çeda's
feet, then her shins, then her thighs. Saliah backed away
and left Çeda standing there, slipping into the sand, alone.
"Wait, can you not come?"

Saliah shook her head. "The Kings are well protected
by the desert gods. But you are one of their own. You, they
cannot see, not easily, in any case."

"Will I see you again?" Çeda asked.

"There will come a day."

"When?"

"Soon." It was one of the loneliest feelings Çeda could
ever remember, knowing the goddess was about to leave
her. "Now trust to the shifting sands."

Çeda continued to sink, and all too soon she had been
swallowed to her waist, then chest and arms, then shoulders. She was towed deeper and deeper, until at last, with
one final breath of the cool night air, she was pulled beneath the surface of the sand.

Despite herself, despite knowing Saliah was doing this
to help her, she fought to free herself from the darkness.
The baked smell. The unyielding tightness of the earth. It
was too much.

She was desperate to breathe, desperate to scream. On
and on it went, the pressure, the scraping, as her lungs
burned, as her skin was scraped raw, until finally she was
free but falling into darkness.

She fell onto a stone floor, one knee cracking painfully
against it, though it was eased by the leather sewn into her

fighting dress. She could see nothing down here. Nothing at all. She rose unsteadily, taking long deep breaths of the chill air. She felt around for a wall, and found it a moment later. She walked the other way and found another wall. A passageway, then. But which way to go?

The question was answered moments later by the sounds of shouting. And then the ring of steel and cries of rage and pain.

And among them, dear gods, she could hear Emre.

Chapter 60

MARCHING AHEAD OF EMRE were Macide and Hamid and Darius. Behind him came a dozen more men and women—soldiers of the Al'Afwa Khadar, the Moonless Host, all of them jogging in order to reach their destination in time. They were all wearing clothes and boots the color of wet earth. Turbans and veils covered their faces to ward against the wind but also to hide their identities.

So far all had gone well. They'd left Sharakhai shortly after sunset and headed northwest, along the same streambed he and Çeda had followed so long ago. Eventually they slowed as they approached the blooming fields. Emre watched carefully for signs of horses or movement along the tops of the dunes or the rocky ridges. He even paid careful attention to the scent on the wind, anything at all that might give him some warning of where Çeda and the Blade Maidens would be.

Macide had agreed to approach any conflict with care should the Maidens discover them, but he gave no guarantees that Çeda wouldn't be harmed. In battle, he'd said, promises are as much use as jewels to a dying man.

They went beyond the blooming fields for a

quarter-league, and then Macide began walking carefully along the right side of the streambed. He checked several large, glinting rocks packed deeply into the earth. He ducked low, searching around them, though for what, Emre couldn't guess.

But when Macide crouched and felt along the base of one particular rock, he then stood and motioned for everyone to come near. "On your bellies." He lay down and slid along the dry earth, and soon he was swallowed by the shallow bank, lost to a gap Emre hadn't realized was there.

Hamid went next, and then it was Emre's turn. He lay flat and sidled into the gap, which was hardly wider than he was. He barely managed to make it into this strange passageway, this natural tunnel into the earth. Embedded in the walls and roof and floor of the passage were sharp crystals. They tore at his hands and knees and, when he wasn't careful, the back of his head. He heard little more than his own breathing, and the breathing of the others, until finally the passage widened, and he heard the trickle of water in the distance.

After a time he was able to rise to a crouch, and then to a full stand. Ahead, Hamid lit three torches he'd brought and handed one to Macide and another to Darius. Golden light played against a cavern whose every surface was covered in clear white crystals. It was as if he were trapped inside a gemstone, like something out of the tales of the vengeful ehrekh.

Macide led them along the sloping cavern in the general direction of the blooming fields. The cavern widened, and then narrowed, then widened again. Several times they were forced to slip sidewise through another gap, or lie on their stomachs, the same as they had done when entering this place. Twice Macide became confused. He would walk around the cavern, examining several of the possible passageways out, eventually choosing one. Once, he backtracked through several caverns before choosing another path. But after a time they came to a tunnel that was formed of solid rock, not crystal. The tunnel widened, became more uniform. Clearly it had been carved by the hands of man. Eventually they reached a passage that ran across theirs.

They stopped at this intersection, and Macide turned to them all and drew one of his two shamshirs. "This is the palace of Külaşan," he said quietly. "We cannot know if there are Maidens here, or Silver Spears, so be careful. Be quiet. Call upon your brothers and sisters if needed."

They broke into three groups from there. Emre went with Hamid and Darius and two others along the left fork. There was a stout man twice Emre's age named Gihran. The other was a woman called Sahbel. They followed the passage and found an arched entryway that opened up on their right. Hamid led the way with one of the torches. The room was small, five paces across, and within it sat a granite sarcophagus with a name carved into its heavy lid. Iyesa Külaşan'ava al Masal.

A daughter, perhaps, or granddaughter, or some other distant relation. The Wandering King had lived for over four centuries, after all.

Around the room were several marble busts and one full-body statue. They were all of the same woman, though at different times in her life. She had been a handsome woman with full lips and a regal brow, and judging from one of the busts that showed her as aged, she had lived a long, long while. There were other adornments in the room as well. A painting of an eagle in flight. A carved ivory horse. A golden necklace with a stunning emerald pendant around the neck of the statue. This last Hamid slipped over the bust's head and into his shirt.

"I don't imagine she'll miss it," he said to Emre as he headed out of the room and along the passageway.

They came across several similar rooms—tombs, in essence, set aside for the Wandering King's loved ones. Most subsumed his name within their own: Külaşan'ava. But there were other names as well. Jalil'ava, Muhsin'ava, Latif'ala. His granddaughters and grandsons, then, or even more distant relations. Külaşan had lived for more than four hundred years. It made sense that his family in Sharakhai was vast.

Eventually they came to a tomb that had no adornments whatsoever. A lone sarcophagus was the only thing occupying the cold, dark space. Unlike the other sarcophagi, however, it was carved with ornate symbols on its lid.

"Seals," Emre said to the cold, echoing darkness. "To keep people out, I suppose."

"No," Hamid replied confidently, "to keep something in." He stepped out into the passage and whistled three times. A few moments later, Emre heard softer whistles answering him. He whistled twice more, perhaps to draw the others to them, now that they'd found what they'd come for.

This was it, then. This was Hamzakiir's tomb.

Emre examined the sarcophagus more carefully. Hamzakiir's name was not written on it. Not that he could tell, anyway. He'd never been good with the old script, but these looked like symbols of power, not a man's name.

He ran his hands across the top of it as Hamid came strolling back in. "All this to speak with a dead man."

Hamid's sleepy eyes rested on him, a knowing smile on his lips.

Emre didn't understand the joke, but then he thought back to what Hamid had said a moment ago. The seals weren't meant to keep something out. They were meant to keep something *in*. To keep *Hamzakiir* in.

By the gods who watch above, they hadn't come merely to speak to Hamzakiir. They'd come to *free* him.

The others filed into the room, Macide leading the way.

Emre took out his iron pry bar, as did Macide and Gihran and Hamid, and then they used them on the lid of the sarcophagus, trying to lever it off.

From outside the room, Emre heard a sharp hiss. Darius rushed in moments later. "Someone's coming," he said.

Macide, working with the others, gave a fierce grunt as the lid shifted. "How many?"

"Not sure yet. A dozen. Maybe more."

"Take six," he said to Darius. "Set the oil at the intersection, and lay the traps beyond it. Light the oil when they come near. Slow them down. Fight them if they cross, but otherwise conserve your strength."

Darius nodded and was gone, taking six of the others with him, leaving only four behind: Macide, Hamid, Emre, and Gihran.

At last they managed to shift the lid off the sarcophagus just enough to see the white shroud covering the form within. Macide pulled the shroud back to reveal a man with horribly tightened skin. He looked as though he'd been lying down here for a thousand years, but the gods had refused to let him rot. His cheeks were so drawn, Emre could make out where jawbone ended and teeth began. His eyes were sunken, looking like grapes waiting to be plucked.

As a shout came from somewhere in the distance, Macide took the blood-red breathstone from within his thawb and placed it against Hamzakiir's emaciated mouth, which was opened slightly, but not wide enough to slip the stone in. "Pry his mouth open," he said to Emre.

Emre reached in and gripped this ancient man's teeth in an attempt at prying his jaw wider.

From the hallway came the sounds of marching at the double, accompanied by the chink of mail, the clatter of shields. It sounded like dozens of Silver Spears were headed toward them. A whooshing sound came from the passageway, and the flicker of flames. Shouts came moments later, then screams of pain.

"Quickly now," Macide said to Emre, nodding for him to try harder.

Emre did, but the man's jaw was slow in moving. He was afraid to tear the tissue and muscle lest he be unable to talk, rendering the stone and its magic useless. Macide pressed the blood-red stone against the corpse's teeth, waiting as Emre struggled. Finally, with a *cluck,* the stone slipped into Hamzakiir's mouth.

And nothing happened.

The sound of steel against steel broke out somewhere down the hall. Men screamed, one calling the name of Külaşan shortly before releasing a cry of anguish that was cut short by a crunching sound. But Hamzakiir remained lifeless.

Emre had released the jaw, but opened it again, which was easier this time, and stuffed the stone further down Hamzakiir's throat.

The throat convulsed, and Macide reached into the sarcophagus and stroked repeatedly under the man's chin. Hamzakiir swallowed again and again, but the stone seemed to be caught there.

"Get him up!" Macide said, beginning to lift him from the sarcophagus. Emre and Hamid moved to help, while Gihran drew the sword from his belt and stood outside the door, ready to protect them should any of the Silver Spears break through. No sooner had he reached the doorway, however, and turned left toward the sound than the spiked head of a morning star crashed into the back of his skull. He crumpled to the stones along the floor, the crown of his head a ruined, reddened mess.

A moment later, a man Emre had never seen before filled the doorway. He was tall and impressive, with a broad chest and a beard and mustache that hung down his chest. He wore a set of polished mail adorned with the sign of a spread-tailed peacock. The mail draped from his conical helm made a *shink* sound as he turned his head to regard Macide and Hamid and Emre.

"You *dare*," King Külaşan said in a deep, scratchy voice as he stepped into the room. "You *dare* tread these halls!"

"Take him," Macide said, leaving Hamzakiir to Hamid and Emre while pulling his twin shamshirs and moving to meet Külaşan.

The two of them clashed. Macide launched a ferocious combination of sword strikes. Külaşan blocked every blow, either with his morning star, Gravemaker, or with a black buckler inlaid with golden crescent moons. Macide's onslaught was so vicious Külaşan was forced back, into the passageway, but only until the attack had played itself out. After blocking two more swings, the King used his morning star from on high, coming at Macide over and over, while keeping his shield at the ready. He pressed Macide into the tomb once more and toward the far corner. "Did you think you could steal into my home and take my son from me?"

Emre and Hamid had managed to lift Hamzakiir out of the sarcophagus. Together they cradled him, for his entire body was stiff. The only evidence that he was alive was his head, twisting from side to side but only marginally, as if it were strapped to a board.

Among the sounds of the battle, Emre heard a wheezing, hardly more than a whisper. Hamzakiir struggled to lift his head. He was trying to speak.

Emre looked at Hamid, but Hamid merely shrugged. "What is it?" Emre asked, leaning his head down to listen. "Tell me!"

He whispered something, but Emre couldn't make it out.

"Louder!"

And then a single word came out in one long rasp, "*Blll-loooooodddd*," making Emre's skin go cold.

"Out," Hamid said. "Get him out of here!"

They began moving toward the passageway, even as Hamzakiir continued to wheeze for blood. But the moment they approached the entryway, Külaşan kicked Macide in the chest. As Macide fell, the King turned and charged Hamid and Emre. With a grunt, Hamid shoved Emre into the hallway, drawing his shamshir and laying his hand across the flat of the blade to block the blow from Külaşan's fearsome morning star.

"*Blood . . .*" Hamzakiir rasped again. "*I need blood.*"

Emre began pulling him to his feet. "We'll get you out," Emre said, "and then we'll find you blood."

To Emre's right, flames were licking up the intersection where Darius had set the trap for the Silver Spears. The rest of Macide's men were engaged with more than a dozen Silver Spears, and more were waiting beyond the flames.

In the tomb, Hamid was momentarily stunned by a backhanded blow from Külaşan's shield. With that one small opening, the King immediately brought Gravemaker down onto Hamid's shoulder, and he crumpled with a cry of pain, his sword clattering to the ground. Macide engaged Külaşan once more, but the King was too fast, blocking blows from Macide's lithe swords with his heavy morning star.

Hamzakiir coughed weakly. "We will never leave this place," he rasped, "unless you give me your blood."

"How?"

In answer, he reached out, took Emre's wrist in his quivering, twig-like hands.

Emre grimaced as, around him, the battle raged on. Things could not last much longer. Macide was looking weak. The men were becoming overpowered, and the flames blocking the advance of the Silver Spears were beginning to fade. Emre looked down at Hamzakiir, who quivered as he stared up into Emre's eyes, looking as though he might fall dead at any moment.

What is a bit of blood for this cause when so much is being shed around me?

He held his arm out, and Hamzakiir wasted no time. He pressed his nail into Emre's arm while Emre gritted his teeth against the hot pain. As Hamzakiir drew Emre's wrist to his mouth and drank, Emre felt himself going instantly chill, from cheeks to fingers to ears to feet. He shivered, felt himself slowly but surely being drained away. He cried out, partly from the pain but more so from the fear of losing himself to Hamzakiir's needs.

How long they stayed like that, Emre couldn't say. Hamzakiir's thirst seemed endless.

The world began to lose focus. The crash of battle and the cries of anguish were fading, becoming more distant as a keen ringing sound replaced them. The flickering light from the burning lamp oil dimmed. His sense of who he was and *where* he was began to distort. It felt as though he were lying on a raft, drifting along the Haddah with Çeda at his side. They'd done that once, when they were younger. Emre had saved coin for weeks to do it, and when the rains had finally come, he'd asked her, and they'd drifted downriver for a day, eating and laughing and admiring the desert, and had then been towed back by one of the long Qaimiri rowing barges headed for the Amber City to trade.

Part of him knew that he wasn't on a river. He was in the catacombs of a lost king, waiting to die. Hamzakiir wouldn't stop until he was dead. He realized that now, and even if he survived the bloodletting, Macide was about to fall. Emre could see it in his slowed movements. He was barely able to fend off Külaşan's attacks.

Suddenly, from his left, something quick and lithe flashed across his vision—a woman holding an ebon blade.

Külaşan blocked her initial swing, but she bulled into him, and sent him reeling. Then she threw something at him. A flower. An adichara bloom. He batted it away with his shield. The bloom flew against the far wall, but a diaphanous, golden-white powder exploded in its wake, and immediately he began to cough—long, wracking coughs that doubled him over.

Hamzakiir released his hold on Emre's wrist and laughed. A rolling, grumbling thing that sounded as though it came not from a man but from a dying god in a dark cave at the lonely edges of the world. Blood slicked his teeth. Emre's blood. It slicked his mouth, as well. Dribbled over his chin. Then he made his way to his feet on shaking limbs, still laughing.

He stared around the room, eyes burning with intense fury, his laugh slowly dying away. As it did, a rumbling filled the air. A groaning of the earth. An awakening of things long forgotten. Dust sifted down from the ceiling. Cracks rent the stone, and chips of it began to fall away.

Ahead, Külaşan, still coughing, launched a series of furious attacks at Macide and the Blade Maiden, who, Emre realized, must be Çeda. The soldiers of the Moonless Host were forced to retreat or be crushed by Gravemaker. The moment they gave ground, he sent one last swipe their way and rushed from the room, heading back the way he'd come.

Emre was still fiercely cold. His arms and legs shook every bit as violently as Hamzakiir's had done moments ago, but he managed to get to his feet by pushing himself up against the rumbling wall.

Çeda started to run from the tomb but stopped when she saw Emre. She glanced at him, at how badly he was shaking, all but her eyes hidden by her black veil. "Get out," she said. "There'll be more Silver Spears coming, and the Maidens have surely been summoned." Then she turned and chased Külaşan.

Macide came from the tomb, Hamid's arm over his shoulder. Hamid seemed to be moving well enough, but his left arm hung limply, and his shoulder was a bloody mess. Macide whistled twice, and his soldiers—the five still standing—beat an orderly retreat down the hall, away from the fire and the Silver Spears.

The rumbling continued. Emre darted into the tomb to grab the torch and led the way down the dark passageway, shivering all the while. They came soon to an intersection. Three tunnels led away from this place and Emre could hear the King's coughing up ahead. He could hear Çeda's rapid footsteps as well. He was ready to head down that hallway, but just then the groaning of the earth intensified. As Emre and the others retreated, rock and rubble fell, crashing down with a sound like the dying of the world. It sent dust everywhere, making the torch gutter, though thankfully their light wasn't extinguished entirely.

Coughing from the cloud of dust, Emre held the torch high to see what state the hallway was in. The rockfall had blocked much of the intersection, though a small gap remained—perhaps enough for a man to slip through. It led only to the leftmost passage, however, not the one Çeda had taken.

Emre crawled through on his belly with the torch, hoping he'd find a gap, even a small hole he could widen, some way to reach Çeda and help her, but there was nothing. The way had been completely blocked.

"Leave her," Macide said, tugging on his sleeve.

Emre knew Macide was right. He knew he couldn't help Çeda, but it burned at him. They'd come all this way, and still Çeda had been there for him. She'd saved him, as she'd done so many times before. He was desperate to even the scales, but there was nothing for it now. He couldn't reach her. So he nodded to Macide and began helping the others through the gap in the rubble. When all the men were through, Darius threw a clay pot down against the stones, coating the way with lamp oil. Emre put the torch to it, and lit the rubble aflame.

It wouldn't last long—the Spears and perhaps the Maidens would be on their trail again soon. But it would block any pursuit for a time.

So on they ran, on toward the crystal caves. On to the desert, and safety.

Chapter 61

RAMAHD WAITED ON A SHALLOW RIDGE, crouching low to the ground with Dana'il at his left and Meryam to his right. Nine of his men waited in a line behind them—Corum and Quezada and Rafiro and the rest. They knelt with bows at the ready, spears on the ground at their sides. They'd been waiting hours beneath the twin moons for Meryam to give them some sign as to what was happening inside Külaşan's hidden palace.

When they'd first arrived, Meryam had stopped them and pointed to a large stone on the other side of the dry streambed. "They entered there," she'd said, and knelt on the ground. She hadn't moved since, remaining in that same position, kneeling on the rocky soil, eyes half-lidded, as the night wheeled slowly by.

"We should scout the cavern," Ramahd had said after hours of waiting.

"We wait," Meryam had replied simply.

"They might leave from a different place altogether."

"Would you rather fight them in cramped quarters or take them unawares from a distance?"

"That isn't the point. I'm worried we've lost them, Meryam."

"I'm not," was all she said, and she refused to say more.

Rhia set, and Tulathan crept ever closer to the western horizon. When the eastern sky began to brighten, Ramahd leaned closer to Meryam. "The sun is set to rise, sister."

But Meryam wouldn't respond. She'd stopped rocking. In fact, she'd gone deathly still.

"Meryam?"

Her jaw was set grimly, her eyes now staring intently at the streambed, not directly to the cavern entrance, but beyond. Ramahd suspected she was looking deeper into the earth, into Külaşan's palace.

"What's wrong?" Dana'il asked him.

"I don't know, but be ready."

Tulathan set, darkening the western sky, but the east continued to brighten. The muscles along Meryam's neck tightened, pulling her lips back in a rictus grin. Her eyes were wide, almost fearful. Or was that anticipation he saw?

Ramahd was just about to call for his men to follow him into the cavern when Meryam's hand snapped out and grabbed his. She held it so tightly it pained him, especially where her nails dug into his skin.

"What's happened?" he asked Meryam.

But Dana'il interrupted them. "They're coming!"

Ramahd pried Meryam's fingers from his wrist and held her hand tightly, shook it fiercely when she didn't respond. "Meryam, what's happened?"

"There is . . ." Meryam's voice trailed off.

Dana'il waved to the men, made sure they were prepared for anything that came.

Ahead, Ramahd could see dark movement near the stone. They were coming from the cavern, a group of men and women warriors scuttling like crabs and coming to a stand as more followed them.

"Meryam, *what?* There is *what?*"

"They've found him. They've raised him from his tomb."

He knew she meant Hamzakiir. "He's dead, Meryam." Meryam tried rising to her feet, but Ramahd pulled her back down. "You told me he was dead."

"I never said that, Ramahd."

"Fucking gods, Meryam, you bloody well never said he was alive, either!"

Before Meryam could reply, a voice called from the stream bed. "Stay where you are! Put not one hand upon your weapons, and you may leave this place unharmed."

Ramahd's skin went cold as the desert wind picked up. It was Macide. He was calling to them, even as more of his people crept out of the caverns.

"Well?" Meryam said. She had a baleful look in her eyes. "He's right there, Ramahd."

She was goading him. She knew something he didn't, but just then he didn't care. "Ready," he called to his men. They nodded grimly as the wind began to blow more fiercely.

Meryam looked like a jungle cat, nostrils flaring, her face filled with ill intent and untamed exhilaration. If he didn't know better, he might say she was eager for this to commence, as if battle were some long lost friend she was keen to embrace once more.

"Now!" Ramahd shouted.

His men all stood, Meryam with them. As she spread her arms wide and the wind rose even higher, Ramahd drew the string of his bow back to his ear.

The wind howled. The sand bit. He loosed his arrow, which flew wide of Macide but struck one of the other men deep in the neck. Other arrows flew, but they were buffeted by the wind and careened wide or short or over their mark. As Ramahd drew another arrow, his thoughts went immediately to Emre, Çeda's love. He might have just killed him, although truly, he had no idea who his arrow had struck. Other than Macide himself—a man he would never fail to recognize—the others were too distant to make out, the morning light too dim.

In the moments it took for him and his men to launch another volley of arrows, the wind had grown stronger. The gale swallowed their arrows, sending them this way or that, into the sand. Whether they struck true he could no longer tell. The air was too thick. He could barely see the dark outlines of Macide and his men, much less an arrow speeding through this sea of swirling sand.

The wind began to play tricks on his eyes. He swore he saw the sand rise up around one of Macide's men, a thin man. Frail. The sand seemed to devour him, his form crumbling as if he were made of nothing more than desert dust.

"Prepare yourselves," Meryam called.

Well behind Ramahd, the sand swirled like a demon, and then resolved into the form of that same thin man. He wore ancient red robes with thread-of-gold embroidery. There were blood stains around his lips, and he was frail as a boneyard shambler.

But his eyes . . . They were wild and mad with a fervent inner spirit that chilled Ramahd to his very core. This was Hamzakiir, reborn, resurrected.

Fear driving him, Ramahd nocked an arrow, lifted it toward this newcomer, and loosed it. It sped straight for Hamzakiir, but before it could strike, a swirl of flame lifted with the sand and caught the arrow. The arrow curled over Hamzakiir, catching fire and leaving a trail of flame that was lost in the haze of the wind. Ramahd's men fired more arrows, and all of them flew wide or well beyond Hamzakiir, trailing intense orange flames as they went.

Then three bolts of fire shot from Hamzakiir's raised palms. One struck Dana'il, another Quezada—

Something punched Ramahd in the chest.

Flame exploded in a fan shape before him. He felt a searing burn and was suddenly flying backward through the air. He lost all sense of direction until he fell hard against the ground, stone gouging his back and hips as his momentum carried him into the sand. A keen ringing drowned out all other sound, as the smell of burnt hair, or burnt skin—he didn't want to think about which—filled his nostrils.

He groaned and managed to raise his head, to look dazedly at the scene unfolding before him. Although Hamzakiir was no longer focused on Ramahd's men, they were in a shambles, several fallen from bolts of flame, others scrambling for cover behind a nearby stand of stones. The blood mage was loosing bolts against Meryam now, but she stood her ground, hands raised, warding off the

incoming bolts one by one, up into the sky or down toward
the ground where it burst in a fiery explosion of sand
and stone.

She took a step toward Hamzakiir. Then another. He
was so emaciated Ramahd had no idea how he still stood,
but he somehow remained upright as he launched ever
more bolts of flame toward Meryam. Any one of them, if
they'd struck, would have dropped her, killing or at the
very least incapacitating her. But Ramahd had never seen
her look so fierce. Her eyes lit with rage and a sickening
sort of glee. This was what she'd been hoping for, not to
catch Macide, but to face Hamzakiir.

Hamzakiir gathered a massive ball of flame between his
hands. It grew and grew as Meryam sprinted toward him,
closing the distance.

"Meryam!" Ramahd called. "No!"

But Meryam didn't listen. She ran straight for her
enemy.

Then Hamzakiir loosed his ball of flame, and it streaked
toward Meryam.

She spun, hair flaring, the skirt of her dark dress spinning like a wheel. She ducked to one side, her leading arm
lifting and warding the fire away, her trailing palm followed, driving it wide of her path with a hammer blow.

As the flame burned an ochre path across his field of
vision, Meryam continued her mad dash, her arms held
chest-high before her, and as she neared Hamzakiir, a ball
of blue flame formed between her palms. It intensified so
quickly it tinged the landscape and the sand-laden air a
bright azure blue.

She released the flame, and it shot forth, striking
Hamzakiir in the chest. He had raised his hands in a warding gesture, perhaps trying to deflect the attack as Meryam
had, but if that were so, he was wholly ineffectual. The ball
of flame struck, a blue diamond bursting over the desert,
sending him flying backward.

Ramahd made his way shakily to his feet, gritting his
teeth against the burning pain along his chest and arms.
The ringing in his ears was beginning to subside, and he
could hear the wind once more, the moaning and

clench-jawed grunts of his men. As he staggered toward
Meryam, he surveyed the damage, his ears still ringing.
Alamante and Corum were dead. Dana'il was unconscious,
his left shoulder and arm burned horribly. Others were con-
scious, but burned and shaken, including Ramahd.

"Drag them behind these stones," Ramahd said to
Quezada and Rafiro. "Tend to them as you can."

As they moved to obey, Ramahd reached Meryam's
side. Hamzakiir was unconscious. His red robes seemed
untouched by flame, but his skin was blackened along his
neck, hands, and wrists. Ramahd wondered how bad it
might be beneath his clothes, as Meryam knelt and began
removing the rings and bracelets from Hamzakiir's hands.
Her own hands were shaking.

"We've lost him," Ramahd said.

"Lost who?" she replied.

"Macide."

When she finished with the rings and bracelets, she
reached for the opaline necklace around his throat, and
began rummaging through the pockets of his robes.

"Meryam, we've lost Macide."

She stuffed all that she'd taken into a bag at her belt.
Only then did she stand and face Ramahd. "Do you really
think Macide has been my only goal these past years?"

"His death has *always* been our goal. Our *only* goal."

"No, it has been *your* only goal. There are more who
must pay. More who were there that day. And others still
who helped Macide, who supplied him with ships, water,
weapons, and food. Those who call themselves his allies."

"I don't care about the entire Host, Meryam."

"I do." She stared intently into his eyes. "They will one
day pay for what they've done, Ramahd Amansir. All of
them. This I swear before my gods and countrymen." With
that she spun and began walking toward the skiff they'd
anchored in a clutch of small scrub trees in the distance,
but Ramahd grabbed her arm and spun her around. "Unhand me!" she shouted, her free hand raised, as if in that
moment she considered him little different than Hamzakiir.

But Ramahd stood his ground. "We cannot chase the
entire Moonless Host, Meryam."

"Ah, but we can, Ramahd." She ripped her arm away and began walking back toward the skiff. "We can, and we will."

The wind was still strong, driving sand across the landscape. As her form was nearly swallowed by the sandstorm, Ramahd turned back toward his men. Dana'il stood there, cradling his left arm, grimacing as he looked from Meryam's dwindling form to Ramahd. "Shall we search for him, my Lord?" He meant Macide.

"No," Ramahd replied. The burn in his chest was coming on stronger now. He was fairly sure the blast had cracked a rib or two. "They're gone, and we're in no shape to engage in any case."

With grimaces and grunts that mirrored one another's, they each took one of Hamzakiir's arms and, following in Meryam's wake, began dragging him toward the skiff. Meryam was little more than a small dark smudge ahead. Dana'il nodded meaningfully toward her. "What will we do now?"

"We'll let Meryam play her game," Ramahd said, "and wait for another chance at Macide. She may wish to destroy the entire Host in revenge for Yasmine and Rehann. She may even think she can do it. But she needs us more than she thinks she does. Once we have Macide, we'll go home, where we belong."

"And if she leads us into the maw of the beast first?"

Ramahd smiled, little better than a sneer, he was sure. "Then we'll fight our way out, as we always have."

Dana'il nodded, but his eyes looked troubled as they walked, dragging the body of Hamzakiir behind them. Ramahd didn't want to show it, but he was every bit as troubled as Dana'il.

Meryam might not be a problem that needed solving today, but one day soon, she would be.

Chapter 62

WHILE SHE STILL HAD LIGHT, Çeda sprinted along the dark passage, chasing Külaşan. The petals she'd consumed still drove her, but their effects had started to wane, and soon she would crash.

Even with the vigor of the petals, even debilitated as Külaşan was from coughing, he was fast as a desert hare, too fast for her to keep up with, especially once the light from the fire faded behind her. The darkness forced her to move carefully, which in turn forced her to trust her heightened senses to pick up Külaşan's trail whenever she came to intersections or forks in the catacombs. The adichara bloom she held in her left hand glowed ever so softly, but it wasn't enough to see by and might give her away were the King lying in wait somewhere ahead, so she hid it behind her back as she treaded forward.

She wished she hadn't had to leave Emre behind—she would have seen them to safety if she could have—but this chance was too rare. She desperately hoped he had escaped the cave-in she'd heard crashing down, but there was nothing she could do about it now. She simply had to trust to Nalamae that he was safe.

Shortly after hearing the distant boom of a door being

slammed shut, and the clatter of something she couldn't identify, she tripped over a set of winding stairs leading up. River's Daughter held ready in her right hand, the adichara bloom in her left, she took the stairs, moving carefully but with some speed lest she lose the Wandering King completely. Light shone down from above, illuminating the curving stairwell in golden light. She watched carefully for anyone lying in wait, but she heard no one, saw no one, and eventually came to a massive foyer with bright mosaics on the ceiling and inlaid marble on the floors. Priceless statues, jewel-encrusted swords, and golden shields stood on pedestals all around the space.

Çeda had no idea how many guardsmen or Blade Maidens might be stationed here on a normal night, but surely most of them would have been dispatched to the catacombs to deal with the Moonless Host. Others would have been sent to Sharakhai to summon help from the Maidens or the Silver Spears, or perhaps there was another way for Külaşan to call for help. Whatever the case, Çeda knew she had little time.

Two wide hallways ran from the foyer, one to her right and one to her left. A set of grand stairs curved up to a pair of doors beneath a grand archway. Another pair of doors were positioned below the stairs, straight ahead.

Where have you gone, my King?

Her hands shook. Her heart pounded, and not simply from the chase. She was as excited and nervous and frightened as she'd ever been. She felt her mother's gaze upon her as she walked over the carpet, looking for any sign of where Külaşan might have gone.

She found nothing, no definitive clue. There were marks—impressions of feet upon the carpeted stairs—but they might have been made an hour ago, or a day, or a week. She began to worry that she'd lost him before the chase had truly begun, and if that were true, the chances that he would expose her was nearly certain. He may not know her identity yet, but when he'd had a chance to think about it, to confer with the other Kings and the Maidens, he would surely piece it together.

But then she heard the distant sound of coughing. It

came from the doors above her, the ones engraved with Külaşan's seal: a peacock in full display. She took the stairs quickly and silently. When she made it to the top, she tried the doors and found them barred from the inside. She sheathed her sword, reached into a pouch at her belt, and retrieved a hook and a length of braided metal with teeth along both sides, a ring saw. After slipping the saw around the stout bar on the far side of the doors and hooking the lower ring, she looped her fingers through the rings and began sawing back and forth. After several minutes of feverish sawing, the door finally gave way.

She drew her ebon blade, her heart thundering in her chest. The door opened soundlessly at her touch, and she stepped inside, closing the door behind her and taking in the stairs that led to a cavernous, lantern-lit room above.

She pulled out one of her three remaining adichara blooms and swung it around fiercely. The telltale signs of the glowing pollen swirled about, filling the space and billowing up through the stairwell. She slapped the flower against the gilt door handles, and the door itself, then the wooden bar she'd sawn through. The bloom now spent of its pollen, she tossed it at the foot of the door and crept up another set of stairs beyond.

She heard coughing somewhere in the distance—not a dry cough, but wet, like a man living his final days. She'd heard such many times in the byways of Roseridge and the Shallows and the Knot, even among the bazaar stalls from time to time. Consumption, the physics called it, but in this case the cause was something entirely different. It wasn't a wickedness of soul, but pollen floating through the air, a weakness this King had lived with for four hundred years.

As she neared the top of the stairs, she wondered whether it had started mildly and over the centuries become worse, or if it had always been this bad.

Always, if the gods are just.

When she reached the top of the stairs, she took in the vast interior, the grand dome high above her.

"What little dove has come?" came a rough voice that echoed through the cavernous chamber. There were many dark corners in the room, spaces hidden by towering potted palms and desert ferns, spaces hidden by freestanding tapestries and vast silk couches and rosewood display cases holding battle-ready swords, long spears, jade vases, and bronze censers.

She listened carefully, turning slowly to take in the entirety of the room, hoping to spot some telltale sign of the King. She pulled out another of the blooms and shook it back and forth, spraying the pollen in a circle, praying it would be enough to keep the King at bay, praying it would weaken him further.

Again the coughing came, though it seemed to move about, flitting around the room like a hummingbird, never in one place overly long.

"Have you come to help me, little dove, while Kings and Maidens abide in Tauriyat?"

Still the voice moved about. She would need to move among the shadows if she hoped to find him. She pulled another bloom from her dress and stepped around a tall stand of armor—a spiked helm with ringmail hauberk and a rune-laden spear.

"The adichara is no friend to me, 'tis true," Külaşan intoned, "but do you think that these fresh blooms will be worse than those that ring this cursed city?"

She finished spreading the pollen and threw the flower to one side, then brought out the last and sent its dust into the air as she had the others. She wished she had more now; the room was large, and she never dreamed she would need so many.

Another coughing fit came, this one much longer, much wetter, than the last. He sounded so close Çeda whirled, striking out with her blade in the hopes of catching the King, but her blade caught only empty air.

"You are new to the House of Maidens. You were brought to us by Zaïde, blessed by Yusam, embraced by Husamettín. But Sümeya had the right of it, did she not? She saw through you."

Out of adichara blooms, Çeda was left feeling utterly alone. She had no idea if the pollen was affecting him or not, and she had no idea how she would find Külaşan.

But she realized there *was* something within her heart:

The adichara in the desert. She felt them after taking the petals of her chosen bloom, and she felt them now, not unlike the sun upon her skin, or the scent of death in the desert—always near to hand, however faint it may be. She had felt the asirim as well, not individually, but as one. A whole. And now, here in the Wandering King's palace, she could feel *him*, a thing apart from the adichara, apart from the asirim, connected yet foreign, hated and despised.

It was a distant feeling, but it was there all the same, and it was fueled by the unending hostility of the asirim. They could not take up swords of their own. They could not move against the King. But Çeda could. And they could speak through her.

As Çeda stepped away from the darkest places of the room and closed her eyes, turning one last time to make sure Külaşan was nowhere near, she reached out, feeling for the heartbeat she knew was there. "Would you cower from one so young as I?" she said, her words echoing.

Külaşan laughed, a ponderous, leaden thing. She felt it in her heart, in her bones. "I see the asirim have taken you beneath their wing, dear child, but who do you think lords over the asirim? Who do you think holds the reins to their yokes?"

She still couldn't sense where he was, but then his wracking coughs suddenly filled the empty air, and his presence became known to her. Like a wight in a boneyard he floated at the very edge of her perception, and he seemed to sense it; for just then he stepped out from behind a tall, empty throne on the opposite side of the room. He wore bright mail armor, a conical helm with a slim nose guard, and fine chain mail that draped along the back of his neck. Çeda's time in the pits had taught her to assess men quickly, and Külaşan was impressive—broad of chest and well proportioned, death on the battlefield were the pollen not hobbling him.

As they stared at one another, she *felt* his heartbeat—so strongly, in fact, that it felt as though *his* heart beat for hers, as if, were he to release her, she would fall to the floor, her heart unable to beat on its own.

Çeda fell to her knees. She was frozen in place. Her

breath came to her as shallow as the water trapped in the salt flats. It felt like the dying of the day over the Amber City, the fading of light. It felt as though, after this one last breath, she would crumble, never to be remembered.

The King strode toward her, embossed buckler in one hand, Gravemaker in the other, a weapon with dozens of nicks along its well-oiled haft. He held the morning star easily, as if he were intimately familiar with its every angle, its every nuance, and he came with intent clear on his youthful face.

He hasn't aged a day. Not a day since they made their foul pact with the desert gods.

That day, the Kings, in order to appease the gods and save the people of Sharakhai, had sacrificed the Thirteenth Tribe. Brother and sister had been sacrificed. Mother and daughter. Father and son. It wasn't just this brutality that fueled a fire deep within her. It was also the laws the Kings had made in the generations that followed, as written in the Kannan.

Thou shalt not cross the threshold of an adulterer, lest thee be stoned by the hand of thine own blood.

Thou shalt not covet thy neighbor's love, lest thine own skin be lashed with sharded whip.

Thou shalt not doubt the word of thy King, lest thee be sent into the desert for seven days and seven nights.

The Kannan's laws were created by those left standing after the slaughter of Beht Ihman. Laws passed down and enforced both vigorously and viciously, to hide their own crimes, even while they celebrated their own moral failures each holy night of Beht Zha'ir. On that night, they called upon their cousins from the lost tribe and paid the price the gods had demanded, proclaiming it a divine honor to be chosen.

They had lied to everyone. To the Tribes who remained. To the people of Sharakhai. To their own blood. The Kings had been desperate, Çeda knew. They would have died had they not done what they'd done—the might of the desert tribes would surely have seen to that—but instead of handing Sharakhai to the enemy and sacrificing themselves, instead of protecting the people they claimed to love, they had chosen to sacrifice an entire tribe of people.

Külaşan was nearly upon her. He slowed and bent over, his body wracked by the coughs that gripped him so completely he couldn't even look at her. In that space, Çeda's heart beat freely, and with it came a surge of pain from her right hand. Another beat, and the pain in her hand blossomed. It was centered on the adichara wound, the thorn that had cut her in the very place that Saliah—the goddess Nalamae herself—had touched her with blood.

It had been a gift all along. Saliah had kissed Çeda that day, blessed her, given her a way to reach the asirim, even trapped as they were in their shriveled forms. Or maybe Saliah had merely seen it, and it had been near enough to grasp all along. Whatever the case, it had allowed her to feel the asirim's rage, their thirst for revenge, and it was this depthless well that let Çeda rise to her feet, to breathe deeply. To lift her sword in her poisoned hand, though the pain was white fire.

Külaşan's coughs finally died away. He pulled himself erect again, their heartbeats still in sync, but the intricacies of their bond had changed. The souls of the asirim reached through her and into Külaşan, governing his breath, the beat of his heart. And they were both slowing.

He wheezed while staring into her eyes. There was a look of shame upon him, a moment of honesty after centuries of ignoring the pain he'd caused. "So many," he said softly. "I had no idea there were still so many."

He raised his morning star and swung at her, but it was child's play for her to slip under it and run the point of her blade deep into his chest.

His weapon clattered to the floor with a sound that seemed strangely crude in this regal place. His blood, dark in the gathered lamplight, flowed from his wound and pattered against the veined white marble. The King fell to his knees, grasped his chest feebly, heedless of the cut that was spilling his lifeblood several inches below.

There was a vast sense of release in Çeda, of a thing that had been building so long—not only within her, but within the asirim—that tears sprung to her eyes. Not tears of joy but of regret. Regret that any of this had come to pass. The tears clouded her vision and almost caused her to miss the movement from the corner of her eye. The soft beat of leather-soled shoes sprinting over marble.

Çeda turned just in time to see a Maiden bring her sword down in a vicious arc. She was barely able to roll to one side, but the Maiden was on her in an instant.

"You dare!" came the Maiden's voice.

It was Jalize. Lithe Jalize. Quick Jalize.

She bore down on Çeda with powerful strokes, parrying Çeda's feeble attempts to stop her.

Çeda's right hand was pain itself. But strangely, she was able to see more through the pain. It was nearly blinding, the outline of Jalize, of the plants and furniture about the room that brightened as she grit her teeth against the agony that burst from her unhealing wound.

"Listen to me," Çeda said as she backed away, desperately fending off Jalize's strikes. She tried to put a massive clay urn between them, but Jalize shattered it with a swift, powerful kick, sending shards flying at Çeda.

She hoped that she could touch Jalize's heart, that she could fend her off as she had the King, using the deep well of hatred the asirim bore for Kings and Maidens both.

But she couldn't. The asirim were so fixated on Külaşan they could think of nothing else.

So she fought, trying in vain to keep Jalize beyond striking range. Jalize was too good, too swift, both in her movements and in her ability to guess Çeda's intentions. She was too in control of her emotions. She sliced Çeda's thigh, gave a shallow cut along her shin, caught Çeda's shoulder with the tip of her blade. Warm blood crept along Çeda's thawb. She could feel it slicking the marble beneath her shoes, making movement treacherous.

Fear, Çeda realized. She could feel it taking root. She might lose everything she had fought for, all that her *mother* had fought for, after coming so close to escaping, and with a King lying dead at her feet.

Enough, Çeda thought. *Enough! Strike the fear from your heart!* If she continued thinking in this way, it would surely be her undoing.

In a flurry of blows, she forced Jalize to retreat, even if only for a moment. When Jalize came in once more, Çeda brought her sword down in a move that seemed to leave an opening for her opponent.

Jalize took the bait. In a move Çeda had honed in the pits time after time, she halted the blade—leaving Jalize off balance—and stepped in, grabbed her wrist, and spun her while lifting Jalize's arm high. Dropping her blade, she controlled Jalize's arm, swinging it around her back and locking it in place, while snaking her free arm around Jalize's neck. Immediately she leaned and pulled Jalize off balance.

Jalize arched her back, trying to grab Çeda's head, but Çeda lifted Jalize's locked arm, hearing a wet crunch as the arm popped out of socket. Jalize screamed, but only for a moment, for Çeda wrenched her neck to one side sharply, and let her fall like a doll of wood and string to the cold marble floor.

Çeda stood there, right hand quivering so badly she had trouble picking up River's Daughter. As she sheathed it, the pain felt like a brand against her skin. She looked down at Jalize for a moment but then knelt by Külaşan's side. He still drew breath, and oddly, it was the breath of the unafflicted. It came easily, if shallowly. He stared at the underside of the dome, at the sweeping mosaics there, rolling hills and a grand sun—the farther fields, as envisioned by some mosaicist who had long since passed to those very same lands—and for a time, Çeda did the same. She hoped it was true. She hoped her mother walked through them, proud of what her daughter had done.

"You saved me."

Çeda looked down at Külaşan. He looked so young. Hardly older than Çeda herself. "What did you say?"

Before he could respond, Çeda felt more than heard others in the room. She looked up and saw Sümeya and Kameyl and Hasenn and a handful of other Maidens.

Sümeya approached, ebon blade in hand. She saw the King still alive, staring with widened eyes, Jalize lying motionless on the floor some distance away, Çeda with weapon sheathed. And then Sümeya lowered her blade.

"Goezhen's dark kiss, what happened?" The words were spoken with the hint of threat. She was confused, and for good reason, and she did not entirely trust Çeda to give her the truth of it. Why would she? Çeda wouldn't believe Sümeya's words had their roles been reversed. But she had to ask. The story had to begin somewhere.

Külaşan lifted an arm and reached for Çeda with quivering hands—one bloody, one not. He took Çeda's poisoned right hand in his own. It pained her, but not so badly as she would have guessed. "Do you understand?" he asked, tears streaming down his face. "You saved me."

He smiled and kissed her hand, breathing deeply as he did so, then fell back, his warm hands still gripping hers, whispering words that Çeda couldn't understand.

"What happened?" Sümeya repeated, looking more confused than angry now.

Çeda swallowed the tightness in her throat. A flood of emotions were welling up inside her, but she choked them back. "I don't understand it all. But there were calls of alarm in the desert. Silver Spears, I suspect. I went to help, but before I could find them, an adichara wrapped its branches around me and brought me down here, into his palace." She stared around the room in wonder. It was only half an act, for she was still astonished at all that had happened. Tears slipped down Çeda's cheeks, hot and biting and beautiful. "The King summoned me—in his desperation, I suppose—and when I came here, I found Jalize standing over him. She'd already delivered the killing stroke."

Külaşan squeezed Çeda's hand tenderly, like a father might his daughter. She wanted to pull away, but she stayed with him and watched as he stroked the tattoos on her right hand.

Then the light in his eyes dimmed. He went limp, his hands fell to the floor, his chest releasing his final breath in one sweet exhalation.

Çeda looked up then, saw the look of confused awe on Sümeya's face. On Kameyl's and Melis's and the others' as well. Sümeya looked between Çeda and Külaşan. Her eyes were alive with uncertainty, her mind clearly trying to weigh the truth in Çeda's words, the truth in Külaşan's words. Then she seemed to come to a decision. She looked into Çeda's eyes with something like embarrassment, and gratitude, and with solemn care took one knee, bowed her head, and brought her closed fist across her chest.

One by one, the others did the same. The last to take a knee was Kameyl, who seemed, if it were possible, even more reverent than Sümeya.

"All hail," Sümeya said.

"All hail," echoed the others.

Chapter 63

ÇEDA WALKED WITH A REAL LIMP NOW, not so different from the one she'd been feigning for years. It was even the same leg, making her wonder if she'd been tempting the gods with her ruse all along.

Her wounds had been slow in healing. She wore not her fighting dress, nor any other raiment of the Blade Maidens, but a simple, clay-colored thawb that faded to blue along the skirt and sleeves. She walked along the Trough with no one the wiser that she was a Maiden, not unless they looked closely. One might be able to tell by the way she carried herself, or the tattoo on her right hand, or the freshly crafted one inked on her left. Sümeya had requested the honor of designing and inking the tattoo herself, and Çeda had granted it to her. She didn't know what design Sümeya would choose, but she would let the history of that night be written upon her, no matter that it came from the leader of the Maidens herself, a woman Çeda had considered her enemy not so long ago.

No longer, though. At least, not in the way she had before joining the Maidens. She had come to realize just how deeply the Kings' lies ran. Who could fight such weight of history? The Maidens had all been raised in deference to the Kings' carefully cultivated tales, a grand tapestry utterly naked of the truth. No wonder they believed in the Kings and their Kannan. How could they not?

But no, Çeda no longer considered them her blood enemies. She would tread carefully in the coming months, but one day she would begin to reveal the truth. She didn't know how—one revelation offered to the wrong woman could mean Çeda's death—but she would find a way.

Sümeya had taken great care in designing Çeda's tattoo, and even more care in inking it onto Çeda's skin. A beautiful peacock wrapped around her wrist, its feathers not in bright display, as the one in Külaşan's seal, but half closed, the bird's head dipped low, as if bowing. Above it, on the back of her hand, surrounded by images of curling leaves and gentle waves of water, were written, in the old signs: *Savior of Sharakhai.*

Just as Sümeya was finishing, Husamettín had come into the room and looked over his daughter's shoulder. When Sümeya was done, she wiped away the ink, leaving it clear for the King of Swords to view. Husamettín had stared at the design, then at Sümeya, then Çeda herself. In that moment, Çeda had been unable to read him, and in the same breath felt laid open by his glare. When he left, Husamettín did not nod to her, did not give any sign of approval. He merely turned and strode from the room, a thing as close to acceptance as she was likely to get from the King of Swords, Sümeya told her afterward.

For two weeks after the attack on Külaşan's palace, the entire city had huddled in fear as the Maidens and Silver Spears had gone door-to-door, turning over the smallest of stones for any clues to the location of the Moonless Host, and any sympathizers who might still be in Sharakhai. Each morning had led to dozens of deaths, some hanging from the gallows at the gates of Tauriyat, but many more dying when the Kings' inquisitors finally finished with them.

As far as Çeda knew, Macide had escaped. Surely she would have heard if he'd been captured or killed by the Kings. Of Emre she'd heard no word. She prayed that he'd escaped as well, and as the days passed, as she looked at those who had been hung at the gates, she began building more and more hope that he was both free and alive.

After passing Bent Man, Çeda turned left onto Highgate Road, and soon after that turned onto Floret Row. She came at last to an apothecary shop. Outside there were spices, a bit of wine, a bit of bread—for Bakhi, for the other gods. Çeda opened the door without knocking and stepped inside to find Dardzada sitting behind his desk, transposing in a ledger figures from a crumpled note he was holding flat with a splayed hand.

He looked up when she came in. He swallowed once, hard, blinking fiercely but then went back to copying, his ever-present frown deepening.

"Have you heard the Maidens took me in?" Çeda asked. "That I am one of them now?"

Dardzada paused to ink his vulture quill. "If you've come only to ask self-evident questions, you may as well turn around and return to them."

"There are changes afoot, Dardzada."

"You think I don't know?"

"I know you know, but it's high time you stopped trying to protect me and started helping me. I am a woman grown now, and whether you like it or not, I am a part of this, as surely as you are, as surely as Macide." She paused. "As surely as my mother was."

With exaggerated care, Dardzada dropped the quill into the inkwell and crossed his arms over the ledger. "And how would you suggest I go about it, Çeda? Ask the Kings to lie down before you so you might slit their collective throats? Demand of the gods that they accede to your will?"

Çeda glanced into the back room, then glanced outside into the street. Finding them clear, she lowered her voice to a near whisper. "I killed one of them, Dardzada." She lifted her right hand and pointed to the puckered wound, which felt almost normal today. "With the help of the asirim, Külaşan lies dead."

Even as she spoke, Dardzada was shaking his head, his heavy double chin waggling from the effort. "It cannot be."

Despite herself, a smile touched her lips. "He was slain by my own hand."

"We would have heard news of it."

"Do you suppose the Kings would have sent their criers to tell every corner of Sharakhai that King Külaşan is dead? They're covering it up, Dardzada. Hiding it. But they can't hide it forever."

"The Kings can do much, Çeda. You of all people should know this."

Çeda nodded. "They can. But the fact remains. One lies dead. Eleven still live. We need clues, Dardzada. We need to find more verses from the poem."

"I have no more rhymes to give you."

"Yes, you do. Ahya gave them to you before she died."

"She did not."

"She told Saliah she had four. One was for Külaşan, so three remain, and she wouldn't have risked their loss after her death. We both know she spoke with you about her plans before she left for Tauriyat that night. There isn't a chance in this wide, grand desert she didn't ask you to keep those secrets safe so that others might continue her work."

Dardzada stared at her. His eyes shifted toward the door, as if he wished she would leave, or that he could flee. But then he visibly deflated. "Külaşan is dead . . ."

"Külaşan is dead."

After gripping the edge of the desk until his knuckles turned white, he stood and lumbered to the stairs that led up to his room. He returned a short while later with a small brass key tied with a purple ribbon. He placed it into Çeda's hands and said, "She gave me this to give to you when I felt you were ready, along with a message."

Çeda stared at the key, wonderingly. "Which was?"

"'The silver moon unlocks the bloody verses.'"

"The silver moon. She meant Rhia, of course, but what did she mean by unlocking the verses? Is there a box? A chest of some kind?"

"No. I never saw her with one, nor had I ever seen the key before she gave it to me."

"This is all she left for me?"

"That and her book and locket, which I've already given you."

"And you've withheld this for eleven years now. What else might she—"

"I've given you everything she gave me, Çeda."

"Why didn't she tell you what she meant?"

"She feared you might be found. That *I* might be found, which would lead them to you. She wanted to leave as few clues as she could."

It made some sense, but it was frustrating to come for answers, only to be given more riddles. She held the key gingerly in one hand. It felt weighty and somehow momentous, as if the gods themselves were waiting to see what she would do with it. "We can bring them down, you know."

There was pride in his eyes now, and a deep-seated fear, one that would probably never leave him. "You'd better go," he said, jutting his chin toward the door.

Çeda stepped toward him, but Dardzada turned away and returned to his seat behind the desk. He resumed scratching away with his quill a moment later.

"I must know something else. The story my mother told herself the night she died. What was it?"

When Ahya and Dardzada had spoken alone in his back room that night, Çeda had eavesdropped and heard Dardzada say to Ahya, *Repeat the story I gave you,* or some such thing. She'd long since realized Ahya's strange behavior was due to hangman's vine, a distillation that allowed one to supplant one's memories, permanently if the draught was strong enough. Most often, the one administering the draught would feed a story to the one drinking it, or one would have been arranged ahead of time.

For a moment Dardzada gave her the same obstinate look he so often chose as his first reaction to her queries, but this was information she wouldn't leave his shop without. Perhaps he sensed this. Or perhaps he thought he owed her this much after the news she'd given him of Külaşan death. Or perhaps he was simply tired of hiding it from her. Whatever the case, he raised his eyebrows as if were surprising even himself and said, "She went to kill a King, Çeda. She told herself she was an assassin, and that the one who'd paid her to do it had been hidden from her. Nearly all other memories would have been stripped from her by the vine. The memories and skills that remained would be those that served the simple story we'd decided upon."

"As simple as that? She was an assassin? She didn't know the identity of her patron?"

"There would have been much more to it by the time she arrived at Tauriyat. It's best to think of that simple narrative as a framework. Hangman's vine draws from your past experiences, some imagined, some dreamed, some real, and fills in that framework, brick by brick, until an edifice has been built, one that looks whole and complete to any who would view it, including and especially the one who swallowed the draught."

"Which King did she go to kill?"

At this Dardzada's mouth straightened into a grim line. "We have to be careful about their names. You shouldn't speak them so easily, as you did with the Wandering King. The chances may be small that the King of Whispers will ever hear us, but it's not a chance I'm willing to take if I can avoid it. Do you understand?"

Çeda nodded. "A clue, then."

He pointed to her right thumb. "The King of that which wounded you."

A thorn. The King of Thorns. He meant King Azad. The very one Nayyan, the leader of Sümeya's hand, had been off to visit when she'd disappeared. Her mother hadn't succeeded—Çeda had seen Azad with her own eyes—but whatever she'd done, it was surely related to Nayyan's disappearance.

"What is it?" Dardzada asked.

"Nothing," she replied.

He stared intently into her eyes, then returned to his ledger. "Have it your way."

"Dardzada?"

"Yes?" he asked, not looking up.

"Do you think my mother would remember me? Given time?"

Dardzada stopped. He looked up, sharing a grief-stricken look with her, and said, "That is my most fervent hope, Çedamihn," and then rededicated himself to his task.

She had asked him this same question when she was

young but hadn't seen then what she saw now: that
Dardzada had harbored as much pain as she over the stories he'd fed to Ahya. And not merely for the part he'd
played in making her forget her child, but also because he'd
made her forget *him* as well. He may have felt some sense
of regret over one, but to have loved her so deeply and to
have then helped her forget him completely before her
death . . . It would be like Çeda making Emre forget her, a
thing she could hardly even imagine.

"Mine as well," she said before stepping up to his desk
and leaning over to kiss his forehead.

He is blood of your blood, her mother had told her long
ago, and Çeda hadn't believed her. She did now, though.
Dardzada had the blood of the thirteenth tribe running
through his veins, and so did many others, most of whom
wouldn't even realize the thirteenth tribe existed. One day
she would find them, though, and she would tell them the
true story of Beht Ihman.

She left Dardzada's apothecary and walked along Floret
Row, wending her way toward the Trough. She might have
gone to her old home, the one she'd shared with Emre, but
he wouldn't be there. The lonely part of her wanted to visit
Osman, to find her way into his arms once more, but she
didn't wish to bring the old shademan to the House of Maidens' attention. She also didn't want Osman to get the impression that she might love him, so she buried the urge and
instead spent her day wandering through the busy streets of
Sharakhai, stopping to partake of thousand-layer sweets
and rosehip tea and a bit of Tehla's crunchy bread, before
finally returning to her new home: the House of Maidens.

In the days that followed, Çeda heard nothing from
Emre. She worried for him so, yet there was nothing to do
but wait. Wait and hope he could find a way to send her a
message.

She continued to struggle with the meaning behind her
mother's message. *The silver moon unlocks the bloody
verses.* What did that have to do with the key she'd given
Çeda? Was there some chest that could only open beneath
Tulathan's light? Some piece of magic that would keep it
safe until Çeda came for it?

She worried that she'd never figure it out, that she'd never find whatever lock the key would open, that she'd not been able to deliver something crucial to Dardzada before she'd died. But when she thought about all her mother had given her, the answer was obvious.

The answer wasn't to do with the key at all, but her mother's book.

That night, when the sun had set, and Rhia had risen in the east, Çeda went to the rooftop of the House of Maidens. When she was sure no one had followed her, she opened her mother's book. She leafed through the pages slowly, seeing nothing at first, yet utterly confident she would.

She found the first poem halfway through the book. On that page, over the other darkly inked words, silvery letters glowed beneath the white light of Rhia, in Ahya's flowing script.

> *Sharp of eye,*
> *And quick of wit,*
> *The King of Amberlark;*
> *With wave of hand,*
> *On cooling sand,*
> *Slips he into the dark.*

> *King will shift,*
> *'Twixt light and dark,*
> *The gift of onyx sky;*
> *Shadows play,*
> *In dark of day,*
> *Yet not 'neath Rhia's eye.*

Several pages later she found another.

> *The King of smiles,*
> *From verdant isles,*
> *The gleam in moonlit eye;*
> *With soft caress,*
> *At death's redress,*
> *His wish, lost soul will cry.*

> *Yerinde grants,*
> *A golden band,*
> *With eye of glittering jet;*
> *Should King divide,*
> *From Love's sweet pride,*
> *Dark souls collect their debt.*

Two, Çeda thought. *Two more poems. Two more riddles. Two more bloody verses.*

She would think on these in the coming days, and she would unlock their secrets. And then she and the others would move once more against the Kings.

But for now, she merely stared at the lines, feeling not the meaning of the words but the weight behind their history. Her mother had found these. She had risked everything to unearth them. Çeda felt so many things as she held that book in her hands.

Relief. Thankfulness. Betrayal, if she was being honest. But more than anything, pride over what her mother had achieved.

"Why didn't you tell me?" she whispered into the night.

But how could she have? How could her mother have explained all of this to an eight-year-old girl? She couldn't, so she had remained silent, and then the world caught up with her. As it still might with Çeda.

"We shall see," she said softly to the pages of the book.

She looked up at Rhia and the firmament beyond, and said once more, "We shall see," then closed the book and went back down, into the House of Maidens.

Acknowledgments

The list of people that helped to get this book where it is now is longer than any book I've written in the past. Why? Because it was the first book in a new series. I was graduating, stepping up, trying to push my boundaries in order (I sincerely hoped) to reach a wider audience. It was very important to me that this first book in a new, expansive series was told well to get the series off to a roaring start. So I threw the net wide, so to speak, and I'd like to thank as many of you as I can. For any omissions, please forgive me. I tried to catch everyone, but realize I may have missed some.

First, I'd like to thank those who read early partials that eventually became part of the proposal package that sold the first three books in the series. Rob Ziegler, Paul Genesse, Robert Levy, Justin Landon, Doug Hulick, Paul Weimer, and Betsy Mitchell. Thank you for your thoughts that helped steer me in the right direction. Also, Patrick Tracy, rivers of gratitude for helping me with the epic poem that became one of the central threads, not just of this book, but the entire series.

To all the folks at the Coastal Heaven writing workshop— Grá Linnaea, Rob Ziegler, Chris Cevasco, Brenda Cooper,

Adam Rakunas, Kris Dikeman, David Levine, Mark Teppo—thank you for helping to sharpen those opening pages. And to my full ms critters, Jennifer Linnaea and Beth Wodzinski, thank you for your insights on the entire (let's face it, rather rough) ms.

Russell Galen, thank you, once again, for guiding my career so expertly. I don't know where I'd be without you.

Betsy Wollheim, thank you for believing in this book. Thank you as well for all your wonderful advice, not just on the ms, but on all the things that surround it as well. The wealth of knowledge you have about this business is invaluable, and I'm grateful to benefit from it. I owe you, the team at DAW Books, and indeed your father, a huge debt of gratitude.

Gillian Redfearn, who provided so many smart comments on this book, thank you for all you did in finding the niggling (and some not so niggling!) problems, and for getting this book ready for the UK market. I've rarely met someone so wholly in love with speculative fiction. It's infectious!

Marylou Capes-Platt, I'm so sorry about all those dashed parentheticals! And the ellipses! And the plenitude of ¶'s! Thank you for lending your expertise to this story. I love your eye for what makes a story work, what a reader will and won't put up with, and the funny comments in the edits!

Adam Paquette, thank you for once again creating a stunning cover for one of my books. Sharakhai is even more beautiful and grand than I had imagined it. The interior artwork turned out wonderfully as well.

Juliette Wade, thanks for providing your insights. I've always appreciated your sensitivity to a wide variety of issues, and you brought that same sensitivity to your review.

Sarah Chorn, thanks for agreeing to my out-of-the-blue request to read the book. It was pretty well baked by the time you read it, but just like it's important to get early feedback on what *isn't* working, it's important to get feedback on what *is* working, so thank you.

Aidan Moher, I'll say it again, thank you for all your feedback, but specifically, for narrowing in on the book of poems, Çeda's relationship with her mother, and the ritual surrounding Çeda and the adichara. Those three things alone opened up so much in the story and made it a much richer tale.

Paul Genesse, who's read so much of my fiction that he knows my strengths and weaknesses. Thanks, Paul, for pushing me to shore up those breaks in the line and to build upon what's already working. Protags have to protag, right? The hinge point of this book changed because of your comments. Thanks for fighting for it!

Rob Ziegler, who read the novel again when it was pretty far along. Thanks for tackling this beast and helping me to narrow in on the things that weren't quite working.

Justin Landon, who read the early partial, but then read the whole book *two more times*. The book is vastly better for your influence. The story really blew up after the first of those reads, but it needed it. Your comments gave me the confidence to break the story up, to tell more of Çeda's backstory, to have parallel threads and to tell the story from additional points of view, and more. Thanks, Justin, for those insights and for plot bashing this with me.

To my fans, especially those who knew about *Twelve Kings* before its publication and cheered me on. You may not have known it, but your support helped keep me going on the long road to publication. The thought of getting this out and into your hands was a comforting feeling. I hope the wait was worth it.

In past books, I've saved the final thank you for my wife, Joanne, who deserved (and deserves) heaps of gratitude for carving out time from her own life to allow me the time to write. Thank you, honey, for all you did to make this possible. But I now have to add my children to this Most Important List. Relaneve and Rhys, thank you for giving up time with daddy to let him chase his dreams.

Bradley P. Beaulieu

The Song of the Shattered Sands

—◆—●—◆—

"Fantasy and horror, catacombs and sarcophagi, resurrections and revelations: the book has them all, and
Beaulieu wraps it up in a package that's as graceful
and contemplative as it is action-packed and pulse-
pounding."   —NPR

TWELVE KINGS IN SHARAKHAI
978-0-7564-0973-9

WITH BLOOD UPON THE SAND
978-0-7564-1406-1

A VEIL OF SPEARS
978-0-7564-0977-7

BENEATH THE TWISTED TREES
978-0-7564-1459-7

"Çeda and Emre share a relationship seldom explored
in fantasy, one that will be tried to the utmost as
similar ideals provoke them to explore different paths.
Wise readers will hop on this train now, as the journey
promises to be breathtaking."   —Robin Hobb

"*The Song of Shattered Sands* series is both gripping
and engrossing."   —*Kirkus*

To Order Call: 1-800-788-6262
www.dawbooks.com

DAW 202